The road, more than the buildings, gave him the eerie feeling of the presence of the temple beyond. He passed along part of a wall, and between the hollow stone buildings, feeling the timeless quality of the place, feeling the life that once was here.

Even now, Richard could almost see it, feel it, sense it, as if his gift were pulling him onward, pulling him home.

Abruptly, he was jerked to a halt.

Ulic on one side of him, and Egan on the other, had seized him under his arms and pulled him back. He looked down, and saw that another step would have taken him out into thin air. Vultures soared in the updraft not twenty feet straight in front of him.

The view was dizzying. He felt as if he were standing at the edge of the world. The hair on the back of his neck stiffened.

More should lie beyond the edge at his feet, he knew it should. But there was nothing there.

The Temple of the Winds was gone.

Terry Goodkind burst upon the fantasy scene with his masterful, bestselling novel *Wizard's First Rule*. He lives in the woods of New England where he is working on the next fantasy in The Sword of Truth sequence.

Available from Millennium

The Sword of Truth series:
Wizard's First Rule
Stone of Tears
Blood of the Fold
Temple of the Winds
Soul of the Fire

Terry Goodkind

TEMPLE OF THE WINDS

A Millennium Paperback
First published in Great Britain by Orion in 1997
This paperback edition published in 1998 by Millennium,
a division of Orion Books Ltd,
Orion House, 5 Upper St Martin's Lane,
London WC2H 9EA

Third impression 2000

A CIP catalogue record for this book
is available from the British Library.

ISBN: 0 75281 678 0

Typeset by Deltatype Ltd, Birkenhead, Merseyside
Printed and bound in Great Britain by
Clays Ltd, St Ives plc.

To my friend Rachel Kahlandt,
who understands

ACKNOWLEDGMENTS

I would like to thank my editor, James Frenkel, for his help and patience; all the hardworking people at Tor; my British editor, Caroline Oakley, for her insights; my agent, Russell Galen, for his guidance and support; my friend, Donald L. Schassberger, M.D., for his expert advice; and Keith Parkinson, for his inspiring cover art.

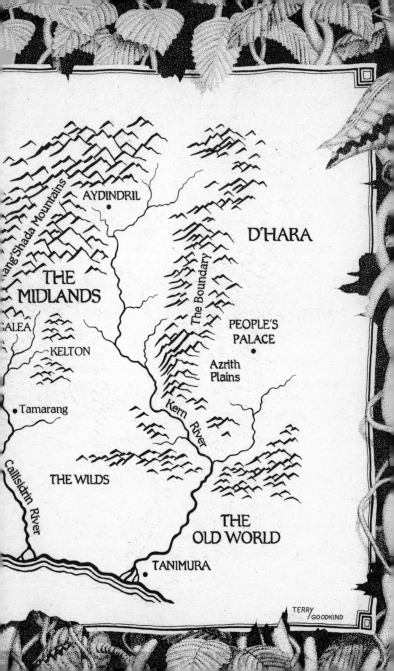

TEMPLE OF THE WINDS

CHAPTER 1

'Let me kill him,' Cara said, her boot strikes sounding like rawhide mallets hammering the polished marble floor.

The supple leather boots Kahlan wore beneath her elegant, white Confessor's dress whispered against the cold stone as she tried to keep pace without letting her legs break into a run. 'No.'

Cara exhibited no response, keeping her blue eyes ahead to the wide corridor stretching into the distance. A dozen leather-and chain-mail-clad D'Haran soldiers, their unadorned swords sheathed, or crescent-bladed battle-axes hooked on belt hangers, crossed at an intersection just ahead. Though their weapons weren't drawn, every wooden hilt was gripped in a ready fist as vigilant eyes scrutinized the shadows among the doorways and columns to each side. Their hasty bows toward Kahlan only briefly interrupted their attention to their task.

'We can't just kill him,' Kahlan explained. 'We need answers.'

An eyebrow lifted over one icy blue eye. 'Oh, I didn't say he wouldn't give us answers before he dies. He will answer any question you have when I'm finished with him.' A mirthless smile ghosted across her flawless face. 'That is the job of a Mord-Sith: getting people to answer questions' – she paused as the smile returned to widen with professional satisfaction – 'before they die.'

Kahlan heaved a sigh. 'Cara, that's no longer your job – your life. Your job now is to protect Richard.'

1

'That is why you should let me kill him. We should not take a risk by letting this man live.'

'No. We first have to find out what's going on, and we're not going to start out doing it the way you want.'

Cara's smile, humorless as it was, had vanished again. 'As you wish, Mother Confessor.'

Kahlan wondered how the woman had managed to change into her skintight red leather outfit so fast. Whenever there was so much as a whiff of trouble, at least one of the three Mord-Sith seemed to materialize out of nowhere in her red leather. Red, as they often pointed out, didn't show blood.

'Are you sure he said that, this man? Those were his words?'

'Yes, Mother Confessor, his exact words. You should let me kill him before he has a chance to try to bring them to pass.'

Kahlan ignored the repeated request as they hurried on down the hall. 'Where's Richard?'

'You wish me to get Lord Rahl?'

'No! I just want to know where he is, in case there's trouble.'

'I would say that this qualifies as trouble.'

'You said that there must be two hundred soldiers holding weapons on him. How much trouble can one man cause with all those swords, axes, and arrows pointed at him?'

'My former master, Darken Rahl, knew that steel alone could not always ward danger. That is why he had Mord-Sith nearby and at the ready.'

'That evil man would kill people without even bothering to determine if they were really a danger to him. Richard isn't like that, and neither am I. You know that if there is a true threat, I'm not shy about eliminating it; but if this man is more than he seems, then why is he so timidly cowering before all that steel? Besides, as a Confessor I am hardly defenseless against threats that steel won't stop.

'We have to keep our heads. Let's not start leaping to judgments that may be unwarranted.'

'If you don't think he could be trouble, then why am I nearly running just to keep up with you?'

Kahlan realized that she was a half a step ahead of the

woman. She slowed her pace to a brisk walk. 'Because it's Richard we're talking about,' she said in a near whisper.

Cara smirked. 'You're as worried as I.'

'Of course I am. But for all we know, killing this man, if he *is* more than he seems, could be springing a snare.'

'You could be right, but that is the purpose for Mord-Sith.'

'So, where is Richard?'

Cara gripped the red leather at her wrist and stretched her armor-backed glove tighter onto her hand as she flexed her fist. Her Agiel, an awesome weapon that appeared to be nothing more than a finger-width foot-long red leather rod, dangled from a fine gold chain at her right wrist, ever at the ready. One just like it, but no weapon in Kahlan's hands, hung on a chain around Kahlan's neck. It had been a gift from Richard, a gift that symbolized the pain and sacrifice they had both endured.

'He is out behind the palace, in one of the private parks.' Cara gestured over her shoulder. 'The one that way. Raina and Berdine are with him.'

Kahlan was relieved to hear that the other two Mord-Sith were watching over him. 'Something to do with his surprise for me?'

'What surprise?'

Kahlan smiled. 'Surely he's told you, Cara.'

Cara snatched a glimpse out of the corner of her eye. 'Of course he has told me.'

'Then what is it?'

'He also told me not to tell you.'

Kahlan shrugged. 'I won't tell him that you told me.'

Cara's laugh, like her smile before, bore no humor. 'Lord Rahl has a peculiar way of finding out things, especially those things you wish him not to know.'

Kahlan knew the truth of that. 'So what's he doing out there?'

The muscles in Cara's jaw flexed. 'Outdoor things. You know Lord Rahl; he likes to do outdoor things.'

Kahlan glanced over to see that Cara's face had turned nearly as red as her leather outfit. 'What sort of outdoor things?'

Cara cleared her throat into her armored fist. 'He is taming chipmunks.'

3

'He's what? I can't hear you.'

Cara waved an impatient hand. 'He said that the chipmunks have come out to test the warming weather. He is taming them.' Her cheeks rounded as she huffed. 'With seeds.'

Kahlan smiled at the thought of Richard, the man she loved, the man who had seized command of D'Hara, and had much of the Midlands now eating out of his hand, having a fine afternoon teaching chipmunks to eat seeds out of his hand.

'Well, that sounds innocent enough – feeding seeds to chipmunks.'

Cara flexed her armored fist again as they swept between two D'Haran guards. 'He is teaching them to eat those seeds,' she said through clenched teeth, 'out of Raina and Berdine's hands. The two of them were giggling!' She aimed a mortified expression toward the ceiling as she threw her hands up. Her Agiel swung on the gold chain at her wrist. 'Mord-Sith – giggling!'

Kahlan pressed her lips tight, trying to keep from breaking into laughter. Cara pulled her long blond braid forward, over her shoulder, stroking it in a way that provoked in Kahlan an unsettling memory of the way Shota, the witch woman, stroked her snakes.

'Well,' Kahlan said, trying to cool the other woman's indignation, 'maybe it's not by their choice. They are bonded to him. Perhaps Richard ordered it, and they're simply obeying him.'

Cara shot her an incredulous look. Kahlan knew that any of the three Mord-Sith would defend Richard to the death – they had shown themselves prepared to sacrifice their lives without hesitation – but though they were bonded to him through magic, they disregarded his orders wantonly if they judged them trivial, unimportant, or unwise. Kahlan imagined that it was because Richard had given them their freedom from the rigid principles of their profession, and they enjoyed exercising that freedom. Darken Rahl, their former master, Richard's father, would have killed them in a heartbeat had he even suspected that they were considering disobeying his orders, no matter how trivial they were.

'The sooner you wed Lord Rahl the better. Then, instead of

4

teaching chipmunks to eat out of Mord-Sith hands, he will be eating out of yours.'

Kahlan exhaled in a soft, lilting laugh, thinking about being his wife. It wouldn't be long, now. 'Richard will have my hand, but you should know as well as anyone that he will not be eating out of it – and I wouldn't want him to.'

'If you regain your senses, come see me, and I will teach you how.' Cara turned her attention to the alert D'Haran soldiers. Men at arms were rushing everywhere, checking every hall and looking behind every door, no doubt at Cara's insistence.

'Egan is with Lord Rahl, too. He should be safe while we see to this man.'

Kahlan's mirth withered. 'How did he get in here, anyway? Did he come in with the petitioners?'

'No.' A professional chill settled back into Cara's tone. 'But I intend to find out. From what I gather, he just walked up to a patrol of guards not far from the council chambers and asked where he could find Lord Rahl, as if just anyone can walk in and ask to see the Master of D'Hara, as if he was a head butcher that anyone can go to if they want a choice cut of mutton.'

'That's when the guards asked him why he wanted to see Richard?'

Cara nodded. 'I think we should kill him.'

Realization wormed up Kahlan's spine in a cold tingle. Cara wasn't simply an aggressive bodyguard, unconcerned about spilling the blood of others – she was afraid. She was afraid for Richard.

'I want to know how he got in here. He presented himself to a patrol inside the palace; he shouldn't have been able to get inside, wandering around unfettered. What if we have a hitherto-unknown breach in security? Wouldn't it be better to find out before another comes without the courtesy of announcing himself?'

'We can find out if you let me do it my way.'

'We don't know enough yet; he could end up dead before we find out anything, then the danger to Richard could become greater.'

'All right,' Cara said with a sigh, 'we will do it your way, as long as you understand that I have orders to follow.'

'What orders?'

'Lord Rahl told us to protect you as we would protect him.' With a toss of her head, Cara flicked her blond braid back over her shoulder. 'If you are not careful, Mother Confessor, and needlessly endanger Lord Rahl with your restraint, I will withdraw my permission for Richard to keep you.'

Kahlan laughed. Her laughter died out when Cara didn't so much as smile. She was never entirely sure when the Mord-Sith were joking and when they were being deadly serious.

'In here,' Kahlan said. 'It's shorter this way, and besides, I want to see what petitioners are waiting, in view of our strange visitor. He could even be a diversion to draw our attention away from someone else – the true threat.'

Cara's brow twitched as if she had been slighted. 'Why do you think I had Petitioners' Hall sealed and ringed with guards?'

'You did it surreptitiously, I hope. There's no need to frighten the wits out of innocent petitioners.'

'I told the officers not to frighten the people in there if they didn't have to, but our first responsibility is to protect Lord Rahl.'

Kahlan nodded. She couldn't argue with that.

Two heavily muscled guards bowed, along with twenty others nearby, before pulling open the tall, brassbound doors leading to an arcaded passageway. A stone rail supported by fat, vase-shaped balusters ran along the white marble pillars. The barrier, separating the petitioners in the hundred-foot-long room from the officials' passageway, was symbolic rather than real. Skylights thirty feet overhead lit the waiting room, but left the length of the passageway to the muted golden light of lamps hung in the peak of each small vault in its ceiling.

It was a long-standing custom for people – petitioners – to come to the Confessors' Palace to seek any number of things, from settlement of disagreements over the rights of peddlers to coveted street corners, to officials of different lands seeking armed intervention in border disputes. Matters that could be handled by city officials were directed to the proper offices. Matters brought by dignitaries of the lands, if those matters were deemed to be important enough, or could be handled in no other way, were taken before the council. Petitioners' Hall was where officers of protocol determined the disposition of requests.

When Darken Rahl, Richard's father, had attacked the Midlands, many of the officials in Aydindril had been killed, among them Saul Witherrin, the Chief cf Protocol, along with most of his office. Richard had defeated Darken Rahl, and being the gifted heir, had ascended to Master of D'Hara. He had ended the bickering and battling among the lands of the Midlands by demanding their surrender in order to forge them all into a force capable of withstanding the common threat from the Old World, from the Imperial Order.

Kahlan found it unsettling to be the Mother Confessor who had reigned over the end of the Midlands as a formal entity, a union of sovereign lands, but she knew that her first responsibility was to the lives of the people, not to tradition; if not stopped, the Imperial Order would cast the world into slavery, and the people of the Midlands would be its chattel. Richard had accomplished what his father could not, but did so for entirely different reasons. She loved Richard and knew his benevolent intent in seizing power.

Soon they would be wedded, and their marriage would unite the Midlands and D'Hara in peace and unity for all time. More than that, though, it would be a personal fulfillment of their love and deepest desire: to be one.

Kahlan missed Saul Witherrin; he had been a capable aide. With the council now dead, too, and the Midlands now a part of D'Hara, matters of protocol were in disarray. A few frustrated D'Haran officers were standing at the railing, attempting to minister to the petitioners' needs.

As she entered, Kahlan's gaze swept the waiting crowd, analyzing the nature of problems brought to the palace this day. By their dress, most appeared to be people from the surrounding city of Aydindril: laborers, shopkeepers, and merchants.

She saw a knot of children she knew from the day before when Richard had taken her to watch them playing a game of Ja'La. It was the first time she had seen the fast-paced game, and it had been an entertaining diversion for a couple of hours:

7

to watch children play and laugh. The children probably wanted Richard to come watch another game; he had been an ardent supporter of each team. Even if he had picked one team to cheer over the other, Kahlan doubted it would have made any difference; children were drawn to Richard, seeming to instinctively sense his kind heart.

Kahlan recognized several diplomats from a few of the smaller lands, who she hoped had come to accept Richard's offer of a peaceful surrender and union into D'Haran rule. She knew the leaders of those lands, and was expecting them to heed her urging to join with them in the cause of freedom.

She recognized, too, a group of diplomats from some of the larger lands that had standing armies. They had been expected, and later that day Richard and Kahlan were to meet with them, along with any other newly arrived representatives, to hear their decision.

She wished Richard would find himself something more suitable to wear. His woods clothes had served him well, but he now needed to present a more fitting image of the position he found himself in. He was so much more than a woods guide now.

Having served nearly her whole life as a person of authority, Kahlan knew that it often smoothed matters of leadership if you matched people's expectations. Kahlan doubted people who needed a woods guide would have followed Richard if he hadn't dressed for the woods. In a way, Richard was their guide in this treacherous new world of untested allegiances and new enemies. He often asked her advice; she was going to have to talk to him about his clothes.

When the people assembled saw the Mother Confessor striding into the passageway, conversation stilled and they began going to a knee in deep bows. Despite the fact that she was of an unprecedentedly young age for the post, there was no one of higher authority in the Midlands than the Mother Confessor. The Mother Confessor was the Mother Confessor, no matter the face of the woman who held the office. People bowed not so much to the woman as to that ancient authority.

Matters of Confessors were an enigma to most people of the Midlands; Confessors chose the Mother Confessor. To Confessors, age was of secondary consideration.

8

Though she was chosen to preserve the freedoms and rights of the people of the Midlands, people rarely saw it in those terms. To most, a ruler was a ruler. Some were good, some were bad. As the ruler of rulers, the Mother Confessor encouraged the good, and suppressed the bad. If a ruler proved bad enough, it was within her power to eliminate them. That was the ultimate purpose of a Mother Confessor. To most people, though, such far removed matters of governance simply seemed the squabbling of rulers.

In the sudden silence that filled Petitioners' Hall, Kahlan paused to acknowledge the gathered visitors.

A young woman standing against the far wall watched as all those around her fell to one knee. She glanced in Kahlan's direction, back to those kneeling, and then followed suit.

Kahlan's brow tightened.

In the Midlands, the length of a woman's hair denoted her power and standing. Matters of power, no matter how trivial they might seem on the surface, were taken seriously in the Midlands. Not even a queen's hair was allowed to be as long as a Confessor's, and no Confessor's hair was as long as that of the Mother Confessor.

This woman had a thick mass of brown hair close to the length of Kahlan's.

Kahlan knew nearly every person of high rank in the Midlands; it was her duty, and she took it seriously. A woman with hair that long was obviously a person of high standing, but Kahlan didn't recognize her. There was likely to be no man or woman in the entire city, other than Kahlan, who would outrank the woman – if she was in fact from the Midlands.

'Rise, my children,' Kahlan said in formal response to the tops of the waiting, bowed heads.

Dresses and coats rustled as everyone began coming to their feet, most keeping their eyes to the floor, out of respect, or needless fear. The woman rose to her feet, twisting a simply made kerchief in her fingers, watching those around her. She turned her brown eyes to the floor, as most of the others were.

'Cara,' Kahlan whispered, 'could that woman there, with the long hair, be from D'Hara?'

Cara had been watching her, too; she had learned some of

the customs of the Midlands. Though Cara's long blond hair was about the length of Kahlan's, she was D'Haran. They didn't live by the same customs.

'Her nose is too "cute" to be D'Haran.'

'I'm serious. Do you think she could be D'Haran?'

Cara studied the woman a moment longer. 'I doubt it. D'Haran women don't wear flower-print dresses, nor are the dresses they do wear of that cut. But clothes can be changed to fit the occasion, or to fit in with local people.'

The dress didn't really fit the local dress of Aydindril, but it might not be so out of place in other, more remote, areas of the Midlands. Kahlan nodded and turned to a waiting captain, motioning him over.

He leaned his head close as she spoke in a low tone. 'There is a woman with long brown hair standing against the wall in the back, over my left shoulder. Do you see who I'm talking about?'

'The pretty one, in the blue kirtle?'

'Yes. Do you know why she's here?'

'She said she wished to speak with Lord Rahl.'

Kahlan's brow drew tighter. She noticed that Cara's did, too. 'What about?'

'She said that she's looking for a man – Cy something – I didn't recognize his name. She said he's been missing since last autumn, and she was told that Lord Rahl would be able to help her.'

'Is that right,' Kahlan said. 'And did she say what business she has with this missing man?'

The captain glanced to the woman and then brushed his sandy hair back from his forehead. 'She said that she's to marry him.'

Kahlan nodded. 'It could be that she's a dignitary, but if she is, I'm embarrassed to admit that I don't know her name.'

The captain glanced at a tattered list with scribbles all over it. He turned the paper and scanned the other side until he found what he was looking for. 'She said her name was Nadine. She gave no title.'

'Well, please see to it that Lady Nadine is taken to a private waiting room where she will be comfortable. Tell her that I will come speak with her and see if I can help. Have dinner brought to her, along with anything else she might require. Give her my apology and tell her that I have something of vital importance that I must attend to first, but I will come see her as soon as I am able, and that I wish to do what I can to help her.'

Kahlan could understand the woman's distress if she really was separated from her love and was searching for him. Kahlan had been in that situation herself and knew well the anguish.

'I'll see to it at once, Mother Confessor.'

'One other thing, captain.' Kahlan watched the woman twisting her kerchief. 'Tell Lady Nadine that there is trouble about, what with the war with the Old World, and that for her own safety we must insist that she remain in the room until I can come to speak with her. Post a heavy guard outside the room. Place archers at a safe distance down the hall to either side of the door.

'If she comes out, insist that she must return to the room at once and wait. If you must, tell her that it is by my command. If she still tries to leave' – Kahlan looked into the captain's waiting blue eyes – 'kill her.'

The captain bowed as Kahlan swept on through the passageway, Cara right at her heels.

'Well, well,' Cara said, once outside Petitioners' Hall, 'at last the Mother Confessor comes to her senses. I knew I had a good reason for allowing Lord Rahl to keep you. You will make him a worthy wife.'

Kahlan turned down the corridor toward the room where guards held the man. 'I haven't changed my mind about anything, Cara. Considering our strange visitor, I'm giving Lady Nadine every chance to live, every chance I can afford to give, but you're mistaken if you think I'll balk at doing whatever it takes to protect Richard. Besides being the man I love more than life itself, Richard is a man of vital importance to the freedom of the people of both D'Hara and the Midlands. There's no telling what the Imperial Order would try in order to get to him.'

Cara smiled, sincerely, this time. 'I know he loves you the same. That's why I don't like you going to see this man; Lord Rahl may separate me from my hide if he thinks I allowed you near danger.'

'Richard is one born with the gift; I, too, have been born with magic. Darken Rahl sent quads to kill the Confessors because there is little danger to a Confessor from one man.'

Kahlan felt the familiar, yet distant anguish of their deaths. Distant, because it seemed so long ago, though it had been hardly a year. For months, in the beginning, she had felt as if she should be dead along with her sister Confessors, and that she had somehow betrayed them by escaping all the traps laid for her. Now, she was the last.

With a flick of her wrist, Cara snapped her Agiel into her fist. 'Even a man, like Lord Rahl, born with the gift? Even a wizard?'

'Even a wizard, and even if, unlike Richard, he knows how to use his power. I not only know how to use mine, I am very experienced at it. I long ago lost count of the number ...'

As Kahlan's words trailed off, Cara considered her Agiel, rolling it in her fingers. 'I guess there is even less than "little" danger – with me there.'

When they reached the richly carpeted and paneled corridor they were seeking, it was thick with soldiers and bristling with steel from swords, axes, and pikes. The man was being held in a small, elegant reading room close to the rather simple one Richard liked to use for meeting with officers and for studying the journal he had found in the Wizard's Keep. The soldiers hadn't wanted to risk an escape attempt and had simply stuffed the man in the room nearest to the spot they found him, pinning him down until it could be decided what was to be done.

Kahlan gently took the elbow of a soldier to urge him back out of the way. The muscles of his bare arm felt as hard as iron. His pike, pointed toward the closed door, could hardly have been more steady had it been embedded in granite. There had to be fifty pikes likewise aimed at the silent door. More men, gripping swords or axes, hunkered beneath the pike points.

The guard turned as Kahlan tugged on his arm. 'Let me through, soldier.'

The man gave way. Others glanced back and began moving aside. Cara shouldered her way ahead of Kahlan, pushing men out of the way. They did so reluctantly, not out of disrespect,

12

but out of concern for the danger that waited beyond the door. Even as they moved aside, they kept their weapons pointed toward the thick oak door.

Inside, the windowless, dimly lit room smelled of leather and sweat. A lanky man squatted on the edge of an embroidered footstool. He seemed too spare, should he make the wrong move, to permit all the steel aimed at him to find a virgin patch to penetrate. His young eyes dithered among the steel and grim glares until he caught sight of Kahlan's approaching white dress. His tongue darted out to wet his lips as he looked up expectantly.

When the burly soldiers in leather and chain mail behind him saw Kahlan and Cara forcing their way into the room, one of them landed the side of his boot on the small of the young man's back, pitching him forward.

'Kneel, you filthy cur.'

The young man, dressed in an outsized soldier's uniform that looked to have been scrounged together from dissimilar sources, peered up at Kahlan, then over his shoulder at the man who had kicked him. He ducked his head of disheveled dark hair and shielded it with a gangly arm, expecting a blow.

'That's enough,' Kahlan said in a quietly authoritative tone. 'Cara and I wish to speak with him. All of you, wait outside, please.'

The soldiers balked, reluctant to lift a weapon from the young man cowering on the floor.

'You heard her,' Cara said. 'Out.'

'But –' an officer began.

'You doubt that a Mord-Sith is capable of handling this one scrawny man? Now, go wait outside.'

Kahlan was surprised that Cara hadn't raised her voice. Mord-Sith didn't have to raise their voices to get people to follow their orders, but still it surprised her, considering Cara's nervousness over the young man before them. The men began withdrawing, turning sideways to eye the intruder on the floor as they filed out the door. The knuckles of the officer's fist around his sword hilt were white. As he backed out last, he gently closed the door with his other hand.

The young man looked up from under his arm to the two

women standing three strides away. 'Are you going to have me killed?'

Kahlan didn't answer the question directly. 'We have come to talk with you. I am Kahlan Amnell, the Mother Confessor –'

'Mother Confessor!' He straightened on his knees. A boyish grin swept onto his face. 'Why, you're beautiful! I never expected you to be so beautiful.'

He put a hand to a knee and began to rise. Cara's Agiel was instantly at the ready.

'Stay where you are.'

He froze, staring at the red Agiel before his face, and then lowered the knee back onto the fringe of the crimson carpet. Lamps on the fluted mahogany pilasters supporting shallow pediments over bookcases to each side of the room cast flickering light across his bony face. He was hardly more than a boy.

'Can I have my weapons back, please? I need my sword. If I can't have that, then I'd like my knife, at least.'

Cara heaved an irritated sigh, but Kahlan spoke first. 'You are in a very precarious position, young man. None of us is in the mood to be indulgent if this is some kind of prank.'

He nodded earnestly. 'I understand. I'm not playing a game. I swear.'

'Then tell me what you said to the soldiers.'

His grin returned as he lifted a hand, gesturing casually toward the door. 'Well, like I was telling those men when I was –'

Fists at her side, Kahlan advanced a stride. 'I told you, this is no game! You're only alive by my grace! I want to know what you're doing here, and I want to know right now! Tell me what you said!'

The young man blinked. 'I'm an assassin, sent by Emperor Jagang. I'm here to kill Richard Rahl. Can you direct me to him, please?'

CHAPTER 2

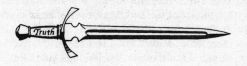

'Now,' Cara said in a dangerous voice, 'can I kill him?'

The incongruous nature of this harmless-looking, skinny young man, kneeling, seemingly helpless, in enemy territory, surrounded by hundreds, thousands of brutish D'Haran soldiers, saying so openly and confidently that he intended to assassinate Richard, had Kahlan's heart hammering against her ribs.

No one was this foolish.

She realized, only after the fact, that she had retreated a step. She ignored Cara's question and kept her attention riveted on the young man.

'And just how do you think you could accomplish such a task?'

'Well,' he said in an offhanded manner as he exhaled, 'I had designs on using my sword, or if I must, my knife.' His smile returned, but it was no longer boyish. His eyes had taken on a steely set that belied his young face. 'That's why I need them back, you see.'

'You'll not be getting your weapons back.'

Disdain powered the dismissive shrug of his shoulders. 'No matter. I have other ways to kill him.'

'You'll not be killing Richard; you have my word on that. Your only hope, now, is to cooperate and tell us everything of your plan. How did you get in here?'

His smirk mocked her. 'Walked. Walked right in. No one paid me any mind. They're not too smart, your men.'

'They're smart enough to have you under their swords,' Cara pointed out.

He ignored her. His eyes remained locked on Kahlan's.

'And if we don't let you have your sword and knife back,' she asked, 'then what?'

'Then things will get messy. Richard Rahl will only suffer greatly. That's why Emperor Jagang sent me: to offer him the mercy of a quick death. The emperor is a man of compassion, and wishes to avoid any undue suffering; he is basically a man of peace, the dream walker, but also one of iron determination.

'I'm afraid I'll have to be killing you, too, Mother Confessor: to spare you the suffering of what's to come if you resist. I have to admit, though, that I don't like the idea of killing such a beautiful woman.' The grin widened. 'Rather a waste.'

Kahlan found his confidence grating. To hear him claim that the dream walker was compassionate turned her stomach. She knew better.

'What suffering?'

He spread his hands. 'I am but a grain of sand. The emperor does not share his plans with me. I am but simply sent to do his bidding. His bidding is that you and Richard are to be eliminated. If you don't let me kill him mercifully, then Richard will be destroyed. I'm told that it won't be pleasant, so why don't you just let me get it over with?'

'You must be dreaming,' Cara said.

His gaze shifted to the Mord-Sith. 'Dreaming? Maybe you're dreaming. Maybe I'm your worst nightmare.'

'I don't have nightmares,' Cara said. 'I give them.'

'Really?' he taunted. 'In that ridiculous outfit? What are you pretending to be, anyway? Maybe you're dressed like that to scare the birds away from the spring planting?'

Kahlan realized that the man didn't know what a Mord-Sith was, but she wondered how she could ever have thought he looked hardly more than a boy; his demeanor was one of age and experience. This was no boy. The air crackled with peril. Remarkably, Cara only smiled.

Kahlan's breathing stilled when she realized the man was standing, and she couldn't recall seeing him come to his feet.

His gaze shifted, and one of the lamps went dark. The

remaining lamp cast harsh, flickering light against one side of his face, letting the other side hide in shadow, but, for Kahlan, that act had brought his nature, his true threat, out of the shadows.

This man commanded the gift.

Her resolve to spare a possible innocent unnecessary violence evaporated with the heat of need to protect Richard. This man had been given a chance; now he was going to confess all he knew – he was going to confess it to a Confessor.

She had but to touch him, and it would be over.

Kahlan had walked among the thousands of corpses of innocent people slaughtered by the Order. When she had seen the women and children in Ebinissia, butchered at Jagang's command, she had sworn undying vengeance against the Imperial Order. This man had proven himself to be part of the Imperial Order, and the enemy of free people. He did the dream walker's bidding.

She focused on the familiar flush of magic deep within herself, always at the ready. A Confessor's magic wasn't released so much as her restraint on it was simply withdrawn. The act was faster even than thought. It was the lightning of instinct.

No Confessor enjoyed using her power to destroy a person's mind, but unlike some Confessors, Kahlan didn't hate what she did, what she was born to; it was simply part of who she was. She didn't maliciously use what she was given, but used her magic to protect others. She was at peace with herself, with what she was and what she could do.

Richard was the first to see her for herself, and care about her despite her power. He didn't irrationally fear the unknown, fear what she was. Instead, he had come to know her, and to love her, Confessor's power and all. For that reason only, he could be with her without her power destroying him when they shared their love.

She intended to use that power, now, to protect Richard, and for that reason it was as close as she ever came to valuing her ability. She had but to touch this man and the threat would be eliminated. Retribution was at hand for a willing minion of Emperor Jagang.

Keeping her gaze firmly fixed on the man, Kahlan held up an admonishing finger to Cara. 'He's mine. Leave this to me.'

But when his squinting gaze sought the remaining lamp, Cara swept between them. The air cracked as she backhanded him with her armored glove. Kahlan nearly screamed in rage at the interference.

Sprawled across the carpet, the man sat up, looking genuinely surprised. Blood ran down his chin from a split in his lower lip. His look changed to genuine displeasure.

Cara towered over him. 'What is your name?' Kahlan couldn't believe that Cara, who had always professed to fear magic, seemed to be deliberately provoking a man who had just shown his command of it.

He rolled away from her and into a crouch. His eyes were on Kahlan, but he spoke to Cara. 'I don't have time for court buffoons.'

With a smile, his gaze flicked to the lamp. The room plunged into darkness.

Kahlan dove for the spot on the floor where he hunkered. She had but to touch him and it would be over.

She caught only air before hitting the empty floor. In the pitch black, she wasn't sure which way he had darted. She snatched wildly, trying to net a part of him. She needed but to touch him, and even his thick clothes wouldn't protect him. She seized an arm, and only an instant before releasing her power realized that it was the leather Cara wore.

'Where are you!' Cara growled. 'You can't get away. Give it up.'

Kahlan scrambled across the carpet. Power or not, they needed light, or they were going to be in a great deal of trouble. She found the bookcase against the wall and felt along its lower ledge until she saw a faint sliver of light coming from beneath the door. Men were banging on the other side, calling out, wanting to know if there was trouble.

Her fingers skimmed up the edge of the molded stile of the door, toward the handle, as she lurched to her feet. She stepped on the hem of her dress and tripped, stumbling forward, landing on her elbows with a bone-jarring thud.

Something heavy smashed into the door where she had almost stood a moment before, and crashed down onto her back. The man laughed in the darkness. As she flailed to shove the thing off, her arms whacked painfully against the sharp edges of the stretcher bars of a chair's legs. She grappled an upholstered armrest and rolled the chair off to the side.

Kahlan heard the air driven from Cara's lungs with a grunt as she slammed into a bookcase on the other side of the room. The men on the other side of the door pounded into it, trying to break it down. The door wasn't budging.

As books across the room were still tumbling and thudding to the floor, Kahlan sprang up and groped for the handle. Her knuckles struck the cold metal of the lever. She slapped her hand over it.

With a shriek, she was thrown back from a sudden flash and landed on her bottom. Like sparks from a flaming log struck with a poker, a shower of flashes from the handle filled the air. Her fingers stung and tingled from touching the shield. Small wonder the men couldn't open the door. As she regained her feet, recovering from the shock, Kahlan could see again by the flickering sparkles of light that still slowly drifted toward the floor.

Suddenly Cara could see, too. She snatched a book and flung it at the man near the center of the small room. He ducked into a squat.

Quick as a slap, Cara spun, catching him off guard. The air resounded with a hard thud as her boot nailed his jaw. The blow drove him backward. Kahlan took aim to leap for him before all the sparks extinguished and it went dark again.

'You die first!' he railed in rage at Cara. 'I'll have no more of your trifling interference! You'll taste my power!'

The air at his fingertips lit with glimmering flashes as he leveled his full attention on Cara. Kahlan had to deal with the threat now, before anything else went wrong.

But before she could leap for him, his curled fingers twitched up. With a contemptuous sneer, he thrust one hand toward Cara.

Kahlan expected Cara to be the one on the floor next. Instead, the young man crumpled with a cry. He tried to stand, but collapsed with a shriek, hugging himself as if he had been stabbed in the gut. The room went black again.

Kahlan reached for the door lever, taking a chance that

whatever Cara had done to him had broken his shield. Wincing against the pain she feared might still be waiting, she seized the handle. The shield was gone. Relieved, she twisted the lever and yanked the door open. Light from behind the crowd of soldiers pierced into the dark room. Confounded faces peered in.

Kahlan didn't need a roomful of men getting themselves killed while trying to save her from things they didn't understand. She shoved the closest man back.

'He has the gift! Stay out!' She knew that D'Harans feared magic. They depended on the Lord Rahl to fight magic. They were the steel against steel, they often said, and Lord Rahl was supposed to be the magic against magic. 'Give me a lamp!'

Men to each side simultaneously snatched lamps from brackets beside the door and held them out. Kahlan grabbed one and kicked the door shut as she turned back to the room. She didn't want a pack of muscle-bound, weapon-wielding men to get in her way.

In the wavering glow from the lamp, Kahlan saw Cara squat down on the crimson carpet beside the man. He clutched his arms across his abdomen as he vomited blood. Her red leather outfit creaked as she rested her forearms on her knees. She was rolling her Agiel in her fingers, waiting.

Once his retching had ceased, Cara snatched a fistful of his hair. Her long blond braid slid across the back of her broad shoulders as she leaned closer.

'That was a big mistake. A *very* big mistake,' she said with silky satisfaction. 'You should never have tried to use your magic against a Mord-Sith. You had it right for a moment, but then you let me make you angry enough to use your magic. Who's the fool now?'

'What's … a … Mord-Sith?' he managed between gasps.

Cara twisted his head upward until he cried out. 'Your worst nightmare. The purpose of a Mord-Sith is to eliminate threats like you.

'I now command your magic. It's mine to use, and you, my pet, are helpless to do anything about it, as you will soon learn. You should have tried to strangle me, or beat me to death, or to run, but you should never, ever, have tried to use magic against me. Once you use your magic against a Mord-Sith, it's hers.'

Kahlan stood transfixed. That was what a Mord-Sith had done to Richard. That was how he had been captured.

Cara pressed her Agiel against the man's ribs. He shivered as he screamed. Blood soaked through his tunic in a spreading stain.

'Now, when I ask a question,' she said in a quiet, authoritative tone, 'I expect an answer. Do you understand?'

He remained silent. She twisted the Agiel. Kahlan winced when she heard his rib pop. He flinched and gasped, holding his breath, unable to scream.

Kahlan felt as if she were frozen in place, unable to move a muscle. Richard had told her that Denna, the Mord-Sith who had captured him, had liked to crack his ribs. It made each breath agony, and screaming, which she soon provoked, excruciating torture. It also left the victim that much more helpless.

Cara rose. 'Stand.'

The man staggered to his feet.

'You are about to find out why I wear bloodred leather.' Unleashing a mighty swing, launched with an angry cry, Cara clouted his face with her armored fist. As he went down, blood sprayed across the bookcase. As soon as he hit the floor, she straddled him, a boot to each side of his hips.

'I can see what you're envisioning,' Cara told him. 'I saw the vision of what you want to do to me. Naughty boy.' She stomped a boot down on his sternum. 'That was the least of what you will suffer for that thought. You had better learn real fast to keep ideas of resistance out of your mind. Got it?'

She bent and drove her Agiel into his gut. 'Got it?'

His scream sent a shiver up Kahlan's spine. She was sickened by what she was watching, having once felt the profoundly painful touch of an Agiel, but worse, knowing that this was what had been done to Richard, and yet she didn't make a move to stop it.

She had offered this man mercy. If he had had his way, he would have killed Richard. He had promised to kill her, too, but it was that threat against Richard that kept her silent, and prevented her from stopping Cara.

'Now,' Cara said with a sneer. She jabbed her Agiel against his cracked rib. 'What is your name?'

'Marlin Pickard!' He tried to blink away the tears. A sheen of sweat covered his face. Blood frothed at his mouth as he panted.

She pressed her Agiel against his groin. Marlin's feet kicked out helplessly as he wailed.

'The next time I ask a question, don't make me wait for an answer. And you will address me as Mistress Cara.'

'Cara,' Kahlan said in a quiet tone, still seeing the vision of Richard in place of the man, 'there is no need to …'

Cara looked over her shoulder, glaring with cold blue eyes. Kahlan turned away and with trembling fingers wiped a tear as it rolled down her cheek. She lifted the glass chimney of the lamp on the wall and used the one she held to light it. When the wick took to flame, she set her lamp down on a side table and replaced its chimney. It was frightening to see the cold look in those Mord-Sith eyes. Her heart pounded at the thought of how many weeks Richard had seen only cold eyes like that looking back as he begged for mercy.

Kahlan turned back to the pair. 'We need answers, nothing more.'

'I'm getting answers.'

Kathlan nodded. 'I understand, but we don't need the screams along with them. We don't torture people.'

'Torture? I have not yet even begun to torture him.' Cara straightened, casting a glance to the shivering man at her feet. 'And if he had managed to kill Lord Rahl first? Would you wish me to leave him be, then?'

'Yes.' Kahlan met the woman's eyes. 'And then I would have done worse to him myself. Worse than you could even conceive of. But he didn't hurt Richard.'

A cunning smile curled the corners of Cara's mouth. 'He intended it. The canon of the spirits says that intent is guilt. Failure to successfully carry out the intent does not absolve the guilt.'

'The spirits also mark a distinction between intent and deed. It was my intent to take care of him, in my way. Was it your intent to disobey my direct order?'

Cara flicked her blond braid back over her shoulder. 'It was my intent to protect you and Lord Rahl. I have succeeded.'

'I told you to let me handle it.'

'Hesitation can be the end of you … or those you care about.' A haunted look passed across Cara's face. Iron quickly repossessed her countenance. 'I have learned never to hesitate.'

'Is that why you were provoking him? To get him to attack you with his magic?'

With the heel of her hand, Cara wiped the blood from a deep cut on her cheek – a cut Marlin had given her when he had struck her and slammed her into the bookcase. She stepped closer. 'Yes.' She took a long lick of the blood from her hand while watching Kahlan's eyes. 'A Mord-Sith can't take a person's magic unless they attack us with it.'

'I thought you feared magic.'

Cara tugged the sleeve of her leather, straightening it down her arm. 'We do, unless it is specifically used by the one who commands it to attack us. Then it's ours.'

'You always claim not to know anything about magic, and yet now you command his? You can use his magic?'

Cara glanced down at the man groaning on the floor. 'No. I can't use it, like he uses it, but I can turn it against him – hurt him with his own magic.' Her brow twitched. 'Sometimes, we feel a bit of it, but we don't understand it the way Lord Rahl understands it, and so we can't use it. Except to give them pain.'

Kahlan couldn't reconcile such contradictions. 'How?'

She was struck by how much Cara's emotionless expression was like a Confessor's face, the face Kahlan's mother had taught her, showing nothing of the inner feelings about what had to be done.

'Our minds are linked,' Cara explained, 'through the magic, so I can see what he's thinking when he is thinking of hurting me, or fighting back, or disobeying my orders, because it contradicts my wishes. Since we are linked to their minds through their magic, our will to hurt them makes it happen.' She looked down at Marlin. He suddenly cried out anew in agony. 'See?'

'I see. Now stop it. If he refuses to give us answers, then

you can … do what it takes, but I won't sanction doing anything that isn't required to protect Richard.'

Kahlan looked up from Marlin's torment to Cara's cold blue eyes. She spoke before she thought. 'Did you know Denna?'

'Everyone knew Denna.'

'And was she as good at … at torturing people as you?'

'Me?' Cara said with a laugh. 'No one was as good at it as Denna. That's why she was Darken Rahl's favorite. I could hardly believe the things she could do to a man. Why, she could …'

With a glance at the Agiel hanging at Kahlan's neck – Denna's Agiel – Cara suddenly caught the meaning behind Kahlan's questions.

'That was in the past. We were bonded to Darken Rahl. We did as we were commanded. We are bonded to Richard, now. We would never hurt him. We would die to keep anyone from hurting Lord Rahl.' Her tone lowered to a whisper. 'Lord Rahl not only killed Denna, but he also forgave her for what she did to him.'

Kahlan nodded. 'So he did. But I have not. Though I understand how she did as she was trained and commanded, and her spirit has been a comfort and an aid to both of us, and I appreciate the sacrifices she has since made on our behalf, in my heart I can't forgive her for the horrifying things she did to the man I love.'

Cara studied Kahlan's eyes a long moment. 'I understand. If you ever hurt Lord Rahl, I would never forgive you, either. Nor would I ever grant you mercy.'

Kahlan held the woman's gaze. 'Likewise. It is said that, for a Mord-Sith, there is no worse death to be had than by the touch of a Confessor.'

A slow smile came to Cara's lips. 'So I have been told.'

'It's fortunate we're on the same side. As I've said, there are things I won't, I can't, forgive. I love Richard more than life itself.'

'Every Mord-Sith knows that the worst pain comes from one you love.'

'Richard need never fear that pain.'

Cara seemed to consider her words carefully. 'Darken Rahl never had to fear that kind of pain; he never loved a woman.

Lord Rahl does. I have noticed that where love is concerned, things sometimes have a way of changing.'

So that was the heart of the matter.

'Cara, I could no more hurt Richard than could you. I would lay down my life first. I love him.'

'As do I,' Cara said, 'if in a different way, but with no less ferocity. Lord Rahl freed us. In his place, anyone else would have had every Mord-Sith put to death. He instead has given us a chance to live up to his expectations.'

Cara shifted her weight to her other foot as her eyes withdrew their cold assessment. 'Perhaps Richard is the only one of us to understand the good spirits' principles – that we can't truly love until we forgive another their worst crimes against us.'

Kahlan felt her face flush at Cara's words. She never thought of a Mord-Sith as having such depth of understanding in matters of compassion. 'Was Denna a friend?' Cara nodded. 'And has your heart forgiven Richard for killing her?'

'Yes, but that's different,' Cara admitted. 'I understand the way you feel about Denna. I don't blame you. In your place, I would feel the same.'

Kahlan stared off. 'When I told Denna – her spirit – that I couldn't forgive her, she said that she understood, and that the only forgiveness she needed had already been granted. She told me that she loved Richard – that even in death she loved him.' Just as Richard had seen in Kahlan the woman behind the magic, he had seen in Denna the person behind the fearsome persona of a Mord-Sith. Kahlan could understand Denna's feelings at having someone finally see her for herself. 'Perhaps the forgiveness of one you love is the only thing in life that really matters – the only thing that can truly heal your heart, heal your soul.'

Kahlan watched her finger as she traced the scoop of a curled leaf carved in the banding of the tabletop. 'But I could never forgive anyone who hurt him.'

'And have you forgiven me?'

Kahlan looked up. 'For what?'

Cara's fist tightened on her Agiel. Kahlan knew that it hurt a Mord-Sith to hold her Agiel in her hand – part of the paradox of being a giver of pain. 'For being Mord-Sith.'

'Why should I have to forgive you that?'

Cara looked away. 'Because if Darken Rahl had commanded me instead of Denna to take Richard, I would have been as merciless as she. As would Berdine, or Raina, or any of the rest.'

'I told you, the spirits mark a distinction between the might have been and the deed. So do I. You cannot be held responsible for what others have done to you, any more than I can be held answerable because I was born a Confessor, and no more than Richard can be held guilty because that murderous Darken Rahl fathered him.'

Still Cara didn't look up. 'But will you ever truly trust us?'

'You have already proven yourselves, in Richard's eyes, and in mine. You are not Denna, nor responsible for her choices.' With a thumb, Kahlan wiped oozing blood from Cara's cheek. 'Cara, if I didn't trust you, all of you, would I allow Berdine and Raina, *two* of you, to be alone with Richard right now?'

Cara glanced again to Denna's Agiel. 'In the battle with the Blood of the Fold, I saw the way you fought to protect Lord Rahl, as well as the people of the city. To be Mord-Sith is to understand that you must sometimes be merciless. Though you are not Mord-Sith, I have seen that you understand this. You are a worthy guardian to Lord Rahl. You are the only woman I know worthy of wearing an Agiel.

'Though to you that may sound reprehensible, in my eyes, it is an honor that you wear an Agiel. Its ultimate purpose is to protect our master.'

Kahlan offered a sincere smile, understanding Cara just a little bit better than she had before. She wondered what the woman behind the appellation had been like before she was captured and trained to become a Mord-Sith. Richard had told her that it was a horror far beyond anything that had been done to him.

'In my eyes, too, because Richard gave it to me. I am his protector, as are you. In that way, we are sisters of the Agiel.'

Cara smiled her approval.

'Does this mean that you'll follow our orders for a change?' Kahlan asked.

'We always follow your orders.'

With a wry smile, Kahlan shook her head.

Cara nodded toward the man on the floor. 'He will answer your questions, as I promised you before, Mother Confessor. I won't practice my skills on him any more than is necessary.'

Kahlan squeezed Cara's arm in sorrow and sympathy for the warped role the woman's life had been twisted into by others. 'Thank you, Cara.'

Kahlan turned her attention to Marlin and the problem at hand. 'Let's try it again. What were your plans?'

He glared up at her. Cara shoved him with a foot.

'You answer truthfully, or I'll start finding some nice, tender places for my Agiel. Understand?'

'Yes.'

Cara squatted down, fanning her Agiel before his face. 'Yes, Mistress Cara.' The sudden threat in her tone seemed to annul everything she had just said. It frightened even Kahlan.

Wide-eyed, he swallowed. 'Yes, Mistress Cara.'

'That's better. Now, answer the Mother Confessor's question.'

'My plans were as I told you: to kill Richard Rahl and you.'

'How long ago did Jagang give you these orders?'

'Nearly two weeks.'

Well, there was that. It could be that Jagang had been killed at the Palace of the Prophets when Richard destroyed it. That was what they had been hoping, anyway. Perhaps he had given the orders before he was killed.

'What else?' Kahlan asked.

'Nothing else. I was to use my talent to get in here and kill the both of you, that's all.'

Cara landed a kick on his cracked rib. 'Don't lie to us!'

Kahlan gently pushed Cara back and knelt beside the choking, gasping young man.

'Marlin, don't mistake my distaste for torture as a lack of resolve. If you don't start telling me what I want to know,' she whispered, 'I'm going to go for a long walk and then to dinner and I'm going to leave you in here all alone with Cara. Crazy as she is, I'll leave you alone with her. And then, when I come back, if you still think to hold out on me, I'm going to use *my* power on you, and you can't even imagine how much worse that will be. Cara can't even come close to what I can do; she can use your magic and your mind. I can destroy it. Is that what you want?'

He shook his head as he clutched his ribs. 'Please,' he begged, tears welling up again, 'don't. I'll answer your questions ... but I don't really know anything. Emperor Jagang comes to me in my dreams and tells me what to do. I know the cost of failure. I do as I'm told.' He paused to gasp a sob. 'He told me to ... to come here and kill you both. He told me to find a soldier's uniform, and weapons, and to come kill you both. He uses wizards, and sorceresses, to do his bidding.'

Kahlan stood, puzzling over Marlin's words. He seemed to have reverted to being hardly more than a boy. Something was missing, but she couldn't imagine what it could be. It made sense on the surface – Jagang sending an assassin – but something deeper didn't tally. She paced to the side table with the lamp and leaned a hip against it. With her back to Marlin, she rubbed her throbbing temples.

Cara inched close. 'Are you all right?'

Kahlan nodded. 'This worry is just giving me a headache, that's all.'

'Maybe you could have Lord Rahl kiss it and make it better.'

Kahlan chuckled silently at Cara's concerned frown. 'That would work.' She waved her hands in the air as if shooing a gnat, trying to chase away the doubts. 'It doesn't make any sense.'

'The dream walker trying to kill his enemy doesn't make sense?'

'Well, think about it.' She glanced over her shoulder to see Marlin hugging his ribs and rocking on the floor. His eyes, even when they were filled with terror, and even, as now, when he wasn't looking her way, for some reason made her skin crawl. She turned back to Cara and lowered her voice. 'Surely Jagang had to know that one man, even a wizard, would fail at such a task. Richard would recognize a man with the gift, and besides, there are too many people here who would be only too ready to kill an intruder.'

'But still, with his gift, he might have a chance. Jagang wouldn't care if the man was killed. He has an abundance of others to do his bidding.'

Kahlan's thoughts flicked about, trying to pick out the nettle of a reason behind her itching doubt.

'Even if he managed to kill some of them with his magic, there are still too many. A whole army of mriswith failed to kill Richard. He can recognize one with the gift, with magic, as a threat. He doesn't know how to command his magic, much as you don't understand how to control Marlin's, beyond giving him pain with it, but his guard would be up, at the least.

'This just doesn't make any sense. Jagang is far from stupid; there has to be more to it. He must have some plan to this. Something more than we're seeing.'

Cara clasped her hands behind her back as she took a deep breath. She turned. 'Marlin.' His head came up, his eyes at attention. 'What was Jagang's plan?'

'To have me kill Richard Rahl and the Mother Confessor.'

'What else?' Kahlan asked. 'What more was there to his plan?'

His eyes flooded. 'I don't know. I swear. I told you as he ordered me. I was to get a soldier's uniform and weapons so I would look like I belonged and could get close. I was to kill you both.'

Kahlan wiped a hand across her face. 'We're not asking the right questions.'

'I don't know what else there could be. He has admitted the worst of it. He told us his goal. What more could there be?'

'I don't know, but there's something still itching at me.' Kahlan sighed in resignation. 'Maybe Richard can reason this out. He is the Seeker of Truth, after all. He'll figure out what it means. Richard will know the right questions to ask so that ...'

Kahlan's head suddenly came up, her eyes wide. She advanced a long stride toward the man on the floor.

'Marlin, did Jagang also tell you to announce yourself when you arrived?'

'Yes. Once inside the palace, I was to give my reason for being here.'

Kahlan stiffened. She snatched Cara's arm and pulled her close while keeping her eyes on Marlin. 'Maybe we shouldn't tell Richard about this. It's too dangerous.'

'I have Marlin's power. He's helpless.'

Kahlan's gaze darted about, hardly hearing what Cara had

said. 'We have to put him somewhere safe. This room won't do.' She put a thumbnail between her teeth.

Cara frowned. 'This room is as safe as anywhere. He can't get away. He's safe in here.'

Kahlan took her thumb from her mouth as she stared at the man rocking on the floor.

'No. We have to find someplace safer. I think we've made a big mistake. I think we're in a lot of trouble.'

CHAPTER 3

'Let me just kill him,' Cara said. 'I have but to touch him in the right place with my Agiel and his heart will stop. He won't suffer.'

For the first time, Kahlan seriously considered Cara's oft-repeated request. Though she had had to kill people before, and had ordered the execution of others, she dismissed the impulse. She had to think this through. For all she knew, that could be Jagang's true plan, though she couldn't imagine what good it would gain him. But he had to have some scheme to what he had ordered. He wasn't stupid; he had to know that Marlin would be captured, at the least.

'No,' Kahlan said. 'We don't know enough yet. For all we know, that could be the worst thing we could do. We can't do anything else until we think it through carefully. We've already walked into a swamp without pausing to think about where we were going.'

Cara sighed at the familiar refusal. 'Then what do you wish to do?'

'I don't know yet. Jagang had to know he would be captured, at the least, yet he ordered it. Why? We have to figure this out. Until we do, we have to put him somewhere safe, where he can't escape and hurt anyone.'

'Mother Confessor,' Cara said with exaggerated patience, 'he cannot escape. I have control of his power. Believe me, I know how to control a person when I have domination over their magic. I have had an abundance of experience. He is incapable of doing anything against my wishes. Here, let me show you.'

She threw open the door. Surprised men reached for weapons as they gazed around the room in silent, professional appraisal. With the extra light from beyond the door, Kahlan could see the true extent of the mess. A spray of blood crossed the bookcase at an angle. Blood soaked the crimson carpet, the spongy, reddish blotch extending past the perimeter of gold banding. Marlin's face was a bloody sight. The side of his beige tunic was dark with a wet stain.

'You,' Cara said. 'Give me your sword.' The blond-haired soldier drew his weapon and handed it over without hesitation. 'Now,' she announced, 'all of you listen to me. I'm going to give the Mother Confessor, here, a demonstration of the power of a Mord-Sith. If any of you go against my orders, you will answer to me' – she gestured back to Marlin – 'just like he did.'

After another glance at the miserable man on the floor, some men nodded and the rest voiced their consent.

Cara pointed with the sword at Marlin. 'If he can make it to the door, you all are to let him go – he is to have his freedom.' The men grumbled objections. 'Don't argue with me!'

The D'Haran soldiers fell silent. A Mord-Sith was trouble enough, but when she had command of a person's magic she was something altogether beyond trouble: she was dealing in magic, and they had no desire to stick their finger in a cauldron of dark sorcery stirred by an angry Mord-Sith.

Cara strode over to Marlin and held the sword down to him, hilt first. 'Take it.' Marlin hesitated, then snatched the sword when she frowned in warning.

Cara looked up at Kahlan. 'We always let our captives keep their weapons. It's a constant reminder to them that they are helpless, that even their weapons will do them no good against us.'

'I know,' Kahlan said in a small voice. 'Richard told me.'

Cara motioned Marlin to his feet. When he didn't move fast enough for her, she punched his cracked rib.

'What are you waiting for! Get up! Now, go stand over there.'

After he had moved off the carpet, she grasped the corner

and flung it aside. She pointed at the polished wood floor and snapped her fingers. Marlin scurried to the spot, grunting in pain with each step.

Cara snatched him by the scruff of his neck and bent him over. 'Spit.'

Marlin coughed blood and spat on the floor at his feet. Cara hauled him up straight, seized the neck of his tunic, and yanked his face close.

She gritted her teeth. 'Now, you listen. You know the kind of pain I can give you if you displease me. Do you need another demonstration?'

He vigorously shook his head. 'No, Mistress Cara.'

'Good boy. Now, when I tell you to do something, that is what I wish you to do. If you do otherwise, if you go against my orders, my wishes, your magic will twist your guts like a washrag. As long as you continue to go against my wishes, the pain will only get worse. I won't let the magic kill you, but you will wish otherwise. You will beg me to kill you in order to escape the pain. I don't grant my pets' requests for death.'

Marlin's face had gone ashen.

'Now, stand on that spot of your spit.' Marlin moved both feet onto the red splat. Cara gripped his jaw in one hand and pointed her Agiel at his face.

'My wish is for you to stand right there, on that spot of your spit, until I tell you otherwise. You are never to so much as lift a finger to harm me, or anyone else, ever again. That is my wish. Do you understand? Do you fully understand my wishes?'

He nodded, as best he could the way her hand clamped his jaw. 'Yes, Mistress Cara. I would never hurt you – I swear. You want me to stand on my spit until you give me permission to do otherwise.' Tears welled up anew. 'I won't move, I swear. Please don't hurt me.'

Cara shoved his face away. 'You disgust me. Men who break as easily as you disgust me. I've had girls last longer under my Agiel,' she muttered. She pointed behind. 'Those men won't hurt you. They will do nothing to stop you. If you get to the door, against my wishes, you are free and the pain will be gone.' She glared at the soldiers. 'You all heard me, didn't you? If he reaches the door, he's free.' The soldiers nodded. 'If he kills me, he's free.'

This time they didn't agree until Cara yelled her order again. Cara turned her hot glare to Kahlan. 'That includes you. If he kills me, or if he makes the door, he's free.'

No matter how improbable, Kahlan wouldn't agree to such a thing. Marlin wanted to kill Richard. 'Why are you doing this?'

'Because you need to understand. You need to trust my word.'

Kahlan forced out a breath. 'Get on with it,' she said, without agreeing to the terms.

Cara turned her back to Marlin and folded her arms. 'You know my wishes, my pet. If you wish to escape, this is your chance. You reach the door, and you're free. If you want to kill me for what I've done to you, now's your chance for that, too.

'You know,' she added, 'I don't think I've seen nearly enough of your blood. When we're done with all this nonsense, I'm going to take you somewhere private, where the Mother Confessor won't be around to intercede on your behalf, I'm going to spend the rest of the afternoon and night punishing you with my Agiel, just because I'm in the mood. I'm going to make you regret the day you were born.'

She shrugged. 'Unless, of course, you kill me, or escape.'

The soldiers stood mute. The room exuded a heavy silence as Cara waited with her arms folded. Marlin carefully looked around, studying the soldiers, Kahlan, and Cara's back. His fingers worked on the hilt of the sword, drawing it tighter into his grip. His eyes narrowed as he considered.

Watching Cara's back, he finally took a small, tentative step to the side.

To Kahlan, it looked as if an invisible club had whacked him in the gut. He doubled over with a grunt. A low groan wheezed from his throat. With a cry of effort, he dived for the door.

He hit the floor screaming. He clutched his abdomen with both arms as he writhed. With fingers curled in agony, he threw himself out flat on the floor and tried to claw his way to the door. It was still a goodly distance. Each inch he gained racked him with ever worse convulsions of pain. Kahlan winced at his panting screams.

In a last, desperate effort, he snatched up the sword again and staggered to his feet, straightening partially, lifting the sword above his head. Kahlan tensed. Even if he couldn't make his arms do his bidding, he could fall and cleave Cara.

The risk to Cara was too great. Kahlan took an urgent step forward as Marlin bellowed and tried to bring the sword down to hack at Cara. Cara, watching Kahlan, held up an admonishing finger, stopping Kahlan where she stood.

Behind her, Marlin's sword clattered to the floor as he crumpled, holding his stomach as he shrieked. He crashed to the floor, his distress obviously growing precipitously with each moment as he writhed on the polished wood floor like a fish out of water.

'What did I tell you, Marlin?' Cara asked in a quiet voice. 'What are my wishes?'

He seemed to grasp the meaning of her words as if they were from a person yelling as he threw a lifeline to a drowning man. His frantic gaze hunted the floor. Finally, he saw it. He clawed his way to the spot of his spit, moving as quickly as the racking pain allowed. At last, he managed to stagger to his feet.

He stood, fists at his side, still shaking and screaming.

'Both feet, Marlin,' Cara said casually.

He looked down and saw that only one foot was on the spit. He jerked the other closer, onto the red spot.

He sagged and finally fell silent. Kahlan felt herself sag with him. His eyes closed, panting, dripping sweat, he stood trembling with the lingering effects of the ordeal.

Cara lifted an eyebrow to Kahlan. 'Understand?'

Kahlan scowled. Cara scooped up the sword and marched it over to the door. As one, the soldiers all backed up a step. She held the sword out, hilt first. Reluctantly, its owner retrieved it.

'Any questions, gentlemen?' Cara asked in an icy voice. 'Good. Now stop banging on the door when I'm busy.' She slammed the heavy door in their faces.

Marlin's lower lip sucked in and out over his teeth with each panting breath. Cara put her face close to his.

'I don't recall giving you permission to close your eyes. Did you hear me say you could close them?'

His eyes opened wide. 'No, Mistress Cara.'

'Then what were they doing closed?'

Marlin's terror quavered through his voice. 'I'm sorry, Mistress Cara. Please forgive me. I won't do it again.'

'Cara.'

She turned, as if she had forgotten Kahlan was even in the room. 'What?'

Kahlan tilted her head in gesture. 'We need to talk.'

'You see?' Cara asked, when she had joined Kahlan at the table with the lamp. 'You see what I mean? He can't hurt anyone. He can't escape. No man has ever escaped a Mord-Sith.'

Kahlan lifted an eyebrow. 'Richard did.'

Cara straightened and let out a noisy breath. 'Lord Rahl is different. This man is no Lord Rahl. Mord-Sith have proven themselves unerring thousands of times. No one but Lord Rahl ever killed his Mistress to reclaim his magic and escape.'

'No matter how improbable, Richard has proven that Mord-Sith aren't infallible. I don't care how many thousands Mord-Sith have subjugated; the fact that one escaped means that it's possible. Cara, I'm not doubting you – it's just that we can't take chances. Something's wrong; why would Jagang throw this lamb in a wolf's lair, and specifically tell him to announce himself?'

'But –'

'It's possible Jagang was killed – he might be dead and we have nothing to fear – but if he's still alive, and anything goes wrong with Marlin, here, it will be Richard who pays the price. Jagang wants Richard dead. Are you so stubborn that you're willing to put Richard at risk for the sake of your pride?'

Cara scratched her neck as she considered. She took a quick glance over her shoulder at Marlin standing on the spot of his spit, his eyes wide open, sweat dripping off the end of his nose.

'What do you want to do? This room has no windows. We can lock and bar the door. Where can we put him that would be safer than this room?'

Kahlan pressed her fingers over the burning ache under her sternum.

'The pit.'

Kahlan twisted her fingers together as she came to a halt before the iron door. Marlin, looking like a frightened puppy, stood silently in the center of a knot of D'Haran soldiers a ways back up the torch-lit hall.

'What's the matter?' Cara asked.

Kahlan flinched. 'What?'

'I asked what was the matter. You look like you're afraid the door is going to bite you.'

Kahlan pulled her hands apart and made herself put them at her sides. 'Nothing.' She turned and lifted the ring with the keys from the iron peg in the coarse stone wall beside the door.

Cara lowered her voice. 'Don't lie to a sister of the Agiel.'

Kahlan mimicked a quick smile of apology. 'The pit is where the condemned await execution. I have a half sister – Cyrilla. She was the queen of Galea. When she was here, when Aydindril fell to the Order, before Richard liberated the city, they threw her in the pit with a gang of about a dozen murderers.'

'*Have* a half sister? She still lives, then?'

Kahlan nodded as the mists of memories swirled before her mind's eye. 'But they had her down there for days. Prince Harold, her brother, my half brother, rescued her when they were taking her to the block to be beheaded, but she's never been the same since. She's withdrawn into herself. On rare occasions she comes out of her stupor, and insists that the people need a queen able to lead them and that I become the queen of Galea in her place. I agreed.' Kahlan paused. 'She screams inconsolably if she comes awake and sees men.'

Cara, hands clasped behind her back, waited without comment.

Kahlan gestured to the door. 'They threw me down there, too.' Her mouth was so dry that it took two attempts before she could swallow. 'With those men who had raped her.' She surfaced from the memories and sneaked a quick glance at

Cara. 'But they didn't do to me as they did to her.' She didn't say how close they had come.

A sly smile came to Cara's lips. 'How many did you kill?'

'I didn't stop to take an exact count as I escaped.' Her brief, flitting smile wouldn't stick. 'But it scared the wits out of me – being down there, alone, with all those beasts.' Kahlan's heart pounded so hard at the memory that it made her sway on her feet.

'Well,' Cara offered, 'do you want to find another place to put Marlin?'

'No.' Kahlan took a purging breath. 'Look, Cara, I'm sorry I'm acting this way.' She peered briefly at Marlin. 'There's something about his eyes. Something strange ...'

She looked back to Cara. 'I'm sorry. It's not like me to be so jittery. You've only known me a short time. I'm not usually so apprehensive. It's just that ... I guess that it's just because it's been so peaceful for the last few days. I've been separated from Richard for so long, and it's been bliss being together. We were hoping Jagang was killed and that the war was ended. We were hoping he was in the Palace of the Prophets when Richard destroyed it ...'

'He still might have been. Marlin said it's been two weeks since Jagang gave him orders. Lord Rahl said Jagang wanted the palace; he was probably with his troops when they stormed it. He's no doubt dead.'

'We can hope. But I'm so afraid for Richard ... I guess it's affecting my judgment. Now that things have come together, I'm terrified that it's going to slip away from me.'

Cara shrugged, as if to dispel Kahlan's need for apology. 'I know how you feel. Now that Lord Rahl has given us our freedom, we have something to fear losing. Maybe that's why I'm so jittery, too.' She flicked her hand toward the door. 'We could find another place. There have to be other places that won't touch painful memories for you.'

'No. Protecting Richard comes above all else. The pit is the safest place in the palace to keep a prisoner. We have no one else down there, now. It's escape-proof. I'm fine.'

Cara lifted an eyebrow. 'Escape-proof? You escaped.'

The memories repressed, Kahlan smiled. With the back of her hand, she gave Cara's stomach a dismissive slap.

'Marlin is no Mother Confessor.' She glanced back up the hall at Marlin. 'But there's something about him – something I can't put my finger on. Something strange. He frightens me, and he shouldn't, not with you controlling his gift.'

'You are right, you shouldn't be concerned. I have complete control of him. No pet has ever slipped from my control. Ever.'

Cara lifted the key ring from Kahlan's hand and unlocked the door. With a tug, it drew open on rusty, squeaking hinges. Dank stench wafted up from the darkness below. The smell clenched Kahlan's stomach muscles with the memories it carried. Cara took a nervous step back.

'There aren't any … rats, down there, are there?'

'Rats?' Kahlan glanced to the dark maw. 'No. There's no way for them to get in. No rats. You'll see.'

Kahlan turned her attention to the soldiers back up the hall, waiting with Marlin, and gestured toward the long ladder resting on its side against the wall opposite the door. Once they had the ladder through the door and it had thudded down in place, Cara snapped her fingers and motioned Marlin forward. He scurried to her without hesitation, anxious to avoid doing anything to displease her.

'Take that torch and get down there,' Cara told him.

Marlin pulled the torch from its rust-encrusted bracket and started down the ladder. With a frown of puzzlement, Cara followed him down into the gloom when Kahlan motioned her to the ladder.

Kahlan turned to the guards. 'Sergeant Collins, you and your men wait up here, please.'

'Are you sure, Mother Confessor?' the sergeant asked.

'Are you eager to be down there, in a small space, with an ill-tempered Mord-Sith, sergeant?'

He hooked a thumb behind his weapons belt as he glanced at the opening into the pit. 'We'll wait up here, as you command.'

Kahlan started backing down the ladder. 'We'll be fine.'

The smooth stone blocks of the walls were so precisely dry-fit that there wasn't so much as a fingernail hold to be had. Looking back over her shoulder, she could see Marlin holding the torch, and Cara, waiting for her nearly twenty feet below.

She carefully put a foot in each rung, mindful not to step on the hem of her dress lest she fall.

'Why are we down here with him?' Cara asked, as Kahlan stepped off the last rung.

Kahlan wiped her hands together, brushing off the grit from the ladder rungs. She took the torch from Marlin and went to the wall before them. She stretched up on her toes and pushed the torch into one of the brackets on the wall. 'Because on the way down here I thought of some more questions to ask him before we leave him here.'

Cara glared at Marlin and pointed to the floor. 'Spit.' She waited. 'Now, stand on it.'

Marlin moved onto the spot, careful to get both feet on it. Cara eyed the empty room, checking the shadows in the corners. Kahlan wondered if she was making sure the place really was free of rats.

'Marlin,' Kahlan said. He licked his lips, waiting for her question. 'When was the last time you received orders from Jagang?'

'Like I told you before, it was about two weeks ago.'

'And he's not sought you out since then?'

'No, Mother Confessor.'

'If he was dead, would you know?'

He didn't hesitate with his answer. 'I don't know. He either comes to me, or he doesn't. I have no way of knowing of him between his calls.'

'How does he come to you?'

'In my dreams.'

'And you've not dreamed of him since you say he last came to you a fortnight ago?'

'No, Mother Confessor.'

Kahlan paced to the wall with the hissing torch and back as she thought. 'You didn't recognize me, when you first saw me.' He shook his head. 'Would you recognize Richard?'

'Yes, Mother Confessor.'

Kahlan frowned. 'How? How would you know him?'

'From the Palace of the Prophets. I was a student there. Richard was brought there by Sister Verna. I knew him from the palace.'

'A student, at the Palace of the Prophets? Then you ... How old are you?'

'Ninety-three, Mother Confessor.'

No wonder he seemed so strange to her, sometimes like a boy and sometimes seeming to have the demeanor of an older man. That explained the sage bearing in his young eyes. There was a presence about those eyes that didn't fit his youthful frame. This would certainly explain it.

The Palace of the Prophets trained boys in their gift. Ancient magic had aided the Sisters of the Light in their task by altering time at the palace so that they would have the time needed, in the absence of an experienced wizard, to teach the boys to control their magic.

That was all ended, now. Richard had destroyed the palace and the prophecies, lest Jagang capture them. The prophecies would have aided him in his effort to conquer the world, and the palace would have given him hundreds of years to rule over those he vanquished.

Kahlan felt the weight of worry lift from her mind. 'Now I know why I felt there was something strange about him,' she said as she sighed her relief.

Cara didn't look so relieved. 'Why did you announce yourself to the soldiers inside the Confessors' Palace?'

'Emperor Jagang didn't explain his instructions, Mistress Cara.'

'Jagang is from the Old World, and no doubt doesn't know about Mord-Sith,' Cara said to Kahlan. 'He probably thought a wizard, like Marlin here, would be able to announce himself, cause a panic, and wreak havoc.'

Kahlan considered the supposition. 'Could be. Jagang has the Sisters of the Dark as his puppets, so he would have been able to get information about Richard. Richard wasn't at the palace long enough to learn much about his gift. The Sisters of the Dark would have told Jagang that Richard doesn't know how to use his magic. Richard is the Seeker, and knows how to use the Sword of Truth, but he doesn't know how to use his gift. Jagang might have thought to send in a wizard, on the chance that he might succeed, and if he didn't ... so what? He has others.'

'What do you think, my pet?'

Marlin's eyes filled with tears. 'I don't know, Mistress Cara. I don't know. He didn't tell me. I swear.' A tremor seeped from his jaw into his voice. 'But it could be. What the Mother Confessor says is true: he doesn't care if we are killed while performing a task. Our lives mean little to him.'

Cara turned to Kahlan. 'What else?'

Kahlan shook her head. 'I can't think of anything else at the moment. I guess it could all make sense. We'll come back later, after I've thought about it. Maybe I'll think of some other questions that might settle it.'

Cara pointed her Agiel at his face. 'You stand right there, on that spot of your spit, until we come back. Whether it's in two hours or two days, it doesn't matter. If you sit down, or any part of you, other than the soles of your feet, touches the floor, you will be down here all alone with the pain it brings for going against my wishes. Understand?'

He blinked as a drop of sweat ran into his eye. 'Yes, Mistress Cara.'

'Cara, do you think it necessary that –'

'Yes. I know my business. Let me do it. You yourself reminded me what was at stake and how we dared not take any chances.'

Kahlan relented. 'All right.'

Kahlan took hold of a rung above her head and started up the ladder. On the second rung, she paused and looked back. Frowning, she stepped back off the ladder.

'Marlin, did you come to Aydindril alone?'

'No, Mother Confessor.'

Cara snatched the neck of his tunic. 'What! You came with others?'

'Yes, Mistress Cara.'

'How many!'

'With one other, Mistress Cara. She was a Sister of the Dark.'

Kahlan's fist joined Cara's on his tunic. 'What was her name!'

Frightened by both women, he tried to back away a bit, but their grip on his tunic wouldn't allow it. 'I don't know her name,' he whined. 'I swear.'

'She was a Sister of the Dark, from the palace, where you

lived for close to a century, and you don't know her name?' Kahlan asked.

Marlin licked his lips, his gaze moving between the two women. 'There were hundreds of Sisters at the Palace of the Prophets. There were rules. We had teachers assigned to us. There were places we didn't go, and Sisters we never came in contact with, like those who handled administration. I didn't know them all, I swear. I saw her before, at the palace, but I didn't know her name, and she didn't tell me.'

'Where is she now!'

Marlin shook in terror. 'I don't know! I haven't seen her for days, since I came to the city.'

Kahlan gritted her teeth. 'What did she look like, then?'

Marlin licked his lips again as his gaze flicked back and forth between the two women. 'I don't know. I don't know how to describe her. A young woman. I don't think she was long out of being a novice. She was young-looking, like you, Mother Confessor. Pretty. I thought she was pretty. She had long hair. Long brown hair.'

Kahlan and Cara shared a look. 'Nadine,' they said as one.

CHAPTER 4

'Mistress Cara?' Marlin called from below.

Cara turned, hanging by one hand on the next rung down from Kahlan. She held the torch out in her other hand. 'What!'

'How will I sleep, Mistress Cara? If you don't come back tonight, and if I have to stand, then how will I sleep?'

'Sleep? That's not my concern. I told you – you must remain on your feet, on that spot. Move, sit, or lie down, and you will be *very* sorry. You will be all alone with the pain. Understand?'

'Yes, Mistress Cara,' came the weak voice from the darkness below.

Once Kahlan was up in the hall, she reached down and took the torch from Cara, freeing the Mord-Sith to use both hands to climb out. Kahlan handed the torch to a relieved-looking Sergeant Collins.

'Collins, I'd like all of you to remain here. Keep the door locked and don't go down there – for anything. Don't let anyone else so much as take a peek.'

'Yes, Mother Confessor.' Sergeant Collins hesitated. 'Is it dangerous, then?'

Kahlan understood his concern. 'No. Cara has control of his power. He's incapable of using his magic.'

She took appraisal of the troops clogging the dingy stone corridor. There had to be close to a hundred.

'I don't know if we'll be back tonight,' she told the sergeant. 'Get the rest of your men down here. Divide them into squads. Take shifts so that there's at least this many down

44

here at all times. Lock all the barricade doors. Post archers at the doors and at each end of this hall.'

'I thought you said there was no need for concern, that he couldn't use his magic.'

Kahlan smiled. 'Do you want to have to explain it to Cara, here, if someone sneaks in and rescues her charge out from under your nose in her absence?'

He scratched his stubble as he glanced at Cara. 'I understand, Mother Confessor. No one will be allowed within shouting distance of this door.'

'Still don't trust me?' Cara asked, when they were out of earshot of the soldiers.

Kahlan offered a friendly smile. 'My father was King Wyborn. He was Cyrilla's father, and then mine. He was a great warrior. He taught me that it's impossible to be too cautious with prisoners.'

Cara shrugged as they passed a sputtering torch. 'Fine by me. It doesn't hurt my feelings. But I have his magic. He's helpless.'

'I still don't understand how you can fear magic, and have such control over it.'

'I told you, only if he specifically attacks me with it.'

'And how do you take control of it? How do you make it yours to command?'

Cara spun the Agiel on the end of the chain at her wrist as she walked. 'I don't know myself. We just do it. The Master Rahl himself takes part in some of the training of Mord-Sith. It is during that phase that the ability is instilled in us. It's not magic from within us, but transferred to us, I guess.'

Kahlan shook her head. 'Yet you don't know, really, what you're doing. And still it works.'

With her fingertips, Cara hooked the iron rail at a corner, swung around it, and followed Kahlan up the stone stairs. 'You don't have to know what you are doing in order for magic to work.'

'What do you mean?'

'Well, Lord Rahl told us that a child is magic: the magic of Creation. You don't have to know what you are doing to make a child.

'One time, this girl – a very naive girl – of about fourteen summers, a daughter of one of the staff at the People's Palace in D'Hara, told me that Darken Rahl – Father Rahl, he liked to be called – had given her a rosebud and it had bloomed in her fingers as he smiled down at her. She said that that was how she had come to be with child – through his magic.'

Cara laughed without humor. 'She really thought that that was how she became pregnant. It never occurred to her that it was because she had spread her legs for him. So you see? She did magic, created a son, and without knowing how she had really done it.'

Kahlan paused on the landing, in the shadows, and seized the crook of Cara's elbow, halting her.

'All Richard's family is dead – Darken Rahl killed his stepfather, his mother died when he was young, and his half brother, Michael, betrayed Richard … allowing Denna to capture him. After Richard defeated Darken Rahl, Richard forgave Michael for what he had done to him, but ordered him executed because his treachery had knowingly caused the torture and death of countless people at the hands of Darken Rahl.

'I know how much family means to Richard. He would be thrilled to come to know a half brother. Could we send word to the palace in D'Hara and have him brought here? Richard would be –'

Cara shook her head and glanced away. 'Darken Rahl tested the child and discovered that he was born without the gift. Darken Rahl was eager to have a gifted heir. He considered anything less deformed and worthless.'

'I see.' Silence filled the stairwell. 'The girl … the mother … ?'

Cara heaved a sigh, realizing that Kahlan wanted to hear it all. 'Darken Rahl had a temper. A sick temper. He crushed the girl's windpipe with his bare hands after he had made her watch him … well, watch him kill her son. When ungifted offspring came to his attention it often made him angry, and then he did that.'

Kahlan let her hand fall away from Cara's arm.

Cara's eyes came up; the calm had repossessed them. 'A few of the Mord-Sith suffered a similar fate. Fortunately, I never came to be with child when he chose me for his amusement.'

Kahlan sought to fill the silence. 'I'm glad Richard freed you from bondage to that beast. Freed everyone.'

Cara nodded, her eyes as cold as Kahlan had ever seen them. 'He is more than Lord Rahl to us. Anyone who ever hurts him will answer to the Mord-Sith – to me.'

Kahlan suddenly saw what Cara had said about Richard being allowed to 'keep' Kahlan in a new light; it was the kindest thing she could think to do for him: allowing him to have the one he loved, despite her concern for the danger to his heart.

'You'll have to wait in line,' Kahlan said.

Cara at last grinned. 'Let us pray to the good spirits that we never have to fight over first rights.'

'I have a better idea: let's keep harm from reaching him in the first place. But remember, when we get up there, that we don't know for sure who this Nadine is. If she is a Sister of the Dark, she is a very dangerous woman. But we don't know for sure that she is. She might be a dignitary: a woman of rank and importance. It could even be that she's nothing more than a rich nobleman's daughter. Maybe he banished her poor, farmboy lover, and she's simply looking for him. I don't want you harming an innocent person. Let's just keep our heads.'

'I'm not a monster, Mother Confessor.'

'I know. I didn't mean to say that you were. I just don't want our desire to protect Richard to make us lose our heads. That includes me. Now, let's get up to Petitioners' Hall.'

Cara frowned. 'Why would we go there? Why not go to Nadine's room?'

Kahlan started up the second flight, two steps at a time. 'There are two hundred eighty-eight guest rooms in the Confessors' Palace, divided among six separate wings at distant points. I was distracted before, and didn't think to tell the guards where to put her, so we have to go ask.'

Cara shouldered open the door at the top of the stairs and, head swiveling, entered the hall ahead of Kahlan, as she liked to do in order to check the way for trouble.

'Seems a poor design. Why would guest rooms be separated?'

Kahlan gestured to a corridor branching to the left. 'This way is shorter.' She slowed as two guards stepped aside to make way for them, and then quickened her pace along the deep blue carpet running down the hall. 'The guest rooms are separated because many diplomats visited the palace on business with the council, and if the wrong diplomats are placed too close together, they could become very undiplomatic. Keeping peace among allies was sometimes a delicate balancing game. That included accommodations.'

'But there are all the palaces – for the representatives of the lands – on Kings Row.'

Kahlan grunted cynically. 'Part of the game.'

When they entered Petitioners' Hall, everyone went to their knees again. Kahlan had to give them the formal acknowledgment before she could speak with the captain. He told her where he had put Nadine, and she was about to leave when a boy, one of the group of Ja'La players waiting patiently in the hall, snatched the floppy wool hat from his head of blond hair and bolted toward them.

The captain caught sight of him trotting across the room. 'He's waiting to see Lord Rahl. Probably wants him to come watch another game.' The captain smiled to himself. 'I told him it would be all right if he waited, but that I couldn't promise that Lord Rahl could see him.' He shrugged self-consciously. 'Least I could do. I was at the game, yesterday, with a crowd of soldiers. The boy and his team won me three silver marks.'

Hat crushed in both little fists, the boy genuflected on the other side of the marble railing from Kahlan.

'Mother Confessor, we'd like to … well … if it's no trouble … we …' His voice trailed off as he gulped air.

Kahlan smiled encouragement. 'Don't be afraid. What's your name?'

'Yonick, Mother Confessor.'

'I'm sorry, Yonick, but Richard can't come watch another game just now. We're busy at the moment. Perhaps tomorrow. I know we both enjoyed it, and we would very much like to come watch again, but on another day.'

He shook his head. 'It's not about that. It's my brother, Kip.' He twisted his hat. 'He's sick. I was wondering if …

48

well, if Lord Rahl could come do some magic and make him better.'

Kahlan gave the boy's shoulder a comforting squeeze. 'Well, Richard's not really that kind of wizard. Why don't you go see one of the healers on Stentor Street. Tell them what he's sick with and they'll give him some herbs to help him feel better.'

Yonick hung his head. 'We don't have no money for herbs. That's why I was hoping … Kip is real sick.'

Kahlan straightened and peered at the captain. His gaze went from Kahlan to the boy and back again. He cleared his throat.

'Well, Yonick, I saw you play, yesterday,' the captain stammered. 'Quite good. Your team was quite good.' Checking Kahlan's eyes again, he stabbed a hand into a pocket and came out with a coin. He bent over the rail and pushed the coin into Yonick's fist. 'I know which one's your brother. He … that was a great play, that goal he made. Take this and get him some herbs, like the Mother Confessor said he needs.'

Yonick stared in astonishment at the silver coin in his hand. 'Herbs don't cost this much, as I hear told.'

The captain waved away the notion. 'Well, I don't have anything smaller. Buy your team a treat, for their win, with the extra. Now take it and be off. We have palace business we must attend to.'

Yonick straightened and clapped a fist to his heart in salute. 'Yes, sir.'

'And practice that kick of yours,' the captain called after the boy as he ran across the hall to his fellows. 'It's a little sloppy.'

'I will,' Yonick shouted over his shoulder. 'Thanks.'

Kahlan watched as he collected his friends and they rushed to the door. 'Very kind of you, captain … ?'

'Harris.' He winced. 'Thank you, Mother Confessor.'

'Cara, let's go see this Lady Nadine.'

Kahlan hoped the captain who came to attention at the end of the hall had had an uneventful watch.

'Has Nadine tried to leave, Captain Nance?'

'No, Mother Confessor,' he said, when he straightened from his bow. 'She seemed grateful that someone was taking an interest in her request. When I explained that there could be trouble about and we needed her to stay in her room, she promised to abide by my instructions.' He glanced at the door. 'She said that she didn't want to get me in 'hot water' and she would do as I asked.'

'Thank you, captain.' She paused before she opened the door. 'If she comes out of this room without us, kill her. Don't stop to ask her any questions, and don't give her any warning, just have the archers take her down.' When his brow twitched, she added, 'If she leaves first, it will be because she has proven she commands magic and has killed us with it.'

Captain Nance, his face gone as pale as year-old straw, clapped a fist to his heart in salute.

The outer sitting room was decorated in red. The walls were a dark crimson, adorned with white crown molding, pink marble baseboard and door casings, and a hardwood floor almost entirely covered with a huge, gold-fringed carpet embellished with an ornate leaf-and-flower motif. The gilded legs of the marble-topped table and of the red velvet, tufted chairs were carved with a matching leaf-and-flower design. Being an interior room, there were no windows. Cut-glass chimneys on the dozen reflector lamps around the room sent sparkles of light dancing across the walls.

To Kahlan's mind it was one of the least tasteful color schemes in the palace, but there were diplomats who specified this color room when requesting accommodations at the palace. They felt it put them in the right frame of mind for negotiations. Kahlan was always wary when hearing the arguments of representatives who had requested one of the red rooms.

Nadine wasn't in the extravagant outer room. The door to the bedroom was ajar.

'Delicious rooms,' Cara whispered. 'Can I have them?'

Kahlan shushed her. She knew why the Mord-Sith would want a red room. With Cara peering over her shoulder, Kahlan cautiously pushed back the bedroom door. Cara's breath tickled her left ear.

If it was possible, the bedroom was more jarring to the

50

senses than the sitting room, with the red theme carried into the carpets, embroidered bedcover, immoderate collection of ornate, gold-fringed crimson pillows, and the swirled, pink marble fireplace surround. Kahlan thought that if Cara was wearing her red leather and ever wanted to hide, she could simply sit in this room and no one would ever find her.

Only half the lamps in the bedroom were lit. Several blown-glass bowls set about on tables and the desk were filled with dried rose petals, their fragrance mingling with the lamp oil to permeate the air with a heavy, sickly-sweet odor.

When the hinges squeaked, the woman resting on the bed opened her eyes, saw Kahlan, and sprang to her feet. Ready to take Nadine with her Confessor's power if she gave the slightest indication of aggression, Kahlan unconsciously held an arm out to her side to keep Cara out of her way. In preparation, her muscles tight as coiled steel, Kahlan was holding her breath. If the woman conjured magic, Kahlan would have to be quick.

Nadine hastily knuckled the sleep from her eyes. By her indecision as to which foot to put forward in the awkward curtsy she performed, Kahlan knew that she was no noble-woman. But that didn't mean she couldn't be a Sister of the Dark.

Nadine gawked at Cara for an instant before smoothing down her dress at her shapely hips and addressing Kahlan. 'Forgive me, Queen, but I've been on a long journey and I was taking a bit of a rest. I guess I must have fallen asleep; I didn't hear you knock. I'm Nadine Brighton, Queen.'

As Nadine dipped into another inelegant curtsy, Kahlan quickly surveyed the room. The washbasin and ewer hadn't been used. The towels beside them on the washstand were clean and still folded. A simple, worn woolen travel bag sat at the foot of the bed. A clothesbrush and a tin cup were the only foreign objects on the overwrought, gilded table to the other side of a red velvet chair beside the fringed canopy bed. Despite the early spring chill and cold hearth, she hadn't pulled down the bedcovers for her nap. Perhaps, thought Kahlan, so as not to become tangled in them if she had to move fast.

Kahlan didn't apologize for entering without knocking.

'Mother Confessor,' she said in a cautious tone, feeling the need to make clear the tacit threat of the power she wielded. 'Queen is one of my less … common, titles. I am more widely known as the Mother Confessor.'

As Nadine blushed, the sprinkling of freckles at the top of her cheekbones and across her delicate nose almost disappeared. Her large brown eyes turned to the floor with unease. She hastily ran her fingers through her thick brown hair, although it didn't look disheveled.

She wasn't as tall as Kahlan, though she looked to be about the same age, or perhaps a year younger. She was a lovely-looking young woman, and cast off no warning signs of threat or danger, but Kahlan wasn't put at ease by a fresh face and innocent demeanor.

Experience had taught Kahlan hard lessons. Marlin, the latest lesson, hadn't appeared, at first, to be anything other than an awkward young man. This young woman's lovely eyes, though, didn't seem to have the same timeless quality to them that had so unnerved Kahlan. Still, her caution wasn't allayed, either.

Nadine turned and hurriedly swept the flats of her hands over the bedcover, pressing out the wrinkles with quick strokes. 'Forgive me, Mother Confessor, I didn't mean to muss your lovely bed. I brushed my dress first, so I wouldn't get road dust on it. I intended to lie on the floor, but the bed looked so inviting I couldn't resist giving it a try. I hope I haven't caused offense.'

'Of course not,' Kahlan said. 'I invited you to use the room as your own.'

Before the last word was out of Kahlan's mouth, Cara had swept around her. Even though there seemed to be no rank among the Mord-Sith, Berdine and Raina always deferred to Cara's word. Among the D'Harans, the rank of the Mord-Sith, and Cara in particular, seemed undisputed, though Kahlan had never heard anyone put definition to it. If Cara said, 'Spit,' people spat.

Nadine let out a wide-eyed squeak when she saw the leather-clad Mord-Sith coming at her.

'Cara!' Kahlan called out.

Cara ignored her. 'We have your friend, Marlin, down in the pit. You'll be joining him shortly.'

Cara jabbed a finger in the hollow at the base of Nadine's neck, causing her to drop backward onto the chair beside the bed.

'Ow!' Nadine shouted as she glared up at Cara. 'That hurt!'

As she bounded up off the chair, Cara sized the young woman's throat in an armored fist. She swept her Agiel up and pointed it between the wide brown eyes. 'I have not yet begun to hurt you.'

Kahlan snatched Cara's braid and gave it a mighty yank. 'One way or the other, you're going to learn to follow orders!'

Cara, still gripping the young woman's throat, turned in surprise.

'Let her go! I told you to let me handle this. Until she makes a threatening move, you will do as you are told, or you can wait outside.'

Cara released Nadine with a shove that plopped her down in the chair again. 'This one's trouble. I can feel it. You should let me kill her.'

Kahlan pressed her lips together until Cara rolled her eyes and grudgingly stepped aside. Nadine came off the chair, slower this time. Her eyes teared as she rubbed her throat and coughed.

'Why'd you do that! I've done nothing to you! I didn't disturb any of your fine things. You people have the worst manners of anyone I've ever seen.' She shook a finger at Kahlan. 'There's no call to treat a person that way.'

'On the contrary,' Kahlan said. 'An innocent enough looking young man showed up at the palace today, also asking to see Lord Rahl. He turned out to be an assassin. Thanks to Cara, here, we were able to stop him.'

Nadine's indignation faltered. 'Oh.'

'That's not the worst of it,' Kahlan said. 'He confessed to having an accomplice – an attractive young woman with long brown hair.'

Nadine's throat-rubbing paused as she looked at Cara, then back to Kahlan. 'Oh. Well, I guess I can understand the mistake …'

'You asked to see Lord Rahl, too. That's made everyone just a little jumpy. All of us are quite protective of Lord Rahl.'

'I guess I can see the reason for the confusion. No offense taken.'

'Cara, here, is one of Lord Rahl's personal guards,' Kahlan said. 'I'm sure you can understand the reason for her belligerent attitude.'

Nadine took her hand away from her throat and rested it on one hip. 'Of course. I guess I landed in the middle of a hornet's nest.'

'The problem is,' Kahlan went on, 'you haven't yet convinced us you are not the second assassin. For your sake, it would be best if you did so at once.'

Nadine's eyes darted between the two women watching her. Her relief reversed to alarm. 'Me? A killer? But I'm a woman.'

'So am I,' Cara said. 'One who is going to have your blood all over this room until you tell us the truth.'

Nadine spun around and snatched up the chair, brandishing its legs toward Cara and Kahlan. 'Stay away! I'm warning you; Tommy Lancaster and his friend Lester once thought to have their way with me, and they now have to eat all their meals without the benefit of their front teeth.'

'Put down the chair,' Cara warned in a deadly hiss, 'or you will be eating your next meal in the spirit world.'

Nadine dropped the chair as if it had caught fire. She retreated until she was up against the wall. 'Leave me be! I didn't do anything!'

Kahlan gently hooked Cara's arm and urged her back. 'Let a sister of the Agiel handle this?' she said in a whisper as she lifted an eyebrow. 'I know I said ''until she makes a threatening move,'' but a chair is hardly the kind of threat I had in mind.'

Cara's mouth twisted in annoyance. 'All right. For the moment.'

Kahlan turned to Nadine. 'I need some answers. Tell the truth, and if you really have nothing to do with this assassin, you will have my sincere apology and I'll do what I can to make up for our inhospitality. But if you lie to me, and you intend to do harm to Lord Rahl, the guards outside have orders not to allow you to leave this room alive. Do you understand?'

Nadine, her back pressed against the wall, nodded.

'You asked to see Lord Rahl.' Nadine nodded again. 'Why?'

'I'm on my way to my love. He's been gone since last autumn. We're to be wed, and I'm on my way to him.' She brushed a strand of hair back from her eyes. 'But I don't know where he is, exactly. I was told to go see Lord Rahl and I would find my betrothed.' Nadine's lower lids brimmed with tears. 'That's why I wanted to speak with this Lord Rahl – to ask if he could help.'

'I see,' Kahlan said. 'I can understand your distress over your love being missing. What is your young man's name?'

Nadine pulled her kerchief from her sleeve and dabbed it at her eyes. 'Richard.'

'Richard. Is there more to his name?'

Nadine nodded. 'Richard Cypher.'

Kahlan had to remind herself to draw a breath through her open mouth, but her mind couldn't seem to make her tongue work.

'Who?' Cara asked.

'Richard Cypher. He's a woods guide where I live in Hartland, that's in Westland, where we live.'

'What do you mean, you're to wed him?' Kahlan finally managed in a whisper. She felt her world threatening to crush in around her as a thousand things all at once whirled chaotically in her mind. 'Did he tell you that?'

Nadine twisted her damp kerchief. 'Well, he was courting me … it was understood … but then he disappeared. A woman came and told me that we're to be married. She said that the sky had spoken to her – she was a mystic of some sort. She knew all about my Richard, how kind and strong and handsome he is and all. She knew all manner of things about me, too. She had that it's my destiny to marry Richard and Richard's destiny to be my husband.'

'Woman?' Kahlan could get out no more than that one word.

Nadine nodded. 'Shota, she said her name was.'

Kahlan's hands balled into fists. Her voice returned with venom. Shota. Did this woman, Shota, have anyone with her?'

'Yes. A strange little … fellow. With yellow eyes. He kind

of scared me, but she said he was harmless. Shota is the one who told me to come see Lord Rahl. She said Lord Rahl could help me find my Richard.'

Kahlan recognized the description of Shota's companion, Samuel. This woman's voice, calling Richard, 'my Richard,' kept thundering around in the storm in Kahlan's head. She worked at making her voice sound calm. 'Nadine, please wait here.'

'I will,' Nadine said, gathering her composure. 'Is everything all right? You believe me, don't you? Every word is true.'

Kahlan didn't answer, but instead pulled her stunned stare from Nadine and marched from the room. Cara closed the door as she followed on Kahlan's heels.

Kahlan staggered to a halt in the outer room, everything swimming in a watery red blur.

'Mother Confessor,' Cara whispered, 'what's wrong? Your face is as red as my leather. Who is this Shota?'

'Shota is a witch woman.'

Cara stiffened at that news. 'And do you know this Richard Cypher?'

Kahlan twice swallowed past the painful lump in the back of her throat. 'Richard was raised by his stepfather. Until Richard found out that Darken Rahl was his real father, his name was Richard Cypher.'

CHAPTER 5

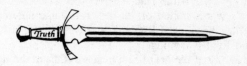

'I'll kill her,' Kahlan rasped in a hoarse voice as she stared off at nothing. 'With my bare hands. I'll strangle the life out of her!'

Cara turned toward the bedroom. 'I will take care of it. Better if you let me take care of her.'

Kahlan hooked Cara's arm. 'Not her. I'm talking about Shota.' She gestured toward the bedroom door. 'She doesn't understand any of this. She doesn't know about Shota.'

'You know this witch woman, then?'

Kahlan bitterly huffed out a breath. 'Oh yes. I know her. She's been trying to prevent Richard and me from being together since the first.'

'Why would she do that?'

Kahlan turned away from the bedroom door. 'I don't know. She gives a different reason every time, but I sometimes fear that it's because she wants Richard for herself.'

Cara frowned. 'How would getting Lord Rahl to marry this little strumpet gain Shota Lord Rahl?'

Kahlan flicked a hand. 'I don't know. Shota is always up to something. She's caused us trouble at every turn.' Her fists tightened with resolve. 'But it won't work, this time. If it's the last thing I do, I'm going to end her meddling. And then Richard and I are going to be married.' Her voice dropped to a whispered oath. 'If I have to touch Shota with my power and send her to the underworld, I will end her meddling.'

Cara folded her arms as she considered the problem. 'What

do you wish done with Nadine?' Her blue eyes turned toward the bedroom. 'It still might be best to … get rid of her.'

Kahlan squeezed the bridge of her nose between a finger and thumb. 'This isn't Nadine's doing. She's simply a pawn in Shota's plotting.'

'One foot soldier can sometimes cause you more trouble than a general's battle plan if he …'

Cara's words trailed off as her arms came unfolded. She cocked her head, as if listening to a wind in the halls.

'Lord Rahl is coming.'

The ability of the Mord-Sith to sense Richard through their bond to him was uncanny, if not unnerving. The door opened. Berdine and Raina, wearing leather of the same cut and skintight style as Cara's, but brown rather than red, strutted into the room.

Both were a bit shorter than Cara, but no less attractive. Where Cara was leggy, muscular, and without a spare ounce of fat, blue-eyed Berdine had a more curvaceous shape. Berdine's wavy brown hair was plaited in the characteristic long braid of a Mord-Sith, as was graceful Raina's fine, dark hair. All three shared the same ruthless confidence.

Raina's incisive, dark-eyed gaze took in Cara's red leather, but she made no comment. Both she and Berdine wore grim, forbidding expressions. The two Mord-Sith turned to face one another from either side of the door.

'We present Lord Rahl,' Berdine said in an officious tone, 'the Seeker of Truth and wielder of the Sword of Truth, the bringer of death, the Master of D'Hara, the ruler of the Midlands, the commander of the gar nation, the champion of free people and bane of the wicked' – her penetrating blue eyes turned to Kahlan – 'and the betrothed of the Mother Confessor.' She lifted an introductory arm toward the door.

Kahlan couldn't imagine what was going on. She had seen the Mord-Sith display a variety of temperaments, from imperious to mischievous, but she had never seen them acting ceremonial.

Richard strode into the room. His raptor gaze locked on Kahlan. For an instant, the world stopped. There was nothing else but the two of them, joined in a silent link.

A smile widened on his lips and gleamed in his eyes. A smile of unbounded love.

There was only her and Richard. Only his eyes.

But the rest of him …

She felt her mouth drop open. In astonishment, Kahlan put a hand over her heart. As long as she had known him, he had worn only his simple woods clothes. But now …

His black boots were all she recognized. The tops of the boots were wrapped with leather thongs pinned with silver emblems embossed with geometric designs, and covered new, black wool trousers. Over a black shirt was a black, open-sided tunic, decorated with symbols snaking along a wide gold band running all the way around its squared edges. A wide, multilayered leather belt bearing several more of the silver emblems and a gold-worked pouch to each side cinched the magnificent tunic at his waist. The ancient, tooled-leather baldric holding the gold and silver wrought scabbard for the Sword of Truth crossed over his right shoulder. At each wrist was a wide, leather-padded silver band bearing linked rings encompassing more of the strange symbols. His broad shoulders bore a cape that appeared to be made of spun gold.

He looked at once noble and sinister. Regal, and deadly. He looked like a commander of kings. And like a vision of what the prophecies had named him: the bringer of death.

Kahlan would never have thought he could look more handsome than he always did. More commanding. More imposing. She was wrong.

As her jaw worked, trying to bring forth words that weren't there, he crossed the room. He bent and kissed her temple.

'Good,' Cara announced. 'She needed that; she had a headache.' She lifted an eyebrow to Kahlan. 'All better now?'

Kahlan, hardly able to get her breath, hardly hearing Cara, touched her fingers to him, as if to test if this was a vision, or real.

'Like it?' he asked.

'Like it? Dear spirits …' she breathed.

He chuckled. 'I'll take that for a yes.'

Kahlan wished everyone was gone. 'But, Richard, what is this? Where did you get all this?'

She couldn't take her hand from his chest. She liked the feel

59

of his breathing. She could feel his heart beating, too. And she could feel her own heart pounding.

'Well,' he said, 'I knew you wanted me to get some new clothes –'

She pulled her gaze from his body and looked up into his gray eyes. 'What? I never said that.'

He laughed. 'Your beautiful green eyes said it for you. When you looked at my old woods outfit, your eyes spoke quite clearly.'

She took a step back and gestured to the new clothes. 'Where did you get all this?'

He clasped one of her hands and with the fingers of his other lifted her chin to gaze into her eyes. 'You're so beautiful. You're going to look magnificent in your blue wedding dress. I wanted to look worthy of the Mother Confessor herself when we're married. I had it made in a hurry so as not to delay our wedding.'

'He had the seamstresses make it for him. It was a surprise,' Cara said. 'I never told her your secret, Lord Rahl. She tried her best to get it out of me, but I didn't tell her.'

'Thank you, Cara.' Richard laughed. 'I bet it wasn't easy.'

Kahlan laughed with him. 'But this is wonderful. Mistress Wellington made all this for you?'

'Well, not all of it. I told her what I wanted, and she and the other seamstresses went to work. I think she did a fine job.'

'I will give her my compliments. If not a hug.' Kahlan tested the cape between a finger and thumb. 'She made this? I've never seen anything like it. I can't believe she made this.'

'Well, no,' Richard admitted. 'That, and some of the other things came from the Wizard's Keep.'

'The Keep! What were you doing up there?'

'When I was there before, I came across these rooms where the wizards used to stay. I went back and had a better look at some of the things that belonged to them.'

'When did you do this?'

'A few days ago. When you were busy meeting with some of the officials from our new allies.'

Kahlan's brow tightened as she appraised the outfit. 'The wizards of that time wore this? I thought wizards always wore simple robes.'

'Most of them did. One wore some of this.'

'What kind of wizard wore an outfit like this?'

'A war wizard.'

'A war wizard,' she whispered in astonishment. Though he largely didn't know how to use his gift, Richard was the first war wizard to have been born in nearly three thousand years.

Kahlan was about to launch into a raft of questions, but remembered that there were more consequential matters at the moment. Her mood sank. 'Richard' she looked away from his eyes 'there is someone here to see you …'

She heard the bedroom door squeak.

'Richard?' Nadine, standing in the doorway, expectantly twisted her kerchief in her fingers. 'I heard Richard's voice.'

'Nadine?'

Nadine's eyes went as big as Sanderian gold crowns. 'Richard.'

Richard smiled politely. 'Nadine.' His mouth smiled, anyway.

His eyes, though, held no hint of a smile. It was as discordant a look as Kahlan had ever seen on his face. Kahlan had seen Richard angry, she had seen him in the lethal rage from magic of the Sword of Truth, when the magic danced dangerously in his eyes, and she had seen him with the deadly calm countenance invoked when he turned the blade white. In the fury of commitment and determination, Richard was capable of looking frightening.

But no look she had ever seen on his face was as terrifying to Kahlan as the one she saw now.

This wasn't a deadly rage that gripped his eyes, or a lethal commitment. This was somehow worse. The depth of disinterest in that empty smile, in his eyes, was frightening.

The only way Kahlan could imagine it being worse would be if such a gaze were directed her way. That look, so devoid of fervor, if directed at her, would have broken her heart.

Nadine apparently didn't know him as well as did Kahlan; she didn't see anything but the smile on his lips.

'Oh, Richard!'

Nadine dashed across the room and threw her arms around his neck. She seemed ready to throw her legs around Richard, too. Kahlan shot an arm out to stop Cara before the Mord-Sith could take more than a step.

Kahlan had to force herself to stand her ground and hold her tongue. Despite everything she and Richard meant to each other, she knew that this was something beyond her say. This was Richard's past, and as well as she knew him, some of that past – his romantic past, anyway – was largely unknown territory. Up until that moment it had seemed unimportant.

Fearing to say the wrong thing, Kahlan said nothing. Her fate was in Richard's hands, and those of a beautiful woman who at that moment had hers around his neck – but worse, her fate seemed once again in Shota's hands.

Nadine began planting kisses all over Richard's neck even as he tried to hold his head away from her. He placed his hands on her waist and pushed her away.

'Nadine, what are you doing here?'

'Looking for you, silly,' she said in a breathless voice. 'Everyone's been puzzled – worried – since you disappeared last autumn. My father missed you – I've missed you. None of us knew what happened to you. Zedd's missing, too. The boundary came down and then you came up missing, and Zedd, and your brother. I know you were upset when your father was murdered, but we didn't expect you to run away.' Her words were running together in breathless excitement.

'Well, it's a long story, and one I'm sure you wouldn't be interested in.'

True to Richard's words, she didn't seem to hear a bit of it, and simply rambled on.

'I had so much to take care of, first. I had to get Lindy Hamilton to promise to get the winter roots for Pa. He's been beside himself without you to bring him some of the special plants he needs that only you can seem to find. I've done my best, but I don't know the woods like you. He's hoping Lindy will be able to fill in until I can get you home. Then I had to think what to take, and how to find my way. I've been looking so long. I came to speak with somebody named Lord Rahl, hoping he could help me find you. I never in all the world dreamed I'd find you before I even talked to him.'

'I am Lord Rahl.'

This, too, she seemed not to hear. She stepped back and

looked him up and down. 'Richard, what are you doing in that outfit? Who are you pretending to be? Get changed. We'll go home. Everything's fine, now that I've found you. We'll be back home soon, and everything will be back to the way it was. We'll be married and –'

'What!'

She blinked. 'Married. We'll be married, and have a house and everything. You can build us a better one – your old house won't do. We'll have children. Lots of children. Sons. Lots of sons. Big and strong like my Richard.' She grinned. 'I love you, my Richard. We're going to be married, at last.'

His smile, as empty as it had been, was gone, and in its place a serious scowl grew. 'Where did you ever get an idea like that?'

Nadine laughed as she playfully ran a finger down his front. She finally glanced about. No one else was so much as smiling. Her laughter died out and she sought refuge in Richard's gaze.

'But, Richard ... you and me. Like it was always supposed to be. We'll be married. At last. Like it was always meant to be.'

Cara leaned toward Kahlan to whisper in her ear. 'You should have let me kill her.'

Richard's glare wiped the smirk from the Mord-Sith's mouth and drained the blood from her face. He turned back to Nadine.

'Where did you get such an idea?'

Nadine was appraising his clothes again. 'Richard, you look foolish dressed like this. Sometimes I wonder if you have a lick of sense. What are you doing playing at being a king? And *where* did you get such a sword? Richard, I know you would never steal, but you don't have the kind of money such a weapon would cost. If you won it in a bet or something, you can sell it so that we –'

Richard gripped her by the shoulders and gave her a shake. 'Nadine, we were never engaged to be married, or even close. Where did you get a crazy idea like that? What are you doing here!'

Nadine finally wilted under his glower. 'Richard, I've come a long way. I've never been out of Hartland before. It was hard

63

traveling. Doesn't that mean anything to you? Doesn't that count for anything? I would never have left except to come get you. I love you, Richard.'

Ulic, one of Richard's two huge personal bodyguards, ducked as he stepped through the doorway. 'Lord Rahl, if you are not busy, General Kerson has a problem and needs to speak with you.'

Richard turned a hot glare toward the towering Ulic. 'In a minute.'

Ulic, not used to Richard directing such a forbidding look, or tone, his way, bowed. 'I will tell him, Lord Rahl.'

Puzzled, Nadine watched the mountain of muscle duck back out the doorway. 'Lord Rahl? Richard, what in the name of the good spirits was that man talking about? What trouble have you gotten yourself into? You were always so sensible. What have you done? Why are you tricking these people? Who are you playing at being?'

He seemed to cool a bit and his voice turned weary. 'Nadine, it's a long story, and one I'm not in the mood to repeat just now. I'm afraid I'm not the same person ... It's been a long time since I've left home. A great many things have happened. I'm sorry you've come a long way for nothing, but what was once between us –'

Kahlan expected a sheepish glance her way. She never got one.

Nadine took a step back. She looked around at all the faces watching her: Kahlan, Cara, Berdine, Raina, and the silent hulk of Egan back near the door.

Nadine threw her hands up. 'What's the matter with all you people! Who do you think this man is? He's Richard Cypher, my Richard! He's a woods guide – a nobody! He's just a simple boy from Hartland, playing at being somebody important. He's not! Are you all blind fools? He's my Richard, and we're to be married.'

Cara finally broke the silence. 'We all know quite well who this man is. Apparently, you do not. He is Lord Rahl, the Master of D'Hara, and the ruler of what was the Midlands. At least, he is the ruler of those who have so far surrendered to him. Everyone in this room, if not this city, would lay down their lives to protect him. We all owe him more than our loyalty; we owe him our lives.'

'We can all only be who we are,' Richard told Nadine, 'no more, and no less. A very wise woman told me that, one time.'

Nadine whispered her incredulity, but Kahlan couldn't hear the words.

Richard put his arm around Kahlan's waist. In that gentle touch, she read the message of comfort and love, and suddenly felt profound sorrow for this woman standing before strangers, exposing such personal matters of the heart.

'Nadine,' Richard said in a quiet tone, 'this is Kahlan, the wise woman I spoke of. The woman I love. Kahlan, not Nadine. Kahlan and I are soon to be married. We're shortly going to leave to be wedded by the Mud People. Nothing in this world is going to change that.'

Nadine seemed afraid to take her eyes from Richard, as if she feared that if she did, it would become true.

'Mud People? What in the name of the spirits are Mud People? Sounds dreadful. Richard, you ...' She seemed to gather her resolve. She pressed her lips together and suddenly scowled. She shook her finger at him.

'Richard Cypher, I don't know what kind of foolish game you're playing, but I'll not have it! You listen to me, you big oaf, you go get your things packed! We're going home!'

'I am home, Nadine.'

Nadine, at last, could think of no counter.

'Nadine, who told you all this ... this marriage business?'

The fire had gone out of her. 'A mystic named Shota.'

Kahlan tensed at the sound of that name. Shota was the true threat. No matter what Nadine said, or wanted, it was Shota who had the power to cause trouble.

'Shota!' Richard wiped a hand across his face. 'Shota. I might have known.'

And then Richard did the last thing Kahlan would have expected: he chuckled. He stood there, with everyone watching him, threw his head back, and laughed aloud.

Somehow, it magically melted Kahlan's fears. That Richard would simply laugh off what Shota might do somehow trivialized the threat. Suddenly, her heart felt buoyant. Richard said that the Mud People were going to marry them, as they both wanted, and the fact that Shota wished otherwise was worth no more than a chuckle. Richard's arm around her waist tightened with a loving squeeze. She felt her cheeks tighten with a grin of her own.

Richard waved an apology. 'Nadine, I'm sorry. I'm not laughing at you. It's just that Shota has been playing her little tricks on us for a long time. It's unfortunate that she's used you in her scheme, but it's just one of her wretched games. She's a witch woman.'

'Witch woman?' Nadine whispered.

Richard nodded. 'She's taken us in with her little dramas in the past, but not this time. I no longer care what Shota says. I'm not playing her games anymore.'

Nadine looked perplexed. 'A witch woman? Magic? I've been plied with magic? But she said that the sky had spoken to her.'

'Is that so. Well, I don't care if the Creator Himself has spoken to her.'

'She said that the wind hunts you. I was worried. I wanted to help.'

'The wind hunts me? Well, it's always something with her.'

Nadine's gaze drifted from his. 'But what about us ... ?'

'Nadine, there is no "us."' The edge returned to his voice. 'You, of all people, know the truth of that.'

Her chin lifted with indignation. 'I don't know what you're talking about.'

He watched her for a long moment, as if considering saying more than he finally did. 'Have it your way, Nadine.'

For the first time, Kahlan felt embarrassed. Whatever the exchange had meant, she felt like an intruder hearing it. Richard seemed uncomfortable, too. 'I'm sorry, Nadine, but I have things I have to take care of. If you need help getting home, I'll see what I can do. Whatever you need – a horse, supplies, whatever. Tell everyone back in Hartland that I'm fine, and I send my best wishes.'

He turned to the waiting Ulic. 'Is General Kerson here?'

'Yes, Lord Rahl.'

Richard took a step toward the door. 'I'd best go see what his problem is.'

General Kerson instead entered from right around the

doorway when he heard his name. Graying, but muscular and fit, and a head shorter than Richard, he cut an imposing figure in his burnished leather uniform. His upper arms bore scars of rank, their shiny white furrows showing through the short chain-mail sleeves.

He clapped a fist to his heart in salute. 'Lord Rahl, I need to speak with you.'

'Fine. Speak.'

The general hesitated. 'I meant alone, Lord Rahl.'

Richard looked in no mood to dally with the man. 'There are no spies here. Speak.'

'It's about the men, Lord Rahl. A great many of them are sick.'

'Sick? What's wrong with them?'

'Well, Lord Rahl, they … that is …'

Richard's brow tightened. 'Out with it.'

'Lord Rahl' – General Kerson glanced among the women before clearing his throat – 'I've got over half my army, well, out of commission, squatting and groaning with debilitating bouts of diarrhea.'

Richard's brow relaxed. 'Oh. Well, I'm sorry. I hope they're better soon. It's a miserable state to be in.'

'It's not an uncommon condition among an army, but to be this widespread it is, and because it is so widespread, something has to be done.'

'Well, be sure they get plenty to drink. Keep me informed. Let me know how they're doing.'

'Lord Rahl, something has to be done. *Now*. We can't have this.'

'It's not like they're stricken with spotted fever, general.'

General Kerson clasped his hands behind his back and took a patient breath. 'Lord Rahl, General Reibisch, before he went south, told us that you wanted your officers to voice their opinions to you when we thought it important. He said that you told him that you may get angry if you didn't like what we had to say, but you wouldn't punish us for voicing our views. He said you wanted to know our opinions because we've had more experience at dealing with troops and with command of an army than you.'

Richard wiped a hand back and forth across his mouth. 'You're right, general. So what is it that's so vital?'

'Well, Lord Rahl, I'm one of the heroes of the Shinavont province revolt. That's in D'Hara. I was a lieutenant at the time. There were five hundred of us, and we came upon the rebel force, seven thousand strong, encamped in a scrag wood. We attacked at first light, and ended the revolt before the day was out. There were no Shinavont rebels left by sunset.'

'Very impressive, general.'

General Kerson shrugged. 'Not really. Nearly all their men had their pants down around their ankles. You ever try to fight when the grips had your guts?' Richard admitted that he hadn't. 'Everyone called us heroes, but it doesn't take a hero to split a man's skull when he's so dizzy with diarrhea that he can hardly lift his head. I wasn't proud of what we did, but it was our duty, and we ended the revolt, and undoubtedly prevented the greater bloodshed that would have occurred if their force had gotten well and escaped us. No telling what they would have done, how many more would have died.

'But they didn't. We took them down because they were sick with dysentery and couldn't keep their feet.' He swept his arm around, indicating the surrounding countryside. 'I've got over half my men down. We've not a full force because General Reibisch went off to the south. What's left isn't in fighting condition. Something has to be done. A sizable enough foe attacks now, and we're in trouble. We're vulnerable. We could lose Aydindril.'

'I'd be grateful if you knew something we could do to reverse the situation.'

'Why are you bringing this to me? Don't you have healers?'

'The healers we have are for those kinds of problems caused by steel. We tried going to some of the herb sellers and healers here in Aydindril, but they couldn't begin to handle the numbers.' He shrugged. 'You're the Lord Rahl. I thought you would know what to do.'

'You're right, the herb dealers wouldn't have anything in that kind of quantity.' Richard pinched his lower lip as he thought. 'Garlic will take care of it, if they eat enough. Blueberries will help, too. Get plenty of garlic into the men, and supplement it with blueberries. There would be enough of those around.'

The general leaned in with a dubious frown. 'Garlic and blueberries? Are you serious?'

'My grandfather taught me about herbs and remedies and such things. Trust me, general, it will work. They've got to drink plenty of tannin tea from quench oak bark, too. Garlic, blueberries, and the quench oak tea should take care of it.' Richard looked over his shoulder. 'Right, Nadine?'

She nodded. 'That would do it, but it would be easier yet if you gave them powdered bistort.'

'I thought of that, but we'll never find any bistort this time of year, and the herb sellers wouldn't begin to have enough.'

'It doesn't take that much in powdered form, and it would work best,' Nadine said. 'How many men, sir?'

'Last report was in the neighborhood of fifty thousand,' the general said. 'By now? Who knows.'

Nadine's eyebrows lifted in surprise at the number. 'I've never seen that much bistort in my life. They'd be old men before that much could be gathered. Richard's right, then: garlic, blueberries, and quench oak tea. Comfrey tea would work, too, but no one will carry that kind of quantity. Quench oak is your best bet, but it's hard to find. If there aren't quench oaks to be had, arrowwood would at least be better than nothing.'

'No,' Richard said. 'I've seen quench oak up in the high ridges, to the north-east.'

General Kerson scratched his stubble. 'What's a quench oak?'

'An oak tree. The kind of oak tree that will be what your men need. It has a yellow inner bark that you use to make the tea.'

'A tree. Lord Rahl, I can identify ten different kinds of steel just from the feel of it between my fingers, but I couldn't tell one tree from another if I had extra eyes.'

'Surely you must have men who know trees.'

'Richard,' Nadine said, 'quench oak is what we call it in Hartland. I've collected roots and plants on my way here that I know the names of, but are called different by the people I've met. If these men drink tea from the wrong tree, the best you can hope for is that it won't harm them, but it won't solve the problem. The garlic and blueberries will help their gut, but they need the liquid for what was drained out of the rest of them; the tea helps stop them from losing all that water and builds their health back up.'

'Yes, I know.' He rubbed his eyes. 'General, get a detachment together, about five hundred men, wagons, and extra packhorses in case we can't get the wagons close. I know where the trees are, I'll lead you up there.' Richard laughed quietly to himself. 'Once a guide, always a guide.'

'The men will appreciate it that Lord Rahl is concerned about their well-being,' the general said. 'I, for sure, appreciate it, Lord Rahl.'

'Thanks, general. Get everything needed together, and I'll meet you out at the stables shortly. I'd like to get up there, at least, before dark. Those passes are no place to be stumbling around in the dark, especially with wagons. The moon is near full, but even that won't help enough.'

'We'll be ready before you can walk out there, Lord Rahl.'

After a quick fist to his heart in salute, the general was gone. Richard flashed Nadine another of his empty smiles. 'Thanks for the help.'

And then he turned his full attention to the Mord-Sith clad in red leather.

CHAPTER 6

Richard gripped Cara's jaw and lifted her face. He turned her head so he could better see the oozing cut on her cheek.

'What's this?'

She glanced to Kahlan when he released his hold on her. 'A man refused my advances.'

'Is that so. Maybe he was put off by your choice of red leather.'

Richard looked to Kahlan. 'What's going on? We've got a palace full of guards so jumpy that they even challenged me when I came in. We've got squads of archers guarding stairwells, and I've not seen so much bared steel since the Blood of the Fold attacked the city.'

His eyes had that raptor gaze again. 'Who's down in the pit?'

'I told you,' Cara whispered to Kahlan. 'He always finds out.'

Kahlan had told Cara not to mention Marlin because she feared he might somehow hurt Richard. But once Marlin had revealed that there was a second assassin, everything changed; she had to tell Richard that there was a Sister of the Dark wandering around loose.

'An assassin showed up to kill you.' Kahlan gestured with a tilt of her head toward Cara. 'Little Miss Magic, here, goaded him into using his gift on her so that she could capture him. We put him down in the pit for safekeeping.'

Richard glanced at Cara before addressing Kahlan. 'Little Miss Magic, eh? Why did you let her do that?'

71

'He said he wanted to kill you. Cara decided to question him in her own fashion.'

'Do you think that was necessary?' he asked Cara. 'We have a whole army. One man couldn't get to me.'

'He also said he intended to kill the Mother Confessor.'

Richard's expression darkened. 'Then I hope you didn't show him your gentle side.'

Cara smiled. 'No, Lord Rahl.'

'Richard,' Kahlan said, 'it's worse than that. He was a wizard from the Palace of the Prophets. He said that he came with a Sister of the Dark. We haven't found her yet.'

'A Sister of the Dark. Great. How did you manage to discover that this man was an assassin?'

'He announced himself, believe it or not. He claims that Jagang sent him to kill you, and me, and that his orders were to announce himself once inside the Confessors' Palace.'

'Then Jagang's plan wasn't really for this man to kill us; Jagang isn't that stupid. What was this Sister of the Dark to do, here in Aydindril? Did he say that she was here to kill us, too, or that she was here for some other purpose?'

'Marlin didn't seem to know,' Kahlan said. 'After what Cara did to him, I believe him.'

'Which Sister is it? What's her name?'

'Marlin didn't know her name.'

Richard nodded. 'That's possible. How long was he in the city before he announced himself?'

'I'm not sure, exactly. I assumed a few days.'

'Then why didn't he come directly to the palace once he arrived?'

'I don't know,' Kahlan said. 'I didn't … ask him that.'

'How long was he with the Sister? What did they do while they were here?'

'I don't know.' Kahlan hesitated. 'I guess I didn't think to ask him.'

'Well, if he was with her, she must have had *something* to say to him. She would have been the one in charge. What did she say to him?'

'I don't know.'

'Did this Marlin see anyone else while he was in the city? Did he meet with anyone else? Where did he stay?'

It was the Seeker questioning her, not Richard. Even though he wasn't raising his voice, or using a threatening tone, Kahlan's ears burned. 'I didn't … think to ask.'

'What did they do while they were together? Did she have anything with her? Did she buy anything, or pick up anything, or talk to anyone else who could end up being another part of a team? Was there anyone else they were ordered to kill?'

'I … didn't …'

Richard combed his fingers through his hair. 'One obviously doesn't send an assassin and have him announce himself to the guards at the intended victim's door. That will only get your assassin killed, instead. Maybe Jagang had this man do something before he came to the palace, and then once the task was done, he wanted Marlin to come here so we would kill him and eliminate any chance we would find out what's going on before this Sister carried out the true plot. Jagang certainly wouldn't care if we killed one of his pawns – he has plenty more, and he doesn't value human life.'

Kahlan twisted her fingers together behind her back. She was feeling decidedly foolish. Richard's furrowed brow over his piercing, gray eyes wasn't helping.

'Richard, we knew that there was a woman up here who was asking to see you, just as Marlin did. We didn't know who Nadine was. Marlin didn't know the Sister's name, but he gave us a description: young, pretty, and with long brown hair. We were worried that Nadine might be the Sister, right here among us, and so we left Marlin down there and came up here at once to see about Nadine. That was our priority: stopping a Sister of the Dark if she was in the palace. We'll ask Marlin all those questions later. He's not going anywhere.'

Richard's raptor gaze softened as he took a contemplative breath. He finally nodded. 'You did the right thing. You're right about the questions being less important. I'm sorry; I should have realized you would do what was best.' He lifted a cautionary finger. 'Leave this Marlin fellow to me.'

Richard turned the raptor gaze on Cara. 'I don't want you and Kahlan down there with him. Understand? Something could happen.'

Cara would offer her life without question to protect his, but by her glare she was apparently beginning to resent having her ability questioned. 'And how dangerous was a big strong man at the end of Denna's leash as she walked him with impunity among the public at the People's Palace in D'Hara? Did she have to do more than tuck the end of her pet's thin chain under her belt to demonstrate her complete control? Did he ever once so much as dare to let tension come to that leash?'

The man at the end of that leash had been Richard.

Cara's blue eyes flashed with indignation, like sudden lightning from a clear blue sky. Kahlan almost would have expected Richard to draw his sword in rage. Instead, he watched her, as if listening dispassionately to her opinion, and waiting to see if she had anything to add. Kahlan wondered if Mord-Sith feared being struck dead, or welcomed it.

'Lord Rahl, I have his power. Nothing can happen.'

'I'm sure you do. I don't doubt your abilities, Cara, but I don't want Kahlan put at risk, no matter how inconceivable the risk, when it isn't necessary. You and I will go question Marlin when I get back. I trust you with my life, but I just don't want to trust Kahlan's to an ugly twist of fate.

'Jagang overlooked the ability of the Mord-Sith, probably because he doesn't know enough about the New World to know what a Mord-Sith is. He's made a mistake. I simply want to make sure we don't make a mistake, too. All right? When I get back we'll question Marlin and find out what's really going on.'

As quickly as it had come, the storm in Cara's eyes passed. Richard's calm demeanor had quelled it, and in seconds it seemed as if nothing had happened. Kahlan almost wasn't sure Cara had actually said the savage things she had heard. Almost.

Kahlan wished she could have thought through the matter of Marlin when she had had the chance. Richard made it all seem so simple to her. She guessed that she was so worried for him that she just wasn't thinking clearly. That was a mistake. She knew she shouldn't allow her concern to cloud her thinking, lest she cause the harm she feared.

Richard held the back of Kahlan's neck as he kissed her brow. 'I'm relieved that you weren't hurt. You frighten me the way you get it in your head to put your life before mine. Don't do it again?'

Kahlan smiled. She didn't promise, but instead changed the subject. 'I'm worried about you leaving the safety of the palace. I don't like you being out there when a Sister of the Dark is about.'

'I'll be all right.'

'But the Jarian ambassador is here, along with representatives from Grennidon. They have huge standing armies. There are a few others here, too, from smaller lands – Mardovia, Pendisan Reach, and Togressa. They're all expecting to meet with you tonight.'

Richard hooked a thumb behind the wide leather belt. 'Look, they can surrender to you. They're either with us, or against us. They don't need to see me, they just have to agree to the terms of surrender.'

Kahlan touched her fingers to his arm. 'But you are Lord Rahl, the Master of D'Hara. You made the demands. They expect to see you.'

'Then they'll have to wait until tomorrow night. Our men come first. General Kerson is right: if the men can't fight, we're in trouble. The D'Haran army is the main reason the lands are ready to surrender. We can't show any weakness in our ability to lead.'

'But I don't want us to be separated,' she whispered.

Richard smiled. 'I know. I feel the same, but this is important.'

'Promise me you'll be careful.'

His smile widened. 'I promise. And you know that a wizard always keeps his promise.'

'All right, then, but hurry back.'

'I will. You just stay away from that Marlin fellow.'

He turned to the others. 'Cara, you and Raina stay here, along with Egan. Ulic, I'm sorry I yelled at you. I'll make it up to you by letting you come with me so you can watch me with those big blue eyes and make me feel guilty.' He turned to the last of them. 'Berdine, since I know that you three will make my life miserable if I don't take at least one of you, you can come with me.'

Berdine turned a grin on Nadine. 'I'm Lord Rahl's favorite.'

Nadine, rather than looking impressed, appeared dumbfounded, as she had throughout most of the preceding conversation. Nadine finally turned a haughty look on Richard. She folded her arms across her breasts.

'And are you going to boss me around, too? Are you going to tell me what to do, like you seem to enjoy doing to everyone else?'

Richard, rather than getting angry, as Kahlan thought he might at the insult, looked more disinterested than ever.

'There are a lot of people fighting for our freedom, fighting to stop the Imperial Order from enslaving the Midlands, D'Hara, and eventually Westland. I lead those willing to fight for their own freedom and on behalf of innocent people who would otherwise be enslaved. I lead because circumstances have placed me in command. I don't do it for power or because I enjoy it. I do it because I must.

'To my enemies, or potential enemies, I deliver demands. To those loyal to me, I issue orders.

'You are neither, Nadine. Do as you wish.'

Nadine's freckles disappeared as her cheeks mantled.

Richard lifted his sword a few inches and let it drop back, unconsciously checking that the blade was clear in its scabbard. 'Berdine, Ulic, get your things and meet me out at the stables.'

Richard scooped up Kahlan's hand and pulled her toward the door. 'I need to talk to the Mother Confessor. Alone.'

Richard took Kahlan down the passageway crowded with muscular D'Haran guards wearing dark leather and chain mail and bristling weapons to an empty side hall. He pulled her around the corner, into the shadow beneath a silver lamp, and backed her up against a wall paneled in age-mellowed cherry.

With a finger, he gently squashed the end of her nose. 'I couldn't leave without kissing you good-bye.'

Kahlan grinned. 'Didn't want to kiss me in front of an old girlfriend?'

'You're the only one I love. The only one I've ever loved.' Richard's features distorted in chagrin. 'You can understand how it would be if one of your old boyfriends showed up.'

'No, I can't.'

His face went blank for just an instant and then went crimson. 'Sorry. I wasn't thinking.'

Confessors had no boyfriends as they grew up.

The deliberate touch of a Confessor destroyed a person's mind, and in its place left only mindless devotion to the Confessor who had touched him with her power. A Confessor always had to restrain her grip on her power, lest it be accidentally released. It generally wasn't difficult; her power grew as she did and, being born with the power, the ability to restrain it came as naturally as breathing.

But in the throes of passion, an experience she hadn't grown up with, it was impossible for a Confessor to maintain that restraint. A lover's mind would unintentionally be destroyed in the distracted, unrestrained apex of a Confessor's passion.

Confessors, even if they wished it, had no friends save other Confessors. People feared them, feared their power. Men, especially, feared Confessors. No man wanted to get within striking distance of a Confessor.

Confessors didn't have lovers.

A Confessor chose her mate for qualities desirable in her daughter, for the father he could be. A Confessor never chose for love, because the act of loving would destroy the person she loved. No one willingly wed a Confessor; a Confessor chose her mate, and took him with her magic before they were wedded. Men feared a Confessor who had yet to choose a mate. She was a destroyer among them, a predator, and men her potential prey.

Only Richard had defeated that magic. His unequivocal love for her had transcended her power. Kahlan was the only Confessor she had ever heard of who had the love of a man, and could reciprocate that love. In her whole life, she had never imagined she would fulfill that most exalted of human desires: love.

She had heard it said that there was only one true love in a person's life. With Richard, that was more than a saying: it was the dead cold truth.

More than any of it, though, she simply loved him, helplessly and completely. That he loved her, and they could be together, sometimes left her numb with disbelief.

She dragged her finger down his leather baldric. 'So, you never think about her? You never wonder ... ?'

'No. Look, I've known Nadine since I was little. Her father, Cecil Brighton, sells herbs and remedies. I'd bring him rare plants now and again. He'd let me know if there was something he wanted but couldn't find. When I went out to guide people, I'd keep an eye out for what he needed.

'Nadine always wanted to be like her father, to learn what herbs helped people and to work in his shop. She'd go with me sometimes, to learn how to find certain plants.'

'She only went with you to look for plants?'

'Well, no. There was a little more to it than that. I – well – sometimes I'd go visit her and her parents. I'd go for walks with her, even if her father hadn't asked me to find some herb. I danced with her at the midsummer festival, last summer, before you came to Hartland. I liked her. But I never led her to think I wanted to marry her.'

Kahlan smiled and decided to end his twisting in the wind. She wrapped her arms around his neck and kissed him. She wondered briefly at something he had said to Nadine, at what more there had been, but then her mind was spinning from the feel of his powerful arms around her, and his soft lips against hers. His tongue glided across the inside of her front teeth, and she sucked it in. A big hand slid down her back and pulled her hard against him.

Then she pushed him away. 'Richard,' she said breathlessly, 'what about Shota? What if she causes trouble?'

Richard blinked, trying to banish the lust from his eyes. 'To the underworld with Shota.'

'But in the past, as much trouble as Shota caused, she always seemed to have a nugget of truth in the trouble she wrapped around it. In her own way, she was trying to do what needed doing.'

'She's not going to keep us from getting married.'

'I know, but –'

'When I get back, we'll get married, and that will be that.' His smile made a sunrise seem boring. 'I want you in that big bed of yours that you keep promising me.'

'But how can we get married, now, unless we do it here? It's a long way to the Mud People. We promised the Bird Man, and Weselan and Savidlin, and all the rest, that we would be wedded as Mud People. Chandalen protected me on my journey here, and I owe him my life. Weselan made me my beautiful blue wedding dress, with her own hands, out of cloth that probably took her years to earn. They took us in. They made us Mud People. The Mud People have sacrificed for us. Many have given their lives for our cause.

'I know it's not the kind of wedding most women dream of – a whole village of half-naked people covered in mud dancing around bonfires, calling the spirits to come join two of their people, having a feast that goes on for days with those strange drums and ritual dancers acting out stories and all the rest … but it's the most heartfelt ceremony we could ever have.

'Right now we can't leave Aydindril to go on a long journey to the Mud People just because we want to. Just for us. Everyone else is depending on us. There is a war going on.'

Richard pressed a gentle kiss against her forehead. 'I know. I want the Mud People to marry us, too. And they will. Trust me. I'm the Seeker. I'm giving it a lot of thought. I have a few ideas.' He sighed. 'But right now I have to go. Take care of things, Mother Confessor. I'll be back tomorrow. Promise.'

She hugged him so tight it made her arms hurt.

He finally separated from her and looked down into her eyes. 'I've got to go, before it gets any later, or I'll have men getting hurt in the dark up in those passes.' He paused. 'If … if Nadine needs anything, would you see that she gets it? A horse, or food, or supplies, or whatever. She's not a bad person. I don't wish her ill. She doesn't deserve what Shota did to her.'

Kahlan nodded and then laid her head against his chest. She could hear his heart beating. 'Thank you for getting this outfit to be married in. You look more handsome than ever.'

She closed her eyes against the pain of the words she had heard back in the red room. 'Richard, why didn't you get angry when Cara said those cruel things?'

'Because I understand what was done to them. I've been in that world of madness. Hate would have destroyed me; forgiveness in my heart was the only thing that saved me. I don't want hate to destroy them. I didn't want to let mere words ruin what I'm trying to give them. I want them to learn to trust. Sometimes you can only gain trust by giving it.'

'Maybe you're having an effect. Despite what Cara said back there, earlier today she said some things that make me think they understand.' Kahlan smiled and tried to lighten the subject of the Mord-Sith. 'I heard you were outside today with Berdine and Raina, taming chipmunks.'

'Taming chipmunks is easy. I was doing something considerably more difficult; I was trying to tame Mord-Sith.' His tone was grave, leading to the impression that his thoughts were far away. 'You should have seen Berdine and Raina. They were giggling, just like little girls. I almost wept at the sight.'

Kahlan smiled to herself in wonder. 'And here I thought you were just out there wasting time. How many more Mord-Sith are back at the People's Palace in D'Hara?'

'Dozens.'

'Dozens.' It was a daunting thought. 'At least chipmunks are plentiful.'

He stroked a hand down her hair as he held her head to his chest. 'I love you, Kahlan Amnell. Thanks for being patient.'

'I love you, too, Richard Rahl.' She clutched his tunic and pressed herself against him. 'Richard, Shota still scares me. Promise me that you really will marry me.'

He let out a little, breathy laugh and then kissed the top of her head.

'I love you more than I could ever tell you. There is no one else, not Nadine, not anyone; I swear an oath on my gift. You are the only one I will ever love. I promise.'

She could hear her heart drumming in her ears. That was not the promise she had asked for.

He pushed away. 'I have to go.'

'But …'

He looked back around the corner. 'What? I have to go.'

She shooed him with a hand. 'Go. Hurry back to me.'

He blew her a kiss and then he was gone. She leaned a shoulder against the corner as she watched his billowing gold cape recede down the hall, and listened to the jangle of chain mail and weapons and thud of boots as a raft of guards trailed in his wake.

CHAPTER 7

The two remaining Mord-Sith and Egan waited in the red sitting room. The door to the bedroom was closed.

'Raina, Egan, I want you to go protect Richard,' Kahlan announced as she walked in.

'Lord Rahl told us to remain with you, Mother Confessor,' Raina said.

Kahlan lifted an eyebrow. 'Since when have you followed Lord Rahl's orders when it comes to matters of protecting him?'

Raina grinned wickedly: a rare sight. 'Fine by us. But he will be angry that we left you alone.'

'I have Cara and a palace packed with guards and surrounded by troops. The biggest danger to me is that one of those hulking guards will step on my foot. Richard has only five hundred men, and Berdine and Ulic. I'm worried for him.'

'What if he sends us back?'

'Tell him … tell him … Wait.'

Kahlan crossed the room to the mahogany writing desk and pulled paper, ink, and pen from under the lid. She dipped the pen, leaned over, and wrote: *Stay warm and sleep snug. It gets cold in the mountains in the spring. I love you – Kahlan.*

She folded the paper and handed it to Raina. 'Follow at a distance. Wait until after they set up camp, then give him this message. Tell him that I told you it was important. It will be dark, and he won't send you back in the dark.'

Raina unfastened two buttons at the side of her leather outfit and slid the note in between her breasts. 'He will still be angry, but at you.'

Kahlan smiled. 'The big fellow doesn't scare me. I know how to cool his scowl.'

Raina smiled conspiratorially. 'I've noticed.' She looked over her shoulder at a pleased-looking Egan. 'Let's do our duty and deliver the Mother Confessor's message to Lord Rahl. We need to find some slow horses.'

After they had departed, Kahlan glanced to a watchful Cara, and then knocked on the bedroom door.

'Come in,' came Nadine's muffled voice.

Cara followed Kahlan in. Kahlan didn't object; she knew that if she had asked her to wait outside, Cara would have ignored the order. The Mord-Sith paid no heed to orders if they thought protecting her or Richard required that they did so.

Nadine was rearranging things in her scruffy travel bag. Her head hung low, looking into the bag, and her thick hair dangled down around her head, hiding her face. Periodically, she pushed her kerchief in under that veil of hair.

'Are you all right, Nadine?'

Nadine sniffled, but didn't look up. 'If you call being the biggest fool the spirits ever saw all right, then I guess I'm just dandy.'

'Shota has played me for a fool, too. I know how you feel.'

'Sure.'

'Is there anything you need? Richard wanted me to see to it that you have anything you need. He's concerned about you.'

'And pigs fly. He just wants me out of your fine room, and on the road home.'

'That's not true, Nadine. He said that you were a nice person.'

Nadine finally straightened and pushed some of her hair back over her shoulder. She wiped her nose and stuffed the kerchief in a pocket in her blue dress.

'I'm sorry. You must hate me. I didn't mean to come busting in here and try to take your man. I didn't know. I swear, I didn't know, or I'd never have done it. I thought ... Well, I thought he wanted ...' The word 'me' was drowned in the sound of her tears.

Trying to imagine the devastation of losing Richard's love stirred Kahlan's sympathy. She gave Nadine a comforting hug and sat her on the bed. Nadine pulled the kerchief back out of her pocket and pressed it against her nose as she wept.

Kahlan sat down on the bed next to the woman. 'Why don't you tell me about it, about you and Richard, if it would make you feel better? Sometimes, it helps to have someone listen.'

'I feel so foolish.' Nadine flopped her arms down in her lap as she made an effort to control her weeping. 'It's my own fault. I always liked Richard. Everybody liked Richard. He's nice to everyone. I've never seen him like he was today. He seems so different.'

'He is different, in some ways,' Kahlan said. 'Even from last autumn, when I first met him. He's been through a lot. He's had to sacrifice his old life, and he's been tested by events. He's had to learn to fight, or die. He's had to face the fact that George Cypher wasn't his real father.'

Nadine looked up in astonishment. 'George wasn't his father? Then who was? Someone named Rahl?'

Kahlan nodded. 'Darken Rahl. The leader of D'Hara.'

'D'Hara. Until the boundary came down, I only thought of D'Hara as an evil place.'

'It was,' Kahlan said. 'Darken Rahl was a violent ruler who sought conquest through torture and murder. He had Richard captured and tortured nearly to death. Richard's brother, Michael, had betrayed him to Darken Rahl.'

'Michael? Well, I guess that really doesn't surprise me. Richard loved Michael. Michael is an important man, but he has a mean streak. If he wants something, he doesn't care who it hurts. Though no one had the nerve to voice it, I don't think anyone was too unhappy when he left and never came back.'

'He died in the fight with Darken Rahl.'

Nadine didn't seem unhappy about this news either. Kahlan didn't say that Richard had had Michael executed for betraying the people he was supposed to be protecting, for his responsibility in the deaths of so many.

'Darken Rahl was trying to use magic that would have enslaved everyone under his rule. Richard escaped and killed his real father, and saved us all. Darken Rahl was a wizard.'

'Wizard! And Richard defeated him?'

'Yes. We all owe Richard a great debt for saving us from what his father would have taken the world into.

'Richard is a wizard, too.'

Nadine laughed at what she thought was a joke. Kahlan didn't so much as smile. Cara stood stone-faced. Nadine's eyes widened.

'You're serious, aren't you?'

'Yes. Zedd was his grandfather. Zedd was a wizard, as was Richard's real father. Richard was born with the gift, but he doesn't know very much about how to use it.'

'Zedd's gone, too.'

'He came with us, in the beginning. He's been fighting with us, and trying to help Richard, but a short time ago, in a battle, he was lost. I fear he was killed up at the Wizard's Keep, up on the mountain above Aydindril. Richard refuses to believe Zedd was killed.' Kahlan shrugged. 'Maybe he wasn't. That old man was the most resourceful person I've ever met, other than Richard.'

Nadine wiped her kerchief across her nose. 'Richard and that crazy old man were best friends. That was what Richard meant, then, when he said that his grandfather taught him about herbs. Everyone comes to my father for remedies. My father knows just about everything about herbs, and I hope someday to know half of what he knows, but my father always said that he wished he knew half as much as old Zedd. I never knew Zedd was Richard's grandfather.'

'No one did, not even Richard. It's a long story. I'll tell you a bit of the more important parts.' Kahlan looked down at her own hands nested in her lap. 'After Richard stopped Darken Rahl, he was taken by the Sisters of the Light to the Old World, so that they could teach him to use his gift. They would have kept him at the Palace of the Prophets, in a web of magic that slowed time. They would have had him there for centuries. We thought he was lost to us.

'The Palace of the Prophets turned out to be infested with Sisters of the Dark, and they wanted to free the Keeper of the Underworld. They tried to use Richard to those ends, but he escaped his confinement and stopped them. In the process, the Towers of Perdition that kept the Old and New Worlds separated were destroyed.

'Now, Emperor Jagang, of the Imperial Order in the Old World, is no longer restrained by those towers and is trying to bring all the world under his rule. He wants Richard dead for thwarting him. Jagang is powerful and has a huge army. We have been unwillingly cast into a war for our destiny, our freedom, and for our very existence. Richard leads us in that war.

'Zedd, acting in his capacity as First Wizard, named Richard the Seeker of Truth. It's an ancient post, created three thousand years ago in the great war that raged at that time. It's a solemn assignment of rectitude granted when there is grave need. A Seeker is above any law but his own, and backs his authority with the Sword of Truth and its attendant magic.

'Fate occasionally touches us all in ways we don't always understand, but it sometimes seems to have a death grip on Richard.'

Nadine, her eyes wide, finally blinked. 'Richard? Why Richard? Why is he in the center of all this? He's just a woods guide. He's just a nobody from Hartland.'

'Just because kittens are born in the hearth oven, that doesn't make them muffins. No matter where they're born, it's their destiny to grow up to go out and kill rats.

'Richard is a very special kind of wizard: a war wizard. He is the first wizard with both sides of the magic, Additive and Subtractive, to be born in three thousand years. Richard didn't choose to do all this; he does this because we are all depending on him to help us remain a free people. Richard isn't one to stand by and watch while people are hurt.'

Nadine looked away. 'I know.' She fumbled with the kerchief in her fingers. 'I kind of lied to you before.'

'About what?'

She heaved a sigh. 'Well, when I told you about Tommy and Lester. I made it sound like it was me who knocked out their front teeth. The truth is, I was on my way to meet Richard. We were to go for a walk and look for some maple-leafed viburnum. My father needed some of the inner bark to make a decoction for a baby with colic, and he had run out. Richard knew where there was a patch.

'Anyway, when I was on my way through the woods, to Richard's place, I came across Tommy Lancaster and his friend Lester on their way back from hunting doves. I'd fended off Tommy's unwanted advances in front of some of his pals, and made him look a fool. I guess I kind of slapped him and called him a name.

'He thought to pay me back when he came across me in the woods. He had Lester hold me down, and he … well, about the time he got his pants pushed down around his knees, Richard showed up. That took the starch right out of Tommy. Richard told them to be off, and said that he was going to tell their fathers.

'Instead of doing the smart thing, and leaving, the two of them decided to put a few bird arrows in Richard to teach him a lesson to mind his own business. That's why Tommy and Lester don't have any front teeth. He told them that that was for what they wanted to do to me. He broke their valuable yew bows, and told them that that was for what they wanted to do to him. He told Tommy that if he ever again tried to do that to me, he'd slice off … well, you know.'

Kahlan smiled. 'That sounds like the Richard I know. It doesn't sound like he's really changed all that much. The Tommys and Lesters are just bigger, now, and meaner.'

Nadine gave a little shrug. 'I guess.' She looked up when Cara held out Nadine's tin cup, which Cara had filled from the ewer on the washstand. Nadine took a sip. 'I can't believe people are really trying to kill Richard. I can't believe anyone would want to kill him.' She smirked. 'Even Tommy and Lester only want to knock out his teeth.' She settled the cup in her lap. 'I can't believe his own father would want to kill him. You said Darken Rahl had Richard tortured. Why did he do that?'

Kahlan glanced up at Cara. 'It's in the past. I really don't want to stir up the memories.'

Nadine reddened. 'Sorry. I almost forgot that he … and you …' She drew her fingers across her cheeks, wiping away a fresh tear. 'It just doesn't seem fair.

'You' – Nadine flicked a hand in frustration – 'you've got everything. You have this, this palace. I never even knew such things existed. It looks like some vision come from the spirit world. And you have such fine things, and magnificent clothes. That dress makes you look like one of the good spirits.'

Nadine looked Kahlan in the eye. 'And you're so beautiful. It doesn't seem fair. You even have beautiful green eyes; I just have dumb brown eyes. You must have had men lined up around the palace your whole life, wanting you. You must have had more suitors than most women can even dream of. You have everything. You could have your pick of any man in the Midlands ... and you pick a man from my home.'

'Love isn't always fair; it just is. And your eyes are lovely.' Kahlan twined her fingers together and hooked her hands over a knee. 'What did Richard mean when he said to you that "there is no 'us,' " and that you of all people should know that?'

Nadine's eyes slid closed as she turned her face away. 'Well, I guess a lot of girls in Hartland wanted Richard, not just me. He wasn't like anyone else. He was special. I remember one time when he was about ten or twelve and he talked two men out of fighting. He always had a way about him. He got the two men to laughing, and they left my pa's shop with an arm over each other's shoulder. Richard was always a rare person.'

'The mark of a wizard,' Kahlan said. 'So, Richard must have had a lot of girlfriends?'

'No, not really. He was nice to everyone, and polite, and helpful, but he never seemed to fall for anyone. That only seemed to make them want him all the more. He didn't have a special person, a love. But a lot of us girls wanted to be the one. After Tommy and Lester tried to ... to ... lay claim to me –'

'To rape you.'

'Yeah. I guess that was what it really was. I never like to think that someone would really do that to me, like that – holding me down and all. But I guess that that's what they were trying to do: rape me.

'Some people don't call it that, though. Sometimes, if a boy does that to a girl, then he's laid claim to her, and the parents say that it was because the girl encouraged it, and so they make the girl and boy get married before she turns up pregnant. I know girls who had to do that.

'Many younglings, mostly those of the country folk, have it already decided for them who they're to marry. But sometimes a boy doesn't like who he's supposed to marry, and so he lays claim to who he wants, like Tommy tried to do to me, in the hope that either he'll get her pregnant and she'll have to marry him, or their parents will make them wed because she's been spoiled. Tommy was supposed to wed skinny Rita Wellington, and he hated her. Sometimes, the girl really does encourage it, because she doesn't like who her parents picked for her. Mostly, though, younglings go along as they're told.

'My parents never decided for me, some parents don't. They say that it's a recipe for trouble as often as it is one for happiness. They said they figured that I'd know for myself what I wanted. A lot of the girls who didn't have it decided for them wanted Richard. Some of them, like me, waited long past when we should have been married and mothers two or three times over.

'After Richard stopped Tommy, Richard kind of always looked out for me. I started to think it was more than him just watching out for me, at last. I started to think that he really wanted to be with me. It seemed like he was really noticing me, as a woman, not as some kid he knew who he was protecting.

'I was sure of it at the midsummer festival last year. He danced with me more than any of the other girls. They were turning green with envy. Especially when he held me close. Right then and there, I wanted him to be the one. No one else.

'I thought that after the festival things would change, that he would tell me that I meant more to him than I had before. I thought he would come around and court me more serious. He didn't.'

Nadine held the cup of water between her knees with one hand as she worked her kerchief in the fingers of her other hand. 'I had other boys who wanted to court me, and I didn't want to throw my future away if Richard was never going to come to his senses, so I got it in my head to give him a shove.'

'A shove?'

Nadine nodded. 'Besides some of the other boys, Richard's brother, Michael, was always after me, too. I think just because he always was jealous of Richard. At the time I wasn't exactly against the idea of Michael courting me. I didn't know him so well, but he was already making somebody of himself. I thought Richard would never be anything more than a woods guide. Not that that's bad. I'm nobody special, either. Richard loved the woods.'

Kahlan smiled. 'He still does. If he could, I'm sure he would like nothing more than being a simple woods guide. But he can't. So, what happened, then?'

'Well, I figured that if I kind of made Richard just a bit jealous, maybe he would get down off the fence and make a move for me. Sometimes men need a shove, my ma always says. So I gave him a good shove.'

Nadine cleared her throat. 'I let him catch me kissing Michael. I made sure he saw that I was having a good time of it.'

Kahlan drew a deep breath as her eyebrows lifted. Nadine may have grown up with Richard, but she certainly didn't know him.

'He never even got angry at me, or jealous, or anything,' Nadine said. 'He was still nice to me, and he still watched out for me, but he never came visiting, and he never asked me to go for walks after that. When I tried to talk to him about it, to explain, he just wasn't interested.'

Nadine stared off. 'He had that look in his eyes, like he did today. That look that means he just doesn't care. I never knew what it meant until I saw it again, today. I think he really had cared and expected me to show him I cared by being loyal, but I'd betrayed him.'

Nadine dabbed at her lower lids as she took labored breaths. 'Shota told me that Richard was going to marry me, and I was so happy that I just didn't want to believe it when he said it wasn't so. I didn't want to believe that look in his eyes, so I pretended to myself that it didn't mean anything, but it does. It means everything.'

'I'm sorry, Nadine,' Kahlan said softly.

Nadine stood and set the tin cup on the side table. Tears streamed down her cheeks and dripped off the side of her jaw. 'Forgive me for coming in here like I did. He loves you, not me. He never loved me. I'm happy for you, Mother Confessor; you have a good man who will watch over you and protect you and always be kind. I know he will.'

Kahlan stood and took Nadine's hand, giving it a comforting squeeze. 'Kahlan. My name is Kahlan.'

'Kahlan.' Nadine still couldn't meet Kahlan's eyes. 'Does he kiss good? I always wondered. When I laid awake in bed, I always wondered.'

'When you love someone with all your heart, their kisses are always good.'

'I guess. I never had a good kiss. One I really enjoyed like the ones I've dreamed about, anyway.' She smoothed the front of her dress as she made an effort to compose herself. 'I wore this because blue is Richard's favorite color. You should know that – blue is his favorite color dress.'

'I know,' Kahlan whispered.

Nadine pulled her bag closer. 'I don't know what I'm thinking, forgetting my profession, while I ramble on about what's over and done.'

Nadine rummaged around in her bag, bringing out a small piece of a sheep's horn with a cork stopper in the square-cut end. The horn was marked with scratches and circles. She pulled the cork stopper and dipped in a finger, then lifted it to Cara.

Cara backed away. 'What do you think you are doing?'

'It's an unguent, made from aum, to take away the sting, and comfrey and yarrow to help stop the bleeding so the wound can heal smooth. The cut on your cheek is still oozing. If this doesn't stop the blood, then I have some foxglove, but I think this will do it. It's not only the ingredients but how much of each, my pa says, that's the secret that makes the medicine work.'

'I don't need it,' Cara said.

'You're very pretty. You don't want to end up with a scar, now do you?'

'I have many scars. You just can't see them.'

'Where are they?'

Cara scowled, but Nadine didn't back away.

'All right,' Cara said at last. 'Use your herbs, if it will get you away from me. But I'm not undressing so you can peer at my scars.'

Nadine smiled assurance and then dabbed the brownish

paste on Cara's cheek. 'This will take away the pain of the cut, but it's going to sting for just a minute, and then it will ease.'

Cara didn't so much as blink. It must have surprised Nadine because she paused and looked at Cara's eyes before resuming her work. When she was finished, Nadine replaced the stopper in the horn and placed it back in her bag.

Nadine glanced around the room. 'I've never seen such a beautiful room. Thank you for letting me use it.'

'Of course. Do you need anything? Some supplies ... anything?'

Nadine shook her head, wiped her nose a last time, and stuffed the kerchief back in the pocket. She remembered the cup, downed the rest of the water, and put it in her bag, too.

'It's a bit of a journey, but I have some silver left. I'll be fine.'

She rested a hand on her bag as she stared down at her trembling fingers. 'I never thought my journey would end like this. I'm going to be the laugh of Hartland, running off after Richard like I did.' She swallowed. 'What's Pa going to say?'

'Did Shota tell him, too, that you were going to marry Richard?'

'No. I hadn't met Shota yet.'

'What do you mean? I thought she was the one who told you to come here – that you were to marry him.'

'Well' – Nadine made a wincing smile – 'that wasn't exactly how it happened.'

'I see.' Kahlan clasped her hands. 'Well, exactly how *did* it happen?'

'It will sound silly – like I'm some moonstruck girl of twelve.'

'Nadine, just tell me.'

Nadine considered a moment before finally sighing. 'I suppose it doesn't matter. I started having these, well, I don't know what to call it. I'd see Richard, or rather, I thought I saw Richard. I'd see him out of the corner of my eye, and I'd turn, but he wouldn't be there. Like one day, when I was walking in the woods looking for new shoots, and I saw him standing beside a tree, so I stopped, but he was gone.

'Every time, I knew he needed me. I didn't know how I

knew, but I knew. I knew it was important, that he was in trouble of some sort. I never questioned it.

'I told my parents that Richard needed me and I had to go help him.'

'And they believed you? They had faith in your visions? They simply let you set out?'

'Well, I never quite explained it to them. I just told them that Richard had sent me a message that he needed my help, and I was going to him. I guess that I, well, I might have kind of made them think I knew where I was going.'

Kahlan was beginning to see that Nadine didn't explain things to anyone very well. 'Then Shota came?'

'No. Then I left. I knew Richard needed me, and so I started out.'

'Alone? You simply thought to march off and search the entire Midlands for him?'

Nadine shrugged self-consciously. 'It never occurred to me to wonder how I would find him. I knew he needed me, and I felt that it was important, so I left to go to him.' She smiled, as if to reassure Kahlan. 'I came right to him – straight as an arrow. It all worked out exactly right.' Her cheeks flushed. 'Except the part about him wanting me, I mean.'

'Nadine, had you been having any … strange dreams? Then, or now?'

Nadine brushed back a thick strand of hair. 'Strange dreams? No, no strange dreams. You know, I mean no stranger than any dreams. Just regular dreams.'

'What kind of "regular" dreams do you have?'

'Well, you know, like when you dream that you're little again, and lost in the woods, and none of the trails lead you where you know they should, or like when you dream that you can't find all the right ingredients for a pie, and so you go to a cave and borrow them from a bear that can talk. Things like that. Just dreams. Dreams that you can fly, or breathe underwater. Crazy things. But just dreams. Like I've always had. Nothing different.'

'Have they changed recently?'

'No. If I remember them, they're the same sort of things.'

'I see. I guess that all sounds pretty normal.'

Nadine pulled a cloak from her bag. 'Well, I guess I'd better get a start. With luck, I'll be home for the spring festival.'

Kahlan frowned. 'You'll be lucky to make midsummer festival.'

Nadine laughed. 'I should think not. It can't take longer back than here. Just two weeks or so. I only left just after the moon's second quarter; it's not yet full.'

Kahlan stared dumbly. 'Two weeks.' It had to have taken Nadine months to travel all the way from Westland, especially in the winter when she would have had to have started, and especially across the Rang'Shada mountains. 'Your horse must have had wings.'

Nadine laughed, then it died out as her smooth brow puckered. 'Funny you should mention that. I don't have a horse. I walked.'

'Walked,' Kahlan repeated incredulously.

'Yes. But since I've left, I've had dreams of flying on a horse with wings.'

Kahlan was having to work at keeping track of the shifting pieces of Nadine's story. She tried to think of how Richard would ask questions. It had made her feel foolish when Richard put words to all the questions she should have asked Marlin, but never thought of. Though he had taken the sting out of it by telling her that she had done the right thing, it still embarrassed her that she had found out next to nothing important from Marlin when she had had her chance.

Confessors didn't need to know much about questioning people; once she had touched a person with her power, a Confessor simply asked the criminal to confess if they had truly committed the crimes they had been found guilty of, and if the answer was yes – which it always was, except in a couple of rare instances – then to recount the details.

There was no art to it, and none needed. It was an infallible way of seeing to it that political dissenters weren't falsely accused and found guilty of crimes they didn't commit, simply to have them eliminated through a convenient execution.

Kahlan was determined to do a better job of asking Nadine questions. 'When did Shota come to see you? You still haven't told me that part.'

'Oh. Well, she didn't exactly come to see me. I came across

93

her up in the mountains. She had a lovely palace, but I never had the chance to go inside. I wasn't there long. I wanted to get to Richard.'

'And what did Shota tell you? What were her words? Her *exact* words?'

'Let's see …' Nadine pressed her first finger to her upper lip as she recollected. 'She welcomed me. She offered me tea – she said that I had been expected – and had me sit with her. She made Samuel leave my bag when he tried to drag it away, and she told me not to be afraid of him. She asked where I was traveling, and I told her that I was going to my Richard – that he needed me. Then she told me things about Richard, things about his past that I would know about. It astonished me that she would know so much about him, but I thought that she must know him.

'And then she told me things about me that she would have no way of knowing. Like longings and ambitions – being a healer, using my herbs, things like that. That's when I realized she was a mystic. I don't remember her exact words about any of that part.

'She told me that it was true about Richard needing me. She said that we were going to be married. She said that the sky had told her it was so.' Nadine looked away from Kahlan's eyes. 'I was so happy. I don't think I'd ever been that happy.'

'The sky. What else?'

'Then she said that she didn't want to delay my journey to Richard. She said the wind hunts him – whatever that means – and that I was right that he needed me, and I should hurry and be on my way. She wished me luck.'

'That's all? She must have said something else.'

'No, that's all.' Nadine buttoned her bag closed. 'Except she said a prayer for Richard, I think.'

'What do you mean? What did she say? *Her exact words*.'

'Well, when she turned away, to go back to her palace as I was getting up to leave, I heard her whisper, real solemn-like, ''May the spirits have mercy on his soul.'' '

Kahlan felt her arms under the white satin sleeves of her dress prickle with gooseflesh. She only remembered to take a breath when she felt her lungs burning for want of air.

Nadine hoisted her bag. 'Well, I've caused you enough grief. I'd best be on my way home.'

Kahlan spread her hands. 'Look, Nadine, why don't you stay here for a while.'

Nadine paused with a bewildered look. 'Why?'

Kahlan desperately searched for an excuse. 'Well, I wouldn't mind hearing stories about Richard when he was growing up. You could tell me about all the trouble he got himself into.' She made herself smile encouragement. 'I'd really like that.'

Nadine shook her head. 'Richard wouldn't want me here. He'll be angry if he comes back and I'm still here. You didn't see the look in his eyes.'

'Nadine, Richard isn't going to throw you out on your ear without letting you have a chance to rest up for a few days before you start back. Richard isn't like that. He said "anything she needs." I think you could use a rest for a few days, more than anything else.'

Nadine shook her head again. 'No. You've already been more kind to me than I've a right to expect. You and Richard belong together. You don't need me around.

'But thank you for the offer. I can't believe how kind you are – it's small wonder Richard loves you. Any other woman in your place would've had me shaved bald and sent out of town in the back of a manure wagon.'

'Nadine, I'd really like you to stay.' Kahlan wet her lips. 'Please?' she heard herself add.

'It might cause hard feelings between you and Richard. I don't want to be the cause of that. I'm not that kind of person.'

'If it was a problem, I wouldn't have asked. Stay. At least for a few days. All right? You could stay right here in this room you like so much. I'd … really like you to stay.'

Nadine studied Kahlan's eyes for a long moment. 'You really want me to stay? Really?'

'Yes.' Kahlan could feel her nails digging into her palms. 'Really.'

'Well, to tell the truth, I'm not in a hurry to go home and confess my foolishness to my parents. All right, then, if you really want me to, I'll stay for a while. Thank you.'

Despite having important reasons for asking Nadine to stay, Kahlan couldn't help feeling like a moth flying into a flame.

CHAPTER 8

Kahlan forced a smile. 'Good, then. You'll stay. It will be …
nice, to have you stay for a visit. We'll talk, you and I. About
Richard. I mean, I'd like to hear your stories about him
growing up.' She realized she must sound like she was
babbling, and made herself stop.

Nadine beamed. 'I can sleep in the bed?'

'Don't be silly. Of course in the bed. Where else?'

'I have a blanket, and could sleep on the carpet so as not
to –'

'No. I won't have it. I've invited you to stay. I want you to
feel at home, just like other guests who use this room.'

Nadine giggled. 'Then I'd be sleeping on the floor. I sleep
on a pallet on the floor in the back room above our shop.'

'Well,' Kahlan said, 'here you will sleep in the bed.' Kahlan
glanced at Cara before going on. 'Later, I'll show you around
the palace, if you'd like, but for now, why don't you just
unpack some of your things and have a rest while Cara and I
go see to some important business.'

'What business?' Cara asked.

The woman is as silent as a stone through all this, Kahlan
thought, and now she has to ask questions.

'Marlin business.'

'Lord Rahl told us to stay away from Marlin.'

'He's an assassin sent to kill Richard. There are things I
need to know.'

'I want to come, too, then,' Nadine said. She looked back
and forth between Kahlan and Cara. 'I can't imagine anyone

wanting to kill a person, much less Richard. I want to see what such a person looks like. I want to look into his eyes.'

Kahlan emphatically shook her head. 'It's not something you want to see. We need to question him, and it isn't likely to be pleasant.'

'Really?' Cara asked, her voice brightening.

'Why?' Nadine asked. 'What do you mean?'

Kahlan held up a finger. 'Enough. I say this for your own good; Marlin is dangerous and I don't want you down there. You are a guest. Please respect my wishes while you are a guest in my home.'

Nadine studied the floor at her feet. 'Of course. Forgive me.'

'I will tell the guards that you are a guest, and if you would like anything – to have some of your things washed, a bath, anything – just ask and they will see that someone from the staff helps you. I'll be back after a while and we can have dinner. We'll talk over dinner.'

Nadine turned to her bag on the bed. 'Sure. I didn't mean to meddle. I don't want to be in the way.'

Kahlan hesitantly touched a hand to the back of Nadine's shoulder. 'I didn't mean to sound like I was ordering you around. This business with someone trying to hurt Richard just has me on edge, that's all. I'm sorry I nearly bit your head off. You're a guest. Please enjoy our home as your own.'

Nadine smiled over her shoulder. 'I understand. Thanks.'

She really was a beautiful young woman: attractive figure and face, and an innocent quality, despite what truths Kahlan feared she danced around. Kahlan could easily see why Richard would have been attracted to her.

She wondered at what random wisp of fate had matched Richard with her, instead of this one. Whatever the reason, she thanked the good spirits that it was so, and prayed fervently that it would remain so.

More than anything, Kahlan wanted this perfidious gift from Shota to vanish. She wanted this tempting, beautiful, dangerous young woman away from Richard, to just send Nadine away. If only she could do so.

After telling the guards that Nadine was a guest, and once Kahlan and Cara had descended the carpeted stairs at the far end of the hall and were alone on the richly appointed landing, Cara seized Kahlan's arm and spun her around to a halt.

'Are you crazy!'

'What are you talking about?'

Cara gritted her teeth as she leaned closer. 'A witch woman sends your man a wedding gift – it's the bride, and you invite her to stay!'

Kahlan rubbed a thumb against the round, polished sphere of ironwood topping the newel post. 'I had to. Isn't it obvious?'

'What is obvious to me is that you should have done as the little strumpet suggested; you should have shaved her bald and sent her away in the back of a manure wagon.'

'She's a victim in this, too. She is Shota's pawn.'

'Her tongue has a distaste for the truth. She still wants your man. If you can't see that in her eyes, then you aren't the wise woman I thought you to be.'

'Cara, I trust Richard. I know he loves me. If there's one thing at the core of Richard's way of looking at things, it's trust and loyalty. I know my heart is safe in his hands.

'How would it look if I acted like a jealous woman and sent Nadine away? If I don't show my trust in him, then I'm not honoring his loyalty to me. I can't afford to even appear to betray his trust in me.'

Cara's scowl didn't so much as soften. 'That bucket won't carry water for me. All that may be true, but that isn't why you asked Nadine to stay. You want to strangle her as much as I do, I can see it in your green eyes.'

Kahlan smiled, trying to see herself in the dark, polished ironwood. She could only see a blur of a reflection. 'Hard to fool a sister of the Agiel. You're right. I had to ask Nadine to stay because there's something going on, something dangerous. The danger won't simply go away if I make Nadine leave.'

With a gloved hand, Cara wiped a strand of blond hair back from her face. 'Dangerous? Like what?'

'Therein lies the problem: I don't know. And don't you *dare* even think of hurting her. I have to find out what's really going on, and in order to do that I may need Nadine. I don't want to have to go hunting her when I could have kept her at hand and in sight in the beginning.

'Look at it this way. Would it have been the right thing to do to simply send Marlin away when he arrived and announced he wanted to kill Richard? Would that have solved the problem? Why are we keeping him around? To find out what's going on, that's why.'

Cara wiped at the unguent on her cheek as if it were a smudge of dirt. 'I think you are inviting trouble to your bed.'

Kahlan had to blink at the burning sensation in her eye. 'I know. Me, too. The obvious thing to do, the thing I ache to do, is to send Nadine away on the fastest horse I can find. But no problem is that easily solved, especially one sent by Shota.'

'You mean what Shota told Nadine, about the wind hunting Lord Rahl?'

'That's part of it. I don't know what it means, but it doesn't sound to me like it's something Shota dreamed up.

'Worse, though, is Shota's prayer: "May the spirits have mercy on his soul." I don't know what she meant by that, but it terrifies me. That, and that I might be making the biggest mistake of my life.

'But what choice do I have? Two people show up on the same day, one sent to kill him and the other sent to marry him. I don't know which is more dangerous, but I do know that neither can be simply dismissed. If someone is trying to stick a knife in your back, closing your eyes doesn't make you safe.'

Cara's face eased from that of a Mord-Sith to the softer features of a woman who understood another woman's fears. 'I will watch your back. If she crawls into Lord Rahl's bed, I will throw her out before he ever finds her there.'

Kahlan squeezed Cara's arm. 'Thanks. Now, let's get down to the pit.'

Cara didn't budge. 'Lord Rahl said he does not want you down there.'

'And since when have you started following orders?'

'I always follow his orders. Especially the ones I know he means. He means this one.'

'Fine. You can watch over Nadine while I go down there.'

Cara snatched Kahlan's elbow as she started to turn away. 'Lord Rahl does not want you in danger.'

'And I don't want him in danger. Cara, I felt a fool when Richard asked me all those questions that we failed to ask Marlin. I want the answers to those questions.'

'Lord Rahl said he would ask them.'

'And he's not going to be back until tomorrow night. What happens in the meantime? What if something is going on and it's too late to stop it by then? What if Richard is killed because we sat on our hands following his orders?

'Richard is afraid for me, and that's keeping him from thinking clearly. Marlin has information about what's going on, and it's foolhardy to let time pass while the danger grows.

'What was it that you said to me, before? Something about hesitation being the end of you? Or the end of those you care about?'

Cara's face went slack, but she didn't answer.

'I care about Richard, and I'm not going to risk his life by hesitating. I'm going to get the answers to those questions.'

Cara smiled at last. 'I like your thinking, Mother Confessor. But then, you are a sister of the Agiel. The orders were ill-advised, if not foolish. Mord-Sith only follow Lord Rahl's foolish orders when his male pride is at stake, not his life.

'We will go have a little discussion with Marlin, and get the answer to every one of those questions, and more. When Lord Rahl comes back, we will be able to give him the information he needs – if we haven't already ended the threat.'

Kahlan popped the palm of her hand against the round newel post. 'That's the Cara I know.'

As they went lower in the palace, below the levels with carpets and paneling, down to the narrow, low-ceilinged halls where light came only from lamps, and even lower, where only torches lit the way, the air went from light and spring-fresh to stale, and then to rank with the heavy smell of damp, moldy stone.

Kahlan had walked those confining halls more times than she wished to recall. The pit was where they took confessions of the condemned. She had taken her first there, from a man who had killed his neighbor's daughters after committing unspeakable acts on them. Of course, each of those times she had been accompanied by a wizard. Now, she was going to see a wizard being held there.

When they had passed out of earshot of a squad of soldiers guarding an intersection with two stairwells, and before they reached the turn that would take them to the pit hall that would be crowded with all the soldiers she had stationed there, Kahlan glanced over. Cara was an attractive woman, but a woman with an air of menace about her as she swept the empty hall with vigilant gazes.

'Cara, can I ask you a personal question?'

Cara clasped her hands behind her back as she strode along. 'You are a sister of the Agiel. Ask.'

'Before, you told me that hesitation can be the end of you, or those you care about. You were talking about yourself, weren't you?'

Cara slowed to a stop. Even in the hissing torchlight, Kahlan could see that her face had paled.

'Now that is truly a personal question.'

'You don't have to tell me. I don't mean it to sound like an order, or anything. I was just wondering, woman to woman. You know so much about me, and I hardly know anything about you, except that you are Mord-Sith.'

'I wasn't always Mord-Sith,' Cara whispered. Her eyes had lost the menace, and she looked like nothing so much as a frightened little girl. Kahlan could tell that Cara was no longer seeing the empty stone hall.

'I guess that there is no reason not to tell you. As you said, I am not to blame for what was done to me. Others were responsible.

'Every year, in D'Hara, they would select a few girls to be trained as Mord-Sith. It is said that the greatest cruelty is drawn from those with the kindest hearts. Rewards were paid for the names of girls who fit the requirements. I was an only child, one of the requirements, and of the right age. The girl, and her parents, are taken, the parents to be murdered in the training of a Mord-Sith. My parents didn't know that our names had been sold to the hunters.'

Cara's face and tone had lost their emotion. She had gone blank, as if she were telling of last year's beet harvest. But her words, if not her tone, carried more than enough emotion.

'My father and I were out back of the house, butchering chickens. When they came, I had no idea what it meant. My

102

father did. He saw them coming down the hill, through the trees. He surprised them. But there were more than he had seen, or could handle, and he had the advantage for only a few moments.

'He screamed at me, ''Cari, the knife! Cari, get the knife!'' I snatched it up because he said to. He was holding three of the men. My father was big.

'He screamed again. ''Cari, stab them! Stab them! Hurry!'' '

Cara looked into Kahlan's eyes. 'I just stood there. I hesitated. I didn't want to stab someone. To hurt someone. I just stood there. I couldn't even kill the chickens. He did that part.'

Kahlan didn't know if Cara was going to go on. In the dead silence, she decided that if she didn't, the questions would end there. Cara looked away from Kahlan's eyes, staring off into the visions, and then she did go on.

'Someone walked up beside me. I'll never forget it as long as I live. I looked up, and there was this woman, this beautiful woman, the most beautiful woman I had ever seen, with blue eyes and blond hair in a long braid. The sunlight coming through the leaves danced in little patches across her red leather outfit.

'She smiled down at me as she took the knife out of my hand. Not a pretty smile, but a smile like a snake. That's what I always called her, in my mind, after that – Snake. When she straightened, she said, ''Isn't that sweet? Little Cari doesn't want to hurt anyone with her knife. That hesitation just made you a Mord-Sith, Cara. It begins.'' '

Cara stood rigid, as if turned to stone. 'They kept me in a little room, with little grates in the bottom of the door. I couldn't get out. But the rats could get in. At night, when I finally could stay awake no longer, and fell asleep, the rats would sneak into my empty little room and bite my fingertips, and my toes.

'Snake beat me nearly to death for blocking the grate. Rats like blood. It excites them.

'I learned to sleep in a ball, with my hands in fists and tucked in against my belly, where they couldn't get at my fingers. But they could usually get at my toes. I tried taking my shirt off, and wrapping it around my bare feet, but then if I didn't sleep on my stomach, they would bite my nipples. Laying bare-chested on the cold stone, with my hands under my stomach, was a torture in itself, but it usually kept me awake longer. If the rats couldn't get at my toes, they would bite me somewhere else – my ears, or nose, or legs – until I woke with a start and scared them away.

'In the night, I could hear the other girls cry out when a rat bit them awake. I could always hear one of them weeping in the night, calling for her mother. Sometimes, I realized it was my own voice I heard.

'Sometimes, I would wake when rats scratched my face with their little claws, their whiskers brushing my cheeks as their cold little noses pressed against my lips, sniffing for a crumb. I thought to stop eating what they brought me, and left the bowl of gruel and slab of bread on the floor, hoping the rats would eat my dinner and leave me alone.

'It didn't work. The food only brought hordes of rats, and then, when it was gone … I always ate every scrap of dinner, after that, when Snake brought it.

'Sometimes she would taunt me when she brought my dinner. She would say, "Don't hesitate, Cara, or the rats will get your dinner." I knew what she meant by saying, "Don't hesitate." It was her way of reminding me what my hesitation had cost me and my parents. When they tortured my mother to death in front of me, Snake said, "See what happens, Cara, because you hesitated? Because you were too timid?"

'We were taught that Darken Rahl was "Father Rahl." We had no father but he. At my third breaking, when they told me to torture my real father to death, Snake told me not to hesitate. I didn't. My father begged for mercy. "Cari, please," he wept. "Cari, spare yourself becoming what they want." But I never hesitated. After that, my only father was Father Rahl.'

Cara brought her Agiel up and stared at it as she rolled it in her fingers. 'I earned my Agiel for that. The very same Agiel they trained me with. I earned the appellation Mord-Sith.'

Cara looked back into Kahlan's eyes, as if from a great distance, not merely the two steps that separated them. From the other side of madness. A madness others had put there. Kahlan felt as if she, too, was turned to stone by what she saw in the depths of those blue eyes.

'I have been Snake. I have stood in the dappled sunlight, over young girls, and taken the knife from their hands when they hesitated, not wanting to hurt anyone.'

Kahlan had always hated snakes. She hated them more now.

Tears tickled her face as they ran down her cheeks leaving wet tracks. 'I'm sorry, Cara,' she whispered. Her stomach roiled. She wanted nothing more than to put her arms around the woman in red leather before her, but she couldn't make herself move so much as a finger.

Torches hissed. In the distance, she heard muffled snippets of conversation from the guards. A soft ripple of laughter floated up the hall. Water weeping from the stone ceiling echoed as it splashed in a little green puddle not far away. Kahlan could hear her own heart pounding in her ears.

'Lord Rahl freed us from that.'

Kahlan remembered Richard telling her that he had almost wept at the sight of the other two Mord-Sith giggling like little girls as they fed seeds to chipmunks. Kahlan understood the leap that was a simple giggle. Richard understood the madness. Kahlan didn't know if these women could ever return from it, but if they were to have a chance, it was only because of Richard.

The iron returned to Cara's grim expression. 'Let's go find out how Marlin planned to harm Lord Rahl. But don't expect me to be gentle if he hesitates in confessing every detail.'

Under Sergeant Collins's watchful eye, a D'Haran soldier unlocked the iron door and backed away, as if the rusty lock was the only thing protecting everyone in the palace from the sinister magic below, in the pit. Two more big soldiers effortlessly dragged the heavy ladder closer.

Before Kahlan could pull open the door, she heard approaching voices and footsteps. Everyone turned to look up the hall.

It was Nadine, with four soldiers escorting her.

Nadine rubbed her hands together, as if to warm them, as she stepped through the ring of hulking, leather-clad guards.

Kahlan didn't return the woman's bright smile.

'What are you doing down here?'

'Well, you said I was a guest. As pretty as your rooms are, I wanted to go for a walk. I asked the guards to show me the way down here. I want to see this killer.'

'I told you to wait upstairs in your room. I told you that I didn't want you coming down here.'

Nadine's dainty brow drew together. 'I'm getting just a little tired of being treated like a backwater bumpkin.' She lifted her delicate nose. 'I'm a healer. I'm respected, where I come from. People listen when I speak. When I tell someone to do something, they do it. If I tell a councilman to take a potion three times a day and to stay in bed, he very well drinks his medicine three times a day from his bed until I tell him he can leave it.'

'I don't care who jumps when you speak,' Kahlan said. 'Here, you jump when I speak. Do you understand?'

Nadine pressed her lips together as she planted her fists on her hips. 'Now, you look here. I've been cold and hungry and scared. I've been played for a fool by people I don't even know. I was minding my own business, going about my life, when I was sent on this pointless journey, only to arrive at a place where people treat me like a leper as my thanks for coming to help. I've been yelled at by people I don't know and humiliated by a boy I grew up with.

'I thought I was going to marry the man I wanted, but I had that rug yanked out from under my feet. He doesn't want me, he wants you. Well, so be it. Now someone is trying to kill the man I traveled all this way to see, and you tell me it isn't any of my business!'

She shook a finger at Kahlan. 'Richard Cypher saved me from Tommy Lancaster laying claim to me. If it wasn't for Richard, I'd be married to Tommy, now. Instead, Tommy had to marry Rita Wellington. If it wasn't for Richard, I'd be the one with black eyes all the time. I'd be barefoot back at his shack and pregnant with the offspring of that pig-faced bully.

'Tommy ridiculed me for fixing herbs to help people. He said it was stupid for a girl to mix herbs. He said my father should have had a boy, if he wanted someone to work in his shop touching herbs that sick people needed. I'd never have any hope of being a healer if it wasn't for Richard.

'Just because I'm not the one to be his wife, that doesn't

mean that I don't care about him. I grew up with him. He's still a boy from my home. We take care of our own, like they're family, even if they aren't. I've a right to know what danger he's in! I've a right to see what sort of man from your world would want to kill a boy from my home who's helped me!'

Kahlan was in no mood to argue. She was also in no mood to spare the woman what she might see.

She studied Nadine's brown eyes, trying to tell if what Cara had said, that Nadine still wanted Richard, was true. If it was, Kahlan couldn't tell simply by looking into her eyes.

'You want to see a man who wants to kill us, Richard and me?' Kahlan gripped the lever and threw open the door. 'Fine. You shall have your wish.'

She gestured to the men with the ladder. They pushed it through the opening and down into the darkness until it thudded in place. Kahlan yanked a torch from a bracket and thrust it in Cara's hand.

'Let's show Nadine what she wishes to see.'

Cara checked Kahlan's resolve, found it rock solid, and then started down the ladder.

Kahlan held her arm out in invitation. 'Welcome to my world, Nadine. Welcome to Richard's world.'

Nadine's determination faltered for only an instant before she huffed and started down the ladder after Cara.

Kahlan glanced around at the guards. 'Sergeant Collins, if he comes up through this door before us, he had better not get out of this hall alive. He wants to kill Richard.'

'On my word as a D'Haran soldier, Mother Confessor, harm won't get a glimpse of Lord Rahl.'

With a hand signal from Sergeant Collins, soldiers drew steel. Archers nocked arrows. Big hands unhooked crescent-bladed axes from weapons belts.

Kahlan gave the sergeant a nod of approval, took another torch, and started down the ladder.

CHAPTER 9

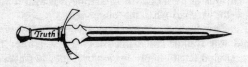

Dank, heavy air wafted up from the pit as Kahlan followed Nadine down the ladder. Using the hand with the torch to also hold the side of the ladder made her have to endure the heat of the flame near the side of her face, but she was almost happy for the smell of pitch because it covered the stink of the air in the pit. Lower down, the wavering light from the torches lit more than the stone walls; they lit the dark figure in the center of the room.

Kahlan stepped off the ladder as Cara rammed her torch into a bracket on the slime-covered wall. Kahlan slipped hers into one on the opposite wall. Nadine stood transfixed, looking at the man covered in dried blood hunched before them. Kahlan stepped past her to stand beside Cara.

Cara's brow drew down as she peered at Marlin.

His head hung forward, and his eyes were closed. His breathing was deep, slow, and even.

'He's asleep,' Cara whispered.

'Asleep?' Kahlan whispered back. 'How can he be asleep while he's standing up like that?'

'I ... don't know. We always make new prisoners stand, sometimes for days. With no one to talk to and nothing to do but consider their doom, it drains their resolve – takes the fight right out of them. It's an insidious form of torment. I have had men beg to be beaten, rather than have to stand, alone, hour after hour.'

Marlin was snoring softly. 'How often does this happen – that they simply fall asleep?'

Cara put one hand on a hip as she wiped her mouth with the other. 'I've had them fall asleep, but that wakes them for sure. If they move from the spot where we've told them to stand, the link brings on the pain. We don't have to be there; the link works no matter where we are. I have never even heard of a man falling asleep and remaining on his feet.'

Kahlan looked over her shoulder, past Nadine, and up the long ladder to the light coming through the doorway. She could see the tops of soldiers' heads, but none were so bold as to stare down into the pit, where there were apt to be deeds of magic.

Nadine stuck her head between them. 'Maybe it's a spell. Magic, of some sort.'

She straightened, pulling her head back, when she received only glares in answer.

More out of curiosity than an attempt to wake him, Cara lightly jabbed Marlin's shoulder. She pushed her finger into his chest, and his stomach.

'Hard as a rock. His muscles are all locked rigid.'

'That must be how he's able to stand there like that. Maybe it's some sort of trick he learned as a wizard.'

Cara didn't seem convinced. With a twitch of her hand so slight Kahlan almost missed it, Cara spun her Agiel up into her fist. The pain Kahlan knew it caused her to hold her Agiel didn't show on her face. It never did.

Kahlan snatched Cara's wrist. 'You don't need to do that. Just wake him. And don't use your link with his mind, his magic, to give him pain, unless it's absolutely necessary. Unless I tell you so.'

Displeasure registered on Cara's face. 'I think it's necessary. I can't have this. I can't hesitate to exert my control.'

'Cara, there is a great gulf between prudence and hesitation. This whole thing with Marlin has been more than odd from the first. Let's just take it one step at a time. You've said that you have control over him; let's not be impetuous. You do have control, don't you?'

A slow smile spread on Cara's lips. 'Oh, I have control, no doubt of that. But if you insist, I will wake him the way we sometimes wake our pets, then.'

Cara bent forward at the waist, slipped her left arm around

his neck, tilted her head, and gently gave Marlin a long kiss on the mouth. Kahlan felt her face go red. She knew that Denna sometimes awakened Richard like that, before torturing him again.

With a satisfied smirk, Cara drew back.

Like a cat coming awake from a nap, Marlin's lids slid open.

His eyes had that quality in them again – that quality that made Kahlan's very soul want to shrink back.

This time, she saw more than she had before. These eyes were not merely those of great age. These were eyes unvisited by fear.

As he regarded the three of them with slow, unflinching, calculating deliberation, he bent his fisted hands back at the wrists and arched his back in a feline stretch. A depraved grin spread onto his face, a taint of wickedness expanding like blood seeping through white linen.

'So. My two darlins have returned.' His disquieting eyes seemed to see more than they should, to know more than they should. 'And they've brought a new bitch with 'em.'

Marlin's voice had been almost boyish, before. Now, it was deep and gravelly, as if coming from a muscled man weighing twice as much – a voice steeped with unquestioned power and authority. It exuded invincibility. Kahlan had never heard such a dangerous voice.

She retreated a step, clutching Cara's arm and pulling her back with her.

Though Marlin didn't move, she felt the coiling of menace.

'Cara' – Kahlan put a hand behind, forcing Nadine back as she withdrew another step – 'Cara, tell me you've got him. Tell me you have control.'

Cara was staring, mouth agape, at Marlin. 'What … ?'

She abruptly unleashed a powerful strike. Her armored fist only snapped his head a few inches to the side. It should have taken him from his feet.

Marlin regarded her with a bloody smile. He spit out broken teeth.

'Nice try, darlin,' Marlin said in a rough voice. 'But I've got control of your link with Marlin.'

Cara rammed her Agiel in his gut. His body flinched with

the jolt, his arms flopping ineffectually. His eyes, though, never lost the deadly look. The smile didn't falter as he watched her.

Cara took two steps back on her own.

'What's going on?' Nadine whispered. 'What's wrong? I thought you said he was helpless.'

'Get out,' Cara whispered urgently to Kahlan. 'Now.' She glanced up the ladder. 'I'll hold him off. Lock the door.'

'Wanting to leave?' Marlin asked in the grating voice as they moved toward the ladder. 'So soon? And before we've had a little talk. I've enjoyed listening to the talks you two have had. I've learned so much. I never knew about Mord-Sith. But I do, now.'

Kahlan halted. 'What are you talking about?'

His predatory gaze moved from Cara to Kahlan. 'I learned of your touching love for Richard Rahl. It was so thoughtful of you to reveal the limits of his gift. I suspected much of it, but you confirmed the extent. You also confirmed my suspicion that he would be able to recognize another with the gift, and that it would raise his suspicions. Even you were able to see something wrong in Marlin's eyes.'

'Who are you?' Kahlan asked as she pushed Nadine back with her toward the ladder.

Marlin shook with a belly laugh. 'Why, none other than your worst nightmare, my little darlins.'

'Jagang?' Kahlan whispered incredulously. 'Is that it? Are you Jagang?'

The belly laugh boomed around the stone walls of the pit. 'You have me cornered. I confess. It is I, the dream walker himself. I've borrowed this poor fellow's mind, just so I could pay you a little visit.'

Cara slammed her Agiel against the side of his neck. A puppet arm swept her aside.

Cara returned almost instantly, crashing into his kidneys, trying to take him down. He didn't budge. With jerky movements, he reached down, caught her braid, and flung her back against the wall behind him as if she were a stick doll. Kahlan winced at the sound of Cara smacking the stone. She rolled facedown on the floor, blood soaking into her blond hair.

Kahlan shoved Nadine toward the ladder. 'Get out!'

Nadine seized a rung on the ladder. 'What are you going to do?'

'I've seen enough. This ends now.'

Kahlan went for Marlin, or Jagang, or whoever it was. She had to end it with her power.

Screaming, Nadine shot past Kahlan and across the floor as if she were sliding across ice. Marlin caught the flailing woman, spun her around, and gripped her by the throat in one hand. Nadine, her eyes wide, choked for air.

Kahlan skidded to a halt as Marlin twitched up a cautionary finger. 'Tut-tut. I'll crush her throat.'

Kahlan retreated a step. Nadine gulped air when he released the pressure.

'One life, for all those you will otherwise kill? Do you think the Mother Confessor would be unwilling to make such a choice?'

At Kahlan's words, Nadine, in renewed panic, writhed in his grip, her fingers digging frantically at his hands. Even if Marlin didn't crush her throat, he was touching her, and if Kahlan took him with her power, Nadine would be lost, too.

'Perhaps you would, but don't you want to know what I'm doing here, darlin? Don't you want to know my plans for your love, the great Lord Rahl?'

Kahlan turned and screamed up the shaft of light. 'Collins! Shut the door! Lock it!'

Above, the door slammed shut. Only the spitting torches remained to light the pit. The sound of the door clanging shut added its echo to the hissing torches.

Kahlan turned back to Marlin. Keeping her eyes on him, she began slowly edging around the room. 'What are you? Who are you?'

'Well, actually, that's a difficult philosophical question to answer in terms you would understand. A dream walker is able to slip into the infinite spaces of time between thoughts, when a person, who they are, their very essence, doesn't exist, and inhabit that person's mind. What you see before you is Marlin, a loyal little lapdog of mine. I'm the flea on his back that he brought into your house with him. He is a host, which I thought to use for … certain things.'

Nadine thrashed against her captor, causing him to squeeze tighter to maintain his grip. Kahlan pursed her lips and urged her to shush. If she continued fighting him, she would get herself strangled. As if snatching the lifeline of Kahlan's command, Nadine stilled in his grip, and was able at last to pull breaths.

'Your host will shortly be a dead host,' Kahlan said.

'He's expendable. Unfortunately, for you, the damage has already been done, thanks to Marlin.'

With a furtive glance to the side, Kahlan checked her slow progress toward the facedown Cara. 'Why? What has he done?'

'Why, Marlin has brought you and Richard Rahl down for me. Of course, you have yet to suffer what I have wrought, but he has done it. I had the privilege of witnessing the glory of it.'

'What have you done? What are you doing here in Aydindril?'

Jagang chuckled. 'Why, I've been enjoying myself. Yesterday, I even went to watch a Ja'La game. You were there. Richard Rahl was there. I saw you both. I wasn't pleased to see that he changed the broc, replacing it with a lightweight one. He's turned it into a game for the weak. It's meant to be played with a heavy ball, and by the strongest, the most aggressive and brutish players – those with the true lust to win.

'Do you know what *Ja'La* means, darlin?'

Kahlan shook her head as she ran through a list of her options and priorities. Foremost on the list was using her power to stop this man before he escaped the pit, but first she had to find out all she could, if they were to stop his plans. She had already failed once at that task. She couldn't fail again.

'It's from my native tongue. The full and proper name is *Ja 'La dh Jin* – The Game of Life. I don't like the way Richard Rahl corrupted it.'

Kahlan had almost reached Cara. 'So you infested this man's mind so that you could come and watch children play a game? I thought that the great and all-powerful Emperor Jagang would have better things to do.'

'Oh, I've had better things to do. Much better.' His grin was maddening. 'You see, you thought I was dead. I wanted you to know that you failed to kill me at the Palace of the Prophets. I

113

wasn't even there. I was enjoying the charms of a young woman, at the time, actually. One of my newly captured slaves.'

'So you aren't dead. You could have sent us a letter, and not have to go to all this trouble. You came for some other reason. You were here with a Sister of the Dark.'

'Sister Amelia had a little task to perform, but I'm afraid she's no longer a Sister of the Dark. She betrayed her oath to the Keeper of the underworld, so that I could destroy Richard Rahl.'

Kahlan's foot touched Cara. 'Why didn't you tell us all this before, when we first captured Marlin? Why wait until now?'

'Ah, well, I had to wait until Amelia returned with what I sent her for. I'm not one to take chances, you see. Not anymore.'

'And what did she steal from Aydindril for you?'

Jagang chuckled derisively. 'Oh, not from Aydindril, darlin.'

Kahlan squatted down beside Cara. 'Why would she no longer be sworn to the Keeper? Not that I'm unhappy about it, but why would she betray her oath?'

'Because I placed her in a double bind. I gave her the choice of being sent to her master, where she would suffer for eternity at his merciless hands for her past failure with your love, or to betray him, and escape his grasp for now, only to intensify his anger for later.

'And, darlin, you should be unhappy about it, very unhappy, as it will be the downfall of Richard Rahl.'

Kahlan forced herself to speak. 'An empty threat.'

'I don't make empty threats.' His smile widened. 'Why do you think I went to all this trouble? To be there at its doing, and to let you know that it is I, Jagang, who has brought it upon you. I'd hate to have you think it was simply chance.'

Kahlan shot to her feet and took an angry stride toward him. 'Tell me, you bastard! What have you done!'

Marlin's hand jerked up, raising one finger. Nadine made a strangling sound. 'Careful, Mother Confessor, or you'll be denying yourself hearing the rest of it.' Kahlan stepped back. Nadine gasped for air. 'That's better, darlin.

'You see, Richard Rahl thought that by destroying the

Palace of the Prophets, he kept me from gaining the knowledge it contained.' Marlin's puppet finger waggled. 'Not so. Prophecies were not unique to the Palace of the Prophets. There have been prophets about, elsewhere, and there are prophecies elsewhere. Here, for example, there are prophecies in the Wizard's Keep. In the Old World, there are prophecies, too. I found a number of them when I excavated an ancient city that once thrived at the time of the great war.

'Among them, I found one that will be Richard Rahl's undoing. It is an extraordinarily rare type of prophecy, called a bound fork. It enforces a double bind on its victim.

'I have invoked the prophecy.'

Kahlan didn't have the slightest idea what he was talking about. She quickly squatted and lifted Cara's head. Cara scowled up at her.

'You idiot,' Cara whispered under her breath, 'I'm fine. Leave me. Get answers. Then signal, and I will use my link to kill him.'

Kahlan dropped Cara's head and stood. She started inching back toward the ladder.

'You're talking babble, Jagang.' She moved more quickly, hoping Jagang would think she had found Cara dead. She was halfway to the ladder, although she had no intention of trying to escape. She intended to unleash her power on him. Nadine, or no Nadine. 'I don't know anything about prophecy. You're making no sense.'

'Well, darlin, it's like this, either Richard Rahl lets the firestorm of what I have wrought rage out of control, fulfilling one fork of the prophecy, in which case it kills him, too, or he tries to stop what I have done, fulfilling the other fork of the prophecy. On that fork, he is destroyed. See? He can't win, no matter which he chooses. Only one of two events can now evolve, only one of the two forks. He has the power to choose which one, but either will be his doom.'

'You are a fool. Richard will choose neither.'

Jagang roared with laughter. 'Oh, but he will. I've already invoked the prophecy, through Marlin. Once invoked, there is no turning back from a bound fork prophecy. But enjoy your delusions, if it will please you. It will make the fall all that much more painful.'

115

Kahlan paused in her tracks. 'I don't believe you.'

'You will. Oh, yes, you will.'

'Empty threats! What proof have you?'

'Proof will come on the red moon.'

'There is no such thing. You are full of empty threats.'

Kahlan lifted a finger toward him as her fear dissolved in the heat of rage. 'But I want you to know of my threat, Jagang, and it is not empty. I have seen the bodies of the women and children you ordered slaughtered in Ebinissia, and I swore undying vengeance on your Imperial Order. Even prophecy will not stop us from defeating you.'

If nothing else, she needed to at least provoke him into revealing the prophecy. If they knew it, perhaps they could thwart it. 'That is my prophecy to you, Jagang. Unlike your pretend prophecy, it has words to it.'

His belly laugh echoed around the pit. 'Pretend? Let me show you the prophecy, then.'

One of Marlin's hands lifted. Lightning exploded in the pit. Kahlan covered her ears as she ducked, hunching to protect her head. Stone chips howled through the air. She felt a sharp pain as one sliced across her arm and another speared the side of her shoulder. She felt the sickening feeling of warm blood soaking down her sleeve.

Above their heads, the lightning jumped and leaped across the wall, incising the stone, leaving in its wake lettering she could just see through the blinding flashes. The crash of lightning cut off, leaving jagged afterimages across her vision, the smell of dust and smoke choking her lungs, and the cacophony echoing in her head.

'There you go, darlin.'

Kahlan rose to her feet, squinting up at the wall. 'Gibberish. That's all it is. It means nothing.'

'It's in High D'Haran. According to the records, in the last war we had captured a wizard, a prophet, and of course since he was loyal to the House of Rahl, my ancestor dream walkers were denied access to his mind.

'So, they tortured him. In a delirious state, and missing half his intestines, he gave forth this prophecy. Have Richard Rahl translate it.' He leaned toward her with a venomous sneer. 'Though I doubt he will want to tell you what it says.'

He pressed a kiss against Nadine's cheek. 'Well, it's been delightful, my little journey, but I'm afraid Marlin must be going. Too bad, for you, that the Seeker wasn't here with his sword. That would have ended it for Marlin.'

'Cara!' Kahlan went for him, mentally beseeching the good spirits' forgiveness for what she was going to have to do to Nadine, too.

Cara sprang up. With impossible strength, Jagang heaved Nadine through the air. The woman cried out as she tumbled violently into Kahlan. Kahlan landed with a grunt onto her back on the stone.

Her vision prickled with floating dots of light. She couldn't feel anything. She feared it might have broken her back. But sensation returned with tingling pain when she twisted to the side. She gasped to get her wind back as she struggled to sit up.

Cara, on the far side of the room, let out a shrill, piercing scream. She crumpled to her knees, covering her ears with her forearms as she shrieked.

Marlin leaped onto the ladder as she and Nadine wrestled to untangle themselves from each other.

Marlin, hands and feet to each side of the ladder, sprang up in spurts, like a cat going up a tree.

The torches puffed out, plunging them into darkness.

Jagang laughed as he ascended. Cara screamed as if she were being torn limb from limb. Kahlan finally managed to shove Nadine aside and shuffle on her hands and knees toward the sound of Jagang's mocking laughter. She could feel blood soaking all the way down her sleeve.

The iron door exploded outward, clanging against the stone on the other side of the hall, the sound resonating with a boom through the halls. A man cried out as it crushed him. With the door gone, a shaft of light bathed the ladder. Kahlan scrambled to her feet and went for it.

As she stretched up for the ladder, the pain in her shoulder caused her to recoil with a cry. She reached up and yanked out the sharp shard of stone. The blood dammed behind it gushed from the wound.

Fast as she could, Kahlan scuttled up the ladder in pursuit of Marlin. She had to stop him. There was no one else who could do it. With Richard gone, she was the magic against magic for all these people. Her wounded arm shook with the effort, and she could barely grasp the ladder.

'Hurry!' Nadine called out from right behind. 'He'll get away!'

From below, Cara's shrieks seared Kahlan's nerves.

Kahlan had once felt the awesome agony of an Agiel for a fraction of a second. Mord-Sith endured the same pain whenever they held their Agiel, yet not the slightest grimace ever registered on their faces. Mord-Sith lived in a world of pain; years of torture had disciplined them in their ability to disregard it.

Kahlan couldn't imagine what it would take to cause a Mord-Sith to scream like that.

Whatever was happening to Cara, it was killing her, there was no doubt in Kahlan's mind.

Kahlan's foot slipped through a rung. Her shinbone whacked painfully against the rung above. She yanked her leg back, in a rush to get to Jagang. Her flesh grazed the side, catching and driving a long splinter into her calf. She cursed in pain and charged up the ladder.

Clambering through the opening at the top, she slipped and fell to her hands and knees in a chaos of viscera. Sergeant Collins stared up at her with dead eyes. Jagged white ends of rib bones stuck up, holding back the ripped leather and mail of his uniform. His entire torso was rent from his throat to his groin.

A dozen or so men writhed in agony on the floor. Others were still as death. Swords were embedded to their hilts in the stone walls. Axes lodged there, too, as if stuck in soft wood.

An enemy with magic had scythed through these men, but not without cost; close by lay an arm, severed above the elbow. By what it was wearing, she recognized it as Marlin's. The fingers of the hand clenched and unclenched with measured regularity.

Kahlan pushed herself up and turned to the door. She clasped wrists with Nadine and helped her up into the hall.

'Careful.'

Nadine gasped at the bloody sight. Kahlan expected her to faint, or scream hysterically. She didn't.

Men bristling swords, axes, pikes, and bows were charging up the hall from the left. The hall to the right was empty, silent, and dark beyond a lone torch. Kahlan went right. To her credit, Nadine chased right after her.

The screams coming from the pit sent shivers up Kahlan's spine.

CHAPTER 10

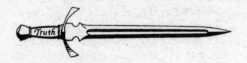

Beyond the last, hissing torch, the hall disappeared into blackness. A soldier lay in a crumpled heap to the side, like dirty laundry waiting to be collected. His blackened sword lay in the center of the hall, its blade fractured into a tangled fray of twisted steel strips.

Kahlan paused and studied the still silence ahead. Just as there was nothing to be seen, there was nothing to be heard. Marlin could be anywhere, hiding around any intersection, crouched in any corner, with Jagang's self-satisfied smirk on his face as he lingered in the darkness to put an end to the pursuit.

'Nadine, stay here.'

'No. I told you, we protect our own. He wants to kill Richard. I'll not let him get away with it, not as long as I have a chance to help.'

'The only chance you will have is to get yourself killed.'

'I'm going.'

Kahlan had neither the time nor desire to argue. If Nadine was going to go, at least she could make herself useful; Kahlan needed her hands free.

'Then grab that torch.'

Nadine yanked it from the bracket and waited expectantly.

'I have to touch him,' Kahlan told her. 'If I touch him, I can kill him.'

'Who, Marlin or Jagang?'

Kahlan's heart pounded against her ribs. 'Marlin. If Jagang could get into his mind, I expect he can get out. But who

120

knows? If nothing else, at least Jagang will be gone, and his minion will be dead. That will end it. For now.'

'That's what you were trying to do back in the pit? What did you mean about making a choice, one life for all the others?'

Kahlan grabbed her face, squeezing her cheeks. 'You listen to me. This isn't just some Tommy Lancaster wanting to rape you; this is a man who is trying to kill us all. I have to stop him. If anyone else is touching him when I do, they will be destroyed along with him. If you or anyone else is touching him, I won't hesitate. Do you understand? I can't afford to hesitate. Too much is at stake.'

Nadine nodded. Kahlan released her. She redirected her anger to the task at hand.

She could feel blood dripping from the ends of the fingers of her left hand. She didn't think she could lift her left arm, and she needed her right arm to touch Marlin. At least Nadine could hold a torch for her. Kahlan hoped that she wasn't making a mistake, hoped that Nadine wouldn't slow her.

She hoped she wasn't letting Nadine come for the wrong reasons.

Nadine took Kahlan's right hand and placed it to her bleeding left shoulder. 'We don't have time to fix this, now. Hold that wound closed as tight as you can, until you need your hand, or you'll lose too much blood and not be able to do what you must.'

A bit chagrined, Kahlan squeezed the wound. 'Thanks. If you're going to come, then stay behind me, and just light the way. If soldiers can't stop him, you can't hope to do better. I don't want you getting hurt for nothing.'

'Got it. Right behind you.'

'Just remember what I said, and don't get in my way.' Kahlan stretched up, looking back behind Nadine to the soldiers. 'Use arrows or spears if you get a shot, but stay behind me. Get some more torches. We need to corner him.'

Some of them ran back to retrieve torches as Kahlan started away. Nadine held her torch out ahead of her as she trotted to keep up. The flame fluttered and roared in the wind of their flight, illuminating the walls, ceiling, and floor for a short distance around them, creating an undulating island of light in a sea of blackness. Close behind, men with torches created their own islands of light. Heavy breathing echoed through the hall as they ran, along with the thud of boots, the jangle of chain mail, the clang of steel, and the roar of flame.

Above it all, in her mind, Kahlan could still hear Cara's screams.

Kahlan halted at an intersection, panting to get her breath as she looked ahead, and then down the corridor that branched to the right.

'Here!' Nadine pointed to blood on the floor. 'He went this way!'

Kahlan looked up the dark hall ahead. It led to the stairwells and up into the palace. The other corridor that branched off to the right led under the palace in a labyrinth of storerooms, abandoned areas once used in the excavation of the bedrock the palace was built atop, access tunnels to inspect and maintain the foundation walls, and drainage tunnels for the springs the builders had encountered. At the ends of the drainage tunnels, massive stone grates let the water out through the foundation walls, but prevented anyone from getting in.

'No,' Kahlan said. 'This way – to the right.'

'But the blood,' Nadine protested. 'He went this way.'

'We've seen no blood until this place. The blood is a diversion. That way leads up into the palace. Jagang went this way, to the right, where there are no people.'

Nadine followed after as Kahlan started down the corridor to the right. 'But why would he care if there are people? He killed and wounded all those soldiers back there!'

'And they managed to take off an arm. Now Marlin is wounded. Jagang won't care if we kill Marlin, but, on the other hand, if he can escape, then he can use Marlin to cause more harm.'

'What more harm could he cause than hurting people? Hurting all those people upstairs and the soldiers?'

'The Wizard's Keep,' Kahlan said. 'Jagang doesn't have command of magic, other than his ability as a dream walker, but he can use a person with the gift. From what I've seen so far, though, he doesn't know much about using another's magic. The things he did back there, simple use of air and heat, are far from inventive for a wizard. Jagang only thinks to do the simplest of things with their magic, things of brute force. That is to our advantage.

'If I were him, I would try to get to the Keep, and use the magic there to cause the most destruction I could.'

Kahlan turned down an ancient stairwell carved from rock, taking the steps two at a time. At the bottom, the rough, tunnel-like hall ran in two directions. She turned to the soldiers still racing down the stairs behind.

'Split up – half each way. This is the lowest level. When you encounter more junctures, cover them all. Remember which way you went at each turn, or you could be lost down here for days.

'You've seen what he can do. If you find him, don't take a chance trying to take him. Post sentries so we know if he backtracks, and then send runners to come get me.'

'How will we find you?' one asked.

Kahlan looked to the right. 'At every choice, I'll take the one to the right, so you can follow where I went. Now hurry. I think he's headed for any opening out of the palace he can find. We can't let him get out. If he gets to the Keep, he can get through shields there that I can't.'

With Nadine and half the men, Kahlan rushed on through the dank hall. They encountered several rooms, all empty, and before long, several more corridors. At every branch, she divided the men and took her continually dwindling force to the right.

'What's the Wizard's Keep?' Nadine asked as they moved on through the darkness.

'It's a massive fortress, a stronghold, where wizards used to live. It predates the Confessors' Palace.' Kahlan lifted a hand, indicating the palace above them. 'In ages long forgotten, nearly everyone was born with the gift. Over the last three thousand years the gift has been dying out in the race of man.'

'What's in the Keep?'

'Living quarters, long abandoned, libraries, rooms of every sort. And things of magic are stored there. Books, weapons, things like that. Shields protect important or dangerous parts of the Keep. Those without magic can't pass through any of the shields. Since I was born with magic, I can pass through some of them, but not all.

'The Keep is vast. It makes the Confessors' Palace look like a cramped cottage, by comparison. In the great war, three thousand years ago, the Keep was filled with wizards and their families. Richard says it was a place filled with laughter and life. At that time, the wizards had both Subtractive and Additive Magic.'

'And now they don't?'

'No. Only Richard has been born with both sides.

'There are places in the Keep that I, and the wizards I grew up with, could not enter because the shields are so powerful. There are other places that have not been entered in thousands of years because they are shielded with both sides of the magic. No one could get past the shields.

'But Richard can. I fear Marlin can, too.'

'Sounds a dreadful place.'

'I've spent a good portion of my life there, studying books of language, and learning from the wizards. I never thought of it as anything but part of my home.'

'Where are these wizards now? Can't they help us?'

'They all killed themselves, at the end of last summer, in the war with Darken Rahl.'

'Killed themselves! How awful. Why would they do that?'

Kahlan was silent for a moment as they moved relentlessly onward into the darkness. It all seemed a dream from another life.

'We needed to find the First Wizard, to have him appoint the Seeker of Truth to stop Darken Rahl. Zedd was the First Wizard. He was in Westland, on the other side of the boundary. The boundary was linked to the underworld, the world of the dead, so no one was able to cross it.

'Darken Rahl was also hunting Zedd. It took all the wizards to conjure magic to get me through the boundary to go after Zedd. If Darken Rahl had captured the wizards, he might have used his vile magic to make them confess what they knew.

'To give me the time to have a chance to succeed, the wizards killed themselves. Darken Rahl still managed to send assassins after me. That was when I met Richard. He protected me.'

'Blunt Cliff?' Nadine said in questioning amazement. 'There were four huge men found dead at the bottom of the cliff. They had leather uniforms, and weapons of every sort. No one had ever seen men like them before.'

'That was them.'

'What happened?'

Kahlan gave her a sidelong glance. 'Something like you and your experience with Tommy Lancaster.'

'Richard did that? Richard killed those men?'

Kahlan nodded. 'Two of them. I took another with my power, and he killed the last. Those were probably the first men Richard had ever encountered who wanted to do more to him than simply give him a beating when he chose to protect someone. To protect me. Richard has had to make a lot of hard choices since that day on Blunt Cliff.'

For what seemed hours, but she knew couldn't be more than fifteen or twenty minutes, they continued on into the dark, stinking halls. The stone blocks were larger, some so huge that single blocks ran from floor to ceiling. They were roughly cut, but fit with no less precision than the other mortarless jointwork elsewhere in the palace.

The halls were wetter, too, with water running down the walls in places, draining into small tiled weep holes at the edges of the floor that had a crown to direct the water to the drains. Some of the drains were plugged with debris, allowing shallow pools to form.

Rats used the tiled drains as tunnels. They squeaked and scurried away at the approach of light and sound, some taking to the drains, some running on ahead. Kahlan thought again of Cara, and wondered if she was still alive. It seemed too cruel that she should die before having a chance to taste life without the madness that shadowed her.

A series of connecting tunnels finally reduced Kahlan's company to Nadine and two men. The way was so narrow that they had to proceed single-file. The low, arched ceiling forced them to trot in a crouch.

Kahlan saw no blood – Jagang probably used his control of Marlin's mind to cut the flow – but in several places she did see that the slime on the wall was smeared in horizontal streaks. As low and narrow as the passageway was, it would be difficult to avoid grazing the close walls. Kahlan brushed against the wall more than she wished to; it hurt her shoulder when the knuckles of her hand over the wound struck the slimy stone. Marlin – Jagang – had to have been through the passageway and brushed against the same wall.

She felt both a rush of heady relief that she was on his tail, and terror at the prospect of catching him.

The arched passageway narrowed again, and the ceiling became even lower. They had to hunch into a deep crouch to proceed. The flames from the torches folded to lap at the stone close overhead, and the smoke billowed along the ceiling, burning their eyes.

As the passageway started into a steep descent, they all slipped and fell more than once. Nadine skinned her elbow as she fell on it while maintaining a grip on the torch. Kahlan slowed, but didn't stop, as one of the soldiers helped Nadine regain her feet. The other three quickly caught up.

Ahead, Kahlan heard the rush of water.

The narrow passageway opened into a large, tubular tunnel. Water rushed in a torrent down the round tunnel that was part of the drainage system below the palace. Kahlan paused at the edge.

'What now, Mother Confessor?' one of the soldiers asked.

'Stick to the plan. I'll go with Nadine downstream, to the right. You two go upstream to the left.'

'But if he's trying to get out, he would have gone to the right,' the soldier said. 'He would hope to get out where the water does. We should go with you.'

'Unless he knows we're after him, and he's trying to send us the wrong way. You two go left. Come on, Nadine.'

'In there? The water must be waist-deep.'

'A little more, I'd say. It's run-off from the spring melt. It's usually no more than a foot or two deep. There are stepping stones along the other side, but they're just underwater now. In the center of where this passageway opens into the drain tunnel there will be an oblong stone to step across on.'

Kahlan stretched and stepped out, putting a foot into the center of the torrent and onto the flat stone just under the surface of the water. She lifted her other leg across the rushing water, testing until her foot found one of the stones against the far wall. She clasped a hand with Nadine and boosted herself across. Standing on the stone, the water was only ankle-deep, but it quickly soaked through the lacing and filled her boots. It was ice cold.

'See?' Kahlan's voice echoed, and she hoped it didn't carry far. 'But be careful; it isn't an unbroken walkway. The stones are spaced apart.'

Kahlan moved to the next stepping stone and gave Nadine a hand across. She gestured to the men to go up the tunnel. They crossed and moved quickly off into the darkness. Soon, the light from the men's torches vanished around a bend, and Kahlan was left with Nadine in the dim light of a single torch. Kahlan hoped it would last long enough.

'Careful, now,' she said to Nadine.

Nadine cupped her ear. It was hard to hear over the roar of the water. Kahlan put her mouth close and repeated the admonition. She didn't want to yell, and alert Jagang, if he was close.

Even if the torch had been brighter, they wouldn't have been able to see far. The drainage tunnel twisted and turned on its way down and out of the palace underground. Kahlan had to put a hand to the cold, slimy stone wall in order to keep her balance.

In several places the tunnel took a steep descent, the stones along the side following it like a stairway down through a roaring rapid. Icy water misted the air and soaked them to the skin.

Even in the flatter sections, running was impossible, as they had to step carefully from stone to stone. If they went too fast and missed a step, they could break an ankle. Down in the tunnel, in the water, with Jagang somewhere about, would be a very bad place to be hurt. The blood running afresh down Kahlan's arm reminded her that she was already hurt. But at least she could walk.

That was when Nadine squealed from behind and went into the water.

'Don't lose the torch!' Kahlan screamed.

Nadine, chest-deep in the rushing water, thrust the torch up in the air to keep it from being doused. Kahlan snatched her wrist and strained against the drag of the water as the current swept Nadine past. There was nothing for Kahlan to grab hold of with her other hand. She hooked the heels of her boots over the edge of the stepping stone to keep from being pulled off.

Nadine thrashed with her other hand, searching for one of the stepping stones. She found one and grasped it. With Kahlan's help, she pulled herself back up.

'Dear spirits, that water is cold.'

'I told you to be careful!'

'Something, a rat, I think, grabbed my leg,' she said, trying to catch her breath.

'I'm sure it was dead. I've seen others float past. Now be careful.'

Nadine nodded in embarrassment. Because she had been swept past Kahlan, Nadine was now in the lead. Kahlan didn't see how they could change places without a struggle, so she motioned Nadine on.

Nadine turned to start out. Suddenly a huge shape erupted from the black depths. Water sluiced from Marlin as he bobbed up and snatched Nadine's ankle with his one hand. She shrieked as she was yanked feet-first into the inky water.

CHAPTER 11

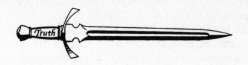

On her way down, Nadine swung the torch and caught Marlin square across the bridge of his nose. He let go of her as he madly groped to wipe the burning pitch from his eyes. The current swept him away.

Kahlan gripped Nadine's arm, still holding the torch above the water, and helped her back up on the stepping stone for a second time. They flattened themselves against the wall, gulping air and shaking in shock.

'Well,' Kahlan said at last, 'at least we know which way he went.'

Nadine was shivering violently from her second dunking. Her hair was plastered to her head and neck. 'I can't swim. Now I know why I never wanted to learn. I don't like it.'

Kahlan smiled to herself. The woman had more pluck than she would have thought. Her smile wilted when she remembered why Nadine was there, and who had sent her.

Kahlan realized that in the surprise of the ambush she had missed her chance to get Jagang.

'Let me go first.'

Nadine held the torch up with both hands. Kahlan put her arms around Nadine's waist as they twisted around on tiptoes to change places on the stone. The woman was as cold as a fish in winter. Kahlan wasn't much warmer from being in the frigid tunnels with the icy water lapping around her ankles. Her toes were numb.

'What if he swims upstream and escapes?' Nadine asked, her teeth chattering.

'I don't think that likely, with only one arm. He was probably holding a stone, keeping just his face above the surface as he lurked in the water, waiting for us.'

'And what if he does it again?'

'I'm in front now. It will be me he grabs hold of, and that will be the last mistake he makes.'

'And what if he waits until you pass, and pops up and grabs me again?'

'Then hit him harder the next time.'

'I hit him as hard as I could!'

Kahlan smiled and gave Nadine a reassuring squeeze on her arm. 'I know you did. You did the right thing. You did well.'

They inched along the wall, passing several more gentle turns, watching the water the whole time for Marlin's face peering up at them. Both started at things they saw in the water, but it always turned out to be nothing more than pieces of flotsam.

The torch was sputtering more, and looked to be near its end. The drains all led outside, and they had traveled a goodly distance in this one. Kahlan knew that the tunnel must end soon.

She realized the thought was more hope than knowledge; as a girl she had explored the tunnels and drains down here, though not when they had been so swollen with run-off, and although she had a good idea of where she was, she didn't know their exact location. She remembered that some drainage tunnels seemed to go on forever.

As they moved along, the sound of the roaring water seemed to change pitch. Kahlan wasn't sure what that meant. Ahead, the tunnel bent to the right.

A thump that she could feel in her chest more than hear made her stop. She held out a hand, not only to halt Nadine, but to signal silence.

The wet stone of the walls ahead brightened, glistening with a reflected bluish glow from something beyond the bend. A low howl rose in pitch until they could hear it clearly over the rush of the water.

A boiling ball of flame exploded from around the bend. Raging yellow and blue flame, filling the entire tunnel, tumbled as it raced toward them with a wail.

Liquid fire seething with all-consuming menace.

Wizard's fire.

Kahlan snatched Nadine by the hair. 'Hold your breath!'

Pulling Nadine with her, Kahlan dived into the water just ahead of the angry fury of roiling flame. The icy water was such a shock that she almost gasped it in.

Under the churning water, it was difficult to tell up from down. Kahlan opened her eyes. She saw the wavering glow of the inferno overhead. Nadine was struggling to get to the surface. Kahlan jammed her left hand against the underside of a stepping stone to hold herself under, and with her good arm held Nadine under with her. Nadine, in the panic of drowning, fought to escape. Panic clawed at Kahlan, too.

When everything went black, Kahlan, her lungs burning for air, thrust her head above the water, pulling Nadine up with her. Nadine choked and coughed as she gasped. Long sodden strands of hair covered both their faces.

Another tumbling ball of wizard's fire raced up the tunnel. 'Get a big breath!' Kahlan screamed.

She sucked a deep breath herself and went under, dragging Nadine down with her. They went under without an instant to spare. Kahlan knew that, given a choice, Nadine would have chosen to die in the fire rather than drown, but the water was their only chance. Wizard's fire burned with deadly determination, with the resolve of the wizard who conjured it.

They couldn't keep doing this. The water was so cold she was shivering uncontrollably already. She knew that cold water, by itself, could kill a person. They couldn't stay in the water; it would end up killing them as sure as the wizard's fire.

They couldn't get to Jagang through Marlin's wizard's fire. If they were to reach him in time, there was only one way: they would have to go under the fire. Under the water.

Kahlan repressed her panic at the thought of drowning, made sure she had a good grip around Nadine's waist, and then pushed away from the stepping stone she had been gripping for dear life.

The wet wrath of water swept them away in its frigid flux.

She could feel herself tumbling under the water as she scraped and bumped along the stone. When her shoulder hit on something, she almost screamed, but the thought of losing her breath instantly locked her throat shut even tighter.

With frenzied need of air, and blackness disorienting her, she knew she had to come up. She was holding Nadine in a death grip with her good arm. With her other hand, she managed to hook a stone. With Nadine's weight in addition to her own, it felt as if the rush of water would rip her arm from its socket.

When her head cleared the surface, there was light. Not twenty feet away was a stone lattice. Late afternoon light poured in through the openings above the water level.

As Kahlan pulled Nadine's head above the water, she clamped a hand over the woman's mouth.

On one of the stepping stones to the side, near the stone grate, facing away, stood Marlin.

Kahlan could see the broken shafts of at least a half dozen arrows sticking from his back. By the way Marlin was staggering as he stepped to the next stone, she knew he couldn't live much longer.

The stump of his left arm wasn't bleeding. If only she could count on him dying before he reached the Keep. Jagang was obviously driving the wounded man relentlessly onward. She had no idea what Jagang was capable of, in controlling the man's mind, to keep him alive and moving. He had no concern for the life he occupied, and she knew he would be willing to let Marlin suffer any damage to accomplish Jagang's wishes.

Marlin lifted a hand, fingers spread, toward the stone grate. Kahlan had grown up around wizards; Marlin was conjuring air. A section of the lattice grate exploded outward in a cloud of dust and stone fragments. More light poured in through the blasted opening.

The suddenly wider spillway let the water flood out with yet greater force. Kahlan's injured arm had no strength, and the mounting might of the discharge tore her away from the stone step. She lost her grip on Nadine.

In the powerful clutch of the water, Kahlan grasped frantically for a handhold, but found none. She twisted and tumbled under the water, trying with her arms and legs to grapple something. She hadn't had a chance to get a good breath, and she struggled, too, to fight her terror at her exigent need for air.

Her fingers caught the sharp stone at the edge of the blasted hole. The water sucked her under and jammed her hard against the lower part of the grate. She could only force her head and part of one shoulder above the surface. It seemed she was breathing more water than air.

Kahlan looked up. Jagang's wicked smile greeted her. He was only a few feet away.

The force of the water ramming against her crushed her tight to the broken grate. She didn't have the muscle to overcome the pounding weight of the water. Try as she might, she couldn't get to him. It was all she could do to get a breath.

She glanced over her shoulder. What she saw took the breath for which she had fought so hard. They were on the east side of the palace – the high side of the foundation. The water roared out of the drainage gateway to plunge for a good fifty feet before crashing to the rocks below.

Jagang chuckled. 'Well, well, darlin, how nice of you to drop by to witness my escape.'

'Where are you going, Jagang?' she managed.

'I thought I'd go up to the Keep.'

Kahlan gasped for air and caught a mouthful of water instead. She coughed and choked it out. 'Why do you want to go to the Keep? What's there that you want?'

'Darlin, you're deluding yourself if you think I would reveal anything I don't want you to know.'

'What did you do to Cara?'

He smiled but didn't answer. He lifted Marlin's hand. A blast of air shattered more of the grate to the side.

The stone she was holding gave way. Her back scraped over the broken edge. Kahlan snatched for a solid piece and just caught it with her fingers before she was ejected from the drain. When she looked down, she was looking at the rocks below the foundation. Water thundered above her.

She worked her fingers over the sharp stone, struggling desperately to pull herself back behind what was left of the grate. Panic powering her effort, she regained the inside of the stone lattice, but she couldn't get away from it. The water kept her pinned.

'Problem, darlin?'

Kahlan wanted to scream at him, but she could only gasp for air as she fought to keep from being swept through the opening. Her arms burned with the effort. She could think of nothing to do to stop him.

She thought of Richard.

Jagang lifted Marlin's hand again, spreading his fingers.

Nadine popped up from the water right behind him. With one hand she held on to a stone step. In her other, she still gripped the dead torch. Looking as if she was at the ragged edge of madness, she took a mighty swing, clubbing him across the back of his knees.

Marlin's legs folded under him and he toppled into the water right in front of Kahlan. He caught himself on the broken grate with his one hand. When he saw what waited outside, he frantically tried to push himself back. Apparently, he hadn't anticipated that there might be no way down from the drain tunnel.

Nadine clutched a stepping stone and held on for dear life.

Kahlan reached behind with her injured arm, stuffed her left hand through a grate opening under the water, and made a fist to lodge it fast.

With her other hand, she seized Marlin by the throat.

'Well, well,' she said through gritted teeth. 'Look what I have here: the great and all-powerful Emperor Jagang.'

He grinned, showing broken teeth. 'Actually, darlin,' he said in Jagang's grating, impudent voice, 'you have Marlin.'

She pulled herself close to his face. 'Think so? Do you know that a Confessor's magic works faster than thought? That's why once we're touching someone, they have no chance. None. The magic bond of my loyalty to Richard Rahl denies a dream walker access to my mind. Marlin's mind is our field of battle now. Do you suppose that my magic might work faster than yours? What do you think? Do you think I can take you, along with Marlin?'

'Two minds at once?' he said with a smirk. 'I don't think so, darlin.'

'We'll see. Maybe I'll get you, too. Maybe we'll end the war, and the Imperial Order, right here and now.'

'Oh, darlin, you are a fool. Man is destined to free his world from the shackles of magic. Even if you could kill me here and now, which you can't, you will not end the Order. It will survive any one man, even me, because it is the struggle of all mankind to inherit our world.'

'Do you really expect me to believe that you don't do this for yourself? For naked power?'

'Not at all. I relish rule. But I simply ride a horse already in full charge. It will run you down. You are a fool who follows the dying religion of magic.'

'A fool who has you by the throat – the great Jagang, who professes to want man to triumph over magic, yet uses magic!'

'For now. But when magic dies, I will be the one with the daring, and the muscle, to rule – without magic.'

Fury erupted through Kahlan. This was the man who had ordered the deaths of thousands of innocent people. This was the butcher of Ebinissia. This was the man who would enslave the world.

This was the man who wanted to kill Richard.

In the silence of her mind, in the core of her power, where there was no cold, no exhaustion, no fear, she had all the time in the world. Though he made no attempt to escape, even if he had, it would have been hopeless. He was hers.

Kahlan did as she had done countless times before – she released her restraint.

For an imperceptible twitch of time, something was different. There was resistance where there had been none before. A wall.

Like hot steel through glass, her power crashed through it.

The magic exploded through Marlin's mind.

Thunder without sound.

Stone chips fell from the ceiling at the concussion. Water droplets danced. Despite the water's rush, a ring of ripples raced outward around the two of them, driving a wall of mist and dust.

Nadine, clinging to the stepping stone, cried out in the pain of being so close to a Confessor's power unleashed.

Marlin's mouth went slack. Once a person's mind had been destroyed by a Confessor, they became a vessel needing her command.

Marlin offered no such abdication.

Blood streamed from his ears and nose. His head lolled to the side in the rushing torrent. His dead eyes stared.

Kahlan released her grip of his throat when his hand went slack on the grate and the water tore him away. Marlin's body tumbled out through the broken stone lattice and plummeted to the rocks below.

Kahlan knew: she had almost had Jagang, but she failed. His thoughts, his ability as a dream walker, had been too fast for her Confessor's magic to catch.

Nadine was reaching toward her. 'Grab my hand! I can't hold on forever!'

Kahlan locked wrists with her. Using her power drained a Confessor of strength. After using her magic, it took even Kahlan, the Mother Confessor, and perhaps the strongest Confessor ever born, several hours before she could use her power again, but longer than that to fully recover her strength. She was exhausted, and couldn't fight the torrent any longer. Without Nadine's hold on her, she would have gone over the edge, too.

With Nadine's help, Kahlan managed to regain the stepping stones. Shivering with the cold, they both dragged themselves up.

Nadine wept at the crest of terror that had passed and had almost taken them. Kahlan was too exhausted to weep, but she knew how Nadine felt.

'I wasn't touching him, when you used magic, but I thought every one of my joints had popped apart. It didn't … do anything to me, did it? Anything magic? Am I going to die, too?'

'No, you're fine,' Kahlan assured her. 'You simply felt the pain because you were too close, that's all. If you had been touching him, though, it would have been inconceivably worse – you would have been destroyed.'

Nadine nodded in mute reply. Kahlan put an arm around her and whispered a thank you in her ear. Nadine smiled the tears away.

'We have to get back to Cara.' Kahlan said. 'We have to hurry.'

'How? The torch is gone. There's no way down the outside, and as soon as we try to go back, it will be pitch black. I don't want to go back there in the dark. It's impossible until the soldiers come with torches to light our way.'

'Nothing is impossible,' Kahlan said wearily. 'We took every turn to the right, so we have only to put a hand on the left wall and follow it to find our way back.'

Nadine threw her hand out, pointing back into the blackness. 'That may be all fine and good in the halls, but when we came into this drainage tunnel, we crossed over to the other side. There aren't steps on that side. We'll never find the opening.'

'The water rushing over the step stone in the center of the tunnel had a different sound. Didn't you notice? I'll remember it.' Kahlan took Nadine's hand to give her encouragement. 'We have to try. Cara needs help.'

Nadine stared in wordless worry for a moment, and then said, 'All right, but wait a moment.'

She tore a strip from the shredded hem of Kahlan's dress and wound it around Kahlan's upper arm, closing the wound as best she could. Kahlan winced when Nadine drew the knot tight.

'Let's go,' Nadine said. 'But be careful until I can sew it closed and put a poultice on it.'

CHAPTER 12

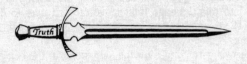

They made excruciatingly slow progress back up the drainage tunnel. The blind trek, groping along the cold, slimy stone, with the water coursing about their ankles, and the constant fear of falling into the raging water in the darkness, was at least devoid of the terror that Marlin might pop up, grab their legs, and pull them in. When Kahlan heard the sound of the water change, and its echo into the hall, she held Nadine's hand and probed with a foot until she found the step stone across the channel.

Partway back through the dark labyrinth of tunnels and halls, the soldiers found them and led the way with torches. In a numb haze, Kahlan followed the wavering flames of the torches as they plunged ever onward into the black nothingness. It was an effort to put one foot in front of the other. Kahlan wished for nothing more than to lie down, even if it were on the cold, wet stone.

Outside the pit, the halls were crowded with hundreds of grim soldiers. Archers all had arrows nocked. Spears were at the ready, as were swords and axes. Other weapons, from the fight with Marlin, were still embedded in the stone. She doubted that anything short of magic would remove them. The dead and wounded had been cleared away, but blood boasted where they had lain.

Screams were no longer coming from the pit.

Kahlan recognized Captain Harris, who had been up in Petitioners' Hall earlier in the day. 'Has anyone gone down there to help her, captain?'

'No, Mother Confessor.'

He didn't even have the decency to look sheepish about it. D'Harans feared magic, and felt no loss of pride admitting it. Lord Rahl was the magic against magic; they were the steel against steel. It was as simple as that.

Kahlan couldn't bring herself to reprimand the men in the hall for leaving Cara alone. They had shown their bravery in the fight with Marlin. Many of them had been killed or seriously injured. Going down into the pit was different from fighting something that came out; defending themselves was different, in their minds, from going out and looking for trouble with magic.

For their part of the bargain, the steel against steel, D'Haran soldiers fought to the death. They expected their Lord Rahl to do his part, and his part was dealing with magic.

Kahlan read the apprehension in all the waiting eyes. 'The assassin, the man who escaped the pit, is dead. It's over.'

Soft sighs of relief could be heard up and down the hall, but by the anxious expression still on the captain's face, she knew she must look quite a mess.

'I think we should get you some help, Mother Confessor.'

'Later.' Kahlan started for the ladder. Nadine followed. 'How long has she been silent, captain?'

'Maybe an hour.'

'That was about when Marlin died. Come with us, and bring a couple more men so we can get Cara out of there.'

Cara was on the far side of the room, near the wall where Kahlan had seen her last. Kahlan knelt on one side, Nadine on the other, as the soldiers held torches so they could see.

Cara was in convulsions of some sort. Her eyes were closed, and she was no longer screaming, but she shook violently, her arms and legs thrashing against the stone floor.

She was choking on her own vomit.

Kahlan gripped the shoulder of Cara's red leather and yanked her onto her side.

'Open her mouth!'

Nadine leaned over from behind and pushed her thumb against the back of Cara's jaw, forcing it forward. With her other hand, she pressed down on her chin, keeping her mouth open. Kahlan swept two fingers through Cara's mouth several times until she had cleared her airway.

'Breathe!' Kahlan yelled. 'Breathe, Cara, breathe!'

Nadine slapped the prone woman on the back, eliciting gurgling, wet, choking coughs that finally brought a semblance of clear, if gasping, breathing.

Although she was able to breathe, it didn't halt the convulsions. Kahlan felt helpless.

'I better go get my things,' Nadine said.

'What's wrong with her?'

'I don't really know. A paroxysm of some sort. I'm no expert, but I think we need to stop it. I might be able to help. I might have something in my bag.'

'You two, go show her the way. Leave a torch.'

Nadine and the two soldiers raced up the ladder after one of them shoved a torch in a bracket on the wall.

'Mother Confessor,' Captain Harris said, 'just a little while ago a Raug'Moss showed up in Petitioners' Hall.'

'A what?'

'A Raug'Moss. From D'Hara.'

'I don't know much about D'Hara. Who are they?'

'They're a secret sect. I don't know much about them myself. The Raug'Moss keep to themselves, and are rarely seen –'

'Get to the point. What's he doing here?'

'This one is the Raug'Moss High Priest himself. The Raug'Moss are healers. He says he sensed that a new Lord Rahl had become Master of D'Hara, and he came to offer his services to his new master.'

'A healer? Well, don't just stand there – go get him. Maybe he can help. Hurry.'

Captain Harris clapped a fist to his heart before racing up the ladder.

Kahlan pulled Cara's shoulders and head into her lap and held her tight, trying to calm her convulsions. Kahlan didn't know what else to do. She knew a lot about hurting people, but little about healing them. She was so sick of hurting people. She wished she knew more about helping people. Like Nadine.

'Hold on, Cara,' she whispered as she rocked the shaking woman. 'Help is coming. Hold on.'

Kahlan's eyes were drawn to the top of the opposite wall. The words incised in the stone stared back. She knew nearly every language in the Midlands, all Confessors did, but she knew nothing about High D'Haran. High D'Haran was a dead language; few people knew the ancient tongue.

Richard was learning High D'Haran. He and Berdine worked together translating the journal they had found in the Keep – Kolo's journal, they called it – which had been written in High D'Haran, in the great war three thousand years before. Richard would be able to translate the prophecy on the wall.

She wished he couldn't. She didn't want to know what it said. Prophecy was never anything but trouble.

She didn't want to believe that Jagang had unleashed some unknown festering plague of torment on them, but she couldn't find a good reason to doubt his word.

She pressed her cheek to the top of Cara's head and closed her eyes. She didn't want to see the prophecy. She wanted it gone.

Kahlan felt tears running down her face. She didn't want Cara to die. She didn't know why she should feel so much for this woman, except perhaps because no one else did. The soldiers wouldn't even come down to see why she had stopped screaming. She could have choked to death on her own vomit. Something as simple as that, not magic, could have killed her because they were afraid, or perhaps because no one cared if she died.

'Hold on, Cara. I care.' She smoothed the Mord-Sith's hair back from her clammy forehead. 'I care. We want you to live.'

Kahlan squeezed the quaking woman, as if trying to squeeze her words, her concern, into her. It occurred to her that Cara wasn't so different from herself; Cara was trained to hurt people.

When it all came down to it, Kahlan was much the same. She used her power to destroy a person's mind. She knew that she was doing it to save others, but it was still hurting people. Mord-Sith hurt people, but to them, it was to help their master, to preserve his life, and that in turn was to save the lives of the D'Haran people.

Dear spirits, was she no more than this Mord-Sith she was trying to bring back from madness?

Kahlan could feel the Agiel hanging around her neck pressing against her chest as she held Cara. Was she a sister of the Agiel in more ways than one?

If Nadine had been killed in the beginning, would she have cared? Nadine helped people; she didn't make a life of hurting them. No wonder Richard had been attracted to her.

She wiped her cheek as the tears ran more freely.

Her shoulder throbbed. She hurt all over. She wanted Richard to hold her. She knew he was going to be angry, but she needed him so badly at that moment. It was hurting her shoulder to hold the trembling woman in her lap, but she refused to let go.

'Hold on, Cari. You're not alone; I'm with you. I won't leave you. I promise.'

'Is she any better?' Nadine asked, as she scurried down the ladder.

'No. She's still unconscious and shaking like before.'

As she knelt, Nadine let her bag drop to the floor beside Kahlan. Things inside banged together with muffled sounds.

'I told those men to wait up there. We don't want to move her until we can bring her out of it, and they'll just be in the way.'

Nadine started pulling things out of her bag, little folded cloth packages, leather pouches with markings scratched on them, and stoppered horn containers, likewise scratched with symbols. She briefly inspected the markings before setting each item aside.

'Blue cohosh,' she mumbled to herself as she squinted at the cryptic marks on one of the leather pouches. 'No, I don't think it would do, and she'd have to drink cups of it.' She took out several more leather pouches, before pausing at another. 'Pearly everlasting. Might work, but we'd have to get her to smoke it, somehow.' She sighed irritably. 'That won't do.' She considered a horn. 'Mugwort,' she muttered as she set it aside. 'Feverfew?' She put that horn in the damp sling of her dress in her lap. 'Yes, betony might be of some good, too,' she said as she considered another. She added the horn to her lap.

Kahlan picked up one of the horns Nadine had set aside and

pulled its cork. The pungent smell of anise made her pull back. She pushed the cork back in and set it down.

She picked up another. Two circles were deeply scratched into the patina of the horn. A horizontal line ran through both circles. Kahlan wiggled the carefully carved wooden stopper, trying to pull it free.

Nadine slapped the horn out of Kahlan's hands. 'Don't!'

Kahlan looked up in surprise. 'Sorry. I didn't mean to snoop in your things. I was –'

'No, it's not that.' She picked up the horn with the two circles struck through with a line and held it up. 'This is powdered canin pepper. If you aren't careful when you open it, you could get it on your hands, or worse, in your face. It's a powerful substance that will immobilize a person for a time. If you had opened it carelessly, you would have been on the floor, blind and gasping for air, convinced you were about to die.

'I thought about using it on Cara, to stop her shaking by paralyzing her, but I decided it best not to. It immobilizes a person partly by interfering with their breathing. It feels like it's burning your eyes out of your head; it blinds you. Your nose feels on fire, you're sure your heart is going to burst, and you can't get your breath. You're helpless. Trying to wash it off only makes it worse, because the powder is oily and just spreads.

'It doesn't cause any real harm, and you'd recover completely in a short time, but until then, you're disabled and totally helpless. I don't think immobilizing Cara in that fashion would be good, since she's already having trouble breathing. In her state, it might make her worse, instead of helping her.'

'Do you know what to do, to help her? You do know what to do, don't you?' Kahlan asked, trying not to sound critical.

Nadine's hand paused on the edge of her bag. 'Well, I … I think I do. It's not so common a problem that I'm sure, but I've heard of it. My father has mentioned it in passing.'

Kahlan wasn't reassured. Nadine found a small bottle in her bag and held it up in the torchlight. She pulled the cork and turned the bottle upside down on a finger.

'Hold her head up.'

'What is it?' Kahlan asked as she turned Cara over. She watched Nadine rub the substance on Cara's temples.

'Oil of lavender. It helps with headaches.'

'I think she has more than a simple headache.'

'I know, but until I find something else, it might help ease the pain, and that might help calm her. I don't think I have any one thing that by itself will do it. I'll need to try to add things together.

'The problem is that with the convulsions we can't get her to drink decoctions or teas. Motherwort and linden help calm people, but we can't get her to drink a whole cup of it in water. Black horehound would help stop the vomiting, but she'd have to drink five cups a day. I don't see how we can get her to drink the first until we stop the convulsions. Maybe we could get her to swallow some feverfew. But there is one thing I'm hoping …'

Nadine's long, damp hair hung around her face as she pawed through her bag. She came up with another small, brown bottle.

'Yes! I did bring it.'

'What is it?'

'Tincture of maypop. It's a strong sedative and also a painkiller. I've heard my pa say that it settles people who are in a state of nervous shakes. I think he may have meant shakes like convulsions. Since it's a tincture, we can put some on the back of her tongue; she'll swallow it, that way.'

Cara shuddered violently in Kahlan's arms. Kahlan embraced her tighter until she settled a bit. She didn't know if she liked the idea of having to rely on Nadine's 'I think,' but Kahlan had no better solution. Something had to be done.

Nadine was working her thumbnail at the wax seal on the little brown bottle of tincture of maypop when the shaft of light coming from the doorway above darkened. Nadine's hands stilled.

A motionless, silhouetted figure filled the doorway, seeming to consider them at length. With nary a flutter of his long cloak, he wheeled and started down the ladder.

In the silence, but for the hissing torch, Kahlan absently stroked a protective hand over Cara's brow as she watched the man in a hooded cloak descend the ladder.

144

CHAPTER 13

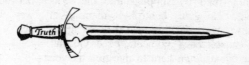

Nadine paused at her work on the wax seal.

'Who ... ?'

'He's some kind of healer,' Kahlan whispered as she watched the man's methodical descent. 'From D'Hara. I was told he came to offer his services to Richard. I think he's an important person.'

Nadine grunted dismissively. 'What's he going to do without any herbs or things?' She leaned closer while watching him. 'He doesn't seem to have anything with him.'

Kahlan shushed her. Stone dust crunched under his boots as he turned, the sound echoing in the hush of the pit. He approached in measured strides. The torch was on the wall behind him, so Kahlan couldn't see his features in the deeply cowled hood of the voluminous, coarse flaxen cloak that hung to the floor.

He was as tall as Richard, with shoulders just as wide.

'Mord-Sith,' he observed in a voice that was smooth and authoritative, something like Richard's, too.

He brought a hand out of his cloak and gestured. Kahlan complied, laying Cara on her back on the stone floor. With the way he seemed to study Cara's shivering, Kahlan didn't want to interrupt for introductions. She just wanted someone to help Cara.

'What happened to her?' he asked from the shadow of the cowl, in a voice just as deep and dark.

'She had control of a man who –'

'He had the gift? She was linked with him?'

'Yes,' Kahlan said. 'That's what she called it.' He made a sound in his throat, as if mentally assimilating the information. 'It turned out that the man was possessed by a dream walker and –'

'What's a dream walker?'

'A person, as I understand it, who can invade another person's mind by slipping into the spaces between their thoughts. He gains control of them in this way. He was covertly possessing this man that she linked with.'

He considered a moment. 'I see. Go on.'

'We came down here to question the man –'

'To torture him.'

Kahlan pulled an irritated breath. 'No. I told Cara that we were simply going to question him to get answers, if we could. The man was an assassin sent to kill Lord Rahl, and if he didn't answer the questions, then Cara was prepared to do what she must to get those answers – to protect Lord Rahl.

'But it never got that far. We discovered that this dream walker had control of him, control of his gift. The dream walker used the man's gift to write a prophecy in the stone behind you.'

The healer didn't turn to look. 'Then what?'

'Then he was going to escape and start killing people. Cara tried to stop him –'

'With her link?'

'Yes. She let out a scream like I've never heard before and fell to the ground holding her ears.' Kahlan inclined her head. 'Nadine here, and I, went after the man when he tried to escape. Fortunately, he was killed. When we got back, we found Cara on the floor, in convulsions.'

'You shouldn't have left her alone. She could have choked to death on her own vomit.'

Kahlan pressed her lips together and remained silent. The man just stood there, watching Cara shudder.

Finally, Kahlan could bear it no longer. 'This is one of Lord Rahl's personal guards. She's important. Do you intend to help her, or you just going to stand there?'

'Quiet,' he commanded in a distracted tone. 'One must observe before one acts, or more harm than help can be the result.'

Kahlan glowered at the shadowed form. At last he sank to his knees and sat back on his heels. He lifted Cara's wrist in one of his big hands, working a finger between her glove and sleeve. He flicked his other hand out over the items on the floor.

'What's all this?'

'They're my things,' Nadine said. Her chin rose. 'I'm a healer.'

Still holding Cara's wrist, the man picked up a leather pouch with his other hand, looking at its markings. He set it down and then scooped the two horns from Nadine's lap.

'Feverfew,' he said as he tossed it back in Nadine's lap. He looked at the symbols on the other. 'Betony.' He tossed it back in her lap with the first.

'You're not a healer,' he said. 'You're an herb woman.'

'How dare you –'

'Did you give her any of your medicines, besides the oil of lavender?'

'How did … I've not had time to give her anything else.'

'Good,' he proclaimed. 'The oil of lavender won't help her, but at least it won't harm her.'

'Well, of course I know it's not going to stop the convulsions. It was just to help ease some of her pain. I was going to give her tincture of maypop for that.'

'Were you now? Fortunate that I arrived in time, then.'

Nadine folded her arms across her breasts. 'Why's that?'

'Because tincture of maypop would likely have killed her.'

Nadine scowled as she unfolded her arms and planted fists on her hips. 'Maypop is a powerful sedative. It would likely have halted her convulsions. If you hadn't interfered, I'd have her recovered by now.'

'Is that so? Did you feel her pulse?'

'No.' Nadine paused warily. 'Why? What difference could that possibly make?'

'Her pulse is weak, staggering, and labored. This woman is struggling with all her strength to keep her heart beating. Had you given her your maypop, it would have done as you said: sedated her. Her heart would have stopped.'

'I … I can't see how …'

'Even a simple herb woman should know to use more caution when dealing with magic.'

'Magic.' Nadine wilted. 'I'm from Westland. I've never seen magic before. I didn't know magic had any effect on healing herbs. I'm sorry.'

He ignored the apology and pointed. 'Undo the buttons and open the top of her outfit.'

'Why?' Nadine asked.

'Do it! Or do you favor watching her die? She can't hold on much longer.'

Nadine leaned forward and began undoing the row of little red leather buttons along the side of Cara's ribs. When she finished, he gestured for her to open it. Nadine glanced up at Kahlan. Kahlan gave her a nod, and she pulled back the supple leather, exposing Cara's chest.

'May I ask your name?' Kahlan asked him.

'Drefan.' Instead of asking hers, he put an ear to the center of Cara's chest, listening.

He shifted around, forcing Kahlan to scoot out of the way, until he was at Cara's head. He briefly inspected the bloody wound above her left ear, and then, seeming to dismiss it as unimportant, went on to systematically probe the base of her neck.

Kahlan could only see the side of his deep cowl, and nothing of his face. The single torch didn't provide much light, anyway.

Drefan leaned forward and gripped Cara's breasts in his big hands.

Kahlan sat up straighter. 'What do you think you're doing?'

'Examining her.'

'Is that what you call it.'

He sat back on his heels. 'Feel her breasts.'

'Why?'

'To see what I discovered.'

Kahlan finally turned from the shadow of his cowl and, rather than grabbing her as he had, put the back of her fingers against the side of Cara's left breast. It was hot – burning with a fever. She felt the other. It was ice cold.

When Drefan gestured, Nadine followed suit. 'What does it mean?' she asked.

148

'I'd like to reserve judgment until I've finished examining her, but it's not good.'

He put his fingers to the side of her neck, feeling her pulse again. He ran his thumbs outward along her forehead. He bent and put his ear to each of hers. He smelled her breath. He carefully lifted her head and rotated it. He spread her arms out to the sides, pulled the red leather outfit open further so that Cara's torso was naked to her waist, and then bent over her and palpated her abdomen and up under her ribs.

With his head bent as if in concentration, he touched his fingers to the front of her shoulders for a moment, the sides of her neck, the base of her skull, her temples, several places on her ribs, and lastly to the palms of her hands.

Kahlan was getting impatient. She was seeing a lot of probing and prodding, but very little healing. 'Well?'

'Her aura is seriously snarled,' he said, as he brazenly thrust a big hand under the red leather at Cara's waist.

Kahlan watched in stunned disbelief as his hand slid down to her crotch. She could see his fingers under the tight leather as he worked them into her sex.

Hard as she could, Kahlan fisted him on the nerve at the side of his upper arm.

He recoiled in pain. He fell to the side of his hip with a groan, covering his arm where she had clouted him.

'I told you, this is an important woman! How dare you grope her like that! I won't have it, do you understand?'

'I wasn't goping her,' he growled.

The heat was still in Kahlan''s voice. 'Then what do you call it?'

'I was trying to determine what this dream walker has done to her. He's greatly disturbed her auras, her energy flows, confusing her mind's control of her body.

'She's not in convulsions, precisely. She's having uncontrolled muscular contractions. I was checking to make sure that he hadn't triggered the part of her brain that controls excitement. I was making sure that he hadn't put her in a state of continual orgasm. I have to know the extent of the blocks and triggers he's disturbed so that I know how to reverse it.'

Nadine, eyes widening, leaned forward. 'Magic can do such a thing? Make a person have … continual …'

He nodded as he flexed his sore arm. 'If the practitioner knows what he's doing.'

'Can you do such a thing?' she breathed.

'No. I don't have the gift, or any other form of magic, but I know how to heal – if the damage isn't too great.' The cowl turned toward Kahlan. 'Now, do you wish me to continue, or do you want to watch her die?'

'Continue. But if you put your hand down there again, you are going to be a one-handed healer.'

'I've already learned what I needed to know.'

Nadine leaned in again. 'Is she … ?'

'No.' He flicked his hand irritably. 'Pull off her boots.'

Nadine shuffled around and did as he had ordered. He turned a bit toward Kahlan, as if peering at her from the depths of his cowl. 'Did you know to hit that particular nerve in my arm with deliberate knowledge, or did you simply get lucky?'

Kahlan studied the shadow, trying to see his eyes. She couldn't. 'I was trained to do such things: to defend myself, and others.'

'I'm impressed. With such understanding of nerves, you could learn to heal instead of hurt.' He turned his attention to Nadine. 'Depress the third anterior axis of the dorsin meridian.'

Nadine made a face. 'What?'

He waggled his hand, pointing. 'Between the tendon at the back of her ankles and the prominent bone sticking out to the sides. Squeeze there with the thumb and one finger. Both ankles.'

Nadine did as she was told while Drefan pressed behind Cara's ears with his little fingers and at the same time on the tops of her shoulders with his thumbs. 'Harder, woman.' He put both palms, one hand atop the other, on Cara's sternum.

'Second meridian,' he murmured.

'What?'

'Move down half an inch and do it again. Both ankles.' He moved his fingers on Cara's skull, concentrating on what he was doing. 'All right. First meridian.'

'Another half inch down?' Nadine asked.

'Yes, yes, hurry.'

He held Cara's elbows between a thumb and finger as he lifted them a few inches.

Finally, he sat back on his heels with a sigh. 'This is astounding,' he muttered to himself. 'This is not good.'

'What is it?' Kahlan asked. 'Are you saying that you can't help her?'

He waved dismissively, as if too distracted to answer.

'Answer me,' Kahlan insisted.

'If I wish you to bother me, *woman*, I will ask.'

Nadine leaned forward, cocking her head. 'Do you have any idea who you're talking to?' She pointed with her chin, indicating Kahlan.

He was feeling Cara's earlobes. 'By the looks of her, I'd say some mucker on the cleaning staff. One in need of a bath.'

'I've just had a bath,' Kahlan said under her breath.

Nadine's voice lowered with import. 'You'd better show some respect, Mister Healer. She's the one who owns this palace. The whole thing. She's the Mother Confessor herself.'

He ran a finger down the inside of Cara's upper arms. 'Is that so? Well, good for her. Now, be quiet, the both of you.'

'She's also the betrothed of Lord Richard Rahl himself.'

Drefan's hands froze. His whole body stiffened.

'And since Lord Richard Rahl is the Master of D'Hara, and you're from D'Hara,' Nadine went on, 'I reckon that makes him the boss of you. If I were you, I'd be showing a lot more respect for Lord Richard Rahl's future wife. He doesn't like it when people don't show respect for women. I've seen him knock out people's teeth for being disrespectful.'

Drefan hadn't moved a muscle.

Kahlan thought Nadine had put it very crudely, but she doubted it could have been any more effective.

'Not only that,' Nadine added, 'but she's the one who killed the assassin. With magic.'

Drefan finally cleared his throat. 'Forgive me, mistress –'

'Mother Confessor,' Kahlan corrected.

'I most humbly beg your forgiveness … Mother Confessor. I had no idea. I had no intention to cause –'

Kahlan cut him off. 'I understand. You were more concerned with healing Cara, here, than with formalities. So am I. Can you help her?'

'I can.'

'Please, get on with it then.'

He immediately turned back to Cara. Kahlan frowned as she watched his hands gliding in patterns over the supine woman, keeping just above her flesh. His hands paused occasionally, fingers trembling with effort at an invisible task.

From Cara's feet, Nadine folded her arms again. 'You call this healing? My herbs would have had a better effect than this piffle, and a lot sooner, too.'

He looked up. 'Piffle? Is that what you think this is? Just some nonsense? Do you have the slightest idea, young lady, what we're dealing with?'

'A paroxysm. It must be ended, not prayed over.'

He rose up on his knees. 'I am the Raug'Moss High Priest. I am not given to praying for my healings.' Nadine snorted derisively. He nodded, as if deciding something. 'You wish to see what we're dealing with? You want proof your simple herb woman eyes can understand?'

Nadine scowled. 'In view of the lack of results, a little proof would be a fine dish.'

He pointed. 'I saw a horn of mugwort. Give it here. I presume you have a taper in that bag; bring it, too, after you light it.'

As Nadine took the candle to the torch to light it, Drefan opened his cloak and took several items from a pouch. Nadine handed him the lit candle. He dripped hot wax on the floor to the side and stuck the taper in it.

Drefan reached under his cloak and pulled out a long, thin-bladed knife. He leaned over and pressed it between Cara's breasts. A ruby drop grew under the point. He set the knife aside and leaned over her. With a long-handled spoon, he skimmed the blood from her flesh.

He sat back, unstopped the horn Nadine had given him, and dumped some mugwort atop the blood in the spoon. 'You call this mugwort! You're only supposed to collect the fluffy underside of the leaf. You've got the whole leaf mixed in with it.'

'It doesn't matter. It's all mugwort.'

'A very low grade, this way. You ought to know to use a

high-grade mugwort. What sort of herb woman are you, anyway?'

Nadine squinted in indignation. 'It works just fine. Are you trying to find an excuse to get out of showing us that you know what you're doing? Are you trying to blame your failure on the grade of mugwort?'

'The grade is more than good enough for my purpose, but not for yours.' His tone turned instructional, if not polite. 'Next time, purify the sample you collect, and you will find it to be of more help to those who need it.'

He hunched over, holding the spoon to the point of the candle flame until the mugwort ignited, giving off a copious amount of smoke and a heavy, musky odor. Drefan circled the smoking spoon over Cara's stomach, letting the layer of smoke build.

He handed the spoon of smoking mugwort to Nadine. 'Hold this between her feet.'

He put his fingers to his temples as he murmured a chant under his breath.

He took his hands from his head. 'Now, watch, and you will see what I can see, what I can feel, without the smoke.'

He put his thumbs to Cara's temples and his little fingers to the sides of her throat.

The thick layer of mugwort smoke jumped.

Kahlan gasped as she saw ropy lines of smoke coiling and snaking all over Cara. Drefan removed his hands and the smoke trails snapped into a still web of lines. Some arched from her sternum to her breasts, her shoulders, her hips, and her thighs. A tangle of lines went from the top half of her head to points all over her body.

Drefan traced one with a finger. 'See this one? From her left temple to her left leg? Watch.' He pressed his fingers to the base of her skull on the left side, and the line of smoke crossed to her right leg. 'There. That's where it belongs.'

'What is all that?' Kahlan asked in astonishment.

'Her meridian lines: the flow of her force, her life. Her aura. It's more than that, too, but it's hard to put it all into a few words for you. What I have done is nothing more than the way a shaft of sunlight shows you the dust motes floating in the air.'

Nadine, her mouth hanging open, sat frozen, holding the smoking spoon. 'How did you make the line move?'

'By using my life force to compel a healing energy shift where it was needed.'

'Then you have magic,' Nadine breathed.

'No, training. Squeeze her ankles, where you did the first time.'

Nadine set the spoon down and squeezed Cara's ankles. The tangle of lines going down Cara's legs twisted and untangled, moving from her hips to her feet in straight lines.

'There,' Drefan said. 'You have just corrected her legs. See how they've stilled?'

'I did that?' Nadine asked incredulously.

'Yes. But that was the easy part. See here?' He indicated the web of lines coming from her head. 'This is the dangerous part of what this dream walker did. It has to be undone. These lines indicate that she can't control her muscles. She can't speak, and she's been blinded. Look here. This line going from her ears outward and then back to her forehead? That's the only one that's correct. She can hear and understand everything we say; she just can't react to it.'

Kahlan's jaw dropped. 'She can hear us?'

'Every word. Rest assured, she knows we're trying to help her. Now, if you please, I need to concentrate. This all has to be done in the correct order or we'll lose her.'

Kahlan whisked her hands toward him. 'Of course. Do what you need to do to help her.'

Drefan hunched to his task, working his way around Cara's body, pressing fingers or the flats of his hands to various places on her. At times he used the knife point. He never drew more than a drop of blood as he pressed it into her flesh. At nearly each thing he did, some of the ropy lines of smoke moved, untangling, some laying down against Cara's body and others curving outward in a smooth arch before returning to a spot he had attended.

When he compressed the flesh between her thumb and first finger, not only did the smoke lines over her arms straighten, but Cara moaned in relief as she twisted her head and rolled her shoulders. It was the first normal response of any kind Cara had given. When he pierced the tops of her ankles with his knife, she gasped and began to breathe with a steady, if rapid, rhythm. Relief and hope flooded through Kahlan.

He at last had moved all the way around her, and was working at her head, pressing his thumbs along the bridge of her nose and across her forehead. Her whole body was still, no longer shaking and quivering. Her chest rose and fell without effort.

He pressed the knife point between her eyebrows. 'That should take care of it,' he murmured to himself.

Cara's blue eyes opened. They searched about until they found Kahlan. 'I heard your words,' she whispered. 'Thank you, my sister.'

Kahlan smiled her relief. She knew what Cara meant. Cara had, after all, heard Kahlan tell her that she wasn't alone.

'I got Marlin.'

Cara smiled. 'You make me proud to serve with you. I regret that you have gone to all this effort healing me for nothing.'

Kahlan frowned, not knowing what she meant. Cara rolled her head back, looking up at Drefan as he hunched over her.

'How do you feel?' he asked. 'Is everything feeling normal now?'

Her brow drew together with a look of foggy confusion bordering on alarm.

'Lord Rahl?' she asked incredulously.

'No, I'm Drefan.'

With both hands, he laid back his cowl. Kahlan's eyes went wide, along with Nadine's.

'But my father, too, was Darken Rahl. I am Lord Rahl's half brother.'

Kahlan stared in wonder. Same size, same muscular build as Richard. Blond hair, like Darken Rahl's, although shorter and not so straight. Richard's hair was darker, and coarser. Drefan's eyes, piercing blue like Darken Rahl's rather than gray like Richard's, nonetheless bore the same cutting, raptor rake. His features possessed that impossibly handsome perfection of a statue that Darken Rahl's had; Richard hadn't inherited that cruel perfection. Drefan's looks, somewhere in the middle, leaned more toward Darken Rahl than Richard.

But while no one would mistake Drefan for Richard, they would have no trouble telling that they were brothers.

She wondered why Cara had made that mistake. Then she saw the Agiel in Cara's fist. That wasn't what Cara had meant by 'Lord Rahl.' In a confused state, looking at him upside down as she regained consciousness, she hadn't thought he was Richard.

She had thought he was Darken Rahl.

CHAPTER 14

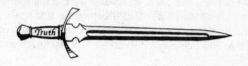

The only sound in the otherwise dead silence was the *click, click, click* of Richard's thumbnail on one of the points of the recurved cross guard on his sword. The elbow of his other arm rested on the polished tabletop while he cradled his head between a thumb under his chin and his first finger along his temple. With a calm face, he did his best to control his anger. He was furious. This time, they had crossed the line, and they knew it.

In his mind he had gone over a whole list of possible punishments, but had rejected them all, not because they were too harsh, but because he knew they wouldn't work. In the end, he settled on the truth. There was nothing harsher than the truth, and nothing else as likely to get through to them.

Before him, in a row, stood Berdine, Raina, Ulic, and Egan. They stood stiffly, their eyes focused at some point over his head and behind him as he sat at the table in the small room he used for meeting with people, reading, and various other work.

To the side of the table hung small landscape paintings of idyllic country scenes, but from the window behind, from which streamed the low-angled rays of morning sunlight, the massive, baleful stone face of the Wizard's Keep glared down on him.

He had been back in Aydindril for only an hour – long enough to discover what had happened after he had left the evening before. All four of his guards had been back since before dawn; he had ordered them to return to Aydindril after Raina and Egan had sauntered into camp the night before.

They had thought he wouldn't make them return in the dead of night. They had been wrong. As brazen as they ordinarily were, the look in his eyes had insured that none of the four dared disobey that order.

Richard had also returned much earlier than he had planned. He had pointed out the quench oak to the soldiers, told them what to collect, and then, instead of overseeing the task, had started back alone for Aydindril before the sun was up. After what he had seen in the night, he'd been too troubled to get any sleep, and had wanted to be back in Aydindril as soon as possible.

Drumming his finger on the tabletop, Richard watched his guards sweating. Berdine and Raina wore their brown leather outfits, their long, braided hair disheveled from their hard ride.

The two great, blond-headed men, Ulic and Egan, wore uniforms of dark leather straps, plates, and belts. The thick leather plates were molded to fit like a second skin over the conspicuous contours of their muscles. Incised in the leather at the center of their chests was an ornate letter 'R,' for the House of Rahl, and beneath that, two crossed swords. Around their arms, just above their elbows, they wore golden bands brandishing razor-sharp projections – weapons for close combat.

No D'Haran but the Lord Rahl's personal bodyguards wore such weapons. They were more than simply weapons; they were the rarest, the highest badges of honor, earned he knew not how.

Richard had inherited the rule of a people he didn't know, with customs that were mostly a mystery to him, and expectations he only partly fathomed.

Since they had returned, these four, too, had discovered what had happened with Marlin the night before. They knew why they had been summoned, but he hadn't said anything to them, yet. He was trying to get a grip on his rage, first.

'Lord Rahl?'

'Yes, Raina?'

'Are you angry with us? For disobeying your orders and coming out to you with the Mother Confessor's message?'

The message had been a pretense, and they knew it as well as he.

Click, click, click, went his thumbnail. 'That will be all. You may go. All of you.'

Their postures relaxed, but none made a move to leave.

'Leave?' Raina asked. 'Aren't you going to punish us?' A smirk spread on her face. 'Maybe clean out the stables for a week, or something?'

Richard pushed back from the table as he ground his teeth. He was not in the mood for their impish humor. He rose behind the table.

'No, Raina, no punishment. You may go.'

The two Mord-Sith smiled. Berdine leaned toward Raina, speaking in a whisper, but loud enough for him to hear.

'He realizes that we know best how to protect him.'

They all started for the door.

'Before you go,' Richard said, as he strolled around the table, 'I just want you to know one thing.'

'What's that?' Berdine asked.

Richard walked past them, pausing long enough to look each in the eye.

'That I'm disappointed in you.'

Raina made a face. 'You're disappointed in us? You're not going to yell or punish us, you're simply disappointed?'

'That's right. You've disappointed me. I thought I could trust you. I can't.' Richard turned away. 'Dismissed.'

Berdine cleared her throat. 'Lord Rahl, Ulic and I went with you by your command.'

'Oh? So if it had been you I'd left here to protect Kahlan, instead of Raina, you would have done as I asked and stayed?' She didn't answer. 'I've counted on all of you, and you've made me feel a fool for trusting you.' He flexed his fists instead of yelling. 'I would have seen to Kahlan's protection if I'd known I couldn't trust you.'

Richard leaned an arm against the window frame and stared out at the cold spring morning. The four behind him shifted their feet uneasily.

'Lord Rahl,' Berdine said at last, 'we would lay down our lives for you.'

Richard rounded on them. 'And let Kahlan die!' He carefully quieted his tone. 'You can lay down your lives for me all you want. Play your games all you want. Pretend you're doing something important. Play at being my guards. Just stay out of my way, and out of the way of people helping me in this effort to stop the Imperial Order.'

He flicked his hand toward the door. 'Dismissed.'

Berdine and Raina shared a look. 'We will be outside, in the hall, if you need us, Lord Rahl.'

Richard gave them such a cold look that it drained the color from their faces. 'I won't be needing you. I don't need people I can't trust.'

Berdine swallowed. 'But –'

'But what?'

She swallowed again. 'What about Kolo's journal? Don't you want me to help you with the translation?'

'I'll manage. Anything else?'

Each of them shook their heads.

They began filing out. Raina, at the end of the line, paused and turned back. Her dark eyes fixed on the floor.

'Lord Rahl, will you be taking us out, later, to feed the chipmunks?'

'I'm busy. They'll manage just fine without us.'

'But … what about Reggie?'

'Who?'

'Reggie. He's the one missing the end of his little tail. He … he … sat in my hand. He'll be looking for us.'

Richard watched her for a silence-filled eternity. He teetered between wanting to hug her and wanting to yell at her. He had tried the hugging, or its equivalent, anyway, and it had nearly gotten Kahlan killed.

'Maybe another day. Dismissed.'

She wiped the back of her hand across her nose. 'Yes, Lord Rahl.'

Raina quietly pulled the door closed behind her. Richard raked back his hair as he flopped down in his chair again. With a finger, he slowly spun Kolo's journal around and around as he ground his teeth. Kahlan could have died while he was off looking for trees. Kahlan could have died while the people he thought were protecting her were instead following their own agenda.

He shuddered to think what the added magic, the added rage, of the sword would do were he to draw it at that moment.

160

He couldn't recall being this angry, without the Sword of Truth in his hand. He couldn't imagine the wrath of the sword's magic on top of this.

The words of the prophecy from the stone wall in the pit ran through his mind with haunting, mocking finality.

A soft knock silenced the hundredth, whispered sound of the prophecy in his head.

This was the knock he had been waiting for. He knew who it was.

'Come in, Cara.'

The tall, muscular, blond-haired Mord-Sith slunk in through the door. She pushed it closed with her back. Her head was bent, and she looked as miserable as he had ever seen her.

'May I speak with you, Lord Rahl?'

'Why are you wearing your red leather?'

She swallowed before answering. 'It's a … Mord-Sith thing, Lord Rahl.'

He didn't ask for an explanation; he didn't really care. This was the one he had been waiting for. This was the one who was at the core of his wrath.

'I see. What do you want?'

Cara approached the table and stood with her shoulders slumped. She had a bandage around her head but he had been told that her head wound wasn't serious. By the red-rimmed look of her eyes, it was obvious that she hadn't slept the night before. 'How is the Mother Confessor this morning?'

'When I left her, she was resting, but she's going to be fine. Her wounds weren't serious, as serious as they easily could have been. She's lucky to be alive, considering what happened. Considering that she wasn't supposed to have been down there with Marlin in the first place, considering that I specifically told you that I didn't want either of you down there.'

Cara's eyes closed. 'Lord Rahl, it was my fault entirely. I'm the one who talked her into it. I wanted to question Marlin. She tried to convince me to stay away, but I went anyway. She only went to try to make me leave him be, as you had instructed.'

Had Richard not been so angry, he might have laughed. Even if Kahlan hadn't admitted the truth to him, he knew her

161

well enough to recognize Cara's confession as pure fiction. But he also knew that Cara hadn't put in much of an effort to keep Kahlan away from the assassin.

'I thought that I had control of him. I made a mistake.'

Richard leaned forward. 'Didn't I specifically tell you that I didn't want either of you down there?'

Her shoulders trembled as she nodded without looking up.

His fist hitting the table made her flinch. 'Answer me! Didn't I specifically tell you that I didn't want either of you down there?'

'Yes, Lord Rahl.'

'Was there any doubt in your mind what I meant?'

'No, Lord Rahl.'

Richard leaned back in his chair. 'That was the mistake, Cara. Do you understand? Not that you didn't have control of him – that was beyond your power. Going down there was a choice you made. That was the mistake you made.

'I love Kahlan more than anything in this world, or anything in any other world. Nothing else is so precious to me. I trusted *you* to protect her, to keep her out of harm's view.'

The sunlight coming through the patterned shears played across her red leather in dappled patches like sunlight coming through leaves.

'Lord Rahl,' she said in a small voice, 'I fully understand the dimensions of my failure, and what it means.

'Lord Rahl, may I be granted a request?'

'What is it?'

She sank to her knees, bending forward in supplication. She took up her Agiel, holding it in both trembling fists.

'May I choose the manner of my execution?'

'What?'

'A Mord-Sith wears her red leather at her execution. If she has previously served with honor, she is allowed to choose the manner of execution.'

'And what would you choose?'

'My Agiel, Lord Rahl. I know how I have failed you – I have committed an unforgivable transgression – but I have served with honor in the past. Please. Allow it to be with my Agiel. It's my only request. Either Berdine or Raina can carry it out. They know how.'

Richard walked around the table. He leaned back against its edge, looking down at Cara's slumped, quivering form. He folded his arms.

'Denied.'

Her shoulders shuddered with a sob. 'May I ask what Lord Rahl will … choose?'

'Cara, look at me,' he said in a soft voice. Her tear-stained face came up. 'Cara, I'm angry. But no matter how angry I was, I would never, ever, have you, any of you, executed.'

'You must. I have failed you. I have disobeyed your orders to protect your love. I have made an unforgivable mistake.'

Richard smiled. 'I don't know that there are unforgivable mistakes. There may be unforgivable betrayals, but not mistakes. If we were going to start executing people for mistakes, I'm afraid I'd have been dead long ago. I make mistakes all the time. Some of them have been pretty big.'

She shook her head as she gazed into his eyes. 'A Mord-Sith knows when she has earned execution. I have earned it.' In those blue eyes he saw the iron of her resolution. 'Either you carry it out, or I will.'

Richard stood for a time, judging the demand of duty to which a Mord-Sith was bound. Judging the madness in those eyes.

'Do you wish to die, Cara?'

'No, Lord Rahl. Since you have been our Lord Rahl, never. That is why I must. I have failed you. A Mord-Sith lives and dies by a code of duty to her master. Neither you nor I can alter what must be. My life is forfeit. You must carry out the execution, or I will.'

Richard knew that she wasn't making a play for sympathy. Mord-Sith didn't bluff. If he didn't somehow change her mind, she would do as she promised.

With comprehension, and the resulting, sickening realization of his only choice, he made the mental leap off the rim of sanity and into the madness, where dwelt part of this woman's mind and, he feared, part of his.

As irretrievable as a heartbeat, the decision had been made.

Muscles flexing with the call, he drew his sword. It sent the soft, matchless ring of steel through the room, through his bones.

With that seemingly simple act, the wrath of the sword's magic was loosed. The lock on the door to death was slipped free. It took his breath like a wall of an acid wind. Storms of rage lifted on that biting wind.

'Magic, then,' he told her, 'will be your judge, and executioner.'

Her eyes squeezed shut.

'Look at me!'

The sword's rage twisted through him, trying to carry him away with it. He fought to maintain his grip of control, as he always had to do when he held the fury unleashed.

'You will look into my eyes when I kill you!'

Her eyes opened. Her brow wrinkled together, tears streaming down her cheeks. Any good she had done, any bravery in the face of danger, any sacrifice to her duty, had been stripped away in the face of her disgrace. She had been denied the honor of a death by her Agiel. For that, and that alone, she cried.

Richard pressed the razor-sharp edge to his forearm, drawing for the blade its taste of blood. He brought the Sword of Truth to his forehead, touching the cold steel, the warm blood, to his flesh.

He whispered his invocation. 'Blade, be true this day.'

This was the person who, for her presumption, and but for luck, would have cost him Kahlan. Cost him everything.

She watched as the blade rose above him. She saw the fury, the righteous rage, in his eyes. She saw the magic dancing there.

She saw death, dancing there.

The knuckles of both fists were white as he gripped the hilt.

He knew he couldn't deny the magic its will – if he was to have a chance. He loosed his wrath at this woman for abandoning her responsibility to protect Kahlan. Her arrogance could have ended Kahlan's life, ended his future, ended his reason for living. He had entrusted his dearest love to her care, and she had failed in her duty to honor his faith.

He could have returned to find Kahlan dead because of this woman on her knees before him. For no other reason.

Their eyes shared the madness of what they were doing, of

what they each had become, of knowing that there was no other way – for either of them.

He committed to cleave her in two.

The sword's wrath demanded it.

He would accept no less.

He envisioned it.

He would have it.

Her blood.

With a scream of rage, with all his strength, with all his fury and anger, he swung the blade down toward her face.

The sword's tip whistled.

In every detail, he could see the light glint off the polished blade as it swept through a streamer of sunlight. He could see drops of his sweat sparkle in the sunlight, as if frozen in space. He could have counted them. He could see where the blade would hit her. She could see where the blade was going to hit her. His muscles screamed with the effort as his lungs screamed with rage.

Between her eyes, an inch from her flesh, the blade stopped as solidly as if it had thunked into an impenetrable wall.

Sweat rolled down his face. His arms shook. The room echoed with the lingering sound of his cry of fury.

At last, he withdrew the blade from over Cara.

She stared up with big, round, unblinking eyes. She was panting in rapid, short breaths through her mouth. A long, low whine came from her throat.

'There will be no execution,' Richard said in a hoarse voice.

'How ...' she whispered, 'how ... could it do that? How could it stop like that?'

'I'm sorry, Cara, but the sword's magic has made the choice. It has chosen that you live. You will have to abide by its decision.'

Her eyes finally turned to look into his. 'You were going to do it. You were going to execute me.'

He slid the sword slowly into its scabbard.

'Yes.'

'Then why am I not dead?'

'Because the magic decided otherwise. We can't question its judgment. We must abide by it.'

Richard had been reasonably sure that the sword's magic

wouldn't harm Cara. The magic wouldn't let him harm one who was an ally. He had been counting on that.

But there had been doubt. Cara had brought Kahlan within danger's grasp, though not intentionally. He wasn't entirely sure that doubt wouldn't cause the blade to take her. That was the way with the Sword of Truth's magic – one wasn't always entirely sure.

Zedd had told Richard when he had given him the sword that therein lay the danger. The sword destroyed an enemy, and spared a friend, but the sword's magic worked as a result of the view of its holder, not the truth. Zedd had told him that doubt could possibly cause the death of a friend, or allow the escape of a foe.

But he did know that if it was to work, he had to commit his entire being to the effort, otherwise Cara wouldn't believe the magic had spared her, and she would have credited it to him. Then she would have been obligated to do as she had promised.

His insides felt as if they were twisted into knots. His knees trembled. He had been sucked into a world of dread; he hadn't been positive that it would work as he had planned.

Worse, he wasn't entirely sure he hadn't made a mistake by sparing her.

Richard cupped Cara's chin. 'The Sword of Truth has made its choice. It chose for you to live, for you to have another chance. You must accept its decision.'

Cara nodded in his hand. 'Yes, Lord Rahl.'

He reached under her arm and helped her to her feet. He could hardly stand himself, and wondered if he had been in her place if he would be able to get to his feet as steadily as she.

'I will do better in the future, Lord Rahl.'

Richard pulled her head to his shoulder and held her tight for a moment, something he had been aching to do. Her arms slipped around him in grateful surrender.

'That's all I ask, Cara.'

As she headed for the door, Richard called her name. She turned back.

'You still must be punished.'

Her eyes turned down. 'Yes, Lord Rahl.'

'Tomorrow afternoon. You will have to learn to feed chipmunks.'

Her gaze came back up. 'Lord Rahl?'

'Do you wish to feed chipmunks?'

'No, Lord Rahl.'

'Then that's your punishment. Bring Berdine and Raina. They, too, are due some punishment.'

Richard closed the door after her, leaned against it, and shut his eyes. The inferno of the sword's rage had consumed his anger. He was left empty and weak. He shook so badly he could hardly stand.

He was almost sick at the vivid memory of looking into her eyes as he brought the sword down with all his strength, expecting that he was going to kill her. He had been prepared for the spray of blood and bone. Cara's blood and bone. A person he cared about.

He had done what he had to, to save her life, but at what cost?

The prophecy reeled through his head, and the nausea took him to his knees in a flash of cold sweat and dread.

CHAPTER 15

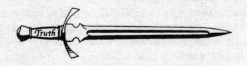

The soldiers he had stationed in the halls around the Mother Confessor's rooms stepped aside, each clapping a fist to the chain mail over his heart as Richard went by. He absently returned the salute as he swept past them, his gold cape billowing out behind. The soldiers crossed their pikes before the three Mord-Sith and two big bodyguards trailing him at a distance. When he had previously stationed the soldiers, he had given them a very short list of who was to be allowed through their positions. His five guards weren't on the list.

He glanced back to see Agiel come up into fists. He met Cara's eyes. The three Mord-Sith reluctantly released their weapons.

His five guards backed away from the challenge and set up their own guard post beyond the soldiers. With a hand signal from Cara, Raina and Ulic swiftly disappeared back down the hall. No doubt she had sent them to find another way around to guard the opposite end of the hall.

When he rounded the next to last corner before Kahlan's room, he saw Nadine sitting on a gilt-legged chair to the side of the hall. She was swinging her legs like a bored child waiting to go outside and play. When she saw him coming, she bounded up out of the chair.

She looked scrubbed and fresh. Her thick hair glistened. His brow twitched; her dress looked tighter than it had the day before. It seemed to fit closer to her ribs and hips, showing her alluring shape more than he remembered. He knew it was the same dress; he thought he must be imagining things. Seeing her figure displayed to such advantage reminded him that there had been a time . . .

She schooled her enthusiasm, twisting a strand of hair with a finger as she affected a smile. Her delight at seeing him faltered as he approached. She took a step back toward the wall as he stopped before her.

Nadine's gaze left his eyes. 'Richard. Good morning. I thought I heard someone say you were back already. I was' – she gestured toward Kahlan's room for an excuse to look away – 'I came . . . to see how Kahlan was doing this morning. I, well, I need to put on a new poultice. I was just waiting until I was sure she was up, and –'

'Kahlan told me how you helped her. Thanks, Nadine. I appreciate it more than you could know.'

She shrugged one shoulder. 'We're Hartlanders, you and I.' In the thick silence she twisted a thread between her fingers. 'Tommy and skinny Rita Wellington got married.'

Richard watched the top of her bowed head as she played with the thread. 'I guess that was to be expected. That was what their parents wanted.'

Nadine didn't look up from her thread. 'He beats the stuffing out of her. I had to give her poultices and herbs one time when he made her bleed . . . you know, down there. People say it's none of their business and pretend not to know it's happening.'

Richard wasn't sure what she was getting at; he certainly wasn't going back to Hartland to rattle a conscience into Tom Lancaster's head. 'Well, if he keeps at it, her brothers might end up giving him a lesson in cracked skulls.'

Nadine didn't look up. 'That could have been me.' She cleared her throat. 'I could have been married to Tommy, crying to anyone who'd listen about how . . . well, it could have been me. It could have been me pregnant, wondering if he'd beat me till I lost this one, too.

'I reckon I owe you, Richard. And you being a boy from Hartland and all . . . I just wanted to help if you were in trouble.' She shrugged her one shoulder again. 'Kahlan's real nice. Most women would have . . . I guess she's about the prettiest woman I ever saw. Nothing like me.'

'I never figured you owed me anything, Nadine; I'd have

done the same no matter who Tom had caught alone that day, but you have my sincere gratitude for helping Kahlan.'

'Sure. I guess that was stupid of me to think you stopped him because …'

Richard realized by the way she sounded on the verge of tears that he hadn't put it very well, so he laid a hand tenderly on her shoulder. 'Nadine, you've grown into a beautiful woman, too.'

She peered up with a growing smile. 'You think I'm beautiful?' She smoothed her blue dress at her hips.

'I didn't dance with you at the midsummer festival because you were still clumsy little Nadine Brighton.'

She started winding the string again. 'I liked dancing with you. You know, I carved the initials "N.C." on my betrothal trunk. For Nadine Cypher.'

'I'm sorry, Nadine. Michael is dead.'

She looked up with a frown. 'Michael? No … that's not what it meant. It meant you.'

Richard decided that this conversation had gone far enough. He had more important things to worry about.

'I'm Richard Rahl now. I can't live in the past. My future is with Kahlan.'

Nadine caught his arm as he started turning away. 'I'm sorry. I know that. I know I made a big mistake. With Michael, I mean.'

Richard caught himself just in time to bite off a caustic retort. What would be the purpose? 'I appreciate that you helped Kahlan. I suppose you'll want to be heading home. Tell everyone I'm well. I'll be back for a visit when –'

'Kahlan invited me to stay a while.'

Richard was caught off guard; Kahlan had neglected to tell him that part of it. 'Oh. And you wish to stay for a day or two?'

'Sure. I thought I'd like that. I've never been away from home before. If it's all right with you, I mean. I wouldn't want to …'

Richard gently pulled his arm from her hand. 'Fine. If she invited you, then it's fine with me.'

She brightened, as if oblivious to the disapproval on his face. 'Richard, did you see the moon last night? Everyone is

170

abuzz about it. Did you see it? Was it as extraordinary, as remarkable, as they say?'

'That, and more,' he whispered, his mood darkening.

Before she could get in another word, he marched off.

His soft knock on the door produced a rotund woman in a staff uniform. Her ruddy face peered out through the narrow crack.

'Lord Rahl. Nancy is just helping the Mother Confessor get dressed. She'll be finished in a minute.'

'Dressed!' he called to the closing door. The latch clicked into place. 'She's supposed to be in bed!' he called through the heavy, ornately carved door.

Getting no response, he decided to wait rather than cause a scene. Once, when he looked up, he saw Nadine peeking around the corner. Her head swiftly disappeared back around the corner. He paced before the door until the rubicund woman finally opened it wide and held an arm out in invitation.

Richard stepped into the room, feeling as if he was entering another world. The Confessors' Palace was a place of splendor, power, and history, but the Mother Confessor's quarters were the place that, more than anywhere else in the palace, reminded him that he was really just a woods guide. It made him feel out of his element.

The Mother Confessor's rooms were a majestic, quiet sanctuary befitting the woman to whom knelt kings and queens. If Richard had seen this room before he came to know Kahlan, he wondered if he would have ever had the nerve to speak to her. Even now, it embarrassed him to recall teaching her to build snares and dig roots when he didn't know who, or what, she was.

It made him smile, though, to remember her eagerness to learn. He was thankful he had come to know the woman before he came to understand the post she filled, and the magic she wielded. He thanked the good spirits she had come into his life, and prayed she would be a part of it forever. She meant everything to him.

The three marble fireplaces in the Mother Confessor's sitting room were ablaze. The heavy drapes on the ten-foot-tall windows hung open slightly, forming tall slits, letting in only enough light, muted by the sheer panels behind, to make lamps unnecessary. He guessed that bright sunlight was inappropriate in a sanctuary. There were only a few houses in Hartland that wouldn't fit in this room alone.

On a glossy, gold-embellished mahogany table to the side sat a silver tray with tea, soup, biscuits, sliced pears, and brown bread. None of it had been touched. The sight reminded him that he hadn't eaten since noon the day before, but failed to summon his appetite.

The three women in crisp gray dresses with white lace collars and cuffs watched him expectantly, as if waiting to see if he would dare to simply walk in on the Mother Confessor, or fall into a show of some other scandalous behavior.

Richard glanced at the door at the far end of the room, his sense of propriety making him ask the obvious. 'Is she dressed?'

The one who had cracked the door before reddened. 'I wouldn't have let you in, sir, had she not been.'

'Of course.' He headed soundlessly across the plush, dark-hued carpets. He stopped and turned back. They watched like three owls. 'Thank you, ladies. That will be all.'

They bowed and reluctantly took their leave. He realized as the last one stole a quick glance over her shoulder while pulling the door closed that they probably considered it the height of indecency for a man engaged to a woman to be alone with her in her bedroom. Doubly so for the Mother Confessor.

Richard forced out an annoyed breath; whenever he was anywhere near the Mother Confessor's rooms, some member of the staff always managed to show up every other minute checking to see if she needed anything. The variety of things they suspected she might be needing never failed to surprise him. He sometimes expected one of them to come right out and ask her if she might need her virtue protected. Outside her rooms the staff was friendly, even joking with him when he put them at ease, or helped them carry things. A few were afraid of him. But not in her rooms. In her rooms, they all turned into bold, protective mother hawks.

Inside the bedroom, against the far paneled wall, stood the huge bed, its four great dark polished posts rising up like columns before a palace. The thick, embroidered bedcover cascaded down the sides of the bed like a colorful waterfall frozen in place. A slash of sunlight cut across the dark, sumptuous carpets and over the lower half of the bed.

Richard remembered Kahlan describing her bed to him, telling him how she couldn't wait to have him in it, when they were married. He very much wanted to be in bed with her; it had been since that night between worlds that he had been alone with her – in that way – but he had to admit that he was intimidated by that bed of hers. He thought he might lose her in it. She had promised there would be no chance of that.

Kahlan was standing at the row of glassed doors before the expansive balcony, looking out past the open curtain. She was staring out over the stone railings and up toward the Keep on the mountainside. The sight of her in her satiny white dress flowing smoothly over her ravishing curves, with her dazzling mane cascading down her back, nearly took his breath. The sight of her made him ache. He decided that the bed would be just fine.

When he tenderly touched her shoulder, she started.

She turned, a beaming smile on her face as she looked up at him. 'I thought you were Nancy, come back in.'

'What do you mean, you thought I was Nancy? You didn't know it was me?'

'How would I know it was you?'

He shrugged. 'Because. I always can tell when it's you who's walked into a room. I don't have to see you.'

Her brow furrowed in disbelief. 'You cannot.'

'Of course I can.'

'How?'

'You have a unique fragrance. I know the sounds you make, the sound of your breathing, the way you move, the way you pause. They're all unique to you.'

Her frown grew. 'You're not kidding? You mean it? You're serious?'

'Of course. Can't you tell me by those things?'

'No. But I guess you've spent much of your life in the woods, watching, smelling, listening.' She slipped her good arm around his. 'I still don't know if I believe you.'

'Then test me some time.' Richard stroked his fingers down her hair. 'How are you feeling? How's your arm?'

'I'm all right. It's not so bad. Not as bad as that time elder Toffalar cut me. Remember? That was worse than this.'

He nodded. 'What are you doing out of bed? You were told to rest.'

She pushed at his stomach. 'Stop. I'm fine.' She looked him up and down. 'And you look more than fine. I can't believe you had that made for me. You look magnificent, Lord Rahl.'

Richard tenderly met her lips. She tried to pull him into a more passionate kiss, but he pulled back.

'I'm afraid I'll hurt you,' he said.

'Richard, I'm fine, really. I was exhausted before because I used my power, along with all the rest of it. People mistook that for me being hurt worse than I was.'

He appraised her for a long moment, before bending to the kind of kiss he had been longing to give her.

'That's better,' she breathed on parting. She pushed back. 'Richard, did you see Cara? You left so quickly, and you had that look in your eye. I didn't have time to really talk to you. It wasn't her fault.'

'I know. You told me.'

'You didn't yell at her, did you?'

'We had a talk.'

She squinted. 'Talk. What did she have to say for herself? She didn't try to tell you that she was … ?'

'What's Nadine still doing here?'

She was looking at him. She snatched his wrist. 'Richard, you have blood on you … your arm …'

She looked up in alarm. 'What did you do? Richard … you didn't hurt her, did you?' She lifted his arm higher into the light. 'Richard, this looks like … like when you …'

She seized his shirt. 'You didn't hurt her? Tell me that you didn't hurt her!'

'She wanted to be executed. She gave me the choice of doing it, or she would. So I used the sword, like that time with the Mud People elders.'

'She's all right? She's all right, isn't she?'

'She's all right.'

Kahlan, concern in her expression, looked into his eyes. 'And you? Are you all right?'

'I've been better. Kahlan, what is Nadine still doing here?'

'She's just staying for a visit, that's all. Have you met Drefan yet?'

Richard held her away when she moved to lay her head to his chest. 'What is she doing here? Why did you invite her to stay?'

'Richard, I had to. Trouble from Shota isn't so easily dismissed. You ought to know that. We have to know what's going on before we can do something to make sure Shota can't cause us trouble.'

Richard went to the glassed door and stared out at the mountain towering over the city. The Wizard's Keep stared back.

'I don't like it. Not one bit.'

'Neither do I,' she said from behind him. 'Richard, she helped me. I didn't think she would have the guts to keep her head, but she did. She's confused by all this, too. Something more than we're seeing is going on, and we have to use our heads, not hide under the blankets.'

He heaved a sigh. 'I still don't like it, but you have a point. I only marry smart women.'

He could hear Kahlan absently smooth her dress behind him. The fragrance of her calmed him.

'I can see why you liked her. She's a lovely woman, besides being a healer. It must have hurt you.'

The Keep seemed to absorb the morning sunlight in its dark stone. He should go up there. 'What must have hurt me?'

'When you caught her kissing Michael. She told me how you caught her kissing your brother.'

Richard wheeled around, staring in slack-jawed disbelief. 'She told you *what?*'

Kahlan gestured back toward the door, as if Nadine might appear to speak for herself. 'She said that you caught her kissing your brother.'

'Kissing him.'

'That's what she said.'

Richard turned his glare back to the window. 'Did she, now?'

'What was she doing, then? You mean you caught –'

'Kahlan, we have sixteen men who died down by the pit last night, and a dozen more who may not live the day. I've got guards I can't trust to protect the woman I love. We've got a witch woman who has made it her life's mission to cause us trouble. We've got Jagang sending us messages in walking dead men. We've got a Sister of the Dark loose somewhere. We've got half the army in Aydindril sick and unable to fight if they have to. We've got representatives waiting to see us. I've got a half brother I never knew I had downstairs under guard. I think we have more important things to discuss than Nadine's ... than Nadine's difficulty with the truth!'

Kahlan's green eyes watched him tenderly for a moment. 'That bad. Now I understand what put that look in your eyes.'

'Remember what you told me one time? "Never let a beautiful woman pick your path for you when there's a man in her line of sight." '

She put a hand over his shoulder. 'Nadine isn't picking my path. I asked her to stay for my own reasons.'

'Nadine sticks to what she wants like a hound on scent, but I'm not talking about Nadine. I'm talking about Shota. She's pointing down a path, and you're walking right down it.'

'We have to find out what's down that path, and Shota's reasons for pointing to it.'

Richard turned back to the glassed door. 'I want to know what else Marlin – Jagang – had to say. Every word. I want you to try to remember every word.'

'Why don't you just yell at me and get it over with?'

'I don't want to yell at you. You scared me to death, going down there. I just want to hold you, to protect you. I want to marry you.' He turned back and looked into her green eyes. 'I think I have a way for it to work. With the Mud People, I mean.'

She stepped closer. 'Really? How?'

'First, you tell me everything Jagang said.'

Richard idly watched the Keep as she went through the whole story: how Jagang said he watched the Ja'La game and that in his native tongue the name meant the Game of Life; that he wanted to witness the glory of what Marlin had done; how he wanted Sister Amelia to return to him before he revealed himself; that he had found prophecies other than those Richard had destroyed, and that he had invoked one called a bound fork prophecy.

'That's all I remember,' she said. 'Why are you watching the Keep so intently?'

'I'm wondering why Sister Amelia went there. And what Marlin was going to do there. Any ideas?'

'No. Jagang wouldn't say. Richard, have you seen the prophecy in the pit?'

His stomach roiled. 'Yes.'

'And? What does it say?'

'I don't know. I'll have to translate it.'

'Richard Rahl, you may be able to tell it's me who has walked into a room without seeing me, but I can tell when you're not telling me the truth without even having to look into your eyes.'

Richard couldn't manage to smile. 'Prophecies are more complicated than their words. You know that. Just hearing their words doesn't mean it's what it sounds like. Besides, just because Jagang found a prophecy, that doesn't mean he can invoke it.'

'Well, that's all true enough. I told him as much myself. He said that proof he had invoked the prophecy would come on a red moon. Not much chance of that –'

Richard spun around. 'What did you say? You didn't tell me that before. What did Jagang say?'

Her face paled. 'I forgot … until you said … I told Jagang that I didn't believe him – about invoking the prophecy. He said that proof would come on the red moon. Richard, do you know what that means?'

Richard's tongue felt thick. He made himself blink.

'The moon was red last night. I've been outdoors my whole life. I've never seen anything even remotely like it. It was like looking at the moon through a glass of red wine. It gave me goose bumps. That was why I came back early.'

'Richard, what did the prophecy say? Tell me.'

He stared at her, trying to think of a lie he could make her believe. He couldn't.

'It said,' he whispered, ''On the red moon will come the firestorm. The one bonded to the blade will watch as his people die. If he does nothing, then he, and all those he loves, will die in its heat, for no blade, forged of steel or conjured of sorcery, can touch this foe.'' '

Silence rang through the still room. Kahlan's face was white.

'What's the rest of it? Jagang said it was a bound fork prophecy. What's the rest of it' – her voice broke – 'the other fork? You tell me, Richard. Don't you lie to me. We're in this together. If you love me, then you tell me.'

Dear spirits, let her hear the words, and not my dread. Let me at least spare her that.

His left hand clutched the hilt of his sword. The raised letters of the word TRUTH bit into his flesh. He blinked his vision clear.

Show no fear.

' "To quench the inferno, he must seek the remedy in the wind. Lightning will find him on that path, for the one in white, his true beloved, will betray him in her blood." '

CHAPTER 16

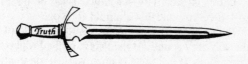

Kahlan could feel tears falling down her cheeks.

'Richard.' She sucked back a sob. 'Richard, you know I would never … You don't believe I could ever … I swear on my life. I would never … You have to believe me …'

He swept her into his arms as she lost control over a wail of anguish.

'Richard,' she sobbed against his chest, 'I would never betray you. Not for anything in this world. Not to spare myself eternal torment in the underworld at the Keeper's hands.'

'I know. Of course I know that. You know as well as I that you can't understand a prophecy by its words. Don't let it hurt you. That's what Jagang wants. He doesn't even know what it means; he just put it down there because the words sounded like what he wanted to hear.'

'But … I …' She couldn't halt her weeping.

'Shhhh.' His big hand held her head against him.

The terror of the night before, and the worse terror of the prophecy, came out in uncontrollable tears. She had never cried in the face of battle, but in the safety of his arms she couldn't control herself. She was swept away by a flood of tears no less powerful than the torrent in the drainage tunnel.

'Kahlan, don't let yourself believe it. Please don't.'

'But it says … I will …'

'Listen to me. Didn't I tell you not to go down there to question Marlin? Didn't I tell you that I would do it when I got back, and that it was dangerous and I didn't want you down there?'

'Yes, but I was afraid for you and I just wanted –'

'You went against my wishes. No matter your reasons, you went against my wishes, didn't you?' She nodded against him. 'That could be the betrayal in the prophecy. You were wounded, you were bleeding. You betrayed me, and you had blood on you. Your blood.'

'I wouldn't call what I did a betrayal. I was doing it for you, because I love you and I was afraid for you.'

'But don't you see? The words of prophecy don't always work the way they sound. At the Palace of the Prophets, in the Old World, both Warren and Nathan warned me that prophecies aren't meant to be understood by the words. The words are only obliquely connected to the prophecy.'

'But I don't see how –'

'I'm just saying that it could be something as simple as that. You can't let a prophecy gain control of your fears. Don't let it.'

'Zedd told me that, too. He said that there were prophecies about me that he wouldn't tell me because the words weren't to be trusted. He said you were right to ignore the words of prophecy. But this is different, Richard. This says I will betray you.'

'I already told you how it could be something simple.'

'Lightning isn't simple. Being struck by lightning is a symbol for being killed, if not an outright declaration of the manner of your death. The prophecy says I will betray you, and because of that, you will die.'

'I don't believe it. Kahlan, I love you. I know it isn't possible. You wouldn't betray me and bring me harm. You wouldn't.'

Kahlan clutched his shirt as she gasped a sob. 'That's why Shota sent Nadine. She wants you to marry someone else, because she knows I will be the death of you. Shota is trying to save you – from me.'

'She thought that once before, and she turned out to be wrong. Remember? If Shota had had her way, we wouldn't have been able to stop Darken Rahl. He would rule us all right now, if we had given in to her reading of the future. Prophecy is no different.' Richard gripped her shoulders and held her at arm's length so that he could look into her eyes. 'Do you love me?'

His grip on her wounded shoulder made it sing with pain, but she refused to pull away from his touch. 'More than life itself.'

'Then trust in me. I won't let it destroy us. I promise. It will all fall into place for the best in the end. You'll see. We can't think of the solution if we're focused on the problem.'

She wiped at her eyes. He sounded so sure of himself. His confidence calmed her and bolstered her spirits. 'You're right. I'm sorry.'

'Do you want to marry me?'

'Of course, but I don't see how we can leave our responsibility for such a long time to travel –'

'The sliph.'

She blinked. 'What?'

'The sliph, up in the Wizard's Keep. I've been thinking about it; we traveled all the way to the Old World and back in her, with her magic, and it took less than a day each way. I can wake the sliph, and we can travel in her.'

'But she would take us to the Old World, to the city of Tanimura. Jagang is somewhere near Tanimura.'

'That's still a lot closer to the Mud People than Aydindril is. Besides, I think the sliph can go other places, too. She asked me where I wished to travel. That means she can go other places. Maybe she can get us a lot closer than Tanimura.'

Kahlan, her tears forgotten at the prospect of their wedding being possible, glanced up at the Keep. 'We might be able to go to the Mud People, be married, and be back in a matter of a few days. We could be gone that long, surely.'

Richard smiled as his arms circled her from behind. 'Surely.'

Kahlan wiped the last of the tears away as she turned in his arms. 'How do you always manage to figure things out?'

He nodded toward her bed. 'I had a great deal of motivation.'

Kahlan, a grin spreading on her face, was just about to reward him with something positively indecent, when there was a knock at the door. It immediately opened without benefit of an answer. Nancy stuck her head in.

'Are you all right, Mother Confessor?' She glanced meaningfully to Richard.

'Yes. What is it?'

'Lady Nadine is asking if she could change the poultice.'

'Is she, now?' Kahlan said in a dark tone.

'Yes, Mother Confessor. But if you are … indisposed, I could ask her to wait until –'

'Send her in, then,' Richard said.

Nancy hesitated. 'We will have to take the top of your dress down, Mother Confessor. To get at the bandage.'

'It's all right,' Richard whispered in Kahlan's ear. 'I have to go talk to Berdine. I have some work for her.'

'I hope it doesn't involve horse manure.'

Richard smiled. 'No. I want her to work on Kolo's journal.'

'Why?'

He kissed the top of her head. 'Knowledge is a weapon. I intend to be formidably armed.' He glanced to Nancy. 'Need me to help with her dress?'

Nancy managed to scowl and turn red at the same time.

'I guess that means you will manage.' At the door, he turned back to Kahlan. 'I'll wait until Nadine's finished with you, and then we better go see this Drefan fellow. I have a task for him. I'd … like you to be with me.'

When he had closed the door, Nancy brushed back her short brown hair and moved around behind Kahlan to help with her dress. 'Your Mother Confessor's dress, the one you were wearing yesterday, was ruined beyond repair.'

'I expected as much.' Confessors had a collection of dresses, all the same. Confessors all wore black dresses; only the Mother Confessor wore white. She thought about the blue wedding dress she would wear. 'Nancy, do you remember when your husband was courting you?'

Nancy paused. 'Yes, Mother Confessor.'

'Then you must know how it would have made you feel if someone were to keep popping in on you when you were alone with him.'

Nancy eased the dress over Kahlan's shoulder. 'Mother Confessor, I was never allowed to be alone with him until we were married. I was young, and ignorant. My parents were right to watch over me and the impulses of youth.'

'Nancy, I'm a grown woman. I'm the Mother Confessor. I can't have you and the other women popping your heads into my room whenever Richard is with me. Ow!'

'Sorry. That was my fault. It isn't proper, Mother Confessor.'

'That's for me to decide.'

'If you say so, Mother Confessor.'

Kahlan held her arm out as Nancy slipped the sleeve over her hand. 'I say so.'

Nancy glanced to the bed. 'You were conceived in that bed. Who knows how many Mother Confessors before you conceived their daughters in that bed. It holds a legacy of tradition. Only wedded Mother Confessors took their men to that bed to conceive a child.'

'And not one of them because of love. I was not conceived through love, Nancy. My child, if I have one, will be.'

'All the more reason that it should be by the grace of the good spirits – in the sanctity of marriage.'

Kahlan didn't say that the good spirits had taken them to a place between worlds to sanctify their union. 'The good spirits know what's in our hearts; there is no one else for either of us, nor will there ever be.'

Nancy busied herself at the bandage. 'And you are eager to get to it. Like my daughter and her young man are.'

If Nancy only knew how eager.

'That's not it. I'm just saying that I don't want you coming in on me when Richard is here with me. We will be wedded soon. We are irreversibly committed to one another.

'There is more to being in love than just jumping into bed, you know. Like just being close, in one another's arms. Can you understand? I can't very well kiss my future husband and have my injuries comforted by him if you keep popping your head in every two minutes, now can I?'

'No, Mother Confessor.'

Nadine knocked at the open door. 'May I come in?'

'Yes, of course. Here, set your bag on the bed. I can manage, now, Nancy. Thank you.'

With a deprecating shake of her head, Nancy shut the door behind herself. Nadine sat on the bed next to Kahlan and worked at finishing unwrapping the bandage. Kahlan frowned at Nadine's dress.

'Nadine, that dress … it is the same one you were wearing yesterday, isn't it?'

'Sure.'

'It seems –'

Nadine looked down at herself. 'The ladies washed it for me but it's … Oh, I know what you're talking about. It was torn in the tunnels, when we went for a swim. Some of the fabric at the seams was ruined, so I had to take it in to save it.

'I haven't had much of an appetite since I left home, thinking about … I mean, what with my travels, I was busy, and I've slimmed down a bit, so I was able to take in the seams and save the dress. It's not too tight. It's fine.'

'In view of your aid, I will see to it that you get another dress that would be more comfortable.'

'No. This one's fine.'

'I see.'

'Well, your cut looks no worse this morning. That's encouraging.' She carefully wiped at the old poultice. 'I saw Richard on the way out. He looked upset. You two haven't had a fight, I hope?'

Kahlan's forbearance evaporated. 'No. He was upset because of something else.'

Nadine paused at her work. She turned to her bag and brought back a horn. The fragrance of pine pitch filled the air when she opened it. Kahlan winced as Nadine dabbed on the poultice. When she was satisfied, she began winding the bandage back around Kahlan's arm.

'There's no need to be embarrassed,' Nadine said in a casual tone. 'Lovers sometimes have spats. They don't always end a relationship. I'm sure Richard will come to his senses. Eventually.'

'Actually,' Kahlan said, 'I told him that I understood about you and him. About what happened. That was why he was so upset.'

Nadine's wrapping slowed. 'What do you mean?'

'I told him what you said about letting him catch you kissing his brother. The little ''shove'' you gave him. Remember?'

184

Nadine brought the tails of the bandage around, her fingers suddenly working swiftly at tying them. 'Oh, that.'

'Yes, that.'

Nadine avoided looking up. She slipped the sleeve of the dress over Kahlan's hand. As soon as she had pulled the dress up over Kahlan's shoulder, she dropped the horn back in her bag.

'That should do it. I should replace the poultice later today.'

Kahlan watched as Nadine hefted her bag and scurried for the door. Kahlan called her name. Nadine reluctantly paused and turned partway back.

'Seems you lied to me. Richard told me what really happened.'

Nadine's freckles vanished in a crimson glow. Kahlan stood and gestured toward a tufted velvet chair.

'Care to set things right? To tell me your side of it?'

Nadine stood woodenly for a moment, then sank into the chair. She folded her hands in her lap and stared down at them. 'I told you, I had to give him a shove.'

'You call that a shove?'

Nadine turned even redder. 'Well.' She flicked a hand. 'I knew how boys lost their heads over … over their lust. I figured that was my best chance of getting him to … to lay claim to me.'

Kahlan was confused, but she didn't let it show. 'Seems it would have been a little late for that.'

'Well, not necessarily. I was bound to end up with one of them when I let Richard catch me like that, naked, atop Michael, having a good time of it. Michael was game for me, that was for sure.'

Kahlan's brow rose. 'How did you figure that –'

'I had it worked out. Richard would come in behind me. He'd see me on Michael's lance, crying out with the pleasure of it, and he'd be taken with lust by the sight, and by my willingness. Then he'd lose his head, his inhibition, and at last he'd have to have me, too.'

Kahlan stared dumbly. 'How was that going to get you Richard?'

Nadine cleared her throat. 'Well, it was like this; I figured that Richard would enjoy having me. I'd make sure of that.

Then, I'd tell him no the next time he wanted me, and he'd want me so much, after he'd had a sampling, that he'd claim me. If Michael wanted to claim me, too, then it's my choice, and I'd choose Richard.

'If Richard didn't claim me, and I got pregnant, then I'd say it was his and he'd marry me because it could be his. If I didn't get pregnant, and he wouldn't claim me, well, then, there was still Michael. I figured second best was better than none.'

Kahlan didn't know what had happened; Richard hadn't said. She feared Nadine would stop her story right there. Kahlan couldn't very well admit she didn't know what happened next, and worse, she feared to hear just how successful Nadine's bizarre plan had been. In the first version, the kissing version, Richard had turned away. But Kahlan now knew that version wasn't true.

She watched the vein in the side of Nadine's neck throb. Kahlan folded her arms and waited.

At last, Nadine collected her voice and continued. 'Well, that was my plan, anyway. It seemed to make sense. I figured I'd get Richard out of it, at best, and Michael at worst.

'It didn't work the way I thought. Richard walked in and froze. I smiled over my shoulder. I invited him to come join the fun, or else to come to me later and I'd see to him, too.'

Kahlan held her breath.

'That was the first time I saw that look in Richard's eyes. He didn't say a word. He just turned and walked out.'

Nadine stuck a hand in under the hair hanging around her face and wiped it across her nose as she sniffled. 'I thought I'd at least have Michael. He laughed at me when I told him he'd claimed me. He just laughed. He never wanted to be with me again after that. He'd gotten what he wanted. I was no use to him after that. He moved on to other girls.'

'But, if you were willing to … Dear spirits, why didn't you simply seduce Richard?'

'Because I was worried he might expect that and have his resistance built up for it. I wasn't the only girl he danced with. I was afraid he wouldn't want to commit, and that if I simply tried to seduce him, he might be ready for that and turn me down. I'd heard a rumor that Bess Pratter tried that. It didn't seem to have worked for her. I was afraid it wouldn't be enough of a shove.

'I figured that jealousy would be the thing that pushed him off the fence. I figured my plan would take him by such surprise that he's just lose his head with jealousy and lust, and then I'd have him. I've heard tell there's nothing more powerful in a man than jealousy and lust.'

With both hands, Nadine pushed her hair back on her head. 'I can't believe Richard told you. I didn't think he would ever tell anyone.'

'He didn't,' Kahlan whispered. 'Richard only stared at me when I told him that you said he caught you kissing his brother. He didn't tell me the story. You just did that all by yourself.'

Nadine's face sank into her hands.

'You may have grown up with Richard, but you didn't know him. Dear spirits, you didn't know the first thing about him.'

'It might have worked. You don't know as much as you think. Richard is just a boy from Hartland who never had anything and has had his head turned by fine things and people doing his bidding. That's why it might have worked – because he just wants what he sees. I was just trying to make him see what I have to offer.'

Kahlan's head throbbed. She pinched the bridge of her nose as she shut her eyes.

'Nadine, as the good spirits are my witness, you have got to be just about the stupidest woman I have ever met.'

Nadine sprang up from the chair. 'You think I'm so stupid? You love him. You want him.' She jabbed her finger at her own chest. 'You know how it feels, in here, to want him. I wanted him no less than you. If you had to, you would do the same thing. Right now, as well as you know him, you'd do the same if you thought it was your only chance. Your only chance! Tell me you wouldn't!'

'Nadine,' Kahlan said in a calm voice, 'you don't know the first thing about love. Love isn't about taking what you want; it's about wanting happiness for the one you love.'

Nadine leaned in with a venomous expression. 'You'd do the same as I did, if you had to!'

The words of the prophecy whispered through Kahlan's head.

Lightning will find him on that path, for the one in white, his true beloved, will betray him ...

'You're wrong, Nadine. I wouldn't. Not for anything in this world would I chance hurting Richard. Not for anything. I would live a life of lonely misery before I would hurt him. I would even let you have him before I would hurt him.'

CHAPTER 17

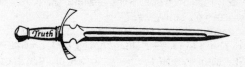

A breathless, beaming Berdine lurched to a halt as Kahlan watched Nadine storm off down the hall.

'Mother Confessor, Lord Rahl wants me to stay up all night and do work for him. Isn't that wonderful?'

Kahlan's brow twitched. 'If you say so, Berdine.'

Grinning, Berdine ran on down the hall in the direction Nadine had gone. Richard was talking to a knot of soldiers just up the hall in the other direction. Beyond the soldiers, a ways further up the hall, Cara and Egan stood watching.

When Richard saw Kahlan, he left the guards and came to meet her. When he was close enough, she twisted a fistful of his shirt and pulled him close.

'Answer me one thing, Richard Rahl,' she hissed through gritted teeth.

'What's that?' Richard asked in innocent bewilderment.

'Why did you ever dance with that whore!'

'Kahlan, I've never heard you use such language.' Richard glanced down the hall in the direction Nadine had gone. 'How did you get her to tell you?'

'I tricked her into it.'

Richard smiled a sly smile. 'You told her that I told you the story, didn't you.'

His smile widened when she nodded. 'I've been a bad influence on you,' he said.

'Richard, I'm sorry I asked her to stay. I didn't know. If I ever get my hands cn Shota, I'm going to strangle her. Forgive me for asking Nadine to stay.'

'Nothing to forgive. My emotions just got in the way of seeing that. You were right to ask her to stay.'

'Richard, are you sure?'

'Shota and the prophecy both mentioned "the wind." Nadine plays some part in this; she has to stay, for now. I'd better have her guarded, so she doesn't leave.'

'We don't need guards. Nadine won't leave.'

'How can you be so sure?'

'Vultures don't give up. They circle as long as they think there are bones to pick.' Kahlan looked back down the empty hall. 'She actually had the nerve to tell me that I would do what she had done, if I had to.'

'I feel a bit sorry for Nadine. She has a lot of good in her, too, but I doubt she will ever truly experience love.'

Kahlan felt the heat of him at her back. 'How could Michael do that to you? How could you ever have forgiven him?'

'He was my brother,' Richard whispered. 'I would have forgiven anything he did against me. Someday I will stand before the good spirits; I didn't want to give them a reason to say I was no better.

'It was what he did to others that I couldn't forgive.'

She put a comforting hand to his arm. 'I guess I see why you want me to go with you to meet Drefan. The spirits tested you with Michael. I think you will find Drefan a better brother. He may be a bit arrogant, but he's a healer. Besides, it would be hard to find two that wicked.'

'Nadine is a healer, too.'

'Not compared to Drefan. His talent borders on magic.'

'Do you think he wields magic?'

'I don't think so, but I have no way of telling.'

'I will know. If he does have magic, I will know.'

Guards at their post near the Mother Confessor's room saluted after Richard gave them instructions. Kahlan walked close at his side as they moved on down the hall. Cara stood up straighter when Richard paused before her. Even Egan perked up expectantly. Kahlan thought Cara looked tired and miserable.

'Cara,' Richard finally said, 'I'm going to see this healer who helped you. I hear he's another bastard son of Darken

Rahl, like me. Why don't you come along. I wouldn't mind having a … friend, with me.'

Cara's brow wrinkled together in near tears. 'If you wish, Lord Rahl.'

'I wish. You, too, Egan. Egan, I told the soldiers that you all are permitted to pass. Go get Raina and Ulic and bring them along, too.'

'Right behind you, Lord Rahl,' Egan said with a rare smile.

'Where did you ask Drefan to wait?' Kahlan asked.

'I told the guards to take him to a guest room in the southeast wing.'

'The opposite end of the palace? Why all the way over there?'

Richard gave her an unreadable look. 'Because I wanted him to remain here, under guard, and that's as far from your rooms as I could get him.'

Cara was still wearing her red leather; she hadn't had time to change. The soldiers guarding the southeast wing of the Confessors' Palace saluted with fists to hearts and moved aside for Richard, Kahlan, Ulic, Egan, and Raina in her brown leather, but they backed away an extra step for Cara. No D'Haran wanted the attention of a Mord-Sith in red leather.

After the brisk march across the palace, they all came to a halt before a simple door flanked by leather and muscles and steel. Richard absently lifted his sword and let it drop back, checking that it was clear in its scabbard.

'I think he's more afraid than you,' Kahlan whispered up to him. 'He's a healer. He said he came to help you.'

'He showed up to help on the same day as Nadine and Marlin. I don't believe in coincidence.'

Kahlan recognized the look in his eyes; he was bleeding a lethal flux of magic from his sword without even touching it. Every inch of him, every ripple of hard muscle, every fluid movement, bespoke the calm coiling death.

Without knocking, Richard threw open the door and stepped into the small, windowless room. Sparsely furnished with a bed, small table, and two simple wooden chairs, it was one of the more utilitarian guest rooms. To the side, the eyes of knots in a plain, pine wardrobe watched them. A small brick hearth provided a modicum of heat to the chill, scented air.

Holding Richard's left arm from a half step behind, knowing better than to get in the way of his sword, Kahlan stayed close. Ulic and Egan stepped to each side, their blond hair nearly brushing the low ceiling. Cara and Raina swept around them, screening Richard and Kahlan.

Drefan knelt before the table against the far wall. Dozens of candles were set randomly about the table. At the sound of all the commotion, he rose smoothly to his feet and turned.

His blue-eyed gaze took in Richard, as if no one else had entered the room with him. Each absorbed in silent thoughts she could only imagine, they appraised one another.

And then Drefan went to his knees, putting his forehead to the floor.

'Master Rahl guide us. Master Rahl teach us. Master Rahl protect us. In your light we thrive. In your mercy we are sheltered. In your wisdom we are humbled. We live only to serve. Our lives are yours.'

Kahlan saw Richard's two huge bodyguards and both Mord-Sith almost drop reflexively to their knees to join in the devotion to the Master of D'Hara. She had seen countless D'Harans in Aydindril give the devotion. She had stood at Richard's side when the Sisters of the Light had knelt and sworn fidelity to him. Richard had told her that at the People's Palace in D'Hara, when Darken Rahl had been there, everyone went to devotion squares twice a day, for two hours each time, and said those same words over and over while touching foreheads to the tiled floors.

Drefan stood once more, assuming a relaxed, self-assured stance. He was dressed nobly in a ruffled white shirt open to mid-chest, high boots turned down just below his knees, and tight, dark trousers that displayed enough of the swell of his manhood that Kahlan could feel her cheeks flush. She forced her eyes to move. She could see at least four leather pouches attached to his wide leather belt, their flaps held closed with carved bone pins. Draped loosely over his shoulders was the simple flaxen cloak she had seen him in before.

The same height and build as Richard, and with the handsome cast of Darken Rahl's features, he cut a striking figure. His tumbledown blond hair made his tanned face look all the better. Kahlan couldn't help staring at the flesh-and-blood twist of Richard and Darken Rahl.

Richard gestured toward all the candles. 'What's this?'

Drefan's blue-eyed gaze stayed locked on Richard. 'I was praying, Lord Rahl. Making my peace with the good spirits, should I be joining them this day.'

There was no timidity in his voice; it was a simple, self-confident statement of fact.

Richard's chest grew with a deep breath. He let it out. 'Cara, you stay. Raina, Ulic, Egan, please wait outside.' He glanced to them as they were leaving. 'Me first.'

They returned grim nods. It was code: if Richard didn't come out of the room first, then Drefan died on his way out – a precaution Kahlan used herself.

'I am Drefan, Lord Rahl. At your service, should you find me worthy.' He bowed his head to Kahlan. 'Mother Confessor.'

'What did you mean about joining the good spirits?' Richard asked.

Drefan slid his hands into the opposite sleeves of the cloak.

'There is a bit of a story to it, Lord Rahl.'

'Take your hands out of your sleeves, and then tell me the story.'

Drefan pulled his hands out. 'Sorry.' He lifted his cloak back with a little finger to reveal the long, thin-bladed knife sheathed at his belt. He pulled the knife free with one finger and a thumb, flipped it in the air, and caught it by the point. 'Forgive me. I meant to set it aside before your visit.'

Without turning, he tossed the knife over his shoulder. The knife stuck solidly in the wall. He bent, pulled a heavier knife from his boot, and tossed that over his shoulder with his other hand as he straightened, sticking it, too, in the wall an inch from the first. He reached behind his back, under the cloak, and came out with a wickedly curved blade. Without looking, he stuck it, too, in the wall behind, between the two blades already there.

'Any other weapons?' Richard asked in a businesslike manner.

Drefan spread his arms. 'My hands, Lord Rahl, and my

knowledge.' He continued to hold his hands out. 'Though even my hands wouldn't be quick enough to defeat your magic, Lord Rahl. Please search my person to assure yourself that I am otherwise unarmed.'

Richard didn't act on the offer. 'So, what's the story?'

'I am the bastard son of Darken Rahl.'

'As am I,' Richard said.

'Not exactly. You are the gifted heir of Darken Rahl. A distinct difference, Lord Rahl.'

'Gifted? Darken Rahl raped my mother. I have often had reason to consider my magic a curse.'

Drefan nodded deferentially. 'As you would have it, Lord Rahl. But Darken Rahl didn't view offspring the way you seem to. To him, there was his heir, and there were weeds. You are his heir; I am but one of his weeds.

'Formalities associated with conception were irrelevant to the Master of D'Hara. Women were ... simply there to bring him pleasure and to grow his seed. Ones who conceived inferior fruit – those without the gift – were barren soil, in his eyes. Even your mother, having produced his prized fruit, would have been no more important to him than the dirt in his most coveted orchard.'

Kahlan squeezed Richard's hand. 'Cara told me much the same. She said that Darken Rahl ... that he eliminated those he found without the gift.'

Richard stiffened. 'He killed my siblings?'

'Yes, Lord Rahl,' Cara said. 'Not in a methodical fashion, but rather on whim, or ill mood.'

'I don't know anything about his other children. I didn't even know he was my father until last autumn. How is it that you're alive?' he asked Drefan.

'My mother wasn't ...' Drefan paused, searching for an inoffensive way to put it. 'She wasn't treated as unfortunately as your cherished mother, Lord Rahl.

'My mother was a woman of ambition and cupidity. She saw our father as a means to gain status. As I have heard it told, she was fair of face and figure, and was one of a few who was called to his bed repeatedly. Most were not. Apparently, she succeeded in cultivating his ... appetite for her charms. To put it bluntly, she was a talented whore.

'She hoped to be the one who bore him a gifted heir, so as to raise her status in his eyes to something more.'

'She failed.' Drefan's cheeks mantled. 'She had me.'

'That may be a failure in her eyes,' Richard said in a quiet tone, 'but not in the eyes of the good spirits. You are no less than I, in their eyes.'

The corners of Drefan's mouth curled in a small smile. 'Thank you, Lord Rahl. Very magnanimous of you to cede to the good spirits that which was always theirs. Not all men do. "In your wisdom we are humbled," ' he quoted from the devotion.

Drefan was managing to be courteously respectful without being servile. He seemed honestly deferential, but without losing his air of nobility. Unlike the way he had been in the pit, he was scrupulously polite, but he nonetheless exuded the bearing of a Rahl: no amount of bowing could alter his aplomb. Like Richard, he carried himself with inherent authority.

'So, what happened then?'

Drefan took a deep breath. 'She took me, as an infant, to a wizard to have me tested for the gift, hoping to present Darken Rahl with the gifted heir that would bring her riches, station, and the fawning adoration of Darken Rahl. Did I also mention that she was a fool?'

Richard didn't answer, and Drefan went on.

'The wizard broke the bad news to her: I was born without the gift. Instead of bearing a pass to a life of ease, she had given birth to a liability. Darken Rahl was known to pull the intestines out of such women – an inch at a time.'

'Obviously,' Richard said, 'you managed not to draw his attention. Why not?'

'My dear mother was responsible for that. She knew that she might be able to raise me, and never be noticed by him, never be killed, but she also knew it would be a hard life of hiding and worry over every knock at the door.

'Instead, she took me, when I was but an infant, to a remote community of healers, hoping that they would raise me in anonymity so that my father would have no reason to come to know of me, and kill me.'

'That must have been hard for her to do,' Kahlan said.

His piercing blue eyes turned on her. 'For her grief, she prescribed herself a potent cure, which was in turn provided by the healers: henbane.'

'Henbane,' Richard said in a flat tone. 'Henbane is poison.'

'Yes. It acts quickly, but has the unfortunate quality of being exquisitely painful at its task.'

'These *healers* provided her with poison?' Richard asked incredulously.

Drefan's raptor gaze, shadowed with admonition, returned to Richard. 'The calling of a healer is to provide the remedy that is warranted. Sometimes, the remedy is death.'

'That doesn't fit my definition of healer,' Richard said, returning the raptor gaze in kind.

'A person who is dying, with no hope of recovery, and in great suffering, can be no better served than by the benevolent act of assisting them in ending their suffering.'

'Your mother wasn't dying with no hope of recovery.'

'Had Darken Rahl found her, her suffering would have been profound, to say the least. I don't know how much you knew about our father, but he was known for his inventiveness at giving pain, and making it last. She lived in shuddering fear of that fate. She was driven nearly insane with dread. She fell to tears at every shadow. The healers could do nothing to prevent that fate, to protect her from Darken Rahl. Had Darken Rahl wanted to find her, he would have. Had she remained with the healers, and been found, he would have slaughtered them all for hiding her. She gave up her life to give me the chance at one.'

Kahlan started when a log in the fire popped. Drefan didn't start, nor did Richard.

'I'm sorry,' Richard whispered. 'My grandfather took his daughter, my mother, to Westland to hide her from Darken Rahl. I guess that he, too, understood the danger she was in. The danger I was in.'

Drefan shrugged. 'Then we are much the same, you and I: exiles from our father. You, however, would not have been killed.'

Richard nodded to himself. 'He tried to kill me.'

Drefan's brow twitched with curiosity. 'Really? He wanted a gifted heir, and then he tried to kill him?'

'He didn't know, as I didn't, that it was he who fathered me.' Richard turned the subject back to the matter at hand. 'So, what's this about you making peace with the good spirits in case you are to join them today?'

'The healers who raised me never kept from me the knowledge of who I was. I have known since I can remember that I was the bastard son of our master, of Father Rahl. I always knew that he could come at any moment and kill me. I prayed each night, thanking the good spirits for another day of life free from my father and what he would do to me.'

'Weren't the healers afraid that he would come and kill them, too, for hiding you?'

'Perhaps. They always discounted it. They said that they were not in fear for themselves, that they could always say I was a babe abandoned to them and they didn't know my paternity.'

'Must have been a hard life.'

Drefan turned his back on them and seemed to stare into the candles for a time before he went on.

'It was life. The only life I knew. But I do know that I was woefully tired of living each day in fear that he might come.'

'He's dead,' Richard said. 'You no longer have to fear him.'

'That is why I'm here. When I felt the bond break, and it was later confirmed that he was dead, I decided that I would end my private terror. I've been guarded since the moment I arrived. I knew I wasn't free to leave this room. I know the reputation of the guards you surround yourself with. That was all part of the chance I took to come here.

'I didn't know if the new Lord Rahl would want me eliminated, too, but I decided to end the constant death sentence hanging over my head. I've come to offer my services to the Master of D'Hara if he will have me; or, if it is his will, that my life be forfeit for my crime of birth.

'Either way, it will be over. I want it over.'

Drefan, his eyes watering, turned to face Richard.

'There you have it, Lord Rahl. Either forgive me, or kill me. I don't know that I much care which anymore, but I beg you to end it – one way or the other.'

His chest rose and fell with labored breaths.

Richard appraised his half brother in the dragging silence.

Kahlan could only imagine what Richard must be thinking, at the emotions of those deliberations, at the painful shadows of the past, and the light of hope for what might be.

At last, he held his hand out.

'I'm Richard, Drefan. Welcome to the new D'Hara, a D'Hara that fights for freedom from terror. We fight that none have to live in fear, as you have done.'

The two men clasped wrists. Their big, powerful hands were the same size.

'Thank you,' Drefan whispered. 'Richard.'

CHAPTER 18

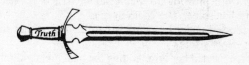

'I heard that you saved Cara's life,' Richard said. 'I want to thank you. It must have been hard, knowing that she was one of my guards who might end up harming you … if things didn't go right for you.'

'I'm a healer. It's what I do – Richard. I'm afraid I may have trouble calling you anything but Lord Rahl – for a time, anyway. I feel the bond to you, to you as the Lord Rahl.'

Richard shrugged self-consciously. 'I'm still having trouble getting used to people calling me Lord Rahl.' He stroked a finger along his lower lip. 'Do we … do you know if we … have any other half brothers, or sisters?'

'I'm sure we must. Some must have survived. I've heard a rumor that we have a younger sister, at least.'

'Sister?' Richard grinned. 'Really? A sister? Where do you think she is? Do you know her name?'

'I'm sorry, Lord … Richard, but all I know is the name: Lindie. The words passed on to me said that if she is still alive, she would be perhaps as much as fourteen years. The person who told me her name said that all he knew was her first name, Lindie, and that she was born in D'Hara, to the southwest of the People's Palace.'

'Anything else?'

'I'm afraid not. You have now heard everything I know.' Drefan turned to Kahlan. 'How are you feeling? Did the herb woman, what was her name, stitch you up properly?'

'Yes,' Kahlan said, 'Nadine did fine. It hurts some, and I have a headache. I guess from everything that's happened. I didn't sleep well last night with the ache of my shoulder, but that's to be expected. I'm fine.'

He moved toward her, and before she knew it, he had her arm in his hand. He lifted it, twisted it, and pulled it, asking each time where it hurt. When he had satisfied himself, he moved around behind her and gripped her collarbone with his fingers while pressing his thumbs to the base of her neck. Pain shot up her spine. The room swam.

He pressed under her arm, and at the back of her shoulder. 'There. How's that?'

Kahlan rotated her arm, finding the pain greatly diminished. 'Much better. Thank you.'

'Just be careful with it; I've numbed some of the pain, but it still must heal before you put it to heavy use. Do you still have the headache?' Kahlan nodded. 'Let me see what I can do for that.'

He pulled her by the hand back toward the table and sat her in a chair. He towered over her, blocking her view of Richard.

Drefan pulled her arms out toward himself, squeezing and manipulating the webs between her first fingers and thumbs. His hands made hers seem so small. He had hands like Richard: big, and powerful, though less callused. He was hurting her, he was pressing so hard, but she didn't voice a complaint, thinking he must know what he was doing.

With him standing right in front of her, she had to turn her eyes up lest she be forced to stare at his tight trousers. Kahlan watched his hands kneading hers – his fingers working over her flesh. She remembered his hand on Cara. She vividly recalled those strong fingers working their way down under Cara's red leather and between her legs. Working into her.

Kahlan abruptly jerked her hands away.

'Thank you, that's much better,' she lied.

He smiled down at her with a penetrating, hawklike, blue-eyed, Rahl gaze. 'I've never healed a headache so quickly. Are you sure it's better?'

'Yes. It was just a little headache. It's gone now. Thank you.'

'Glad to help,' he said. He watched her for a long moment, the little smile still on his lips. Finally, he turned to Richard.

'I was told that you are to be wedded to the Mother

Confessor, here. You are a very different sort of Lord Rahl from our father; Darken Rahl would never have considered marriage for himself. Of course, he probably was never tempted into marriage by one so beautiful as your betrothed. May I offer my congratulations? When's the wedding?'

'Soon,' Kahlan interjected as she moved to Richard's side.

'That's right,' Richard said. 'Soon. We don't know the exact date, yet. We … have a few things to work out.

'Look, Drefan, I could use your help. We have a number of wounded men, and some of them are in grave condition. They were wounded by the same man who hurt Cara. I'd really appreciate it if you'd see what you could do to help them.'

Drefan retrieved his knives, slipping them away without having to look at what he was doing. 'That's what I'm here for: to help.' He headed for the door.

Richard caught his arm. 'You'd better let me go first. Until I change the orders, you will die if you step out of a room before me. We don't want that.'

As Richard took Kahlan's arm and turned toward the door, she met Cara's eyes for an instant. Her hearing wasn't affected, Drefan had said. She could hear everything, even though she couldn't react. She had to have heard Kahlan warn him not to put his hand on her there again. She had to have known what Drefan had been doing, but she had been unable to do anything to stop him. Kahlan's face heated at the memory.

She turned and hugged Richard's waist as they went through the door.

Richard looked up and down the quiet hall, and when he saw no one, he backed her to the paneled wall outside her rooms and pressed a kiss to her lips. She was glad that Drefan had eased the pain in her arm earlier in the day; it hardly hurt to circle both arms around Richard's neck.

She moaned against his mouth. She was tired from the long day, and her arm did still hurt just a bit, but it wasn't weariness or discomfort that drove out the moan – it was longing.

He drew her into his arms and turned so that he was leaning his back against the wall instead. His powerful arms crushed her to him, almost lifting her toes from the floor as his kiss became more insistent. She returned it in kind. She pulled his lower lip through her teeth and then backed away for a breath.

'I can't believe Nancy or one of her women isn't here, waiting for us,' Richard said.

He had left their guards farther up the hall, around the corner. They were at last alone – a rare luxury. Even though she had grown up with people always around, she now found their constant presence wearing. There was great value in simply being alone.

Kahlan gave his lips a quick lick and a kiss. 'I don't think Nancy will be bothering us.'

'Really?' Richard asked with a sly grin. 'Why, Mother Confessor, who will protect your virtue?'

Her lips brushed his. 'Dear spirits, no one, I pray.'

He surprised her with an abrupt change of topic. 'What do you think of Drefan?'

That was a question she was not prepared to answer. 'What do you think of him?'

'I'd like to have a brother I could trust and believe in. He's a healer. The surgeon was impressed with the way he helped some of those men. He said that at least one of them will live only because of what Drefan did for him. Nadine was more than a little curious about some of the compounds he carried in the leather pouches at his belt. I'd like to think that I have a brother who helps people. Nothing seems so noble as that.'

'Do you think he has magic?'

'I didn't see any trace of it in his eyes. I'm sure I would have been able to tell. I can't explain how I can sense magic, now, how I can see it sometimes sparkle in the air about a person, or show in their eyes, but I didn't see any of that with Drefan. I think that he is simply a talented healer.

'I'm grateful that he saved Cara. At least he said he saved her. What if she had recovered on her own after Marlin was dead and her link with him was broken?'

Kahlan hadn't thought of that. 'So, you don't trust him?'

'I don't know. I still don't believe in coincidence.' He sighed in frustration. 'Kahlan, I need you to be honest, and not let me be blinded because he's my brother and I want to trust him. I haven't proven a very good judge of brothers. If you have any reason to doubt him, I want to hear about it.'

'All right. That seems fair.'

He tipped his head toward her. 'For example, you can tell me why you lied to him.'

Kahlan frowned. 'What do you mean?'

'About your headache being gone. I could see that he didn't make it any better. Why did you tell him that it was gone?'

Kahlan cupped a hand to the side of his face.

'I'd like you to have a brother you could be proud of, Richard, but I want it to be real. I guess what you said about coincidence has made me wary, that's all.'

'Anything other than simply what I said, about coincidence?'

'No, I hope he can bring a little brotherly love to your heart. I pray that it is nothing more than simple coincidence.'

'Me, too.'

She gave his arm an affectionate squeeze. 'I know he has the women on the staff all aflutter. I suspect he will soon be breaking hearts, what with all the swooning looks I've seen.

'I promise to let you know if he gives me reason to suspect something amiss.'

'Thanks.'

He didn't smile at what she said about the women all liking Drefan. Richard had never displayed any jealousy, he didn't have reason to, even if she hadn't been a Confessor, but still, there was a painful history with Michael that she realized could make reason less than relevant. She wished she hadn't mentioned it.

He ran his fingers back into her hair, holding the sides of her head as he kissed her. She pulled back.

'Why did you take Nadine with you this afternoon?'

'Who?'

He leaned toward her again. She pulled back. 'Nadine. Remember her? The woman in the tight dress?'

'Oh, that Nadine.'

She poked his ribs. 'So, you noticed her dress.'

His brow drew together. 'Did you think there was something different about it, today?'

'Oh yes, there was something different about it. So, why did you take her with you?'

'Because she's a healer. She's not an evil person – she has good qualities. I thought that as long as she was going to be here, she might as well make herself useful. I thought that that might make her feel better about herself. I had her check that the men were making the quench oak tea properly, that it was strong enough. She seemed happy to help.'

Kahlan remembered Nadine's smile when Richard had asked her to go with him. She had been happy, all right, but not simply to help. The smile was for Richard, as was the dress.

'So,' Richard said, 'you think Drefan is handsome, as all the other women do?'

She thought his trousers were too tight. She pulled Richard into a kiss, hoping he wouldn't notice her face flushed and misunderstand the reason for it.

'Who?' she breathed dreamily.

'Drefan. Remember him? The man in the tight pants?'

'Sorry, I don't remember him,' she said as she kissed his neck, and she nearly didn't. She ached for Richard and nothing else.

There was no room in her mind for Drefan. Almost the only thing in her thoughts was the time she had been with Richard in that strange place between worlds where they had been together, truly together, as never before or since. She wanted him that way again. She wanted him that way now.

With the way his hands were slipping down her back, and the urgency of his lips on her neck, she knew he wanted her the same way, and just as badly.

But she also knew that Richard didn't want to even appear to be like his father. He didn't want anyone to think she was no more than Darken Rahl's women had been: an amusement for the Master of D'Hara. That was why he always let the women on the staff so easily keep him at bay; despite his frustrated objections, he never overruled them when they shooed him away.

The three Mord-Sith, too, always seemed to be protecting Kahlan from being seen as less than the true betrothed to the Master of D'Hara. Whenever she and Richard thought to go to his room at night, even just to talk, either Cara, or Berdine, or Raina was always there, asking some pointed question that seemed to keep them apart. When Richard scowled, they reminded him that he had instructed them to protect the Mother Confessor; he never countermanded the orders.

Today, the three Mord-Sith were scrupulously following his orders, and when he had told Cara and Raina to guard him from around the corner and down the hall, they had remained there without objection.

With their wedding so soon, Kahlan and Richard had decided to wait, even though they had already been together once. That time seemed somehow unreal – in a place between worlds, in a place with no heat, no cold, no source of light, no ground, and yet they could see, and they had lain in dark space firm enough to support them.

More than anything, she remembered the feel of him. They had been the source of all heat, all light, all feeling, in that strange place between worlds where the good spirits had taken them.

She was feeling that heat, now, as she ran her hands over the muscles of his chest and stomach. She could hardly get her breath with the feel of his lips on her. She wanted his mouth everywhere on her. She wanted hers everywhere on him. She wanted him on the other side of her door.

'Richard,' she whispered in his ear, 'please, stay with me tonight.' His hands were making her lose all sense of restraint.

'Kahlan, I thought …'

'Please, Richard. I want you in my bed. I want you in me.'

He moaned helplessly at her words, and at her hands.

'I hope I'm not interrupting,' came a voice.

Richard jerked up straight. Kahlan spun around. With the thick carpets, they hadn't heard Nadine's silent approach.

'Nadine,' Kahlan said, catching her breath. 'What … ?'

Kahlan self-consciously clasped her hands behind her back, wondering if Nadine had seen where they had just been. She had to have seen where Richard's had been. Kahlan felt her face going red.

Nadine's cool gaze moved from Richard to Kahlan. 'I didn't mean to interrupt. I just came to change your poultice. And to apologize.'

'Apologize?' Kahlan asked, still gulping air.

'Yes. I said some things to you earlier, and I guess I was a bit … out of sorts at the time. I thought I may have said some things I shouldn't have. I thought I should apologize.'

'That's all right,' Kahlan said. 'I understand how you felt at the time.'

Nadine lifted her bag and her eyebrows. 'The poultice?'

'My arm is fine for tonight. You could change the poultice for me tomorrow, though.' Kahlan sought to fill the dragging silence. 'Drefan did some of his healing on it earlier … so it's fine for tonight.'

'Sure.' She lowered her bag. 'You two off to bed, then?'

'Nadine,' Richard said in a restrained tone, 'thanks for checking on Kahlan. Good night.'

Nadine regarded him with a cold glower. 'Don't even plan to get married first? Just going to throw her down on the bed and lay claim to her, like some girl you come across in the woods? Seems a bit crude for the high and mighty Lord Rahl. And here you were pretending you were better than us common folk.'

She glanced down at Richard and then turned her glare on Kahlan. 'Like I said before, he wants what he's shown. Shota told me about you. I guess you know about what pushes men off the fence, too. It seems you *would* do anything to have him, after all. Like I said before, you're no better than me.'

Bag in hand, she turned and marched off down the hall.

Kahlan and Richard stood in the uncomfortable silence, watching the empty hall.

'Out of the mouths of whores,' Kahlan said.

Richard wiped his hands back across his face. 'Maybe she has a point.'

'Maybe she does,' Kahlan admitted reluctantly.

'Well, good night. Sleep well.'

'You too. I'll be thinking about you in that little guest room you use.' He bent and kissed her cheek. 'Not going to bed right off.'

'Where are you going?'

'Oh, I thought I'd go dunk myself in a horse trough.'

She caught him by the wide, leather-padded band around his wrist. 'Richard, I don't know if I can stand this much longer.

Are we ever going to get married before something else happens?'

'We'll go wake the sliph just as soon as we make sure everything here is in order. I promise. Dear spirits, I promise.'

'What things?'

'Just as soon as we know that the men are getting better, and I'm satisfied about a few other things. I want to make sure that Jagang can't make good on his threats. A couple of days and the men should be better. A couple of days. I promise.'

She held one of his fingers in each of her hands as she stared longingly into his gray eyes. 'I love you,' she whispered. 'In a few days, or after an eternity, I'm yours. Words spoken over us or not, I'm forever yours.'

'We are already one, in our hearts. The good spirits know the truth of that. They want us to be together, they've already proven it, and will watch over us. Don't worry, we'll have the words said over us.'

He started away, but turned back with a haunted look in his eyes. 'I only wish Zedd could be there when we're married. Dear spirits, I wish he could. And that he was here to help me, now.'

When he looked back from the corner at the end of the hall, Kahlen threw him a kiss. She shuffled into her empty, lonely rooms and threw herself on her big bed. She thought about what Nadine said: 'Shota told me about you.' Kahlen wept in frustration.

'So, you're not going to be sleeping … up here, tonight,' Cara said when he walked past.

'And what would make you think I was?' Richard asked.

Cara shrugged. 'You made us wait around the corner.'

'Maybe I just wanted to kiss Kahlan good night without you two passing judgment on my skill.'

Cara and Raina both smiled, the first he had seen from them all day.

'I have already seen you kiss the Mother Confessor,' Cara said. 'You appear quite talented at it. It always leaves her breathless and wanting more.'

Even though he didn't feel like smiling, he did anyway

because he was glad to see them smiling. 'That doesn't mean I'm talented, it just means she loves me.'

'I've been kissed,' Cara said, 'and I've seen you kiss. I believe I can say with some authority that you are talented at the task. We watched you from around the corner tonight.'

Richard tried to look indignant as he felt his face going red. 'I gave you orders to stay down here.'

'It is our responsibility to watch over you. To do that, we can't let you out of our sight. We can't follow such orders.'

Richard shook his head. He couldn't be angry over the violation of orders. How could he, when they were risking his anger to protect him? They hadn't endangered Kahlan in doing so.

'What do you two think of Drefan?'

'He is your brother, Lord Rahl,' Raina said. 'The resemblance is obvious.'

'I know the resemblance is obvious. I mean, what do you think of him.'

'We don't know him, Lord Rahl,' Raina said.

'I don't know him, either. Look, I'm not going to be angry if you tell me you don't like him. In fact, I'd really like to know if you don't. What about you, Cara? What do you think of him?'

She shrugged. 'I've never kissed either of you, but from what I have seen, I would rather kiss you.'

Richard put his hands on his hips. 'What does that mean?'

'I was hurt, yesterday, and he helped me. But I don't like the fact that master Drefan came now, when Marlin and Nadine came.'

Richard sighed. 'My thoughts, too. I ask people not to judge me because of who my father was, and I find myself doing that with him. I'd really like to trust him. Please, both of you, if you have any reason for concern, don't be afraid to come and tell me.'

'Well,' Cara said. 'I don't like his hands.'

'What do you mean?'

'He has hands like Darken Rahl. I have already seen them caressing fawning women. Darken Rahl did that, too.'

Richard threw his hands up. 'When did he have time to do that? He was with me most of the day!'

'He found the time, when you were talking to soldiers and when you were out checking on the men with Nadine. It didn't take him long. The women found him. I have never seen so many women batting their lashes at a man. You have to admit, he is fine to look upon.'

Richard didn't see what was so especially fine about his looks. 'Have any of these women not been willing?'

Her answer was a long moment in coming. 'No, Lord Rahl.'

'Well, I guess I've seen other men who acted like that. Some of them have been my friends. They liked women, and women liked them. As long as the women are willing, I can't see that it's any of my business. I'm more concerned about other things.'

'Like what?'

'I wish I knew.'

'If you learn that he is here innocently, and only means to help, as he says, then you can be proud of him, Lord Rahl. Your brother is an important man.'

'He is? How important is he?'

'Your brother is the leader of his sect of healers.'

'He is? He never told me that.'

'No doubt he did not wish to vaunt himself. Humility before the Lord Rahl is the way of D'Harans, and one of the tenets of that ancient sect of healers.'

'I suppose. So he leads these healers?'

'Yes.' Cara said. 'He is the High Priest of the Raug'Moss.'

'The what?' Richard whispered. 'What did you call them?'

'The Raug'Moss, Lord Rahl.'

'Do you know the meaning of the words?'

Cara shrugged. 'Just that it means "healers," that's all. Does it have some meaning to you, Lord Rahl?'

'Where's Berdine?'

'In her bed, I would suppose.'

Richard started down the hall, calling orders back to them as he went. 'Cara, post a guard for the night around Kahlan's room. Raina, go wake Berdine and ask her to meet me in my office.'

'Now, Lord Rahl?' Raina asked. 'This late?'

'Yes, please.'

Richard took the steps two at a time on the way to his office where waited the journal, Kolo's journal, written in High D'Haran.

In High D'Haran, *Raug'Moss* meant 'Divine Wind.'

Both Shota's warning to Nadine for Richard, 'the wind hunts him,' and the words from the prophecy down in the pit, 'he must seek the remedy in the wind,' spun through his mind.

CHAPTER 19

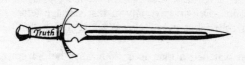

'This time,' Ann warned, 'you had better let me do the talking. Understand?'

Her eyebrows drew so tight together Zedd thought they might touch. She leaned close enough that he could smell the lingering aroma of sausage on her breath. With a fingernail she tapped his collar – another warning, albeit a wordless one.

Zedd blinked innocently. 'If it would please you, by all means, but my tales always have your best interest, and our purpose, at heart.'

'Oh, of course, and your clever wit is always a delight, too.'

Zedd felt that her affected smile was overdoing it; the sardonic praise would have been quite enough. There were accepted customs to such things. The woman really did need to learn where the line was.

Zedd's gaze again focused beyond her, to the problem at hand. He passed a critical eye over the inn's dimly lit door. It was across the street and at the end of a narrow, board walk. Above the alleyway that ran between two warehouses hung a small sign: '*Jester's Inn.*'

Zedd didn't know the name of the large town they had come to in the dark, but he did know that he would have preferred to pass it by. He had seen several inns in the town; this wasn't the one he would have chosen, had he a choice.

Jester's Inn looked as if it had either been an afterthought meant to use available space in the back, or else its proprietors wanted to shelter it from the scrutiny of honest people and the critical eye of authority. From the customers Zedd had already

211

seen, he was leaning in the direction of the second guess. Most of the men looked to be mercenaries or highwaymen.

'I don't like it,' he muttered to himself.

'You don't like anything,' Ann snapped. 'You're the most disagreeable man I've ever met.'

Zedd's eyebrows went up in true surprise. 'Why would you say that? I've been told that I'm a most pleasant traveling companion. Do we have any of that sausage left?'

Ann rolled her eyes. 'No. What is it you don't like this time?'

Zedd watched a man look both ways before going to the door at the back of the dark alleyway. 'Why would Nathan go in there?'

Ann looked over her shoulder, across the deserted street of rutted, frozen slush. She fingered a stray wisp of graying hair into the loose knot tied at the back of her head.

'To get a hot meal and some sleep.' She scowled back at Zedd. 'That is, if he's even in there.'

'I've shown you how to sense the thread of magic I used to hook the tracer cloud to him. You've felt it, felt him.'

'True enough,' Ann admitted. 'Yet now that we finally catch him, and know that he's in there, you suddenly don't like it.'

'That's right,' he said distantly. 'I don't like it.'

The scowl on Ann's face lost its heat and turned serious. 'What is it that bothers you?'

'Look at the sign. After the name.'

A pair of woman's legs pointed up in the shape of a V.

She turned back and peered at him as if he were daft. 'Zedd, the man has been locked up in the Palace of the Prophets for almost a thousand years.'

'You just said it: he's been locked up.' Zedd tapped the collar, called a Rada'Han, around his own neck, the collar she had put on him to capture him and make him do her bidding. 'Nathan is not inclined to be locked up in a collar again. It probably took him hundreds of years of planning, and the right turn of events, to get out of his collar and to escape. I dread to consider how that man may have influenced or even directly altered events through prophecy to bring to pass the turn of fate that allowed him the opportunity to get off his collar.

'Now you expect me to believe he would go in there just to

212

be with a woman? When he has to know you're chasing after him?'

Ann stared in stunned disbelief. 'Zedd, are you saying that you think Nathan may have influenced events – prophecies – just to get his collar off?'

Zedd looked across the road and shook his head. 'I'm just saying I don't like it.'

'He probably wanted what's in there enough that it distracted him from worrying about me. He simply wanted some female companionship, and ignored the dangers of being caught.'

'You have known Nathan for over nine centuries. I've only known him a short time.' He leaned down closer to her and lifted an eyebrow. 'But even I know better than that. Nathan is anything but stupid. He is a wizard of remarkable talent. You make a serious mistake if you underestimate him.'

She watched his eyes a moment. 'You're right; it may be a trap. Nathan wouldn't kill me to escape, but beyond that … You may be right.'

Zedd harrumphed.

'Zedd,' Ann said, after a long, uncomfortable silence, 'this business with Nathan is important. He must be caught. He's helped me in the past when we have discovered danger in the prophecies, but he is still a prophet. Prophets are dangerous. Not because they deliberately wish to cause trouble, but because of the nature of prophecy.'

'You don't need to convince me of that. I know well the dangers of prophecy.'

'We have always kept prophets confined at the Palace of the Prophets because of the potential for catastrophe should they roam free. A prophet who wanted mischief could have it. Even a prophet who doesn't wish mischief is dangerous, not only to others but to himself; people usually extract vengeance on the bringer of truth, as if knowing the truth as its cause. Prophecy is not meant to be heard by untrained minds, those having no understanding of magic, much less prophecy.

'One time, as we sometimes did at his request, we let a woman visit Nathan.'

Zedd frowned at her. 'You took prostitutes to him?'

Ann shrugged self-consciously. 'We knew the loneliness of

his confinement. It wasn't the most desirable solution, but yes, we brought him companionship from time to time. We weren't heartless.'

'How magnanimous of you.'

Ann glanced away from his eyes. 'We did what we had to, by locking him in the palace, but we felt sorrow for him. It wasn't his choice to be born with the gift of prophecy.

'We always warned him not to tell the women any prophecy, but one time he did. The woman ran screaming from the palace. We never knew how she escaped before we could stop her.

'She spread word of the prophecy before we could find her. It started a civil war. Thousands died. Women and children died.

'Nathan sometimes seems crazy, out of his senses. Sometimes he seems to me to be the most dangerously unbalanced person I've ever known. Nathan views the world not only by what he sees around him, but through the filter of prophecy that visits his mind.

'When I confronted him, he professed not to remember the prophecy, or having told the young woman anything. I only found out much later, when I was able to link several prophecies, that one of the children who died was a boy named in prophecy as one who would go on to rule through torture and murder. Untold tens of thousands would have died had that boy lived and grown into a man, but Nathan had choked off that dangerous fork in prophecy. I have no idea how much that man knows but won't disclose.

'A prophet has the potential to just as easily cause great harm. A prophet who wished power would have a fair chance of ruling the world.'

Zedd was still watching the door. 'So you lock them away.'

'Yes.'

Zedd picked at a thread on his maroon robes. He looked down at her squat form in the dim light. 'Ann, I am First Wizard. If I didn't understand, I wouldn't be helping you.'

'Thank you,' she whispered.

Zedd considered their options. There weren't many. 'What you are saying, if I understand you, is that you don't know if

Nathan is sane, but even if he is, he has the potential to be dangerous.'

'I guess so. But Nathan has often helped me to spare people suffering. Hundreds of years ago, he warned me about Darken Rahl, and told me of a prophecy that a war wizard would be born – that Richard would be born. We worked together to see to it that Richard would be safe from interference as he grew, so that you would have the time to help raise your grandson into the kind of man who would use his ability to help people.'

'For that, you have my gratitude,' Zedd offered. 'But you put this collar around my neck, and I don't like that one bit.'

'I understand. It's not something I liked doing, nor am I proud of what I did. Sometimes, desperate need calls for desperate acts. The good spirits will have the final say on my actions.

'The sooner we get Nathan, the sooner I will take the Rada'Han from your neck. I don't enjoy holding you prisoner by that collar and making you help me, but in view of the dire consequences should I fail to get Nathan, I do as I feel I must.'

Zedd aimed a thumb over his shoulder. 'I also don't like that.'

Ann didn't look; she knew what he was pointing at. 'What does a red moon have to do with Nathan? It's most peculiar, but what does one have to do with the other?'

'I'm not saying it has anything to do with Nathan. I just don't like it.'

With the thick clouds of the last few days, they had been slowed at night, both by the darkness and also by the difficulty of seeing the tracer cloud he had hooked to Nathan. Fortunately, they had been close enough to sense the link of magic without having to see the tracer cloud; the tracer cloud was only used to get its tracker close enough to sense the link.

Zedd knew they were very near to Nathan – within a few hundred feet. This close to the object of the trace, the link's magic distorted Zedd's senses, his ability to judge with the aid of his magic, his capacity to access his familiar ability with his gift. This close, his magic was like a bloodhound on scent, so concentrated on the object of its search that it disregarded anything else but the trail. It was an uncomfortable form of blindness, and another reason for his unease.

He could break the link, but that was risky before they actually had Nathan; once broken, it couldn't be reestablished without physical contact.

The snow flurries of the last few days had slowed them and made the going cold and miserable. Earlier in the day the clouds had at last cleared away, even if they had left behind the bitter wind to vex them. They had been looking forward to the moonrise, and the light it would provide as they closed in on Nathan.

They had both watched in stunned silence when the moon had risen: It had risen red.

At first, they thought that it might be a lingering haze that was causing it, but with the moon well overhead, Zedd knew it was not being caused by some innocent atmospheric event. Worse, with the recent cloud cover, he didn't know how long it had been since the moon had turned red.

'Zedd,' Ann finally asked into the brooding silence, 'do you know what it means?'

Zedd looked away, pretending to scan the shadows. 'Do you? You've lived a lot longer than I. You must know something about such a sign.'

He could hear her fussing with her wool cloak. 'You are a Wizard of the First Order. I would defer to your expertise in such matters.'

'You all of a sudden think my judgment worthwhile?'

'Zedd, let's not joust with words about this. I know that such a sign is without precedent in my experience, but I do recall a reference to a red moon in an ancient text, a text from the great war. The book didn't say what it meant, only that it brought great alarm.'

Zedd squatted in the shadow of the corner of the building they hid behind. He leaned his back against the clapboards and held a hand out in invitation. Ann sat beside him, deeper in the shadow.

'In the Wizard's Keep there are dozens of libraries, huge libraries, most at least as large as the vault of books at the Palace of the Prophets, many a great deal larger. There are also many books of prophecy there.'

There were books of prophecy at the Keep that were considered so dangerous that they were kept locked behind the powerful shields protecting the First Wizard's private enclave. Not even the old wizards who had lived at the Keep when Zedd was young were allowed to read those prophecies. Even though he had access to them after he became First Wizard, Zedd had not read nearly all of them; the ones he had read left him in sleepless sweats.

'Dear spirits,' he went on, 'there are so many books at the Keep that I've not even read all the titles. There used to be staffs of curators for each library. Each knew the books in his section of the stacks. Long ago, well before my time, these curators were gathered when an answer was sought. Each knew his own books and could speak up if his particular books held information on the subject in question. In this way it was a relatively simple task to locate the reference volumes or prophecies that might help with the problem at hand.

'When I was very young, there were only two wizards left acting as curators. Two men could not begin to tap the knowledge held there. A plethora of information is held in those books, but finding a specific bit of it is a formidable challenge. The guidance of the gift is needed to even begin to narrow the search.

'Needing information from the libraries is like being adrift in the ocean and needing a drink of water. Information is in overabundance, yet you can die of thirst for it before you can locate it. When I was young, I was guided as to what were the more important books of history, magic, and prophecy. I mostly confined my studies to those books.'

'What about the red moon?' Ann asked. 'What did the books you read say of it?'

'I only recall once reading about a red moon. What I read wasn't very explicit, mentioning it only obliquely. I wish I had thought to inquire into the subject further, but I didn't. There were other matters in the books that were of greater importance at the time and demanded my attention – matters that were real, and not hypothetical.'

'What did this book say?'

'If I recall correctly, and I'm not saying that I do, it said something about a breach between worlds. It said that in the event of such a breach, the warning would be three nights of a red moon.'

'Three nights. For all we know, with the clouds we've had, we could already have had our three nights. What if there were clouds all the time? The warning would be missed.'

Zedd squinted in concentration as he tried to recall what he had read. 'No … no, it said that the one to whom the warning was directed would see all three nights of the warning – all three nights of the red moon.'

'What exactly is meant by such a warning? What kind of breach could there be between worlds?'

'I wish I knew.' Zedd thumped his head of wavy white hair back against the wall. 'When the boxes of Orden were opened by Darken Rahl, and the Stone of Tears came into this world from another, and the Keeper of the underworld was near to coming into our world through the breach, there was never a red moon.'

'Then, maybe the red moon doesn't mean that there is a breach. Perhaps you recall it wrongly.'

'Perhaps. What I recall most vividly are my thoughts at the time. I remember picturing a red moon in my mind, and telling myself to remember such an image, and that if I ever saw it for real, I must remember that it was grave trouble, and I must at once search out the meaning of the sign.'

Ann touched his arm, an act of compassion she had never done before. 'Zedd, we almost have Nathan. We'll have him tonight. When we do, I'll take the Rada'Han from your neck so that you can hurry to Aydindril and see to this matter. In fact, as soon as we have Nathan, we will all go. Nathan will understand the seriousness of this, and will help. We'll go to Aydindril with you and help.'

Although Zedd didn't like that this woman had insisted he come with her to capture Nathan, he had come to understand how afraid she was of what could happen with Nathan free, and that she needed his help. At times he had difficulty maintaining his indignation. He knew how desperate she was to keep the prophecies from being loosed along with Nathan.

Zedd knew how dangerous it could be if people were exposed to raw prophecy. He had been lectured since he was a boy on the dangers of prophecy, even for a wizard.

'Sounds like a worthwhile bargain to me; I help you get

218

Nathan back, and you two help me find the meaning of the red moon.'

'A bargain, then – we work together willingly. I must admit, it will be a pleasant change of affairs.'

'Is that so?' Zedd asked. 'Then why don't you take this collar off me?'

'I will. Just as soon as we have Nathan.'

'Nathan means more to you than you have admitted.'

She was silent a moment. 'He does. We have worked together for centuries. He can be trouble on two legs, but somewhere in all that bluster, Nathan has a noble heart.' Her voice lowered as she turned her head away. Zedd thought she wiped a hand at her eyes. 'I care greatly for that incorrigible, wonderful man.'

Zedd peeked around the corner at the inn's silent door.

'I still don't like it,' he whispered. 'Something about this is wrong. I wish I knew what it was.'

'So,' she finally asked, 'what are we going to do about Nathan?'

'I thought you wanted to do the talking.'

'Well, I guess you have convinced me that we should be careful. What do you think we should do?'

'I'll go in there alone and ask for a room. You wait outside. If I find him before he leaves, I'll surprise him and put him down. If he comes out before I find him, or if something … goes wrong, you seize him.'

'Zedd, Nathan is a wizard; I'm only a sorceress. If he had his Rada'Han around his neck I could easily control him, but he is without it.'

Zedd mulled it over for a moment. They couldn't take a chance on his getting away. Beyond that, Ann could be hurt. They would have a difficult time of finding Nathan again; once he knew they were onto him, he might figure out the tracer cloud and possibly unhook it. That was not likely, though.

'You're right,' he said at last. 'I'll cast a web outside the door, so that if he comes out it will hobble him, and then you can snap that infernal collar around his neck.'

'That sounds a good idea. What sort of web will you use?'

'As you've said yourself, we can't fail.' He studied her eyes in the dim light. 'Bags! I can't believe I'm actually doing this,' he muttered. 'Give me the collar for a moment.'

Ann searched under her cloak for the pouch at her waist. When her hand came out, the light of the red moon glinted dully off the Rada'Han.

'This is the same one he wore?' Zedd asked.

'For almost a thousand years.'

Zedd grunted. He took the collar in his hands and let his magic flow into the cold object of subjugation, let it mingle with the magic of the collar. He could feel the warm hum of the Additive Magic the collar possessed, and he could feel the icy tingle of its Subtractive Magic.

He handed back the collar. 'I've keyed the spell to his Rada'Han.'

'What spell are you going to weave?' she asked in a suspicious tone.

He considered the resolve in her eyes. 'A light spell. If he comes out without me ... You will have twenty of his heartbeats to get that around his neck, or the light web will ignite.'

If she didn't get the collar around his neck in time to extinguish the spell, Nathan would be consumed by it. Without the collar, there would be no escape for Nathan from such a spell. With it, he would escape the spell but then there would be no escape from her.

A double bind.

At that moment, Zedd didn't much like himself.

Ann took a deep breath. 'Someone else coming out won't trigger it, will they?'

Zedd shook his head. 'I will link it to the tracer cloud. The spell will recognize him and only him by that and that alone.'

His voice lowered in warning. 'If you don't get it around him in time, and it ignites, then others beside Nathan will be hurt or killed if they're close enough. If you can't get that around his neck for any reason, then you make sure you get away in time. He may prefer death over having that around his neck again.

CHAPTER 20

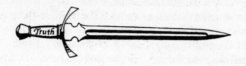

As he ambled in, surveying the gloomy room, Zedd realized that his heavy maroon robes with black sleeves and cowled shoulders were out of place. The mellow lamplight showed off the three rows of silver brocade at each cuff, and the thicker gold brocade running around the neck and down the front. A red satin belt set with a gold buckle cinched the waist of the rich robes.

Zedd missed his simple robes, but they were long gone – at Adie's insistence. The old sorceress had chosen his new disguise; for powerful wizards, simple accoutrements were the equivalent of military dress. Zedd suspected she just didn't like his old robes, and preferred him in this.

He missed Adie, and felt sorrow for the heartache she must feel at believing him dead. Nearly everyone thought he was dead. When they had time, maybe he would have Ann write a message in her journey book, letting Adie know he was alive.

He felt the most sorrow, though, for Richard. Richard needed him. Richard had the gift, and without proper instruction he was as helpless as an eaglet fallen from the nest. At least Richard had the Sword of Truth to help protect him, for now. Zedd intended to go to Richard just as soon as they had Nathan. It wouldn't be long, and then he could hurry on his way to Richard.

The innkeeper eyed Zedd's flashy outfit, his gaze snagging on the gold belt buckle. A collection of scraggy patrons dressed in furs, tattered leather, and ragged wool watched from a few booths at the wall to the right. The two plank tables sat empty on the straw-covered floor, waiting for diners, or drinkers.

'Rooms are a silver,' the innkeeper said in a disinterested tone. 'If you'd like company, it's an extra silver.'

'It would appear that my choice of outfits has turned out to be rather costly,' Zedd observed.

The burly innkeeper smiled with one side of his mouth as he held out a meaty hand, palm up. 'The price is the price. You want a room, or not?'

Zedd dropped a single silver in the man's hand.

'Third door on the left.' He nodded his head of curly brown hair toward the hall in the back. 'Interested in company, old man?'

'You'd have to share it with the lady who called. I was thinking you might be interested in a bit more profit. A considerable bit more.'

The man's brow twitched with curiosity as he closed his fist around the silver coin.

'Meaning?'

'Well, I heard a dear old friend of mine has been known to stop here. I've not seen him in quite a while. If he were here, tonight, and you could direct me to his room, I'd be so overwhelmed with joy and happiness to see him again that I'd foolishly part with a gold piece. A full gold piece.'

The man looked him up and down again.

'This friend of yours have a name?'

'Well,' Zedd said in a low voice, 'like many of your other patrons, he has a problem with names – he can't seem to remember them for very long, and has to keep thinking up new ones. But I can tell you that he's tall, older, and with white hair down to his broad shoulders.'

The man stroked his tongue across the inside of his cheek. 'He's … busy at the moment.'

Zedd produced the gold piece, but pulled it back when the innkeeper reached for it. 'So you say. I'd like to decide for myself just how busy he is.'

'Then it's another silver.'

Zedd forced himself to keep his voice down. 'For what?'

'For the lady's time and company.'

'I've no intention of availing myself of your lady.'

'So you say. When you see her with him, you might have a change of mood, and decide to try to rekindle your ... youth. It's my policy to collect the money first. If she tells me you gave her no more than a smile, then you can have the silver back.'

Zedd knew there was no chance of that. It would be his word against hers, and her word would carry the sweet ring of extra profit, if not the truth. But in the scheme of things, the price was of no consequence, no matter how much it irked him. Zedd dug into an inner pocket and handed over the silver coin.

'Last room on the right,' the innkeeper said as he turned away. He turned back to Zedd. 'And we have a guest in the next room who doesn't want to be disturbed.'

'I won't bother your guests.'

He gave Zedd a cunning grin. 'Plain as she is, I offered her a little companionship – no extra charge – and she told me that if anyone disturbed her rest, she'd skin me alive. A woman with enough brass to come in here alone, I believe her. I'm not giving her her silver piece back if you wake her. I'll take it out of your hide. Understand?'

Zedd nodded absently as he gave brief consideration to asking for a meal – he was hungry – but reluctantly dismissed the thought.

'Would you happen to have a back door, in case I ... need some night air?' Zedd didn't want Nathan slipping out the wrong door. 'I'd understand if it cost extra.'

'We're backed up to the blacksmith's shop,' the innkeeper said as he walked away. 'There's no other door.'

Last room on the right. Only one way in. One way out. Something about this was wrong. Nathan wouldn't be so foolish. Yet Zedd could feel the air crackling with the magic of his link.

As dubious as he was that Nathan would be so conveniently bedded down for them, he moved silently down the dark hall. He listened intently for anything out of the ordinary, but heard only the well-practiced, feigned sounds of passion from a woman in the second room to the left.

The end of the hall was lit by a single candle on a wooden bracket to the side. From the next to last room Zedd could hear the soft snores of the brassy lady who didn't want to be disturbed. He hoped it wouldn't come to that, and that she would sleep through the whole thing.

Zedd put his ear close to the last door on the right. He heard soft, throaty laughter from a woman. If this went wrong, she might be hurt. If it went very wrong, she might be killed.

He could wait, but having Nathan distracted would certainly be convenient. The man was a wizard, after all. Zedd didn't know how strongly Nathan felt about being captured.

Zedd knew how he would feel about it. That decided him. He couldn't afford not to take the opportunity of the distraction.

Zedd threw open the door, casting a hand out, igniting the air with silent, confusing flashes of heat and light.

The naked couple on the bed cringed away, covering their eyes. With a fist of air, Zedd threw Nathan off the woman and over the far side of the bed. With Nathan grunting and flailing at the air, Zedd seized the woman's wrist and threw her back out of the way. She snatched a sheet with her.

As the flashes of light sparked out, and before she was even able to throw the sheet around herself, Zedd loosed a web, paralyzing her where she stood. Almost simultaneously, he cast a similar web at the man behind the bed, except this web was laced with serious consequences should he try to fend it off with magic of his own. This was no time to be polite, or indulgent.

With hardly a sound, other than a bit of thumping onto the floor, the gloomy room was suddenly silent. Only a single candle on a washstand flickered weakly. Zedd was relieved it had gone so well, and he hadn't had to hurt the woman.

He rounded the bottom of the bed to see the man on the floor, frozen in place, his mouth opened in the beginning of a scream, his hands clawed to defend himself.

It wasn't Nathan.

Zedd stared in disbelief. He could feel the magic of the hook in the room. He knew this was who he had been chasing.

He leaned over the man. 'I know you can hear me, so listen carefully. I'm going to release the magic holding you, but if you cry out I will put it back on and leave you like that forever. Think carefully before you dare to call for help. As you may have already surmised, I'm a wizard, and anyone who comes will not be able to do anything to save you, should you displease me.'

Zedd passed his hand before the man, pulling back the veil of the web. The man scooted back to the wall, but he remained silent. He was older, but not as old as Nathan appeared. His hair was white, but wavy, rather than Nathan's straight hair. It wasn't as long, either, but the short description Zedd had given the innkeeper would have been close enough for him to think this was the man Zedd sought.

'Who are you?' Zedd asked.

'William's my name. You'd be Zedd.'

Zedd straightened. 'How do you know that?'

'The fellow you'd be looking for told me.' He gestured toward the nearby chair. 'Mind if I pull on my trousers? I have a feeling I'll not be needing them off anymore tonight.'

Zedd tilted his head toward the chair, signaling for William to go ahead. 'Talk while you do it. And keep in mind what I told you about my being a wizard. I know when a man is telling me a lie. Keep in mind, too, that I'm suddenly in a very foul mood.'

Zedd wasn't exactly telling the truth about being able to detect a lie, but he reasoned that the man didn't know that. He was, however, telling the truth about his mood.

'I ran into the man you were chasing. He didn't tell me his name. He offered me …' William glanced to the woman as he pulled the trousers up. 'Can she hear this?'

'Don't you worry about her. Worry about me.' Zedd gritted his teeth. 'Talk.'

'Well, he offered me …' He peered at the woman. Her wrinkled face was frozen in a startled expression. 'He offered me a … purse, if I'd do him a favor.'

'What favor.'

'Taking his place. He told me to ride like the Keeper himself was after me until I got at least this far. He said that when I got here, I could slow, rest, or stop, whatever my choice. He told me that you'd be catching up with me.'

'And he wanted that?'

William buttoned his trousers, plopped back into the chair, and started pulling on his boots. 'He said I wouldn't be able to

225

lose you, that sooner or later you'd catch up with me, but he didn't want that to happen until at least after I arrived here. Fast as I was moving, I must admit that I didn't think you'd be so close on my heels, so I thought to enjoy some of my profits.'

William stood and stuffed an arm into his brown wool shirt. 'He told me that I was to give you a message.'

'Message? What message?'

William tucked in his shirt and then reached into a trouser pocket and pulled out a leather purse. It looked to be heavy with coins.

William fingered open the purse. 'It's in here, with what he gave me.'

Zedd snatched the purse from the man. 'I'll take a look.'

The purse held mostly gold coins, with a few silver. Zedd felt one of the gold coins between a finger and thumb. He could feel the slight after-tingle of magic. The coins had probably started out as coppers, and Nathan had changed them to gold with magic.

Zedd had been hoping that Nathan didn't know how to do that. Changing things to gold was dangerous magic. Zedd only did it himself if there was no other choice.

Inside the purse, besides the coins, was a folded piece of paper. He pulled it out and turned it over in his fingers, giving it a good look in the dim light, wary of any form of magic snare that might be attached to it.

William pointed. 'That's what he gave me. He told me to give it to you when you caught me.'

'Anything else? Did he tell you anything else, besides to give me this message?'

'Well, as we were parting, he paused and looked up at me. He said, ''Tell Zedd it's not what he thinks.'' '

Zedd mulled this over for a moment. 'Which way did he go?'

'I don't know. I was atop my horse, and he was still afoot. He told me to ride, then he slapped my horse's rump and I rode.'

Zedd tossed the purse to William. While keeping a wary eye on the man, he unfolded the paper. He squinted in the dim light of the single candle as he scanned the message.

Sorry, Ann, but I have important business. One of our Sisters is going to do something very stupid. I must stop her, if I can. In case I die, I want you to know I love you, but I guess you knew that. I could never say it as long as I was your prisoner. Zedd, if the moon rises red, as I expect it to, then we are all in mortal danger. If the moon rises red for three nights, it means Jagang has invoked a bound fork prophecy. You must go to the Jocopo treasure. If you instead waste precious time coming after me, we will all die, and the emperor will have the spoils. The bound fork prophecy enforces a double bind on its victim. Zedd, I am sorry, but the victim named is Richard. May the spirits have mercy on his soul. If I knew the meaning of the prophecy, I would tell you, but I don't – the spirits have denied me access to it. Ann, go with Zedd. He will need your help. May the good spirits be with you both.

As Zedd blinked, trying to clear his watery vision, he noticed a smudge. He turned the message over and realized that the smudge was wax residue. The messge had been sealed, but in the poor light he hadn't noticed before.

Zedd looked up to see William's club. He flinched back, but felt the stunning pain of a blow. The floor crashed against his shoulder.

William pounced atop him, holding a knife to his throat.

'Where's this Jocopo treasure, old man! Talk, or I'll slit your throat!'

Zedd tried to hold on to his vision as he felt the room spinning and tilting. Nausea gagged him. He was in an instant sweat.

William's eyes were wild above him. 'Talk!'

The man stabbed him in the upper arm. 'Talk! Where's the treasure?'

A hand reached down and snatched William by the hair. It was a middle-aged woman in a dark cloak. Zedd couldn't seem to make sense of who she was, or what she was doing there. With surprising strength, the woman threw William back. He crashed against the wall beside the open door and slumped to the floor.

She sneered down at Zedd. 'You have made a big mistake, old man, letting Nathan get away. I suspected that following that old crone would net me the prophet, so I've followed you two until I could sense your link with him. Yet what do I find at the end of your magic hook but this fool here, instead of Nathan? So, now I have to make things unpleasant for you. I want the prophet.'

She turned and cast a hand out toward the naked woman frozen in place. The room erupted with thunder as a midnight-black discharge of lightning arced from her hand. The deathlike bolt of lightning sliced the woman and the sheet she held cleanly in half. Blood splattered the wall. The top half of her toppled to the floor like a statue cleaved in two. Her insides spilled across the floor as her torso hit the ground, but her limbs remained frozen in the same pose.

The woman hovering above him turned back. Her eyes were molten rage.

'If you would like a taste of Subtractive Magic, one limb at a time, then just give me a reason. Now, let me see the message.'

Zedd opened his hand to her. She reached out. He focused his mind through the dizziness. Before she could snatch the paper, he ignited it. It went up in a bright yellow flash.

With a cry of fury, she spun to William. 'What did it say, you little worm!'

William, until that instant rigid in panic, flung himself through the door and bolted down the hall.

Her stringy hair whipped around her face as she spun back to Zedd. 'I'll be back to get answers from you. You will confess everything before I kill you.'

As she lunged for the door, Zedd felt an unfamiliar composition of magic ram through his hasty shield. Pain erupted in his head.

Trying to gather his senses, he fought through the grip of blinding agony. He wasn't paralyzed, but he was unable to think of how to make himself get up. His arms and legs battled the air as ineffectively as a turtle on its back.

The searing pain made it difficult to do much more than maintain consciousness. He pressed his hands against the sides of his head, feeling as if it was going to come apart and he had to hold it together. He could hear himself gasping for breath.

The sudden thud of a concussion jolted the air and briefly lifted him clear of the floor.

A blinding flash lit the room as the roof tore open, the ripping roar of splintering wood and snapping beams was nearly lost in a deafening boom of thunder. The pain extinguished.

The light web had ignited.

Dust billowed through the air as smoking debris rained down around him. Zedd drew into a ball and covered his head as boards and bits of rubble peppered him. It sounded like being under a kettle in a hailstorm.

When silence settled over the scene, Zedd finally took his hands from his head and looked up. To his surprise, the building was still standing – after a fashion. The roof was mostly gone, letting the wind pull the dust away into the dark night above. The walls were holed like moth-eaten rags. Nearby lay the gory remains of the woman.

Zedd took assessment of himself, and was surprised to find he was in remarkably good condition, considering. Blood was running down the side of his head from where William had clubbed him, and his arm was throbbing where he had been stabbed, but other than that, he seemed uninjured. Not a bad bargain, in view of what could have been, he decided.

Moans drifted in from outside. A woman screamed hysterically. Zedd could hear men throwing wreckage aside, calling out names as they searched for the injured or dead.

The door, hanging crookedly from one hinge, suddenly exploded open as someone kicked it in.

Zedd sighed in relief as he saw a familiar, squat form rush in, her red face etched with concern.

'Zedd! Zedd, are you alive?'

'Bags, woman, don't you think I look alive?'

Ann knelt beside him. 'I think you look a mess. Your head is bleeding.'

Zedd grunted in pain as she helped him sit up. 'I can't tell you how glad I am to see you alive. I feared you might have been too close to the light spell when it ignited.'

She pawed through his blood-matted hair, inspecting the

wound. 'Zedd, that wasn't Nathan. I almost snapped the collar around that man's neck when he ran into the spell. Then Sister Roslyn came flying out the door. She threw herself on him, screaming something at him about a message.

'Roslyn is a Sister of the Dark. She didn't see me. My legs aren't what they used to be, but I ran like a girl of twelve when I saw her trying to use Subtractive Magic to undo the spell.'

'I guess it didn't work,' Zedd muttered. 'I guess she never encountered a spell cast by a First Wizard. But I certainly didn't make it that big. Using Subtractive Magic on the light spell expanded its power. It cost innocent people their lives.'

'At least it cost that evil woman hers, too.'

'Ann, heal me, and then we have to help these people.'

'Zedd, who was that man? Why did he set off the spell? Where is Nathan?'

Zedd held out his hand and opened his tightly closed fist. He let the warmth of magic flow into the ashes in his hand. The powdery black residue began clumping together as the inky ashes lightened to gray. When the charred ruins reconstituted itself into the paper it had been, it finally returned to pale brown.

'I've never seen anyone able to do such a thing,' Ann whispered in astonishment.

'Be thankful that Sister Roslyn hadn't, either, or we would be in even more trouble than we are. Being First Wizard has its advantages.'

Ann lifted the crumpled paper from his palm. Her lower lids brimmed with tears as she read the message from Nathan. By the time she had finished, silent tears were running down her round cheeks.

'Dear Creator,' she breathed at last.

His own eyes stung with tears. 'Indeed,' he whispered in response.

'Zedd, what is the Jocopo treasure?'

He blinked at her. 'I was hoping you would know. Why would Nathan tell us to go protect something, and not tell us what it is?'

People outside were crying in pain and calling for help. In the distance, a wall, or perhaps a piece of roof, crashed to the ground. Men were yelling directions as they dug through the rubble.

'Nathan forgets that he is different from other people. Just as you recall things from a few decades ago, he also recalls what was, except what he recalls is sometimes not a couple of decades ago, but a couple of centuries.'

'I wish he would have told us more.'

'We have to find it. We will find it. I have a few ideas.' She shook her finger at him. 'And you are coming with me! We still haven't got Nathan. That collar stays on for now. You're going with me, do you understand? I'll hear none of your arguing!'

Zedd reached up and unstrapped the collar around his neck.

Ann's eyes went wide and her jaw dropped.

Zedd tossed the Rada'Han into her lap. 'We have to find this Jocopo treasure that Nathan spoke of. Nathan is not playing games about this. This is deadly serious. I believe what he wrote in that message. We are in a lot of trouble. I'm going with you, but this time we must be more careful. This time we must cover our trail with magic.'

'Zedd,' she finally whispered, 'how did you get that collar off? It's impossible.'

Zedd scowled at her to keep himself from weeping at the thought of the prophecy trapping Richard. 'Like I said, being First Wizard has its advantages.'

Her face flushed crimson. 'Did you just … How long have you been able to take off the Rada'Han?'

Zedd shrugged a bony shoulder. 'It took me a couple of days to figure it out. Since then. Since after the first two or three days.'

'Yet you went with me? You still went with me? Why?'

'I guess I like women who do things out of desperation. Shows character.' He balled his trembling hands into fists. 'Do you believe everything Nathan said in that message?'

'I wish I could say no. I'm sorry, Zedd.' Ann swallowed. 'He said, "May the spirits have mercy on his soul," meaning Richard. Nathan didn't say "good spirits," he just said "spirits."'

Zedd wiped his sticklike fingers across his face. 'Not all spirits are good. There are evil spirits, too. What do you know about double fork prophecies? About prophecy that enforced a double bind?'

'Unlike your collar, there is no escape from one. The cataclysm named has to be brought about to invoke the prophecy. Whatever it is, the event has already happened. Once invoked, the nature of the cataclysm is self-defining, meaning that the victim has only the choice of one of the two forks in the prophecy. The victim can choose only which way he would rather ... Surely you must know this? As First Wizard, you would have to know.'

'I had been hoping you would tell me I was wrong,' Zedd whispered. 'I wish Nathan would have at least written the prophecy for us to see.'

'Be thankful he didn't.'

CHAPTER 21

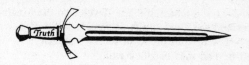

Clarissa gripped the weathered sill of the window in the stone tower of the abbey in an effort to control her quaking. She clutched her other hand over her thundering heart. Even with the acrid smoke burning her eyes, she had to force herself to blink as she stood transfixed, watching the tumult in the city, and the square below.

The noise was deafening. The invaders screamed battle cries as they charged ahead, swinging swords, axes, and flails. Steel clashed and rang. The air hissed with arrows. Horses screamed in panic. Balls of light and flame wailed in from the distant countryside and exploded through the stone walls. The grisly invaders blew shrill horns and bellowed like beasts as they poured through the rents in the city walls, their impossible numbers darkening the streets in a sooty flood. Flames whooshed and roared and snapped.

Townsmen wept unashamedly as they begged for mercy, their hands outstretched, imploring, even as they were put to the sword. Clarissa saw the bloody body of one of the assembly of seven being dragged down the street on a rope behind a horse.

The shrill screams of women pierced through it all as their children, their husbands, their brothers and fathers were murdered before their eyes.

The hot wind carried the jumbled smells of a burning city, pitch and wood, oil and cloth, hide and flesh, but laced through it all, in every breath she pulled, was the gagging stench of blood.

It was all happening, just as he had said it would. Clarissa had laughed at him. She didn't think she would ever be able to laugh again as long as she lived. At the thought of how short a time that might be, her legs nearly gave way.

No. She wouldn't think that. She was safe here. They wouldn't violate the abbey. She could hear the throng seeking safety in the great room below weeping and crying out in terror. This was a sacred place, devoted to the worship of the Creator and the good spirits. It would be blasphemy even for these beasts to spill blood in such a sanctuary.

Yet, he had told her they would.

Below, out in the streets, the army's resistance had been crushed. The Renwold defenders had never before let an invader set foot inside the walls. It was said the city was as safe as if the Creator Himself defended it. Invaders had tried before, and had always departed bloodied and dispirited. No horde from the wilds had ever breached the city walls. Renwold had always stood safe.

This day, as he had said it would, Renwold had fallen.

For their audacity at refusing to surrender the city and its spoils peacefully, without a fight, the people of Renwold were being shown no mercy.

Some had urged surrender, arguing that the red moons of the previous three nights had been an ill omen. But those voices were few; the city had always been held safe before.

The good spirits and the Creator Himself, had turned away from the people of Renwold this day. What their crime was, she couldn't fathom, but, surely, it must be terrible indeed to warrant no mercy from the good spirits.

From her vantage point at the top of the abbey, she could see the people of Renwold being herded into clusters in the streets, the market district, and courtyards. She knew many of the people being forced at the point of steel into the square below. The invaders, clad in foreign outfits of studded metal, and spiked leather straps and belts, and layers of hides and fur, looked to her the way she imagined savages from the wilds.

The invaders began sorting through the men, pulling aside those with trades: smiths, bowyers, fletchers, bakers, brewers, butchers, millers, carpenters – anyone of a craft or trade who might be put to use. Those men were chained together, to be marched off as slaves. The very old, young boys, and those seemingly without useful trades, like valets, yeomen, inn-keepers, city officials, and merchants, were slaughtered on the spot – a sword hacked to the side of the neck, a spear through the chest, a knife in the gut, a flail across the skull. There was no system to the slaughter.

Clarissa stared as an invader clubbed the head of a man on the ground who wouldn't seem to die. It reminded her of a fisherman, clubbing a catfish on the bank – *thunk, thunk, thunk.* The man doing the clubbing didn't seem to think any more of it than a fisherman would. Dumb Gus, the poor half-wit who ran errands for merchants, shopkeepers, and inns, his work paid for with food and a bed and watered ale, kicked one last time as his thick skull gave way with a resounding crack.

Clarissa put trembling fingers over her mouth as she felt the contents of her stomach lurch up into the back of her throat. She swallowed it back down and gasped for air.

This wasn't happening, she told herself. She was dreaming. She repeated the lie over and over in her head. *This isn't happening. This isn't happening. This isn't happening.*

But it was. Dear Creator, it was.

Clarissa watched as the women were culled from the men. The old women were summarily put to death. The women judged worth keeping were shoved, screaming and crying for their men, into a group. Invaders sorted through them, further winnowing them according to age and, apparently, looks.

Laughing invaders held the women as others of the beasts methodically went from woman to woman, seized them by their lower lip, and poked it through with a thin spike. A ring was pushed through each woman's lip, its split opening efficiently closed with the aid of the invader's teeth.

He had told her this, too: the women would be marked into slavery. This, too, she had laughed at. And why not? He seemed to her as daft as dumb Gus, expounding his crazy, preposterous ideas and nonsense.

Clarissa squinted, trying to see better. It appeared that the different groups of women had different-colored rings put through their lips. One group of older women of every shape looked to have copper-colored rings. Another group of younger women screamed and fought as silver rings were put upon them. They stopped fighting and meekly submitted after a few who fought the hardest were run through with swords.

The smallest group of the youngest, prettiest women were in the grip of the greatest terror as they were surrounded by a gang of burly invaders. These women received gold rings. Blood ran down their chins and onto their fancy dresses.

Clarissa knew most of these young women. It was hard not to remember people who regularly humiliated you. Being in her early thirties, and unmarried, Clarissa was the object of scorn among many women, but these young women were the cruelest, giving her smirking sidelong glances as they passed, referring to her as 'the old maid,' 'or 'the hag,' among themselves, but just loud enough that she could hear them.

Clarissa had never planned to be this age and without a husband. She had always wanted a family. She wasn't entirely sure how life and time had rolled on without providing her with the opportunity for a husband.

She wasn't ugly, she didn't think, but she knew she was no more than plain, at best. Her figure was satisfactory; she had meat on her bones. Her face wasn't twisted, or shriveled, or grotesque. Whenever she looked at her reflection while passing a window at night, she didn't think an ugly woman stared back at her. She knew it wasn't a face that inspired ballads, but it wasn't repulsive.

Yet with more women than men to be had, being merely 'not ugly' wasn't adequate. The pretty, younger women didn't understand; they had men in abundance courting them. The older women understood, and were kinder; but still she was an unfortunate in their eyes, and they feared to be overly friendly, lest they catch the unseen, unknown taint that kept her unwed.

No man would want her now; she was too old. Too old, they would fear, to give them sons. Time had trapped her, alone and an old maid. Her work filled her time, but it never made her happy the way she suspected a family would have.

As much as the sting of those young women's words hurt, and as much as she had often wished them to experience humiliation, she would never wish them this.

The invaders laughed as they ripped the bodices of the fine dresses, inspecting the young women like livestock.

'Dear Creator,' she wept in prayer, 'please don't let this be because I wished them to feel the shame of degradation. I never wished them this. Dear Creator, I beg you forgive me ever wishing them ill. I didn't want this for them, I swear on my soul.'

Clarissa gasped and leaned out the little window for a better view when she saw a band of invaders running forward with a log. They disappeared beneath an overhang below.

She felt the building reverberate with a dull thud. People in the great room screamed. Another thud. And another, followed by splintering wood. The underworld's own pandemonium broke out below.

They were violating the sanctity of the Creator's abbey.

Just as the prophet had said they would.

Clarissa clutched her dress over her heart in both hands as she heard the slaughter begin anew below. She shuddered uncontrollably. They would soon come up the stairs, and find her.

What was to happen to her? Was she to be marked with a ring through her lip, and cast into slavery? Would she have the courage to fight, and be killed, rather than submit?

No. She knew the answer would be no. In the face of it, she wanted to live. She didn't want to be butchered like one of the people in the square had been, or like poor dumb Gus. She feared death more than life.

She gasped as the door banged open.

The Abbot burst into the small room. 'Clarissa!' Neither young nor fit, he huffed from running up the stairs. His portly shape could not be disguised beneath his dull brown robes.

His round face was as ashen as a three-day-dead corpse.

'Clarissa! The books,' he panted. 'We must run away. Take the books with us. Take them and hide!'

She blinked dumbly at him. The room of books would take days to pack, and several wagons to lug them away. There was nowhere to hide. There was nowhere to run. There was no way to escape through the throng of invaders.

It was a ludicrous command born of mad terror.

'Abbot, there is no way we can escape.'

He rushed to her and took her hands. He licked his lips. His eyes darted about. 'They won't notice us. Pretend we are just going about our business. They won't question us.'

She didn't know how to answer such delusion, but was denied an attempt. Three men in blood-splattered leather and hides and fur stepped through the door. They were so big, and the room so small, that it took them only three strides to close the distance to the Abbot.

Two had greasy, curly, matted hair. The third was shaved bald, but had a thick beard like the other two. Each wore a gold ring through his left nostril.

The one with the shiny head snatched the Abbot by his fringe of white hair and yanked his head back. The Abbot squealed.

'Trade? Do you have a trade?'

The Abbot, his head bent back so that he could look only at the ceiling, spread his hands in supplication.

'I am the Abbot. A man of prayer.' He licked his lips and added in a shout, 'And books! I care for the books!'

'Books. Where are they?'

'The archives are in the athenaeum.' His head tilted back, he pointed blindly. 'Clarissa knows. Clarissa can show you. She works with them. She can show you. She cares for them.'

'No trade, then?'

'Prayer! I'm a man of prayer! I'll pray to the Creator, and the good spirits, for you. You'll see. I'm a man of prayer. No donation required. I'll pray for you. No donation.'

The man with the shaved head, his sweat-slicked muscles bulging, pulled the Abbot's head back further and with a long knife sliced down through his throat. Clarissa felt warm blood splatter her face as the Abbot exhaled through the gaping wound.

'We don't need a man of prayer,' the invader said as he tossed the Abbot aside.

Clarissa stared in wide-eyed horror as she saw blood spread under the Abbot's brown robes. She had known him for nearly her whole life. He had taken her in years ago, and kept her from starving by giving her work as a scribe. He had taken pity on her because she could find no husband, and she had no skill, except that she could read. Not many could read, but Clarissa could read, and it provided her with bread.

That she had to endure the Abbot's pudgy hands and slobbering lips was an onus she had to abide if she wanted to keep her work and feed herself. It hadn't been that way right from the first, but after she came to know her work and feel safe in being able to meet her needs, she came to understand that she had to tolerate things she didn't like.

Long ago, when she had begged him to stop and that hadn't worked, she had threatened him. He told her that she would be banished if she made such scandalous accusations against a respected Abbot. How would a single woman, alone in the countryside, survive? he had asked. What truly terrible things would she suffer then?

She supposed it wasn't the worst of things. Others went hungry, and pride didn't fill their bellies. Some women suffered worse at the hands of men. The Abbot never struck her, at least.

She had never wished him harm. She only wished him to leave her be. She never wished him harm. He had taken her in, and given her work and food. Others gave her only scorn.

The brute with the knife stepped to her, startling her from her shock at seeing the Abbot murdered. He slid the knife behind a belt.

He gripped her chin with callused, bloodstained fingers and turned her head side to side. He looked her up and down. He pinched her waist in evaluation. She felt her face burn with humiliation at being scrutinized so.

He swung to one of the others. 'Ring her.'

For a moment, she didn't understand. Her knees began trembling as one of the burly men came forward, and she realized what he had meant. She feared to cry out. She knew what they would do to her if she resisted. She didn't want her throat slit like the Abbot, or her head bashed in like poor dumb Gus. Dear Creator, she didn't want to die.

'Which one, Captain Mallack?'

The bald man looked into her eyes. 'Silver.'

Silver. Not copper. Silver.

A maniacal laugh cavorted through the back of her mind as the man gripped her lower lip between a thumb and knuckle. These men, these men who were experienced at judging the worth of flesh, had just valued her more highly than her own people. Even if it was as a slave, they had given her value.

She clenched shut the back of her throat to hold in the

scream as she felt the pick stab into the margin of her lip. He twisted the pick until it poked through. She blinked, trying to see through the tears of pain.

Not gold, she told herself, of course not gold, but not copper, either. They thought her worth a silver ring. Some part of her was disgusted at her vainglory. What else did she have, now?

The man, stinking of sweat, blood, and soot, shoved the split silver ring through her lip. She grunted in helpless pain. He leaned in and closed the ring with his crooked yellow teeth.

She made no effort to wipe the dripping blood from her chin as Captain Mallack looked her in the eyes again.

'You are now the property of the Imperial Order.'

CHAPTER 22

Clarissa thought she might faint. How could a person be the property of anyone? With shame, she realized that she had let herself be little more to the Abbot. He had been kind to her, after a fashion, but in return, he had viewed her as his property.

She knew these beasts were not going to be kind. She knew what they were going to do with her, and it was going to be something considerably worse than the Abbot's drunken, impotent affections. The look of steel in the man's eyes told her that they were men who would have no difficulty following through with what they wanted.

At least it was silver. She didn't know why that mattered to her, but it did.

'You have books here,' Captain Mallack said. 'Are there prophecies among them?'

The Abbot should have kept his mouth closed, but she didn't want to die to protect the books. Besides, these men would tear the place apart and find them anyway; the books weren't hidden. The city had been thought safe from invasion, after all.

'Yes.'

'The emperor wants all books brought to him. You will show us where they are.'

Clarissa swallowed. 'Of course.'

'How's it going, boys?' came an amicable voice from behind the men. 'Everything in order? You look to have matters well in hand.'

The three men turned. A vigorous older man filled the doorway. A full head of straight white hair hung to his broad shoulders. He was wearing high boots, brown trousers, and a ruffled white shirt under an open dark green vest. The hem of his heavy, dark brown cape hovered just above the floor. A sword was sheathed in an elegant scabbard at his hip.

It was the prophet.

'Who are you?' Captain Mallack growled.

The prophet casually flipped his cape back over a shoulder.

'A man in need of a slave.' He shouldered one of the men out of his way as he strode up to Clarissa. He grasped her jaw in a big hand and turned her head this way and that. 'This one will do. How much do you want for her?'

The bald-headed Captain Mallack snatched a fistful of white shirt. 'The slaves belong to the Order. They are all the property of the emperor.'

The prophet scowled down at the hand on his shirt. He slapped it away. 'Mind the shirt, friend; your hands are dirty.'

'They're going to be bloody in a moment! Who are you? What's your trade?'

One of the other men put a knife to the prophet's ribs. 'Answer Captain Mallack's question, or die. What's your trade?'

The prophet dismissed the question with a flip of a hand.

'Not one you would be interested in. Now, how much for the slave? I can pay handsomely. You boys might as well make something for yourselves out of it. I never begrudge a man his profit.'

'We have all the plunder we want. It's here for the taking.' The captain glanced to the man who had put the ring through her lip. 'Kill him.'

The prophet casually swept a staying hand before them. 'I mean you no harm, boys.' He leaned down a little closer to their faces. 'Won't you reconsider?'

Captain Mallack opened his mouth, but then he paused. No words came out. Clarissa heard distressed, liquid rumbling from the guts of the three men. Their eyes widened.

'What's wrong?' the prophet asked. 'Is everything all right? Now, how about my offer, boys? How much do you want for her?'

The three men's faces twisted with discomfort. Clarissa smelled an unpleasant odor.

'Well,' Captain Mallack said in a strained voice, 'I think ...' He grimaced. 'We, ah, we have to go.'

The prophet bowed. 'Why, thank you, boys. Off with you, then. Give my regards to my friend, Emperor Jagang, won't you?'

'But what about him?' one of the men asked the captain as they edged away.

'Someone else will be along shortly and kill him,' the captain said, as all three of them shuffled bow-legged through the door.

The prophet turned to her, his smile evaporating as he regarded her with a hawklike gaze.

'Well, have you reconsidered my offer?'

Clarissa stood quivering. She wasn't sure who she feared more, the invaders or the prophet. They would hurt her. She didn't know what the prophet would do to her. He might tell her how she was to die. He had told her how a whole city was going to die, and it was coming to pass. She feared that if he said something, he could make it happen. Prophets commanded magic.

'Who are you?' she whispered.

He bowed dramatically. 'Nathan Rahl. I have already told you that I am a prophet. Forgive me for overlooking the introductions, but we don't exactly have a great deal of time.'

His penetrating blue eyes frightened her, but she made herself ask, 'Why do you want a slave?'

'Well, not for the same as they.'

'I don't want –'

He snatched her arm and forced her to the window. 'Look out there. Look!'

For the first time, she lost control of the tears, and they poured out in forlorn sobs. 'Dear Creator ...'

'He's not coming to help you. No one can help those people, now. I can help you, but you have to agree to help me in return. I'll not risk my life and lives of tens of thousands of others on you if you are of no use to me. I'll find another who would rather go with me than be a slave to these beasts.'

She made herself look into his eyes. 'Will it be dangerous?'

'Yes.'

'Will I die helping you?'

'Maybe. Maybe you'll live. If you die, you will die doing something noble: trying to prevent suffering worse than this.'

'Can't you help them? Can't you stop this?'

'No. What is done is done. We can only strive to shape the future – we cannot alter the past.

'You have an inkling of the dangers in the future. You once had a prophet living here, and he wrote down some of his prophecies. He was not an important prophet, but he left them here, where you fools view them as revelation of divine will.

'They are not. They are simply the words of potential. The same as if I tell you that you have it within your power to choose your destiny. You can stay and be a whore to this army, or you can risk your life doing something worthwhile.'

She trembled under his powerful grip on her arm. 'I … I'm afraid.'

His azure eyes softened. 'Clarissa, would it help if I told you that I am terrified?'

'You are? You seem so sure of yourself.'

'I am only sure of what I can try to do to help. Now, we must go to your archives before these men get a look at the books.'

Clarissa turned, glad for the excuse to withdraw from his gaze. 'Down here. I'll show you the way.'

She led him down the spiral stone steps at the back of the room. They weren't often used because they were so narrow and hard to negotiate. The prophet who had constructed the abbey was a slight man, and the stairs were built to suit him. As tight as they were for her, she couldn't imagine how this prophet could pass down them, but he did.

On the dark landing below, he lit a little flame above his palm. She paused in astonishment, wondering at why it did not burn his flesh. He urged her to hurry on. The low wooden door opened into a short hall. The stairs at the center led down to the archives. The door at the end of the hall led to the main room of the abbey. Beyond that door, people were being murdered.

She turned down the stairs, taking them two at a time. Nathan caught her arm when she slipped, keeping her from a fall. He made a gentle joke about that not being the danger he'd warned her about.

In the dark room below he cast out a hand, and the lamps hanging on wooden pilasters sprang to flame. His brow drew down as he surveyed the shelves lining the walls of the room. Two sturdy but unexceptional tables provided a place to read and to write.

While he strode to the shelves on the left, she frantically tried to think of a place she could hide from the men of the Order. There must be some place. Surely the invaders would leave, sooner or later, and then she could come out and be safe.

She was afraid of the prophet. He expected things of her. She didn't know what those things were, but she didn't think she had the courage to do them. She just wanted to be left alone.

The prophet strode past the shelves, stopping here and there to put a finger atop a spine and pull out a volume. He didn't open the books he removed, but tossed them on the floor in the center of the room and went on to the next. The books he pulled out all contained prophecies. He didn't select all the books of prophecy, by any means, but prophecies were the only ones he chose.

'Why me?' she asked as she watched him. 'Why do you want me?'

He paused with a finger on a large leatherbound volume. He watched her, the way a hawk watched a mouse, as he withdrew the book. He took it to the pile of eight or ten already on the floor, set it down, and picked up one already there.

He paged through it after he stopped before her.

'Here. Read this.'

She lifted the heavy book from his hands and read where he pointed:

Should she go freely, one ringed will be able to touch that long trusted into the winds alone.

Long trusted into the winds alone. The very idea of such an incomprehensible thing made her want to run.

'One ringed,' she said. 'Does that mean me?'

'If you choose to go freely.'

'What if I choose to stay, and hide? Then what?'

He lifted an eyebrow. 'Then I will find another who wants

to escape. I offered you the chance first for my own reasons, and because you can read. I'm sure there are others who can read. If I have to, I will find another.'

'What is it "one ringed" can touch?'

He took the book from her tremulous hands and snapped it shut. 'Don't try to understand what the words mean. I know that you people try to do that, but I am a prophet, and I can tell you with a great deal of authority that such an endeavor is futile. No matter what you think, what you fear, you will be wrong.'

Her resolve to leave with him weakened. Despite his seeming kindness in saving her up in the tower, the prophet frightened her. A man who knew things such as he could know frightened her.

They had put a silver ring through her lip. Not copper. Maybe that meant she would be treated better. At least she would live. They would feed her, and she would live. She wouldn't have to fear some terrifying, unknown death.

She started when he spoke her name.

'Clarissa,' he said again. 'Go get some of the soldiers. Tell them that you are to lead them to the archives, down here.'

'Why? Why do you want me to get them?'

'Do as I say. Tell them that Captain Mallack said you were to lead them down to the books. If you have any trouble, tell them he also said to "get their sorry hides down to the books right now or the dream walker would pay them a visit they would regret." '

'But, if I go up there …'

Her words trailed off in the grip of his gaze. 'If you have trouble, tell them those words, and you will be all right. Lead them down here.'

She opened her mouth to ask why he wanted them to come down to the books, but his expression changed her mind. She dashed up the stairs, glad to be away from the prophet, although she realized that she would have to face the brutes.

She paused before the door to the great room. She could run away. She remembered the Abbot suggesting the same thing, and she remembered knowing how foolish the idea was. There was nowhere to run. She had a silver ring; maybe that would be good for something. These men valued her at least that much.

She opened the door and took one step before the sight brought her to a wide-eyed halt. The double door to the street was splintered and broken in. The floor was strewn with the bodies of men who had run to the abbey for shelter.

The great room was packed with invaders. Among the bloody bodies of the dead, the women were being raped. Clarissa stood frozen, her mouth agape.

Men stood in groups, waiting their turn. The largest groups were for the women with gold rings. The things being done to those women brought vomit up into Clarissa's mouth. She covered her mouth and forced herself to swallow it.

She stood transfixed, unable to turn her eyes away from a naked Manda Perlin, one of the young women who had frequently tormented her. Manda had married a wealthy, middle-aged man who lent money and invested in cargos. Her husband, Rupert Perlin, lay close by, his throat so viciously cut that his head had been nearly severed from his body.

Manda wailed in terror as the brutes held her down. The men roared with laughter at her wails, but they could hardly be heard above all the noise. Clarissa felt her eyes water. These were not men. They were wild animals.

A man snatched Clarissa by the hair. Another hooked her leg with an arm. They laughed as her scream joined all the others. Before she landed on her back, they had her dress up.

'No!' she cried out.

They laughed at her, as the others were laughing at Manda.

'No – I was sent!'

'Good,' one man said. 'I was tired of waiting my turn.'

He smacked her when she fought off his hands. The pain of the wallop stunned her, and made her ears hum.

She had a silver ring. That meant something. She had a silver ring.

She heard a woman not two feet away grunt as a man flopped down on her back. Her silver ring did her no good, either.

'Mallack!' Clarissa screamed. 'Captain Mallack sent me!'

The man put a fist in her hair and crushed a grimy, bristly

kiss to her lips. Her wound, from the ring through her lip, sang with pain and she could feel blood gush anew across her chin.

'My thanks to Captain Mallack,' he said. He bit her ear, making her scream again as the other man pawed at her small clothes. She tried desperately to remember what the prophet had told her to say.

'Message!' she cried out. 'Captain Mallack sent me with a message! He said I'm to lead you down to the books. He said to tell you to get your sorry hides down to the books right now or the dream walker would pay you a visit you would regret.'

The men cursed obscenely, then pulled her to her feet by her hair. She smoothed her dress down with trembling hands. The half dozen men around her laughed. One slid a hand back up between her legs.

'Well, don't just stand there enjoying it, bitch. Get going. Lead the way.'

Her legs had all the starch of wet rope and she had to hold the rail on the way down the stairs. Visions of what she had seen flashed through her mind in a jumble as she led the half dozen men down to the archives.

The prophet met them at the door, as if he were about to leave.

'There you are. About time,' the prophet said in an irritable voice. He gestured back to the room. 'Everything is in order. Start packing them up before anything happens, or the emperor will be using us as firewood.'

The men frowned in confusion. They glanced about the room. In the center, where Clarissa had seen the prophet stack the books he had taken from the shelves, there was only a stain of white ash. The empty places where he had pulled out books had been closed up, so it didn't appear that any had been removed.

'I smell smoke,' one of the men said.

The prophet thunked the man's skull. 'Idiot! Half the city is ablaze. At last, you begin to smell smoke? Now, get to it! I have to report on the books I found.'

One of them snatched Clarissa's arm as the prophet started leading her out. 'Leave her. We'll be needing some entertainment.'

The prophet glared at them. 'She's a scribe, you fool! She

knows all the books. We have more important work for her than amusing you lazy oafs. There are women enough when you finish your work, or would you rather have me report you to Captain Mallack?'

Even though they were confused by who Nathan was, they decided to get to work. Nathan closed the door behind him. He pushed Clarissa on ahead.

On the steps, alone with him in the silence, she halted, leaning against the railing for support. She felt lightheaded and sick to her stomach. He put his fingers to her cheek.

'Clarissa, listen to me. Slow your breathing. Think. Slow it down, or you will faint.'

Tears coursed down her face. She lifted a hand toward the room she had gone to to get the men. 'I ... I saw ...'

'I know what you saw,' he said in a soft voice.

She slapped him. 'Why did you send me up there? You didn't need those men!'

'You think you will be able to hide. You won't. They will search every hole in this city. When they are finished, they will burn it all to the ground. There will be nothing of Renwold left.'

'But I ... I could ... I'm afraid of going with you. I don't want to die.'

'I wanted you to know what will happen to you should you choose to stay here. Clarissa, you are a lovely young woman.' He pointed with his chin toward the great hall. 'Believe me, you do not want to be here to experience what is going to happen to the women here over the next three days, and then as slaves to the Imperial Order. Please believe me, you don't want that.'

'How can they do such things? How can they?'

'This is the unspeakable reality of war. There are no rules of conduct except those the aggressor makes, or those the winner can enforce. You can either fight against this, or submit to it.'

'Can't ... can't you do anything to help these people?'

'No,' he whispered. 'I can only help you, but I'm not going to waste precious time doing it unless you are worth saving. The dead here died a quick death. Terrible as it was, it was quick.

'Vast numbers of people, many times as many people as

lived in this city, are about to die horrible, suffering, lingering deaths. I can't help these people, but I can try to help those others. Is freedom worth having, life worth living, if I don't try?

'It is time for you to decide if you will help, if your life is worth living, worth the Creator's gift of your soul.'

Visions of what was happening up in the great hall, out in the streets, and to her whole city flashed chaotically through her mind. She felt as if she were already dead. If she could have a chance to help others, and to live again, she must take it. This was the only chance she would get. She knew it was.

She wiped the tears from her eyes, and the blood from her chin. 'Yes. I'll help you. I swear on my soul that I will do what you ask, if it means a chance to save lives, and a chance at my freedom.'

'Even if I ask you to do something that you fear? Even if you think you will die doing it?'

'Yes.'

His warm smile made her heart lift. Surprisingly, he drew her to him and gave her a comforting hug. She had been a child the last time she had been comforted with a hug. It made her weep.

Nathan put his fingers to her lip, and she felt a warm sensation of succor. Her terror eased. Her memories of what she had seen now gave her the determination to stop the men who did this, to prevent them from visiting suffering on others. Her mind filled with hope that she might do something important that would help other people to be free, too.

Clarissa felt her lip after Nathan had taken his hand away. It no longer throbbed. The wound was healed around the ring.

'Thank you – Prophet.'

'Nathan.' He ran a hand down her hair. 'We must go. The longer we stay here, the greater the chance of never getting away.'

Clarissa nodded. 'I'm ready.'

'Not yet.' He cupped his big hands to her cheeks. 'We must walk through the city, through it all, to get away. You have seen too much already. I don't want you to see any more, or hear any more. I would spare you that much, at least.'

'But I don't see how we can ever get past the Order.'

'You let me worry about that. For now, I am going to put a spell over you. You will be blind, so that you don't have to see any more of what is happening to your city, and you will be deaf, so that you don't have to hear any more of the suffering and death that now possesses this place.'

She suspected that he feared she might panic and get them caught. She didn't know that he might not be right.

'If you say so, Nathan. I will do as you say.'

Standing there in the dim light, two steps below her so that his face was closer to hers, he gave her a warm smile. For as old as he was, he was a strikingly handsome man.

'I have chosen the right woman. You will do well. I pray the good spirits grant you freedom in return for your help.'

Holding his hand as they walked was her only connection to the world. She couldn't see the slaughter. She couldn't hear the screams. She couldn't smell the fires. Yet she knew that those things had to be happening around her.

In her silent world, she prayed as she walked, prayed that the good spirits would keep safe the souls of those who had died here this day, and for those who still lived she prayed for the good spirits to give them strength.

He guided her around rubble, and around the heat of fires. He held her hand tight when she stumbled over debris. It seemed they walked for hours through the ruins of the vast city.

Occasionally they stopped, and she lost the connection to his hand as she stood still and alone in her silent world. She could neither see nor hear, so she didn't know the exact reason for the stop, but she suspected that Nathan was having to talk their way out. Sometimes those stops dragged on and on, and her heart raced at the thought of what unseen danger Nathan warded. Sometimes, the stop was followed by his arm around her waist pulling her into a run.

She felt confident in his care, and comfort, too.

Her hip sockets ached from walking, and her weary feet throbbed. He at last placed both hands on her shoulders, turned her, and helped her sit. She felt cool grass under her.

Her vision suddenly returned, along with her hearing and sense of smell.

Rolling green hills spread away before her. She looked around and saw only countryside. There were no people anywhere. The city of Renwold was nowhere to be seen.

She dared to feel the budding of sweet relief, not only at having escaped the slaughter but at having escaped her old life.

The terror had burned so deep into her soul that she felt as if she had been recast in a furnace of fear, and had come out a shiny new ingot, hardened for what lay ahead.

Whatever she had to face, it could be no worse than what she would have faced had she stayed. If she had chosen to stay, it would have been a turning away from helping others, and from herself.

She didn't know what he was going to ask her to do, but every day of freedom she had was one she wouldn't otherwise have had if not for the prophet.

'Thank you, Nathan, for choosing me.'

He was staring off in thought, and didn't seem to hear her.

CHAPTER 23

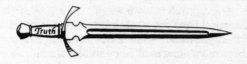

Sister Verna turned to the commotion and saw a scout leaping from his lathered horse before it had skidded to a stop in the near darkness. The scout panted, trying to catch his breath, at the same time as he relayed his report to the general. The general's tense posture visibly relaxed at the report. He gestured in a jaunty fashion for his officers to stand down their concern, too.

She couldn't hear the scout's report, but she knew what it would be. She didn't have to be a prophet to know what the scout would have seen.

The fools. She had told him as much.

The smiling General Reibisch approached her, his heavy eyebrows arched with his good humor. When he came into the ring of firelight, his grayish-green eyes searched her out.

'Prelate! There you are. Good news!'

Verna, her mind on other, more important matters, loosened the shawl around her shoulders.

'Don't tell me, general; my Sisters and I won't have to spend the whole night calming nervous soldiers and casting spells to tell you where panicked men have run off to hide while they await the end of the world.'

He scratched his rust-colored beard. 'Ah, well, I do appreciate your help, Prelate, but no, you won't. You're right, as usual.'

She snorted an I-told-you-so.

The scout had been watching from atop the hill, and from

253

there could see the moonrise before any of them down in the valley.

'My man said that the moon didn't rise red, tonight. I know you told me it wouldn't, and that three nights of it was all there would be, but I can't help being relieved to know things are back to normal, Prelate.'

Back to normal. Hardly.

'I'm glad, general, that we will all get a good night's sleep for a change. I hope, too, that your men have learned a lesson, and that in the future, when I tell them that the underworld isn't about to swallow us all, they will have a little more faith.'

He smiled sheepishly. 'Yes, Prelate. I believed you, of course, but some of these men are more superstitious than is healthy for their hearts. Magic scares them.'

She leaned a little closer to the man and lowered her voice. 'It should.'

He cleared his throat. 'Yes, Prelate. Well, I guess we better all get some sleep.'

'Your messengers haven't returned yet, have they?'

'No.' He traced a finger down the lower part of the white scar running from his left temple to his jaw. 'I don't expect they've even reached Aydindril yet.'

Verna sighed. She wished she could have heard word first. It might have made her decision easier.

'I suppose not.'

'What do you think, Prelate? What's your advice? North?'

She stared off, watching the sparks from the fire spiral up into the darkness, and feeling its heat on her face. She had more important decisions to make.

'I don't know. Richard's exact words to me were, "Head north. There's an army of a hundred thousand D'Haran soldiers heading south looking for Kahlan. You'll have more protection with them, and they with you. Tell General Reibisch that she is safe with me." '

'It would have made things easier if he would have said for sure.'

'He didn't say for us to go north, back to Aydindril, but it was implied. I'm sure he thought that's what we would do. However, I take seriously your advice in matters such as this.'

He shrugged. 'I'm a soldier. I think like a soldier.'

Richard had gone to Tanimura to rescue Kahlan, and had managed to destroy the Palace of the Prophets, along with its vault of prophecies, before Emperor Jagang could capture it. Richard had said that he had to return to Aydindril at once, and that he didn't have time to explain, but only he and Kahlan had the magic required that would allow their immediate return. He said he couldn't take the rest of them. He had told her to go north to meet up with General Reibisch and his D'Haran army.

General Reibisch was reluctant to return north. He reasoned that with a force this large already this far south, it would be strategically advantageous to blunt an invasion of the New World before it could drive into the populous areas.

'General, I have no argument with your motives, but I fear that you underestimate the threat. From the information I've managed to gather, the Imperial Order's forces are large enough to crush even an army of this size without losing stride. I don't doubt your men's ability, but by sheer numbers alone the Order will swallow you whole.

'I understand your reasoning, but even with as many men as you have, it won't be enough, and then we wouldn't have them to lend their weight to a gathering of a larger force that might have a chance against the Order.'

The general smiled reassuringly. 'Prelate, what you say makes sense. I've listened to reasoned arguments like yours my whole career. The thing is, war isn't a reasonable pursuit. Sometimes, you simply have to take advantage of what the good spirits give you and throw yourself into the fray.'

'Sounds like a good way to be annihilated.'

'Well, I've been doing it a long time, and I'm still alive. Just because you choose to meet the enemy, that doesn't mean you have to stick your chin out and let him have a good swing at it.'

Verna squinted at the man. 'What have you in mind?'

'Seems to me that we're already here. Messengers can move a great deal faster than an army. I think we should move to a more secure location, one more defendable, and sit tight.'

'Where?'

'If we go east, into the high country of southern D'Hara, then we could be in a better position to react. I know the country there. If the Order tries to come up into the New

255

World through D'Hara, the easy way through the Kern River valley, then we are there to stop them. We can fight on more equal terms in tighter country like that. Just because you have more men, that doesn't mean you can use them all. A valley is only so wide.'

'What if they go more to the west as they move north, skirt the mountains and head up through the wilds?'

'Then we have this army to sweep in behind them when our other forces are sent south to meet them. The enemy would have to split their force and fight against us on two fronts. On top of that, it would limit their options by making it difficult for them to move freely.'

Verna considered his words. She had read of battles in the old books, and understood the sense of his strategy. It seemed more prudent than she had thought at first. The man was bold, but he was no fool.

'With our troops in a strategic location,' he went on, 'we can send messengers to Aydindril and the People's Palace in D'Hara. We can get reinforcements from D'Hara, and from the lands of the Midlands that join with us, and Lord Rahl can send us his instructions. If the Order invades, well, then, we're already here to know about it. Information is a valuable commodity in war.'

'Richard may not like it that you hunker down here, instead of returning to protect Aydindril.'

'Lord Rahl is a reasonable man –'

Verna interrupted with a guffaw. 'Richard, reasonable? Now you stretch my credulity, general.'

He frowned at her. 'As I was saying, Lord Rahl is a reasonable man. He told me that he wants me to speak up with my advice, when I think it important. I think it's important. He considers my advice on matters of war. The messengers are already on their way with my letter. If he doesn't like my advice, then he can say so and order me north and I will go; but until I know for sure that he wishes it, I think we should do our job and defend the New World from the Imperial Order.

'I asked your advice, Prelate, because you command magic. I don't know anything about magic. If you or the Sisters of the Light have something to say that would be important to us in our struggle, then I'm listening. We're on the same side, you know.'

Verna relented. 'Forgive me, general. I guess I sometimes forget that.' She offered him a smile. 'The last few months have turned my life upside down.'

'Lord Rahl has turned the whole world upside down. He has reordered everything.'

She smiled to herself. 'That he has.' She looked back at the general's grayish-green eyes. 'Your plan makes sense – at the very worst it would slow the Order, but I'd like to talk to Warren first. He … he sometimes has surprising insights. Wizards are like that.'

The general nodded. 'Magic is not my part. We have Lord Rahl for that. And you, too, of course.'

Verna repressed a laugh at the idea of Richard being the one to wield magic for them. The boy could hardly get out of his own way where magic was concerned.

No, that wasn't entirely true; Richard often did surprising things with his gift. The problem was that it usually surprised him, too. Still, he was a war wizard, the only to be born in the last three thousand years, and all their hopes hung on his leadership in this war against the Imperial Order.

Richard's heart, and his determination, were in the right place. He would do his best. It was up to the rest of them to help him, and to keep him alive.

The general shifted his weight and scratched under his chain-mail sleeve. 'Prelate, the Order claims to want to end magic in this world, but we all know that they use magic in their attempt to crush us.'

'That they do.'

She knew Emperor Jagang had most of the Sisters of the Dark at his beck and call. He had young wizards to do his bidding, too. He had also captured a number of the Sisters of the Light, and dominated them through his ability as a dream walker. It was this that nettled her conscience; as Prelate, it was ultimately up to her to see to the safety of the Sisters of the Light. Some of her Sisters were anything but safe in the hands of Jagang.

'Well, Prelate, seeing as how their troops are likely to be accompanied by those with magic, I'm wondering if I can count on you and your Sisters to be the counter to them. Lord Rahl said: "You'll have more protection with them, and they with you." That sounds to me like he intended you to use your magic to help us against the Order's army.'

Verna would like to think the general wrong. She would like to think that Sisters of the Light, those charged with doing the Creator's work, would be above bringing harm to anyone.

'General Reibisch, I don't like it; however, I'm afraid that I concur. If we lose this war, we all lose, not simply our troops on the field of battle; all free people will be slaves to the Order. If Jagang wins, the Sisters of the Light will be executed. We all must fight or die.

'The Order would not want to fall into your plans so conveniently. They may try to sneak past undetected – farther to the west, possibly even to the east of you. The Sisters can be of use in detecting the movements of the enemy, should they advance into the New World and try to slip past you.

'If those with magic mask the Order's movements from you, our Sisters will know it. We will be your eyes. If fighting comes, the enemy will use magic to try to defeat you. We will have to use our power to thwart that magic.'

The general considered the flames for a moment. He glanced off toward the men bedding down for the night.

'Thank you, Prelate. I know that decision can't be easy for you. Since you've all been with us, I've come to know the Sisters as gentle women.'

Verna barked a laugh. 'General, you have not come to know us at all. The Sisters of the Light are many things, but gentle is not one of them.' She flicked her wrist. Her dacra sprang into her hand. A dacra resembled a knife but had a sharpened rod instead of a blade.

Verna twirled the dacra. 'I have had to kill men before.' Reflected flashes of firelight sparkled and danced as she spun the weapon with graceful ease, walking it over her knuckles and back. 'I can assure you, general, I was anything but gentle.'

He lifted an eyebrow. 'A knife in talented hands, such as yours, is trouble, but it's hardly a match for the weapons of war.'

She smiled politely. 'This is a weapon possessing deadly

magic. If you see one of these coming for you, run. It only must penetrate your flesh – even if it's your little finger – and you will be dead before you can blink.'

He straightened, and his chest grew with a deep breath. 'Thanks for the warning. And thanks for your help, Prelate. I'm glad to have you on our side.'

'I regret that Jagang has some of our Sisters of the Light under his control. They can do the same as I, maybe more.' She gave him a reassuring pat on the shoulder when she saw that his face had paled. 'Good night, General Reibisch. Sleep well – the red moons are gone.'

Verna watched the general make a zigzag course through his officers, speaking with them, checking on his men, and issuing orders. After he had disappeared into the darkness, she turned to her tent.

Deep in thought, she idly cast her Han and lit the candles inside the small field tent the men had provided for her use. With the moon up, Annalina – the real Prelate – would be waiting.

Verna pried the little journey book from its secret pouch in her belt. Journey books had magic that allowed a message written in one to appear simultaneously in its twin. Prelate Annalina had the twin to Verna's. She sat cross-legged on her blankets and opened the book in her lap.

There was a message waiting. Verna pulled a candle closer and bent in the dim light to better see the writing in the journey book.

Verna, we have trouble here. We finally caught up with Nathan, at least who we thought was Nathan. The man we had been pursuing turned out not to be Nathan. Nathan tricked us. He is gone, and we don't know where he went.

Verna sighed. She had thought it had sounded too good to be true when Ann told her that they were closing in on the prophet.

Nathan left us a message. The message is more trouble than the thought of Nathan being on the loose. He said that he had important business – that one of 'our Sisters' was going to do something very stupid, and that he must stop her if he could. We have no idea where he went. He also confirmed what you told me Warren said, that the red moon means Jagang has

259

invoked a bound fork prophecy. Nathan said that Zedd and I must go to the Jocopo treasure, and that if we wasted time going after him instead, we would all die.

I believe him. Verna, we must talk. If you are there, reply. I will be waiting.

Verna pulled the stylus from the spine of the journey book. Moonrise was the time they had agreed upon to communicate through the journey books if they needed to. She bent closer and wrote in her book:

I am here, Ann. What happened? Are you all right?

In a moment, words began appearing in the book.

It's a long story, and I don't have time for it now, but Sister Roslyn was hunting Nathan, too. She was killed, along with at least eighteen innocent people. We can't be sure of the true number consumed in the light spell.

Verna's eyes widened at hearing that people were killed so. She wanted to ask what they were doing casting such a dangerous web, but decided not to ask as she read on.

First of all, Verna, we need to know if you have any idea what the 'Jocopo treasure' is. Nathan didn't explain.

Verna put a finger to her lips as she squeezed her eyes closed, trying to remember. She had heard the name before. She had been on her journey to the New World for twenty years, and she had heard of it there.

Ann, I think I recall hearing that the Jocopo were a people living somewhere in the wilds. If I recall correctly, they are all dead – exterminated in a war. I believe all traces of them were destroyed.

The wilds, you say. Verna, are you sure it was the wilds?

Yes.

Wait a moment while I tell Zedd this news.

The minutes dragged by as Verna watched the blank place at the end of the writing. At last, words began to appear.

Zedd has succumbed to a bout of loud cursing and arm flailing. He is swearing oaths about what he intends to do to Nathan. I am quite sure that he will find most of his intentions to be physically impossible. The Creator is humbling me for complaining to him that Nathan was incorrigible. I think I am being taught a lesson as to the true meaning of incorrigible.

Verna, the wilds are a big place. Any idea where in the wilds?

No. Sorry. I only recall hearing the Jocopo mentioned once. Somewhere in southern Kelton I once admired a pottery relic in a shop of curiosities. It was purported by the proprietor to have been made by a disappeared culture from the wilds. He called them the Jocopo. That's all I know. I was hunting Richard at the time, not vanished cultures. I will check with Warren. He might know something from the books.

Thank you, Verna. If you find anything, send word at once. Now, do you have any idea what stupid thing it is that Nathan thinks a Sister is going to do?

No. We are all here with the D'Haran army. General Reibisch wants to stay to the south so as to thwart the Order should they invade. We await word from Richard. But there are Sisters of Light being held captive by Jagang. Who can tell what he will make them do?

Ann, did Nathan say anything of the bound fork prophecy? Warren might be able to help if you would tell me the words of the prophecy.

There was a pause before Ann's writing began again.

Nathan didn't tell us the words. He said that the spirits denied him access to its meaning. He did say, though, that the victim of the double bind in the prophecy is Richard.

Verna gasped in some saliva. She coughed violently trying to get it back out of her lungs. Her eyes watering as she coughed, she held the book up and read the last message again. She finally got her lungs and throat clear.

Ann, you wrote 'Richard.' Did you really mean Richard?
Yes.

Verna closed her eyes with a whispered prayer, fighting down the flutter of panic.

Anything else? Verna wrote.

Not for now. Your information about the Jocopo will help. We will be able to narrow our search now, and know the questions to ask. Thank you. If you learn more, let me know. I had better go. Zedd is complaining of life-threatening hunger.

Ann, is everything all right with you and the First Wizard?
Ducky. He has his collar off.

*You took off his collar? Before you find Nathan? Why would
you do such a thing?*

I didn't. He did.

Verna's eyes widened at this news. She feared to ask how
he could accomplish such a thing, so she didn't. Verna thought
she could read in Ann's message that it was a sore subject.

And yet he is going with you?

*Verna, I am not quite sure who is going with whom, but for
now we both understand the dire nature of Nathan's warning.
Nathan isn't always irrational.*

*I know. No doubt that old man is right now smiling at a
woman, trying to make her swoon and fall into his bed.* Verna
wrote. *May the Creator hold you safely in his care, Prelate.*

Ann was really the Prelate, but had named Verna Prelate
when she and Nathan had faked their deaths and gone on an
important mission. For now, everyone thought Ann and
Nathan dead, and that Verna was Prelate.

*Thank you, Verna. One other thing. Zedd is concerned for
Adie. He wishes you to take her aside and let her know that he
is alive and well, but 'in the hands of a crazy woman.'*

*Ann, do you wish me to tell the Sisters that you are alive and
well?*

The message took a moment to resume.

*No, Verna. Not just now. It helps you, and them, that they
have you as Prelate. With what Nathan has told us, and what
we must do, it would be inadvisable to tell them that I live,
only to have to turn around and tell them that I am dead, after
all.*

Verna understood. The wilds were a dangerous place. That
was where Verna had had to kill people. And she hadn't been
trying to get information out of them; she had been trying to
avoid contact with people there. Verna had been young and
fast at the time. Ann was nearly as old as Nathan. But she was
a sorceress, and she did have a wizard with her. While Zedd
was not young, either, he was far from helpless. The fact that
he had managed to remove his Rada'Han spoke volumes about
his ability.

*Ann, don't say that. You be careful. You and Zedd must
protect each other. We all need you back.*

Thank you, child. Take care of the Sisters of the Light, Prelate. Who knows, I may want them back, someday.

Verna smiled at the comfort of consulting with Ann, and at her humor in dire circumstance. Verna wished she had a sense of humor like Ann. The smile faded when she remembered that Ann had told her that Richard was the victim named in the deadly prophecy.

She thought about what Nathan had warned, that one of the Sisters was going to do something stupid. She wished that Nathan had been more specific. He could mean almost anything by 'stupid.' Verna wouldn't be inclined to believe just anything Nathan said, but Ann knew him much better than did Verna.

She thought about the Sisters Jagang was holding. Some were Sisters of the Light, and a few were Verna's dear friends, and had been since they were novices. The five of them – Christabel, Amelia, Janet, Phoebe, and Verna – had grown up together at the palace.

Of those, Verna had named Phoebe one of her administrators. Only Phoebe was with them, now. Christabel, Verna's dearest friend, had turned to the Keeper of the Underworld; she had bcome a Sister of the Dark, and had been captured by Jagang. The last two of Verna's friends, Amelia and Janet, had been taken by Jagang, too. Janet had remained loyal to the Light, Verna knew, but she wasn't sure about Amelia. If she was still loyal ...

Verna pressed trembling fingers to her lips at the thought of her two friends, two Sisters of the Light, being slaves to the dream walker.

In the end, that decided her.

Verna peeked into Warren's tent. Unbidden, a smile came to her lips when she saw his shape on his blankets in the darkness, probably pondering some young prophet's thoughts. She smiled at how much she loved him, and at knowing how much he loved her.

Verna and Warren, having both grown up at the Palace of the Prophets, had known each other nearly their whole lives. Her gift as a sorceress was destined to be used to help train young wizards, while his gift as a wizard destined him toward prophecy.

Their paths didn't cross in a serious way until after Verna returned to the palace with Richard. Because of Richard and his huge impact on life at the palace, events brought Verna and Warren together, and their friendship grew. After Verna was named Prelate, during their struggle against the Sisters of the Dark, she and Warren had depended on each other for their very lives. It was during that struggle that they had become more than friends. After all those years in the palace, only now had they really found each other, and found love.

At the thought of what she had to tell him, her smile faded.

'Warren,' she whispered, 'are you awake?'

'Yes,' came a quiet reply.

Before he could have a chance to rise and take her into his arms and she lost her nerve, she stepped into his tent and blurted it out.

'Warren, I've made my decision. I'll have no argument from you. Do you understand? This is too important.' He was silent, so she went on. 'Amelia and Janet are my friends. Besides being Sisters of the Light in enemy hands, I love them. They would do the same for me, I know they would. I'm going after them, and any others I can rescue.'

'I know,' he whispered.

He knew. What did that mean? Silence dragged on in the darkness. Verna frowned. It wasn't like Warren not to argue about such a thing. She had been ready for his argument, but not his calm acceptance.

Using her Han, the force of life and spirit through which the magic of the gift worked, Verna lit a flame in her palm and passed it to a candle. He was huddled on his blanket, his knees pulled up and his head resting in his hands.

She knelt down before him. 'Warren? What's wrong?'

His face came up. His blue eyes were rimmed with red. His face was sickly pale.

Verna clutched his arm. 'Warren, you don't look well. What's wrong?'

'Verna,' he whispered, 'I have come to realize that being a prophet is not the wonder I had imagined.'

Warren was the same age as Verna, but looked younger

because he had remained at the Palace of the Prophets, under its spell that retarded aging, while she went on her twenty-odd-year journey to find Richard. Warren didn't look so young at the moment.

Warren had only recently had his first vision as a prophet. He had told her that the prophecy came as a vision of events, accompanied by words of the prophecy. The words were what were written down, but it was the vision that was the true prophecy. That was why it took a prophet to truly understand the meaning of the words; they invoked the vision that was being passed on from another prophet.

Hardly anyone knew this; everyone tried to understand prophecy by the words. Verna now knew, from what Warren had told her, that this method was inadequate at best and dangerous at worst. Prophecy was meant to be read by other prophets.

She frowned. 'Have you had a vision? Another prophecy?'

Warren ignored the question, and asked one of his own.

'Verna, do we have any Rada'Han with us?'

'The collars around the young men who escaped with us are the only ones. We didn't have time to bring any extras. Why?'

He put his head back in his hands.

Verna shook a finger at him. 'Warren, if this is some trick to try to get me to stay here with you, it won't work. Do you hear me? It won't work. I'm going, and I'm going alone. That's final.'

'Verna,' he whispered, 'I have to go with you.'

'No. It's too dangerous. I love you too much. I won't risk anyone else. If I have to, I will order you, as Prelate, to stay here. I will, Warren.'

His head rose again. 'Verna, I'm dying.'

Icy goose bumps tingled across her arms and thighs.

'What? Warren –'

'I'm having the headaches. The headaches from the gift.'

Verna was choked silent with the realization of the deadly nature of what he had just said.

The whole reason the Sisters of the Light took boys born with the gift was to save their lives. Unless schooled, the gift could kill him. The headaches were a manifestation of the fatal nature of the gift going awry. Besides providing the Sisters with control over the young wizards, the most important function of the collar was its magic, which protected the life of the boy until he could learn to control his gift.

Because of all that had happened, Verna had taken Warren's collar off long before it was customary.

'But, Warren, you've studied a long time. You know how to control your gift. You shouldn't need the Rada'Han for protection any longer.'

'If I was an ordinary wizard, that may be true, but my gift is for prophecy. Nathan was the only prophet at the palace in centuries. We don't know how the magic works in a prophet. I only recently had my first prophecy. It signifies a new level of my ability. Now, I'm having the headaches.'

Verna was suddenly in a panic. Her eyes were tearing. She threw her arms around him.

'Warren, I'll stay. I won't go. I'll help you. We'll do something. Maybe we could take a collar off one of the boys and you could share it. That might work. We'll try that first.'

His arms pulled her tight. 'That won't work, Verna.'

A sudden thought flashed into her mind, making her gasp with relief. It was so simple.

'Warren, it's all right. It is. I just realized what we can do. Listen to me.'

'Verna, I know what –'

She shushed him. She held him by the shoulders and looked into his blue eyes. She brushed back his wavy blond hair. 'Warren, listen. It's simple. The reason the Sisters were founded was to help boys born with the gift. We were given Rada'Han to protect them while we teach them to control their gift.'

'Verna, I know all that, but –'

'Listen. We have the collars to help them because we don't have wizards who can do what is needed. In the past, greedy wizards refused to help those born with the gift. An experienced wizard can join with your mind and pass on the protection – show you how to put the gift right. It's simple for a wizard to do, but not a sorceress. We need only to visit a wizard.'

Verna pried the journey book from her belt and held it before his eyes. 'We have a wizard – Zedd. All we have to do is talk to Ann, and have her and Zedd meet us. Zedd can help you, and then you'll be all right.'

Warren stared into her eyes. 'Verna, it won't work.'

'Don't say that. You don't know. You don't know, Warren.'

'Yes I do. I have had another prophecy.'

Verna sat back on her heels. 'You have? What was it?'

Warren pressed his fingertips to his temples. She could see that he was in pain. She knew that the pain of the headaches from the gift were excruciating. In the end, if not corrected, they were fatal.

'Verna, now you listen to me for a change. I have had a prophecy. The words aren't important. The meaning is.' He took his hands away from his head and looked her in the eye. In that moment, he looked very old to her. 'You must do what you plan, and go after the Sisters. The prophecy didn't say whether you will succeed, but I must go with you. If I do anything else, I will die. It's a forked prophecy – an "either-or" prophecy.'

She cleared her throat. 'But ... surely, there must be something ...'

'No. If I stay, or if I try to go to Zedd, I will die. The prophecy doesn't say that if I go with you I will live, but it does say that going with you is my only chance. End of discussion. If you make me stay, I will die. If you try to take me to Zedd, I will die. If you want me to have a chance to live, then you must take me with you. Choose, Prelate.'

Verna swallowed. As a Sister of the Light, a sorceress, she could tell by the distinctive murky cast to his eyes that he was in the pain of a headache from the gift. She also knew that Warren would not lie to her about a prophecy. He might pull some trick to go with her, but he would not lie about a prophecy.

He was a prophet. Prophecy was his life. Maybe his death.

She took his hand up in hers. 'Get some supplies together. Get two horses. I have to go tell Adie something, and then I must talk to my advisors, let them know what to do while we're gone.'

Verna kissed his hand. 'I won't let you die, Warren. I love

you too much. We'll do this together. I'm not sleepy. Let's not wait till morning. We can be on our way in an hour.'

Warren drew her to him in a thankful embrace.

CHAPTER 24

From the solace of the shadows, he watched as the middle-aged man closed the door and stood in the dim hall a moment to tuck in his shirt over his potbelly. The man chortled to himself and then thumped off down the hall to disappear as he descended the stairs.

It was late. It would be several hours yet before the sun was up. With the walls painted red, the candles set before silvered reflectors at either end of the narrow hall were able to provide precious little useful light. He liked it that way – the way the comforting cloak of shadows in the pit of the night lent its mood to such nefarious needs.

Debauchery was best indulged in the night. In the darkness.

He stood awhile in the quiet obscurity of the hall, savoring his desire. It had been too long. He let his lust have rein, and felt its glorious, wanton ache fill him.

He closed his mouth and breathed through his nose to better experience the range of aromas, both transcendent and abiding. He put his shoulders back and used his abdominal muscles to draw slower, deeper breaths.

He counted a variety of scents, from the smells men carried in and took away with them back to their own lives, the smells of their work – horse, clay, grain dust, the lanolin soldiers used in the care of leather uniforms, and the oil they used for sharpening their weapons, to a redolent wisp of almond oil, and the stale dirt and wet wood of the building.

It was an afferent feast that was only just beginning.

He glanced the length of the hall again, checking. He heard

no sounds of lust coming from any of the other rooms. It was late, even for an establishment like this. The fat, potbellied man was probably the last of them, except for himself.

He liked to be last. The evidence of the events before he arrived, and the lingering smells, gave him a rush of sensation. His senses were always heightened in his aroused state, and he valued all the details.

He closed his eyes for a moment, feeling the throbbing of his need. She would help him. She would sate his desire; that was what they were here for. They offered themselves willingly.

Other men, like the potbellied man, simply threw themselves on a woman, grunted in a moment of satisfaction, and it was over. They never gave thought to what the woman was feeling, to what she needed, to giving her satisfaction. Those men were no more than rutting beasts, ignorant of all the details that could add to the climax for both. Their mind's eye was too focused on the object of their lust; they didn't see the integral parts of the wider setting that led to true satisfaction.

It was the fleeting, the ephemeral, that created a transcendent experience. Through uncommon perception, and his singular awareness, he could net such evanescent events and commemorate them forever in his memory, thus giving the transient nature of satisfaction permanence.

He felt fortunate that he could see such things, and that he, at least, could bring fulfillment to women.

At last, he took a settling breath and then advanced silently down the hall, marking the way the shadows and tiny rays of light mirrored off the silvered candle reflectors slipped across his body. He thought that if he was mindful, he might someday be able to feel the touch of the light, and of the dark.

Without knocking, he opened the door the potbellied man had come from and stepped into her room, gratified to see that it was nearly as dim as the hall. With a finger, he shut the door.

Behind the door, the woman was just pulling her panties up her legs. She spread her knees and squatted a bit, drawing them up tight against herself. When her sky-blue eyes finally turned up to look at him, her only reaction was to toss the sides of her robe together over the rest of her bare body and casually flip the silk belt together into a loose knot.

The air carried the odor of the hot coals in the warming pan under the bed, the weak but clean aroma of soap, the light fragrance of body powder, and the cloying scent of a sickly sweet perfume. But pervading it all, like the darkness that shaped shadows, was the lingering smack of lust, pointed with the arresting scent of semen.

The room had no windows. The bed, covered with stained, rumpled sheets, was pushed into the far corner. Even though it wasn't large, the bed took up a good part of the room. Against the wall, beside the head of the bed, sat a small, simply made pine chest, probably for personal items. On the wall over the head of the bed hung an ink drawing of two people coupled in passion. It left nothing to the imagination.

A washbasin sat centered on a wobbly-looking cabinet beside her, behind the door. In its edge, the white washbasin had a stained, kidney-shaped chip, with a crack that looked like an artery coming from the kidney. The cloth hanging over the side of the basin still dripped. The milky water in the basin gently sloshed from side to side. She had just washed herself.

They each had their own habits. Some didn't bother to wash, but they were usually the older, unattractive ones who were paid little, and cared little. He had noticed that the younger, prettier, more expensive women washed after each man. He preferred the ones who washed before he came to them, but in the end, his lust overrode such trivial matters.

He idly wondered if those he had been with who were not professionals ever gave thought to such things. Probably not. He doubted that others pondered such curious particulars. Others gave little thought to the texture of details.

Other women, women looking for love, satisfied him, but not in the same way. They always wanted to talk, and to be wooed. They wanted. He wanted. In the end, his want overrode what he would prefer, and he gave them some of what they wanted before his needs could be satisfied.

'I thought I was finished for the night,' she said. Her words came out silky smooth, with a pleasant, pert lilt, but bore no real interest at the prospect of another man this late.

'I think I'm the last,' he said, trying to sound apologetic so as not to anger her. It wasn't as satisfying if they were angry. He liked nothing more than when they were eager to please.

271

She sighed. 'All right, then.'

She showed no fear at having a man simply walk into her room without knocking, even though she was hardly wearing anything, nor did she make any demands for money. Silas Latherton, downstairs, with his cudgel and a long knife in his belt, made sure the women had nothing to fear. He also didn't let anyone go up the stairs unless they paid in advance, so the women didn't have to be bothered with the trouble of collecting money. It insured that he, rather than they, kept control of the income, and its distribution.

Her short, straight blond hair was disheveled, from mister potbelly, no doubt, but he found its disorder alluring. It was a suggestive indication of what she had just been doing. It lent her an erotic look – a look he very much liked.

Her body was shapely and firm, with long legs and wonderfully formed breasts, at least what he had seen of her body before she had thrown closed her robe. He would see it again, and could wait.

The anticipation added to his excitement. Unlike her other men, he was in no rush to have it over. Once it began, it would be over all too quickly. He could never stop himself, once it began. For the moment, he would relish all the little details, so that he could capture them in his memory for all time.

She was more than simply pretty, he decided. She was a creature possessed of features that would fire men's minds with obsessive memories of her, and make them return time and time again to try, if only for fleeting moments, to possess her. The confidence with which she carried her body told him that she knew this. The frequency with which men spent money to have her was a constant reinforcement of that confidence.

Those features, though, no matter their grace and haunting beauty, had an acidic edge to them, a harshness that betrayed her true character. No doubt other men saw only the sweet face and never noticed.

He noticed. He noticed such subtle things, and he had seen this detail often. It always looked the same. It was a baseness her fair features couldn't hide from one such as himself.

'Are you new?' he asked, even though he knew she was.

'First day here,' she said. He knew that, too. 'Aydindril is big enough to mean clients for me, but with a huge army here, it's all the better. Blue eyes around here aren't all that common; my blue eyes remind the D'Haran soldiers of girls from home. So many extra men mean women like me are in greater demand.'

'And it insures a better wage.'

She allowed herself a small, smug, knowing smile. 'If you couldn't afford it, you wouldn't be up here, so cut the complaints.'

He had only meant to make an observation, and regretted the way she took it. Her voice betrayed an underlying, acerbic temperament. He sought to smooth away the ripple of her displeasure with him.

'Soldiers can sometimes get rough with a young woman as attractive as you.' The compliment didn't register in her sky-blue eyes. She had probably heard it so often that she was numb to such praise. 'I'm glad you came to Silas Latherton,' he went on. 'He doesn't let any of his clients rough up the young ladies. You'll be safe, here, under his roof. I'm glad you came here.'

'Thanks.' Her tone carried no warmth, but the ripple, at least, had been smoothed. 'I'm glad to hear his reputation is known to his clients. I got slammed around, once. I didn't like it. Besides the pain, I couldn't work for a month.'

'That must have been terrible. The pain, I mean.'

She tilted her head toward the bed. 'You going to take off your clothes, or what?'

He said nothing, but gestured to her robe. He watched her slip loose the knot from the satin belt.

'Have it your way,' she said, as she shrugged the robe open just enough to tempt him into getting on with it.

'I'd like … I'd like you to enjoy it, too.'

She lifted an eyebrow. 'Darling, don't you worry about me. I'll enjoy it just fine. You'll no doubt thrill me. But you're the one who paid for it. Let's just worry about your pleasure.'

He liked to hear the tempered thread of sarcasm in her voice. She cloaked it well with a breathy tone, and others might have missed it, but he had been listening for it.

Carefully, slowly, one at a time, he placed four small gold coins on the washstand beside her. It was ten times what Silas

Latherton, downstairs, charged for his women's company, and probably thirty times what he gave her for each man. She watched the coins as he withdrew his hand, as if counting them to herself to make sure she was seeing what she thought she was seeing. It was a great deal of money.

She gave him a questioning look.

He liked the twitch of confusion in her eyes. Women like this weren't often confused by money, but she was young, and probably never had a man bestow such largess on her before. He liked it that it impressed her. He knew that few things would.

'I'd like you to enjoy yourself. I'm willing to pay to see you enjoying yourself.'

'Darling, for that much, you'll remember my screams until you're an old man.'

Of that, he was sure.

She smiled her best smile, and slipped off the robe. Gazing at him with her big, sky-blue eyes, she blindly hung the robe on a peg in the back of the door.

She stroked his chest and then circled her arms around his waist. Gently but deliberately, she squashed her firm breasts against him.

'So what is it you want, darling? Some nice clawmarks down your back to make your young lady jealous?'

'No,' he said. 'No, I just want to see you enjoying it. You're so fair of face and figure. I think that if you're paid well enough, you'll enjoy your part, that's all. I want to know that you're enjoying yourself.'

She eyed the coins and then smiled up at him. 'Oh, I will, darling. I promise. I'm a very talented whore.'

'That was what I was hoping.'

'I want you to be so pleased with my charms that you will want to return to my bed.'

'You seem to be reading my mind.'

'My name is Rose,' she whispered in her breathy voice.

'A name as beautiful as you are.' And as unoriginal.

'And yours? What should I call you when you call on me regularly, as I'm already aching for you to do?'

'I like the name you've already given me. I like the sound of it on your lips.'

274

She licked her lips for him. 'Glad to meet you, darling.'

He slipped a finger under the waist of her panties.

'Can I have these?'

She ran her fingers down his belly, performing a moan at the feel of him.

'It's the end of a long day. These aren't exactly … clean. I have some clean ones in my trunk. For what you've paid, you can have as many of them as you wish. Darling, you can have them all, if you wish.'

'These will do fine. I only need these.'

She smirked up at him. 'I see. Like that, is it?'

He didn't answer.

'Why don't you take them off me,' she teased. 'Take your prize.'

'I'd like to watch you do it.'

Without hesitation, she slipped them down her legs as dramatically as she could. She pressed herself up against him again and, looking into his eyes, stroked his cheek with her panties. She smiled wickedly and then pushed them into his hand.

'Here you go. Just for you, darling. Just the way you like them – with the scent of Rose.'

He worked them in his fingers, feeling the warmth of her still in them. She stretched up to kiss him. If he hadn't known better, known what she was, he might have thought she wanted him more than anything else in life. But he would please her.

'What do you want me to do for you?' she whispered. 'Name it, and it's yours – and I don't make that offer to my other men. But I want you so badly. Anything. Just tell me.'

He could smell the sweat of the other men on her. He could smell the stink of their lust on her.

'Let's just see how things work out, shall we, Rose?'

'Anything you say, darling.' She smiled dreamily. 'Anything.'

She winked at him as she swept the four gold coins from the washstand. She swayed provocatively as she went to the small trunk. She squatted down before it. He had been wondering if she would squat, or bend at the waist. He was satisfied at the detail, at the remnant of a demure past.

As she pushed the coins under some of her clothes in the

chest, he saw atop her things a small pillow decorated with a dash of red. Such a detail intrigued him. It seemed out of place.

'What's that?' he asked, knowing that the money had earned her indulgence.

She held it up for him to see. It was a small pillow, an item of decoration, a frivolity. It had a red rose embroidered on it.

'I made it, when I was younger. I stuffed it with cedar shaving, so it would smell nice.' She glided her fingers lovingly over the rose. 'My namesake – a rose. For Rosa. My father named me. He was from Nicobarese. *Rosa* means "rose" in his language. He always called me his little Rosa, and said that I grew in the garden of his heart.'

The detail astonished him. He was thrilled to know something so intimate about her. He felt as if he already possessed her. The pleasure of knowing such a small, seemingly insignificant thing pounded through his veins.

As he watched her replace the little packet of her past into her trunk, he wondered at her father, wondered if he knew where she was, or if perhaps he had sent her away in revulsion, his rose wilted in his heart. He imagined an angry scene. He wondered at her mother – if her mother understood her choice in life, or cried at a daughter lost.

Now he, too, was playing a part in who she was, in her life.

'May I call you Rosa?' he asked, as she closed the lid of her trunk. 'It's such a lovely name.'

She looked back over her shoulder. Her eyes watched his fingers working her underpants into a tight ball.

She returned to him, smiling as she came. 'You're my special man, now. I've never told another man my true name. It would give me pleasure to hear my given name on your lips.'

His heart pounded, and he swayed on his feet with his need. 'Thank you, Rosa,' he whispered, and he truly meant it. 'I want so much to please you.'

'Your hands are trembling.'

They always did, until he started. Then, they were rock steady. Once he started, he would be steady. It was just the anticipation.

'I'm sorry.'

A throaty, lusty laugh came from deep in her throat. 'Don't be. It excites me that you would be nervous.'

He wasn't nervous, not in the least, but he was excited.

Her hands found that he was. 'I want to taste you.' She licked his ear. 'I have no one else tonight. We have all the time we want to enjoy this.'

'I know,' he whispered back. 'That's why I wanted to be last.'

'Yes,' she teased, 'I want it to last, too. Can you make it last, darling?'

'I can, and I will,' he promised. 'A long time.'

She let out a purr of satisfaction at his promise, and turned in his arms, pressing her bottom against him. She arched her back and rocked her head against his chest as she moaned again. He kept the smirk from his face as he looked down into her sky-blue eyes.

Yes, she was a talented whore.

He slid his hand down her lower spine, counting her vertebrae, fingering the spaces between them. She moaned urgently at his touch.

Because of the way she swayed her bottom, he missed the spot he wanted.

She staggered.

The second time he slammed the knife into her lower back, he hit the right spot, between the vertebrae, severing her spinal cord.

He swept an arm around her middle to hold her up. The shocked, grunting moan was real, this time. Anyone in the other rooms wouldn't think it any different from the sounds she regularly made for men. Others didn't notice such details.

He did, and savored the difference.

As her mouth widened to scream, he stuffed it full with the wadded ball of her dirty underpants. He timed it just right, so only the cry of the gasp sounded, before the pitch rose. He yanked the silk tie from her robe on the peg beside him and whirled it around her head four times to hold the gag in her mouth. With one hand, and the aid of his teeth, he drew it tight and knotted it.

He would have liked to have listened to her heartfelt screams, but that would bring a premature end to their pleasure. He loved the screams, the cries. They were always sincere.

He pressed his mouth against the side of her head. He could smell the sweat of men in her hair.

'Oh, Rosa, you are going to please me so. You are going to give me more pleasure than you've ever given any man before. I want you to enjoy it, too. I know this is what you always wanted. I'm the man you've been waiting for. I've come at last.'

He let her slip to the floor. Her legs were useless, now. She wasn't going anywhere.

She tried to punch him between his legs. He caught her dainty little fist in his hand. He watched her wide, sky-blue eyes as he pressed open her fist. He held her palm between his thumb and a finger, and bent it down until the bones in her wrist snapped.

He used the arms of her robe to bind her hands, so that she couldn't pull the gag from her mouth. His heart hammered as he listened to her muffled wails. He couldn't understand the words against the gag, but they heightened his excitement because he could feel their pain.

A storm of emotion rampaged through his mind. At least the voices were silent, for now, leaving him to his lust. He wasn't sure what the voices were, but he was sure that he was only able to hear them because of his singular intellect; he was able to seine such evanescent messages from the ethers because of his incomparable perception, and because he minded the details.

Tears flooded down her face. Her perfectly plucked brows bunched together, lifting in the middle, furrowing the skin on her forehead into neat rows. He counted them, because he was special.

With wide, anguished, sky-blue eyes, she watched as he removed his clothes and set them aside. It wouldn't do to have them soaked in blood.

The knife was rock steady in his hand now. He stood above her, naked and erect, to show her what a good job she was doing for him, so far.

And then he began.

CHAPTER 25

Kahlan, with Cara following behind, came to the door of the small room Richard used as an office at the same time as a young woman with short, black hair arrived carrying a small silver tray with hot tea. Raina, standing guard beside the door along with Ulic and Egan, yawned.

'Richard ask for tea, Sarah?'

The young woman curtsied, as best she could holding the tray. 'Yes, Mother Confessor.'

Kahlan lifted the tray from the woman's hands. 'That's all right, Sarah. I'm going in – I'll take it in to him.'

Sarah blushed, trying to hold on to the tray. 'But, Mother Confessor, you shouldn't have to do that.'

'Don't be silly. I'm perfectly capable of carrying a tray for ten feet.'

Kahlan backed away a step, gaining full possession of the tray. Sarah didn't know what to do with her hands, so she bowed.

'Yes, Mother Confessor,' she said before departing. Rather than being pleased to have been relieved of a small task, she looked as if she had just been ambushed and robbed. Sarah, like most of the staff, was fiercely vigilant about her duties.

'Has he been up long?' Kahlan asked Raina.

Raina gave her a sullen look. 'Yes. All night. I finally left a squad of guards and went to bed. He had Berdine up with him all night, too.'

The reason, no doubt, for the sullen look.

'I'm sure it was important, but I'll see if I can't get him to stop at night for some sleep, or at least let Berdine get hers.'

'I would appreciate it,' Cara muttered. 'Raina gets grumpy when Berdine doesn't come to bed.'

'Berdine needs her sleep,' Raina said defensively.

'I'm sure it was important, Raina, but you're right; if people don't get enough sleep, they won't be any good to him. I'll remind him – he sometimes gets lost in what he's doing and forgets about what other people need.'

Raina's dark eyes brightened. 'Thank you, Mother Confessor.'

Kahlan balanced the tray in one hand as she opened the door. Cara took up station beside Raina, peering after Kahlan, to make sure she didn't have any trouble with the tray, and then closed the door.

Richard had his back to her as he stared out the window. A low fire in the hearth did a poor job banishing the chill from the room.

Kahlan smirked to herself. She would put the lie to his boast. Before she had a chance to set the tray on the table, and let the cup *ping* against the pot to catch his attention and make him think it was the serving woman, Richard spoke without turning.

'Kahlan, good, I'm glad you came.'

Frowning, she set down the tray.

'You have your back to the door. How could you know it was me, and not the woman bringing the tea you ordered?'

Richard turned around with a puzzled look. 'Why would I think it was the woman with the tea, when it was you bringing it in?' He truly looked bewildered by her question.

'I swear, Richard, sometimes you give me the shivers.'

She decided that he had to have seen her reflection in the window.

He lifted her chin with a finger and kissed her. 'I'm glad to see you. It's been lonely without you.'

'Sleep well?'

'Sleep? I … I guess not. But at least the riots seem to have ceased. I don't know what we would have done if the moon had risen red again. I can't believe people would go wild simply because of something like that.'

'You have to admit that it was odd … frightening.'

'I do, but that didn't make me want to run screaming through the streets breaking windows and setting fires.'

'That's because you're Lord Rahl, and you have more sense.'

'I'll have some order, too. I'll not have people doing that kind of damage, to say nothing of injuring innocent people. The next time it happens I'm going to have the soldiers put it down immediately, rather than wait, hoping people will be suddenly stricken with reason. I have more important matters to worry about than childish reactions to superstition.'

Kahlan could tell by his smoldering tone that he was on the verge of losing his temper.

His eyes were bleary. She knew that if a person didn't get enough sleep, forbearance could quickly evaporate. One night was one thing, but three in a row was quite another. She hoped it wasn't affecting his judgment.

'More important matters. You mean your work with Berdine?'

He nodded. Kahlan poured a cup of tea and held it out to him. He stared at the cup a moment before taking it.

'Richard, you have to let the poor woman get more sleep. She'll be no good to you if you don't let her have enough sleep.'

He took a sip. 'I know.' He turned to the window and yawned. 'I had to send her over to my room to take a nap. She was making mistakes.'

'Richard, you need to get some sleep, too.'

He stared out the window toward the massive stone walls of the Wizard's Keep up on the mountain. 'I think I may have found out what the red moon meant.'

The somber quality in his voice gave her pause.

'What?' she finally asked.

He turned to the table and set down the cup. 'I had Berdine looking for places where Kolo used the word *moss,* or maybe mentioned a red moon, hoping that we might find something to help us.'

He flipped open the journal on the table. He had found the journal up in the Keep, where it had been sealed in for three thousand years, along with the man who had written it. Kolo had been keeping watch over the sliph, the strange creature that could take some people great distances, when the towers separating the Old and New Worlds were completed. When the towers were activated, Kolo had been sealed in, trapped, and had died there.

The journal had already proven an invaluable source of information, but it was written in High D'Haran, which complicated matters. Berdine understood High D'Haran, but not such an ancient form of it. They had to use another book written in almost the same ancient form of High D'Haran to aid them. Richard's childhood memory of that book's story helped Berdine to translate words, which they used as a cross reference in order to work out the translation of the journal.

As they went along, Richard was learning much of both the vernacular High D'Haran and also the much older, argot form, but it was still frustratingly slow going.

After Richard had brought Kahlan back to Aydindril, he told her how he had used the information in the book to find a way to rescue her. He said that sometimes he could seem to read with ease, but then at other places he and Berdine became bogged down. He said that at times he was able to unravel a page in a few hours, and then they would spend a whole day trying to translate one sentence.

'*Moss?* You said you had her checking for the word *moss*. What's that mean?'

He took a sip of tea and set the cup back down. '*Moss?* Oh, it means "wind" in High D'Haran.' He opened the pages to a marker. 'Since it was taking so much time to translate the journal, we've just been looking for key words, and then concentrating on those passages, hoping to get lucky.'

'I thought you said that you were translating it in order, to better understand the way Kolo uses the language.'

He sighed in annoyance. 'Kahlan, I don't have the time for that. We had to change our tactics.'

Kahlan didn't like the sound of that.

'Richard, I was told that your brother is the High Priest of an Order called the *Raug'Moss*. Is that High D'Haran?'

'Means "Divine Wind," ' he muttered.

He tapped the book, not seeming to want to discuss it. 'See here? Berdine found where Kolo was talking about a red moon. He was really upset about it. The whole Keep was in an uproar. He writes that they were betrayed by the "team." He said that the team was to be put on trial for their crimes. We haven't had time to look into that, yet. But ...'

Richard flipped the book back toward the front where one of their written translations was inserted, and read her the passage:

' "Today, one of our most coveted desires, possible only through the brilliant, tireless work of a team of near to one hundred, has been accomplished. The items most feared lost, should we be overrun, have been protected. A cheer went up from all in the Keep when we received word today that we were successful. Some thought it was not possible, but to the astonishment of all, it is done: The Temple of the Winds is gone." '

'Gone?' Kahlan asked. 'What's the Temple of the Winds? Where did it go?'

Richard shut the book. 'I don't know. But later in the journal, Kolo says that this team who had done it had betrayed them all. High D'Haran is an odd language. Words have different meanings depending on how they're used.'

'Most languages are that way. Our own is.'

'Yes, but sometimes, in High D'Haran, a word that ordinarily has different meanings according to its usage is intended to have multiple meanings. You can't have one meaning without all the rest. That makes translating it all the more difficult.

'For example, in the old prophecy that names me the bringer of death, the word "death" means three different things, depending on how it's used: the bringer of the underworld, the world of the dead; the bringer of spirits, spirits of the dead; and the bringer of death, meaning to kill. Each meaning is different, but all three were intended. That was the key.

'The prophecy was in the book we brought with us from the Palace of the Prophets. Warren was only able to translate the prophecy after I told him that all three meanings were true. He told me that because of that, he was the first in thousands of years to know the true meaning of the prophecy, as it was written.'

'What does this have to do with the Temple of the Winds?'

'When Kolo says "winds," I think that he sometimes just means the wind, like when you say that the wind is blowing today, but sometimes when he says "winds," I think he means the Temple of the Winds. I think he used it as a short way of referring to the Temple of the Winds, and at the same time as a way to differentiate it from other temples.'

Kahlan blinked. 'Are you saying that you think Shota's message, that the wind hunts you, means that the Temple of the Winds is really somehow hunting you?'

'I don't know, for sure.'

'Richard, that's a pretty big leap of reasoning, if that's what you're really thinking – to take Kolo's short way of referring to the Temple of the Winds and infer that Shota is talking about the same place.'

'When Kolo talks about how everyone was in an uproar, and these men were to be put on trial, he makes it sound as if the winds have a sense of perception.'

Kahlan cleared her throat this time. 'Richard, are you trying to tell me that Kolo claims that this place, the Temple of the Winds, is sentient?'

She wondered how long it had been since he had gotten any sleep. She wondered if he was thinking clearly.

'I said I wasn't sure.'

'But that's what you mean.'

'Well, it sounds … absurd, when you say it like that. It doesn't sound the same when you read it in High D'Haran. I don't know how to explain the difference, but there is one. Maybe it's just a difference of degree.'

'Difference of degree or not, how can a place have a sense of perception? Be sentient?'

Richard sighed. 'I don't know. I've been trying to figure that out myself. Why do you think I've been up all night?'

'But such a thing is not possible.'

His defiant gray eyes turned to her. 'The Wizard's Keep is just a place, but it knows when someone violates it. It reacts to that violation by stopping the person, even killing them if it must, to prevent an unauthorized person from entering a place they don't belong.'

Kahlan made a face. 'Richard, that's the shields. Wizards placed those shields to protect important or dangerous things from being stolen, or to prevent people from going where they could be hurt.'

'But they react without anyone having to tell them to, don't they?'

'So does a leg-hold trap. That doesn't make them sentient. You mean that the Temple of the Winds is protected by shields. That's all you're saying, then – that it has shields.'

'Yes, and no. It's more than simply shields. Shields only ward. The way Kolo talks about it makes it sound like the Temple of the Winds can ... I don't know, like it can think, like it can decide things when it must.'

'Decide things. Like what?'

'When he wrote how everyone was in a panic about the red moon, that was when he said that the team who had sent the Temple of the Winds away had betrayed them.'

'So ... what?'

'So I think that the Temple of the Winds made the moon turn red.'

Kahlan watched his eyes, transfixed by the look of conviction in them. 'I won't even ask how such a thing would be possible, but for the moment, let's just say you're right. Why would the Temple of the Winds make the moon turn red?'

Richard held her gaze. 'As a warning.'

'Of what?'

'The shields in the Keep react by warding. Almost no one can pass through them. I can, because I have the right kind of magic. If someone who wants to do harm has enough magic, and knowledge, they too can get by the shields. What happens, then?'

'Well, nothing. They get through.'

'Exactly. I think the Temple of the Winds can do more. I think it can know if someone has violated its defenses, and send a warning.'

'The red moon,' she whispered.

'It makes sense.'

She put a hand tenderly to his arm. 'Richard, you need to get some rest. You can't infer all this from Kolo's journal alone. It was just one journal, written a long time ago.'

He yanked his arm away. 'I don't know where else to look.

Shota said the wind was hunting me! I don't need to go to sleep to have nightmares.'

In that instant, Kahlan knew that it wasn't Shota's message that was driving him. It was the prophecy down in the pit.

The first part of the prophecy said: *On the red moon will come the firestorm.*

It was the second part that truly terrified her.

To quench the inferno, he must seek the remedy in the wind. Lightning will find him on that path, for the one in white, his true beloved, will betray him in her blood.

She realized that the prophecy frightened him more than he had admitted.

Someone knocked at the door.

'What!' Richard yelled.

Cara opened the door and poked her head in. 'General Kerson would like to see you, Lord Rahl.'

Richard raked his fingers back through his hair. 'Send him in, please, Cara.'

Richard put a hand to Kahlan's shoulder as he stared off toward the window. 'I'm sorry,' he whispered. 'You're right. I need some sleep. Maybe Nadine can give me some of her herbs to put me to sleep. My mind doesn't seem to want to allow it when I try.'

She would sooner let Shota give him something. Kahlan answered with a tender touch, fearing to test her voice at that moment.

General Kerson, wearing a wide grin, marched into the room. He saluted with a fist over his heart before coming to a halt.

'Lord Rahl. Good morning. And a good morning it is, thanks to you.'

Richard took a sip of his tea. 'Why's that?'

The general slapped Richard on the shoulder. 'The men are all better. The things you ordered – the garlic, blueberries, quench oak tea – it worked. They're all well again. I've got a whole army of bright-eyed men who're ready and able to do as ordered. I can't tell you how relieved I am, Lord Rahl.'

'Your smile just did, general. I'm relieved, too.'

'My men are uplifted that their new Lord Rahl is a worker of great magic, able to turn death from their door. Every one of

286

those men would like to buy you an ale and toast your health and long life.'

'It wasn't magic. It was simply things that ... Thank them for the offer, but I ... What about the riots? Were there any more last night?'

General Kerson grunted dismissively. 'It's mostly finished. The worry went out of people when the moon returned to normal.'

'Good. That's good news, general. Thanks for the report.'

The general rubbed a finger along his smooth jaw. 'Ah, there was one other thing, Lord Rahl.' He glanced at Kahlan. 'If we could talk ...' The man let out a sigh. 'A ... woman was murdered last night.'

'I'm sorry. Was it someone you knew?'

'No, Lord Rahl. She was a ... a woman who ... she accepted money in return for ...'

'If you're trying to say she was a whore, general,' Kahlan said, 'I've heard the word before. I won't faint if I hear it again.'

'Yes, Mother Confessor.' He turned his attention back to Richard. 'She was found dead this morning.'

'What happened to her? How was she killed?'

The general was looking more uncomfortable by the moment. 'Lord Rahl, I've been looking at dead people a lot of years. I can't remember the last time I vomited when I saw one.'

Richard rested a hand on one of the leather pouches on his wide belt. 'What was done to her?'

The general glanced to Kahlan as if to beg her indulgence as he put an arm around Richard's shoulder and pulled him aside. Kahlan couldn't hear the whispered words, but the look on Richard's face told her she didn't want to know.

Richard went to the hearth and stood staring into the flames. 'I'm sorry. But you must have men who can look into it. Why are you bringing this to me?'

The general grimaced and cleared his throat. 'Ah, well, you see, Lord Rahl, it was, well, it was your brother who found her.'

Richard turned with a dark frown. 'What was Drefan doing at a house of prostitution?'

287

'Ah, well, I asked him that myself, Lord Rahl. He doesn't seem to me a man who would have any trouble' – the general wiped a hand across his face – 'I asked him, and he said that it was his business, not mine, if he wanted to go to whorehouses.'

Kahlan could see the tightly controlled anger etched in Richard's expression. He abruptly snatched his gold cloak from a chair.

'Let's go. Take me there. Take me where Drefan goes. I want to talk to the people there.'

Kahlan and General Kerson rushed after Richard as he swept out the door. She caught his sleeve and glanced to the general.

'General, could you give us a moment, please?'

After he moved down the hall, Kahlan pulled Richard in the other direction, away from Cara, Raina, Ulic, and Egan. She didn't think that Richard was in any mood at the moment to be looking into such a thing. Besides, she had come to him for a reason.

'Richard, there are representatives waiting to meet with us. They've been waiting days.'

'Drefan is my brother.'

'He's also a grown man.'

Richard rubbed his eyes. 'I need to see about this, and I have a lot of other things on my mind. Would you mind talking to the representatives? Tell them that I was called away on important matters, and that they can just as easily give their land's surrender to you and then all the arrangements of command can begin to be coordinated?'

'I can. I know that some of them would be just as happy to talk to me and not have to face you, even in surrender; they're terrified of you.'

'I wouldn't hurt them,' Richard objected.

'Richard, you frightened the wits out of them, before, when you demanded their surrender. You promised to annihilate them if they dared join with the Imperial Order.

'They fear you might do it anyway, on a whim. The reputation of the Master of D'Hara precedes you, and you fed their fears. You can't expect that they'll suddenly be at ease around you just because they agree to your terms.'

He leaned down and whispered in her ear. 'Well, just tell them how lovable I am.'

'I can tell them that you look forward to working with them for our mutual peace and prosperity,' she said with a smile. 'They trust me, and will listen.

'But Tristan Bashkar, the Jarian minister, is here, along with a pair from the royal house in Grennidon. These three are the important ones, the ones with huge standing armies. They're expecting to meet with you. It is they who may not be satisfied to surrender to me. They will want to discuss terms.'

'Make them satisfied.'

'Tristan Bashkar is not an affable man but a tough negotiator, as are Leonora and Walter Cholbane, from Grennidon.'

'That's one reason I ended the Midlands alliance: too many wish to argue and posture. Arguing and posturing are over. The terms of surrender are unconditional.' Richard hooked a thumb behind his wide leather belt. His expression hardened. 'The terms are fair to all, the same for all, and are not subject to discussion. They're either with us or against us.'

Kahlan dragged a finger down the black sleeve of his shirt, over the rise and fall of his muscles. He'd been busy with the journal. It had been too long since she'd been in those arms.

'Richard, you depend on me for advice. I know these lands. Just having them agree is not the only aim. There will be need for sacrifice. We need their full cooperation in this war.

'You are Lord Rahl, the Master of D'Hara. You made the demands. You said that surrender, while unconditional, will be handled with respect for their people. I know these representatives. They will expect to see you, as a matter of your respect for them.'

'You are the Mother Confessor. We are one, in this as in everything else. You led these people long before I came along. You have no less standing than I. You have had their respect a good long time. Remind them of that.'

Richard directed a brief gaze up the hall to the waiting general, and the others. He looked back into her eyes.

'It may not be any of General Kerson's business, as far as Drefan is concerned, but it is mine; I'll not be deceived by another brother. From what you've said, and others have told me, he already has women in the palace fawning over him. If he catches something from those whores and then gives it to the young women here ... that's my business.

'I'll not have it be my brother bringing diseases to innocent women here who trust him because he's my brother.'

Sarah, the woman who had been bringing tea to Richard, was young and trusting. She was one of the women captivated by Drefan.

Kahlan rubbed his back. 'I understand. If you promise you will get some sleep, I'll go talk with the representatives. When you have time to talk to them, then you will talk to them. They have no choice but to wait. You are the Lord Rahl.'

Richard bent and kissed her cheek. 'I love you.'

'Then marry me.'

'Soon. We'll go wake the sliph soon.'

'Richard, you be careful. Marlin said that the Sister of the Dark – I don't remember her name – left Aydindril and returned to Jagang, but he may be lying. She could still be out there.'

'Sister Amelia. You know, I remember her. When I first went to the Palace of the Prophets, she was one of Verna's friends who met us: Sisters Phoebe, Janet, and Amelia. I remember Amelia's tears of joy at seeing Verna after all those years.'

'Jagang has her now.'

He nodded. 'Verna must be heartbroken that her friend is in Jagang's hands, and worse, that she's a Sister of the Dark. If Verna even knows.'

'You be careful. Despite what Jagang says, she may still be lurking in Aydindril.'

'I doubt it, but I'll be careful.'

He turned and signaled to Cara. She sprinted up the hall.

'Cara, I'd like you to go with Kahlan. Let Berdine get some rest. I'll take Raina, Ulic, and Egan with me.'

'Yes, Lord Rahl. I will keep her safe.'

Richard smiled. 'I know you will, Cara, but that's not going to get you out of your punishment.'

She betrayed no emotion. 'Yes, Lord Rahl.'

'What punishment?' Kahlan asked when they were out of earshot.

'An unjust one, Mother Confessor.'

'That bad. What is it?'

'I am to feed seeds to his chipmunks.'

Kahlan suppressed a smile. 'That doesn't sound so bad, Cara.'

Cara flipped her Agiel up into her fist. 'That is why it is unjust, Mother Confessor.'

CHAPTER 26

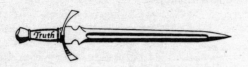

Kahlan sat alone in the ornate chair of the Mother Confessor, the tallest one behind the semicircular dais, under the ornate fresco of Magda Searus, the first Mother Confessor, and her wizard, Merritt. They were painted onto the dome that capped the enormous council chambers. Kahlan watched the representatives approaching across the expanse of marble before her.

From her place of honor overhead, Magda Searus had witnessed the long history that was the Midlands alliance. She had witnessed, too, Richard ending it. Kahlan prayed that Magda Searus's spirit would understand and approve of his reasons; they were benevolent, despite what it must seem to some.

Cara stood behind Kahlan's right shoulder. Kahlan had hastily gathered a number of administrators to handle matters of state, such as the signing of documents of surrender and trade instructions, and several D'Haran officers to oversee matters of command. They all waited silently behind her left shoulder.

Kahlan tried to focus her mind on the things she must say and do, but Richard's words about the Temple of the Winds made it hard to think of anything else. He thought the Temple of the Winds was sentient. The winds were hunting Richard. The Temple of the Winds was hunting him. That threat lurked in every dark corner of her mind.

Footsteps of the representatives and boot strikes of the soldiers escorting them echoed off vast expanses of marble, and brought her out of her brooding. The approaching knot of people strode through glaring shafts of sunlight that streamed in through round windows at the lower edge of the dome. Kahlan put on her Confessor's face, as her mother had taught her, a face that showed nothing, and masked what was inside.

Arched openings around the room covered stairways up to colonnaded balconies edged with polished mahogany railings, but this day no observers stood behind the railing.

The group, flanked by D'Haran soldiers, came to a halt before the resplendent, carved desk. Tristan Bashkar of Jara and Leonora and Walter Cholbane of Grennidon stood at the fore. Behind them waited ambassadors Seldon from Mardovia, Wexler from Pendisan Reach, and Brumford from Togressa.

Kahlan knew that Jara and Grennidon, lands of vast wealth and large standing armies, were likely to be the most obstinate about retaining their prerogative of status in return for their surrender. She knew she must shake their confidence first. Having served in a position of authority and power most of her life, first as a Confessor, then as the Mother Confessor, Kahlan knew the task well. She knew these people, knew how they thought; surrender was acceptable, as long as they could retain station above certain other lands, and as long as they could be assured of unfettered authority in their own business.

That kind of attitude was no longer acceptable. It couldn't be tolerated if all of them were to have a chance against the Imperial Order. Kahlan had to uphold Richard's word and conditions of surrender. The future of every land in the Midlands depended on this.

In order for this new union to prevail against the Imperial Order, there could no longer be sovereign lands, each with its own agenda. They must now all be one, under one authority of command, working together as one people, not a coalition that could fragment at a critical moment, letting the Imperial Order snatch freedom from all.

'Lord Rahl is occupied with matters of our mutual safety in our struggle. I have come in his place to hear your decisions. Your words will be passed on to him as you speak them to me. As Mother Confessor, Queen of Galea, Queen of Kelton, and betrothed of the Master of D'Hara, I have the authority to speak on behalf of the D'Haran empire. My word is as final as would be Lord Rahl's.'

The words had come out unbidden, but that was what it was – the D'Haran empire. Richard was its supreme leader, its supreme authority.

The representatives bowed and mumbled that they understood.

Wanting these people of authority to know that the order of things was no longer how it had been in these chambers in the past, Kahlan reversed the order of how such matters were handled.

'Ambassador Brumford, please step forward.'

Tristan Bashkar and Leonora Cholbane immediately began objecting. It was unheard of to have a lesser land speak first.

Kahlan's glare brought them to silence. 'When I ask you to speak for your people, then you may speak. Not before. Until a land joins with us through surrender of their sovereignty, they have no standing before me.

'Do not expect that your presumption will be excused, as was customary in the past in the alliance of the Midlands. The Midlands alliance is no more. You now stand in the D'Haran empire.'

An icy silence settled over the chambers.

Kahlan had been devastated when she had first heard that Richard had spoken much the same words in this very chamber to representatives of the Midlands. She had come to understand that there was no other way.

Tristan Bashkar and the Cholbanes, to whom she had directed her words, stood red-faced but silent. When she moved her gaze to Ambassador Brumford, he remembered her orders and scurried forward.

The amicable Ambassador Brumford gathered his voluminous violet robes in one hand and put a knee to the marble floor as he sank into a deep bow.

'Mother Confessor,' he said as he straightened, 'Togressa stands ready to join with you and all free people in our alliance against tyranny.'

'Thank you, Ambassador. We welcome Togressa as a member of the D'Haran empire. The people of Togressa will have standing equal to any among us. We know your people will do their part.'

'They will. Thank you, Mother Confessor. Please relay my word to Lord Rahl that we are joyful to be a part of D'Hara.'

Kahlan smiled sincerely. 'Lord Rahl and I share your joy, Ambassador Brumford.'

He moved to the side as Kahlan called forward the muscled, short, fiery-eyed Ambassador Wexler from Pendisan Reach.

'Mother Confessor,' he said upon arising, tugging his leather surcoat straight, 'Pendisan Reach is a small land, with a small legion of men at arms, but we are fierce fighters, as any who have come against our swords can attest.

'The Mother Confessor has always fought for us with the same fierceness. We have always held with the Midlands and with the Mother Confessor, and so we accord your words great weight. With the greatest respect, we heed your counsel to join with D'Hara.

'Our swords are lowered to you and Lord Rahl. The people of Pendisan Reach, both those of simple muscle and bone, and those with magic's talents, wish to be at the van of battle against the horde from beyond the wilds, so that the enemy may have a bitter taste of our ferocity. We will be known to all from this day forward as the D'Harans from Pendisan Reach, if it so pleases you.'

Touched by his words, Kahlan bowed her head to him. The people of Pendisan Reach did have a flair for the dramatic, but they were no less wholehearted for it. As small as their land was, they were not to be taken lightly; the ambassador's bold claim of their ferocity was no idle boast. If only their numbers were as great as their fortitude.

'I can't promise you the van, Ambassador Wexler, but we will be honored to have your people with us in our struggle. We will value them regardless of how they serve.'

She turned a dispassionate face to the ambassador from Mardovia. The Mardovian people were proud, too, and no less fierce. They had to be for their survival in tough country among the wilds, though they, also, were a small land.

'Ambassador Seldon, please come forward and deliver Mardovia's decision.'

Ambassador Seldon glided forward, wearily eying the others. He bowed from the waist, his white hair falling forward over the gold braiding on the shoulders of his red coat as he did so.

'Mother Confessor. The assembly of seven of Mardovia in our mother city of Renwold has charged me with the duty of the long journey to Aydindril to relay their decision. The assembly of seven has no desire or intention to relinquish rule over our beloved people to outlanders, whether they be from D'Hara or from the Imperial Order.

'Your war with the Imperial Order is not our war. The assembly of seven has ruled that Mardovia will remain sovereign and will remain neutral.'

Behind her, in the silence, a soldier coughed. The sound of it echoed around the stone chamber.

'Ambassador Seldon, the land of Mardovia lies among the eastern wilds, not far from the Old World. You will be vulnerable to attack.'

'Mother Confessor, the walls surrounding our mother city of Renwold have stood the test of time. As you say, we lie among the people of the wilds. Those people in the past have tried to exterminate us. None ever succeeded in so much as breaching the walls, much less overcoming our stalwart defenders. Instead, the various peoples of the wilds now trade with us, and Renwold is a center of commerce in the eastern wilds of the Midlands, respected by all who once sought to conquer us.'

Kahlan leaned forward. 'Ambassador, the Order is no tribe from the wilds. They will crush you. Doesn't the assembly of seven have the sense to realize that?'

Ambassador Seldon smiled indulgently. 'Mother Confessor, I understand your concern, but as I have said, Renwold's walls have stood us in good stead. Be assured, Renwold will not fall to the Order.' His expression hardened. 'Nor will it fall to this new alliance you form with D'Hara.

'Numbers do not mean much against a knob of stone in the wilds. Would-be conquerors soon tire of breaking their teeth on so small a morsel. Our small size, our location, and our walls make us less than worth the trouble. Should we join with you, then we would be vulnerable because we would represent resistance.

'Our neutrality is not of hostile intent. We will be willing to trade with your alliance, as we will be willing to trade with the

Imperial Order. We wish harm to no one, but we will defend ourselves.'

'Ambassador Seldon, your wife and children are in Renwold. Don't you understand the danger to your family?'

'My beloved wife and children are safe behind the walls of Renwold, Mother Confessor. I fear not for them.'

'And will your walls stand against magic? The Order uses those with magic! Or are you too drunk with the past to see the threat to your future?'

His face had reddened. 'The decision of the assembly of seven is final. We don't fear for our safety. We have people of magic in turn to protect the walls from magic. Neutrality is not a threat. Perhaps you should pray to the good spirits for mercy, since it is you who sues for war. To live by violence is to invite it.'

Kahlan drummed her fingernails against the desktop as everyone awaited her words. She knew that even if she could convince this man, it would do no good; the assembly of seven had made its decision, and he could not change it even if he wanted.

'Ambassador Seldon, you will leave Aydindril by the end of the day. You will return to the assembly of seven in Renwold, and tell them that D'Hara does not recognize neutrality. This is a struggle for our world – whether it is to thrive in the Light, or wither under the shadow of tyranny. Lord Rahl has decreed that there are no bystanders. I have decreed no mercy against the Order. We are of one mind in this.

'You are either with us, or you stand against us. The Imperial Order views it the same.

'Tell the assembly of seven that Mardovia now stands against us. One of us, either D'Hara or the Order, will conquer Mardovia. Direct them to pray to the good spirits, and ask that it is we who conquer you and take Renwold instead of the Order. We will impose harsh sanctions for your resistance, but your people will live. Should the Order set upon you first, they will annihilate your defenders and enslave your people. Mardovia will be ground into the dust of the past.'

His indulgent smile widened. 'Fear not, Mother Confessor. Renwold will stand against any land, even the Order.'

Kahlan regarded him with cold ire. 'I have walked among

the dead inside the walls of Ebinissia. I have seen the slaughter at the hands of the Order. I have seen what they did to the living, first. I will pray for those poor people who will suffer because of the mad delusions of the assembly of seven.'

Kahlan angrily gestured to the guards to escort the man from the chambers. She knew what would happen to the Mardovian people if the Order attacked first. She knew, too, that Richard could not risk the lives of allies simply to take Renwold in order to protect it. It was too distant a land. She would advise against it, as would any of his generals.

Mardovia was lost; their neutrality would draw the Order as the scent of blood drew wolves.

She had walked through the gates in the massive walls of Renwold. The walls were impressive. They were not invincible. The Order had wizards, like Marlin. The walls would not stand against wizard's fire, despite those of magic's talent defending Renwold.

Kahlan tried to put the fate of Mardovia from her mind as she called the pair from the royal house in Grennidon forward.

'How does Grennidon stand?' she growled.

Walter Cholbane cleared his throat. His sister spoke.

'Grennidon, a land of great importance, a land of vast fields which produce –'

Kahlan cut her off. 'I asked how Grennidon stands.'

Leonora dry-washed her hands as she considered the resolve in Kahlan's eyes.

'The royal house offers its surrender, Mother Confessor.'

'Thank you, Leonora. We are gladdened for you and for your people. Please see to it that my officers here are granted any information they need so that your army can be brought under coordination of our central command.'

'Yes, Mother Confessor,' she stammered. 'Mother Confessor, are our forces to be bled against the walls of Renwold to bring them down?'

Grennidon was north of Mardovia, and in the best position to attack, but Kahlan knew that Grennidon would not relish attacking a trading partner. Moreover, some of the family of the assembly of seven had married into the royal house of Cholbane.

'No. Renwold is a city of the walking dead. The vultures

will pick it clean. In the meantime, trade with Mardovia is forbidden. We trade only with those who join us.'

'Yes, Mother Confessor.'

'Mother Confessor,' Walter, her brother, interjected, 'we wish to discuss some of the terms with Lord Rahl. We have things of value to offer, and matters of interest to us that we wish to bring to his attention.'

'Surrender is unconditional. There is nothing to discuss. Lord Rahl has instructed me to remind you that there will be no negotiations. Either you are with us, or you are against us. Now, do you wish to withdraw your offer of surrender before you sign the documents and instead cast your fate with Mardovia?'

He pressed his lips together as he took a deep breath. 'No, Mother Confessor.'

'Thank you. When Lord Rahl has the time, soon, I hope, he would very much like to hear what you have to say, as a valued member of the D'Haran empire. Just remember that you are now part of D'Hara, and he is the Master of D'Hara, the master of that empire.'

She had treated them with less respect than the two small lands who had offered their surrender; not to do so would have resulted in emboldening them, and inviting trouble. These two were among those who always requested red rooms.

Walter and Leonora seemed to relax, now that Kahlan had their acquiescence. The Cholbanes could be tenacious and stubborn to the end, but once an agreement was reached and their word given, they never looked back, never second-guessed what might have been. It was a quality that made dealings with them bearable.

'We understand, Mother Confessor,' Walter said.

'Yes,' his sister added. 'And we look forward to the day that the Imperial Order no longer threatens all our people.'

'Thank you, both of you. I know this must seem harsh to you, but know that we rejoice to count you and your people among us.'

As they moved off to sign the papers and talk with the officers, Kahlan turned her attention to Tristan Bashkar, of Jara.

'Minister Bashkar, how stands Jara?'

Tristan Bashkar was a member of the royal family of Jara. In Jara, the position of minister was one of high rank and trust. Of those gathered, he was the only one with the authority to change his land's commitment without returning home for consultation. If he thought there was reason enough, he could alter the royal family's instructions, and thus, Jara's stand.

Hardly out of his thirties, he wore his age well. He also used his looks to distract people from his quick mind. After people had been disarmed by his likable smile, bright brown eyes, and smooth-spoken flattery, he would extract concessions before they realized they had parted with them.

He brushed a thick lock of dark hair back from his forehead – a compulsive habit. Or possibly a way to draw interest to his eyes, where people were often distracted.

He spread his hands apologetically. 'Mother Confessor, I'm afraid it's not as easy as a simple yes or no, although I wish to assure you that we are in harmony with the great empire of D'Hara, and admire the wisdom of both Lord Rahl, and of course, yourself. We have always put the advice of the Mother Confessor above all others.'

Kahlan sighed. 'Tristan, I'm in no mood for your usual games. You and I have sparred in these chambers more times than I can remember. Don't test me today. I'll not have it.'

Being a member of the royal family, he was well trained in all the arts of war, and had fought with distinction in the past. Broad-shouldered and tall, he cut a handsome figure. His easy smile always carried a playful twist that cloaked any threat, were there one, and there sometimes was. Kahlan never turned her back, so to speak, on Tristan Bashkar.

He casually unbuttoned his dark blue coat and rested a hand on his hip. The ploy revealed an ornate knife sheathed at his belt. Kahlan had heard it whispered that, going into battle, Tristan Bashkar preferred to draw his knife rather than his sword. It was whispered, too, that he got sadistic pleasure from slicing the enemy.

'Mother Confessor, I admit that in the past I've been reticent to reveal our exact position in order to best protect our people from the avarice of other lands; but it isn't like that this time. You see, the way we view the situation –'

'I'm not interested. I want only to know if you stand with us or against us. If you stand against us, Tristan, I give you my word that by morning we will have troops riding for the royal palace in Sandilar, and they will return with either unconditional surrender, or the heads of the royal family.

'General Baldwin is here in Aydindril with a sizable Keltish force. I'll send him – Keltans never let down their queen, nor rest until she is satisfied. I am now the queen of Kelton. Do you wish a fight with General Baldwin?'

'Of course not, Mother Confessor. We wish no fight, but if you will hear me out –'

Kahlan slapped a hand to the desk, silencing him. 'When the Imperial Order held Aydindril, before Richard liberated it, Jara sat on the council, allied with the Order.'

'As was D'Hara, at the time,' he gently reminded her.

Kahlan glared at him. 'I was brought before the council, and convicted of the very crimes committed by the Order. Wizard Ranson, from the Order, called for a death sentence. The councilor from Jara sat at this desk and voted to have me beheaded.'

'Mother Confessor …'

Kahlan turned a finger to her right. 'He sat right there and called for me to be put to death.'

She looked back to Tristan's brown eyes. 'If you look closely, I think you will still be able to pick out a stain down the front of the desk over there. When Richard liberated Aydindril, he executed those traitorous councilors. The stain was left by the Jarian councilor. I heard that Richard cleaved the man nearly in two, he was so angered by the betrayal to me, and to the people of the Midlands.'

Tristan stood politely, showing nothing of his emotions. 'Mother Confessor, it was not by the choice of the royal family that that councilor spoke for Jara. He was a puppet of the Order.'

'Then join with us.'

'We want to, and we intended to. In fact, I was sent with authorization to make it so.'

'Whatever it is you want, Tristan, you'll not get it. We make the same offer to all, and no special terms for any.'

'Mother Confessor, would it be considered a special term to hear me out?'

Kahlan sighed. 'Make it short, and keep in mind, Tristan, that your smile has no effect on me.'

He smiled anyway. 'As a member of the royal family, I have the authority, and authorization, to surrender Jara and join with you. Given a choice, that is what we wish.'

'Then do it.'

'The red moon interrupts those plans.'

Kahlan sat up straighter. 'What does that have to do with it?'

'Mother Confessor, Javas Kedar, our star guide, holds great sway with the royal family. He has read the stars in the matter of our surrender, and has given his opinion that the stars hold this action with favor.

'Before I left home, Javas Kedar told me that the stars would give sign if circumstances changed, and to heed any sign. The red moon has given me pause in our plans.'

'The moon is not the stars.'

'The moon is in the sky, Mother Confessor. Javas Kedar councils on the meaning of moon symbols, also.'

Kahlan pinched the bridge of her nose between a thumb and finger as she sighed. 'Tristan, are you going to allow harm to visit your people on the basis of such superstition?'

'No, Mother Confessor. But I am bound by my honor to give heed to the beliefs of our people. Lord Rahl said that surrender would not mean that we had to give up our customs and beliefs.'

'Tristan, you have an annoying habit of leaving out things you wish to ignore. Richard said that a land wouldn't have to give up its customs as long as they brought harm to no one, and broke no laws common to all. You are stepping over a dangerous line.'

'Mother Confessor, we in no way wish to circumvent his words or to step over any line. I wish only some time.'

'Time. Time for what?'

'Time, Mother Confessor, to assure myself that the red moon isn't a sign that we have reason to fear joining with D'Hara. Now, I can either travel back to Jara and consult with Javas Kedar, or I can simply wait here for a while, if you would prefer, to assure myself that the red moon is not a sign of danger.'

Kahlan knew that the Jarians, and the royal family in particular, were fervent believers in guidance from the stars. As much effort as Tristan devoted to chasing skirts, Kahlan knew that were a beautiful woman to offer him her charms, he would flee from her if he believed the stars were against it.

It would take him at least a month to return to Jara, consult the star guide, and return to Aydindril.

'How long would you have to wait in Aydindril before you felt comfortable and could in good conscience surrender?'

He frowned thoughtfully for a moment. 'If Aydindril remained safe for a couple of weeks after such a significant sign, then I would feel safe in knowing that the sign was not a bad portent.'

Kahlan drummed her fingers.

'You have two weeks, Tristan. Not one day more.'

'Thank you, Mother Confessor. I pray that in two weeks we can consummate our union with D'Hara.' He bowed. 'Good day, Mother Confessor, and I look forward to the stars remaining fair for us.'

He took a step away, but turned back. 'By the way, would you happen to know of a place I can stay for such a length of time? Our palace was burned down in your battle with the Blood of the Fold. What with all the damage to Aydindril, I'm having difficulty in finding accommodations.'

She knew what he was angling for – to be close so he could see if the stars struck out against D'Haran rule. The man thought too much of himself, thought himself more clever than he was.

Kahlan smiled. 'Oh yes, I know a place. You will stay right here, where we can keep an eye on you until the two weeks are up.'

He buttoned his blue coat. 'Why, thank you, Mother Confessor, for your hospitality. It is most appreciated.'

'And, Tristan, while you are a guest under my roof, if you lay a finger, or anything else, on any of the women living and working here, I will see to it that the anything else is cut off.'

He laughed good-naturedly. 'Mother Confessor, I never knew you believed the gossip about me. I'm afraid that I often have to resort to the charms of coin for company, but I'm flattered that you would think me so talented at wooing young ladies. If I should break your rules, I would expect to be put on trial and subjected to your choice of punishment.'

Trial.

Richard said that the people who sent the Temple of the Winds away were put on trial. In the Wizard's Keep there were records of all trials held there. She had never read any of those books, but she had been told of them. Maybe they could find out from the records of the trial what happened to the Temple of the Winds.

As Kahlan watched Tristan Bashkar departing behind a pair of guards, she thought about Richard, and wondered what he would find. She wondered if he was about to lose another brother.

Kahlan knew most of the women working at the Confessors' Palace. The women at the palace respected Richard as a man of honor. She wouldn't like to think that they would be prey to a man who would win them by trading on their trust of Richard.

She felt a pang of sadness for Richard. She knew he was hoping that Drefan would be a brother he could be proud of. Kahlan hoped that Drefan didn't turn out to be trouble. She remembered his hand on Cara.

Kahlan turned to the Mord-Sith. 'Three more with us, one lost, and one yet to decide ...

Cara smiled conspiratorially. 'A sister of the Agiel must be able to strike fear into people's hearts. Mother Confessor, you wear the Agiel well. I thought I could hear some of their knees knocking all the way up here.'

CHAPTER 27

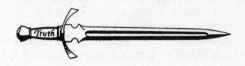

Armor and weapons clattered and clanged as the soldiers following behind marched up the steep cobbled street. Narrow houses, mostly three and four stories, sat cheek by jowl, with the upper floors overhanging the lower so that the topmost almost closed off the sky. It was a gloomy part of the city.

Soldiers throughout the city had cheered their thanks as Richard passed, wishing him good health and long life. Some had wanted to buy him a drink. Some had run up to bow before him and give the devotion: 'Master Rahl guide us. Master Rahl teach us. Master Rahl protect us. In your light we thrive. In your mercy we are sheltered. In your wisdom we are humbled. We live only to serve. Our lives are yours.'

They had hailed him as a great wizard for protecting them and healing their sickness. Richard felt more than a little uncomfortable at their acclaim; he had, after all, simply instructed them to take well-known cures for intestinal distress. He hadn't worked any magic.

He had tried to explain it wasn't magic; that the things they ate and drank had cured them. They would hear none of it. They had expected magic from him, and, in their eyes, they had gotten it. He had finally given up on explaining and took to waving his thanks for their praises. Had they gone to an herb seller, they would no doubt be just as healthy, and complaining about the price.

He had to admit, though, that it did make him feel good to know that he had helped people for a change instead of hurting them. He understood a little of what Nadine must feel when she helped people with her herbs.

He had been warned of a wizard's need for balance. There was balance in all things, but especially in magic. He could no longer eat meat – it made him sick – and suspected it was the gift seeking balance for the killing he sometimes had to do. He liked to think that helping people was part of the balance in being a war wizard.

Sullen people, going about their business, moved to the side of the cramped street, tramping through the dirty snow still in the sheltered places in order to squeeze past the soldiers. Grim-looking groups of older boys and young men watched warily and then vanished around corners as Richard and his escort approached.

Richard absently touched the gold-worked leather pouch on his belt. It contained white sorcerer's sand that had been in the pouch when he found the belt in the Keep. Sorcerer's sand was the crystallized bones of the wizards who had given their lives into the Towers of Perdition separating the Old and New Worlds. It was a sort of distilled magic. White sorcerer's sand gave power to spells drawn with it – good and evil. The proper spell drawn in white sorcerer's sand could invoke the Keeper.

He touched the other gold-worked pouch on his belt. A little leather purse tied securely inside contained black sorcerer's sand. He had gathered that sorcerer's sand himself from one of the towers. No wizard since the towers were built had been able to gather any black sorcerer's sand; it could only be taken from a tower by one with Subtractive Magic.

Black sorcerer's sand was the counter to the white. They nullified each other. Even one grain of the black would contaminate a spell drawn with the white, even one drawn to invoke the Keeper. He had used it to defeat Darken Rahl's spirit and send him back to the underworld.

Prelate Annalina had told him to guard the black sand with his life – that a spoonful of it was worth kingdoms. He possessed several kingdoms' worth. He never let the little leather purse containing the black sand out of his sight or his reach.

Children, layered with ragged clothes for warmth against the cold spring day, played catch-the-fox in the tightly hemmed street, running from doorway to doorway, giggling with glee at the prospect of finding the fox, and more so at seeing the impressive procession coming up their very own street.

Even seeing happy children didn't bring a smile to Richard's face.

'This one, Lord Rahl,' General Kerson said.

The general lifted a thumb to a door on the right, set back a few feet into the clapboard face of a building. The faded red paint was flaking off the bottom of the door where the weather worked on it the most. A small sign said: 'Latherton Rooming House.'

A big, stocky man inside didn't look up from a chair behind a rickety table set with dry biscuits and a bottle. He stared at nothing with red-rimmed eyes. His hair was disheveled and his clothes rumpled. He seemed in a daze. Beyond him was a stairway, and beside that a narrow hall that ran back into darkness.

'Closed,' he murmured.

'Are you Silas Latherton?' Richard asked, his gaze sweeping the clutter of dirty clothes and bed sheets awaiting washing. A half dozen empty ewers sat against the wall, along with a stack of washrags.

The man peered up from behind a puzzled frown. 'Yeah. Who are you? You look familiar.'

'I'm Richard Rahl. Perhaps you see a resemblance to my brother, Drefan.'

'Drefan.' The man's eyes widened. 'Lord Rahl.' His chair rasped noisily against the floor as he shoved it back and stood to bow. 'Forgive me. I didn't recognize you. I've never seen you before. I didn't know that the healer was your brother. I beg the Lord Rahl's forgiveness ...'

For the first time, Silas noticed the dark-haired Mord-Sith at Richard's side, the muscled general at the other side, Richard's two huge bodyguards towering behind him, and the phalanx of soldiers spilling out the doorway and into the street. He raked his greasy hair back and stood up straighter.

'Show me the room where the ... where the woman was murdered,' Richard said.

Silas Latherton bowed twice before hurrying to the stairs, tucking in his shirt as he went. Checking over his shoulder to make sure Richard was following, he climbed the stairs two at a time. They objected to his weight with creaks and groans.

He finally came to a halt before a door partway down a narrow hall. With the walls painted red, the candles at either end of the hall provided little illumination. The place stank.

'In here, Lord Rahl,' Silas said.

When he moved to open the door, Raina snatched his collar and pulled him back out of the way. She planted him in place with a sinister look. A look like that from Raina was enough to give an angry cloud pause.

She opened the door and, Agiel in hand, stepped into the room before Richard. Richard waited a moment while Raina checked the room for threat; it was easier than objecting. Silas stared at the floor while Richard and General Kerson went into the little room. Ulic and Egan took up posts beside the door and folded their massive arms.

There wasn't much to see: a bed, a small pine chest beside it, and a washstand. A dark stain discolored the unfinished spruce floorboards. The bloodstain ran under the bed and covered nearly the entire floor.

The size of it didn't surprise him. The general had told him what had been done to the woman.

The water in the washbasin looked to be at least half blood. The rag hanging over its side was red with it. The killer had washed the blood from himself before he left. He must either be neat or, more likely, didn't want to walk out past Silas Latherton dripping blood.

Richard opened the pine chest. It contained orderly stacks of clothes, and nothing else. He let the lid drop back down.

Richard leaned a hand against the doorway. 'No one heard anything?' Silas shook his head. 'A woman is mutilated like that, has her breasts cut off, and is stabbed hundreds of times, and no one heard a thing?'

Richard realized that his exhaustion was putting an edge to his voice. His mood wasn't helping, either, he guessed.

Silas swallowed. 'She'd been gagged, Lord Rahl. Her hands were tied, too.'

Richard scowled. 'She must have kicked her feet. No one heard her kicking? If someone was slicing me up, and I was gagged and my hands were tied, I'd have kicked the washstand over at least. She must have kicked her feet trying to get someone's attention.'

'I didn't hear it if she did. None of the other women heard it, either. Least, they never mentioned it, and I'd think they would have come got me if they'd heard anything like that. If there was trouble, they always came to me. They always did. They know I'm not shy about protecting them.'

Richard rubbed his eyes. The prophecy wouldn't leave him be. He had a headache.

'Bring the other women here. I want to talk to them.'

'They left me, after –' Silas gestured vaguely. 'Except Bridget.'

He hurried to the end of the hall and knocked on the last door. A woman with rumpled red hair peered out after he spoke quietly to her. She withdrew back into her room and in a moment emerged, pulling a cream-colored robe closed. She tossed a quick knot in the tie as she followed Silas up the hall to Richard.

Standing in the belly of a stinking whorehouse, Richard was getting more angry with himself by the moment. Despite trying to be objective, he had begun to let himself be happy about having a brother. He was beginning to like Drefan. Drefan was a healer. What could be more noble?

Silas and the woman bowed. They both looked the way Richard felt: dirty, tired, and distraught.

'Did you hear anything?' Bridget shook her head. Her eyes looked haunted. 'Did you know the woman who died?'

'Rose,' Bridget said. 'I only met her once, for a few minutes. She just came here yesterday.'

'Do either of you have any idea who murdered her?'

Silas and Bridget shared a look.

'We know who did it, Lord Rahl,' Silas said, a smoldering tone welling in his voice. 'Fat Harry.'

'Fat Harry? Who's that? Where can we find him?'

For the first time, Silas Latherton's features twisted in anger. 'I shouldn't have let him come here anymore. The women didn't like him.'

'None of us girls would take him anymore,' Bridget said. 'He drinks, and when he drinks, he gets mean. There's no need to put up with that, not with the army …' Her words died out as she glanced to the general. She resumed with a different tack. 'We have enough clients nowadays. We don't have to put up with mean drunks like fat Harry.'

'The women all told me that they wouldn't see Harry no more,' Silas said. 'When he came last night, I knew that they would all say no. Harry was real insistent, and seemed sober enough, so I asked Rose if she'd see him, as she was new and …'

'And didn't know she was in danger,' Richard finished.

'It wasn't like that,' Silas said defensively. 'Harry didn't seem to be drunk. I knew the other women wouldn't take him, though, sober or not, so I asked Rose if she was interested. She said she could use the money. Harry was the last one with her. She was found a little while later.'

'Where can we find this Harry?'

Silas's eyes narrowed. 'In the underworld, where he belongs.'

'You killed him?'

'No one saw who slit his fat throat. I wouldn't know who done it.'

Richard glanced at the long knife tucked behind Silas's belt. He didn't blame the man. If they had captured fat Harry, he would get the same for his crime as had already been done. Although he would have had a trial first, and he could have confessed, just to be sure it was he who had done it.

That was why they used Confessors: to be sure they had convicted the guilty man. Once touched by her magic, a criminal would confess all that he had done. Richard wouldn't want Kahlan to hear what had been done to this woman, Rose. Especially not from the beast who had done it.

It made him sick to his stomach to think of Kahlan having to touch a man like that, a man who had killed a woman in such a brutal fashion. He feared he would have killed Harry himself to keep Kahlan from having to touch the flesh of a man like that.

He knew she had touched other men who were no better. He didn't want her to ever have to do that again. He knew it had to hurt her to hear such perverted crimes confessed in detail. He feared to think what terrible memories haunted her and visited her dreams.

Richard forced his mind off it and looked at Bridget. 'Why did you stay when the others ran off?'

She shrugged. 'Some of them had children, and feared for them. I don't fault them their fears, but we were always safe here. Silas has always been fair to me. I've been hurt other places, but never here. It wasn't Silas's fault that a crazy killer did this. Silas always respected our wishes when we said we wouldn't see a man again.'

Richard felt his stomach tighten. 'And you saw Drefan?'

'Sure. All the girls saw Drefan.'

'All the girls,' Richard repeated. He held a tight grip on his anger.

'Yeah. We all saw him. Except Rose. She never got a chance, 'cause she ...'

'So, Drefan didn't have a ... favorite?' Richard had been hoping that Drefan had confined himself to one woman he liked, and that maybe she would be one who was healthy, at least.

Bridget's brow wrinkled up. 'How can a healer have a favorite?'

'Well, I mean, was there one he preferred, or did he just take who was available?'

The woman stuck a finger into her mat of red hair and scratched her scalp.

'I think you got the wrong idea about Drefan, Lord Rahl. He never touched us ... in that way. He only came here to do his healing.'

'He came here to heal?'

'Yeah,' Bridget said. Silas nodded his agreement. 'Half the girls had something or other. Rashes and sores and such. Most people who sell herbs and cures don't want to help our kind, so we just live with our ailments.

'Drefan told us how he wanted us to wash. He gave us herbs, and unguents to put on the sores. He came twice before, real late, after we was done, so as not to interfere with us earning a living. He checked on the girls' children, too. Drefan was special kind with the children. One had a bad cough, and he got better after Drefan gave him something to take.

'He came checking on us early this morning. After he saw one of the girls, he went to Rose's room, to check on her.

311

That's when he found her. He came flying out of her room after what he saw and was calling out' – she pointed at the floor at Richard's feet – 'between throwing up. We all rushed out in the hall and saw him there, on his knees, heaved his guts out right there.'

'So he didn't come here to … to … and he never –'

Bridget guffawed. 'I offered – no charge, since he helped me and all with what he gave me. He said that that wasn't why he had come. He said he only wanted to help, that he was a healer.

'I offered, mind you, and I can be very persuasive' – she winked – 'but he said no. He has a real handsome smile, he does. Just like yours, Lord Rahl.'

'Enter,' came the response to Richard's knock.

Drefan was kneeling before his array of candles set about on the table against the wall. His head was bowed, and his hands were folded in supplication.

'I hope I'm not interrupting,' Richard said.

Drefan looked back over his shoulder and then stood. His eyes reminded Richard of Darken Rahl. Drefan had the same blue eyes, with the same indefinably odd, unsettling look in them. Richard couldn't help being disquieted by them. It sometimes made him feel as if Darken Rahl himself were staring at him.

People who had lived in fear of Darken Rahl were probably terrified when they looked into Richard's eyes, too.

'What are you doing?' Richard asked.

'Praying to the good spirits to watch over the soul of someone.'

'Whose soul?'

Drefan sighed. He looked tired and doleful.

'The soul of a woman no one cared about.'

'A woman named Rose?'

Drefan nodded. 'How did you know about her?' He waved off his own question. 'Forgive me – I wasn't thinking. You're the Lord Rahl. I expect you get reports of such things.'

'Yes, well, I do hear about things.' Richard spotted

something new in the room. 'I see you've taken to brightening up the decor.'

Drefan saw where Richard was looking, and went to the chair beside the bed. He returned with a small pillow. He ran his fingers lovingly over the rose embroidered on it.

'This was hers. They didn't know where she came from, so Silas – he's the man who runs the house – Silas insisted I take this for the small help I offer the women there. I won't accept their money. If they had money to spare, they wouldn't be doing what they do.'

Richard wasn't an expert, but the embroidered rose looked to be done with care. 'Do you think she made it?'

Drefan shrugged. 'Silas didn't know. Maybe she did. Maybe she saw it somewhere and bought it because it had a rose on it, like her name.'

He gently rubbed his thumb back and forth across the rose as he stared at it.

'Drefan, what are you doing going to … to places like that? There's no shortage of people needing healing. We have soldiers here who were wounded down by the pit. There's plenty for you to do. Why were you going to whorehouses?'

Drefan dragged a finger down the stem of green thread. 'I'm seeing to the soldiers. I go on my own time, before people are up and need me.'

'But why go there at all?'

Drefan's eyes welled with tears as he stared at the rose on the pillow.

'My mother was a whore,' he whispered. 'I am the son of a whore. Some of those women have children. I could have been any one of them.

'Just like Rose, my mother took the wrong man to her bed. No one knew Rose. No one knew who she was, or where she came from. I don't even know my own mother's name – she wouldn't tell the healers she left me with. Only that she was a whore.'

'Drefan, I'm sorry. That was a pretty stupid question.'

'No, it was a perfectly logical question. No one cares about those women, I mean cares about them as people. They get beaten bloody by the men who come to them. They catch terrible diseases. They're scorned by other people.

'Herb sellers don't want them coming into their shops – it gives them a reputation and then decent people won't come around. Many of the things those women have, even I don't know how to cure. They suffer sad, lingering deaths. Just for money. Some of them are drunks, and the men prostitute them and pay them with liquor. They're drunk all the time and don't know the difference.

'Some of them think they'll find a rich man and be his mistress. They think they will please him and gain his favor. Like my mother. Instead, they have bastard children, like me.'

Richard was mentally wincing. He had been ready to believe that Drefan was an unfeeling opportunist.

'Well, if it makes you feel any better, I'm the son of that bastard, too.'

Drefan looked up and smiled. 'I guess so. At least your mother loved you. Mine didn't. She didn't even leave me her name.'

'Don't say that, Drefan. Your mother loved you. She took you to a place where you would be safe, didn't she?'

He nodded. 'And left me there with people she didn't know.'

'But she left you because she had to, so that you would be safe. Can you imagine how that must have hurt her? Can you imagine how it must have broken her heart to leave you with strangers? She must have loved you a great deal to do that for you.'

Drefan smiled. 'Wise words, my brother. With a mind like that, you might make something of yourself, someday.'

Richard returned the smile. 'Sometimes, we have to do desperate things to save the ones we love. I have a grandfather who has great admiration for acts of desperation. I think, with your mother, I'm beginning to understand what he means.'

'Grandfather?'

'My mother's father.' Richard idly stroked a finger along the raised gold wire spelling out the word TRUTH on the hilt of his sword. 'One of the greatest men I've ever had the honor of knowing. My mother died when I was young, and my father – the man I thought was my father – was often gone on his business as a trader. Zedd practically raised me. I guess I'm more Zedd than anyone else.'

Zedd had the gift. Richard had inherited the gift not only from Darken Rahl, but also from Zedd, from his mother's side as well as his father's. From both bloodlines. Richard found comfort in knowing that the gift of a good man flowed in his veins, and not just that of Darken Rahl.

'Is he still living?'

Richard looked away from Drefan's blue, Darken Rahl eyes. 'I believe he is. I don't think anyone else does, but I do. Sometimes I feel like if I don't believe, then he will be dead.'

Drefan laid a hand on Richard's shoulder. 'Then keep believing; you may be right. You're fortunate to have a family. I know, because I don't.'

'You do now, Drefan. You have a brother, at least, and soon a sister-in-law.'

'Thanks, Richard. That means a lot to me.'

'How about you? I hear you have half the women in the palace chasing after you. Any of them special?'

Drefan smiled distantly. 'Girls, that's all. Girls who think they know what they want and are impressed by foolish things that shouldn't matter. I see them all batting their eyelashes at you, too. Some people are drawn to power. People like my mother.'

'Me! You're seeing things.'

Drefan turned serious. 'Kahlan is beautiful. You're a fortunate man to have a woman of such substance and noble character. A woman like that only comes along once in a lifetime, and then only if the good spirits smile on you.'

'I know. I'm the luckiest man alive.' Richard stared off, thinking about the prophecy, and the things he had read in Kolo's journal. 'Life wouldn't be worth living without her.'

Drefan laughed and slapped Richard on the back. 'If you weren't my brother, and a good one besides, I'd steal her from you and have her for myself. On second thought, you'd better be careful, I may yet decide to have her.'

Richard smiled with him. 'I'll be careful.'

Drefan pointed an admonishing finger at Richard. 'You treat her right.'

'I'd not know how to do otherwise.' Richard swept a hand out, indicating the small, simple room, and changed the subject. 'What are you still doing here? We can find you better quarters than this.'

Drefan gazed about at his room. 'This is a king's room compared to my quarters at home. We live simply. This room is almost more ostentation than I can bear.' His brow drew down. 'It isn't what kind of house you have that matters. This is not happiness. It's what kind of mind you have, and how you care for your fellow man – what you can do to help others who can be helped by no one else.'

Richard adjusted the bands at his wrists. They made him sweat under the leather pads. 'You're right, Drefan.'

He hadn't even realized it, but he had come to be used to his surroundings. Since he had left Hartland, he had seen many splendid places. His own home, back in Hartland, wasn't nearly as nice as this plain room, and he had been happy there. He had been happy being a woods guide.

But, as Drefan said, a person had to help others who could be helped in no other way. He was stuck with being Lord Rahl. Kahlan was the balance. Now, all he had to do was find the Temple of the Winds before he lost it all.

At least he had a woman he loved more than he would ever have thought possible, and now, too, he had a brother.

'Drefan, do you know the meaning of *Raug'Moss?*'

'I was taught that it's old High D'Haran, meaning "Divine Wind." '

'Do you know High D'Haran?'

Drefan brushed back his tumbled-down blond hair. 'Just that word.'

'I hear that you're their leader. You've done well for yourself to become the leader of a community of healers.'

'It's the only life I've ever known. Being the High Priest, though, mostly means that they have someone to blame when things go wrong. If someone we try to help doesn't get better, the healers point in my direction and say, "He is our leader. Talk to him." Being High Priest means I have to read the reports and records, and try to explain to distraught relatives that we are only healers, and we can't revoke the Keeper's call. Sounds more impressive than it is, really.'

'I'm sure you exaggerate. I'm proud that you've done well. What are the Raug'Moss? Where do they come from?'

'Legend has it that the Raug'Moss were founded thousands of years ago by wizards whose gift was for healing. The gift began dying out in the race of man, and wizards, especially ones gifted for healing, became more and more rare.'

Drefan told Richard the story of how the community of the Raug'Moss started to change as wizards began dying out. Worried that their work would die out with them, the healers, the wizard healers, decided to take in apprentices without the gift. Over time, there were fewer and fewer wizards to oversee the work, until long ago the last of the wizards died.

It sounded to Richard much like reading in Kolo's journal how different the Keep had been in that time long past when it was filled with wizards and their families.

'Now, there are no gifted among us,' Drefan said. 'The Raug'Moss were taught many keys of health and healing, but we have nowhere near the talent of the wizards of old; we have no magic to aid us. We do what we can, with the teachings the true healers of old passed down, but we can only do so much. It's a simple life, a hard life, but it has rewards that comforts of belongings can't provide.'

'I understand. It must be the best feeling in the world to help people.'

Drefan's face took on a curious set. 'What of you? What is your gift? Your talent?'

Richard looked away from Drefan's eyes. His hand tightened on the hilt of his sword.

'I was born a war wizard,' he whispered. 'I have been named *fuer grissa ost drauka*, High D'Haran for "the bringer of death." '

The room fell quiet.

Richard cleared his throat. 'I was pretty distraught by that, at first, but since then I've come to understand that being a war wizard means that I have been born to help others, by protecting them from those who would enslave them. From those like our bastard father – Darken Rahl.'

'I understand,' Drefan said into the uneasy silence. 'Sometimes the best use of our ability is to kill – such as to end a life that has no hope but pain, or to end the life of one who would bring endless pain to others.'

Richard rubbed a thumb over the symbols on the silver

317

bands at his wrist. 'Yes. I understand what you mean by that, now. I don't think I did, before. We both must do things that we don't like, but which must be done.'

Drefan smiled a small smile. 'Not many, other than my healers, ever understand it. I'm glad you do. Sometimes killing is the greatest of charity. I am careful to whom I speak those words. It is good to have my brother understand them.'

'The same with me, Drefan.'

Before Richard could ask more, they were interrupted by a knock at the door. Raina poked her head in. Her long, dark braid fell forward over her shoulder.

'Lord Rahl, do you have a moment?'

'What is it, Raina?'

Raina rolled her eyes, indicating someone behind her. 'Nadine wishes to see you. She seems upset about something, and will only speak to you.'

When Richard gestured, Raina opened the door a little wider and Nadine pushed her way in, oblivious to Raina's scowl.

'Richard. You have to come with me.' She took up his hands in both of hers. 'Please? Please, Richard, come with me? There's someone here who desperately needs to see you.'

'Who?'

She looked to be genuinely troubled. She tugged on his hand. 'Please, Richard.'

Richard was still wary. 'Mind if I bring Drefan along?'

'Of course not. I was going to ask that you did.'

'Let's go, then, if it's really important.'

She held his hand tight and dragged him behind her.

CHAPTER 28

Richard spotted Kahlan coming down the hall toward him. She
frowned at seeing Nadine pulling him along by the hand.
Drefan, Raina, Ulic, and Egan trailed behind him as they all
wove their way past palace staff going about their chores, and
soldiers on patrol. Richard shrugged to Kahlan.

Nadine glared at Kahlan before turning down the hall
toward her room. He wondered what that was all about.
Annoyed, Richard yanked his hand away from Nadine's grip,
but kept following. Nadine skirted a walnut table against the
wall beneath an old tapestry with a herd of white-tailed deer
grazing before white-peaked mountains in the background.
She checked over her shoulder to make sure Richard was still
with her.

Kahlan and Cara caught up. Kahlan fell in beside him.

'Well,' Cara said from behind, as she stroked her thick
braid, 'doesn't this look interesting?'

Richard shot her a scowl. Nadine turned and impatiently
snatched his hand again.

'You promised. Come on.'

'I promised nothing. I said I'd go with you,' Richard
complained. 'I didn't say I would run.'

'Big strong Lord Rahl can't keep up with me?' Nadine
taunted. 'The woods guide I remember could walk faster than
this when he was half asleep.'

'I am half asleep,' he muttered.

'The guards told me you were back, and had gone to

Drefan's room,' Kahlan whispered to him. 'I was on my way to meet you there. What's this business with Nadine?'

Her whispered question was laced with aggravation. He noticed her quick glance to Nadine's hand gripping his.

'Beats me. She wants me to see someone.'

'And must you hold her hand to do it?' she growled under her breath.

He yanked his hand away again.

Kahlan stole a quick peek at Drefan, back behind Cara and Raina. She twined her arm through Richard's. 'How are you doing? What did you … find out?'

Richard put his hand over hers and gave it a squeeze. 'Everything is fine,' he whispered to her. 'It wasn't what I thought. I'll tell you about it later.'

'What about the murderer? Has anyone found him yet?'

'Yes, someone found him, and murdered him for his crime,' Richard told her. 'What about the representatives? Did you take care of it?'

Her answer was a moment in coming. 'Grennidon, Togressa, and Pendisan Reach surrendered. Jara may yet, but they wish to wait for two weeks for a sign from the sky.' Richard frowned. 'Mardovia refused to join with us. They choose to remain neutral.'

Richard jerked to a halt. 'What!'

Everyone marching behind almost lurched into him.

'They refuse to surrender. They claim to be neutral.'

'The Order doesn't recognize neutrality. Neither do we. Didn't you tell them that?'

Kahlan's face showed nothing. 'Of course I did.'

Richard hadn't meant to yell at her. He was angry at Mardovia, not her.

'General Reibisch is in the south. Maybe we could have him take Mardovia before the Order grinds them into carrion.'

'Richard, they were given a chance. They are now the walking dead. We can't waste the lives of our soldiers to take Mardovia just so that we might protect them. It would serve no purpose and it would weaken our effort.'

Nadine pushed between them and glared at Kahlan. 'You talked to that evil Jagang. You know what he's like. Those people will all die if you leave them to the Order. You just don't care about the lives of innocent people. You're heartless.'

From the corner of his eye, Richard saw a red flash as Cara's Agiel spun up into her hand.

Richard shoved Nadine on ahead of him. 'Kahlan is right. It just took a moment for it to sink in through my thick skull. Mardovia has chosen their own path; they must walk it. Now, if you want to show me someone, then show me. I have important things to do.'

Nadine huffed, flipped her thick brown hair back over her shoulder, and marched on. Cara and Raina were scowling at the back of her head. A scowl from a Mord-Sith was more often than not prelude to a serious consequence. Richard had probably just spared Nadine that consequence. Someday, he was going to have to do something about Shota. Before Kahlan tried.

Richard leaned toward Kahlan. 'I'm sorry. I'm dead tired and I just wasn't thinking.'

She squeezed his arm. 'You promised you would get some sleep, remember?'

'Soon as I see to this business with Nadine, whatever it is.'

At the door to her room, Nadine snatched Richard's hand again and tugged him in. Before he could object, he saw the boy sitting on a red chair. Richard thought he recognized him as one of the Ja'La players he had watched.

The boy was shuddering in tears. When he saw Richard coming into the room, he jumped down off the chair and swiped the floppy wool hat from his head of blond hair. He stood crushing his hat in his fists, trembling expectantly, tears coursing down his face.

Richard crouched down before the boy. 'I'm Lord Rahl. I hear you need to see me. What's your name?'

He wiped his nose. The tears kept coming. 'Yonick.'

'There now, Yonick, what's the matter?'

He could only get out the word 'brother' before succumbing to gasping sobs. Richard took the boy in his arms and comforted him. He wept in racking sobs as he clung to Richard. His misery was heartbreaking.

'Can you tell me what's the matter, Yonick?'

'Please, Father Rahl, my brother's sick. Real sick.'

Richard stood the boy on his feet before him. 'He is? What's he sick with?'

'I don't know,' Yonick cried. 'We bought him herbs. We tried everything. He's so sick. He's just been getting worse since I came to see you before.'

'Since you came to see me before?'

'Yes,' Nadine snapped. 'He came begging for your help a few days ago.' Nadine thrust a finger at Kahlan. 'She sent him away.'

Kahlan's face went crimson. Her jaw worked, but no words came out.

'All she cares about are her armies and fighting wars and hurting people. She doesn't care about a miserable little boy who's sick. She would only care if he was some fancy, important diplomat. She doesn't know what it is to be poor and sick.'

With a glare, Richard froze Cara's advance. He turned and glared at Nadine.

'That's enough.'

Drefan laid a hand on Kahlan's shoulder. 'I'm sure you had a good reason. You couldn't have known how sick his brother was. No one is blaming you.'

Richard turned back to the boy. 'Yonick, my brother here, Drefan, is a healer. Take us to your brother, and we'll see if we can't help him.'

'And I have herbs,' Nadine said. 'I'll help your brother, too, Yonick. We'll do everything we can. We promise.'

Yonick wiped his eyes. 'Please hurry. Kip is real sick.'

Kahlan looked on the verge of tears. Richard put a hand tenderly to her back. He could feel her trembling. He feared how sick the boy's brother might be, and wanted to spare her seeing it. He feared she might blame herself.

'Why don't you wait here while we see to this.'

Her wet green eyes flashed up at him. 'I'm going,' she said through gritted teeth.

Richard gave up trying to remember the warren of narrow streets and twisting alleys they went down, and simply noted where the sun was in the sky in order to keep his bearings as

Yonick led them through a maze of buildings and walled courtyards hung with laundry.

Chickens flapped and squawked as they scattered out of the way. Some of the tiny, walled courtyards held a few goats, or sheep, or a pig or two. The animals seemed incongruous amid the tightly packed buildings.

Overhead, people carried on conversations from opposing windows. Some leaned out on elbows to have a look at the procession led by a boy. It created quite a stir. Richard knew that it was the sight of Lord Rahl, dressed in his black war wizard's outfit with a gold cloak billowing out behind, and the Mother Confessor in her pristine white dress, that was the object of wonder, rather than the knot of soldiers or two Mord-Sith – soldiers were common, and the city people probably didn't have a clue as to who the two women in brown leather were.

People in the streets and alleyways pushed their carts of vegetables, wood, or household goods to the side to get out of the way. Others stood against the walls and watched, as if it were a miniature, impromptu parade unexpectedly coming through their neighborhood.

At intersections, soldiers on patrol cheered their Lord Rahl, and called out their thanks for his curing their ailment.

Richard held a tight grip on Kahlan's hand. She hadn't spoken a word since they left the palace. He had made Nadine walk behind, between the two Mord-Sith. He hoped Nadine knew enough to keep her mouth shut.

Yonick pointed. 'Just up there.'

They followed him as he turned from the street down a narrow alley between stone walls forming the bottom floors of houses, with wood above for the second story. Water dripping from melting snow overhead splashed mud from the alley a few feet up onto the stone. With one hand, Kahlan held Richard's, and with the other she held the hem of her dress up as she followed him down the line of boards laid in the mud.

Yonick paused at a door under a small shed roof. People peered out windows to each side. When Richard caught up, Yonick opened the door and ran up the stairs, calling out for his mother.

A door at the top of the stairs squeaked open. A woman in a

brown dress and white apron stared down at the boy running up the stairs.

'Ma – it's Lord Rahl! I brought Lord Rahl!'

'The good spirits be praised,' she said.

She rested a weary hand on her son's back as he threw his arms around her waist. She lifted her other hand toward a doorway at the rear of the small room used as kitchen, dining room, and living area.

'Thank you for coming,' she mumbled to Richard, but she broke down in tears before she could finish.

Yonick ran for the back room. 'This way, Lord Rahl.'

Richard squeezed the woman's arm to reassure her as he swept past, following Yonick. Kahlan still gripped his other hand. Nadine and Drefan followed on their heels, with Cara and Raina close behind. Yonick balked at the bedroom door as the rest of them entered.

A single candle on a small table struggled to ward off the shroud of darkness. A basin of water and soapy rags stood vigil beside the candle. The rest of the room, mostly taken up with three pallets, seemed to be waiting for the candle's diligence to flag, so night could seize the room.

A small figure lay on the far pallet. Richard, Kahlan, Nadine, and Drefan crowded in beside it. Yonick and his mother, silhouetted by the light from beyond the door, stood at the brink of the darkness, watching.

The room stank like rotting meat.

Drefan pushed back the hood of his flaxen cloak. 'Open the shutters so I can see.'

Cara drew both open and folded them against the wall, allowing the light to flood into the tiny room and reveal a blond-headed boy covered to his neck with a white sheet and blanket. The side of his neck, just above the sheet, was grossly distended. His uneven breaths rattled.

'What's his name?' Drefan called back to the mother.

'Kip,' she said in a whining cry.

Drefan patted the boy's shoulder. 'We're here to help you, Kip.'

Nadine leaned in. 'Yes, Kip, we'll have you up and about in no time.'

She put her hand back over her mouth and nose against the smell of rot that gagged them all.

The boy didn't respond. His eyes were closed. His sweaty hair was plastered against his forehead.

Drefan drew the bed covers down to Kip's waist, below his hands resting on his stomach. The boy's fingertips were black.

Drefan stiffened. 'Dear spirits,' he breathed.

He rocked back on his heels and touched the back of his hand to the legs of the two Mord-Sith towering behind them.

'Get Richard out of here,' he whispered urgently. 'Get him out, now.'

Without questioning, Cara and Raina thrust hands under Richard's arms and started to pull him up. Richard jerked away from their grip.

'What's going on?' he demanded. 'What's the matter?'

Drefan wiped a hand across his mouth. He glanced over his shoulder at the mother and Yonick. His gaze took in the rest of them before settling on Richard. He leaned closer.

'This boy has the plague.'

Richard stared at him.

'What do we have to do to cure him?'

Drefan lifted an eyebrow. He turned back to the boy, elevating a little hand. 'Look at his fingers.' The fingertips were black. He pulled the bedcover aside. 'Look at his toes.' His toes were black. He opened the boy's trousers. 'Look at his penis.' The tip of it was black, too.

'That's gangrene. It rots the extremities. This is why they call it the black death.'

Richard cleared his throat. 'What can we do for him?'

Drefan's voice lowered even more with incredulity. 'Richard, did you hear what I said? Black death. People sometimes recover from the plague, but not when it's this advanced.'

'If we would have gotten to him sooner ...' Nadine's imputation trailed off.

Kahlan's grip on Richard's forearm tightened painfully. He heard her stifle a cry.

Richard glared at Nadine. She looked away.

'And do you know how to cure the plague, herb woman?' Drefan sneered.

325

'Well, I –' Nadine blushed and fell silent.

The boy's eyes fluttered open. His head rolled toward them. 'Lord … Rahl,' he said with a shallow breath.

Richard put a hand on his shoulder. 'Yes, Kip. I came to see you. I'm here.'

Kip nodded the slightest bit. 'I waited.' His chest rested longer between each breath.

'What can you do to help?' came a tearful question from the doorway. 'How soon will he be well again?'

Drefan opened the collar of his white, ruffled shirt as he leaned close to Richard. 'Say something comforting to the boy – that's all we can do. He won't last long. I'll go talk to the mother. It's part of the job of healer.'

Drefan stood, pulling Nadine away with him. Kahlan was leaning against Richard's shoulder. He feared looking at her, lest she break down in tears. Lest he break down in tears.

'Kip, you'll be up and playing Ja'La soon. You'll be getting over this any day now. I'd like to come watch another of your Ja'La games. I promise to come, just as soon as you're better.'

A faint smile passed over the boy's face. His eyelids closed partway. His ribs sank as breath abandoned his lungs.

Richard crouched, feeling his heart pounding, as he waited for the boy's lungs to fill again. They didn't.

Silence settled into the room, patiently waiting for darkness to return.

Richard could hear the wheels of a handcart outside squeaking, and the distant, raucous cry of ravens. The music of children's laughter drifted in the air.

This child would never laugh again.

Kahlan's head fell against his shoulder. Soft sobs claimed her as she clutched his sleeve.

Richard reached over to pull the sheet over the body.

The boy's hand rose slowly off his stomach. Richard froze.

The hand floated purposefully to Richard's throat. The black fingers curled, gathering Richard's shirt in a death grip.

Kahlan had fallen silent.

They both knew that the boy had died.

The boy's hand drew Richard closer. The long-silent lungs filled once more with a breath.

Richard, the hair at the base of his neck stiffening, put his ear close.

'The winds,' the dead boy whispered, 'hunt you.'

CHAPTER 29

Richard stared in a daze as Drefan wrapped the dead boy in the sheet. Only Richard and Kahlan had seen what had happened – had heard what the dead boy had said. Behind him, in the outer room, the mother wailed in anguish.

Drefan leaned close to him. 'Richard.' Drefan touched his arm. 'Richard.'

Richard started. 'What?'

'What do you want to do?'

'Do? What do you mean?'

Drefan glanced over his shoulder at the rest of them back by the door. 'What do you want to tell people about this? I mean, he died of the plague. Do you want to try to keep it a secret?'

Richard couldn't seem to make his mind work.

Kahlan leaned past Richard. 'A secret? Why would we want to do that?'

Drefan took a deep breath. 'Well, word of a plague might cause a panic. If we let people know, believe me, word of it will beat us back to the palace.'

'Do you think others have it?' she asked.

Drefan shrugged. 'I doubt there would be only one isolated case. We have to bury or burn the body at once. His bedcovers, bed, and anything else he touched should be burned. The room should be treated with smoke.'

'Won't people want to know why that's being done?' Richard asked. 'Won't they guess the reason?'

'Probably.'

'Then how could it be kept a secret?'

'You're the Lord Rahl. Your word is law. You would have to suppress any information. Arrest the family. Accuse them of a crime. Have them held until this is over. Have the soldiers carry off all their possessions to be burned and shut up their home.'

Richard closed his eyes and pressed his fingertips to them. He was the Seeker of Truth, not the suppressor of it.

'We can't do that to a family who just lost a boy. I won't do that. Besides, wouldn't it be better if people knew? Don't people have a right to know of the danger they're in?'

Drefan nodded. 'If it were my decision, I would want people to know. I've seen the plague before, in small places. Some have tried to suppress the knowledge of it to prevent panic, but when more people started dying, it couldn't be kept a secret.'

Richard felt as though the sky had fallen on him. He struggled to make his mind work, but the dead boy's words kept echoing around in his head. *The winds hunt you.*

'If we try to lie to people, they won't believe anything we say. We have to tell them the truth. They've a right to know.'

'I agree with Richard,' Kahlan said. 'We shouldn't try to deceive people, especially about something that could endanger their lives.'

Drefan nodded his concurrence. 'We're fortunate, at least, with the time of year. Plague is worst in the heat of summer. It could run rampant if this were summer. In the colder weather of the spring it shouldn't be able to get a good foothold. With luck, the outbreak of plague will be weak and soon over.'

'Luck,' Richard muttered. 'Luck is for dreamers; I only have nightmares. We have to warn people.'

Drefan's blue eyes looked to each in turn. 'I understand, and I agree with your reasoning. The problem is, there's not much to be done, other than burying the dead quickly and burning their things. There are remedies, but I fear they are of limited value.

'I just want to warn you: news of plague will spread like a firestorm.'

Richard's flesh prickled with goose flesh.

On the red moon will come the firestorm.

'Dear spirits spare us,' Kahlan whispered. She was thinking the same as he.

Richard sprang up. 'Yonick.' He crossed the room, rather than make the boy come to his dead brother.

'Yes, Lord Rahl?' His brow creased as he struggled to hold back his tears.

Richard put one knee to the floor and held the boy's shoulders.

'Yonick, I'm so sorry. But your brother isn't suffering any longer. He's with the good spirits now. He's at peace, and hoping we will remember the good times with him, and not be too sad. The good spirits will watch over him.'

Yonick brushed his blond hair aside. 'But … I …'

'I don't want you to blame yourself. Nothing could have been done. Nothing. Sometimes people get sick, and none of us has the power to make them well. No one could have done anything. Even if you had brought me right at the first, we couldn't have done anything.'

'But you have magic.'

Richard felt heartsick. 'Not for this,' he whispered.

Richard hugged Yonick for a moment. In the room beyond, the mother wept onto Raina's shoulder. Nadine was wrapping up some herbs for the woman, and giving her instructions. The woman nodded against Raina's shoulder as she listened and sobbed.

'Yonick, I need your help. I need to go see the other boys on your Ja'La team. Can you take us to their homes?'

Yonick wiped his sleeve across his nose. 'Why?'

'I'm afraid they might be sick, too. We have to know.'

Yonick glanced back at his mother with unspoken concern. Richard gestured for Cara.

'Yonick, where's your father?'

'He's a felt maker. He works down the street and three over to the right. He works until late every day.'

Richard stood. 'Cara, have some soldiers go and get Yonick's father. He should be here with his wife right now. Have a couple of soldiers take his place for today and tomorrow and help out as best they can, so that his family won't lose the income. Tell Raina to stay here with her until Yonick's father comes home. It shouldn't be long, then she can catch up with us.'

At the bottom of the stairs, Kahlan clutched his arm, holding him back, and asked Drefan and Nadine to wait outside with Yonick while Cara went to find his father. Kahlan closed the door to the alley, leaving Richard alone with her at the bottom of the dim stairwell.

She wiped the tears from her cheeks with trembling fingers. Her green eyes let slip more.

'Richard.' She swallowed and gasped a breath. 'Richard, I didn't know. There was Marlin, and the Sister of the Dark … I never knew that Yonick's brother was so sick, or I would never –'

Richard held up a finger to silence her. He realized, though, by the dread in her eyes, that his scowl was what had silenced her.

'Don't you *dare* dignify Nadine's cruel lies with an explanation. Don't you dare. I know you, and would never believe such things about you. Never.'

She closed her eyes with relief and fell against his chest. 'That poor child,' she wept.

He stroked a hand down her long, thick hair. 'I know.'

'Richard, we both heard what that boy said after he died.'

'Another warning that the Temple of the Winds has been violated.'

She pushed herself back. Her green eyes searched his.

'Richard, we have to reconsider everything now. What you were telling me about the Temple of the Winds was only one source and not an official one at that. It was just a journal kept by one man to keep himself occupied while he guarded the sliph. Besides that, you've only read parts of it, and it's in High D'Haran, which is difficult to translate accurately. You may have been getting the wrong idea about the Temple of the Winds from the journal.'

'Well, I don't know that I would agree –'

'You're dead tired. You're not thinking. We now know the truth. The Temple of the Winds isn't trying to send a warning – it's trying to kill you.'

Richard took pause at the concern on her face. Besides the grief he saw in her eyes, he saw disquiet. Disquiet for him.

'Kolo didn't make it sound like that was what was happening. From what I've read, I think the red moon is a warning that the Temple of the Winds has been violated. When the red moon came before –'

'Kolo said everyone was in an uproar. He didn't explain the uproar, did he? Maybe it was because the temple was trying to kill them. Kolo said that the team who had sent the Temple of the Winds away had betrayed them.

'Richard, face the facts. That dead boy just delivered a threat from the Temple of the Winds: "The winds hunt you." You hunt something when you want to kill it. The Temple of the Winds is hunting you – trying to kill you.'

'Then why didn't it kill me, instead of the boy?'

She didn't have an answer.

Out in the alley, Drefan's blue, Darken Rahl eyes watched Richard and Kahlan returning over the boards in the mud. It seemed as if the process of deep reflection could be glimpsed through those eyes. Richard guessed that healers had to be keen observers of people, but those eyes made him feel somehow naked. At least he saw no magic in them.

Nadine and Yonick waited in mute anxiety. Richard whispered to Kahlan to wait with Drefan and Yonick. He took Nadine's arm.

'Nadine, would you come with me a moment, please?'

She beamed up at him. 'Sure, Richard.'

He helped her step up into the stairwell. As Richard closed the door, she fussed with her hair.

When the door was shut, he turned to the smiling Nadine and slammed her back against the wall so hard it drove the wind from her lungs.

She pushed off the wall. 'Richard –'

He seized her by the throat and smacked her against the wall again, holding her there.

'You and I were never going to be married.' The sword's magic, its fury, was bleeding into his voice. It was coursing through his veins. 'We never are going to be married. I love Kahlan. I am going to marry Kahlan. The only reason you are still here is because you are somehow tangled in this. You are going to remain here, for now, until we can figure it out.

'I can, and I have, forgiven you for what you did to me, but if you ever again say or do anything so cruel and deliberately hurtful to Kahlan, you will spend the rest of your time in Aydindril down in the pit. Do you understand me!'

Nadine put her fingers tenderly to his forearm. She smiled patiently, as if she thought he didn't fully grasp the situation, and she would make him see her reasoned side of it.

'Richard, I know you're upset right now, everyone is, but I was only trying to warn you. I didn't want you to be unaware of what had happened. I only wanted you to know the truth about what she had –'

He slammed her against the wall again. 'Do you understand me!'

She watched his eyes a moment. 'Yes,' she said, as if believing that there was no use in trying to reason with him until he cooled off.

It only made Richard more angry. He struggled to rein it in so that he could get across to her that this was more than anger and that he meant what he was saying.

'I know you have good in you, Nadine. I know that you care about people. We were friends back in Hartland, so I'm going to let this go with a warning. You had better mind my words. There is trouble about. A lot of people are going to need help. You always wanted to help people. I'm giving you your chance to do that. I can use your help.

'But Kahlan is the woman I love and the woman I'm going to marry. I won't have you trying to change that, or trying to hurt her. Don't you so much as *think* to test this again, or I will find another herb woman to help. Are you clear on that?'

'Yes, Richard. Whatever you say. I promise. If she's what you really want, then I'll not interfere, no matter how wrong –'

He held up a finger. 'Your toe is on the line, Nadine. If you step over it, I swear there will be no coming back.'

'Yes, Richard.' She smiled in an understanding, patient, long-suffering way. 'Whatever you say.'

She seemed to be satisfied that he had paid attention to her. It reminded him of a child who misbehaved so that a beloved parent would notice her. He glared at her until he was sure she would not say another word, and only then did he open the door.

Drefan was squatted down, whispering words of comfort to Yonick while he rested a hand on the boy's shoulder. Kahlan's green eyes watched as Nadine reached back for Richard's hand to help her balance as she stepped onto the narrow board in the mud.

'Drefan,' Richard said when he had joined them, 'I need to talk to you about some of the things you said in there.'

Drefan rubbed Yonick's back and then stood. 'What things?'

'About how you wanted Cara and Raina to get me out of there, for one thing. I want to know why.'

Drefan considered Richard a moment, and then Yonick. He drew open his cloak, hooking it behind one of the leather pouches on his belt. He opened the pouch at the front of his belt and poured some dried powder from a leather purse onto a piece of paper. He twisted the paper closed and handed it to the boy.

'Yonick, before we go to see the other boys, would you please take this up to your mother and tell her to steep it in hot water for a couple of hours to make a tea, and then strain it and see that everyone in your family drinks it tonight? It will help build up your family's strength to keep them well.'

Yonick looked at the paper in his hand. 'Sure. I'll be back as soon as I tell my mother.'

'No rush,' Drefan said. 'We'll be waiting when you're through.'

Richard watched Yonick close the door. 'All right, I know you wanted me out of there because of the danger of catching the plague from the sick boy. But we're all in danger, aren't we?'

'Yes, but I don't know how much. You are the Lord Rahl. I wanted you as far away as possible.'

'How do you catch the plague?'

Drefan glanced to Kahlan and Nadine, and then to Ulic and Egan back with the soldiers guarding either end of the alley. He took a deep breath.

'No one knows how the plague is passed from one person to the next, or even if that is the way it spreads. There are some who believe that it's the wrath of the spirits brought down on us, and the spirits decide who they will smite. There are others who argue that the effluvia infest the very air of a place, of a city, endangering everyone. Others insist that it can only be caught by inhaling the infectious steams of the body of a sick person.

'I can only assume, for the sake of caution, that, like fire, the closer you are, the more dangerous it is. I didn't want you close to that danger, that's all.'

Richard was so tired that he felt sick. Only his terror kept him on his feet. Kahlan had been near the boy, too.

'So, you're saying that it's possible we could all get it just from being in the same house as someone who has it.'

'It's possible.'

'But the sick boy's family doesn't have it, and they lived with him. His mother tended to him. Wouldn't she have it, at least, if that were true?'

Drefan considered his words carefully. 'Several times I have seen isolated outbreaks of the plague. One time, when I was young and in training, I went with an older healer to a town, Castaglen Crossing, that had been visited with the plague. From this place, I learned much of what I know about the sickness.

'It started when a merchant came with his wagon of goods to sell. It was reported that when he arrived, he was coughing, vomiting, and complaining of agonizing headaches. In other words, the plague was already upon him before he arrived in Castaglen Crossing. We never knew where he came to have it, but it could have been that he drank envenomed water, stayed with a sick farmer, or that the spirits chose to strike him with it.

'The townspeople, wishing to do a trusted merchant a kindness, put him up in a room, where he died the next morning. Everyone remained well for a time, and they thought the danger had passed them by. They soon forgot about the man who had died among them.

'Because of the confusion brought on by the sickness and death by the time we arrived, the accounts were varied, but we were able to determine that the first townsperson became sick with the plague at least fourteen days, by some accounts, or as many as twenty days, by others, after the merchant arrived.'

Richard pinched his lower lip as he thought. 'Kip was well at the Ja'La game a few days back, so that would mean that he really became ill with it sometime before.'

Despite being mournful over the boy's death, Richard felt great relief that what he had been thinking didn't seem to be plausible. If Kip got the plague long before the Ja'La game, then Jagang didn't have anything to do with it. The prophecy wasn't involved.

But then, why the warning of the winds hunting him?

'That would also mean,' Drefan said, 'that the dead boy's family may yet become sick. They look well at the moment, but they may already be fatally infected with plague. Just as were the people of Castaglen Crossing.'

'Then,' Nadine said, 'we may all have caught it just from being in the room with the boy. That awful smell was his sickness. We may all have the plague from breathing it in, but won't know it for a couple of weeks yet.'

Drefan shot her a condescending look. 'I can't deny that it's possible. Do you wish to run away, herb woman, and spend the next two or three weeks preparing for death by living out the things you always wanted to do?'

Nadine lifted her chin. 'No. I'm a healer. I intend to help.'

Drefan smiled in that private, knowing way he had. 'Good, then. A true healer is above the phantom evils he chases.'

'But she may be right,' Richard said. 'We may all already be infected with the plague.'

Drefan lifted a hand, warding off the concern. 'We mustn't let fear rule us. When I was in Castaglen Crossing, I cared for many people who were in death's grip, people just like that boy. So did the man who took me there. We never became sick.

'I was never able to determine any pattern to the plague. We touched the sick every day and never became sick. Possibly because we were with the sick so much that our bodies knew it well, and were able to strengthen us against its corruption.

'Sometimes, a member of a family would come down sick and thereafter every member of the family, even those who stayed away from the sick room, succumbed to the plague and all died. In other homes, I witnessed, one, or even several, children come down sick with the plague and die, yet their mothers who tended them nearly every moment never became ill, nor did any other member of the household.'

Richard sighed in frustration. 'Drefan, all this isn't very

helpful. Maybe this, maybe that, sometimes yes, sometimes no.'

Drefan wiped a hand wearily across his face. 'I'm just telling you what I've seen, Richard. There are people who will tell you for sure that it is this or it is that. Shortly, there will be people in the streets who will be selling indisputable cures, unquestionable preservatives against the plague. Hucksters all.

'What I am telling you is that I don't know the answers. Sometimes knowledge is beyond our limited understanding. It's one of our tenets, as healers, that it is a wise man who admits the limits of his knowledge and skill, and that pretending either causes harm.'

'Of course.' Richard felt foolish to have pressed for answers that weren't there. 'You're right, of course. It's better to know the truth than hang hope on lies.'

Richard looked to see where the sun was in the sky, but clouds were moving in, obscuring it. A cold wind was coming up. At least it wasn't hot. Drefan had said that the plague spread worst in heat.

He looked back at Drefan. 'Are there any herbs – or anything – that you do know will help prevent it, or cure it?'

'A standard precaution is to treat the home of sick people with smoke. It is said the smoke may purge the air of the effluvia. There are herbs that are recommended for smoking sick rooms. I would think it a wise precaution, at least, but I wouldn't count on it.

'There are other herbs that can help with the complaints of the plague – the headaches, sickness of the stomach, things like that – but none that I know of that will cure the plague itself. Even with these treatments, the person will likely die just the same, but they may have some comfort from the herbs before they pass.'

Kahlan touched Drefan's arm. 'Do all the people who come down with the plague die? Are all who catch it doomed?'

Drefan smiled in reassurance to her. 'No, some recover. In the beginning not as many, and in the end of the outbreak more. Sometimes, if the infection can be urged to a head and the poison drained away, then the person will recover, but will complain for the rest of their life about the torture of the treatment.'

Richard saw Yonick come out the door. He put his arm around Kahlan's waist and pulled her close.

'So we all may already be infected.'

Drefan watched his eyes a moment. 'It's possible, but I don't believe it so.'

Richard's head was pounding, but it wasn't from any plague; it was from lack of sleep, and dread.

'Well, then, let's go to the other boys' homes and see what we can find out. We need to know as much as we can.'

CHAPTER 30

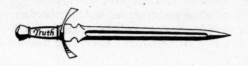

The first boy they went to see, Mark, was fine. Mark was happy to see Yonick, and wondered why he hadn't seen him and his brother, Kip, for the last few days. The young mother was frightened by the important strangers who had appeared at her door inquiring after the health of her son. Richard was relieved that Mark, who had been in the Ja'La game with Yonick and his brother, wasn't sick.

So far, only one boy who had been at the Ja'La game had become sick. It was looking more and more as if his fears about Jagang were just panicked inferences. Richard was beginning to feel the warmth of hope.

Yonick told a stunned Mark of Kip's death. Richard told the mother to send for Drefan if any of the family fell ill. Richard left the home feeling much better.

The second boy, Sidney, had been dead since morning.

By the time they found the third boy lying in blankets at the rear of a one-room house, Richard's hopes had faded.

Bert was gravely ill, but at least his extremities weren't black, as Kip's had been. His mother told them that he had a headache, and had been throwing up. While Drefan saw to the boy, Nadine gave the woman herbs.

'Sprinkle these on the fire,' Nadine told Bert's mother. 'It's mugwort, fennel, and hussuck. They'll smoke and help drive away the sickness. Bring hot coals to your boy, put a pinch of the herbs on the coals, and fan the smoke at your son to insure that he breathes enough of it. It will help drive the sickness from him.'

'Do you think that will really help?' Richard whispered when Nadine returned to his side, near the boy. 'Drefan said he doesn't know if it will.'

'I was taught that it was said to help serious sickness, like the plague,' she said in a low voice, 'but I've never seen anyone with the plague before, so I can't say for sure. Richard, it's all I know to do. I have to try.'

Even though he was dead tired, and had a headache, Richard had no trouble sensing the helplessness in her voice. She wanted to help. As Drefan had said, maybe it would do some good.

Richard watched as Drefan pulled a knife from his belt. He gestured for Cara and Raina, who had both caught up with them after taking care of Richard's instructions, to hold down the sick boy. Raina gripped Bert's chin with one hand, and held his forehead with the other. Cara pressed his shoulders into the blankets.

With a steady hand, Drefan lanced the swelling at the side of the boy's throat. Bert's screams seared Richard's nerves. He could almost feel the knife slicing his own throat. The mother wrung her hands as she stood off a ways, watching with unblinking eyes.

Richard remembered Drefan saying that if the person lived, they would complain the rest of their life about the torture of the treatment. Bert would have cause.

'What did you give Kip's mother?' Kahlan asked Nadine.

'I gave her some herbs to smoke the house, the same as I gave this woman,' Nadine said. 'And I made her a pouch of hop cone, lavender, yarrow, and lemon balm leaves to put in her pillow so that she might sleep. Even so, I don't know that she will be able to sleep, after …' Her eyes turned away. 'I know that I wouldn't be able to,' she whispered, almost to herself.

'Do you have any herbs that you think might prevent the plague?' Richard asked. 'Things that would keep people from catching it?'

Nadine watched Drefan mopping blood and pus from the boy's throat. 'I'm sorry, Richard, but I don't know enough about it. Drefan might be right; he seems to know a lot. There may be no cure, or preventative.'

Richard went to the boy and squatted down beside Drefan, watching his brother work. 'Why are you doing that?'

Drefan glanced over as he folded the rag to a clean place. 'As I said before, sometimes, if the sickness can be brought to a head and drained, they will recover. I have to try.'

Drefan gestured to the two Mord-Sith. They gripped the boy again. Richard winced as he watched Drefan slide the sharp knife deeper into the swelling, bringing forth more blood and yellowish-white fluid. Mercifully, Bert passed out.

Richard wiped sweat from his own brow. He felt helpless. He had his sword to defend against attack, but it could do no good against this. He wished it was something he could fight.

Behind him, Nadine spoke to Kahlan in a soft voice, but loud enough for Richard to hear.

'Kahlan, I'm sorry about what I said before. I've devoted my life to helping sick people. It makes me so upset to see people suffer. That's what I was angry about. Not you. I was frustrated at Yonick's grief, and I lashed out at you. It wasn't your fault. Nothing could have been done. I'm sorry.'

Richard didn't turn. Kahlan said nothing, but she might have offered Nadine a smile to accept the apology.

Somehow, Richard doubted it.

He knew Kahlan, and he knew that she expected as much from others as she expected from herself. Forgiveness was not forthcoming simply because someone asked for it. The transgression was weighed into the equation, and there were transgressions that outweighed absolution.

The apology hadn't been for Kahlan, anyway; it had been for Richard's benefit. Like a child who had been upbraided, Nadine was on her best behavior, trying to impress him with how good she could be.

Sometimes, even though she had once brought him pain, a part of him was comforted to have Nadine around; she reminded him of home, and his happy childhood. She was a familiar face from a carefree time. Another part of him was troubled over what her real purpose was in coming. Despite what she might believe, she hadn't decided it on her own. Someone, or something, had precipitated her actions. Another part of him wanted to skin her alive.

After they left Bert's home, Yonick led them down a

cobbled alley to a yard behind where Darby Anderson's family lived. The small yard of mud churned with wood shavings was cluttered with cutoffs and scraps, several stickered stacks of lumber protected by tarps, some old, rusty two-man rip saws, two carving benches, and warped, split, or twisted boards leaning up against the buildings to the side.

Darby recognized Richard and Kahlan from the Ja'La game. He was astonished that they had come to his home. To have them come to see a Ja'La game was a cause of great pride, but to have them come to his home was beyond belief. He frantically brushed sawdust from his short brown hair and dirty work clothes.

Yonick had told Richard that the whole Anderson family – Darby, his two sisters, his parents, father's parents, and an aunt – lived over their small workshop. Clive Anderson, Darby's father, and Erling, his grandfather, made chairs. Both men, having heard the commotion, had come to the wide, double doors and were bowing.

'Forgive us, Mother Confessor, Lord Rahl,' Clive said after Darby had introduced his father, 'but we didn't know you were coming, or we would have made preparations – I'd have had my wife make tea, or something. I'm afraid that we're just simple folk.'

'Please don't be concerned about any of that, master Anderson,' Richard said. 'We came because we were concerned about your son.'

Erling, the grandfather, took a stern step toward Darby. 'What's the boy done?'

'It's nothing like that,' Richard said. 'You have a fine grandson. We watched him play Ja'La the other day. One of the other boys is sick. Worse, two others of them have died.'

Darby's eyes widened. 'Died? Who?'

'Kip,' Yonick said, his voice choking off.

'And Sidney,' Richard added. 'Bert is very ill, too.'

Darby stood in shock. His grandfather put a comforting hand to the boy's shoulder.

'My brother, Drefan' – Richard lifted a hand to the side – 'is a healer. We're checking on all the boys on the Ja'La team. We don't know if Drefan can help, but he would like to try.'

'I'm fine,' Darby said in a shaky voice.

Erling, an unshaven, scrawny man, had teeth so crooked Richard wondered how he managed to chew his food. He noticed Kahlan's white dress and Richard's gold cloak billowing in the cold wind, and gestured toward the shop.

'Please, won't you all step inside? The wind is biting today. It's warmer inside, out of the weather. I think we'll have snow tonight, the way it looks.'

Ulic and Egan took up posts near the back gate. Soldiers milled about in the alley. Richard, Kahlan, Nadine, and Drefan went into the shop. Cara and Raina shadowed them inside, but remained on guard near the doors.

Old chairs and templates hung from pegs on the dusty walls. Cobwebs in all the corners, that in a forest would have netted dew, here netted loads of sawdust. The workbench held chair pieces being glued up, a fine-toothed saw, a variety of smaller finishing and beading planes, and a number of chisels. Several jack and long joiner planes hung on the wall behind the bench along with hammers and other tools.

Partially finished chairs, cinched tightly together in twisted ropes as they were being finished, or drying in peg-and-wedge clamps, sat about the floor. A carving horse where the grandfather had been when they came into the yard held a split billet of ash he had been working with a drawknife.

Clive, a broad-shouldered young man, seemed content to let his father do the talking.

'What's ailing these children?' Erling asked Drefan.

Drefan cleared his throat but let Richard answer.

Richard was so tired he could hardly stand anymore. He almost felt as if he were asleep, and this was just a bad dream.

'The plague. I'm relieved to see that Darby, here, is well.'

Erling's scruffy jaw dropped. 'Dear spirits spare us!'

Clive turned white. 'My daughters are sick.'

He turned suddenly and ran for the stairs, but stopped abruptly. 'Please, master Drefan, will you see them?'

'Of course. Show the way.'

Upstairs, Darby's mother, grandmother, and aunt had been making meat pies. Turnips were boiling in a pot hung in the hearth, and the boiling water had steamed the windows over.

The three women, alarmed by Clive's calls, were waiting wide-eyed in the center of the upstairs common room. They were shocked by the sight of the strangers, but bowed the instant they saw Kahlan's white dress. Kahlan, in the dress of the Mother Confessor, needed no introduction to anyone in Aydindril, or most of the Midlands, for that matter.

'Hattie, this man here, master Drefan, is a healer, and has come to see the girls.'

Hattie, her short, sandy-colored hair tied back with a head wrap, wiped her hands on her apron. Her gaze darted among all the people standing in her home. 'Thank you. This way, please.'

'How do they fare?' Drefan asked Hattie on their way back to the bedroom.

'Beth has complained since yesterday of her head hurting,' Hattie said. 'She was sick at her stomach, earlier. Common children ailments, that's all.' It sounded to Richard more like a plea than a statement of fact. 'I gave her some black horehound tea to settle her.'

'That's good,' Nadine assured her. 'An infusion made of pennyroyal might help, too. I have some with me I'll leave in case she needs it.'

'Thank you for the kindness,' Hattie said, her concern growing with each step she took.

'What of the other girl?' Drefan asked.

Hattie had almost reached the doorway. 'Lily's not so sick, but just feeling out of sorts. I suspect she's just looking for sympathy because her older sister is getting attention and honey tea. That's the way of children. She has some little, round sores on her legs.'

Drefan missed a step.

Beth was fevered, but not gravely so. She had a wet cough, and complained that her head hurt. Drefan all but ignored her. He watched Lily, in that analytical way of his, as she sat in her blankets, carrying on an earnest conversation with her rag doll.

The grandmother fussed with her collar and watched from the doorway as Hattie fussed with Beth's covers. The aunt mopped Beth's brow with a wet cloth while Nadine spoke words of comfort to the girl. Nadine really did have a soothing, kind way about her. She selected herbs from leather pouches in her bag and wrapped them up in several cloth packets, giving the intent, nodding mother instructions.

Richard and Kahlan moved with Drefan over to the younger girl. Kahlan squatted down and talked to her, telling her what a lovely doll she had, so as to keep her from being frightened by Richard and Drefan. Lily cast worried looks in their direction as she chattered with Kahlan. Kahlan hugged an arm around Richard's waist to show Lily that he wasn't anyone to be afraid of. Richard made himself smile.

'Lily,' Drefan said with forced cheerfulness, 'could you show me your doll's sores?'

Lily held the doll upside down and pointed out spots on the inside of the doll's thighs.

'She has ouches here, and here, and here.' Her big, round eyes turned up to Drefan.

'And do they hurt her?'

Lily nodded. 'She goes "ouch" when I touch them.'

'Really? Well, that's too bad. I'll bet she's better, soon, though.' He squatted down so that he wasn't towering over her, circling an arm around Kahlan's waist and pulling her back down with him. 'Lily, this is my friend, Kahlan. Her eyes aren't so good. She can't see the sores on your doll's legs. Could you show Kahlan here the ones on your legs?'

Nadine was still talking to the mother about the other girl. Lily glanced in their direction.

Kahlan brushed Lily's hair back and told her what a pretty doll she had. Lily grinned. She was fascinated by Kahlan's long hair. Kahlan let her feel it.

'Can you show me the ouches on your legs?' Kahlan asked.

Lily hiked up her white nightdress. 'Here they are, just like my doll's ouches.'

She had several dark spots, the size of pennies, on the inside of each thigh. Richard could tell when Drefan gently touched them that they were hard as calluses. Kahlan straightened Lily's nightdress back down and drew the blanket back over her lap as Drefan patted her cheek, telling her what a good girl she was, and that her doll's ouches would be better by morning.

'I'm glad,' Lily said. 'She doesn't like them.'

Erling was absently planing a chair seat at the workbench. Richard could see that he wasn't paying any attention to what he was doing, and was ruining it. He didn't look up when they came down the stairs. At Richard's urging, Clive had stayed upstairs with his wife and daughters.

'Do they have it?' Erling asked in a hoarse voice.

Drefan laid a comforting hand on the old man's shoulders. 'I'm afraid so.'

Erling took a shaky, crooked stroke with his plane.

'When I was young, I lived in the town of Sparlville. The plague came one summer. It took a good many people. I hoped never to see such a thing again.'

'I understand,' Drefan said in a soft voice. 'I, too, have seen it visit places.'

'They're my only granddaughters. What can we do to help them?'

'You can try to smoke the house,' Drefan offered.

Erling grunted. 'We did that in Sparlville. Bought cures and preventatives, too, but people died just the same.'

'I know,' Drefan said. 'I wish there was something I could do, but I've never heard of a sure cure. If you know of anything that you think helped when you were young, then try it. I don't know of all the treatments, by any means. At worst, it could do no harm, and at best may help.'

Erling set the plane aside. 'Some folk burned fires hot that summer, trying to drive the sickness from their blood. Some said it was because their blood was too hot already with the high summer heat and with the fever on top of that, and tried to fan their loved ones to cool their blood. Which would you advise?'

Drefan shook his head. 'I'm sorry, but I just don't know. I've heard of people recovering when each was tried, and I've heard of people dying just the same with each. Some things are out of our hands. No one can stay the Keeper's hand when he comes.'

Erling rubbed his scruffy chin. 'I'll pray that the good spirits spare the girls.' His voice caught. 'They're too good, too innocent, for the Keeper to touch them just yet. They've brought untold joy to this house and family.'

Drefan returned his hand to Erling's shoulder. 'I'm sorry, master Anderson, but Lily has the tokens upon her.'

Erling gasped and gripped the bench. Drefan had been ready and caught him under his arms to keep him from falling when his knees gave out. Drefan helped him to sit on the carving horse.

Kahlan turned her face away and put it to Richard's shoulder when Erling covered his tears with both hands. Richard felt numb.

'Grandpa,' Darby called from the steps, 'what's wrong?'

Erling straightened. 'Nothing, boy. I'm just worried about your sisters, that's all. Old men get foolish, that's all.'

Darby eased the rest of the way down the stairs. 'Yonick, I'm real sorry about Kip. If your pa needs anything, I'm sure my pa would let me leave my work and go help.'

Yonick nodded. He looked in a daze, too.

Richard squatted down before the boys. 'Did either of you see anything strange at the Ja'La game?'

'Strange?' Darby asked. 'Strange like what?'

Richard combed his fingers back through his hair. 'I don't know. Did you talk to any strangers?'

'Sure,' Darby said. 'There were lots of people there we didn't know. Soldiers were there watching the game. Lots of people I didn't know came to congratulate us after we won.'

'Do any of them stand out in your mind? Anything odd about any of them?'

'I saw Kip talking to a man and a woman after the game,' Yonick said. 'More than like they were just congratulating him. They were leaning down talking to him, showing him something.'

'Showing him something? What?'

'I'm sorry,' Yonick said, 'but I didn't see. I was too busy getting slapped on the back by soldiers.'

Richard was trying not to frighten the boy with his questions, but he had to press for answers. 'What did this man and woman look like?'

'I don't know,' Yonick said. His eyes were filling with tears at remembering his brother alive. 'The man was skinny, and young. The woman was young, too, but not as young as he. She was kind of pretty, I guess. She had brown hair.' He pointed at Nadine. 'Like hers, but not as thick, or as long.'

Richard glanced up at Kahlan. By the stricken look on her face, he knew she was fearing the same thing as he.

'I remember them,' Darby said. 'My sisters talked to that man and woman, too.'

'But neither of you talked to them?'

'No,' Darby said. Yonick shook his head. 'We were jumping around, excited that we'd won the game in front of Lord Rahl. A lot of the soldiers were congratulating us, and so were a lot of other people; I never talked to those two.'

Richard took Kahlan's hand. 'Kahlan and I have to go ask Beth and Lily a question,' he said to Drefan. 'We'll be right back.'

Pressed close together, seeking support in each other's touch, they climbed the stairs. Richard was dreading what he might hear from the girls.

'You ask them,' Richard whispered to her. 'They're afraid of me. They'll talk easier to you.'

'Do you think it could have been them?'

Richard didn't need to ask who she was talking about. 'I don't know. But you told me that Jagang said he had watched the Ja'La game – through Marlin's eyes. Sister Amelia was with Marlin. They were doing something here in Aydindril.'

Richard reassured the women that they just had a small question to ask the girls. The women busied themselves with their work while he went with Kahlan back into the bedroom. Richard doubted they were paying any more attention to their meat pies than Erling had been with the chair seat he had been planing.

'Lily,' Kahlan asked the younger girl first in a soft voice as she smiled, 'do you remember when you went to watch your brother play Ja'La?'

Lily nodded. 'He won. We were real happy that he won. Pa said Darby scored a point.'

'Yes, we saw him play, and we were happy for him, too. Do you remember the two people you talked to? A man and a woman?'

She frowned. 'When Ma and Pa were cheering? That man and woman?'

'Yes. Do you remember what they said to you?'

'Beth was holding my hand. They asked if it was my brother we was cheering for.'

'That's right,' Beth said from the other bed. She had to stop talking as she was taken with a bout of coughing. When she recovered and caught her breath, she went on. 'They said Darby played really good. They showed us the pretty thing they had.'

Richard stared at her. 'Pretty thing?'

'The shiny thing in the box,' Lily said.

'That's right,' Beth said. 'They let me and Lily see it.'

'What was it?'

Beth frowned through her headache. 'It was … it was … I don't know exactly. It was in a box that was so black you couldn't see its sides. The shiny thing inside was pretty.'

Lily nodded her agreement. 'My doll saw it, too. She thought it was real pretty, too.'

'Do you have any idea what it was?'

They both shook their heads.

'It was in a box that was as black as midnight. To look at it is like looking down a dark hole.' Richard said.

They both nodded.

'Sounds like the night stone,' Kahlan whispered to him.

Richard knew well that blackness. Not only the night stone had been like that, but also the outer covering of the boxes of Orden. It was a color so sinister that it seemed to suck the very light from a room.

In Richard's experience, that void of light was only associated with immensely dangerous things. The night stone could bring beings forth from the underworld, and the boxes of Orden held magic that, if used for evil, could destroy the world of life. The boxes could open a gateway to the underworld.

'And inside was something shiny,' Richard said. 'Was it like looking at a candle, or the flame of a lamp? That kind of shiny?'

'Colors,' Lily said. 'It was pretty colors.'

'Like colored light,' Beth said. 'It was sitting on white sand.'

Sitting on white sand. The hairs on the back of Richard's neck stood on end. 'How big was the box?'

Beth held her hands not quite a foot apart. 'About this big on a side. But it wasn't very thick. Kind of like a book. It was almost like they opened a book. That's what the box reminded me of – a book.'

'And inside, the sand that was inside, did it have lines drawn in it? Kind of like if you were to draw lines in dry dirt with a stick?'

Beth nodded as she succumbed to a bout of rattling coughs. She panted, catching her breath, when they finally ceased.

'That's right. Neat lines, in patterns. That's just what it was like. It was a box, or maybe a big book, and when they opened it to show us the pretty colors, it had white sand in it with careful lines drawn in it. Then we saw the pretty colors.'

'You mean, there was something sitting in the sand? This thing that made the colored light was sitting in the sand?'

Beth blinked in confusion, trying to remember. 'No ... it was more like the light came out of the sand.' She flopped back on her bed and rolled on her side, in obvious distress from her sickness.

From the plague. From black death.

From a black box.

Richard stroked a hand tenderly down her arm and pulled the blanket back up over her as she moaned in pain. 'Thank you, Beth. You rest now, and get yourself better.'

Richard couldn't thank Lily. He dared not trust his voice.

Lily lay back. Her tiny little brow puckered. 'I'm tired.' She pouted, near tears. 'I don't feel good.'

She curled up and put her thumb in her mouth.

Kahlan tucked Lily in, and promised her a treat as soon as she was well. Kahlan's tender smile brought a small smile to Lily's mouth. It almost made Richard smile. Almost.

In the alley, after they had left the Anderson house, Richard pulled Drefan aside. Kahlan told the others to wait, and then she joined them.

'What are tokens?' Richard asked. 'You told the grandfather that the youngest had tokens on her.'

'Those spots on her legs are called tokens.'

'And why was the old man nearly struck down with dread when he heard you say the girl had them?'

Drefan's blue eyes turned away. 'People die of the plague in different ways. I don't know the reason, except to imagine it has something to do with their constitution. The strength and vulnerability of everyone's aura is different.

'I've not seen with my own eyes all manner of death the

350

plague causes, as, thankfully, it is a rare occurrence. Some of what I know I learned from the records that the Raug'Moss keep. The plagues I've seen have been in small, remote places. In the past, many centuries ago, there have been a few great plagues in large cities, and I've read the records of those.

'With some people it comes on of a sudden – very high fevers, intolerable headaches, vomiting, searing pains in their backs. They are out of their minds with the agony of it for many days, even weeks, before they die. A few of these recover. Beth is like that. She will get much worse, yet. I have seen people like her recover. She has a small chance.

'Sometimes, they look like the first boy, with the black death overwhelming them and rotting their bodies. Others are tortured with horribly painful swellings in their neck, armpits, or groin, they suffer miserably until they finally die. Bert is like that. If the distemper can be brought to a head, and encouraged to break and run, then they occasionally recover.'

'What about Lily?' Kahlan asked. 'What about these tokens, as you called them?'

'I've never seen them before, with my own eyes, but I've read about them in our records. The tokens will appear on the legs and sometimes on the chest. People who have the tokens rarely know they are sick, until the end. They will one day discover to their horror that they have the tokens upon them, and be dead shortly thereafter.

'They die with little or no pain. But they all die. No one with tokens on them ever lives. The old man must have seen them before, because he knew this.

'The plagues I've seen, as violent as the outbreaks were, never displayed the tokens. The records say that the worst of the great plagues, the ones that brought the most widespread death, were marked with the tokens. Some people thought they were visible signs of the Keeper's fatal touch.'

'But Lily is just a little girl,' Kahlan protested, as if arguing could change it, 'she doesn't seem so sick. It isn't possible for her to ...'

'Lily is feeling out of sorts. The tokens on her legs are fully developed. She will be dead before midnight.'

'Tonight?' Richard asked in astonishment.

'Yes. At the very latest. More likely within hours. I think perhaps even ...'

A woman's long, shrill scream came from the house. The horror in it sent a shiver through Richard's bones. The soldiers who had been talking in low voices off at the end of the alley fell silent. The only sound was a dog barking down the next street.

A man's anguished cry came from the house.

Drefan closed his eyes. 'As I was about to say, even sooner.'

Kahlan buried her face against Richard's shoulder. She clutched his shirt. Richard's head spun.

'They're children,' she wept. 'That bastard is killing children!'

Drefan's brow bunched. 'What's she talking about?'

'Drefan' – Richard tightened his arms around Kahlan as she shook – 'I think these children are dying because a wizard and a sorceress went to a Ja'La game a few days back and used magic to start this plague.'

'That's not possible. It takes longer than that for people to fall sick.'

'The wizard was the one who hurt Cara when you first arrived. He left a prophecy on the wall in the pit. It begins: "On the red moon will come the firestorm." '

Drefan regarded him with a dubious frown. 'How can magic start a plague?'

'I don't know,' Richard whispered.

He couldn't bear to speak aloud the next part of the prophecy. *The one bonded to the blade will watch as his people die. If he does nothing, then he, and all those he loves, will die in its heat, for no blade, forged of steel or conjured of sorcery, can touch this foe.*

Kahlan trembled in his arms, and he knew she was agonizing over the final part of the prophecy.

To quench the inferno, he must seek the remedy in the wind. Lightning will find him on that path, for the one in white, his true beloved, will betray him in her blood.

CHAPTER 31

At the edge of the expansive palace grounds, a patrol of D'Haran soldiers spotted them and snapped to attention. Just beyond the soldiers, in the streets of the city, Kahlan could see people everywhere going about their business pause to bow to the Mother Confessor and the Lord Rahl.

Although the activities of commerce, on the surface, seemed like any other day, Kahlan thought she could detect subtle differences: men loading barrels into a wagon scrutinized people who passed close by; shopkeepers appraised customers carefully; people walking on the street skirted those stopped in conversation. The knots of people gossiping seemed more numerous. Laughter was conspicuously absent from the streets.

After they had solemnly saluted with fists to the leather armor and chain mail over their hearts, the patrol of soldiers not far off broke into good-natured grins.

'Huzzah, Lord Rahl!' they cheered as one. 'Huzzah, Lord Rahl!'

'Thank you, Lord Rahl,' one of the soldiers shouted toward them. 'You cured us! Restored our health! We're well because of you. Long live the great wizard, Lord Rahl!'

Richard froze in midstride, not looking at the soldiers, but staring at the ground before him. His cloak, snared in a gust of wind, embraced him, shrouding him in its golden sparkles.

The others joined in. 'Long live Lord Rahl! Long live Lord Rahl!'

Hands balled in fists, Richard started out once more without looking their way. Kahlan, her arm around his, slid her hand down and urged his fist open to twine her fingers in his. She gave his hand a squeeze of silent understanding and support.

From the corner of her eye, Kahlan could see Cara, back behind Drefan and Nadine, gesturing angrily at the patrol to silence them and move them along.

In the distance before them, on a gentle rise, the expanse of the Confessors' Palace rose up in all its splendor of stone columns, vast walls, and elegant spires, standing out a pristine white against the darkening sky. Not only was the sun going down but murky clouds scudded by, messengers, delivering a vow of a storm. A few errant snowflakes flitted past on the wind, scouting for the horde to come. Spring had not yet prevailed.

Kahlan gripped Richard's hand as if clutching at life itself. In her mind's eye, she saw nothing but sickness and death. They had seen near to a dozen sick children, stricken with plague. Richard's pallid face looked hardly better than the six dead faces she had seen.

Her insides ached. Holding back her tears, her cries, her screams, had cramped her stomach muscles. She had told herself that she couldn't lose control and cry in front of mothers who were terrified that their sick children might be sicker than they had imagined, or as sick as they knew, but refused to believe.

Many of those mothers were hardly older than Kahlan. They were just young women, faced with a crushing plight, who fell to piteous prayer for the good spirits to spare their precious children. Kahlan couldn't say that she wouldn't have been reduced to the same state in their place.

Some of the parents, like the Andersons, had older members of their families to rely on for advice and support, but some of the mothers were young and alone, with only husbands hardly more than boys themselves, and no one to turn to.

Kahlan put her free hand over the painful spasm in her abdomen. She knew how devastated Richard felt. He had more than enough to carry on his shoulders. She had to be strong for him.

Majestic maple trees stood to each side, the bare thicket of branches laced together over their heads. It wouldn't be long before they budded. They passed out from the tunnel of trees, onto the winding promenade that led up to the palace.

Behind them, Drefan and Nadine carried on a whispered discussion of herbs and cures to be tried. Nadine would propose something, and Drefan would give his opinion as to whether it would be useless or might be worth trying. He would gently lecture her on the paths of infirmity, and the causes of breaks in the body's defenses that allowed an affliction to gain hold.

Kahlan got the vague impression that he almost seemed to view those who fell sick with contempt, as if because they took so little care with their auras and flows of energy that he talked about all the time, it was only to be expected that they would succumb to a pestilence unworthy of those like himself who minded their bodies better. She guessed that one with his knowledge of healing people must get frustrated with those who brought disease upon themselves, like the prostitutes and the men who went to them. She was relieved, at least, that he wasn't one of those.

Kahlan wasn't sure if she felt Drefan was justified in some of the things he was saying, or if it was simple arrogance. She herself had felt frustration at people who flouted dangers to their health. When she was younger, there was a diplomat who became ill every time he ate rich sauces with certain spices. They always left him with difficulty breathing. He loved the sauces. Then one time, at a formal dinner, he gorged himself on the sauces he loved, and fell dead at the table.

Kahlan could never understand why the man would bring such sickness on himself, and had trouble feeling sorry for him. In fact, she always viewed him with contempt when he came to a formal dinner. She wondered if Drefan didn't feel much the same way about some people, except that he knew much more of what made people sick. She had seen Drefan do remarkable things with Cara's aura, and she knew, too, that sickness could sometimes be influenced by the mind.

Kahlan had on a number of occasions stopped in a small place called Langden where lived a very superstitious and backward people. It was decided by their powerful local healer that the headaches that so bothered the people of Langden must be caused by evil spirits possessing them. He ordered white-hot irons put to the bottoms of the feet of those with headaches to drive out the evil spirits. It was a remarkable cure. No one in Langden was ever possessed again. The headaches vanished.

If only the plague could vanish so easily.

If only Nadine could vanish so easily. They couldn't send her away, now, when there would be so much need among the people. Like it or not, Nadine was going to be around until this was over. Shota seemed to be tightening her clutches around Richard.

Kahlan didn't know what Richard had said to Nadine, but she could imagine. Nadine had suddenly been stricken with overt politeness. Kahlan knew Nadine's apology hadn't been sincere. Richard had probably told her that if she didn't apologize, he would boil her alive. With the way Cara's gaze so often passed over Nadine, Kahlan suspected that Nadine had more to worry about than Richard.

Kahlan and Richard led the rest of their group between the towering white columns set to each side of the entrance, through the open doors carved with geometric designs, and into the palace. The cavernous grand hall inside was lit by windows of pale blue glass set between polished white marble columns topped with gold capitals, and by dozens of lamps spaced along the walls.

A leather-clad figure in the distance wandered toward them across the black-and-white marble squares. Someone else approached from the right side, from the guest rooms. Richard slowed to a stop and turned.

'Ulic, would you please go find General Kerson. He might be at the D'Haran headquarters. Does anyone know where General Baldwin is?'

'He's probably at Kelton's palace, on Kings Row,' Kahlan said. 'He's been staying there since he arrived and helped us defeat the Blood of the Fold.'

Richard nodded wearily. Kahlan didn't think she had ever seen him looking worse. His spiritless eyes stared out from an ashen face. He swayed on his feet as he squinted, looking for Egan not ten feet away.

'Egan, there you are. Go get General Baldwin, please. I don't know where he is, but you can ask around.'

Egan cast a quick, uneasy glance toward Kahlan. 'Would you like us to bring anyone else, Lord Rahl?'

'Anyone else? Yes. Tell them to bring their officers. I'll be in my office. Bring them there.'

Ulic and Egan both clapped fists to hearts before turning to their duties. As they departed, they conveyed a message through quick hand signals to the two Mord-Sith. In response, Cara and Raina maneuvered closer to Richard, screening him as Tristan Bashkar came to a wary halt.

Berdine meandered up on the other side, her rapt attention on the open journal in her hands. She seemed completely absorbed in what she was studying, and oblivious to anything around her. Kahlan put out a hand to stop her before she bumped into Richard. She rocked to a halt like a rowboat that had drifted in and grounded on the shore.

Tristan bowed. 'Mother Confessor. Lord Rahl.'

'Who are you?' Richard asked.

'Tristan Bashkar, of Jara, Lord Rahl. I'm afraid we haven't been formally introduced.'

Life sparked into Richard's gray eyes. 'And have you decided to surrender, minister Bashkar?'

Tristan had been about to bow again at an expected formal introduction. He hadn't expected Richard's questions to come first. He cleared his throat and straightened. His easy smile welled onto his face.

'Lord Rahl, I do appreciate your indulgence. The Mother Confessor has graciously granted me two weeks to observe the signs from the stars.'

Power came to Richard's voice. 'You risk your people seeing swords, instead of stars, minister.'

Tristan unbuttoned his coat. From the corner of her eye, Kahlan saw Cara's Agiel twitch up into her hand. Tristan didn't notice. His gaze stayed on Richard while he drew his coat back, holding it open casually by resting his fist on his hip. It exposed the knife at his belt. Raina flicked her Agiel up into her hand.

'Lord Rahl, as I explained to the Mother Confessor, our people looked forward with great joy to joining with the D'Haran empire.'

'D'Haran empire?'

'Tristan,' Kahlan said, 'we're rather busy at the moment. We have discussed this already, and you have been given two weeks. Now, if you will excuse us?'

Tristan brushed back a lock of his hair, his bright brown eyes taking her in. 'I'll get to the point, then. I've heard rumors that plague is loose in Aydindril.'

Richard's raptor glower was suddenly in full form. 'It's not just a rumor. It's true.'

'How much danger is there?'

Richard's hand found the hilt of his sword. 'If you join with the Order, minister, you will wish it was the plague on you, instead of me.'

Kahlan had rarely seen two men so instantly and intently dislike each other. She knew Richard was exhausted, and in no mood, after having just seen so many seriously ill or dead children, to be challenged by a noble such as Tristan inquiring after his own hide. Jara had also been on the council that had condemned Kahlan to death. Although it wasn't Tristan who had voted to behead her, it had been a councilor from his land. Richard had killed that Jarian councilor.

Kahlan didn't know why Tristan took such an instant dislike to Richard, except for the fact that this was the man who had demanded Jara's surrender. She guessed that was reason enough; if she were in his place, she might feel the same.

Kahlan was expecting the two men to draw steel any second. Drefan stepped between them.

'I'm Drefan Rahl, High Priest of the Raug'Moss community of healers. I've had some experience with the plague. I suggest that you confine yourself to your room and avoid contact with strangers. Especially prostitutes. Beyond that, you should get enough sleep and proper, healthful food.

'Those things will help to keep your body strong against the distemper. Also, I will be speaking to the staff, here at the palace, on strengthening oneself against illness. You're welcome to come and hear my guidance, as is anyone else of a mind.'

Tristan had listened earnestly to Drefan. He bowed, thanking him for his advice. 'Well, I appreciate the truth, Lord Rahl. A lesser man might have tried to deceive me about such a serious problem. I can see why you're so busy. I'll take my leave so that you may see to your people.'

Berdine nudged up beside Richard as he glared after Tristan's departing back. As intently as she had been studying the journal, muttering to herself, testing the pronunciation of High D'Haran words, Kahlan doubted she had heard anything that had been said.

'Lord Rahl, I need to talk to you,' Berdine mumbled.

Richard put a hand on her shoulder in a signal for her to wait. 'Drefan, Nadine, do either of you have anything for a headache? A really bad headache?'

'I have some herbs that will help, Richard,' Nadine offered.

'I have something better.' Drefan leaned closer to Richard. 'It's called sleep. Perhaps you recall having experienced it in the past?'

'Drefan, I know that I've been awake for a while, but –'

'Many days and nights.' Drefan held up a finger. 'If you try to mask the outcome of lack of sleep with so-called remedies, you do yourself no service. The headache will return, worse than before. You will ruin your strength. You will be no good to yourself, or anyone else.'

'Drefan is right,' Kahlan said.

Without looking up, Berdine turned the page she was reading in the journal.

'I agree. I feel much better since I got some sleep.' Berdine seemed to have finally noticed that there were other people around. 'Now that I'm alert, I can think better.'

Richard warded their insistence with a lifted hand. 'I know. Soon, I promise. Now, what was it you wanted to tell me, Berdine?'

'What?' She was reading again. 'Oh. I found out where the Temple of the Winds is.'

Richard's brow went up. 'What?'

'After I got some sleep, I could think more clearly. I realized that we were limiting our search by looking for a limited number of key words, so I tried to think of what the old wizards would do in their situation. I reasoned that –'

'Where is it!' Richard bellowed.

Berdine finally looked up and blinked. 'The Temple of the Winds is located atop the Mountain of the Four Winds.'

Berdine noticed Raina for the first time. The two women smiled in greeting, their eyes sharing a private warmth.

Kahlan shrugged to Richard's questioning look. 'Berdine, that's not much help unless you can tell us where it is.'

Berdine frowned a moment, and then waved in apology. 'Oh. Sorry. That's the translation' – she frowned again – 'I think.'

Richard swiped a hand across his face. 'What does Kolo call it?'

Berdine flipped the page back and turned the book, tapping a finger at a place in the writing.

Richard squinted. '*Berglendursch ost Kymermosst,*' he read from the journal. 'Mountain of the Four Winds.'

'Actually,' Berdine said, '*Berglendursch* means more than just mountain. *Berglen* is "mountain," and *dursch* can sometimes mean "rock," though it can also mean other things, like "strong-willed," but in this case I think it means something more along the lines of rock mountain, or great mountain made of rock. You know, rocky mountain of the four winds … something like that.'

Kahlan shifted her weight on her tired feet. 'Mount Kymermosst?'

Berdine scratched her nose. 'Yes. That sounds like it could be the same place.'

'That has to be the same place,' Richard said, looking hopeful for the first time in hours. 'Do you know where it is?'

'Yes. I've been on Mount Kymermosst,' Kahlan said. 'There's no doubt about its being windy up there – and rocky. There are some old ruins atop the mountain, but nothing like a temple.'

'Maybe the ruins are the temple,' Berdine offered. 'We don't know how big it is. A temple can be small.'

'No, I don't think so, in this case.'

'Why?' Richard asked. 'What's up there? How far is it?'

'It's not far to the northeast. Maybe a day's ride, depending. Two at the most. It's a pretty inhospitable place. As treacherous as the old trail going up and over the mountain is, going over Mount Kymermosst prevents you from having to go through some very difficult country and saves days of travel.

'At the top is the site of some old ruins. Just some kind of outbuildings, from the look of them. I've seen a lot of grand places; I recognize, architecturally, that what's up there isn't the main structure. They're something like the outbuildings here, at the Confessors' Palace. There's a road through the buildings, a bit like the grand promenade here going through the outbuildings.'

Richard hooked a thumb behind his wide leather belt. 'Well, where does it go, this grand road?'

Kahlan stared into his gray eyes. 'Right to the edge of a cliff. The buildings are at the edge of a cliff. That sheer stone wall drops off for maybe three or four thousand feet.'

'Is there any kind of stairway carved in the cliff? Something leading down to the temple itself?'

'Richard, you don't understand. The buildings are hard on the edge of the cliff. It's obvious that the buildings, walls, and the road itself went on, because they're sheared off abruptly right at the edge. There used to be more of the mountain there. It's gone now. It's all fallen away. A rockslide, or something. What was beyond the ruins, the main structure and the mountain, is gone.'

'That's what Kolo said. The team returned, and the Temple of the Winds was gone.' Richard looked devastated. 'They must have used magic to tear away the side of the mountain, to bury the Temple of the Winds so no one could ever go there again.'

'Well,' Berdine sighed, 'I'll keep looking in the journal to see if he says anything about the Temple of the Winds falling in a rockslide, or avalanche.'

Richard nodded. 'Maybe there's more about it in the journal.'

'Lord Rahl, will you have time to help me before you go off to be married?'

A chill silence filled the grand hall.

'Berdine –' Richard's mouth worked, but no more words were forthcoming.

'I heard the soldiers are well,' Berdine said, looking briefly at Kahlan and then back at Richard. 'You told me that you and the Mother Confessor would be leaving to be wedded just as soon as the soldiers were well. The soldiers are well.' She grinned. 'I know that I'm your favorite, but you haven't changed your mind, have you? Gotten cold feet?'

She waited expectantly, seeming not to notice that no one was smiling at her joke.

Richard looked numb. He couldn't say it. Kahlan knew that he feared speaking the words, feared he would break her heart.

'Berdine,' Kahlan said into the heavy hush, 'Richard and I won't be going away to be married. The wedding is called off. For now, anyway.'

Even though she had whispered the words, they seemed to echo off the marble walls as if she had shouted them.

Nadine's intently blank face spoke more than if she had grinned. It was somehow worse that she didn't, because it made it all the more obvious that she was schooling her expression, yet no one could have cause to reproach her.

'Called off?' Berdine blinked in astonishment. 'Why?'

Richard stared down at Berdine, not daring to look at Kahlan. 'Berdine, Jagang started a plague in Aydindril. That's what the prophecy down in the pit was about. Our duty is to the people here, not to our own … How would it look if… ?'

He fell silent.

The journal in her hands lowered. 'I'm sorry.'

CHAPTER 32

Kahlan stared out the window at the falling night, at the falling snow. Behind her, Richard sat at his desk, his gold cloak laid over the arm of his chair. He was working on the journal with Berdine while he waited for the officers to arrive. Berdine did most of the talking. He grunted occasionally when she told him what she thought a word meant, and why. Kahlan didn't think that as tired as he was he was much use to Berdine.

Kahlan glanced back over her shoulder. Drefan and Nadine were huddled together beside the hearth. Richard had asked them to come along to answer any questions the generals might have. Nadine confined her attention to Drefan, scrupulously avoiding looking at Richard, and especially at Kahlan. Probably because she knew that Kahlan would detect the glint of triumph in her eyes.

No. This wasn't a triumph for Nadine – for Shota. This was only a postponement. Just until ... until what? Until they could halt a plague? Until most of the people of Aydindril died? Until they themselves got the plague and died, as the prophecy foretold?

Kahlan went to Richard and laid a hand on his shoulder, desperately needing his touch. Thankfully, she felt him put a hand over hers.

'Just a postponement,' she whispered as she leaned close to his ear. 'This doesn't change it, Richard. This only delays it for a little while, that's all. I promise.'

He patted her hand as he smiled up at her. 'I know.'

Cara opened the door and leaned in. 'Lord Rahl, they're coming now.'

'Thanks, Cara. Leave the door open and tell them to come in.'

Raina lit a long splinter in the hearth. She put a hand to Berdine's shoulder to balance herself as she leaned past to light another lamp at the far end of the table. Her long, dark braid slipped over her shoulder, tickling Berdine's face. Berdine scratched her cheek and gave Raina a brief smile.

To see those two touch or even acknowledge one another in front of others was rare in the extreme. Kahlan knew that it was because of the things Raina had seen that day. She, too, was feeling lonely, and in need of comfort. As deadening as their training had been, as numb as they were to agony, their human feelings were beginning to be rekindled. Kahlan could see in Raina's dark eyes that witnessing children suffer and die had affected her.

Kahlan heard Cara, out in the hall, telling men to go in. Muscular, graying General Kerson, looking as imposing as ever in his burnished leather uniform, marched through the doorway. Muscles bulged under the chain mail covering his arms.

Behind him came the commander of the Keltish forces, the robust General Baldwin. He was an older man with a white-flecked dark mustache, the ends of which grew down to the bottom of his jaw. As always, he looked distinguished in his green silk-lined serge cape, fastened on one shoulder with two buttons. A heraldic emblem slashed through with a diagonal black line dividing a yellow and blue shield was emblazoned on the front of his tan surcoat. Lamplight flashed off his ornate belt buckle and silver scabbard. He looked as fierce as he was dashing.

Before the phalanx of officers accompanying them had all entered the room, both generals were bowing. In the lamplight, General Baldwin's pate shone through his thinning gray hair as he bent low.

'My queen,' General Baldwin said. 'Lord Rahl.'

Kahlan bowed her head to the man as Richard stood, pushing his chair back. Berdine scooted her chair over, to be out of his way. She didn't bother to look up. She was Mord-Sith, and busy besides.

'Lord Rahl,' General Kerson said with a salute of his fist to his heart after he had straightened. 'Mother Confessor.'

Behind them, the officers were all bowing. Richard waited patiently until it was all finished. Kahlan imagined that he couldn't be eager to start.

He did so simply. 'Gentlemen, I regret to inform you that there is a plague upon Aydindril.'

'A plague?' General Kerson asked. 'A plague of what?'

'A distemper. A plague that makes people sicken and die. That kind of plague.'

'The black death,' Drefan put in with a somber voice from behind Kahlan and Richard.

The men all seemed to take a collective breath. They waited in silence.

'It started not long ago,' Richard said, 'so, fortunately, we will be able to take a few precautions. As of this moment, we know of less than a couple of dozen cases. Of course, there is no telling how many have it and have yet to fall ill. Of the ones we know were stricken, almost half are already dead. By morning, the number will grow.'

General Kerson cleared his throat. 'Precautions, Lord Rahl? What precautions are there to be taken? Do you have another cure for the men? For the people of the city?'

Richard rubbed his fingertips on his forehead as his eyes turned to the desk before him.

'No, general, I have no cures,' he whispered. Everyone heard his words, though; it was that silent in the room.

'Then what… ?'

Richard straightened himself. 'What we need to do is to separate the men. Disperse them. My brother has seen the plague before, and has read of great plagues in the past. We believe that it's possible that it spreads from person to person, much as when one person in a family has a sore throat, chest congestion, and stuffed nose, then the others in the family, from their proximity to the sick person, come down with the same illness.'

'I've heard that the plague is caused by bad air in a place,' one of the officers in the back put in.

'I am told that this, too, is possible,' Richard said. 'I have also been told that it could be caused by any number of other things: bad water, bad meat, heated blood.'

'Magic?' someone asked.

Richard shifted his weight. 'That, too, is a possibility. It is said by some that it could be a judgment by the spirits on our world, and a punishment for what they find. I, myself, don't believe such a thing. I've been out this afternoon, seeing innocent children suffering and dying. I can't believe that the spirits would do such a thing, no matter how displeased.'

General Baldwin rubbed his chin. 'Then what do you think it is that spreads it, Lord Rahl?'

'I'm no expert, but I lean toward my brother's explanation that it's like any other sickness, that it can be passed from person to person through odors in the air or close contact. This makes the most sense to me, although this sickness is much more serious. The plague, I am told, is almost always fatal.

'If it is, in fact, passed from person to person, then we must not delay. We must do what we can to keep the plague from our forces. I want the men split up into smaller units.'

General Kerson spread his hands in frustration. 'Lord Rahl, why can't you simply use your magic and rid the city of this plague?'

Kahlan touched Richard's back, reminding him to hold his temper. He seemed, though, to have no anger in him.

'I'm sorry, but right now, I don't know what magic can cure this plague. I don't know that any wizard has ever before cured a plague through the use of magic.

'You have to understand, general, that just because a person can command magic, that doesn't mean that they can stay the Keeper himself, when the time for his touch has come. If wizards could do that, I assure you, graveyards would vanish for want of clients. Wizards have not the power of the Creator.

'Our world has balance to it. Just as we all, especially soldiers, can aid the Keeper in bringing death, we all can also be a part of the Creator's work of creating life. We know, better than most, perhaps, that soldiers are charged with protecting peace and life itself. The balance to that is that we sometimes must take life to stay an enemy who would do greater harm. For this, we are remembered, not for the lives we try to preserve.

'A wizard, too, must be in balance, in harmony, with the world he lives in. The Creator and the Keeper both have a part to play in our world. It is not within the power of a mere wizard to dictate to them what shall be. He can work for events to combine toward a result – a marriage, for example, but he cannot direct the Creator Himself to bring forth a life as a result of that marriage.

'A wizard must remember always that he works within our world, and must do his best to help people, just as a farmer would help a neighbor who has a harvest to bring in, or a fire to douse.

'There are things a wizard can do that those without magic cannot, much the same as you men are strong and can wield a heavy battle-axe, whereas an old man could not. Even though you have the muscle to do this, that doesn't mean that your muscles can do what they aren't meant to do, such as exercise wisdom the old man has from his experience. He may defeat you in battle through his knowledge, rather than his muscle.

'No matter how great a wizard may be, he could not bear a new life into this world. A young woman, without magic, experience, or wisdom, could do such a thing, but he could not. Perhaps she has more to do with magic than he, in the end.

'What I'm trying to tell you men is that just because I have been born with the gift, that doesn't mean that the gift can stop this plague. We can't depend on magic to solve all our problems. Knowing the limitations of his power is just as important for a wizard as knowing the limitations of his men is for an army officer.

'Many of you have seen what my sword can do against the enemy. Yet as awesome a weapon as it is, it cannot touch this invisible enemy. Other magic may prove as impotent.'

' "In your wisdom we are humbled." ' General Kerson quoted softly from the devotion.

Men voiced their agreement and nodded at the logic of Richard's explanation. Kahlan was proud of him, that at least he had convinced them. She wondered if he had convinced himself.

367

'It's not so much wisdom,' Richard murmured, 'as it is simple common sense.

'Please be assured, all of you,' he went on, 'that that doesn't mean I have no intention of trying to find a way to end this plague. I am looking into every possible means of stopping it.' He laid a hand on Berdine's shoulder. She glanced up. 'Berdine is helping me with the old books from wizards past, to see if they left us any wisdom.

'If there is a way for magic to stop it, then I will find that way. For now, though, we must use other means at our disposal to protect people. We need to have the men split up.'

'Split up, and then what?' General Kerson asked.

'Split up and get out of Aydindril.'

General Kerson stiffened. The links of his chain mail reflected the lamplight, so that he seemed to sparkle like a vision of a spirit. 'Leave Aydindril undefended?'

'No,' Richard insisted. 'Not undefended. What I propose is to have our forces divide up, so there is less chance of the plague spreading among them, and move to separate positions around Aydindril. We can put detachments of our forces at all the passes, all the roads and access valleys. That way, no force can advance against us.'

'What if one does?' General Baldwin asked. 'Then those smaller, separate forces may be insufficient to drive off an attack.'

'We will have sentries and scouts. We'll have to increase them so that we don't have any surprises. I don't think there are any forces of the Order this far north yet, but if any attack does come, then we will have warning and can gather our forces quickly. We don't want them too far apart to be able to defend the city if they must, but they must be far enough apart to keep from passing the plague throughout the whole of the army.

'Any ideas you men have would be valued. That's one reason I asked you here. If you have ideas about any of this, then please feel free to speak up.'

Drefan stepped forward. 'It needs to be done quickly. The sooner the men are away, the better the chance that none of them will have come in contact with the sickness.'

The officers all nodded as they pondered.

'The officers who went with us today should remain here,' Drefan said. 'They may have come in contact with someone who has the plague. Make a list of any they work closely with, and have them isolated here in Aydindril, too.'

'We'll see to it at once,' General Kerson said. 'Tonight.'

Richard nodded. 'Each group of our forces must communicate with the others, of course, but messages must be spoken only. No written messages passing from hand to hand. The papers could carry the plague. These men who pass commands and messages should talk at a distance. At least the way we are here, in this room, with me at this end and you at the other.'

'Isn't that a rather extraordinary precaution?' one of the officers asked.

'I have heard,' Drefan said, 'that people who have the plague, but have not yet fallen sick and therefore don't know of their affliction, can be detected by the distinctive odor of the plague on their breath.' Men nodded with interest. 'But to smell that fatal odor would infect you with the plague, and you, too, would be stricken and die.'

Mumbling spread back through the men.

'That's why we don't want the messengers to get too close to one another,' Richard said. 'If one were to already have the plague, we don't want him spreading it to another group of our forces. There is no use in going to all of this trouble if we aren't scrupulous in our attention to everything.

'This is a deadly poison. If we act quickly, and act as wisely as we know how, we may spare a great many people from death. If we don't take these precautions seriously, nearly every one of the people in this city, and every one of our men, could be dead within weeks.'

Serious, worried talk swept back through the room.

'We are giving you the worst look at it,' Drefan said, bringing their attentive gazes back. 'We don't want to pretend the danger is less than it is. But there are things in our favor. The most important is the weather. The plagues I have seen, and read about, spread worst in the high heat of summer. I don't think it will be able to get a foothold in the cool weather of this time of year. We have that much.'

Men sighed with renewed hope. Kahlan didn't.

'One other thing,' Richard said as he looked from eye to

eye. 'We are D'Harans. We are people of honor. Our men will act accordingly. I don't want any of us lying to people about the danger, telling people that there is no risk, and on the other hand, I don't want anyone deliberately panicking people. Everyone will be frightened enough as it is.

'You are also soldiers. This is no less a battle than if any other enemy attacked our people. This is part of our job.

'Some of the men will have to stay in the city to help. There may need to be men at arms to hold down any uprising that may be stirred up. If there are any riots, like there were with the red moon, I want them put down at once. Use whatever force is necessary, but no more. Remember, the people of this city are our people – we are their protectors, not their wardens.

'We will need men to help with digging graves. I don't think we can be burning that many dead, if the plague gets hot among the population.'

'How many do you think could die, Lord Rahl?' one of the officers asked.

'Thousands,' Drefan answered. 'Tens of thousands.' His blue-eyed gaze took them all in. 'If it gets bad enough, more. I read of a plague that in three months took the life of nearly three of every four people in a city of close to half a million.'

A low whistle came from an officer in back.

'One other thing,' Richard said. 'Some people will panic. They will want to run from Aydindril to remove themselves from the danger. Most will want to stay, not only because this is the only home they know, but because their livelihood is here.

'We can't allow people to flee Aydindril and spread the plague to other places in the Midlands, or even beyond, to D'Hara. It must be confined here. If people want to rush away from the city and go to the surrounding hills, separating themselves from their neighbors who they fear have the plague upon them, we must be understanding of their fears.

'They are to be allowed to run to the countryside if they wish, but they must remain in the area. I want our soldiers who will be in these separate units to ring the city and surrounding country, protecting all routes to and from Aydindril. The people must stay within these limits.

'Any person fleeing could be infected with the plague and

not know it, thus endangering people in other places. As a last resort, force must be used to prevent them from taking the plague abroad. Please keep in mind that these are not malevolent people, but simply people frightened for the lives of their families.

'The ones who flee the city to wait out the plague will soon be short of food and succumb to starvation. Remind people to take food, as they are not likely to find it in the countryside. They will be no less dead if they die of hunger rather than plague. Remind them of this, and that looting of farms will not be tolerated. We will not allow anarchy.

'Well, I guess that's about all I have to say. What are your questions?'

'Will you be leaving tonight, my queen, Lord Rahl, or in the morning?' General Baldwin asked. 'And where will you be staying?'

'Richard and I won't be leaving Aydindril,' Kahlan said.

'What? But you must get away,' General Baldwin insisted. 'Please, both of you must escape this. We need you to lead us.'

'We didn't know what we were dealing with until it was too late,' Kahlan said. 'We may have already been exposed to the plague.'

'We don't think that likely,' Richard said, wanting to assuage their fears. 'But I must stay to see if there is any magic that will stop this plague. I will need to be going up to the Keep. If we're up in the hills we can't be of any use, and I might miss a chance of finding a solution. We will remain here and oversee the command of the city.

'Drefan is the High Priest of the Raug'Moss healers, from D'Hara. The Mother Confessor and I could be in no better hands. He and Nadine will be staying, too, to see what relief can be brought to people.'

As the men asked questions and discussed matters of food and supplies, Kahlan moved to the window, watching the snow and wind build in the spring storm. Richard was speaking to his men the way a commander spoke on the eve of a battle, to instill in them a sense of purpose, to harden them to the battle ahead. As in any battle, death would run rampant.

Despite what Drefan believed about the plague not being

able to build to full strength in the cold weather, Kahlan knew that it wasn't true in this case.

This was no ordinary plague. This was a plague started by magic, by a man who wanted to kill them all.

Down in the pit, Jagang had called it *Ja'La dh Jin* – The Game of Life. Jagang was incensed that Richard had changed the ball to a lighter one so that all the children could enjoy playing, instead of just the strongest, the most brutal. Jagang started the killing with those children. It was no accident; it was a message.

It was the game of life.

This would be Jagang's world, ruled by such savagery, if he won.

CHAPTER 33

For the next hour, the men asked questions, mostly of Drefan. The two generals offered suggestions to Richard regarding command and logistics. Options were briefly discussed, plans were made, and officers were assigned duties. The army was to begin moving that very night. There were a great many Blood of the Fold who had surrendered, and although they had since sworn loyalty to Richard, it was still thought wise to divide them, too, sending some with each unit, rather than letting them remain together. Richard concurred with the suggestion.

When at last they had all departed to begin the work, Richard dropped heavily into his chair. He had come a long way from being a woods guide.

Kahlan was proud of him.

She opened her mouth to say so, but Nadine spoke the words in her stead.

Richard mumbled a flat 'Thanks.'

Nadine tentatively touched her fingertips to the back of his shoulder. 'Richard, you were always … I don't know … Richard, to me. A boy from home. A woods guide.

'Today, and especially tonight, with all those important men, I think I saw you differently for the first time. You really are this Lord Rahl.'

Richard put his elbows on the table before him and his face in his hands. 'I think I'd rather be at the bottom of the cliff, buried with the Temple of the Winds.'

'Don't be silly,' she whispered.

Bristling, Kahlan moved to his side. Nadine glided away.

'Richard,' Kahlan said, 'you have to get some sleep. Now. You promised. We need you strong. If you don't get some sleep –'

'I know.' He pushed away from the table and stood. He turned to Drefan and Nadine. 'Do either of you have anything to make a person go to sleep? I've tried … Lately, I just lie there. My mind won't be quiet.'

'A Feng San disharmony,' Drefan announced at once. 'You bring it on yourself with the way you push past the limits of your body. There are bounds to what we can do, and if –'

'Drefan,' Richard said, cutting him off with a gentle voice, 'I know what you mean, but I do what I must. You just have to understand that. Jagang is trying to kill us all. It will do me no good to be as high-spirited as a squirrel in spring if it means we all end up dead.'

Drefan grunted. 'I understand, but that doesn't get you strong.'

'So, I'll try to be good later. What about going to sleep tonight?'

'Meditation,' Drefan said. 'That will calm your energy flows, and begin bringing them into harmony.'

Richard rubbed his brow. 'Drefan, hundreds of thousands of people are in danger of dying because Jagang wants to put the whole of the world under his boot. He's shown us that he has no bounds to his determination.

'He's starting the killing with children.' Richard's knuckles turned white as his hands fisted. 'Just to send me a message! Children!

'He has no conscience. He's showing me what he's willing to do to win. To make me surrender! He thinks it will break me!'

In contrast to his knuckles, Richard's face had gone scarlet. 'He's wrong. I'd never give our people over to that kind of tyrant. Never! I'll do whatever I must to stop this plague! I swear it!'

The room rang with the sudden silence. Kahlan had never seen Richard angry in quite this way. When he had the deadly fury of the Sword of Truth's magic in his eyes, the object of his rage was usually at hand; the rage was invoked by and directed at a palpable threat.

This was frustrated anger at an invisible enemy. There was no threat he could get his hands on, now. He had no direct way to fight it. Kahlan could see in his eyes that this anger wasn't the magic of the sword. This was purely Richard's rage.

His face finally cooled. He took a calming breath as he wiped a hand across his face. He regained control of his voice.

'If I try to meditate, I will only see those sick and dead children again in my mind. Please, I can't bear to see that in my sleep. I need to go to sleep and not have dreams.'

'Go to sleep and not have dreams? You are bothered by dreams?'

'Nightmares. I have them all day, too, when I'm awake, but they're real. The dream walker can't enter my dreams, but he has found a way to give me nightmares, nonetheless. Please, dear spirits, at least when I'm asleep, grant me some peace.'

'A sure sign of a Feng San meridian disharmony,' Drefan confirmed to himself. 'I can see that you are going to be a difficult patient, but not without a cause.'

He slipped the bone pin from the loop of leather and opened the flap on one of the pouches at his belt. He pulled out a few leather purses. He put one back. 'No, that will kill pain, but not be much aid to sleep.' He sniffed another. 'No, that will make you vomit.' He searched his other things and finally closed the flaps on the pouches. 'I'm afraid I didn't bring anything so simple with me. I only brought rare items.'

Richard sighed. 'Thanks for trying, anyway.'

Drefan turned to Nadine. She was bottled zeal, pressing her lips together with restrained delight as the others talked.

'The things you gave Yonick's mother wouldn't be strong enough for Richard,' Drefan said to her. 'Do you have any hops?'

'Sure,' she said calmly, but obviously pleased that someone had at last asked her. 'In tincture, of course.'

'Perfect,' Drefan said. He slapped Richard on the back. 'You can meditate another time. Tonight, you will be asleep in no time. Nadine will fix you a preparation. I'll go start checking with the staff and giving them my recommendations.'

'Don't forget to meditate,' Richard muttered as Drefan departed.

Berdine remained behind, studying the journal, as Nadine, Cara, Raina, Ulic, Egan, and Kahlan all followed Richard to his room, not far away. Ulic and Egan took up posts outside in the hall. The rest of them went into the room with Richard.

Inside, Richard tossed his gold cloak over a chair. He pulled the baldric over his head and laid the Sword of Truth atop it. He wearily drew his gold-trimmed tunic over his head, and removed his shirt, leaving him with a black, armless undershirt.

Nadine watched from the corner of her eye while she softly counted each drop aloud as it dripped into a glass of water.

Richard flopped down on the edge of the bed. 'Cara, would you pull my boots off for me, please?'

Cara rolled her eyes. 'Do I look like a valet?'

She squatted to the task when Richard smiled.

He leaned back on his elbows. 'Tell Berdine that I want her to look for any reference to this Mountain of the Four Winds place. See what else she can find out about it.'

Cara looked up from his feet. 'What a brilliant idea,' she said with mock enthusiasm. 'I bet she would never have thought of that on her own, all-wise and knowing master.'

'All right, all right. I guess I'm not needed. How's my magic potion coming over there?'

'Just finished,' Nadine said in a cheery voice.

Cara grunted as she yanked off his other boot. 'Undo your pants, and I'll pull them off, too.'

Richard scowled down at her. 'I'll manage, thank you.'

Cara smirked to herself as he rolled off the bed and went to Nadine. She handed him the glass of water with the tincture of hops. She had put something else in the glass of water, too.

'Don't drink it all. I put in fifty drops. That's way more than you should need, but I wanted to leave you with extra. Drink about a third, and then if you wake in the night, you can always drink another swallow or two. I put in some valerian and skullcap, too, to help insure you go into a deep and dreamless sleep.'

Richard downed half of it. His face contorted. 'As bad as this tastes, it will put me to sleep or else kill me.'

Nadine smiled at him. 'You'll sleep like a baby.'

'Babies don't sleep all that well, from what I've heard.'

Nadine laughed in a soft lilt. 'You'll sleep, Richard. I promise. If you wake too early, just take a little more.'

'Thanks.' He sat down on the edge of the bed, looking from one woman to the next. 'I'll manage with my pants. I swear.'

Cara rolled her eyes and headed for the door, urging Nadine along before her. Kahlan kissed his cheek.

'Get in bed. I'll come back in and tuck you in and kiss you good night as soon as I see to the guards.'

Raina followed Kahlan out and closed the door. Nadine was waiting, rocking back and forth on her heels.

'How's the arm? Do you need a poultice?'

'My arm is much better,' Kahlan said. 'I think it's fine, now. But thank you for asking.'

Kahlan clasped her hands and stood watching Nadine. Cara watched Nadine. Raina watched Nadine.

Nadine's gaze moved from one woman to the next. She glanced to Ulic and Egan, who were watching her, too. 'All right, then. Good night.'

'Good night,' Kahlan, Cara, and Raina said as one.

They watched as Nadine strolled off.

'I still say you should have let me kill her,' Cara said under her breath.

'I may yet let you,' Kahlan said. She knocked on the door. 'Richard? You in bed?'

'Yes.'

Cara started to follow as Kahlan opened the door.

Kahlan turned. 'I'll only be a minute. I don't think he can spoil my honor in a minute.'

Cara frowned. 'With Lord Rahl, anything is possible.'

Raina laughed and slapped Cara's arm, making her leave Kahlan be.

'I wouldn't worry. With what we've seen today, neither of us would be in the mood,' Kahlan said. She shut the door.

A single candle was lit. Richard was covered to his stomach. Kahlan sat on the edge of the bed and took his hand. She held it to her heart.

'Are you terribly disappointed?' he asked.

'Richard, we will be married. I've waited my whole life for you. We're together; that's all that really matters.'

Richard smiled. His tired eyes sparkled. 'Well, not all.'

Kahlan couldn't help smiling herself. She kissed his knuckles.

'Just as long as you know that I understand,' she said. 'I didn't want you to go to sleep thinking I was heartbroken that we can't be married just now. We'll be married when we can.'

He put his other hand to the back of her neck and pulled her into a gentle kiss. She laid a hand on his bare chest, feeling his warm flesh, his breathing, his heartbeat. If she hadn't been so devastated by the suffering children she had seen that day, the feel of him would have ignited longing in her own breast.

'I love you,' she whispered.

'I love you, now, and always,' he whispered back.

She blew out the candle. 'Sleep well, my love.'

Cara eyed Kahlan suspiciously as she closed the door. 'That was two minutes.'

Kahlan ignored Cara's little jab. 'Raina, would you guard Richard's room until you go to bed, and then have a guard posted?'

'Yes, Mother Confessor.'

'Ulic, Egan, with that sleep potion, Richard may not be able to awake if he were in danger. I'd like one of you to be here when Raina goes to bed.'

Ulic folded his massive arms. 'Mother Confessor, neither of us has any intention of leaving this spot as long as Lord Rahl is asleep.'

Egan pointed at the floor against the opposite wall. 'One of us can take a nap if need be. We'll both be here. Don't be concerned for Lord Rahl's safety while he is sleeping.'

'Thank you, all of you. One other thing: Nadine isn't to be allowed into his room – for any reason. None whatsoever.'

They all nodded in satisfaction. Kahlan turned to the blond-headed Mord-Sith.

'Cara, go get Berdine. I'm going to get a cloak. Both of you should bring your cloaks, too. It's a foul night.'

'And where are we going?'

'I'll meet you both out in the stables.'

'The stables? Why do you want to go out there? It's time for dinner.'

Cara would never really balk at a duty over a matter so petty as dinner. She was suspicious.

'Grab something from the kitchens that we can take with us, then.'

Cara clasped her hands behind her back. 'Where are we going?'

'For a ride.'

'A ride. Mother Confessor, where are we going?'

'The Wizard's Keep.'

Both Cara and Raina lifted an eyebrow.

Cara's surprise turned to a frown of disapproval. 'Does Lord Rahl know that you want to go up to the Keep?'

'Of course not. If I had told him why I'm going, he would have insisted on going, too. He needs sleep, so I didn't tell him.'

'And why are we going?'

'Because the Temple of the Winds is gone. The wizards who did it were put on trial. There are records in the Keep of all the trials held there. I want to find that record. Tomorrow, Richard can read it over, after he's gotten some sleep. It could help him.'

'Makes sense, going to the Wizard's Keep after dark. I will go get Berdine and some food and meet you in the stables. We'll make a picnic of it,' Cara said with blithe sarcasm.

CHAPTER 34

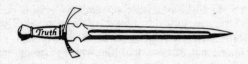

Kahlan batted the big, wet snowflakes from her lashes and pulled the hood of her cloak forward as she considered the foolishness of not thinking to change out of her white Confessor's dress. She stood in the stirrups, reached between her legs, and pulled more of the back of the dress under her bare legs to protect them from the cold saddle. Fortunately, her boots were high enough that hiking up the dress to sit in the saddle didn't expose her calves to the wind. She was glad, though, to be back on Nick, the big warhorse her Galean soldiers had given her. Nick was an old friend.

Cara and Berdine looked just as uncomfortable as she, but Kahlan knew that it was because they feared going to a place of magic. They had been in the Wizard's Keep before. They didn't want to return. Back at the stables they had tried to talk her out of it. Kahlan had reminded them of the plague.

Nick's ears twitched even before the dark shapes of soldiers appeared out of the swirling snow to challenge them. Kahlan knew they had reached the stone bridge; the soldiers were posted just to the city side of it.

The men sheathed their swords when Cara growled at them, pleased to have someone handy upon whom to vent her foul mood.

'Terrible night to be out, Mother Confessor,' one of the soldiers said, happy to address someone other than the Mord-Sith.

'Terrible night to be stationed out here,' she said.

The man looked back over his shoulder. 'Any night you're stationed on watch up here at the Keep is a terrible night.'

Kahlan smiled. 'The Keep looks sinister, soldier, but it's not so bad as it looks.'

'If you say so, Mother Confessor. Myself, I think I'd just as soon stand guard over the underworld itself.'

'No one has tried to get in the Keep, have they?'

'If they had, you'd have heard about it, or found our bodies, Mother Confessor.'

Kahlan urged her big stallion on. Nick snorted and surged ahead on the slick snow. She trusted him in such conditions and let him lead the way. Cara and Berdine both swayed easily in their saddles as they followed behind. Back in the stables, Cara had snatched her horse's bit, looked the animal in the eye, and ordered it not to give her any trouble. Kahlan had the odd feeling that the bay mare understood the warning.

Kahlan could just see the stone walls at the sides of the bridge. Just as well that the horses couldn't see the chasm beyond. She knew Nick wouldn't spook, but she wasn't sure about the other two. The sheer rock walls of the yawning abyss dropped for thousands of feet. Unless you had wings, there was only this one way into the Wizard's Keep.

In the snowy darkness, the vast Keep, its soaring walls of dark stone, its ramparts, bastions, towers, connecting passage-ways, and bridges all blended into the inky darkness of the side of the mountain into which it was built. To those without magic or those who didn't understand magic, the Keep presented an unmistakable spectacle of sinister menace.

Kahlan had grown up in Aydindril and had been up to the Keep uncountable times, more often than not, alone. Even as a child, she had been allowed to go alone to the Keep, as were the other young Confessors. When she was little, wizards had tickled her and chased her through the halls, laughing with her. The Keep was a second home to her: comfortably safe, welcoming, and protective.

She knew, though, that there were dangers in the Keep, just as in any home. A home could be a safe, welcoming place, as long as one wasn't foolish enough to walk into the hearth. There were places in the Keep you didn't walk into, either.

It was only when she was older that she no longer went to

the Keep alone. When a Confessor became older, it was dangerous to go anywhere alone. After a Confessor had begun taking confessions, it wasn't safe for her to be without the protection of her wizard.

When she was older, a Confessor earned enemies. Family of the condemned rarely believed that a loved one had committed violent crimes, or they blamed Confessors for the man's death sentence, even though she was only the means of confirming its justice.

There were always attempts on the lives of Confessors. There was no shortage of people, from commoners to kings, wanting a Confessor dead.

'How are we going to go through the shields without Lord Rahl?' Berdine asked. 'His magic enabled us to pass through, before. We won't be able to get through the shields.'

Kahlan smiled assurance to the two Mord-Sith. 'Richard didn't know where he was going. He just blundered through the Keep, going where he needed to go on instinct. I know the ways to go that don't require magic to pass. There may be a few mild shields that will keep people out, but I can pass those. If I can pass, then I can get you through them by touching you when you pass through, the same way Richard took you through the more powerful shields.'

Cara grunted disagreeably. She had been hoping that the shields would stop them.

'Cara, I've been in the Keep thousands of times. It's perfectly safe. We're just going to the libraries. Just as you are my protector out in the world, in the Keep I will be yours. We are sisters of the Agiel. I won't let you get anywhere near dangerous magic. Trust me?'

'Well … I guess you are a sister of the Agiel. I can trust a sister of the Agiel.'

They passed under the huge portcullis and onto the Keep grounds. Once inside the massive outer walls, the snow melted as it touched the ground. Kahlan pushed back her hood. Inside the walls, it was warm and comfortable.

She shook the snow from her cloak and took a deep breath of the spring-fresh air, filling her lungs with the familiar, soothing scent. Nick whinnied agreeably.

Kahlan led the two Mord-Sith across the stretch of gravel

and stone chips to the arched opening in the wall that tunneled under part of the Keep. As they passed through the long passageway, the lamps hanging from Cara and Berdine's saddles lit the arched stone around them in an orange glow.

'Why are we going through here?' Cara asked. 'Lord Rahl took us in that big door back there.'

'I know. That's one reason you're afraid of the Keep. That was a very dangerous way to go in. I'm taking us to the way I usually enter. It's much better. You'll see.

'It's not the way visitors entered, either, but the way used by those who lived and worked here. The public came in at a different door, a place where they were greeted by a guide who saw to their wants.'

Beyond the tunnel, all three horses eyed the expansive paddock lush with grass. The gravel road ran beside the wall that held the main entrance to the Keep, with a fence on the other side of the road enclosing the paddock. To the left, part of the paddock was bounded by the walls of the Keep rather than a fence. At the rear were stables.

Kahlan dismounted and opened the gate. After removing saddles and tack, all three of them turned their horses loose in the paddock, where they could crop grass and frisk in the mild air if they wished.

A dozen wide granite steps, worn smooth and swayback over the millennia, led up into a recessed entryway, to the simple but heavy double doors into the Keep proper. Cara and Berdine followed behind with the lamps. The anteroom swallowed the lamplight into its vast space, only allowing the weak flames to hint at the columns and arches.

'What's that?' Berdine asked in a low whisper. 'It sounds like a storm drain.'

'There aren't … rats in here, are there?'

'Actually, it's a fountain,' Kahlan said, her voice echoing into the distance. 'And yes, Cara, there are rats in the Keep, but not where I'm taking you. Promise. Here, give me your lamp. Let me show you the bones of this menacing dungeon.'

Kahlan took the lamp and strode to one of the key lamps on the wall to the right. She could walk there without the aid of the lamp, she had done it so often, but she needed the lamp's flame. She found the key lamp, tilted back the tall chimney, and lit it with the flame from Cara's lamp.

The key lamp took to flame. With a succession of whooshing sounds, the rest of the lamps in the room lit – hundreds of them – two at a time, in pairs, one to each side. Each *whoosh* was followed almost simultaneously by another, as the lamps around the huge room took to flame from the key lamp. The light in the room grew; the effect was like turning up the wick on a lamp.

In a span of seconds, the anteroom was nearly as bright as day, bathed in the mellow yellow-orange glow of all the flames. Cara and Berdine stood slackjawed at the sight.

A hundred feet overhead the glassed roof was dark, but in the day, it flooded the room with warmth and light. At night, if the sky was clear, you could turn down the lamps and gaze at the stars, or let the moonlight wash the room.

In the center of the tiled floor stood a clover leaf-shaped fountain. Water shot fifteen feet into the air above the top bowl, to cascade down each successive tier into ever wider, scalloped bowls, finally running from evenly spaced points in the bottom one in perfectly matched arcs into the lower pool. An outer wall of variegated white marble was wide enough to act as a bench.

Berdine stepped down one step of the five that ringed the room. 'It's beautiful,' she whispered in astonishment.

Cara gazed about at the red marble columns holding the arches below the balcony that ran all the way around the oval-shaped room. She had a smile on her lips.

'This is nothing like the place Lord Rahl took us.' Cara frowned. 'The lamps. That was magic. There is magic in here. You said you would keep us away from magic.'

'I said I would keep you away from dangerous magic. The lamps are kind of like a shield, except in reverse. Instead of keeping people out, they're an enabling shield, to welcome and help them enter. It's a friendly kind of magic, Cara.'

'Friendly. Sure.'

'Come on, we came here for a purpose. We have work to do.'

Kahlan took them to the libraries via the elegant, warm halls, rather than the frightening way they had gone before.

They encountered only three shields. Kahlan's magic allowed her to pass these, and by holding Cara and Berdine's hands, it was possible to get them through, too, though both complained about a tingling sensation.

These shields didn't guard dangerous areas, and so were weaker than others in the Keep. There were shields that Kahlan couldn't pass, like the ones Richard had taken her through to go down to the sliph, though Kahlan thought there might be other ways to get down there. There were shields which Richard had gone through that in her experience no wizard had ever crossed before.

They came to an intersection with a hall of light pink stone running down both sides. At places, the hall opened into commodious rooms ringed with padded benches for conversing or reading. Beyond double doors in each of these large outer rooms was a library.

'I've been here,' Berdine said. 'I remember this.'

'Yes. Richard brought you here, but by a different route.'

Kahlan continued on to the eighth sitting room, and went through the double doors into the library there. She used her lamp to light the key lamp, and as before, all the rest lit, lifting the room out of its pitch blackness, bringing it to life. The floors were polished wood, with walls paneled in the same honey-colored oak. During the day, glassed windows on the far wall bathed the room with light and provided a beautiful view of Aydindril. Now, through the snow, Kahlan could only occasionally see the lights of the city below.

She strode down the aisle between the reading tables and the rows upon rows of bookshelves, looking for the one she remembered. In this room alone, there were one hundred and forty-five rows of books. There were comfortable chairs to use while reading, but tonight they would need the tables to lay out the books.

'So this is the library,' Cara said. 'In D'Hara, at the People's Palace, there are libraries much larger than this.'

'This is only one of twenty-six rooms like this. I can only imagine how many thousands of books are here in the Keep,' Kahlan said.

'Then how are we ever going to find the ones we're looking for?' Berdine asked.

'It shouldn't be as hard as it sounds. The libraries can be a bewildering maze when you wish to find something. I used to know a wizard who searched on and off his whole life for a bit of information he knew was in the libraries. He never found it.'

'Then how can we?'

'Because there are a few things that are specialized enough that they are kept together. Books of language, for example. I can take you to all the books on any specific language, because they're not about magic and so they're in one place. I don't know how books on magic and prophecy are organized, if they even are.

'Anyway, this library is where certain records are kept, such as the records of trials held here. I've not read them, but I was taught about them.'

Kahlan turned and led them between two rows of shelves. Nearly midway down the fifty-foot-long aisle, she came to a halt.

'Here they are. I can see by the writing on the spines that they're in different languages. Since I know all the languages but High D'Haran, I'll search all the ones in other languages. Cara, you look at the ones in ours, and Berdine, you take the ones in High D'Haran.'

The three of them started picking books from the shelves and carrying them to the tables, separating them into three stacks. There weren't as many as Kahlan had feared. Berdine had only seven books, Cara had fifteen, and Kahlan eleven, in a variety of languages. For Berdine, it would be slow going translating the D'Haran, but Kahlan was fluent in the other languages, and she would be able to help with Cara's stack as soon as she finished her own.

As Kahlan started in, she quickly found that it was going to be easier than she'd first thought. Each trial began with a statement of the type of crime, making it simple to eliminate those that had nothing to do with the Temple of the Winds.

There were charges against the accused ranging from the taking of a cherished object of little worth to murder. A sorceress was accused of casting a glamour, but was found innocent. A boy of twelve was accused of starting a fight in which another boy's arm was broken; because the aggressor

386

had used magic to cause the injury, the sentence was the suspension of his training for a period of one year. A wizard was accused of being a drunkard, a third offense, the prior punishments having failed to halt his belligerent behavior. He was found guilty and sentenced to death. The sentence was carried out two days later, when he had sobered.

Habitually, drunken wizards were viewed not with tolerance but as the true dangers they were, capable, in their inebriated state, of causing mass injury and death. Kahlan herself had seen wizards drink to excess only one time.

The accounts of the trials were fascinating, but the seriousness of their purpose kept Kahlan skimming through the books, looking for a reference to the Temple of the Winds, or to a team charged with a crime. The other two were making quick progress, too. In an hour, Kahlan had finished all eleven books in the other languages, Berdine had only three left, and Cara six.

'Anything?' Kahlan asked.

Cara lifted an eyebrow. 'I just found an account of a wizard who fancied hiking up his robes in front of women in the market on Stentor Street and commanding them to "kiss the serpent." I never knew wizards could get themselves in such a variety of trouble.'

'They're people, just like any other people.'

'No, they're not. They have magic,' Cara said.

'So do I. Have you found anything, Berdine?'

'No, not what we're looking for. Just common crimes.'

Kahlan reached for one of the books Cara hadn't been through, but paused.

'Berdine, you were down in the room with the sliph.'

Berdine made a show of shivering and producing a sound of revulsion from deep in her throat. 'Don't remind me.'

Kahlan shut her eyes, trying to remember the room. She remembered Kolo's bones, and she remembered the sliph, but she only vaguely recalled what else was in the room.

'Berdine, do you remember if there were any other books down there?'

Berdine bit down on the end of a fingernail as she squinted in concentration. 'I remember finding Kolo's journal open on the table. An inkwell and pen. I remember Kolo's bones, lying on the floor next to the chair, with most of his clothes long ago rotted away. His leather belt was still around him.'

Kahlan remembered much the same thing. 'But do you remember if there were any books on the shelves?'

Berdine turned her eyes up as she thought. 'No.'

'No there weren't, or no you don't remember?'

'No, I don't remember. Lord Rahl was really excited about finding Kolo's journal. He said it was something different from the books in the library, and he felt it was what he had been searching for: something different. We left right after that.'

Kahlan stood. 'You two keep looking through these books. I'm going down there and have a look, just to be sure.'

Cara's chair clattered against the floor as she stood. 'I will go with you.'

'There are rats down there.'

Her expression vexed, Cara put a hand on her hip. 'I've seen rats before. I will go with you.'

Kahlan remembered well Cara's story about the rats. 'Cara, there's no need. I don't need your protection in the Keep. Outside, yes, but in here I know the dangers better than you.

'I told you I wouldn't take you near dangerous magic. Down there is dangerous magic.'

'Then there is danger to you.'

'No, because I know about it. You don't. The danger would be to you, not me. I grew up here. My own mother let me have the run of the Keep when I was a little girl because I was taught about the dangers and how to avoid them. I know what I'm doing.

'Please stay here with Berdine and finish going through the books. It will save us time, and it's important. The sooner we find the one we're looking for, the sooner we can get home to watch over Richard. That's where our real concern is.'

Cara's leather creaked as she shifted her weight. 'I guess you would know the dangers of the magic here better than I. I think you're right about getting home. Nadine is back there.'

CHAPTER 35

Kahlan tried to overlay her mental map of the Keep on the passageways, stairwells, and rooms she traversed as she wound her way lower. Rats squeaked and skittered away from her lamp.

Although she had often seen the tower outside Kolo's room from the ramparts and walkways up on top of the Keep, she had never been down inside it until Richard had taken her there. Unfortunately, Richard had taken her there by way of dangerous passages, through shields she would never be able to get through on her own.

She was confident that there were other routes down to Kolo's room. There were vast areas of the Keep that weren't protected by any shields at all. She had only to find a way without shields, or with shields that her magic would be able to pass. The areas that Richard had taken her, protected by dangerous shields, she didn't know at all, since she had never been beyond those before, but she was familiar with a myriad of ways to get around them.

Oftentimes the 'hard shields,' as the wizards used to call them, were meant to protect something just beyond, rather than specifically to prevent passage to another area. Many of the rooms Richard had taken her through were like that: places of menacing magic she had never seen before. They oftentimes provided a more direct route, but required special magic.

If she was correct, that Richard had traversed a maze through dangerous places, rather than going through hard shields specifically protecting the tower, then there would be a way around the dangerous areas and into the tower room. In her experience, that was the way the Keep worked; if the tower room was meant to be off-limits, then it would be protected by its own hard shields. If it wasn't forbidden, then there would be at least one way she could enter. She had but to find it.

Even though she had spent a great deal of time in the Keep, much of that time was spent in the libraries studying. She had explored, of course, but the Keep was almost inconceivably vast. Not only was the part that could be seen from the outside immense, but much more of the Keep was burrowed into the mountain. The outer walls were only the tip of the Keep, the visible part of the tooth, with much more of the root hidden beneath.

Kahlan went through an empty room, chiseled from bedrock, to one of the passages on the other side. There were numerous empty rooms in the Wizards' Keep. Some of them, like the one she had just passed through, seemed nothing more than junctions where various passages connected, possibly enlarged to provide reference points.

The square-sided passage through the rock ahead appeared carefully cut and smoothed. Her lamp illuminated bands of symbols incised in the granite, with round areas in the field of swirling carvings polished to a high luster. Each encircling band marked the location of a mild shield that tingled against her flesh as she passed through.

Ahead, she saw the hall split into three passageways. Before she reached the junction, the air about her suddenly hummed. It took two steps before she could halt her onward rush. Each of those two steps caused the hum to raise in pitch to an uncomfortable buzzing. Her long hair lifted from her shoulders and back to stand straight out in all directions. The band carved in the stone ahead immediately began to glow red.

Kahlan retreated several paces. The humming lowered in pitch. Her hair settled down.

She cursed under her breath. A humming shield was an urgent warning to stay away. The red glow displayed the region of the shield itself. The hum warned that you were entering the field of a dangerous shield.

Some of these hard shields would actually prevent a person without the required magic from getting too close, by making

390

the very air get as thick as mud, and then stone. Some of the humming shields didn't prevent entry, but walking into one would sear the flesh and muscle right off a person's bones. The lesser shields were meant to keep people without magic, and thus knowledge, from getting close to the danger.

Kahlan turned and held up the lamp as she quickly retraced her steps to the room. She took a different passageway that ran in the general direction she wanted to go. It was a much more congenial-looking hall, with whitewashed walls and ceiling, making the lamp better able to brighten her way.

She encountered no shields at all in the white hall. A stairway took her lower into the Keep. Another stone hall at the bottom provided quick travel devoid of shields. In her mind, she was retracing the halls, rooms, stairs, and cramped tunnels, and was pretty sure that, by eliminating the false routes she had taken, there was a way to get to and from the tower without encountering any shields.

Kahlan threw open the door at the end of the stone hall and stepped out onto a walkway with an iron railing. She held the lamp up in front of her. She stood at the bottom level of the tower.

The walkway ringed the hall. Stairs wound their way up around the inside of the immense stone tower, with landings at other doors along the way. In the center, at the bottom of the tower, lurked a pool of black water. Rocks broke the surface of the water here and there. Bugs skittered across the inky surface of the pool. Salamanders rested on the rocks, their eyes rolling to watch her.

This was the place where she and Richard had fought the mriswith queen. Her stinking, broken eggs still littered the rock. Small bits of the door blasted from Kolo's room still floated in the pool, providing islands for fat bugs that hissed at the intrusion.

Across the water, on the opposite side of the round tower room, was the opening to Kolo's room.

Kahlan quickly made her way around the walkway to the wide platform outside Kolo's room. The doorway had been blown open, leaving blackened, jagged edges. In some places the stone itself was melted like candle wax. The tower wall outside the doorway was streaked with blackened lines of soot from the unleashed power that had opened Kolo's room for the first time in millennia.

When Richard had destroyed the Towers of Perdition, it had destroyed the magic seal on this room, too. The towers had sealed the Old World away from the New in the great war three thousand years before. They had also sealed the room with the sliph, and sealed in the man who had been unfortunate enough to be the one guarding her at the time.

Stone fragments crunched under her feet as Kahlan stepped into the room where Kolo had died, the room where dwelled the sliph. The silence was oppressive. It droned in her ears, making her welcome the relief of her footsteps.

Richard had awakened the sliph after thousands of years. The sliph had taken Richard to the Old World, and had brought him and Kahlan safely back to Aydindril. When they returned, Richard had put the sliph back to sleep. All the years Kahlan had spent in the Keep, and she had never known the sliph was there.

Kahlan couldn't even imagine the magic the wizards of old could use to conjure a being such as the sliph, or how they could have put her to sleep for all that time, so that she could wake again. Only at the fringes of her imagination could she conceive of the power Richard wielded, but didn't comprehend.

What would the war wizards of old, who knew their gift well, have been able to do with such unfathomable magic? What terrors would a war among those with that kind of power have been like?

The very thought gave her shivers.

It would have been things like the plague that had been set upon them, now. They could do those kinds of things.

The lamplight fell across Kolo's bones beside the chair. The pen and inkwell still sat on the dusty table. The round room, nearly sixty feet across, was capped with a high-domed ceiling, itself nearly as tall as the room was wide.

In the center was a round stone wall, like a well, twenty-five or thirty feet across. There dwelled the sliph. Kahlan held the light over the wall of the well, and glanced briefly down the smooth stone walls of the dark shaft that fell away seemingly forever.

The walls of the room were scorched in ragged lines as if lightning had gone wild in the place – another result of the same magic Richard had invoked when he destroyed the towers and when the doorway had been blasted open. Kahlan strode quickly around the room, checking to see if there was anything that might be useful. There was nothing in the room, other than the table, chair, and Kolo, except for a dusty set of shelves.

Kahlan was disappointed to find that there were no books on the shelves. There were three faded blue, glazed, lidded containers, probably once holding water or soup for the wizard on duty guarding the sliph. A white, glazed bowl held a silver spoon. A neatly folded cloth, or embroidery of some sort, sat on one of the shelves. When she touched it, it disintegrated into dust and little flakes where her fingers contacted it.

Kahlan bent lower, seeing that the bottom shelf held only a few spare candles and a lamp.

An abrupt sensation of icy alarm inundated her.

She was being watched.

She froze, holding her breath, telling herself that it was just her imagination. The fine hairs at the back of her neck stiffened. She felt a cold wave of gooseflesh run up her arms.

She strained to hear a-telling sound. Her toes cringed inside her boots. She feared to move. Carefully, quietly, she let her lungs draw a needed breath.

Slowly, ever so slowly, so as not to make a sound, she straightened a little. She dared not move her feet lest the stone chips crunch.

Courage, as thin as eggshells, urged her to hide behind the wall of the sliph's well. From there, she could determine if it was only her imagination spooking her. Perhaps it was just a rat.

She twisted to check the distance to the stone wall.

Kahlan sucked a cry as she flinched back.

C H A P T E R   3 6

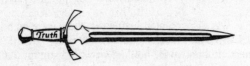

The quicksilver face of the sliph had risen above the edge of the stone wall and was watching her.

The glossy metallic female features of the sliph reflected the lamplight and the room in a living mirror. It was obvious why Kolo called the sliph 'she.' The sliph was a silver statue. Except it moved with liquid grace.

Kahlan pressed a hand to her hammering heart as she panted, getting her breath. The sliph watched her, as if curious about what Kahlan might do next. Kolo often said in his journal that 'she' was watching him.

'Sliph …' Kahlan stammered. 'What are you doing – awake?'

The face distorted into a puzzled frown. 'Do you wish to travel?' The eerie voice echoed around the room. Her lips hadn't moved as she spoke, but she smiled pleasantly.

'Travel? No.' Kahlan took a step toward the well. 'Sliph, Richard put you to sleep. I was here.'

'Master. He woke me.'

'Yes, Richard woke you. He traveled in you. He rescued me, and I traveled back with him … in you.'

Kahlan recalled that strange experience with a certain fondness. To travel in the sliph, you had to breathe her in. It was frightening at first, but with Richard there holding her hand, Kahlan had been able to do it, and had discovered the enthralling sensation of 'traveling.'

To breathe the sliph was rapture.

'I remember,' the sliph said. 'Once you are in me, I remember.'

'But don't you remember Richard putting you to sleep again?'

'He woke me from the sleep of ages, but he did not put me back into the long sleep. He put me at rest, until I was needed.'

'But we thought – we thought you had gone back to sleep. Why are you not at … rest, now?'

'I felt you near. I came to look.'

Kahlan stepped to the stone wall. 'Sliph, has someone traveled in you since Richard and I last did?'

'Yes. I was used.'

Suddenly realization broke through her surprise. 'A man and a woman. They traveled in you, didn't they?'

The sliph's smile turned sly, but she didn't answer.

Kahlan touched her fingers to the stone wall. 'Who was it, sliph, who traveled in you?'

'You should know that I never betray those I hold within me.'

'I should know? How would I know?'

'You have traveled in me. I would not reveal you. I never betray my clients. You traveled, so you must understand.'

Kahlan licked her lips patiently. 'Sliph, I'm afraid that I don't know anything about you, really. You are from a time before my time – from another age. I only know that you can travel, and that you helped me before. You were a valuable aid in defeating some very bad people.'

'I am glad that you were pleased with me. Perhaps you would like to be pleased again? Would like to travel again?'

A shiver ran up Kahlan's spine. This had to be why Marlin was trying to get to the Keep. He and Sister Amelia must have come to Aydindril from the Old World in the sliph. Jagang had said he had waited to reveal himself until she returned. How else could she have returned to him so fast, except in the sliph?

Kahlan swept out an imploring arm. 'Sliph, some very evil people …'

She halted, sucking a breath through her open mouth. Her eyes widened.

'Sliph,' she whispered, 'you took me to the Old World before.'

'Ah. I know the place. Come, we will travel.'

'No, no, not there. Sliph, can you travel other places?'

'Of course.'

'Where?'

'Many places. You must know. You have traveled. Name the place that would pleasure you, and we will travel.'

Kahlan leaned toward the alluring, smiling silver face.

'The witch woman. Can you take me to the witch woman?'

'I do not know this place.'

'It's not a place. It's a person. She lives in the Rang'Shada mountains. In a place called Agaden Reach. Can you go there, to Agaden Reach?'

'Ah. I have been there.'

Kahlan touched her trembling fingers to her lips.

'Come, and we will travel,' the sliph said, her haunting voice echoing around the ancient stone walls. The sound died out slowly, letting silence settle once more, covering everything, like the veil of dust in the room.

Kahlan cleared her throat. 'I have to go do something, first. Will you still be here when I get back? Will you wait for me?'

'If I am at rest, you can let me know of your need, and we will travel. You will be pleased.'

'You mean, if you're not right here, I should call down to you, and you will come to me, and we will travel?'

'Yes. We will travel.'

Kahlan rubbed her hands together as she backed away. 'I'll be back. I'll be back soon, and we will travel.'

'Yes,' the sliph said, watching Kahlan retreat, 'we will travel.'

Kahlan snatched the lamp from where she had set it on the floor near the shelves. She paused at the door, looking back at the quicksilver face floating in the gloom.

'I'll be back. Soon. We will travel.'

'Yes. We will travel,' the sliph said as Kahlan started running.

Kahlan had to struggle to think where she was going as she ran. Her mind spun with arguments. While she grappled with her alternatives, she also tried to pay attention as she turned down halls, raced through rooms, and dashed upstairs.

She seemed to reach Library Hall before she was ready.

Huffing, she realized that she couldn't run in on Cara and Berdine in such a state. They would know something was wrong.

Not far from the library where the two Mord-Sith waited, Kahlan collapsed onto a padded bench, letting the lamp slip to the floor. She leaned back against the wall and stretched out her aching legs. She fanned her face with one hand. She gulped air, and tried to convince her heart to slow down. She knew her face must be red as an apple.

She couldn't walk in on the other two like this. Kahlan made plans as she rested, waiting for her heart to slow, her lungs to recover, her face to cool.

Shota knew something about the plague. Kahlan was sure of it. Shota had said about Richard, 'May the spirits have mercy on his soul.'

Shota had sent Nadine to marry Richard. Kahlan vividly recollected Nadine's tight dress, her flirtatious smiles, her accusations, telling Richard that Kahlan was heartless. The look in Nadine's eyes when she talked to him.

Kahlan thought about what she must do. Shota was a witch woman. Everyone feared the witch woman. Even wizards feared Shota. Kahlan had never done anything against her, but that had never stopped Shota from hurting her.

Shota might kill her.

Not if Kahlan killed her first.

The distraction of making plans had allowed her to regain her composure. She stood, smoothed down her dress, and took a deep, settling breath.

Kahlan put on her Confessor's face and strode through the doors to the library where the other two waited.

Cara and Berdine popped out from behind a row of bookshelves. The books were gone from the table.

Cara eyed Kahlan suspiciously. 'You've been gone long enough.'

'It took me a while to find a way with shields I could pass.'

Berdine came out from behind the shelves. 'Well? Did you find anything?'

'Find anything? Like what?'

Berdine spread her hands. 'Books. You went to look for books.'

'No. Nothing.'

Cara was frowning. 'Did you have any problems?'

'No. I'm just upset about all this … about everything. The plague and all. I'm upset that I couldn't find anything to help. What about you two?'

Berdine swiped a stray strand of hair back from her face. 'Nothing. Nothing about the Temple of the Winds or the team who sent it away.'

'I don't understand,' Kahlan said, mostly to herself. 'If there was a trial, as Kolo said, then there should be a record of it.'

'Well,' Berdine said, 'we were looking through the other books to see if we missed any of the records of the trials. We didn't find any. Where else can we look?'

Kahlan sagged in disappointment. She had been sure they would find a record of the trial for Richard.

'Nowhere. If it isn't here, then there must be no record of the trial, or else it was destroyed. From what Kolo said, the Keep was in an uproar at the time; they may have been too busy to keep a record.'

Berdine cocked her head. 'But we're going to keep looking for part of the night, at least.'

Kahlan looked about the library. 'No. It would be a waste of time. The time would be better spent if you kept working on Kolo's journal. If we don't have the record of the trial, translating the journal would be the best help to Richard. Maybe you can find something important in the journal.'

In the brightness of the library, Kahlan's resolve was beginning to falter. She began to reconsider her plan.

'Well,' Cara said, 'I guess we better get back, then. No telling what Nadine will be up to. If she gets into Lord Rahl's room, she'll get blisters kissing him while he's asleep and helpless.'

Berdine pressed her lips tight and smacked Cara's shoulder. 'What's the matter with you? The Mother Confessor is a sister of the Agiel.'

Cara blinked in surprise. 'Forgive me. I was only making a joke.' She touched Kahlan's arm. 'You know that I will kill Nadine if you wish – you have but to ask. Don't worry, Raina would not let Nadine into his room.'

Kahlan wiped a tear from her cheek. 'I know. It's just that with all that's going on – I know.'

Her mind was made up. It might help Richard find an answer. It might help Richard discover something that would stop the plague. Kahlan knew she was only making excuses to herself. She knew why she was going.

'Did you find what you were looking for?' Raina asked as Kahlan, Cara, and Berdine approached.

'No,' Kahlan said. 'There was no record of the trial.'

'I'm sorry,' Raina said.

Kahlan gestured to the door. 'Has anyone tried to bother him?'

Raina smirked. 'She came by. She wanted to check on Lord Rahl. To make sure he was sleeping, she said.'

Kahlan didn't have to ask who came by. Her blood heated. 'And you let her in?'

Raina smiled that dark smile of hers. 'I put my head in, saw that Lord Rahl was asleep, and told her so. I didn't let her have so much as a peek at him.'

'Good. But she'll probably be back.'

Raina's smile widened. 'I don't think so. I told her that if I caught her in this hall again tonight, she would feel my Agiel against her bare bottom. When she left, there was no doubt in her mind that I meant it.'

Cara laughed. Kahlan couldn't.

'Raina, it's late. Why don't you and Berdine go get some sleep.' Kahlan caught the quick glance to Berdine. 'Berdine, just like Lord Rahl, needs to get some rest so that she can work on the journal tomorrow. We all need some rest. Ulic and Egan here will watch over Richard.'

Raina slapped the back of her hand against Ulic's stomach. 'You boys up to it? Can you handle it without me?'

Ulic scowled down at the Mord-Sith. 'We are the Lord Rahl's bodyguards. If anyone tried to get into his room, there wouldn't be enough left for you to pick your teeth with.'

Raina shrugged. 'I guess the boys can handle it. Let's go, Berdine. It's about time you got a good night's sleep for a change.'

Cara stood beside Kahlan as she watched Berdine and Raina stride off down the hall, passing a critical eye over soldiers on patrol.

'You are right about rest. You need to get some sleep, too, Mother Confessor,' Cara said. 'You don't look well.'

'I … I want to check on Richard first. I'll be able to sleep better if I know he's all right. I'll be back out in a minute.' She gave Cara a firm look to discourage any ideas she might have about going in with her. 'Why don't you go get some sleep, too?'

Cara clasped her hands behind her back. 'I will wait.'

Richard's room was dark, but the light coming from the window proved enough to find the bed. Kahlan stood beside him and listened to his even breathing.

She knew how distressed Richard was by recent events. She felt the same pain. How many families were suffering in grief this night? How many more would be suffering the next, and the night after?

Kahlan sat lightly on the edge of the bed. She slipped an arm under his shoulders and strained to gently lift him. He murmured her name under his breath in his sleep, but didn't wake as she sat him up a bit and leaned the heavy weight of him against her.

Kahlan reached behind and picked up the glass with the sleeping potion Nadine had made. It was still half full. She held it to his mouth and tipped it, letting the potion slide to his lips. He stirred slightly, and swallowed as she tipped the glass higher.

'Drink, Richard,' she urged in a whisper. She kissed his forehead. 'Drink, my love. It will help you sleep.'

She tipped the glass a little more each time he swallowed, forcing him to drink more. When he had taken most of it, she set it behind once more. He murmured her name again.

Kahlan hugged his head, holding his cheek to her breast. She pressed her cheek to the top of his head as a tear rolled over the bridge of her nose and fell into his hair.

'I love you so much, Richard,' she whispered. 'No matter what, don't ever doubt how much I love you.'

He mumbled something she couldn't understand, except for the word 'love.' Kahlan eased him back onto the pillow and slipped her arm out from underneath him. She pulled up his covers.

She kissed her finger, and gently pressed the kiss to his lips, before she left the room.

On the way to her own room, she again told Cara that she should go get some sleep.

'I will not leave you unguarded,' Cara insisted.

'Cara, you need sleep, too.'

Cara glanced over out of the corner of her eye. 'I have no intention of letting Lord Rahl down again.' When Kahlan started to protest, Cara spoke over her words. 'I will be posting soldiers outside your room, too. I can nap there, and if anything happens I will be at hand. I'll get enough sleep.'

Kahlan had things to do. She needed Cara out of her hair. 'You saw how Richard was when he didn't get enough sleep.'

Cara let out a dismissive chuckle. 'Mord-Sith are stronger than men. Besides, he was like that because he hadn't slept for days. I slept last night.'

Kahlan didn't want to argue. She was frantically trying to think of how to overcome this obstacle in skintight leather. She couldn't let Cara know what she was doing. Sister of the Agiel or not, Cara would tell Richard; there was no doubt of that.

That was the last thing Kahlan wanted. Under no circumstances did she want Richard knowing what she was going to do. She would have to think of a new plan.

'I don't know if I'm ready for bed. I'm kind of hungry.'

'You look tired, Mother Confessor. You need sleep, not food. You won't sleep as well if you eat right before bed. I want you to get a good sleep, like Lord Rahl. You can sleep well knowing that Nadine will not be going near him. I have a good idea of what Raina said to Nadine, and I can assure you that as brazen as that strumpet is, she has enough sense to heed a warning from Raina. You have no cause for fear tonight, so you can sleep well.'

'Cara, what are you afraid of? Besides magic, and rats.'

Cara scowled. 'I don't like rats. I am not afraid of them.'

Kahlan didn't believe a word of it. She waited until they

were out of earshot of a patrol passing in the opposite direction.

'What scares you? What do you fear?'

'Nothing.'

'Cara,' Kahlan admonished, 'it's me, Kahlan, a sister of the Agiel. Everyone is afraid of something.'

'I wish to die in battle, not weak and sick in a bed, at the hands of some unseen foe. I fear Lord Rahl getting the plague, and leaving us without a Master of D'Hara.'

'I'm afraid of that, too,' Kahlan whispered. 'I'm afraid of Richard getting the plague, and everyone else I love. You, Berdine, Raina, Ulic, Egan, and everyone I know here at the palace.'

'Lord Rahl will find a way to stop it.'

Kahlan hooked some hair behind her ear. 'Are you afraid of not finding a man who will love you?'

Cara flashed Kahlan an incredulous look. 'Why would I be afraid of that? I have but to give any man permission to love me, and he would.'

Kahlan let her gaze drift from Cara to the columns at the sides of the room they were passing through. Their boot strikes echoed off the marble floor.

'I love Richard. A Confessor's magic will destroy a man if she loves him – you know, when they're … together. Only because Richard is special, has special magic, can he love me in return. I'm terrified of losing him. I want no one but Richard – ever – but even if I wanted, I couldn't. No other man could express his love for me except Richard. I could never have anyone else.'

Cara's voice softened in sympathy. 'Lord Rahl will find a way to stop the plague.'

They passed from the marble floor onto the quiet of carpets running up the stairs toward Kahlan's room.

'Cara, I'm terrified of losing Richard to Nadine.'

'Lord Rahl does not care for Nadine. I can see it in his eyes that he has no interest in her. Lord Rahl only has eyes for you.'

Kahlan ran her fingers along the smooth marble railing as she ascended the stairs. 'Cara, a witch woman sent Nadine.'

Cara had no answer for that; magic was involved.

When they came at last to the door to her rooms, Kahlan paused. She looked into Cara's blue eyes.

'Cara, will you make me a promise? As a sister of the Agiel?'

'If I can.'

'With all that's going on – so much has gone wrong already. Will you promise me that if … if something happens, if I somehow make a mistake, the worst mistake I've ever made, and I somehow get things wrong … will you promise me that you won't let it be her, instead of me, who has Richard?'

'What could happen? Lord Rahl loves you, not that woman.'

'Anything could happen. The plague – Shota – anything. Please, Cara. I couldn't bear to think that if anything happened, Nadine would have my place with Richard.' Kahlan clutched Cara's arm. 'Please, I'm begging you. Promise me?'

Cara's intent blue eyes stared back. Mord-Sith didn't take oaths lightly. Kahlan knew that she was asking for something of solemn importance; she was asking Cara to swear her life on this, for that was what it meant for a Mord-Sith to give her word.

Cara brought her Agiel up in her fist. She kissed it.

'Nadine will not have your place with Lord Rahl. I swear it.'

Kahlan nodded, words failing her for a moment.

'Get some sleep, Mother Confessor. I will be here, watching your rooms. No one will bother you. You can sleep well, knowing that Nadine will never take your place. You have my oath.'

'Thank you, Cara,' Kahlan whispered in gratitude. 'You truly are a sister of the Agiel. If you ever want a favor in return, you have but to name it.'

CHAPTER 37

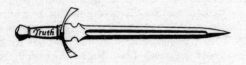

Kahlan was finally able to send away Nancy and her helper, telling them that she was exhausted and wanted only to go to bed. She had to decline an offer of a bath, having her hair brushed, a massage, and food; but she let Nancy help her with her dress so as not to raise the woman's suspicion.

Kahlan rubbed her bare arms in the chill after she was alone at last. She tested her wound, under the bandage. It was healing well, and hardly hurt her anymore. Drefan had helped it, and she supposed that Nadine's poultices had been a benefit, too.

Kahlan slipped on a dressing gown and went to the writing desk beside one of the hearths. The heat felt good, but it only warmed one side of her. She pulled paper and pen from a drawer. As she took the silver lid from the ink bottle, she tried to organize her thoughts, and what she would write.

At last, she dipped the pen.

My dearest Richard,

I have something important to do, and I have to do it alone. I am serious about this. Not only because I respect you, but because you are the Seeker, I bow to what you sometimes do that I wish would be otherwise. I understand that I must sometimes allow you to do what you know you must. I am the Mother Confessor; you must understand that I must sometimes do what I must. This is one of those times. Please, if you love me, then you will respect my wishes, not interfere, and leave me to do what I must.

I have had to trick Cara, which I greatly regret. She does not know anything of what I plan. She did not know I was leaving. If you hold her liable for this, I will view it with the greatest displeasure.

I don't know when I will return, but I expect that I will be gone for a few days. I am doing this to help our situation. I beg you to understand and not be angry with me – I must do this.

Signed, the Mother Confessor, your queen, your love for all time, in this world and those beyond – Kahlan.

Kahlan folded the letter and wrote Richard's name on the outside. She opened it and read it again, just to be sure she hadn't revealed anything she didn't want him to know. She was satisfied with 'to help our situation.' It was vague enough to mean anything. She hoped she wasn't being too harsh with the way she insisted he not interfere.

Kahlan brought a candle close and heated the end of a stick of colored sealing wax from the drawer. She watched the wax drip onto the letter, making a red pool, and then pressed the Mother Confessor's seal – twin lightning bolts – into the warm wax. She kissed the letter, blew out the candle, and propped the letter against it so it couldn't be missed.

She never used to know why the Mother Confessor's seal was twin lightning bolts, but she did now; it was the symbol of the Con Dar – the Blood Rage – an ancient component to a Confessor's magic. It was magic so rarely invoked that she had never known of it; her mother had died before she could teach Kahlan to call it forth if needed.

After she had met Richard and fallen in love with him, she had invoked it by instinct. In the grip of that magic, she had painted a lightning bolt on each cheek as a warning to others not to get in her way. A Confessor in the Con Dar couldn't be reasoned with.

The Blood Rage was the Subtractive side of a Confessor's magic, invoked for retribution. Kahlan had brought it to life within herself when she thought Darken Rahl had killed Richard. It was called forth on behalf of someone, and could only be used to defend that person. It couldn't be used to defend herself.

Like her Confessor's power, which she had always felt in the core of her being, the Con Dar was always there, now, just below the surface, a menacing storm cloud on the horizon. She had felt it instantly rip through her when she needed it to protect Richard: blue lightning that destroyed all before it.

Without the Subtractive as well as the common Additive Magic, a person couldn't travel in the sliph. The Sisters of the Dark, and the wizards who had become the Keeper's minions, could call on Subtractive Magic, too.

Kahlan went into her bedroom. She stripped off the dressing robe and tossed it on the bed. She pulled open the bottom drawer of the ornately carved chest and pawed through her things, looking for what she needed.

Inside were clothes she had worn before, when she had been on her journeys, better suited to what she was going to do than was her white Mother Confessor's dress. She stepped into dark green pants. She pulled out a heavy shirt and threw it on, buttoning it up with shaking fingers. She tucked in the shirt and buckled the wide belt. She left the waist pouch.

From the back of the drawer, Kahlan retrieved an object carefully wrapped in a square of white cloth. She set it on the floor and, crouching over it, laid back the corners of the cloth.

Even though she knew what it was, and what it looked like, she couldn't help feeling a shiver when she actually saw it again.

Atop the cloth sat the spirit knife Chandalen had given her. It was a weapon made from the arm bone of his grandfather.

This knife had saved her life before. She had used it to kill Prindin, a man who had been her friend, but who had turned to the Keeper.

At least, she thought she had killed him; she didn't remember exactly what had happened that day. She had, at the time, been under the influence of the poison Prindin had been giving her. She wasn't entirely sure that it wasn't the spirit of Chandalen's grandfather who had saved her. Prindin had lunged atop her, and the knife seemed just to be there, in her hand. She remembered his blood running down the knife and over her fist.

Inky black raven feathers spread in a fan from the round

knob of bone at the top. Raven was powerful spirit magic to the Mud People; it was associated with death.

Chandalen's grandfather had sought the aid of the spirits to protect his people from slaughter by another people of the wilds who had gone mad with the blood lust of war. No one knew the reason, but the result was a bloodbath.

Chandalen's grandfather had called a gathering to ask the spirits for their help. His people were peaceful, and didn't know how to defend themselves. The spirits had taught Chandalen's grandfather how to kill the Jocopo, and in so doing, they became the Mud People. The Mud People defended themselves, and eliminated the threat.

There were no more Jocopo.

Chandalen's grandfather had taught his son to be a protector of his people, and Chandalen's father had in turn taught Chandalen. Kahlan knew few men who were as good protectors of their people as Chandalen. In a battle with the army of the Imperial Order, Chandalen had been death itself. So had she.

Chandalen wore this spirit knife made from his grandfather's bones, and one made from his father's. Chandalen had given Kahlan the one made from his grandfather, so that it might protect her. Indeed, it once had. Maybe it would again.

Kahlan reverently lifted the bone knife in her hands.

'Grandfather of Chandalen, you helped me before. Please protect me now.' She kissed the sharpened bone.

If she was to face Shota, Kahlan didn't want to do it unarmed. She could think of no better weapon to carry.

She tied the band made of woven prairie cotton around her arm and slipped the knife through it. It lay against her upper arm, with the black feathers draped down over it. It was a surprisingly quick weapon to draw, held to her arm as it was. Even though she was going to see a woman she feared, Kahlan felt decidedly better with grandfather's spirit knife.

Kahlan pulled a light tan cloak from another drawer. She would have liked to have taken one that was heavier, considering the spring snowstorm, but she wasn't liable to be out in it all that long. Agaden Reach wouldn't be cold, as it was in Aydindril.

She was hoping that the light color would help her slip

unnoticed past the guards up at the Keep, and besides, with the light cloak, she could draw the knife faster.

She wondered if it was folly to think she could draw her bone knife faster than Shota could cast a spell, or if such a weapon would even be of any use against a witch woman. She threw the cloak around her shoulders. The knife was all she had.

Other than her Confessor's power. Shota was wary of a Confessor's power: no one was immune to the touch of a Confessor. If Kahlan could touch Shota, that would be the end of her. Shota had magic that in the past had prevented Kahlan from getting close enough to use her power, though.

But Kahlan wouldn't have to be touching Shota for the blue lightning of the Con Dar to work. She gave a mental sigh; she couldn't invoke the Con Dar to defend herself. Kahlan had defended Richard with the lightning before when the screeling had attacked him, and when the Sisters of the Light had come to take him.

Kahlan felt a wave of realization course through her mind. Richard loved her and wanted to marry her; to be with her always. Shota had defied his wishes and sent Nadine to marry him. He didn't want that.

Even disregarding the fact that Richard loved Kahlan, Nadine had caused him anguish, hurt him. He didn't want to be with her, and only tolerated her presence because Shota was up to something and he feared to let that threat out of his sight. But he desperately didn't want to be forced to marry her.

Shota was harming Richard.

Richard was in danger because of Shota. Kahlan could call the Con Dar to defend him. She had done it before at the threat of the Sisters taking Richard against his wishes. Kahlan could use the blue lightning to stop Shota. Shota had no defense against that kind of magic.

Kahlan knew how magic worked. This was magic from within her. Like the magic of Richard's sword, it worked through perception. If Kahlan felt justified in its use to defend Richard, the Con Dar would do her bidding. She knew Richard didn't want Shota using him, controlling him, dictating what his life would be.

Kahlan had justification: Shota was harming Richard. The Con Dar would work against her.

Kahlan paused, sitting back on her heels, and prayed to the good spirits that they would guide her. She wouldn't want to think she was doing this for vengeance, or that she was setting out to murder someone. She didn't want to think that she intended to kill Shota. She wondered if she was trying to put justification to something that couldn't be justified.

No, she wasn't going with the intention of killing Shota. She was just going to get to the bottom of this business with Nadine, and to find out what Shota knew about the Temple of the Winds.

But if she had to, Kahlan intended to defend herself. Moreover, she intended to defend Richard against Shota – against her plans to ruin his future. Kahlan had had enough of being at the unfavorable end of Shota's capricious ire. If Shota tried to kill her, or tried to force this suffering on Richard, then Kahlan would end the threat.

Kahlan already missed Richard. For so long they had struggled to be together, and here she was leaving him. If the situation were reversed, would she be as understanding as she was expecting him to be?

At the thought of Richard, she slowly pulled open the top drawer to her most prized of possessions. Reverently, she lifted her blue wedding dress from its place as the only item in the drawer. Her thumbs stroked the fine fabric. Kahlan clutched the dress to her breast as tears took her.

She carefully set the dress back in its place in the drawer before she got tears on it. For a long moment, she stood there with one hand on the dress.

She pushed the drawer closed. She had a job to do. She was the Mother Confessor, whether she liked it or not; Shota lived in the Midlands, and was therefore one of her subjects.

Kahlan didn't want to die and never see Richard again, but she could no longer tolerate Shota's meddling in their lives – her tampering with their future. Shota had sent another woman to marry Richard. Kahlan wouldn't allow that kind of interference to go unchecked.

Her resolve hardened. She reached into the back of a wardrobe and pulled a knotted rope from a peg. It was there in case of fire, so that the Mother Confessor could escape from the balcony.

Opening the glass doors gave her a shock of snarling wind and snow. Kahlan squinted against the storm and pulled the doors shut behind her. She drew up the hood and stuffed her hair inside it. It would do no good to have people recognizing the Mother Confessor – if anyone was even out on a night like this. But she knew that the guards up at the Wizards' Keep would be.

She quickly secured the rope around one of the vase-shaped stone balusters and tossed the rest of the heavy coil out over the railing. In the darkness, she couldn't see if it reached to the ground. She would have to trust that whoever had put the rope in the wardrobe had checked to make sure that it was long enough.

Kahlan swung a leg over the stone railing, gripped the rope in both hands, and started down.

Kahlan had decided to walk. It wasn't that far, and besides, if she took a horse, she would have to leave it at the Keep and it might be found, giving her away, or else she'd have to turn it loose before she got there, only raising fears as to what had happened to her. A horse would also make it more difficult to get past the guards up at the Keep. The good spirits had provided her with a spring snowstorm; the least she could do was take advantage of it.

Tramping through the heavy, wet snow, she was beginning to wonder if going on foot was the wise thing to do. She stiffened her resolve. If she was already beginning to second-guess her decisions, she had no business going through with the rest of it.

Most of the buildings were shuttered. The few people she encountered were too worried about making their own way to be concerned with a huddled figure struggling into the wind. In the darkness, no one would even be able to tell if she was a man or a woman. Before long, she was out of the city and on the deserted road up to the Keep.

All the way up the road, she pondered the best way past the guards. These were D'Haran soldiers. It was always a mistake to underestimate D'Haran soldiers. It wouldn't do to have them recognize her. They would report it.

Killing sentries was the easiest way to get past them, but she couldn't do that; they were her men, now, fighting for their cause against the Imperial Order. Killing them was out of the question.

Whacking them across the skull to knock them unconscious was no good, either. That was never a dependable way to silence someone. In her experience, hitting a man across the head rarely had the desired result. Sometimes they would not be knocked unconscious and would scream at the top of their lungs before anything else could be done, raising an alarm and bringing other guards ready to kill the intruder.

Besides, she had seen men suffer and die from a blow on the head. She didn't want that. You only hit someone on the head if you intended to kill them, because you most likely would.

The Sister and Marlin had probably used magic to get by the guards unseen. She didn't have any magic that could do that. Her magic would destroy their minds.

That left either a trick, or stealth. D'Haran sentries were trained in every kind of trick, and probably knew more of them than she could even imagine.

She was down to stealth.

She wasn't sure exactly where she was, but she knew she was getting close. The wind was coming from the left, so she stayed to the right of the road, downwind of them, crouching lower as she went on. When she got close enough, she would have to crawl.

If she laid down on the snow, spread her cloak out over her, and waited for a short time, the snow would cover her back and hide her. Then she would have to proceed slowly, and if she saw a soldier, simply lie still until he passed. She wished she had remembered to bring gloves.

Deciding that she was as close as she dared get, she moved off the right side of the road. She knew that the bridge would be the hardest part; it would funnel her into a relatively narrow space, with no option of moving away from the soldiers. But the soldiers feared the magic of the Keep, and would probably not be close to the bridge. They had been twenty or thirty feet from it when she had seen them before, and in the darkness and snow, visibility wasn't great.

She was beginning to feel better about her chances of getting by unseen. The snow would provide enough cover.

Kahlan froze in her tracks as a sword blade appeared in front of her face. A darting glance revealed a sword to each side. Another man rested a lance on her back, at the base of her neck.

So much for stealth.

'Who goes there?' came a gruff voice from the man in front of her.

Kahlan had to think of a new plan, and fast. She quickly settled on a bit of truth, mixed in with their fear of magic.

'Captain, you nearly scared me to death. It's me, the Mother Confessor.'

'Show yourself.'

Kahlan pushed back her hood. 'I thought I'd be able to get past you unnoticed. I guess D'Haran sentries are even better than I thought.'

The men lowered their weapons. Kahlan was the most relieved to feel the lance lift from the back of her neck. That was the killing weapon in a challenge.

'Mother Confessor! You gave us a fright, you did. What are you doing up here again tonight? And on foot, no less?'

Kahlan sighed in resignation. 'Get all your men together and I'll explain.'

The captain tilted his head. 'Over here. We have a shelter to get you out of the wind.'

Kahlan let them lead her to the other side of the road, where stood a simple three-sided structure meant to give some relief from wind and wet weather. It wasn't big enough for her and all six men. They insisted she take the driest spot, farthest inside.

She was torn between satisfaction that even in a snowstorm no one got past D'Haran guards, and wishing she had. It would have made it much easier. Now, she was going to have to talk her way out of it.

'All of you, listen carefully,' she began. 'I don't have a lot of time. I'm on an important mission. I need your confidence. All of you. You all know about the plague?'

The men grunted and nodded that they did, shifting their weight uncomfortably.

'Richard, Lord Rahl, is trying to find a way to stop it. We don't know if there is a way, but he won't give up, you know that. He would do anything it takes to save his people.'

The men were nodding again. 'What's that got to do with –'

'I'm in a hurry. Lord Rahl is sleeping right now. He's exhausted from trying to find a cure for the plague. A cure that involves magic.'

The men straightened a bit. The captain rubbed his chin. 'We know that Lord Rahl won't let us down. He cured me a few days back.'

Kahlan looked to all the eyes watching her. 'Well, what if Lord Rahl comes down with the plague himself? Before he can find an answer? Then what? We're all dead, that's what.'

The anxiety on their faces was clear. For D'Harans to lose a Lord Rahl was a calamitous event. It cast all their futures into doubt.

'What can be done to protect him?' the captain asked.

'What can be done is up to you men, here, tonight.'

'What can we do?'

'Lord Rahl loves me. You men all know how he protects me. He has those Mord-Sith shadowing me all the time. He sends guards with me wherever I go. He won't let danger come within miles of me. He won't let harm even get a view of me.

'Well, I don't want him harmed, either. What if he gets the plague? Then we all lose him.

'I may have a way to help him stop the plague before it can touch us all – before he can get it, as surely he will.'

They gasped. 'What can we do to help?' the captain asked.

'What I'm doing involves magic – very dangerous magic. If I'm successful, I may be able to protect Richard from the plague. Protect all of us from the plague. But, like I said, it's dangerous.

'I need to go away for a few days, with the aid of magic, to see if I might be able to help Lord Rahl stop the plague. You men know how he guards me. He would never let me go. He would rather die than let me be exposed to danger. He can't be reasoned with when it comes to my being in danger.

'That's why I tricked the Mord-Sith and my other guards. No one knows where I'm going. If anyone finds out, then Richard will come after me, and be in the same danger as me. What good will that do? If I'm killed, then he would be killed, too. If I'm successful, there's no reason to expose him to the danger.

'I intended for no one to find out where I went tonight, but you men are better than I gave you credit for. Now, it's up to you. I'm risking my life to protect Lord Rahl. If you want to protect him, too, then you must swear to secrecy. Even if he looks you in the eye, you must tell him that you haven't seen me, that no one came up here.'

The men shuffled their feet, cleared their throats, and looked at one another.

The captain's fingers fretted with his sword hilt. 'Mother Confessor, if Lord Rahl looks us in the eye and asks us, we can't lie to him.'

Kahlan leaned closer to the man. 'Then you may as well slay him on the spot. That's what you'll be doing. Do you want to endanger your Lord Rahl's life? Do you want to be responsible for his dying?'

'Of course not! We'd all lay down our lives for him!'

'I'm offering to lay down my life, too. If he finds out what I'm doing, where I went this night, then he will come after me. He can be of no help and he may die because of it.'

Kahlan pulled her arm out from under her cloak and passed a finger before each man's face. 'You will be responsible for endangering Lord Rahl's life. You will be exposing him to harm's view to no purpose. You may be killing him.'

The captain looked into the eyes of each of his men. He straightened and rubbed his face as he considered. At last he spoke.

'What is it you wish us to do? Swear on our lives?'

'No,' Kahlan said. 'I want you to swear on Lord Rahl's life.'

At the captain's lead, the men all went to one knee.

'We give our oath on Lord Rahl's life to tell no one that we saw you again tonight, and further to swear that no one went up to the Keep, except you and your two Mord-Sith earlier.' He looked about at his men. 'Swear it.'

414

When they had all sworn, the men stood. The captain placed a fatherly hand on Kahlan's shoulder.

'Mother Confessor, I don't know anything about magic, that's Lord Rahl's business, and I don't know what you're up to tonight, but we don't want to lose you, either. You're good for Lord Rahl. Whatever you're about to do, please be careful.'

'Thank you, captain. I think you men are the most danger I'll see tonight. Tomorrow is another matter.'

'If you are killed, it ends our oath. If you die, we will have to tell Lord Rahl what we know. If that happens, we will be executed.'

'No, captain. Lord Rahl wouldn't do something like that. That's why we have to do what we must to protect him. We all need him, lest we be ruled by the Imperial Order. They have no respect for life – it is they who started this plague. They started it among children.'

Kahlan swallowed as she stared into the silver face of the sliph.

'Yes, I'm ready. What do you want me to do?'

A lustrous metallic hand rose up from the pool and touched the top of the wall. 'Come to me,' the voice said, echoing around the room. 'You do not do. I do.'

Kahlan climbed up onto the wall. 'And you're sure you can take me to Agaden Reach?'

'Yes. I have been there. You will be pleased.'

Kahlan didn't know about being pleased. 'How long will it take?'

The sliph seemed to frown. Kahlan could see herself reflected in the shiny surface of the sliph's face.

'From here to there. That long. I am long enough. I have been there.'

Kahlan sighed. The sliph didn't seem to understand that she had been asleep for three thousand years, either. What was a day, more or less, to her?

'You won't tell Richard where you took me, will you? I don't want him to know.'

The silver face distorted into a sly smile. 'None who know me wish others to know. I never betray them. Be at ease; no one will know what we do together. No one will know of your pleasure.'

Kahlan's face assumed a perplexed expression. The liquid silver arm came up and slipped around her. The warm, undulating grip held her tight.

'Do not forget: you must breathe me,' the sliph said. 'Do not be afraid. I will keep you alive when you breathe me. When we reach the other place, you must then breathe me out and breathe in the air. You will be just as afraid to do that as you will be to breathe me, but you must do it or you will die.'

Kahlan nodded as she panted. She rocked from one foot to the other. 'I remember.' She couldn't help fearing to be without air. 'All right, I'm ready.'

Without further word, the sliph's arm lifted her gently from the wall and plunged with her down into the quicksilver froth.

Kahlan's lungs burned. Her eyes were squeezed shut. She had done it before, and knew she must, but she was still terrified to breathe in this liquid silver. Richard had been with her the last time. Alone this time, panic snatched at her.

She thought about Shota sending Nadine to marry Richard.

Kahlan let the air go from her lungs. She pulled a deep breath, inhaling the sliph's silken essence.

There was no heat, no cold. She opened her eyes and saw light and dark in a single, spectral vision. She felt movement in the weightless void, at once fast and slow, rushing and drifting. Her lungs swelled with the sweet presence of the sliph. It felt as if she were taking the sliph into her soul. Time meant nothing.

It was rapture.

CHAPTER 38

Through the warm swirl of color, Zedd could hear Ann calling his name. It was a distant plea, even though she stood only a short distance away. In the flux of power atop his wizard's rock, it might as well have come from another world.

In many ways, it did.

Her voice came again, irritating, insistent, urgent. Zedd all but ignored her as he lifted his arms into the rotating smoke of light. Shapes before him hinted at their spirit presence. He was almost through.

Abruptly, the wall of power began to collapse. The sleeves of his robes slipped down his arms as Zedd threw his contorted hands higher, trying to coerce more puissance into the field of magic, trying to stabilize it. He was madly hauling a bucket from the well, and finding it empty.

Sparkles of color fizzled. The twisting eddy of light degenerated into a muddy gloom of color. With gathering speed, it slumped, foundering impotently.

Zedd was dumbfounded.

With a thump that shook the ground, the whole elaborately forged warp in the world of existence extinguished.

Zedd's arms windmilled as Ann snatched the back of his collar and yanked him from atop his wizard's rock. He tumbled back, knocking them both to the ground.

Deprived of enlivening magic, the rock, too, collapsed. Zedd hadn't done it; his wizard's rock had reverted to its inert state of its own accord. Now he truly was baffled.

'Bags, woman! What's the meaning of this!'

'Don't you curse at me, you contrary old man. I don't know why I bother trying to save your skinny hide.'

'Why did you interfere? I was almost through!'

'I didn't interfere,' she growled.

'But if it wasn't you' – Zedd shot a glance at the dark hills. 'You mean… ?'

'I suddenly lost the link with my Han. I was trying to warn you, not stop you.'

'Oh,' Zedd said in a thin voice. 'That's very different.' He stretched out and snatched up his wizard's rock. 'Why didn't you say so?' He slipped the rock into an inner pocket.

Ann scanned the darkness. 'Did you find out anything before you lost contact?'

'I never made contact.'

Her gaze shot back at him. 'You never … what do you mean, you never made contact? What were you doing all that time?'

'Trying,' he said as he reached for a blanket. 'Something was wrong. I couldn't reach through. Get your things. We'd better get out of here.'

Ann scooped up a saddlebag and began stuffing their gear into it. 'Zedd,' she said in a worried tone, 'we were counting on this. Now that you have failed –'

'I didn't fail,' he snapped. 'At least, it wasn't my fault that it wasn't working.'

She slapped his hands away when he pushed her toward her horse. 'Why wouldn't it work?'

'The red moons.'

She twisted and stared at him. 'You think …'

'It's not something I do often, or lightly. I've only made contact with the spirit world a handful of times in the whole of my life. My father warned me, when he gave me the rock, that it must only be used in the most dire of circumstances. Such contact risks letting the wrong spirits through, and worse, tearing the veil. When I had trouble making contact in the past, it was because of a disharmony. The red moons were a warning of disharmony, of a sort.'

'We're running out of things to try.' She yanked her arm from his grip. 'What's gotten into you?'

Zedd grunted. 'What's this you said about not being able to touch your Han?'

Ann stroked a hand along the flanks of her horse, letting it know she was close to its hindquarters. The horse pawed a front hoof as it whickered.

'When you were up on your rock, I was casting sensing webs to make sure no one was near. This is the wilds, after all, and you were making quite a show with all the light. All of a sudden, when I reached to touch my Han again, it was like falling on my face.'

Zedd flicked his hand, casting a simple web to flip over a fist-sized rock lying at his feet. Nothing happened. It felt rather like trying to lean against something, and finding out too late that it wasn't there. Like falling on his face.

Zedd reached into an inner pocket and pulled out a pinch of concealing dust. He cast it in the direction they had come. The breeze carried it away. It didn't sparkle.

'We're in trouble,' he whispered.

She huddled close to him. 'You wouldn't mind being more specific, would you?'

'Leave the horses.' He took her arm again. 'Come on.'

This time she didn't object as he took her arm and led her at a trot. 'Zedd, what is it?' she whispered.

'This is the wilds.' He stopped, lifted his nose, and sniffed the air. 'My guess would be Nangtong.' He pointed in the dim moonlight. 'Down here, in this ravine. We must do our best to stay out of sight. We may have to split up and try to escape in separate directions.'

Zedd held her arm, helping her as her feet slipped on the dewy grass and wet clay of the steep sides.

'Who are the Nangtong?'

Zedd reached the bottom first. He put his hands on her wide waist and helped her down. Her legs were short, and she didn't have the reach with them that he had with his. Without the aid of magic, her weight almost toppled him. With a hand, she caught a tangled mat of bur bush roots to steady herself.

'The Nangtong,' Zedd whispered, 'are a people of the wilds. They have magic of their own. They can't exactly use their magic for anything, the way we use it, but it leaches the strength right out of other magic. Like rain on a campfire.

419

'That's the trouble with the wilds. There are any number of people in the wilds who cause odd things to go wrong with your attempts to use magic. There are creatures and places here, too, that are trouble in ways you don't expect. It's best to stay clear of the wilds.

'That's why I was so perturbed when after Nathan said we had to go to the Jocopo Treasure, Verna told us that the Jocopo used to live somewhere in the wilds. Nathan might as well have told us to reach into a roaring fire and pull out a hot coal. There are hazards everywhere in the wilds; the Nangtong are only one of them.'

'So what makes you think it's these Nangtong people who are causing the trouble with our magic?'

'With most peoples of the wilds who have this effect, it steals the strength out of our magic, but my concealing dust would still have worked. It doesn't. The Nangtong are the only ones I know of who can do that.'

Ann held her arms out to the sides to help balance herself and keep her footing as she crossed behind him on a fallen log. The moon slipped behind the clouds. The return of darkness pleased Zedd, because it helped hide them, but it made it nearly impossible to see where to step. They would be no less dead if they fell and broke their necks than if they were run through with a poison arrow or spear point.

'Maybe we could show them that we're friendly,' Ann whispered from behind him. She nabbed his robes so she could follow in the dark as he hurried along the flat beside the stream. 'You're always boasting and telling me to let you do the talking, as if you have a magic, honeyed tongue, to hear you tell it. Why don't you simply tell these Nangtong that we're looking for the Jocopo, and we would appreciate their help? Many people who would seem to be trouble turn out to be reasonable if you only talk with them.'

He turned his head back so he could keep his voice low and she would still be able to hear him. 'I agree, but I don't speak their language, so I can't win them over.'

'If these people are so dangerous, and you know it, then why would you be so foolish as to take us right into them?'

'I didn't. I skirted their lands by a wide margin.'

'So you say. It would appear you've gotten us lost.'

'No, the Nangtong are seminomadic. They have no exact, permanent home, but they stay within their own homelands. I stayed out of their homelands. It's probably a spirit raiding party.'

'A what?'

Zedd halted and crouched low, studying the lay of the land. He couldn't see anyone in the faint light, and he could only vaguely detect the foreign smell of sweat. It could be that it had been carried on the breeze for miles.

'A spirit raiding party,' he said as he put his mouth close to her ear. 'It's a long story, but the ending is that they offer sacrifices to the spirit world.

'It is their belief that the newly departed spirit will carry the Nangtongs' respects and requests to their departed ancestors, and in return the spirits will look kindly upon them. The hunting parties hunt things to sacrifice.'

'People?'

'Sometimes. If they can get away with it. They aren't very brave when they encounter strong opposition – they would rather run than have a fight – but they will gladly pick off the weak or defenseless.'

'In the name of Creation, what kind of place is this Midlands, letting people get away with such things? I thought you people were more civilized than that. I thought you had this alliance through which everyone in the Midlands cooperated and saw to the common good.'

'The Confessors come here, to try to insure the Nangtong don't murder people, but it's a remote place. The Nangtong are always servile when a Confessor comes; her magic is one of the few not altered by the Nangtongs' power. It could be that because a Confessor's power has an element of the Subtractive to it, it isn't altered.'

'Why would you fools leave these people to their own devices, if you know what they are capable of?'

Zedd scowled at her in the darkness. 'Part of the reason for the Midlands alliance was to protect those with magic who would be slaughtered by stronger lands.'

'They don't have magic. You said they couldn't do anything with magic.'

'Since they can nullify magic, make it impotent, then that

means that they have magic. Those without magic could not do such a thing. It's part of the way these people defend themselves. It's their teeth, so to speak, used to defend themselves against those with powerful magic who would subjugate or destroy them.

'We leave alone people and creatures with magic. They have as much right to exist as we, but we try to insure that they don't murder innocent people. We may not like all forms of magic, but we don't believe in exterminating the Creator's beings to make a world in the image of those with the most power.'

She remained silent, so he went on. 'There are creatures that can be dangerous, such as a gar, but we don't go out and kill all the gars. Instead, we leave them be, let them have their own lives, the way the Creator intended. It is not up to us to judge the wisdom of Creation.

'The Nangtong are diffident when challenged by strength, but deadly when they think they have the upper hand. They're a kind of scavenger – like vultures, or wolves, or bears. It wouldn't be right to eliminate those creatures. They have a part to play in the world.'

She put her face close so she could express her displeasure without yelling. 'And what part do the Nangtong play?'

'Ann, I am not the Creator, nor do I have conversations with Him to discuss His choices in creating life and magic. But I am respectful enough to allow that He may have a reason, and it isn't my place to say He is wrong. That would be naked arrogance.

'In the Midlands, we allow all forms of Creation to exist, and if it's dangerous, we simply keep away from it. You, of all people, with your dogmatic teachings of your version of the Creator, should be able to sympathize with this view.'

Ann's words, whispered though they were, became heated. 'Our duty is to teach heathens such as this to respect the Creator's other beings.'

'Tell that to the wolf, or the bear.'

Her growl could have been either.

'Sorceresses and wizards are meant to be custodians of magic, to protect it, just as a parent protects a child,' Zedd said. 'It is not up to us to decide which are good enough to have a right to exist, which is worthy of life.

'Down that path lies Jagang's view of all magic. He thinks we are dangerous, and that we should be eliminated for the good of all. You seem to be siding with the emperor.'

'If a bee stings you, do you not swat it?'

'I didn't say we shouldn't defend ourselves.'

'Then why haven't you defended yourselves and eliminated such threats? In the war with Darken Rahl's father, Panis, your own people called you the wind of death. You knew how to eliminate a threat then.'

'I did what I had to do to protect innocent people who would have been slaughtered – who were being slaughtered. I will do the same against Jagang if I must. The Nangtong haven't warranted annihilation; they don't try to rule others through murder, torture, and enslavement. Their beliefs result in harm only if we are careless enough to intrude.'

'They're dangerous. You should never have let the threat continue.'

He shook a finger at her. 'And why haven't you killed Nathan, to eliminate the threat he represents?'

'Would you equate Nathan with those who sacrifice people for heathen beliefs? And I can tell you that when I get my hands on Nathan again, I will set him on the right path!'

'Good. But in the meanwhile, this is a poor time to debate theology.' Zedd smoothed back his wavy hair. 'Unless you wish to begin teaching the Nangtong your beliefs, I would suggest we follow mine, and remove ourselves from their hunting grounds.'

Ann sighed. 'Perhaps you have a point or two. Your intentions, at least, were benevolent.'

With a shooing motion, she signaled for him to get going. Zedd followed the twisting gorge, trying to stay out of the sluggish ribbon of water running through it.

The ravine led southwest. He knew that would take them away from the Nangtong homeland. He hoped it would also conceal them while they fled. The Nangtong had spears and arrows.

When the moon came out between a break in the clouds, Zedd put out a hand to stop Ann, and squatted down to take a quick appraisal of the landscape while there was light enough for a moment. He saw little but the eight- to ten-foot-high walls of the banks and, beyond, the nearly barren hills. There were scattered copses on distant hills.

In the low valley ahead, the stream ran into a thicket of woods. Zedd turned back to tell Ann that their best bet might be to hide in the brush and woods. The Nangtong might be leery of a trap, and stay out of such a place.

The moon was still out. He saw behind them their perfect pair of tracks through the mud. He had forgotten that he couldn't hide their trail. He pointed, so she would see them, too. She gestured with a thumb, indicating that they should get out of the muddy gully.

Twin, reed-thin screams in the distance cut through the stillness.

'The horses,' he whispered.

The screams silenced abruptly. Their throats had been cut.

'Bags! Those were good horses. Do you have anything with which to defend yourself?'

Ann flicked her wrist and brought forth a dacra. 'I have this. Its magic won't work, but I can still stab them. What do you have?'

Zedd smiled fatalistically. 'My honeyed tongue.'

'Maybe we should split up, before your weapon gets me killed.'

Zedd shrugged. 'I wouldn't hold it against you if you wish to strike out alone. We have important business. Maybe it would be better if we split up to give a better chance of at least one of us making it.'

She smiled. 'You just want me to miss out on all the fun. We'll get away. We're a goodly distance from the horses. Let's stay together.'

Zedd squeezed her shoulder. 'Maybe they only sacrifice virgins.'

'But I don't want to die alone.'

Zedd chuckled softly as he moved on, searching for a place ahead where he could take them up and out of the ravine. He finally found a cut through the bank. Roots of gnarled bushes hung down like hair, providing handholds. The moon slid behind a thick cloud. In the inky darkness, they climbed slowly, blindly, feeling their way with their hands.

Zedd could hear a few bugs buzzing about and, in the distance, the mournful call of a coyote. Other than that, the night was still and silent. Hopefully, the Nangtong would be busy picking through Zedd and Ann's things back with the horses.

Zedd reached the top and turned to help pull Ann up. 'Stay on your hands and knees. We'll crawl or at least crouch as we go.'

Ann whispered her agreement. She made her way atop the bank with him. They struck out, away from the gully. The bright moon came out from behind the cloud.

In a semicircle right in front of them, blocking their way, stood the Nangtong.

There were perhaps twenty of them. Zedd reasoned that there were more about nearby; Nangtong hunting parties were larger.

They were not tall, and were nearly naked, wearing only a thong and a pouch of sorts that held their manhood. Necklaces made of human finger bones hung around their necks. Heads were shaved bald. They all had sinewy arms and legs and pronounced bellies.

The Nangtong had all smeared white ash over their entire body. The area around their eyes was painted black, giving them the appearance of living skulls.

Zedd and Ann peered up at spears, their barbed, steel points glinting in the moonlight. One of the men chattered an order. Zedd didn't understand the words, but he had a good idea of what it meant.

'Don't use the dacra,' he whispered over to Ann. 'There's too many. They'll kill us on the spot. Our only chance is if we can stay alive and think of something.'

He saw her slip the weapon back up her sleeve.

Zedd grinned up at the wall of grim faces. 'Would any of you men happen to know where we could find the Jocopo?'

A spear jabbed at him, then signaled them to stand. He and Ann reluctantly complied. The men, not up to Zedd's shoulders, but about as tall as Ann, crowded in around them, suddenly jabbering all at once. Men pushed and poked at them.

Their arms were pulled back and their wrists tightly bound.

'Remind me again,' Ann said to him, 'about the wisdom of leaving these heathens to their unenlightened practices.'

'Well, I heard from a Confessor, once, that they are quite good cooks. Perhaps we will sample something new and delightful.'

Ann stumbled but caught herself as she was pushed on ahead. 'I'm too old,' she muttered to the sky, 'to be mucking about with a crazy man.'

An hour of brisk marching brought them to the Nangtong village. Broad, round tents, perhaps thirty of them, made up the mobile community. The low tents hunkered close to the ground, presenting the least possible purchase to the wind. Enclosures made of tall stick fences held a variety of livestock.

Chattering people, wrapped head to toe in unadorned cloth to hide their identities from the sacrificial offerings about to take their prayers to the spirit world, turned out to watch Zedd and Ann being prodded at spearpoint through the village. Their captors, covered in the white ash and with their eyes painted black, were hunters in the guise of the dead, so there would be no danger of their being recognized as one of the still living.

Zedd was jerked to a halt before a pen while men undid the rope tie at the gate. The gate swung open in the moonlight. It seemed that the whole Nangtong village had followed behind. They hooted and hollered as the two prisoners were hustled through the gate, apparently wanting to give messages to the two spirits about to go speak on the Nangtongs' behalf to their ancestors.

Zedd and Ann, their wrists still bound behind their backs, both fell when they were forcefully shoved into the pen. It was a muddy landing. Snorting shapes loped away. The pen was occupied by pigs. The way they had churned the ground into a quagmire, the village must have occupied this place for at least the past few months. It smelled like what it was.

The spirit hunting party, nearly fifty, as Zedd had guessed, split up. Some went back to tents, surrounded by gleeful children and stoic women. Others of the hunters encircled the pen to stand guard. Most of the people who stood around watching were calling out to the prisoners, giving their messages for the spirit world.

'Why are you doing this?' Zedd called to their guards. He nodded his head and inclined it toward Ann. 'Why?' He shrugged.

One of the guards seemed to understand. He made a cutting gesture across his throat, and then indicated the imaginary blood running from the pretend wound. With his spear, he pointed at the moon.

'Blood moon?' Ann asked under her breath.

'Red moon,' Zedd whispered in realization. 'The last I'd heard, the Confessors had secured a pledge from the Nangtong that they would no longer sacrifice people. I was never sure if they held to their promise. Just the same, people stayed away.

'The red moon must have frightened them, made them think the spirit world was angry. That's probably why we're to be sacrificed: to placate the angry spirits.'

Ann squirmed uncomfortably in the mud beside him. She gave Zedd a murderous look.

'I only pray that Nathan's situation is worse than ours.'

'What was it you said,' Zedd asked absently, 'about mucking about with a crazy man?'

CHAPTER 39

'What do you think?' Clarissa asked.

She turned a little one way and then the other, trying to mimic a natural stance while feeling anything but natural. She wasn't sure what to do with her hands, so she clasped them behind her back.

Nathan was lounging in a chair as splendid as any she had ever seen, its padded seat and back covered with striped tan and gold fabric. His left leg was draped casually over one of the chair's ornately carved arms as he slouched with his elbow propped on the chair's other arm. His chin rested thoughtfully in the heel of his hand. His sword's finely crafted silver scabbard hung down, so that its point touched the floor in front of the chair.

Nathan smiled that smile he had that said he was sincerely pleased.

'My dear, I think you look lovely.'

'Really? You're not just saying that? You really like it? I don't look ... silly?'

He chuckled. 'No, most definitely not silly. Ravishing, perhaps.'

'But I feel ... I don't know ... presumptuous. I've never even seen clothes so fine, much less tried them on.'

He shrugged. 'Then it's about time you did.'

The dressmaker, a thin, neat man with only a wisp of long gray hair covering the bald expanse atop his head, returned through the curtained doorway. He gripped each end of the tape measure draped around his neck, seesawing it nervously back and forth.

'Madam finds the dress acceptable?'

Clarissa remembered how Nathan had instructed her to conduct herself. She smoothed the rich blue satin at her hips.

'It's not the best fit –'

The dressmaker's tongue darted out to wet his lips. 'Well, madam, had I known you were to grace my shop, or if you had sent the measurements on ahead, I would certainly have made the appropriate alterations.' He glanced to Nathan. His tongue darted out again. 'Be assured, madam, I can make any necessary minor adjustments.'

The man bowed to Nathan. 'My lord, what think you? I mean, if it were altered to suit you.'

Nathan folded his arms as he studied Clarissa the way a sculptor studied a work in progress. He squinted as he considered, rolled his tongue around inside his cheek, and made little sounds in his throat as if unable to decide. The dressmaker twiddled with the end of his tape measure.

'Like madam says, it fits a little sloppily at the waist.'

'Sir, have no fear.' The dressmaker whisked around behind her, tugging sharply at the material. 'See here? I have but to take a dart or two. Madam is graced with an exquisite figure. I rarely have ladies so fine of form, but I can have the dress altered in a matter of hours. I would be most honored to do the work this very night and have it delivered to you at – at – where would you be staying, my lord?'

Nathan flicked a hand. 'I've yet to seek accommodations. Any place you could recommend with confidence?'

The dressmaker bowed again. 'The Briar House would be the finest inn in Tanimura, my lord. If you wish, I'd gladly have my assistant run over there and make arrangements for you and … madam.'

Nathan straightened himself in the chair and fingered a gold coin from his pocket. He flipped the coin to the man, followed by a second, and then a third.

'Yes, thank you, that would be very kind of you.' Nathan frowned in thought, and then tossed the man another gold coin. 'It's late, but I'm sure you could convince them to keep their dining room open until we arrive. We've been on the road all day and could use a decent meal.' He shook a finger at the man. 'Their best rooms, mind you. I'll not have them sticking me in some cramped little sty.'

'I assure you, my lord, the Briar House has no room that could remotely be considered a sty, even by one such as yourself. And how long shall I have my assistant tell them you will be staying at their establishment?'

Nathan stroked the ruffles on the front of his shirt. 'Until Emperor Jagang requires me, of course.'

'Of course, sir. And would you like the dress, my lord?'

Nathan hooked a thumb in the little pocket in the front of his green vest, letting his hand hang. 'It will have to do for common wear. What do you have that would be more elegant?'

The dressmaker smiled and bowed. 'Let me bring some others for your approval, and madam can try on the ones you fancy.'

'Yes,' Nathan said. 'Yes, that would be best. I'm a man of wide experience and refined taste. I'm used to better. Bring something to dazzle me.'

'Of course, my lord.' He bowed twice and rushed off.

Clarissa grinned in wonder after the man had gone. 'Nathan! This is the finest dress I've ever seen, and you wish him to show us something better?'

Nathan lifted an eyebrow. 'Nothing is too good for a concubine to the emperor, the woman carrying the emperor's child.'

Her heart fluttered to hear the prophet say that again. Sometimes, when she looked into his azure eyes, she almost saw something there, almost had the vaguest impression, if only for an instant, that Nathan was quite beyond mad. But when that serene smile of his came to his face, she melted in his confidence.

He was more daring than any man she had ever met. His daring had saved her from the brutes back in Renwold. Since then, his daring had saved them in circumstances that to her seemed worse than hopeless.

There had to be a grain of madness in daring that far beyond bold.

'Nathan, I trust in you, and will do whatever you ask of me,

430

but please, would you tell me if this is just a story to pass us here, or do you really see such a horrid thing for my future?'

Nathan brought his leg down and rose to his full, towering height. He lifted one of her hands, bringing it to his heart as if it were the most fragile of blossoms. His long silver hair slipped over the front of his shoulder as he stood ever so close to her and looked into her eyes.

'Clarissa, it is just a tale to accomplish my goals. It in no way reflects anything I see about the future. I won't lie to you and tell you that there are not dangers ahead, but be at ease for now, and enjoy this much of it. We must wait for a while, and I wanted you to have an enjoyable time of it.

'You are pledged to do what you must. I trust in your word. In the meantime, I wanted nothing more than to do you a simple kindness.'

'But shouldn't we hide where people won't know of us? Somewhere alone and out of sight?'

'That is the way criminals or unskilled runaways would hide. That's why they get caught. It makes people suspicious. If anyone is hunting them, they look in all the dark holes, never thinking to look in the light. As long as we must hide, the best place to hide is in the open.

'The story is too preposterous for people not to believe in its truth. No one would ever consider that anybody would have the audacity to invent such a tale, and so no one will question it.

'Besides, we aren't really hiding; no one is hunting us. We simply don't want to make people suspicious. Hiding would make them so.'

She shook her head. 'Nathan, you are a marvel.'

Clarissa eyed the bodice of the beautiful dress, what she could see of it, anyway, beyond the exposed flesh of her breasts, which were pushed up so high that they nearly tumbled out. She tugged at the bone stays lying against her ribs under her bosom. She had never worn such strange and uncomfortable undergarments. She couldn't imagine why they were all required. She smoothed the silken skirt of the dress.

'Does it look good on me? I mean, honestly. Tell me the truth, Nathan. I'm just a plain woman. Doesn't it look silly on a plain woman?'

Nathan's eyebrow arched. 'Plain? Is that what you think?'

'Of course. I'm no fool. I know I'm not –'

Nathan waved her to silence. 'Maybe you should have a look for yourself.'

He pulled the sheet off the standing mirror. This was a showing room for gentlemen. When he had instructed her on matters of decorum and propriety, he had told her that the mirrors in such a place were rarely used, and she wasn't to look in one unless asked. It was the look in the gentleman's eyes that mattered in such an exclusive shop, not the look in the mirror.

Nathan gently took her elbow and walked her before the mirror. 'Forget what you see in your mind, and look at what others see when they look at you.'

Clarissa's fingers fidgeted over the bunched frills at her waist. She nodded at Nathan, but feared to look in the mirror and be disappointed by what she always saw when she looked at herself. He gestured again. Wincing just a little out of embarrassment, she turned to gaze at her reflection.

Her jaw dropped at what she saw.

Clarissa didn't recognize herself. She was not this young-looking. A woman – not a young, fickle woman, but a woman in the full glory of her maturity, a woman of elegance and bearing – stared back.

'Nathan,' she whispered, 'my hair … my hair wasn't this long. How did the woman who worked on it this afternoon make it longer?'

'Ah, well, she didn't. I used some magic to do it. I thought it would look better if it was just a bit longer. You don't object, I pray?'

'No,' she whispered. 'It's lovely.'

Her soft brown hair was done in ringlets, with delicate violet ribbons tied into them. She moved her head. The ringlets sprang up and down, and swayed side to side. Clarissa had once seen a woman of standing come to Renwold, and she had hair like this. It was the most beautiful hair Clarissa had ever seen. Now, Clarissa's hair looked just like that.

She stared at herself in the mirror. Her shape was so … shapely. All those hard, tight things under her dress had somehow rearranged her figure. Clarissa's face blushed to see her bosom straining up the way it did, half exposed for all to see.

She had always known, of course, that women like Manda Perlin weren't really shaped as they appeared. She knew that when they had their clothes off, their shapes were not a great deal different from any other woman's, but Clarissa had never known just how much of it was due to the dresses those attractive women wore.

In the mirror, in this dress, with her hair done in such a fashion and with the paint on her face, she looked the equal of any of them. Perhaps older, but that age seemed only to add bearing to what she saw; not a spent, unattractive quality, as she had always thought.

And then she saw the ring in her lip.

It was gold, not silver.

'Nathan,' she whispered. 'What happened to the ring?'

'Oh, that. Well, it wouldn't do to have you supposedly a concubine to the emperor himself and carrying his little emperor heir, and have a silver ring through your lip. Everyone knows that the emperor only brings those with gold rings to his bed.

'Besides, you were wrongly marked with a silver ring. It should have been gold from the beginning. Those men were just plain blind.' He gestured in a grand fashion. 'I, of course, am a man of vision.' He held his hand out toward the mirror. 'Look for yourself. That woman is too beautiful to wear anything but a gold ring.'

In the mirror, the woman staring back was getting tears in her eyes. Clarissa wiped a finger across her lower lids. She feared to ruin the paint the woman had put on her face when her hair was being curled.

'Nathan, I don't know what to say. You have done magic. You have made a plain woman into something ...'

'Beautiful,' he finished.

'But why?'

His face screwed up with an odd expression. 'Are you daft? I couldn't very well have you looking plain,' He swept a hand down, indicating himself. 'No one would believe a man as dashing as myself would be seen with a woman any less stunning.'

Clarissa grinned. He didn't look so old to her as he had seemed when she had first met him. He really did look dashing. Dashing, and distinguished.

'Thank you, Nathan, for having faith in me, in more ways than one.'

'It's not faith; it's vision for what others are too blind to see. Now they do.'

She glanced to the curtain where the dressmaker had disappeared. 'But this is all so very expensive. This dress alone would cost me near to a year's wages. And all the other things: the lodging; the coaches; the hats; the shoes; the women who did my hair and face. It all costs so much. You are spending money like a prince on holiday. How can you possibly afford it?'

The sly smile oozed back onto his face. 'I'm good at ... making money. I could never spend all I can make. Don't be concerned about it; it means little to me.'

'Oh.' She glanced back at the mirror. 'Of course.'

He cleared his throat. 'What I mean is that you are more important than petty matters of gold. People are more important than such considerations. If it was my last copper, I would have spent it with no less enthusiasm, or greater worry.'

When the dressmaker finally returned with a selection of stunning dresses, Nathan chose a number for her to try on. Clarissa went into the dressing room with each, and with the aid of the dressmaker's woman, tried on each. Clarissa didn't think she would have been able to lace, tie, and button any of them by herself.

Nathan smiled at each dress she came out in, and told the dressmaker he would buy it. By the end of the next hour, Nathan had selected a half dozen dresses, and had passed a handful of gold to the dressmaker. In all her life, she had never imagined a place of such wealth that dresses were already made. It was another measure of how much her life had changed with Nathan; only the very rich, or royalty, would buy dresses this way.

'I will make the necessary alterations, my lord, and have the dresses delivered to the Briar House.' He darted a look at Clarissa. 'Perhaps my lord would wish me to leave several of them loose-fitting, to accommodate madam, when she grows with our emperor's child?'

Nathan waved a hand dismissively. 'No, no. I enjoy having her look her best. I will have a seamstress let them out when necessary, or simply purchase others to fit her then.'

It suddenly embarrassed Clarissa to realize that this dressmaker thought that she was concubine not only to the emperor but to Nathan. The ring through her lip, gold though it was, still meant she was nothing more than a slave. A slave would mean little to the emperor, with child or not, gold ring or not.

Nathan boldly told people that he was Emperor Jagang's plenipotentiary, which kept them furiously bowing and scraping. Clarissa was merely property, shared with the emperor's trusted agent.

The dressmaker's sidelong glance finally struck home. She was a whore in his eyes. Maybe a whore in a fine dress, and maybe not a whore by choice, but a whore nonetheless. A whore who was enjoying herself, being dressed in fine clothes and kept by an important man at the finest inn in the city.

The fact that Nathan didn't think the same thing was all that kept her from running from the dress shop in humiliation.

Clarissa reproached herself. This was the pretense Nathan had crafted for them, to keep them safe. It kept the soldiers they encountered at every turn from hauling her away to a tent. Deprecating glances were a small thing indeed for her to bear in return for all that Nathan had done for her, and for the respect he always showed her. It was what Nathan thought that mattered.

Besides, she was used to disapproving looks – looks of sympathy at best, scorn at worst. People had never looked upon her with favor. Let these people think what they would. She knew she was doing something worthwhile, for a man of worth.

Clarissa lifted her chin as she strutted to the door.

The dressmaker bowed again as they stepped out into the dark street to the waiting carriage. 'Thank you, Lord Rahl. Thank you for allowing me to serve the emperor in my small way. The dresses will be delivered before morning, you have my word.'

Nathan waved an offhanded dismissal to the man.

In the dim dining room of the elegant Briar House, Clarissa sat across a small table from Nathan. She now noticed the surreptitious glances she got from the staff. She sat up straighter and put her shoulders back, defying them to have a good look at her bosom. She reasoned that in the murky candlelight, and under all the face paint, they wouldn't be able to see her face reddening.

The wine warmed her, and the roasted duck finally sated her gnawing hunger. People kept bringing food – fowl and pork and beef, along with gravies and sauces and a variety of side dishes. She nibbled at a few, not wanting to appear a glutton, and afterward she was satisfied.

Nathan ate with zeal, but didn't overeat. He enjoyed the different dishes, wanting to try them all. The staff hovered around him, slicing meat, pouring sauces, and moving plates and platters around as if he were helpless. He encouraged them, asking for things, sending others away, and in general made himself appear an important man in their midst.

She guessed that he was. He was the emperor's plenipotentiary; a man not to be crossed. No one wanted Lord Rahl to be anything but most pleased. If his pleasure required seeing to Clarissa's desires, they did that, too.

Clarissa was relieved when they were finally shown to their rooms, and Nathan had at last closed the door. She sagged, at last unburdened of the responsibility of acting a fine lady, or a fine whore; she wasn't exactly sure how to play the part. She did know that she was glad to be away from the eyes that played over her.

Nathan strode around the two rooms, inspecting the painted walls with gold molding applied to form huge, sweeping panels with reverse-curved corners. Rich carpets in deep colors covered nearly every inch of floor. Everywhere there were couches and chairs. One room had several tables, one for taking meals there, another, with a slant top, for writing. The writing table held neatly arranged sheets of paper, silver pens, and gold-topped ink bottles with various colors of ink.

In the other room was the bed. Clarissa had never seen a bed like it. Four elaborately turned posts held up a canopy of lace and rich red fabric with gold designs splashed boldly over it.

The bed cover matched. It was a huge bed. She had trouble imagining why such an expanse of bed was needed.

'Well,' Nathan said as he strolled back into the room with the bed, 'I guess it will have to do.'

Clarissa giggled. 'Nathan, a king would be delighted to sleep in such a room.'

Nathan's expression contorted in a casual manner. 'Perhaps, but I am more than a king. I am a prophet.'

Her smile faded as her mood turned earnest. 'Yes, you really are more than a king.'

Nathan went around the room blowing out most of the dozen lamps. He left the one beside the bed, and the one on the dressing stand.

He half-turned, and gestured to the other room. 'I'll sleep on a couch in there. You may have the bed.'

'I'll take the couch. I wouldn't be comfortable in such a bed. I'm a simple woman, not accustomed to such grand things. You are. You should have the bed.'

Nathan cupped her cheek. 'Get used to them. Take the bed. It would be uncomfortable for me, knowing such a lovely lady was sleeping on a couch. I'm a man of the world, and such things don't faze me.' He bowed grandly from the doorway. 'Sleep well, my dear.' He paused with the door half closed. 'Clarissa, I apologize for the looks you had to endure, and for what people might have thought of you, because of my story.'

He truly was a gentleman.

'No apology is necessary. It was rather fun pretending, as if I were in a play on a stage.'

He laughed with that sparkle in his blue eyes as he flung his cape around himself. 'It was fun, wasn't it, having those people think we were other than we were?'

'Thank you for everything, Nathan. You made me feel pretty, today.'

'You are pretty.'

She smiled. 'That was just the clothes.'

'Beauty comes from within.' He winked. 'Sleep well, Clarissa. I've left a protective shield on the door so no one can enter. Be at ease here; you will be safe.' He closed the door gently.

Feeling a warm glow from the wine, Clarissa ambled about

the room, inspecting all the fine things. She ran her fingers over the inlaid silver on the small tables beside the bed. She touched the cut glass on the lamps. She ran her hand over the finely woven bed covers when she turned them down.

Standing in front of the dressing table, she looked at herself in the mirror as she unlaced the bodice of her dress. She almost hated to take off the dress and be just herself again, although she wouldn't be unhappy about being free of the bone stays that confined her.

With the laces loose, she was at last able to take a full breath. She slipped the top of the dress off her shoulders. The things still pressing from underneath held the dress up over her bosom. She sat on the edge of the bed as she tried to reach the buttons up the back. Some of them were too high. Sagging in frustration, she settled on removing her new shoes, made of supple, napped leather. She rolled off her stockings and wiggled her toes, glad to have them free.

Clarissa thought about home. She remembered her cozy bed, little as it was. She missed home, not because she was so happy there, but simply because it was home, and all she knew. As fancy as this place was, it felt cold to her. Cold and frightening. She was someplace she didn't know, and she could never go home again.

Suddenly Clarissa was very lonely. With Nathan, she felt the comfort of his confidence. He always knew where he was going, what to do, and what to say. He never seemed to have any doubts. Clarissa was full of them, now that she was alone in the bedroom.

It was odd, but she missed Nathan more than home, and he was right in the next room. Nathan was almost her home, now.

The carpet felt good under her bare feet as she went to the door. Gently, she rapped against the white panel in the center of the gold molding. She waited a moment, and then knocked again.

'Nathan?' she called softly.

She knocked and called his name once more. When still no answer came, she cracked the door open and peeked in. Only a single candle cut the still gloom.

Nathan was in one of his trances again. He was sitting in a

chair, staring blankly at nothing. Clarissa stood at the door for a time, watching his steady breathing.

She had been frightened the first time she found him stiff and unblinking, but he had assured her that it was something he had done nearly his whole life. He hadn't gotten angry, that first time, when she shook him, thinking there was something wrong.

Nathan never got angry with her. He always treated her with respect and kindness – two things she had always longed for, but had never gotten from her own people, and here was a stranger who gave them without effort.

Clarissa called his name again. Nathan blinked and looked up at her.

'Is everything all right?' he asked.

'Yes. I hope I'm not disturbing you in your reflection?'

Nathan waved away her concern. 'No, no.'

'Well, I was wondering, could you help me … undo my dress? I can't reach the buttons in the back and I seem to be stuck in it. I didn't want to lie down in it and ruin it.'

Nathan followed her back into the bedroom. She had blown out the lamp on the dressing table so that she wouldn't be embarrassed. Only the one beside the bed allowed him to see what he was doing.

With both hands, Clarissa held her hair up out of the way as his strong fingers worked their way down the buttons. It felt good to have him near.

'Nathan?' she whispered when he had reached the last of them at her waist.

He made a questioning sound in response. She feared he would ask what the thumping sound was, and she would have to tell him that it was her heart.

Clarissa turned, having to hold the dress over her breasts, now that it was undone.

'Nathan,' she said, as she gathered her courage and looked up into his beautiful eyes, 'Nathan, I'm lonely.'

His brow drew together as he gently laid one of his big hands on her bare shoulder. 'No need, my dear. I'm right in the next room.'

'I know. But I mean that I'm lonely in a bigger way than that. I mean, I'm lonely for the way you … I don't know how to say it. When I'm alone, I start thinking about what I will have to do to help those people you talked about, and all kinds of fearful things come into my head, and before I know it, I'm sweating in a terror.'

'It's often more worrisome to ponder something than it is to actually do it. Just don't think about it. Try to enjoy the big bed, and the fine room, if you can. Who knows, one day we may have to sleep in a ditch.'

She nodded. She had to look away from his eyes, lest she lose her courage.

'Nathan, I know I'm a plain woman, but you make me feel special. No man ever made me feel pretty, feel … desirable.'

'Well, as I said before –'

She reached up and put her fingers to his lips to silence him. 'Nathan, I really …' She looked up into his wonderful eyes. She swallowed and changed what she was going to say. 'Nathan, I'm afraid you are just too dashing a man for me to resist. Will you come spend the night in this big bed with me?'

He smiled with one side of his mouth as she took her fingers away. 'Dashing?'

She nodded. 'Very.' She could feel the curls springing.

He rested his arms around her waist. It made her heart beat even faster.

'Clarissa, you owe me nothing. I saved you from what was happening in Renwold, but you in return have promised to help me. You owe me nothing beyond that.'

'I know. It's not –'

She wasn't making herself clear, she knew.

She stretched up on her tiptoes, her arms circling his neck, and pressed her lips to his. His arms drew her tight. She abandoned herself in those arms, and to those lips.

He pulled back. 'Clarissa, I'm old. You're a young woman. You don't want someone who's as old as I.'

How long had she hurt because she thought she was too old to have someone? How often had she felt forlorn because she was too old? And now this man, this wonderful, vibrant, handsome man, was telling her she was too young.

'Nathan, what I want is to be thrown on the bed, to have this fancy, expensive dress pulled off me, and for you to have your way with me until I hear the spirits sing.'

In the silence, Nathan stared at her. At last he reached down, put an arm behind her legs, and swept her off her feet. He carried her to the bed, but instead of throwing her onto it, as she had suggested, he set her down gently.

His weight sank into the bed as he reclined beside her. His fingers stroked her forehead. They looked into each other's eyes. Tenderly, he kissed her.

Since her dress was all untied and unbuttoned, it easily slipped down to her waist. She ran her fingers through his long silver hair as she watched him lovingly kiss her breasts. His lips were warm against her. For some reason, she found that surprising, and marvelous. A soft moan escaped her throat at the feeling of her nipples being kissed in such a manly, passionate fashion.

Nathan may have lived longer than she, but he was not an old man in her eyes. He was dashing, daring, and thoughtful, and he made her feel beautiful. She found herself panting at the sight of him without his clothes.

No man had ever touched her with such tender purpose, and the sureness of that touch further heated her passion.

His kisses trailed down the front of her, each making her gasp to catch her breath in sweet, startled desire.

When he at last took his place atop her, she totally and unashamedly succumbed to her need. She felt cradled not only in the canopy bed but in his ardent embrace. At long last, as her whole body stiffened with her cry of release, she could hear the spirits sing.

CHAPTER 40

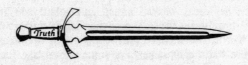

Like a hawk in a dive, Kahlan silently shot ahead, and at the same time, like an eagle in an updraft, she serenely hovered in place. Light and dark, heat and cold, time and distance, had no meaning, yet they meant everything. It was a marvelous confusion of sensations, heightened by the sweet presence of the sliph each time Kahlan drew the living quicksilver into her lungs, into her soul.

It was rapture.

With an abrupt explosion of perception, it ended.

Light erupted in Kahlan's vision. Sounds of birds, breezes, and bugs hurt her ears. Trees draped with streamers of moss, rocks incrusted with lichen and snarled in roots and vines, and patches of damp, dark mist crowded in all around. The overpowering presence of it all terrified her.

Breathe, the sliph told her.

The thought horrified her. *No.*

The sliph's voice seemed to sear through Kahlan's mind. *Breathe.*

Kahlan didn't want to be thrust from the serene womb of the sliph into this garish, loud world.

She remembered Richard, and with Richard, the threat to him: Shota.

Kahlan expelled the sliph from her lungs. The liquid silver sloughed from her, yet she was not wet. She gasped a deep breath of the strange, sharp air. She covered her ears and shut her eyes as the sliph set her on the edge of the well.

'We are where you wished to travel,' the sliph said.

Kahlan reluctantly opened her eyes and lowered her hands. The living world seemed to slow and settle into harmony with what she expected it to be. The comforting hand of the sliph slipped from Kahlan's waist.

'Thank you, sliph. It was … a pleasure.'

The sliph's fluid face smiled. 'I am pleased that you found it pleasurable.'

'I hope not to be long, and then we must travel back.'

'I will be ready when you wish to travel again,' the sliph said, her voice echoing out into the gloom. 'I am always ready to travel, if I am awake.'

Kahlan swung her legs down off the stone wall of the sliph's well. Parts of an ancient structure were visible, but it seemed mostly to have crumbled into the damp, tangled forest. She could see a bit of a wall here, half of a column there, some paving stones on the ground, all covered with vines and roots and leaves.

Kahlan didn't know exactly where she was, but she knew she was in the somber woods around the witch woman's home. Kahlan remembered going through this dangerous, mysterious forest when Shota had captured her and taken her to Agaden Reach in order to draw Richard there.

Jagged peaks, like a wreath of thorns, sheltered the murky forest high up in the vast spine of the Rang'Shada mountains. The dark and dangerous woods, in turn, surrounded and protected Shota's remote home. These woods kept people away from Agaden Reach, away from the witch woman.

Whoops, clicks, and calls echoed through the stagnant stink. Kahlan rubbed her arms, even though the air was damp and warm. Her chill came from within.

Through small, rare gaps in the forest canopy, Kahlan could detect the pink glow of the sky. It must be just dawn. She knew that the brightening day would bring no relief to the gloom of these woods. On the sunniest day, this morose place was never anything more than dismally dark.

Kahlan stepped carefully, watching the forest floor, the hanging vines, and the drifting fog that seemed to conceal creatures issuing strings of hissing clicks and hooting calls. In the expanses of stagnant water lurking under the thick vegetation, she could see eyes just breaking the surface.

Kahlan took another careful step and then paused. She realized that in the directionless forest, she didn't know where she was going. There was no telling north from south, east from west. This wood looked the same in all directions.

She realized, too, that she didn't even know if Shota was home. The last time Richard and Kahlan had seen Shota was at the Mud People's village. Shota had been driven from her home by a wizard aligned with the Keeper. Shota might not be here.

No, Nadine had visited her. Shota was here. Kahlan took another step.

Something snatched her ankle and yanked her feet from under her. She landed on her back with a hard thud.

A heavy, dark shape sprang onto her chest, driving the wind from her lungs.

A hiss, carried on fetid breath, came from between sharp teeth packed with gray, spongy filth.

'Pretty lady.'

Kahlan gasped to catch her breath.

'Samuel! Get off me!'

Powerful fingers squeezed her left breast. Bloodless lips drew back with a wicked grin. 'Maybe Samuel eat pretty lady.'

Kahlan pressed the point of the bone knife up into the folds of skin at Samuel's neck. She seized one of his long fingers and bent it back until he squealed and released her breast.

She jabbed the knife against his throat. 'Maybe I'll feed you to the things in the water over there. What do you think? Shall I slit your throat? Or do you want to get off me?'

The hairless, splotchy gray head drew back. Yellow eyes, like twin lanterns in the dim light, glared hatefully down at her. He carefully rolled to the side to let her up. Kahlan kept the bone knife trained on him.

Dead leaves and forest debris stuck to his waxy skin. A long arm lifted to point off into the dark mist.

'Mistress wants you.'

'How does she know I'm here?'

The grotesque face split with a hissing grin. 'Mistress knows everything. Follow Samuel.' He skittered a few steps and then stopped to look back over his shoulder. 'When mistress is finished with you, Samuel will eat you.'

'I may just have something for Shota she isn't expecting. She's made a mistake this time. When I'm finished with her, you may not have a mistress.'

The squat figure stared, appraising her. His bloodless lips pulled back and he hissed.

'Your mistress is waiting. Get going.'

The stocky, hairless, long-armed figure finally moved on through the undergrowth. He skirted dangers Kahlan didn't see, and grudgingly pointed at things for her to avoid. Vines he circumvented reached for her as she passed, but she was too far away for them to catch her. Roots Samuel bypassed snarled up, trying to snare her.

The short figure, dressed only in pants held up with straps, glanced over his shoulder occasionally to make sure she followed. A couple of times, he gurgled his odd laugh as he bounded along.

After a time, they picked up a trail of sorts, and not long after that the light coming through the tangled mass of branches overhead became brighter. As Kahlan followed the repulsive little creature, they came at last to the edge of the dark wood, and the edge of a cliff.

Far below lay the verdant valley where lived the witch woman. That it was as beautiful a place as any in the Midlands didn't ease the anxious knot in Kahlan's stomach. All around the valley the massive rocky peaks of the surrounding mountains soared nearly straight up. The budding trees in the placid valley below swayed gently in the early morning breeze.

Descending the sheer walls of rock looked to be impossible, but Kahlan knew from being here before that there were steps carved in the rock. Samuel led her through a morass of brush, tight trees, and fern-covered boulders, to a place that would be nearly impossible to find without him to guide her. A trail hidden behind rocks, trees, ferns, and vines ran to the edge of the precipice and the steps leading down the cliff walls.

Samuel pointed off, down into the valley. 'Mistress.'

'I know. Get moving.'

Kahlan followed Samuel down the cliff's edge. Part of it was a narrow trail, but most of the way down was comprised of thousands of steps cut into the rugged rock wall. They twisted and turned downward, sometimes spiraling back under ones above.

Below, far off in the center of the valley, among the streams, grand trees, and rolling fields, sat Shota's graceful palace. Colorful flags flew atop towers and turrets as if to announce a festival. Kahlan could hear the distant flags snapping in the wind. She had trouble seeing it for the splendid place it was. She saw it as the center of the spiderweb. A place where threat lurked. Threat for Richard.

Samuel sprang down the steps ahead, happy to be going back to the protection of his mistress, no doubt thinking about cooking Kahlan in a stew when his mistress was finished with her.

Kahlan hardly noticed the hateful glances from the big yellow eyes. She, too, was lost in a world of loathing.

Shota wanted to harm Richard. Kahlan kept that thought foremost in her mind; it was key. Shota wanted to deny Richard happiness. Shota wanted Richard to suffer.

Kahlan could feel angry power welling up inside her, ready to do her bidding and eliminate the threat against Richard. Kahlan had at last found the way to defeat Shota. Shota had no shield against Subtractive power. It would slice through any magic she threw out.

Kahlan had found the path, the gateway, through the labyrinth of protection layered over her magic, to the core of its power. This side of her magic was protected by precepts that governed its use. Like the Wizards' Keep, protected by shields of all kinds, there was a way to get through. She had found a way to get through the Keep, and she had used her reason to find the justification that traced its way through the maze of rationale forbidding this magic's use.

She had tapped its ancient strength, its destructive power.

Kahlan felt the power coursing up through her and down her arms. Blue light snarled and snapped around her fists.

She was nearly lost in a trance of purpose.

For the first time, Kahlan wasn't afraid of the witch woman. If Shota didn't swear to leave Richard alone, to let him have his own life, Shota was going to be dust before this day was out.

At the bottom of the cliff, Kahlan followed behind Samuel

as he bounded along the road among tree-dotted hills and green fields. Snow-capped peaks all around soared up past a scattering of clouds. Blue deepened in the sky as the sun rose over those peaks.

Kahlan felt as if she had enough power blazing within her to level those peaks. Shota had only to say or do the wrong thing – to prove herself a threat to Richard – and she would be no more.

The road led up a gentle rise from which Kahlan could see the spires of the palace through the trees ahead. Samuel glanced back to make sure she was still following, but Kahlan didn't need his direction; she knew that Shota waited in the grove of trees below.

The witch woman was the last person Kahlan ever wanted to see again, but if it was to be, then, this time, she intended it to be on her terms.

Samuel halted and pointed with a long finger. 'Mistress.' Yellow eyes glowered back at Kahlan. 'Mistress wants you.'

Kahlan lifted a warning finger to his face. Threads of blue light crackled around the finger.

'If you get in my way, or interfere, you will die.'

He glanced from her finger back into her eyes. His bloodless lips drew back as he hissed, and then he skittered off into the trees.

In a cocoon of seething magic, Kahlan advanced down the slope toward the waiting witch woman. The breeze was spring-warm, the day bright and cheerful. Kahlan felt no cheer.

Sheltered among the towering maples, ash, and oak, sat a table covered with a white cloth and set with food and drink. Beyond the table, atop three square white marble platforms, stood a massive throne carved with gold-leaf vines, snakes, and other beasts.

Shota sat regally, one leg crossed casually over the other, her ageless almond eyes watching Kahlan's approach. Shota's arms rested on the chair's high, widely spaced arms, with her hands draped arrogantly over gold gargoyles. The gargoyles nuzzled her hands, as if hoping to be stroked. A rich canopy draped with heavy red brocade and trimmed with gold tassels shaded the throne's occupant from the morning sun, yet her luxuriant auburn hair shimmered as if touched by streamers of sunlight.

Kahlan halted, not far away, under the witch woman's rock-hard, penetrating gaze. The blue lightning screamed for release.

Shota clicked her lacquered fingernails together. A self-satisfied smile spread across her full red lips.

'Well, well, well,' Shota said in her velvety voice. 'The child assassin arrives at last.'

'I am not an assassin,' Kahlan said. 'Nor am I a child. But I have had enough of your games.'

Shota's smile slipped away. She put her hands to the chair's arms and stood. Points of her wispy, low-cut, variegated gray dress lifted in the gentle breeze. Her gaze never left Kahlan as she gracefully descended the three white marble platforms.

'You're late.' Shota held a hand out to the table. 'The tea is getting cold.'

Kahlan flinched when a bolt of lightning struck from the blue sky, hitting the teapot. Amazingly, it didn't shatter.

Shota glanced down at Kahlan's hands, and then back to her eyes. 'There, I believe it's hot, now. Please, won't you have a seat? We will have tea and … conversation.'

Knowing Shota had seen the ominous blue light, Kahlan returned the self-assured smile in kind. Shota drew out a chair and sat. She again held out a hand in invitation.

'Please, have a seat. I imagine you have things you wish to discuss.'

Kahlan slid into a chair as Shota poured tea, holding on the white top with her other hand as she did so. Steam rose from the cups. The tea was indeed hot. Shota lifted a gold-trimmed platter, offering Kahlan toast. Kahlan warily pulled a golden-crisp slab from the platter. Shota slid a bowl of honeyed butter across the table.

'Well,' Shota said. 'Isn't this unpleasant.'

Against her will, Kahlan smiled. 'Very.'

Shota picked up her silver knife and spread honeyed butter across her slice of toast. She took a sip of tea.

'Eat, child. Murder is always best accomplished on a full stomach.'

'I have not come to murder you.'

Shota's sly smile returned. 'No, I suppose you have managed to justify it to yourself. Retribution, is it? Or perhaps self-defense. Punishment? Recompense? Justice?' The smooth smile widened. An eyebrow arched. 'Bad manners?'

'You sent Nadine to marry Richard.'

'Ahh. Jealousy, then.' Shota leaned back as she sipped her tea. 'A noble motive, were it justified. I hope you realize that jealousy can be a cruel taskmaster.'

Kahlan nibbled her crunchy toast. 'Richard loves me, and I love him. We're engaged to be married.'

'Yes, I know. For one who professes to love him, I would think you would be more understanding.'

'Understanding?'

'Of course. If you love someone, you want them to be happy. You want what's best for them.'

'I make Richard happy. He wants me. I'm best for him.'

'Yes, well, we can't always have what we want, now can we?'

Kahlan sucked honeyed butter from her finger. 'Just tell me why you wish to hurt us.'

Shota looked genuinely surprised. 'Hurt you? Is that what you think? You think I am being spiteful?'

'Why else would you always try to keep us apart, to hurt us?'

Shota took a dainty bite of toast. She chewed for a moment. 'Has the plague come, yet?'

The cup paused partway to Kahlan's lips. 'How do you know about that?'

'I'm a witch woman. I see the current of events. Let me ask you a question. If you visited a young child sick with the plague, and the child's mother asked you if her child was going to recover, and you told her the truth, would you be guilty of causing the child's death because you foretold it?'

'Of course not.'

'Ah. It is only I, then, who am to be judged by different standards.'

'I'm not judging you. I simply want you to stop interfering with Richard's and my life together.'

'A messenger is often blamed for the message.'

'Shota, the last time we saw you, you said that if we stopped

449

the Keeper, you would owe us a debt. You asked me to help Richard. We stopped the Keeper. It cost us dearly, but we did it. You owe us.'

'Yes, I know,' Shota whispered. 'That is why I sent Nadine.'

Kahlan could feel the rage of power surge within her. 'Seems a strange way to show your appreciation – sending someone to try to ruin our lives.'

'No, child,' Shota said gently. 'You see things through blind eyes.'

Kahlan had to help Richard by finding out all she could, but she would defend herself and Richard if she had to. Until that became necessary, she could endure this wandering conversation, if it would help get the answers they needed. And they did need answers.

'What do you mean?'

Shota sipped her tea. 'Have you lain with Richard?'

Kahlan was taken off guard by the question, but she recovered quickly. She shrugged one shoulder in an offhanded manner. 'Yes, as a matter of fact, I have.'

Shota's gaze rose from her tea. 'You're lying.'

Pleased by the smoldering tone in Shota's voice, Kahlan lifted an eyebrow. 'It's the truth. You don't like the message, and so now you hold malice toward the messenger?'

Shota's eyes narrowed. Her gaze locked on Kahlan as if drawing a bow and aiming an arrow.

'Where, Mother Confessor? Where did you lie with him?'

Kahlan felt triumphant at Shota's obvious displeasure.

'Where? What difference does that make? Have you turned from witch woman to gossip, now? I was with him … in that way, and that's the truth, whether you like it or not. I'm no longer a virgin. I was with Richard; that's all that matters.'

Shota's gaze turned dangerous. 'Where?' she repeated.

Shota's tone was so threatening that Kahlan forgot she needn't be afraid of the witch woman.

'In a place between worlds,' Kahlan said, suddenly embarrassed to reveal the details. 'The good spirits … took us there,' she stammered. 'The good spirits … they wanted us to be together.'

'I see.' Shota's gaze cooled. Her small smile returned. 'I'm afraid that doesn't count.'

'Doesn't count! What in the name of all that's good does that mean? I was with him. That's all that matters. You're just vexed because it's true.'

'True? You were not with him in this world, child. This is the world we live in. You were not with him here, where it counts. In this world, you are still a virgin.'

'That's absurd.'

Shota shrugged. 'Think what you will. I am satisfied that you have not been with him.'

Kahlan folded her arms. 'This world, or another, it doesn't matter. I was with him.'

Shota's smooth brow puckered with mirth restrained. 'And if you have been with him in the place between worlds, where the good spirits took you, then why have you not been with him in this world, since you are no longer a virgin, here, as you say?'

Kahlan blinked. 'Well, I … we … thought it best to wait until we were wedded, that's all.'

Shota's soft, exultant laugh drifted out through the morning air. 'You see? You know the truth of what I say.' She held the teacup between the tips of the fingers of both hands as she sipped, more balmy laughter escaping between each sip.

Kahlan fumed, somehow feeling she had lost the argument. She tried to look confident as she leaned back and took a drink of her own tea.

'If it pleases you to delude yourself with punctilios, then be my guest. I know what we did,' Kahlan said. 'I don't know why it's any concern of yours, anyway.'

Shota looked up. 'You know why it's my concern, Mother Confessor. Every Confessor bears a Confessor. If you have his child, it will be a boy. I told you both to remember that before you lay together. Lust dims thoughts of the consequences.

'From you, the boy would be a Confessor. From Richard, he would have the gift. Such a dangerous melding has never taken place before.'

With a patient, reasoned tone, meant almost as much for herself as for the witch woman, Kahlan hid her inner terror at Shota's prediction.

'Shota, you are a witch woman of great talent, and you may know it would be a boy, I grant you that, but you could not know he would be like most of the male Confessors born in the past. Not all were like that. You have as much as admitted that you don't know if it would be so. You are not the Creator; you can't know what He will choose to do – if He even chooses to give us a child.'

'I don't need to see the future in this. Almost every male Confessor was like that. They were beasts without conscience. My mother lived in the dark times caused by a male Confessor. You would visit upon the world not only a male Confessor, but one with the gift. You cannot even envision such a cataclysm.

'It is for this very reason that Confessors are not supposed to love their mates. If she bears a male child, she must ask the husband to kill the baby. You love Richard. You would not ask that of him. I have warned you that I have the strength to do what you will not. I also told you that it will not be personal.'

'You talk about the distant future as if it has come to pass. It has not,' Kahlan said. 'Events do not always unfold as you say. Yet, other things have already come to pass. Because of Richard, you still live. You told us that if Richard and I were able to close the veil, saving you and everyone else from the Keeper, you would be forever grateful to us both.'

'And so I am.'

Kahlan leaned forward. 'You show your gratitude not only by threatening to murder my child should I have one, but also by trying to kill me when I come to ask your help?'

Shota's brow twitched. 'I have made no attempt on your life.'

'You sent Samuel up there to attack me, and then you have the effrontery to rebuke me for coming prepared to defend myself. The little monster threw me on the ground and attacked me. If I hadn't had a weapon, who knows what he would have done. This is your gratitude? He said that when you were through with me, you would let him eat me. And then you expect me to believe in your benevolence? You dare to profess gratitude?'

Shota's gaze shifted toward the trees. 'Samuel!' She set down her teacup. 'Samuel! Come here at once!'

The squat figure loped out of the trees, using his knuckles to help himself bound across the grass. He ran to Shota and nuzzled against her legs.

'Mistress,' he purred.

'Samuel, what did I tell you about the Mother Confessor?'

'Mistress told Samuel to go get her.'

Shota looked into Kahlan's eyes. 'What else did I tell you?'

'To bring her to you.'

'Samuel,' she said with rising inflection.

'Mistress said not to harm her.'

'You attacked me!' Kahlan put in. 'You threw me on the ground and jumped on me! You said you were going to eat me when your mistress was through with me.'

'Is that true, Samuel?'

'Samuel not hurt pretty lady,' Samuel grumbled.

'Is what she says true? Did you attack her?'

Samuel hissed at Kahlan. Shota thunked him on the head with a finger. He shrank back against her leg.

'Samuel, what did I tell you? What were my instructions?'

'Samuel must guide Mother Confessor back. Samuel must not touch Mother Confessor. Samuel must not hurt Mother Confessor. Samuel must not threaten Mother Confessor.'

Shota drummed her fingers on the table. 'And did you disobey me, Samuel?'

Samuel hid his head under the hem of her dress.

'Samuel, answer my question at once. Is what the Mother Confessor says true?'

'Yes, mistress,' Samuel whined.

'I'm very disappointed in you, Samuel.'

'Samuel sorry.'

'We will discuss this later. Leave us.'

The witch woman's servant skittered away into the trees. Shota turned back to face Kahlan's eyes.

'I told him not to harm or threaten you. I can understand why you would be upset and think I meant you harm. Please accept my apology.' She poured Kahlan more tea. 'You see? I have no intention of hurting you.'

Kahlan took a sip from her full cup. 'Samuel is the least of it. I know you want to hurt me and Richard, but I'm not afraid of you anymore. You can no longer harm me.'

Shota's smug smile returned. 'Really?'

'I'd suggest you not try to use your power against me.'

'My power? All things I do, all things everyone does, is using their power. To breathe is to use my power.'

'I'm talking about hurting me. If you dare try it, you'll not survive the attempt.'

'Child, I have no wish to harm you, despite what you think.'

'A brave thing to say, now that you know you can't.'

'Really? Did you ever think that the tea might be poisoned?' Her smile widened when Kahlan stiffened. 'You …?'

'Of course not. I told you, I have no wish to harm you. If I wished to harm you, I could do any number of things. I could have simply put a viper behind your heels. Vipers dislike sudden movement.'

If there was one thing Kahlan hated, it was snakes, and Shota knew it.

'Relax, child. There is no viper under your chair.' Shota took a bite of her toast.

Kahlan eased her breath out. 'But you wished to make me think there might be.'

'What I wished is for you to realize that confidence can be overrated. If it will please you, I will tell you that I have always regarded you as singularly dangerous for any number of reasons. That you have found a way to tap the other side of your magic means little to me.

'It is the other things you do that frighten me. Your womb frightens me. Your arrogant certitude frightens me.'

Kahlan nearly leaped to her feet in anger, but then she suddenly thought of the children dying back in Aydindril. How many of them hung near death, shivering in fear for their lives, while Kahlan stubbornly debated fault and imputation with Shota. Shota knew something about the plague, and about the winds hunting Richard. What significance was Kahlan's pride in the face of that?

She remembered, too, part of the prophecy: … *no blade, forged of steel or conjured of sorcery, can touch this foe.*

In much the same way, crossing swords with Shota wasn't

going to work. This was serving no purpose, and worse, solving nothing.

Kahlan admitted to herself that she had come for vengeance. Her true duty should be to help people who were suffering and dying. How would anything but pride be satisfied by striking out at Shota? She was stubbornly putting herself and her insecurity above innocent lives. She was being selfish.

'Shota, I came with hurt in my heart because of Nadine. I wanted you to leave Richard and me be. You say you have no wish to harm us, and that your intent is to help. I also wish to help people who are desperate and dying. Why don't we, for the moment at least, agree to take each other's word as true?'

Shota watched over her teacup. 'What an outrageous concept.'

Kahlan reasoned with her inner fear, her inner rage. Her anguish at the things Nadine did made Kahlan want to strike out at Shota. What if it wasn't Shota's fault? What if Nadine was acting on her own, much the same way as Samuel had? What if Shota was telling the truth, if she had not meant to cause harm?

If that were true, then Kahlan was guilty of a grievous wrong in wanting to strike out at Shota.

Kahlan admitted to herself that Shota had been right, that she had been justifying vengeance simply to be able to tap her deadly power. She hadn't been willing to listen.

Kahlan placed her hands on the table. Shota sipped her tea as she watched the blue glow around Kahlan's hands fade and finally extinguish. Kahlan didn't know if she would be able to call it forth should Shota strike, but she realized it didn't matter.

Failure in her true task was too great a price to pay for pride.

Kahlan felt that this was the only thing that could truly have a chance of saving her future, of saving Richard, and of saving those innocent people back in Aydindril. Richard always said to think of the solution, not the problem.

She would trust in Shota's word.

'Shota,' Kahlan whispered, 'I always thought the worst of you. Fear has been only part of it. As you warned, jealousy has been my taskmaster. I beg you forgive my obstinacy and insolence.

'I know that you have tried to help people before. Please, help me, now. I need answers. Lives depend on this. Please, talk with me. I'll try to hear with an open mind the things you say, knowing that you are the messenger, and not the cause.'

Shota set down her teacup. 'Congratulations, Mother Confessor. You have earned the right to ask me questions. Have the courage to hear the answers, and they will be of aid to you.'

'I swear to do my best,' Kahlan said.

CHAPTER 41

Shota poured them more tea. 'What do you wish to know?'

Kahlan reached for her cup. 'Do you know anything about the Temple of the Winds?'

'No.'

Kahlan paused, cup in hand. 'Well, you told Nadine that the winds hunt Richard.'

'I did.'

'Could you explain that? What you meant?'

Shota lifted a hand in a vague gesture. 'I don't know how to explain to a woman who is not a witch how I see the flow of time, the passing of future events. I guess you could say that it's something like memories. When you think about a past event, or a person, say, the memory comes to you. Sometimes you more vividly remember past events. Some things you can't recall.

'My talent is like that, except I am also able to do the same with the future. To me, there is little difference between past, present, and future. I ride a current of time, seeing both upstream and down. To me, seeing the future is as simple as it is for you to remember the flow of past events.'

'But sometimes I can't remember things,' Kahlan said.

'It is the same with me. I can't recall whatever happened to a bird my mother would call when I was very young. I remember it sitting on her finger as she spoke soft, tender words to it. I don't remember if it died, or if it flew away.

'Other events, such as the death of a loved one, I remember vividly. I remember the texture of the dress my mother wore

457

on the day she died. Even today, I could measure out for you the length of the loose thread on the sleeve.'

'I understand.' Kahlan stared down into her tea. 'I, too, remember well the day my mother died. I remember every horrid detail, even though I wish I could forget.'

Shota placed her elbows on the table and twined her fingers together. 'The future is that way with me. I can't always see pleasant future events that I wish to see, and I sometimes can't avoid seeing those things I abhor. Some events I can see with clarity, and others, despite how much I wish to see them, are only shadows in the fog.'

'What about the winds hunting Richard?'

With a distant look, Shota shook her head. 'That was disturbing. It was as if someone else's memory was being forced on me. As if someone else was using me to pass on a message.'

'Do you think it was a message, or a warning?'

A thoughtful frown creased Shota's brow. 'I wondered that, myself. I don't know the answer. I passed it on through Nadine because I thought Richard should know, in either case.'

Kahlan rubbed her forehead. 'Shota, when the plague started, it started among children who had been playing or watching a game.'

'Ja'La.'

'Yes, that's right. Emperor Jagang –'

'The dream walker.'

Kahlan looked up. 'You know of him?'

'He visits my future memories occasionally. He plays tricks, trying to get into my dreams. I won't allow it.'

'Do you think it possible that it was the dream walker who gave you this message about the winds hunting Richard?'

'No. I know his tricks. Take my word; it was not a message from Jagang. What of the plague and the Ja'La game?'

'Well, Jagang used his ability as a dream walker to slip into the mind of a wizard he sent to assassinate Richard. He was at the Ja'La game. The wizard, I mean. Jagang saw the game through this wizard's eyes.

'Jagang was incensed that Richard had changed the rules so that all the children could play. The plague started among those children. That's one reason we think Jagang was responsible.

'The first child we went to see was near death.' Kahlan closed her eyes and covered them with her fingertips at the memory. She took a settling breath. 'While Richard and I knelt at his side, he died. He was just a boy. An innocent boy. His whole body was rotting from the plague. I can't imagine the suffering he endured. He died before our eyes.'

'I'm sorry,' Shota whispered.

Kahlan composed herself before looking up. 'After he had died, his hand reached up and grabbed ahold of Richard's shirt. His lungs filled with air, he pulled Richard close, and he said, "The winds hunt you."'

A troubled sigh came from across the table. 'Then I was right; it was not something I saw, but a message sent through me.'

'Shota, Richard thinks it means that the Temple of the Winds is hunting him. He has a journal from a man who lived during the great war of three thousand years ago. The journal tells of how the wizards of that time placed things of great value, and great danger, in the temple, and then they sent the temple away.'

Frowning, Shota leaned forward. 'Away? Away where?'

'We don't know. The Temple of the Winds was atop Mount Kymermosst.'

'I know the place. There is no temple there, only a few bits of old ruins.'

Kahlan nodded. 'It's possible the wizards used their power to blast the side of the mountain away and bury the temple in a rockslide. Whatever they did, it's gone. From information in the journal, Richard believes that the red moons were a warning from the temple. He further believes that the Temple of the Winds is also known more simply as "the winds."'

Shota tapped a finger against the side of her teacup. 'So the message could have come directly from the Temple of the Winds.'

'Do you think that possible? How could a place send a message?'

'The wizards of that time could do things with magic we can only wonder at. The sliph, for example. From what I know, and what you have told me, my best guess would be that Jagang has somehow stolen something deadly from the Temple of the Winds, and used it to start the plague.'

Kahlan felt a cold wave of fright flood through her. 'How could he do such a thing?'

'He is a dream walker. He has access to untold knowledge. Despite his crude objectives, he is anything but stupid. I have been touched by his mind in my sleep, when he hunts in the night. He is not to be underestimated.'

'Shota, he wishes to extinguish all magic.'

Shota lifted an eyebrow. 'I have already told you I will answer your questions. There is no need to convince me of my own interest in this matter. Just as the danger from the Keeper, Jagang is no less a threat to me. He promises to eliminate magic, but to accomplish those ends he uses magic.'

'But how could he have stolen this plague from the Temple of the Winds? Do you think it even possible? Really?'

'I can tell you that the plague did not start of its own account. Your guess is correct. It was ignited through magic.'

'How can we stop it?'

'I know of no cure for plague.' Shota took a sip of her tea. She glanced up at Kahlan. 'On the other hand, how could a plague be started?'

'Magic.' Kahlan frowned. 'You mean . . . you mean that if magic could start it, even though we don't know how to cure the plague, magic may be able to stop it? Is that what you're suggesting?'

Shota shrugged. 'I know no more how to start a plague than to cure it. I know magic started this one. If magic started it, then it would stand to reason that magic could halt it.'

Kahlan straightened. 'Then there is hope we can stop it, and save all those people from dying.'

'Possibly. If we were to put the pieces together, it would at least suggest that Jagang stole from the Temple of the Winds magic to start the plague, and that the temple is trying to warn Richard of the violation.'

'Why Richard?'

'Why do you think? What makes Richard different from anyone else?'

Kahlan felt transfixed by Shota's small, sly smile.

'He's a war wizard. He has Subtractive Magic. It's how he defeated the spirit of Darken Rahl and stopped the Keeper. Richard is the only one with the power to do whatever it is that can help.'

'Keep that in mind,' Shota whispered into her teacup.

Kahlan was suddenly getting the feeling that she was being led down a path. She dismissed the feeling. Shota was trying to help.

Kahlan gathered her courage. 'Shota, why did you send Nadine?'

'To marry Richard.'

'Why Nadine?'

Shota's lips spread in a sad smile. It was the question for which she had been waiting.

'Because I care about him. I wanted it to be someone in whom he could find at least some small comfort.'

Kahlan swallowed. 'But he finds comfort in me.'

'I know. But he is to marry another.'

'The flow of the future tells you this? Your future ... memory?' Shota gave her a single nod. 'It wasn't your idea? You didn't simply want to send someone to marry him so I wouldn't?'

'No.' Shota leaned back in her chair and stared off into the trees. 'I saw that he will marry another. I see great pain for him in this. I exerted all my influence so that it would be someone he knew, someone in whom he would find at least some solace. I wanted to spare him as much pain in it as I could.'

Kahlan didn't know what to say. She felt as she had when she was struggling against the flow of water down in the drainage tunnel when she was fighting Marlin. She remembered the weight of the water, the way it pinned her in place.

'But I love him,' was all she could think to say.

'I know,' Shota whispered back. 'It was not my choice to have him marry another. I was only able to influence who it would be.'

Kahlan struggled to pull a shaky breath as she looked away from the witch woman's ageless eyes.

'I had no say,' Shota added, 'in who would be your husband.'

Kahlan's gaze returned to Shota. 'What? What do you mean?'

'You are to be wedded. It is not Richard. I could not influence that part of it. That is not a good sign.'

Kahlan felt stunned. 'What do you mean?'

'The spirits are somehow involved in this. They would only accept limited influence. They have their reasons for the rest of it. Those reasons are veiled from me.'

Kahlan felt a tear run down her cheek. 'Shota, what am I to do? I'll lose my only love. I could never love anyone but Richard, even if I wished it. I'm a Confessor.'

Shota sat still as stone as she watched Kahlan. 'The good spirits have granted us all they could in allowing me to have a say in who will be Richard's bride. I searched, and could find no other woman for whom he feels even this limited empathy. She was the best I could do.

'If you truly love Richard, then you should try to find comfort in the fact that he will have Nadine, a woman he knows and for whom he at least has some feeling, however small. Perhaps, with a woman such as this, he will someday find happiness and come to love her.'

Kahlan put her trembling hands in her lap. She felt sick to her stomach. It would do no good to argue with Shota. This wasn't her doing. The spirits were involved.

'To what purpose? What good will it do for him to marry Nadine? For me to be mated to one I don't love?'

Shota's voice came soft and compassionate. 'I don't know, child. Just as some parents, for a variety of reasons, choose their children's spouses, so have the spirits chosen for you and Richard.'

'If the spirits were involved, why would they desire our misery? They took us to that place so we could be together.' Kahlan struggled against the weight of the floodwaters. 'Why would they want to do this to us?'

'Perhaps,' Shota whispered as she watched Kahlan, 'it is because you will betray him.'

Kahlan's throat clenched shut, locking her breath in her lungs. The prophecy screamed through her head.

*... for the one in white, his true beloved, will betray him in
her blood.*

Kahlan shot to her feet. 'No!' Her hands balled into fists. 'I would never hurt him, I would never betray him!'

Shota calmly sipped her tea.

'Sit down, Mother Confessor.'

Kahlan fought to keep the tears back as she sank into her chair.

'I don't control the future memories any more than I control the past. I told you, you must have the courage to hear the answers.' She tapped a finger to her temple. 'Not only here' – she tapped the finger over her heart – 'but here, too.'

Kahlan made herself take a deep breath. 'Forgive me. It's not your fault. I know that.'

Shota lifted an eyebrow. 'Very good, Mother Confessor. Learning to accept the truth is the first step to gaining control of your destiny.'

'Shota, I don't mean this to sound disrespectful, but seeing the future does not provide all the answers. Before, you told me that I would touch Richard with my power. I thought that would destroy him. I tried to kill myself to prevent your words from coming to pass, to prevent myself from hurting him.

'Richard wouldn't allow me the chance at suicide. As it turned out, your seeing of the future was true, but there was more to it, and it turned out differently than we thought.

'I touched Richard, but his magic protected him, and my touch didn't harm him.'

'I didn't see the result of the touch. Only that you would touch him. This is different. I see you both being wedded.'

Kahlan felt numb. 'Who is it to be that I will marry?'

'I see only a misty form. I cannot see the person. I do not know his identity.'

'Shota, I was told that a witch woman's seeing of future events is a form of prophecy.'

'Who told you this?'

'A wizard. Zedd.'

'Wizards,' Shota muttered. 'They don't know what is in a witch woman's mind. They think they know everything.'

Kahlan pushed her long hair back over her shoulder. 'Shota, we were going to be honest with each other, remember?'

Shota let out a dainty grumble. 'Well, I guess that in this case, they may be mostly right.'

'Prophecy does not always turn out how it seems. The dire dangers can be avoided, or changed. Do you think there is any way I can change the prophecy?'

Shota frowned. 'The prophecy?'

'The one you mentioned. Betraying Richard.'

Shota's frown deepened into suspicion. 'Are you saying that this was also foretold in a prophecy?'

Kahlan's eyes turned away from the witch woman's intense gaze. 'When the wizard came, with Jagang possessing his mind, Jagang said that he had invoked a prophecy to trap Richard. It, too, says I will betray him.'

'Do you remember this prophecy?'

Kahlan rubbed her finger around the rim of her teacup. 'It's one of those memories that we spoke of, the memories we wish we could forget, but we can't.

'"On the red moon will come the firestorm. The one bonded to the blade will watch as his people die. If he does nothing, then he, and all those he loves, will die in its heat, for no blade, forged of steel or conjured of sorcery, can touch this foe.

'"To quench the inferno, he must seek the remedy in the wind. Lightning will find him on that path, for the one in white, his true beloved, will betray him in her blood."'

Shota leaned back, taking her teacup with her. 'It is true, as you say, that the events in prophecy can be altered, or avoided, but not in a double bind prophecy. This one is such a prophecy, a trap that ensnares its victim. The red moon proves that the trap has sprung.'

'But there must be a way –' Kahlan pushed her hands back into her hair. 'Shota, what am I to do?'

'You are to be wedded to another,' she whispered, 'as is Richard. What is beyond, I don't see, but this much of it is the future.'

'Shota, I know you're speaking the truth, but how can it be that I would betray Richard? I'm telling you the truth; I would die before I would betray him. My heart won't allow me to betray him. I couldn't.'

Shota smoothed a loose wisp of her dress. 'Think, Mother Confessor, and you will see that you are wrong, just as I showed you that you were wrong that I could no longer harm you.'

'How? How could I do such a thing, when I know it isn't in me – for any reason – to betray him?'

Shota took a patient breath. 'It is not nearly so difficult as you wish to think. What if you knew, for example, that you had only one way to save his life, and that way was to betray him, but in so doing, you would lose his love? Would you make the sacrifice of his love to preserve his life? The truth, now.'

Kahlan swallowed past the lump in her throat. 'Yes. I would betray him if it was to save his life.'

'So, you see, it is not as impossible an event as you imagined.'

'I guess not,' Kahlan said in a small voice. She pushed at a few crumbs, on the table. 'Shota, what is the purpose of all this? Why would the future hold that Richard will marry Nadine, and that I will marry another man? There must be a reason. It goes against everything we both want, so there must be some force pushing events down that path.'

Shota said after a moment's deliberation. 'The Temple of the Winds hunts Richard. The spirits have a hand in this.'

Kahlan's face sank wearily into her hands.

'You said to Nadine, "May the spirits have mercy on him." What did you mean by that?'

'The underworld contains more than just the good spirits. The spirits – good, and the evil – are all involved in this.'

Kahlan didn't want to talk anymore. It was too painful, talking about the ruination of her dreams and hopes as if they were pieces on a game board.

'To what purpose?' she mumbled.

'The plague.'

Kahlan looked up. 'What?'

'It has something to do with the plague, and the thing of magic the dream walker stole from the Temple of the Winds.'

'You mean that it could be that this could somehow be part of our attempt to find the magic to stop the plague?'

'I believe it is so,' the witch woman said at last. 'You and Richard are desperately seeking a way to stop the plague and save the lives of countless people. I see in the future that you each wed other people.

'For what other reason would both of you make such a sacrifice?'

'But why would it be necessary –'

'You seek something I cannot answer. I cannot alter what will be, nor do I know the reason for it. We are forced to consider the possibilities. Think.

'If the only way to save all those people from dying in a firestorm of plague were for Richard and you to sacrifice your life together, perhaps, say, to prove your true devotion to protecting innocent lives, would you both do such a thing?'

Kahlan put her trembling hands in her lap, under the table. She had seen the pain in Richard's eyes when he had watched that boy die. She knew her own pain. They had both seen innocent, sick children, who were going to die. How many more would die?

She would never be able to live with herself if the only way to save those children was to sacrifice her love, and she refused.

'How could we not? Even if it would kill us, how could we not? But how could the good spirits demand such a price?'

Kahlan suddenly remembered Denna's spirit taking the Keeper's mark from Richard, and freely choosing to go in Richard's place to eternal torment at the Keeper's hands. That it turned out that Denna didn't have to face that fate didn't matter; she thought that she would, and had sacrificed her soul in the place of one she loved.

The branches of a nearby maple tree clacked together in the gentle breeze. Kahlan could hear the flags atop Shota's palace snapping in the wind. The air tasted of spring. The grasses were a bright, new green. Life was beginning to bud all around.

Kahlan's heart felt like dead ashes.

'Then I will tell you one other thing,' Shota said, as if from a great distance. Kahlan listened from the bottom of a well of despair. 'You have not heard the last message from the winds. You will receive one more, involving the moon. This will be the consequential communion.

'Do not ignore it, nor dismiss it. Your future, Richard's

future, and the future of all those innocent people will hinge on this event. Both of you must use all you have learned in order to comprehend the chance you will be offered.'

'Chance? Chance for what?'

Shota's gaze riveted Kahlan. 'The chance to carry out your most solemn duty. The chance to save all the innocent lives of those who depend upon you to do what they cannot.'

'How soon?'

'I only know it will not be long.'

Kahlan nodded. She wondered why she wasn't crying. It seemed as if this was the most devastating personal tragedy she could imagine – losing Richard – and yet, she wasn't crying.

She guessed she would, but not now, not here.

Kahlan stared at the table. 'Shota, you would try to stop us from having a child, wouldn't you? A boy child?'

'Yes.'

'You would try to kill our son, if we had one, wouldn't you?'

'Yes.'

'Then how do I know that this isn't just some plot on your part to prevent us from having a child?'

'You will have to judge the truth of my words with your own mind and heart.'

Kahlan remembered the dying boy's words, and the prophecy. Somehow, she had known all along that she would never marry Richard. It was all just an impossible dream.

When she was young, Kahlan had asked her mother about growing up and having a love, a husband, a home. Her mother had stood before her, beautiful, radiant, statuesque, but wearing her Confessor's face.

Confessors don't have love, Kahlan. They have duty.

Richard was born a war wizard. He had been born for a purpose. Duty.

She watched the breeze roll a few of the crumbs from the table. 'I believe you,' Kahlan whispered. 'I wish I didn't, but I do. You're telling me the truth.'

There was nothing else to say. Kahlan stood. She had to lock her knees to stay upright on her trembling legs. She tried to remember where the sliph's well was, but she couldn't seem to make her mind work.

'Thank you for the tea,' she heard herself say. 'It was lovely.'

If Shota answered, Kahlan didn't hear it.

'Shota?' Kahlan grasped the back of the chair to steady herself. 'Could you point me in the right direction? I can't seem to remember . . .'

Shota was there, taking her arm. 'I will walk partway with you, child,' Shota said in a soft, compassionate voice, 'so you may find your way.'

They walked the road in silence. Kahlan tried to find cheer in the warm spring morning. It was still so cold in Aydindril. It had been snowing when she left. Still, she couldn't find any cheer in the fine day.

As they climbed the stone steps cut into the cliff, Kahlan fought to regain a sense of purpose. If she and Richard could somehow save all those people from the plague, it would be a wonderful thing. Most wouldn't care about the sacrifice they made, but that wouldn't lessen the relief she would feel in the sound of a child's laughter, or the sight of a mother's joy in her child's safety.

There would still be things to live for. She could fill the void with the happiness to be seen in the eyes of her people. She would have done something no other could do. She and Richard would have stopped Jagang from harming all those people.

Near the top of the cliff, Kahlan paused at a turn in the steps and looked out at Agaden Reach. It truly was a beautiful place, this valley nestled among the peaks of jagged mountains.

She remembered that the Keeper had sent a wizard and a screeling to kill Shota. Shota had barely escaped with her life. She had vowed to regain her home.

'I'm glad you got your home back. I'm glad for you, Shota. I really am. Agaden Reach belongs to you.'

'Thank you, Mother Confessor.'

Kahlan looked to the witch woman's almond eyes. 'What did you do to the wizard who chased you out?'

'What I said I would do. I tied him up by his thumbs, and I

skinned him alive. I sat back and watched as his magic bled from his skinless carcass.' She turned and gestured back down into the green valley. 'I covered the seat of my throne with his hide.'

Kahlan remembered that that was precisely what Shota had promised to do. It was small wonder that even wizards rarely dared to enter Agaden Reach; Shota was more than a match for a wizard. One wizard, at least, had learned that lesson too late.

'I can't say I blame you – the Keeper sending him to kill you and all. If the Keeper had gotten you, well, I know how much you feared that.'

'I owe you and Richard a debt. Richard prevented the Keeper from having us all.'

'I'm glad the wizard didn't send you to the Keeper, Shota.'

Kahlan really meant it. She still knew Shota was dangerous, but the witch woman seemed also to have a compassion that Kahlan hadn't expected.

'Do you know what he said to me, this wizard?' Shota asked. 'He said he forgave me. Can you believe it? He granted me forgiveness. And then he begged mine.'

The wind carried some of Kahlan's hair across her face. She pulled it back. 'Seems a strange thing for him to say, considering.'

'The Wizard's Fourth Rule, he called it. He said that there was magic in forgiveness, in the Fourth Rule. Magic to heal. In forgiveness you grant, and more so in the forgiveness you receive.'

'I guess the Keeper's minion would say anything to try to get away with what he had done, and to get away from you. I can understand you not being in the mood to forgive him.'

Light seemed to vanish into the ageless depths of Shota's eyes. 'He forgot to place the word "sincere" before "forgiveness."'

CHAPTER 42

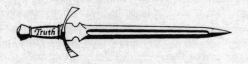

Kahlan watched the witch woman disappear back into the gloomy forest. Vines hanging down from craggy branches reached out to touch their mistress as she passed, while tendrils and roots stretched up to brush her leg. She vanished into a shroud of mist. Unseen creatures called in low whistles and clicks from the direction she had gone.

Kahlan turned back to the moss-covered boulder Shota had shown her and, just beyond, found the sliph's well. The silver face of the sliph rose from beyond the round, stone wall, to watch as Kahlan approached. Kahlan almost wished the sliph hadn't come, as if somehow, if Kahlan couldn't get back, none of the things she had learned would come to pass.

How was she going to look into Richard's eyes and not scream in anguish? How was she ever going to be able to go on? How would she find the will to live?

'Do you wish to travel?' the sliph asked.

'No, but I must.'

The sliph frowned, as if well puzzled. 'If you wish to travel, I will be ready.'

Kahlan sank to the ground, put her back to the sliph's well, and folded her legs under herself. Was she to give up this easily? Was she to submit meekly to the fates? She didn't have a choice.

Think of the solution, not the problem.

Somehow, things didn't seem as desperate as they had back in the reach. There had to be a way to solve this. Richard would not so easily give in. He would fight for her. She would

470

fight for him. They loved each other, and that was more important than anything else.

Kahlan's mind felt as if it were in a fog. She tried to focus with more resolve. She couldn't just give up. She had to face this with her old determination.

She knew that witch women bewitched people. They didn't necessarily do it out of malice; it was just the way they were. It was like a person not being able to help the fact that they were tall, or short, or the color of their hair. Witch women bewitched people because that was the way their magic worked.

Shota had bewitched Richard, to an extent. Only the magic of the Sword of Truth saved him the first time.

The Sword of Truth.

Richard was the Seeker. This was the kind of thing a Seeker did: solved problems. She was in love with the Seeker. He would not so easily give up.

Kahlan plucked a leaf and tore little strips from it as she began to reconsider everything she had been told by Shota. How much of it dare she believe? It was all beginning to seem like a dream, from which she was just coming awake. Matters could not possibly be as desperate as she had thought.

Her father had told her never to give up, to fight with every breath, with the last breath if need be. Nor would Richard give in easily. This wasn't ended yet. The future was still the future, and despite what Shota said, the matter was not yet decided.

Something at her shoulder was bothering her. As she thought, she flicked her hand at it, and then went back to tearing strips off the big leaf. There had to be a way to solve this.

When she swatted at her shoulder again, her fingers hit the bone knife. It felt warm.

Kahlan drew the knife and held it in her lap. The knife was warm. It seemed to pulse and vibrate. It grew so hot that it became uncomfortable to hold.

Kahlan watched, wide-eyed, as the black feathers stood up. They danced and waved and twisted in a breeze. Her hair hung limp. The air was dead still. There was no breeze.

Kahlan shot to her feet.

'Sliph!'

The sliph's silver face was right there, close. Kahlan backed away a bit.

'Sliph, I need to travel.'

'Come, we will travel. Where do you wish to go?'

'The Mud People. I need to go to the Mud People.'

The liquid features contorted in thought. 'I do not know this place.'

'It's not a place. They're people. People –' Kahlan tapped her chest – 'they're people, like me.'

'I know different peoples, but not these Mud People.'

Kahlan pushed back her hair, trying to think. 'They live in the wilds.'

'I know places in the wilds. Which one do you wish to travel to? Name it, and we will travel. You will be pleased.'

'Well, it's a place that's flat. It's a grassland. Flat grassland. No mountains, like here.' Kahlan gestured around, but realized that the sliph could see only trees.

'I know several places like that.'

'Which places? Maybe I'll recognize them.'

'I can travel to a place overlooking the Callisidrin River –'

'To the west of the Callisidrin. The Mud People are farther west.'

'I can travel to Tondelen Vale, the Harja Rift, Kea Plains, Sealan, Herkon Split, Anderith, Pickton, the Jocopo Treasure –'

'The what? What was the last one?' She knew most of the rest of the places the sliph named, but they weren't close to the Mud People.

'The Jocopo Treasure. Do you wish to travel there?'

Kahlan held out the warm bone knife – grandfather's knife. Chandalen had told her how the Jocopo had made war on the Mud People, and the ancestor spirits had guided Chandalen's grandfather in how to defend his people against the Jocopo. Chandalen had said they used to trade with the Jocopo, before their war. The Jocopo had to be close to the Mud People.

'Say the last place again,' Kahlan said.

'The Jocopo Treasure.'

At the echoing words, the black feathers danced and twisted. Kahlan shoved the bone knife back in the band around her upper arm. She sprang up onto the stone wall.

'That's where I wish to go: the Jocopo Treasure. I wish to travel to the Jocopo Treasure. Can you take me there, sliph?'

A silver arm swept her off the stone wall. 'Come. We will travel to the Jocopo Treasure. You will be pleased.'

Kahlan gasped one quick breath before she was plunged into the quicksilver froth. She let the breath go, and inhaled the sliph, but this time, numbed by troubling thoughts of losing Richard, of his marrying Nadine, she felt no rapture.

Zedd cackled like a madman. Ann was upside down in his vision. He stuck out his tongue at her and blew, making a long, crude sound.

'You needn't attempt to pretend,' she growled. 'It seems to be your natural state.'

Zedd moved his legs as if trying to walk upside down through the air. The blood was rushing to his head.

'Do you wish to die with your dignity?' he asked her. 'Or would you rather live.'

'I'll not play a fool.'

'That's the word – play! Don't just sit there in the mud. Play in it!'

She leaned over, putting her head close to his. He was standing on it in the mud. 'Zedd, you can't possibly think such a thing would work.'

'You said it yourself. You are mucking about with a crazy man. It was your suggestion.'

'I suggested no such thing!'

'Perhaps you didn't suggest it, but you were the one who gave me the inspiration. I'll be happy to give you full credit, when we tell people the story.'

'Tell people! In the first place, it won't work. In the second place, I realize full well that you would be only too delighted to tell people. That's just one more reason why I won't do it.'

Zedd howled like a coyote. He stiffened his legs and his spine, letting himself topple like a felled tree. Mud splashed on Ann. Fuming, she wiped a small splat from her nose.

At the tall stick fence, grim-faced Nangtong guards watched the two prisoners, the two sacrifices. Zedd and Ann had sat in the mud with their backs to one another and untied the ropes binding their wrists. The guards, armed with spears and bows, didn't seem to care; the prisoners couldn't get away. Zedd knew they were right.

Happy people had begun to stop by the pigpen at dawn. As the morning wore on, the crowd grew as more people stopped by to chatter with the guards and take a look at the fine offerings. Apparently, everyone was in a good mood because they now had a sacrifice for the spirits. Their lives would be safe after the unhappy spirits were appeased.

The guards and the people of the Nangtong village, watching from the other side of the fence, were now looking less pleased. They fidgeted with the cloth covering their faces, making sure it hid enough, and that it was secure. The guards began wiping more ash on their faces and bodies. Apparently, one couldn't be too careful, lest the spirits recognize them.

Zedd tucked his head down between his knees and rolled himself through the wet, sticky slop. He laughed maniacally as he rolled in a circle around Ann's squat figure sitting on the cold ground.

'Would you stop that!'

Zedd spread supine in the mud before her. He swept his rigid arms and legs through the mud.

'Ann,' he said in a low tone, 'we have important business. I think we might have better success if we attempt to carry out those tasks in this world, rather than in the underworld, after we are dead.'

'I know we can't help if we're dead.'

'It would stand to reason, then, that we need to get away, now, wouldn't it?'

'Of course it would,' she grumbled. 'But I don't think –'

Zedd plopped himself down in her lap. She winced in disgust. Her nose wrinkled when he rested his muddy arms around her neck.

'Ann, if we do nothing, we die. If we try to fight these people, we will die. Without the use of our magic, we can't escape them. Our only option is to convince them to let us go. We can't speak their language, and even if we could, I doubt we would be able to persuade them.'

'Yes, but –'

'We have only one chance, as I see it. We must convince them that we are quite loony. This sacrifice is a sacred service to their spirit ancestors. Look at the guards behind my back. Do they look happy?'

'Well, no.'

'If they believe that we're crazy, then they just might think twice before sacrificing us to their spirits. Wouldn't the spirits be insulted to receive a lunatic as a sacrifice? Wouldn't that be disrespectful? We have to make them fear insulting their spirits with two loony people.'

'But that's … crazy.'

'Look at it this way. A sacrifice is something like a treaty wedding between two peoples. The bride is the sacrifice of one people to another, in the flesh of the new husband, all in the hope for a peaceful and productive future. The bride's new people treat her with respect. The bride's people treat the husband and his people with respect. It's all an arrangement symbolizing unity, continuity, and hope for the future.

'We are like the bride, being offered to the spirits. How would it look if the Nangtong offered an unworthy, demented bride? If you were one of the spirits, wouldn't you be offended?'

'If I got you in the bargain, I would be.'

Zedd howled at the sky. Ann winced and pulled away from him.

'It's our only chance, Ann.' He leaned close, whispering in her ear. 'I swear an oath as First Wizard that I will never tell anyone how you behaved.'

He drew back and grinned at her. 'Besides, it's fun. Remember how much fun it was as a child to play outside? To play in the mud? Why, it was the grandest of things.'

'But it might not work.'

'Even if it doesn't, wouldn't you rather die having fun on the last day of your life, instead of sitting here, afraid and cold and dirty? Wouldn't you rather have some childlike fun one last time? Let yourself go, Prelate, and recall what it was to be a child. Let yourself do anything that comes into your head. Have fun. Be a child.'

With a serious expression, Ann considered his words.

'You won't tell anyone?'

'You have my word. You can act with childish glee, and no one but I will ever know – and the Nangtong, of course.'

'Another of your acts of desperation, Zedd?'

'The time for desperation is upon us. Let's play.'

Ann smiled a sly smile. She stiff-armed him in the chest, knocking him back into the mud. With a riot of laughter, she leaped on top of him.

They wrestled like children, rolling through the slop. After a half dozen turns, Ann was a mud monster with arms, legs, and two eyes. The mud split, revealing a pink mouth as she howled with him at the sky.

They made mudballs and used the pigs as targets. They chased the pigs. They flopped onto the hard, round backs of the squealing creatures, riding them around until they were tossed off into the mud. Zedd doubted that Ann had ever been this dirty in her nine centuries of life.

He realized, while they were having a one-legged game of tag that involved more falling in the mud than hopping progress, that her laughter had changed.

Ann was having fun.

They stomped through puddles. They chased the pigs. They ran around the enclosure rattling sticks against the fence.

And then they hit upon the idea of making faces at the guards. They drew whimsical expressions on each other's faces in mud. They made every rude noise they could think of. They jumped and laughed and pointed at the solemn guards.

Ann and Zedd got to laughing so hard that they couldn't stand, and like two drunks, they rolled on the ground, holding their sides.

The crowd grew. Worried whispers swept through the onlookers.

Ann stuck her thumbs in her ears and wiggled her fingers as she made faces at them. Zedd stood on his head and sang a few lewd ballads. he knew. Ann laughed hysterically as he mispronounced key words.

Zedd fell to laughing, and then fell in the mud, and then Ann fell on him. She sat on his stomach, pinning him to the ground as she tickled him under his arms, while he gasped for breath between laughter and tickled her ribs. The two of them had never had so much fun. The pigs cowered in the corner.

Suddenly, buckets of water were dumped over the both of them as they were furiously engaged in trying to find each other's most ticklish spots. They looked up. More water rained down on them.

As fast as the mud was washed off them, they dived back into it. Ash-covered guards seized them by the arms and held them at spearpoint while they were once again washed off. Zedd peered over at Ann. She peered back. She looked ridiculous, her face emerging from streamers of slop. He giggled and made a face at her. She giggled and made a face back. The men yelled.

Zedd's cheeks puffed with attempts to halt his laughing. The guards shoved them forward, spears poking in their backs. It reminded him of being tickled, and they both laughed.

It was as if once uncorked, the laughter had a life of its own. If they were to be sacrificed, what difference did it make? They might as well have the last laugh.

The crowd of shrouded figures parted as the two prisoners were led out of the pigs' pen.

Giggling, Zedd held his arm high and waved. 'Wave at the people, Annie.'

She made faces instead. Zedd liked the idea and imitated her. People shrank back, as if seeing a horrifying sight. Some of the women wept and wailed. Zedd and Ann laughed and pointed at them as the women ran from the crowd, seeking refuge from the lunatics.

The tents and onlookers were soon left behind as their captors prodded them on with spears. Before long, the two dirty, smelly, happy sacrifices were out in the hills. Thirty-five or forty Nangtong spirit hunters, all holding ready spears or bows, followed behind. Zedd noticed that some of them had brought packs and provisions.

First Wizard Zeddicus Zu'l Zorander and Prelate Annalina Aldurren skipped along ahead of the spears, laughing and making outrageous, ever-increasing claims as to how many onions they could eat without producing tears.

Zedd hadn't a clue where they were going, but it was a fine morning to be going there, wherever it was.

*

'It's kind of funny, Lord Rahl,' Lieutenant Crawford said.

Richard gazed out over the boulder field. 'What's funny about it?'

The lieutenant bent his head back to peer up the cliff. 'Well, I meant it's odd. I grew up in rugged mountains, so I've seen places like these mountains my whole life, but this place is odd.' He turned and pointed. 'See that mountain over there? You can see where the rockslide came from.'

Richard put a hand over his brow to shield his eyes from the low afternoon sun. The mountain the lieutenant was pointing to was rugged and covered with trees, except for the uppermost reaches. On the steep side facing them, a part of it had given way, leaving naked rock to scar the mountain where the rock had broken off. At the bottom of the barren scar lay a boulder field.

'What about it?'

'Well, look at all the rock at the bottom. That's the portion that broke off the face of the mountain.' He gestured to the boulder field they stood atop. 'This isn't the same.'

Another soldier approached and saluted with a fist to his heart. He cast a wary glance at Ulic and Egan, who were standing with their arms folded, while he waited silently.

'Nothing, Lord Rahl,' he said when Richard acknowledged him. 'Not so much as a flake of rock that's been worked with tools.'

'Keep looking. Try the outer fringes of the boulder field. Look for places where you can crawl down under some of the larger boulders and check under there, too.'

The soldier saluted and hurried off. There wasn't much of the day left. Richard had told them that he didn't want to stay the next day. He wanted to get back to Aydindril. Kahlan would probably be back that night, or possibly tomorrow. He wanted to be there.

If she came back. If she was still alive.

He broke out in a sweat at the very thought. His knees felt weak.

He banished the thought. She would be back. That was all there was to it. She would be back. He made himself quit thinking about it, and put his mind to the problem at hand.

'So what do you think, lieutenant?'

Lieutenant Crawford pitched a stone, watching it bounce first off one boulder, and then another. The sharp sound echoed off the cliff behind them.

'It could be that the face of this mountain broke off much longer ago. Then, over all that time, things started growing in, dying, making soil for larger things to grow, and then they died, making yet more soil. It could be that it's been covered over.'

Richard knew what Lieutenant Crawford was talking about. He knew how a forest, in time, could cover over rockslides. If you dug in the forest at the bottom of a cliff, you often encountered the bones of the fallen mountain.

'I don't think so, in this case.'

The lieutenant looked over at him. 'May I ask why you think not, Lord Rahl?'

Richard stared across the rift to the next mountain. 'Well, look at that cliff. The face of it is rough and uneven, yet the rock of the mountain left behind after the face fell away is weathered now, so much of it isn't sharp. It's been worn by time.

'Some of it is sharp, though. Water gets in the cracks, freezes, and breaks off more of the rock with time. You can see some of those sharp places; but most of it has a softer look.

'It has the look to me that it happened long before this slide here, yet you can still see most of the rock lying at the bottom of the cliff. Here, there's much less scree.'

Egan unfolded his arms and brushed back his blond hair. 'Could just be the lay of the land. This cliff faces south, letting the sun in to help things grow, whereas that one faces north, so it's in shade most of the time. The forest wouldn't grow in as well over there, and that would leave the scree exposed.'

Egan had a point.

'There's more to it.' Richard tilted his head back and looked up the thousands of feet of sheer cliff face towering above them. 'Half this mountain is gone. That one over there is just a small slide, in comparison.

'Look up at this mountain, and try to imagine what it would have looked like before this happened. It's cleaved from the very top all the way down, like a log round split in half. All the rest of the mountains around here are more or less cone-shaped. This one is only half a cone.

'Even if I'm wrong, and half the mountain isn't gone, and it used to be shaped much as we see it now, there would still be an immense amount of rock down here. I mean, even if it used to be much this shape, and only a shell of rock ten or twenty feet thick collapsed, by the towering height alone there would have to be a huge pile of rubble.

'This rock is sharp, so it might be pieces broken off by the working of water freezing, but probably, since I can't see any time-worn places, it happened more recently. Yet I just don't see any evidence of the mass of rock that would have had to come off this mountain. Even if it had been covered over in time, I'd think that where we're standing would be a huge mound.'

The lieutenant glanced about. 'You have a point. This is pretty much level with the bottom of the rift. If all that rock broke off, there's no mound under the forest down here.'

Richard watched the soldiers all about searching through the rock and woods for any sign of the Temple of the Winds. None looked to be finding anything.

'I can't see that it's down here. I just don't see any reason to believe that the mountain fell down here.'

Ulic and Egan folded their arms again, the matter settled as far as they were concerned.

Lieutenant Crawford cleared his throat. 'Lord Rahl, if the half of Mount Kymermosst that used to be there isn't down here, then where is it?'

Richard shared a long look with the man. 'That's what I'd like to know. If it isn't down here, then it must be someplace else.'

The blond-headed lieutenant shifted his weight to his other foot. 'Well, it didn't just get up and walk away, Lord Rahl.'

Richard turned his scabbard out of the way as he started climbing down off the rocks. He realized he was frightening the man; Richard seemed to be suggesting something that hinted at magic.

'It must be as you say, lieutenant. It must have fallen and grown over. Perhaps the cleft between the mountains was deeper back then, and the fall simply filled it in, rather than making a mound.'

The lieutenant liked the idea. It gave him a rock solid reality.

Richard didn't believe it. The cliff face looked peculiar to him. It was too smooth, as if cleaved with a huge sword. Yes, there were jagged places, but that would explain the rock that was at the bottom. It looked to him as though the mountain had been cut off and taken away, and over time water and ice had worked at the smooth face of the cliff, breaking off pieces and making it more craggy; but it was nowhere near as rough as the other cliffs round about.

'That might explain it, Lord Rahl,' the lieutenant said. 'If that's true, though, that would mean that the temple you're looking for must be buried deep underground.'

With his two huge guards right at his heels, Richard made for the horses. 'I want to have a look up on top. I want to see the ruins up there.'

Their guide, a middle-aged man named Andy Millett, was waiting with the horses. He wore simple wool clothes of browns and greens, much like Richard used to wear. His shaggy brown hair hung past his ears. Andy was immensely proud that Lord Rahl had asked him to guide them to Mount Kymermosst. Richard felt a bit sheepish about that; Andy was simply the first person Richard found who knew where it was.

'Andy, I'd like to go up to the ruins on top.'

Andy handed Richard the reins to the big roan. 'Sure enough, Lord Rahl. There's not much up there, but I'd be glad to show you, just the same.'

Big as his two guards were, they mounted lightly, their horses hardly moving under the sudden weight. Richard swung up into the saddle and wiggled his right boot into the stirrup.

'Can we get up there before dark? Most of that spring snowstorm is melted. The trail should be open.'

Andy glanced at the sun, which was just about touching a mountain. 'With the way you ride, Lord Rahl, I'd say long before. Usually, important people slow me down. I think I'm the one slowing you down.'

Richard smiled. He remembered the same thing himself.

The more important the person he guided, the slower they went, it seemed.

The sky was streaked with golds and reds by the time they reached the ruins. The surrounding mountains were cast in deep shadow. The ruins seemed to glow in the honeyed light.

There were some once elegant structures, now crumbling, that looked to have been a part of a larger place, just as Kahlan had said. Here and there on the barren mountaintop, parts of walls still stood, their stones not covered by vine and wood, as they would have been down below, but covered with a rust of lichens instead.

Richard dismounted and handed his reins to Lieutenant Crawford. The building to the left of the broad road was large by any standards Richard had grown up with, but compared to castles and palaces he had seen since, it was an insignificant structure.

The doorway stood empty. Crumbling evidence of a doorframe remained, still partly covered with gold leaf. Inside, the walls echoed with his footsteps. A stone bench sat in one room of the roofless building. In another room a stone fountain held snowmelt.

A twisting hall with most of its barrel ceiling still in place led Richard past a warren of rooms. The hall split, leading, he surmised, to rooms at either corner of the building. He followed the left branch to the room at the end.

Like all the rooms on this side, it faced the cliff. Hollow rectangles gaped where windows once shielded the room from wind and rain. Beyond, through the openings, was a view past the edge of the cliff to the blue haze of the mountains beyond.

This was the place where visitors and supplicants to the temple would have awaited admittance. During their wait, they would have had a glorious view of the Temple of the Winds. If they were turned away, they left with at least that much. He could almost see what those who had stood in this very spot had seen.

It was his gift, he knew, that was telling him this, much the way the spirits of those who once held the Sword of Truth guided him when he used that magic.

As he stood staring, he could almost imagine it there, just beyond the edge, a place of grandeur and might. This was where the wizards had taken things of powerful magic for safekeeping. The wizards of old, some of them Richard's ancestors, had probably stood where he stood, looking out at the Temple of the Winds.

Richard strolled around outside in the fading light, past the stately columns, peering into guard huts and once magnificent garden structures, touching the deteriorating walls. Even though it all was now crumbling, it was easy for him to imagine the majestic scene it must once have been.

He stood in the center of the broad road that ran through the crumbling ruins, feeling his gold cloak billowing out behind in the wind, trying to visualize the place as it had been, trying to get the feel of it. The road, more than the buildings, gave him the eerie feeling of the presence of the temple beyond. This road had once led right into the Temple of the Winds.

He strode the wide roadway, imagining striding toward the Temple of the Winds, the winds that had said they were hunting him. He passed along part of a wall, and between the hollow stone buildings, feeling the timeless quality of the place, feeling the life that once was here.

But where had it gone? How was he to find it? Where else could he look?

It had been here, and even now, Richard could almost see it, feel it, sense it, as if his gift were pulling him onward, pulling him home.

Abruptly, he was jerked to a halt.

Ulic on one side of him, and Egan on the other, had seized him under his arms and pulled him back. He looked down, and saw that another step would have taken him out into thin air. Vultures soared in the updraft not twenty feet straight in front of him.

He felt as if he was standing at the edge of the world. The view was dizzying. The hair on the back of his neck stiffened.

More should lie beyond the edge at his feet; he knew it should. But there was nothing there.

The Temple of the Winds was gone.

CHAPTER 43

Breathe.

Kahlan did as she was told, expelling the sliph, and pulling in the sharp, cold air.

The sound of a hissing torch roared in her ears. Her own breath echoed painfully. But she knew what to expect by now, and calmly waited for the world around her to twist back to normal.

Except this was not normal. At least it was not the normal she expected.

'Sliph, where are we?' Her voice reverberated around her.

'Where you wished to travel: the Jocopo Treasure. You should be pleased, but if you are not, I will try again.'

'No, no, it isn't that I'm not pleased, it's just that this wasn't what I expected.'

She was in a cave. The torch wasn't the familiar kind she was accustomed to, a length of wood with pitch at the head, but instead was made of bundled reeds. The ceiling nearly brushed her head as she swung her legs down from the sliph's well and stood.

Kahlan pulled the bundled-reed torch from where it was wedged in a split in the rough stone wall.

'I'll be back,' she told the sliph. 'I'll have a look around, and if I don't find a way out, I'll come back and we'll go somewhere else.' She realized that there must be a way out, or the torch wouldn't have been there. 'Or else, when I'm through finding what I'm looking for, I'll be back.'

'I will be ready when you wish to travel. We will travel again. You will be pleased.'

Kahlan nodded to the silver face reflecting the dancing torchlight, then stepped into the cave. There was only one way out of the room she was in, a wide, low passageway, so she went through it, following it as it twisted and turned through the dark brown rock. There were no other corridors, or rooms, so she kept going.

The passageway led to a broad room, perhaps fifty or sixty feet across, and she found out why this place was called the Jocopo Treasure. Torchlight reflected back in thousands of golden sparkles. The room was filled with gold.

Some was stacked in crude ingots, or spheres, as if the molten metal had been poured into pots, the pots then broken away. Simple boxes were piled high with nuggets. Other boxes, with handles at both ends so they could be carried by two men, held a rubble of golden objects.

There were several tables, still holding gold disks, and shelves along one wall. The shelves held several gold statues, but were filled mostly with rolled vellum scrolls. Kahlan wasn't interested in the Jocopo Treasure; she didn't take time to inspect the objects all around and, instead, made for the corridor on the other side of the room.

She didn't want to linger in the room because she was worried and wanted to get to the Mud People, but even if she had been interested in looking around, she wouldn't have stayed long; the air smelled awful, and made her gag and cough. The foul stench made her head spin and start to hurt.

The air in the passageway was better, though not what she would call good. She reached over and felt the bone knife, and found it still warm. At least it wasn't hot, as it had been.

The tunnel began slanting upward as it twisted along. As she went higher, the dark rock became dirt, in places held back with beams. She didn't see any other passages branching off until she began to smell fresh air. One tunnel branched left, and in a few paces, another right. She felt cool air drifting down from the one straight ahead, and so went that way.

The flame of the torch whipped and fluttered as she stepped out into the night. The sky glittered with stars. A figure not far away sprang up. Kahlan backed a few paces into the cave, glancing both ways to see if there was anyone else waiting outside.

'Mother Confessor?' came a voice she knew.

Kahlan took a step forward and held out the torch into the night air.

'Chandalen? Chandalen, is it you?'

The muscular figure rushed into the torchlight. He had no shirt, and was smeared with mud. Grass bundles were tied to his arms and head. His straight black hair was slicked down with the sticky mud the hunters used. Even though his face was also smeared with the mud, she recognized the familiar, wide grin.

'Chandalen,' she said with a sigh of relief. 'Oh, Chandalen, I'm so happy to see you.'

'And I you, Mother Confessor.'

He advanced toward her, to slap her face in the traditional Mud People greeting to show respect for another's strength. Kahlan held her hands out, warding him.

'No! Stay away!'

He straightened to a halt. 'Why?'

'Because there was sickness where I came from – in Aydindril. I don't want to get too close to any of you, for fear I might pass the fever on to you and our people.'

The Mud People were, indeed, her people. She and Richard had been named Mud People by the Bird Man and the other elders, and were now members of the village, even though they lived apart.

Chandalen's pleasure at seeing her faded. 'There is sickness here, too, Mother Confessor.'

Kahlan's torch lowered. 'What?' she whispered.

'Much has happened. Our people are afraid, and I cannot protect them. We called a gathering. Grandfather's spirit came to us. He said that there was much trouble.

'He said he must speak with you and that he would send you a message to come to us.'

'The knife,' she said. 'I felt his call through the knife. I came right away.'

'Yes. Just before dawn, he told us this. One of the elders came out of the spirit house and said I was to come to this

486

place to wait for you. How did you come to us from the hole in the ground?'

'It's a long story. It was magic … Chandalen, I don't have the time to wait until we can call another gathering to speak with the ancestor spirits. There's trouble. I can't afford to wait three days.'

He lifted the torch from her hand. His face was grim under the mud mask.

'There is no need to wait three days. Grandfather waits for you in the spirit house.'

Kahlan's eyes widened. She knew that a gathering lasted only through the one night it was called.

'How can that be?'

'The elders still sit in the circle. Grandfather told them to wait for you. He, too, waits.'

'How many are sick?'

Chandalen held all his fingers up once, and then only one hand a second time. 'They have great pain in their heads. They empty their stomachs even though they have nothing in them. They burn with fever. Some begin to turn black on their fingers and toes.'

'Dear spirits,' she whispered to herself. 'Have any died?'

'One child died this day, just before grandfather sent me here. He was the first to become sick.'

Kahlan herself felt sick. Her head spun as she tried to come to grips with what she was hearing. The Mud People didn't usually tolerate other people coming to their village, and they rarely ventured from their lands. How could this have happened?

'Chandalen, have any outsiders come?'

He shook his head. 'We would not allow it. Outsiders bring trouble.' He seemed to reconsider. 'One may have tried to come. But we would not allow her to come to the village.'

'Her?'

'Yes. Some of the children were playing at hunting out in the grassland. A woman came to them, asking if she could come to the village. The children ran back to tell us. When I took my hunters to the place, we could not find her. We told the children that their spirit ancestors would be angry if they played such tricks again.'

Kahlan feared to ask, because she feared the answer. 'The child who died today, he was one of those children who said they saw the woman, wasn't he?'

Chandalen cocked his head. 'You are a wise woman, Mother Confessor.'

'No, I'm a frightened woman, Chandalen. A woman came to Aydindril, and talked to children. They have begun to die, too. Did the boy who died say that she showed him a book?'

'When I went on my journey with you, you showed me these things called books that you use to pass on knowledge, but the children here do not know of such things. We teach our children with living words, as our ancestors taught us.

'The boy did say that this woman showed him pretty colored lights. That does not sound like the books I remember.'

Kahlan put a hand to Chandalen's arm, a touch that once would have frightened him with the implied threat of a Confessor's power, but now worried him for other reasons.

'You said we should not be close.'

'It doesn't matter, now,' she reassured him. 'I can cause no further harm; the same sickness is here that is in Aydindril.'

'I am sorry, Mother Confessor, that this sickness and death should visit your home, too.'

They embraced in friendship, and shared fear.

'Chandalen, what is this place? This cave?'

'I told you of it once. The place with the bad air and the worthless metal.'

'Then we're north of your home?'

'North, and some west.'

'How long will it take us to get back to the village?'

He gave his own chest a thump with a fist. 'Chandalen is strong and runs fast. I left our village as the sun was going down. It takes Chandalen only a couple hours. Even in the dark.'

She surveyed the moonlit grassland beyond the low, rocky hill on which they stood. 'There is enough moon to see our way.' Kahlan managed a small smile. 'And you ought to know that I'm as strong as you, Chandalen.'

Chandalen returned the smile. It was a wonderful sight to see, even under the circumstances.

'Yes, I remember well your strength, Mother Confessor. We will run, then.'

The moonlight conveyed intimately the ghostly, boxy shapes of the Mud People's village lying hidden on the dark, grass-covered plain. Few lights burned in the small windows. At this late hour not many people were out, and Kahlan was glad for that; she didn't want to see the faces of these people, see the fear and sorrow in their eyes, and know that many of them would die.

Chandalen took her directly to the spirit house, among the communal buildings at the north side of the village. Most of these buildings were bunched close together, but the spirit house sat apart. Moonlight reflected off the tile roof Richard had helped to make. Guards, Chandalen's hunters, ringed the windowless building.

Outside the door, on a low bench, sat the fatherly figure of the Bird Man. His silver hair hanging down around his shoulders shone in the moonlight. He was naked. Black and white mud covered his body and face in a tangle of whorls and lines: a mask all in the gathering wore so the spirits could see them.

Two pots, one with white mud and the other holding black, sat on the ground at the Bird Man's feet. She could tell by the glazed look in his eyes that he was in a trance, and speaking would do her no good. She knew what was required.

Kahlan unbuckled her belt. 'Chandalen, would you mind turning your back, please? And ask your men to do the same.' It was the greatest concession to her modesty that circumstances would allow.

Chandalen called out the order to his men in his own language.

'My men and I will guard the spirit house while you and the elders are inside,' Chandalen said to her over his shoulder.

When she had slipped off all her clothes and at last stood naked in the cool night air, the silent Bird Man began applying the gooey mud so that the spirits might see her, too. Sleepy chickens sat watching from the nearby low wall. The wall still bore a slash from Richard's sword.

She knew she had to do this, to go in and speak with the spirits, but she wasn't eager; speaking with the spirit ancestors was only done in times of dire need, and while the results sometimes brought the answers needed, they never brought joy.

When the Bird Man had finished covering Kahlan with the black and white mud, he silently led her inside. The six elders sat in a circle around the skulls of ancestors arranged in the center. The Bird Man took his place, sitting cross-legged on the floor. Kahlan sat in the circle, opposite him, to the right of her friend Savidlin. She didn't speak to him; he, too, was in a trance, seeing the spirit in the center of the circle that she could not yet see.

A woven basket sat behind her. Knowing why it was there, she picked it up and reached inside. Hesitantly, she seized a squirming red spirit frog and pressed its back between her breasts – the one place she wasn't painted.

The slime from the frog tingled against her skin. She released the spirit frog and took up hands with the elders to either side. It wasn't long before she felt herself spiraling into a daze.

The room began its dizzying spin. She was lifted away from the world she knew, and carried into a revolving vortex of light, shadow, aroma, and sound. The skulls spun with her.

Time twisted, much as it did in the sliph, but not in the same comforting way. This was a disorienting experience that brought sweat to her brow.

It also brought the spirit.

His glowing form was before her, yet she couldn't recall when it had appeared to her. It was simply there.

'*Grandfather,*' she whispered in the tongue of the Mud People.

Chandalen had said that it was his grandfather who had come in the gathering, but she recognized him on a more visceral level; he had become her protector. She felt the connection to the bone that had been his in life.

'*Child.*' The unearthly sound of his voice coming through the Bird Man tingled against her flesh. '*Thank you for heeding my call.*'

'*What does our ancestor's spirit wish of me?*'

The Bird Man's mouth moved with the spirit's voice. *'That which has been partly entrusted to us has been violated.'*

'Entrusted to you? What was entrusted to you?'

'The Temple of the Winds.'

Kahlan's naked flesh prickled with goose bumps.

Entrusted to the spirits? The implications made her head swim. The spirit world was the underworld, the world of the dead. How could something like a temple, built mostly of inert materials like stone, be sent to the underworld?

'The Temple of the Winds is in the spirit world?'

'The Temple of the Winds exists partly in the world of the dead, and partly in the world of life. It exists in both places, both worlds, at once.'

'Both places, both worlds, at once? How could such a thing be possible?'

The glowing form, like a shadow made of light, lifted a hand. *'Is a tree a creature of the soil, like the worms, or is it a creature of the air, like the birds?'*

Kahlan would have preferred a simple answer, but she knew better than to argue with the dead.

'Honored grandfather, I guess the tree is of neither world, yet exists in both.'

The spirit seemed to smile. *'So it does, child,'* the spirit said through the Bird Man. *'As does the Temple of the Winds.'*

Kahlan leaned forward. 'You mean, the Temple of the Winds is like the tree, with its roots in this world, and its branches in your world?'

'It exists in both our worlds.'

'In this world, in the world of life, where is it?'

'Where it always was, on the Mountain of the Four Winds. You know it as Mount Kymermosst.'

'Mount Kymermosst,' Kahlan repeated in a flat tone. 'Honored grandfather, I have been to that place. The Temple of the Winds is no longer there. It's gone.'

'You must find it.'

'Find it? It looks to have been there at one time, but the rock of the mountain where the temple used to be has collapsed. The temple is gone, except for a few of its outbuildings. There is nothing to find. I'm sorry, honored *grandfather, but in our world, the roots have died and crumbled.'*

The spirit stood silently. Kahlan feared it might become angry.

'Child,' the spirit said, but not through the Bird Man. The voice came from the spirit itself. The sound was so painful it was almost more than she could bear. She felt as if the flesh would burn from her bones. *'Something was stolen from the winds and taken to your world. You must help Richard, or all my blood in your world, all our people, will die.'*

Kahlan swallowed. How could something be stolen from the spirit world, the world of the dead, and be brought back to the world of the living?

'Can you help me? Can you tell me anything that might help me to know how to find the Temple of the Winds?'

'I have not called you here to tell you how to find the winds. The way of the winds will come with the moon. I have called you here to see the extent of what has been released, and what will become of your world should this be allowed to stand.'

Grandfather's spirit spread his arms. Soft light cascaded from them, like water coming over a ledge. The light spread in her vision until she saw only white light.

The light cleared, and she saw death. Corpses, like leaves littering the ground in the autumn, lay everywhere. They were strewn in the street where they fell. They sat on steps, slumped against railings. They lay in doorways and on dead-carts.

Kahlan's vision was carried through windows, as if on the wings of a bird. Bodies lay rotting in homes. She saw them in beds, in chairs, in halls, stretched out on floors, and slumped over one another.

The stench gagged her.

With her floating vision, Kahlan swept to towns and cities she knew, and everywhere it was the same. Death had taken nearly everyone, their bodies black and rotting even before they had died. The few still living, wherever she viewed, wept in unrelieved anguish.

Her floating vision returned to the Mud People's village. She saw the corpses of people she knew. Beside dead cook fires lay dead mothers holding dead children in their arms. Dead husbands held dead wives. Here and there, orphaned children with tear-stained faces wailed hysterically beside the corpses of parents. Everywhere, the stench was so thick it made her eyes water.

Kahlan gasped back a sob as she closed her eyes. It did no good. The sight of the dead burned through to the vision in her mind.

'This,' the spirit said, 'is what will come to pass if that stolen from the winds isn't halted.'

'What can I do?' Kahlan whispered through the tears.

'The winds have been violated. That which was entrusted was taken. The winds have decided that you are the path of the price. I have come to show you the results of this violation and to beg you, on behalf of my living descendants, to fulfill your part, when you are asked.'

'And what is the price?'

'I have not been shown the price, but I forewarn you that I do know that there is no way for you to circumvent or avoid it. It must be as it will be revealed to you, or all will be lost. I ask that when the winds show you the path, you take it, lest what I have shown you comes to be.'

Kahlan, tears streaming down her cheeks, didn't have to consider. 'I will, grandfather.'

'Thank you, child. There is one other thing I would tell you. In our world, where the souls of those departed from your world now reside, there are those existing in the Light with the Creator, and those who are forever shadowed from His glory by the Keeper.'

'You mean that there are both good and evil spirits in this?'

'That is an oversimplification that nearly obscures the truth, but it is as near as you, in your world, would be able to come to comprehending this world. In this, our world, all make it what it is. The winds must allow all to mark out the path.'

'Can you tell me how the magic was stolen from the winds?'

'The path was betrayal.'

'Betrayal? Who did they betray?'

'The Keeper.'

Kahlan's jaw dropped. She immediately thought of the Sister of the Dark who had been in Aydindril: Sister Amelia. It had to be her. 'The Sister of the Dark has betrayed her master?'

'This soul's path was to enter the Temple of the Winds through the Hall of the Betrayer. That is the only way to achieve the initial breach. It was created as a precaution.

'To tread the Hall of the Betrayer, a person must betray completely and irrecoverably that in which they believe. Since they have irreparably betrayed their cause, they would no longer have reason to enter.

'The dream walker found a prophecy that could be used to defeat his foe, but to ignite it, he needed magic from the winds.

'The dream walker found a way to force this soul to betray her master, the Keeper, yet still carry out the dream walker's wishes. He did this by at first allowing her to maintain her oath to the Keeper and by relegating himself to the role of her secondary master, her master in your world alone. Then, with the use of a double bind, he forced her to betray her primary master. She was able to tread Betrayer's Hall, with her charge from the dream walker, and her obligation to it, intact. In this way, the dream walker violated the winds and obtained what he wanted.

'Those who sent the temple into the winds did, however, make contingency plans, should such a thing happen. The red moon was the ignition of these plans.'

The very word 'betray' had made Kahlan's heart pound. 'Is this the way we must gain entrance to the winds?'

The spirit considered her, as if weighing her soul. 'Once the Temple of the Winds has been violated, that path is closed, and another must be used. But this is not your concern; the winds will issue their requirements in conjunction with the precepts of balance. The five spirits guarding the winds will dictate the path accordingly.'

'Honored grandfather, how can a place issue instructions? You make it seem as if the winds are alive.'

'I no longer exist in the world of life, yet, when called, I can pass information through the veil.'

Kahlan's head hurt from trying to understand. She wished Richard were here to ask questions. She feared to miss the important one.

'But, honored grandfather, you can do this because you are a spirit. You lived once. You have a soul.'

The spirit began fading.

'The boundary, the veil, was damaged by this event in the winds. I can remain no longer. The skrin, the guardians of the boundary between worlds, pull me back. Because the violation in the winds altered the balance, we cannot return again in a gathering unless the balance is restored.' The spirit faded until she could hardly see it.

'Grandfather, I must know more. Is the plague itself magic?'

The voice came from a great distance. *'The magic sent into the winds is of vast power. To use it fully requires vast knowledge. It was used without understanding what was released, or how to control it. The plague was begun by this magic, much as a bolt of lightning from a wizard is magic, but if the lightning strikes a tinder grassland, the resulting firestorm is not magic. The plague is like this. It was begun with magic, but it is now simply a plague, as others before – random and unpredictable – yet heated by magic.'*

'The plague is in Aydindril, and here. Will it stay confined?'

'No.'

Jagang didn't realize what he had done. This could end up killing him, too, if allowed to burn out of control.

'Is it, as you showed me, already in other places? Has it already been started in these other places, too?'

The light of the spirit extinguished like the weak flame of a lamp gone out.

'Yes,' came the distant, echoing whisper.

They had hoped that they could confine the plague to Aydindril. That was hope lost. The whole of the Midlands, the whole of the New World, was about to be consumed in the firestorm started by that spark of magic from the Temple of the Winds.

In the center of the circle, where the spirit had been, the air swirled as the spirit vanished back into the underworld.

In the distance, in the underworld, Kahlan heard the soft echo of laughter from a different spirit. The malevolent chuckle made her skin crawl.

As Kahlan came out of the trance of the gathering, the elders were there, standing around her. They were more used to this altered state than she; her head still spun sickeningly. Elder Breginderin reached down, offering her his hand to help her up.

As she took his hand, under the covering of black and white mud, she saw the tokens on his legs. She gazed up into his face, at his kindly smile of assurance. He would be dead within the day.

Her friend, Savidlin, was there, holding out her clothes. Kahlan, despite the mud, suddenly felt very naked. She started pulling on her clothes, trying not to betray her embarrassment, and at the same time chiding herself for such mundane concerns in the face of the impending catastrophe. The gathering was about calling the spirits of the dead, not about being man or woman. Still, she was the only one of the latter, and they were all the former.

'Thank you for coming, Mother Confessor,' the Bird Man said. 'We know this homecoming is not the one of joy we all wished.'

'No,' she whispered, 'it's not. My heart sings to see my people again, but the song is tempered by sadness. You know, honored elders, that Richard and I will do what we must. We will not rest until this is stopped.'

'Do you think you can stop such a thing as a fever?' Surin asked.

Savidlin placed a hand on her shoulder as she buttoned her shirt. 'The Mother Confessor and Richard with the Temper have helped us before. We know their hearts. Our ancestor said that this is a fever caused by magic. The Mother Confessor and the Seeker have great magic. They will do what they must.'

'Savidlin is right. We will do what we must.'

Savidlin smiled at her. 'And then, when you have finished, you will come home to your people and be wedded, as you planned? My wife, Weselan, wishes to see her friend, the Mother Confessor, wedded in the dress she made for you.'

Kahlan swallowed back a cry. 'There is nothing I could wish that would bring me greater joy, except to see all our people well.'

'You are a great friend to all our people, child,' the Bird

Man said. *'We look forward to the wedding, when you have finished with these matters of the spirits and magic.'*

Kahlan glanced at all the eyes watching her. She didn't think these men had witnessed the visions of death she had been shown, or the true nature or dimensions of the epidemic they faced. They had all seen fevers come before, but never one like the plague.

'Honored elders, if we fail … if we …'

Her voice faltered. The Bird Man came to her rescue.

'If you should fail, child, we know it will not be because you didn't do everything you could. If there is a path, we know you will do all you can to find it. We trust in you.'

'Thank you,' she murmured.

Tears were watering her vision. She forced herself to hold her chin up. She would only frighten these people if she showed her fear.

'Kahlan, you must wed Richard with the Temper.' The Bird Man chuckled softly as if trying to cheer her. *'He escaped wedding a Mud Woman before, as I had planned for him. He will not escape wedding you, if I have any say. He must marry a Mud Woman.'*

She felt too numb to return the smile.

'Will you stay the rest of the night?' Savidlin asked. *'Weselan would find joy in seeing you.'*

'Forgive me, honored elders, but if I am to save our people, I must return at once. I must go to Richard and tell him what I have learned with your help.'

CHAPTER 44

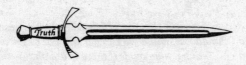

A woman stepped out of a doorway into the narrow, deserted alleyway. He had to stop, or collide with her. Under her shawl she wore a thin dress, and he could tell by the way her nipples stood out with the cold that she wore nothing underneath the dress.

She thought his smile was for her; it wasn't. It was amusement at the way opportunity sometimes stepped into his path when he least expected it. He guessed it was his extraordinary nature that drew such events to him.

Expecting it or not, he was never unprepared to bend events to his advantage.

She returned the smile as she ran her hand up his chest and with a single finger stroked the bottom of his chin.

'There, there, love. Care for a bit of pleasure?'

She wasn't attractive; nonetheless, the nature of the chance opportunity instantly ignited his need. He knew what this was about. By the way she stood close, commanding his attention, he knew. He had had this kind of encounter before. In fact, he sometimes sought it out. It was more of a challenge. With challenge came a rare form of fulfillment.

It wasn't an ideal situation – there were distinct disadvantages, such as not being able to allow her screams to bring attention, yet there were still pleasures to be had, even like this. His senses opened to it. Already, he was taking in the details, like dry earth took in a soaking rain.

He let the lust take him.

498

'Well,' he said, drawing the word out, 'do you have a room?'

He knew she wouldn't have one. He knew what this was about.

She rested a wrist over his shoulder. 'Don't need no room, love. Just a half silver.'

Discreetly as possible, he swept his gaze over the close buildings. The windows were all dark. Only a few lights in the distance reflected off the wet stone. This was a warehouse district; no one lived in these buildings. There weren't likely to be many people about, except passersby, like himself. Still, he knew he had to temper his lust with prudence.

'A little cold to be undressing out here on the cobblestones, isn't it?'

She put one hand on the side of his face to keep his attention focused on her. Her other hand touched him between his legs. She purred with satisfaction at what she found.

'Not to worry, love. For a half silver I'll have someplace warm for you to put it.'

He was enjoying the game. It had been too long. He put on his most innocent, inexperienced expression for her.

'Well, I don't know. This seems somewhat crude to me. I usually like it best when there's time for the young lady to enjoy it, too.'

'Oh, I do enjoy it, love. You don't think I do this just for the half silver, do you? 'Course not. I enjoy it. It's my pleasure.'

She was backing toward the doorway she had come from. He let her fingers, curled behind his neck, guide him with her.

'I don't carry any money that small.' He could almost see her eyes light with her luck. She had yet to learn that her luck this night was going to be bad.

'You don't?' she said, as if preparing to withdraw her offer now that she thought she had snared him with tempting thoughts of what she was offering. 'Well, a lady has to earn a living. I guess I'll have to move along and see if I can find …'

'The smallest I have is a silver. But I'd be willing to give you the whole silver if it would mean you took your time and enjoyed it, too. I like lovely young ladies like you to enjoy it. That's what pleases me.'

'What a love,' she said with clumsy, exaggerated delight as she took the silver coin when he held it out.

She stank. Her smile brought no beauty to her face, yet he reveled in the details: coarse hair, the smell of her body, the humped nose, and small eyes. She was common, less than a man of his stature was used to, but this had its own delights to offer.

He listened carefully as he watched her. Other details were even more important, if he was to have his full pleasure from this.

She backed into the shallow doorway and sat on a stool waiting there. The doorway was just deep enough to hold them both, with his back to the alleyway as he stood before her.

It aggravated him that she thought him so ignorant, so foolish, so impetuous. She would learn just how wrong she was.

She planted a kiss on the front of his trousers as she fumbled with his belt. It wouldn't be long. She wouldn't want it to take too long, before she moved on to another place, reaping all the coin she could in the cloak of night.

Before she undid his trousers, he gently took her wrists in one hand. It wouldn't do to have his trousers down around his knees when it started. No, that wouldn't do at all.

She smiled up at him, clearly puzzled, but just as clearly sure she was bewitching him with her smile. He wouldn't have to suffer it for long. It wouldn't be long.

It was dark enough. Too dark to see for sure what he was doing. People saw what they expected.

While she still smiled at him, before she had time to question, he reached down with his other hand and gripped her neck. She thought he simply wished to hold her while she performed her service.

The way her head was tilted back was perfect.

With a thumb, and a small grunt of effort, he crushed her windpipe.

The smile transferred to his face. The choking sound wouldn't immediately raise suspicions. People heard what they expected to hear, just as they saw what they expected to see. He hunched over her, to make it look as expected, while he crushed the life out of her.

'Surprise,' he whispered to her bulging eyes.

He luxuriated in her startled, strangled expression. When her arms went limp, he let them drop, and held her up by a fistful of her hair. He bent her head back over his thigh to help hold her up as he waited.

He had to wait only seconds before he heard the careful footsteps approaching from behind. More than one man, as he had expected. He knew what this was about: robbery.

Mere seconds more, and they had closed the distance. To him, time stretched with the anticipation, with the details of sights, sounds, and smells. He was the most rare of men. He owned time. He owned life. He owned death.

And now it was time for the rest of his pleasure.

He pushed his knee up against her spine and, with a quick yank, snapped her neck over his leg. He spun, bringing his knife up into the man right behind, slicing him open from his groin to his sternum. He spun past the man as guts slopped out into the alley.

He expected another man. There were two. A woman like this usually had two men to rob the man. He had never before seen three. The unexpected danger of this development made him reel with lust.

The second man on the right swung an arm. He saw the knife in the fist, and with a step back, escaped the sweep of the blade. As the third man advanced, he drove him back with a boot to the point at the base of the breastbone. The man smacked the wall behind and stumbled to his knees with a grunt of pain, unable to regain his breath.

The man on the right froze. In that instant, it was one on one. The face was that of a boy, really. Hardly a man, yet. With a boy's courage, he broke and ran.

He smiled. There was no more perfect target as they ran than a person's head. The head remained nearly still while the arms and legs flailed furiously. That target was a core of stability in his vision.

He loosed his knife. The boy ran as fast as his rapidly pumping legs would carry him. The knife was faster, hitting home with a solid thunk. The young thief went down instantly.

The third man was coming up from his knees. He was older, muscled, heavy, and violently angry. Good.

501

A side kick broke the man's nose. Howling in pain and rage, the man sprang forward. He saw a flash of steel and dodged to the side as he swept a leg beneath the man, taking his feet from under him. It all happened in a blink. It was a glorious event, this dangerous, raging bull charging madly.

He pulled in the details: the man's clothes, the small rip in the back of his coat, his bald spot reflecting the distant light, his curly, greasy hair, the nick missing out of his right ear, the way he flopped when the boot landed between his shoulders.

It was when he was twisting the man's arm behind his back that he saw the blood. Blood was something he kept careful track of. This blood surprised him. He hadn't cut the man – yet. Nor was this blood from the man's crushed nose.

He rarely had a thrill of surprise such as this unexpected blood brought.

He realized the man was screaming in pain. He screamed louder when the shoulder joint popped. He dropped onto the man's back and smacked his head with the heel of a hand, breaking the man's teeth against the cobbles and quieting him, somewhat.

He gripped the greasy hair in a fist and pulled the man's head back, listening to the sound of the grunts.

'Robbery is a dangerous business. Time you paid the price.'

'We wouldn't have hurt you,' the man burbled. 'Just robbed you, you bastard.'

'Bastard, is it?'

Carefully, slowly, enjoying the detail of every inch, he slit open the man's throat as he thrashed.

What unexpected pleasure this night had brought. He lifted his hands, curling his fingers, slowly sweeping the quintessence of death from the air, capturing the silken substance of it as it lifted in the darkness, and pulled it back to himself.

He was the fulfillment of their lives. He was the balance. He was death. He savored seeing that awareness in their eyes. He liked it best when he could bask in that look, that knowledge … that terror. It brought him fulfillment. It made him complete.

He stood, swaying in ecstasy at the cloying scent of blood. He regretted it hadn't lasted longer. He regretted not being able to enjoy prolonged screams. Screams were rapture. He craved them, needed them, lusted after them. Screams fulfilled him, made him whole. He needed the screams, not the actual sound of them – he often gagged his partners – but the attempt at them, and what they represented: terror.

Being denied the chance to leisurely enjoy the screaming terror left him unfulfilled, his lust unsated.

He glided up the alley and found that his skill was as sharp as ever, as was his knife; it had found its target. The boy lay crumpled on his side. He looked delicious with the knife buried to the cross guard at the back of his head, and the point of the heavy blade jutting from his forehead, just slightly off center.

Immersed in a pool of sensation, he realized he felt a new one: pain.

Surprised, he inspected his arm, and discovered the source of the unexpected blood. He had a gash a good six inches long on the outside of his right forearm. It was deep. It would need to be stitched.

The pleasure of such an unexpected occurrence made him gasp.

Danger, death, and damage – all in one night, in one chance encounter. This was nearly too much.

The voices had been right about coming to Aydindril.

Still, he hadn't had what he needed – the prolonged terror, the careful cutting, the slicing, the binge of blood, the giving of endless, exquisite pain, the orgy of frenzied stabbing at the end.

But the voices from the ethers promised him he would have those things, promised him he would have the ultimate conquest, the ultimate balance, the ultimate pairing.

They promised him he would have the ultimate consummation of debauchery.

They promised him he would have the Mother Confessor.

His time was coming.

Her time was coming.

Soon.

When Verna dabbed the wet cloth against Warren's forehead, his eyes opened. She let out a long breath of relief.

'How are you feeling?'

He tried to sit up. With a firm hand on his chest, she gently pushed him back down into the hay.

'Just you lay there and rest.'

He winced in pain and then smacked his lips. 'I need a drink.'

Verna twisted and lifted the dipper from the bucket. She held it to his lips. His hands cupped the dented bowl of the dipper as he greedily gulped down all the water.

He panted, catching his breath after the long drink. 'More.'

Verna dragged the dipper through the bucket and let him drink his fill.

She smiled down at him. 'Glad to see you awake.'

It looked to be an effort for him to return the smile. 'Glad to be awake. How long have I been out, this time?'

She shrugged, discounting his concern. 'A few hours.'

He glanced around the inside of the barn. Verna lifted the lamp so he could see his surroundings. Rain drummed against the roof, making it feel cozy inside.

Verna set down the lamp and rested on an elbow beside him. 'Not fancy lodging, but at least it's dry.'

He had been nearly unconscious when they found the farm. The family who owned the farm was sympathetic. Verna had refused the offer of their bed, not wanting to force them to sleep in their own barn.

On her journey of over twenty-odd years, Verna had often slept in such places, and found the accommodations agreeable, if a little rough. She liked the smell of hay. When she was on her journey, she had thought she hated it, but once returned to the cloistered life at the Palace of the Prophets, she changed her opinion, and found herself longing for the smell of hay, dirt, grass, and rain-clean air.

Warren laid a gentle hand over hers. 'Verna, I'm sorry I'm slowing us down so.'

Verna smiled. She recalled a time when her impatient nature would have had her pacing and fretting. Warren, and his love, brought out a little of her calmer nature. He was good for her. He was everything to her.

She pushed back his curly blond hair and kissed his forehead. 'Nonsense. We had to stop for the night anyway.

The rain would have made traveling slow and miserable. A good rest will result in more progress in the end. Take my word; I've had plenty of experience at such things.'

'But I feel so – useless.'

'You are a prophet. That provides us with information that is far from useless. That in itself has saved us from traveling days in a wrong direction.'

His troubled blue eyes turned to the rafters. 'The headaches are coming more often with time. I fear to think that when I close my eyes, I may never come awake again.'

She scowled for the first time that night. 'I'll not hear that sort of talk, Warren. We will make it.'

He hesitated, not wanting to argue with her. 'If you say so, Verna. But I'm slowing us down more all the time.'

'I've taken care of that.'

'You have? What have you done?'

'I hired us transportation. For a ways, at least.'

'Verna, you said you didn't want to hire a coach, that it would draw attention to us. You said you didn't want to risk being recognized, and you didn't want nosy people inquiring as to who was riding a coach.'

'Not a coach. And I don't want to hear a string of objections. I hired this farmer to take us south for a ways in his hay cart. He said we could lay in the back and you could rest. He'll cover us with hay so we won't have to worry about people bothering us.'

Warren frowned. 'Why would he do this for us?'

'I paid him well. More than that, though, he and his family are loyal to the Light. He respects the Sisters of the Light.'

Warren relaxed back into the hay. 'Well, I guess that sounds good. You're sure he's willing? You didn't twist his nose, did you?'

'He was going anyway.'

'Really? Why?'

Verna sighed. 'He has a sick daughter. She's only twelve. He wants to go to get some tonic for her.'

Suspicion darkened Warren's expression. 'Why didn't you cure the girl?'

Verna held his gaze. 'I tried. I couldn't cure her. She has a high fever, she's cramping and vomiting. I tried my best. I would have given nearly anything to have been able to cure that poor child of her suffering, but I couldn't.'

'Any idea why not?'

Verna shook her head sadly. 'The gift doesn't cure everything, Warren. You know that. If she had a broken bone, I could help her. If she had any number of ills, I could help her, but the gift is of limited use for fever.'

Warren looked away. 'Seems unfair. They offer to help us, and we can do next to nothing for them.'

'I know,' Verna whispered.

She listened to the rain against the roof for a time.

'I was able to ease the pain in her gut, at least. She'll rest a little more comfortably.'

'Good. That's good, at least.' Warren fussed with a piece of straw. 'Have you been able to get in contact with Prelate Annalina? Has she left you a message in the journey book yet?'

Verna tried not to betray how troubled she was. 'No. She hasn't answered my messages, nor has she sent one of her own. She's probably busy. She doesn't need to be bothered by our little problems. We'll hear from her when she has time.'

Warren nodded. Verna blew out the lamp. She snuggled up to him, putting her forehead against his shoulder. She rested her arm across his chest.

'We best get some sleep. At sunrise we'll be moving on.'

'I love you, Verna. If I die in my sleep, I want you to know that.'

Verna's fingers stroked the side of his face in answer.

Clarissa rubbed the sleep from her eyes. Dawn was leaking in around the edges of the heavy, dark green drapes. She sat up in the bed. She didn't think she had ever awakened feeling this good. She reached over to tell Nathan as much. Nathan wasn't with her.

Clarissa sat up and swung her legs over the edge of the bed. When she stretched, her leg muscles protested; they were sore from the night's activities. She guessed it was simply the thought of the cause that made her smile at the mild ache. She had never known that sore muscles could be so pleasant.

She stuffed her arms through the lovely pink robe Nathan had bought for her. She snugged the ruffles up around her neck and then tied the silk belt. She wiggled her toes in the thick carpet, luxuriating in the feeling.

Nathan was at the writing desk, bent over a letter. He smiled up at her as she stood in the doorway.

'Sleep well?'

Clarissa half-closed her eyes and sighed. 'I should say so.' She grinned. 'What sleep I got, anyway.'

Nathan winked at her. He dipped the pen in a bottle of blue ink and went back to his scratching. Clarissa strolled around behind him and put her hands on his shoulders. He was wearing his trousers, and nothing else. With her thumbs she kneaded the muscles at the base of his neck. He made an agreeable sound deep in his throat, so she continued. She liked to hear his sounds of pleasure, and liked even more being their cause.

As her thumbs worked along the muscles of his shoulders, she glanced down at what he was writing. Scanning the letter, she saw that it was instructions about moving troops to places she had never heard of. Nathan wrote on, admonishing a general about the bond to the Lord Rahl, and the dire repercussion should he ignore it. The tone of the letter was the same authoritative tone he used when he expected people to treat him as the man of importance that he was. He signed the letter: 'Lord Rahl.'

Clarissa bent and nuzzled his neck, giving his ear a little nip.

'Nathan, last night was beyond wonderful. It was magic. You were magnificent. I'm the luckiest woman in the world.'

He gave her a roguish grin. 'Magic. Yes, there was some of that in it, too. I'm an old man; I need to use what I've got.'

She combed her fingers through his hair, ordering it. 'Old man? I don't think so, Nathan. I hope I was half as pleasing to you as you were to me.'

He laughed as he folded his letter. 'I guess I did manage to keep up with you.' He slipped a hand inside her robe and pinched her bare bottom. She jumped with a squeak. 'It was one of the high points of my life, to be with such a beautiful and loving woman.'

She hugged his head to her breasts. 'Well, we're still alive. No reason we can't reach for some more of those high points.'

His sly smile grew as he put his hand back on her bare bottom and gave it a squeeze. He had that lusty twinkle in his eye.

'Let me dispense with this bit of business, and we'll see about getting our money's worth out of that big bed.'

With a diminutive copper spoon, he scooped little nuggets of red wax from a tin and dumped the tiny spoonful on the folded letter.

'Nathan, silly, you're supposed to melt the sealing wax onto the letter.'

One of his eyebrows arched. 'You should know by now, my dear, that my way is better.'

She let out a throaty laugh. 'My mistake.'

He twirled a finger over the nuggets of wax. Sparkles of light danced from his finger onto the lumps of wax. They glowed briefly and then melted into a red puddle on the letter. She gasped with delight. Nathan was one never-ending little surprise after another. She felt her cheeks warm as she remembered that his fingers were magic in more ways than one.

She bent and whispered intimately in his ear. 'I'd like you and that magic finger of yours back in bed with me, Lord Rahl.'

Nathan lifted his magic finger in proclamation. 'And it shall be, my dear, just as soon as I send this letter on its way.'

He again twirled the finger over the letter, and it lifted off the desk as if of its own accord. Clarissa's eyebrows rose in astonishment. The letter floated in the air ahead of him as he walked to the door. He twirled his other hand dramatically, and the door glided open.

A soldier, sitting on the floor in the hall, leaning against the opposite wall, rose to his feet. He saluted with a fist to his heart.

Nathan, standing there in only his trousers, with his white hair hanging down to his shoulders, had the look of a wild man. She knew he wasn't, but standing there, as tall as he was, as commanding as he was, she knew he must look that way to others.

People were afraid of Nathan. She could see it in their eyes. She could understand their fear, though; she remembered how much she had feared him, before she had come to know him. She could hardly remember, now, just how much the sight of the towering prophet had terrified her.

When he turned those azure eyes on people, and his hawklike brow lowered in displeasure, she thought he could make a whole army turn and run.

Nathan stretched his arm out, and the letter floated to the grim-faced soldier. 'You remember all my instructions, don't you, Walsh?'

The soldier snatched the letter out of the air and stuffed it inside his tunic. This soldier, though respectful, didn't seem intimidated by Nathan.

'Of course. You know me better than that, Nathan.'

Nathan lost a bit of his lofty attitude and scratched his head. 'I guess I do.'

Clarissa wondered where Nathan had found the soldier, and when he had had time to give him instructions. She guessed he must have gone out while she was asleep.

This soldier looked to be somewhat different from most of the others she had seen. He had a traveling cloak, with leather packs at his belt, and his clothes were of a higher quality than those of the regular soldiers she was getting used to seeing. His sword was shorter, too, and his knife longer. He was not a small man, either. He was as big as Nathan, but Nathan's bearing made him seem bigger than anyone to her.

'Give the letter to General Reibisch,' Nathan said. 'And don't forget, if any of those Sisters start asking you questions, you warn them about what I said, and tell them that Lord Rahl ordered you to keep what you were told to yourself. That will keep their jaws locked tight.'

The soldier smiled knowingly. 'I understand … Lord Rahl.'

Nathan nodded. 'Good. What about the others?'

Soldier Walsh gestured vaguely. 'Bollesdun will be around to let you know what he finds out. I'm pretty sure it was only Jagang's expeditionary force, but Bollesdun will find out for sure. Large as it was, it wasn't much compared to the main force. I don't see any evidence that his main force down near Grafan Harbor has come north yet.

'From what I've heard, Jagang is content to sit and wait for something. I don't know what that something is, but he's not rushing troops north, into the New World.'

'He thrust the army I saw deep into the New World.'

'I still think it was just his expeditionary force. Jagang is a patient man. It took him years to conquer and consolidate the Old World under his rule. He used much the same tactics: sending out the expeditionary force to take a key city, or capture information of one sort or another, mostly records and books. Those men are brutal, that's part of their purpose, too, but it's the books they're sent to get.

'They would send back whatever they captured, and wait to go wherever Jagang sends them next. Bollesdun has some of our men checking into it, but they have to be careful, and it may take them awhile, so just enjoy the wait.'

Nathan stroked his chin as he pondered. 'Yes, I imagine Jagang isn't eager to send his army into the New World, yet.' He returned his gaze to Walsh. 'You'd best be on your way.'

Walsh nodded. His gaze shifted and his eyes met Clarissa's. He looked back to Nathan, a small smile coming to his lips.

'A man after my own heart.'

Nathan chuckled softly. 'One of nature's wonders, matters of the heart.'

The way Nathan said the words made Clarissa's own heart swell with pride to be included in matters of his heart.

'You be careful, here in the rat's nest, eh, Nathan? I'd not like to hear that you don't have eyes in the back of your head, after all.' He patted his tunic where he had put the letter. 'Especially not after I deliver this.'

'I will, lad. You just be sure you get that letter delivered.'

'You have my word.'

After Nathan shut the door, and business was finished, he turned to her. He had that twinkle in his eye. That lusty twinkle. His sly smile returned.

'Alone at last, my dear.'

Clarissa squealed and ran for the bed in mock fright.

C H A P T E R 4 5

'What do you think is going on?' Ann asked.

Zedd stretched his head up to try to see. It was hard to get much of a look past the wall of legs around them. The Nangtong spirit hunters jabbered orders, which he couldn't understand, but some of the spears pointing down from the circle surrounding them settled on his shoulders, delivering an unequivocal message that he had better stay where he was.

He and Ann sat cross-legged on the ground, guarded by a ring of Nangtong, while others of them were sitting in conference a ways off with a party of Si Doak.

'They're too far away to hear clearly, but even if we could hear them, it probably wouldn't help much. I only speak a few words of Si Doak.'

Ann plucked a long blade of grass and wound it around a finger. She didn't glance over at Zedd. They didn't want to give their captors the idea that they were sane and capable of plotting.

Ann let out a high-pitched cackle, just to keep up appearances. 'What you know about these Si Doak?'

Zedd flapped his arms like a bird about to take to wing. 'I know they don't sacrifice people.'

A guard thunked a spear shaft on Zedd's head, as if to discourage him from any ideas of flying off. Zedd howled with laughter, instead of cursing, which he was longing to do.

Ann glanced over out of the corner of her eye. 'Beginning to reconsider your attitude about letting these Nangtong live as they wish?'

Zedd smiled. 'If I wanted to let them live as they wish, we'd be in the spirit world by now. Just because you believe in letting wolves be, that doesn't mean you have to let them eat your flock at will.'

She grunted to concede the point.

Off in the distance, beside a slight rise, the negotiations dragged on. About ten of the Nangtong and an equal number of the Si Doak sat cross-legged in a circle. The Nangtong counted out loud, accompanied by exaggerated arm movements. They pointed Zedd's way. They made unintelligible but seemingly heartfelt speeches.

Zedd leaned toward Ann and whispered, 'The Si Doak are peaceful enough, as far as I know; I've never heard of them making war or using force against neighbors, even weaker neighbors, but when it comes to matters of trade, they're ruthless. Most people in this part of the wilds would just as soon bargain with a wolf. Other peoples teach their young people to fight; the Si Doak teach them to barter.'

Ann looked off in the other direction, as if disinterested. 'What makes them so good at it?'

Zedd glanced up at their guards. They were all watching the bargaining, and paying little attention to the helpless prisoners.

'They have the rare ability to walk away from a deal. Others get their mind set on something and soon start settling for less, just to have a deal. The Si Doak won't do that. They'll simply walk. When need be, they'll cut their losses without regret and move on to something else.'

One of the Si Doak, the one wearing a rabbit fur over his head, slapped a pile of blankets in the center of the circle. He pointed off to a small heard of goats and made an offer Zedd understood to include two of the animals.

The offer seemed to incense the Nangtong. Their chief negotiator leaped to his feet and stabbed his spear at the sky repeatedly, apparently to express his outrage at the low price. Zedd noted that he didn't walk away. There was honor involved; the Nangtong had that much invested.

Zedd nudged Ann. He tilted his head back and howled like a coyote. Ann, getting the message, joined in. They both yelped and bayed as loud as they could.

512

The negotiators fell silent as they all looked toward the prisoners. The head Nangtong negotiator sat back down.

A thunk on both their heads silenced Zedd and Ann. Talking resumed over at the bartering session. A Nangtong emissary was sent to have a better look at the goats.

Zedd scratched his shoulder. The dry mud was getting uncomfortable. He guessed it was less uncomfortable than having his heart cut out, or his head cut off, or whatever it was the Nangtong did to sacrifices.

'I'm hungry,' he muttered. 'They haven't fed us all day. It's near to mid-afternoon, and they haven't fed us.'

He barked at his captors to show his displeasure. The negotiations halted for a moment while they once again looked toward the prisoners. The Si Doak all folded their arms and remained silent as they stared at the Nangtong.

The Nangtong quickly resumed talking, their tone changing, becoming conciliatory. Chuckling interspersed their casual chatter. The Si Doaks' response was short and curt. The one with the rabbit skin on his head gestured toward the afternoon sun and then off toward his home.

The Nangtong man in charge pulled a blanket from the stack in the center and inspected it with grudging admiration. He passed the blanket to his fellows. They nodded with appreciation of its worth, as if just discovering it. The man sent to have a look at the goats returned with two. He showed them off to his associates, and they oohed and aahed, as if realizing for the first time that these goats were much more impressive than they had at first thought, and not at all the scraggly animals they had expected to find.

The Nangtong had apparently decided that, no matter what, they didn't want to return home with the prisoners. Any useful commodities were better than two crazy people. They couldn't very well send the spirits two crazy people. Any exchange for them was better than nothing, especially in view of the waning interest of the Si Doak.

The Si Doak remained stone-faced. The Nangtong had made a mistake; they had betrayed their need to sell what they had. There was nothing the Si Doak valued more than a motivated seller.

A price, whatever it was Zedd couldn't tell, was suddenly

513

agreed upon. The head Si Doak and the head Nangtong stood, hooked arms at the elbows, and turned around each other three times while so locked together. When they parted, both sides fell to happy chatter. A bargain had been struck.

The Nangtong started lifting blankets. The goats were tethered. The Si Doak headed for their prizes. The guards thunked Zedd and Ann on the head as the Si Doak approached, apparently in warning not to spoil the deal.

Zedd had no intention of spoiling the deal. The Si Doak didn't sacrifice people. As far as he knew, they were gentle people; the worst punishment they dispensed to someone who committed a grievous wrong was banishment. A banished Si Doak sometimes starved to death because he was so heartsick at being sent from the only home he knew. A misbehaving child was set straight by everyone ignoring him for a day. It was a horrifying punishment to a Si Doak child, and resulted in best behavior for a good long time after.

Of course, Zedd and Ann weren't members of the Si Doak community, so it was entirely possible, in fact probable, that such treatment didn't extend to them.

Zedd leaned toward Ann and whispered, 'I don't think these people would hurt us, so keep that in mind. If they decide not to take us, the Nangtong may just slit our throats rather than have to suffer the humiliation of having to return with two crazy people.'

'First you want me to play in the mud, and now you want me to be a good little girl?'

Zedd smiled at her sarcasm. 'Just until our new keepers take us away from the old.'

The Si Doak elder, the one with the rabbit fur over his head, squatted before his new acquisitions. He reached out and felt Zedd's arm muscles. He grunted disapprovingly. He felt Ann's arms and made a sound as if pleased at what he found.

Ann lifted an eyebrow to Zedd. 'Seems I'm more agreeable to them than a skinny old man.'

Zedd smiled. 'I think they find you better suited as a human oxen. They'll give you the hard work.'

Her satisfied expression vanished. 'What do you mean?'

He shushed her. Another Si Doak squatted down beside the elder. He had goat antlers fixed to his head. He wore what had to be a hundred necklaces over his buckskin tunic. The necklaces, some hanging to his crotch, others tight at his throat, and the rest every length in between, held teeth, beads, bones, feathers, pottery shards, metal disks, gold coins, small leather pouches, and carved amulets. He was the Si Doak shaman.

The shaman took Zedd's hand and gently held his arm out. He released it. Zedd let it drop. The shaman chattered his disapproval. Zedd understood enough to gather that he was supposed to hold his arm up. He didn't let on that he understood any of the words, and instead let the shaman lift the arm out again, and use a hand signal to indicate he meant Zedd to hold it there.

While the Nangtong guards still held spears on the two prisoners, the shaman retrieved long, coiled stalks of grass from one of the pouches at his waist. He chanted as he wove the grass around Zedd's wrist. When finished, he wove the grass around Zedd's other wrist, and then did the same to Ann.

'Any idea what this is about?' she asked.

'It binds our magic. The Nangtong need do nothing to render our magic useless, but the Si Doak have to use some kind of magic of their own to suppress ours. This shaman is a man of magic. He has the gift. He's something like the Si Doaks' wizard.' Zedd glanced at her out of the corner of his eye. 'Or maybe you could say he's like the Sisters of the Light, with their collars. Like the collars, we won't be able to get these wristbands off.'

Once they had the grass woven around their wrists, the Nangtong withdrew their weapons, picked up their portion of the blankets, collected their two goats, and quickly made good their escape.

The elder, the one with the rabbit skin on his head, leaned toward Zedd and spoke. When Zedd frowned and shrugged that he didn't understand, the man added sign language seemingly invented on the spot. He indicated chores to be done, and time, by showing the seasons: digging at the ground and pretending to plant, the heat of summer, and the freezing of winter. Zedd couldn't understand a great deal of it, but he understood enough.

He turned to Ann. 'I believe that these fellows here have

purchased us out of our death sentence. We are to be in servitude to them for a period of about two years, to repay them for our cost, plus a profit for their trouble.'

'We've been sold into slavery?'

'It would appear so. But only for a couple of years. Quite generous of them, actually, considering that the Nangtong were going to kill us.'

'Maybe we could buy our way out.'

'To the Si Doak, this is a personal debt we owe them, and can only be repaid with personal servitude. To their way of looking at it, they have returned our lives to us, and so we must use part of those lives to show our gratitude. And to clean up after them.'

'Clean up? We're to scrub floors to repay our debt?'

'I imagine they'll want us to cook, carry things, sew, care for their animals, those sorts of things.'

As if to confirm what Zedd had told her, the Si Doak began pulling the thongs holding their waterskins off over their heads and passing them to Zedd and Ann.

'What do they want?' Ann asked him.

Zedd lifted an eyebrow. 'They want us to carry their water.'

Three more of the Si Doak appeared with the remaining blankets, divided them, and handed them to their new bearers.

'Do you mean to tell me,' Ann growled, 'that the First Wizard of the Midlands and the Prelate of the Sisters of the Light have been sold into slavery for the price of some blankets and two goats!'

With a shove from behind, Zedd staggered after the departing Si Doak.

'I know what you mean,' he said over his shoulder. 'For the first time I know of, the Si Doak have overpaid.'

Zedd stumbled and dropped half his load of waterskins. As he regained his balance, he stepped on one that had snagged a thorny berry bush. Bending to retrieve the waterskins, his stack of blankets toppled into the mud puddle created by the burst waterskin. He put a knee to the ground to regain his balance as he gathered up the scattered waterskins. His knee squashed the berries under the blanket.

'Oops.' He waved an apology to the Si Doak. 'Sorry.'

The Si Doak leaped about in agitation, demanding he pick

everything up at once. The man whose waterskin Zedd had ripped open over a thorn bush pointed angrily at his damaged property while jabbering demands of recompense.

'I said I was sorry,' Zedd protested, even though they couldn't understand him. He bent to gather up the wet blankets. He lifted one up high and held it out between his widespread arms, inspecting it.

'Oh dear. Look at that. We'll never get that stain out.'

CHAPTER 46

'Lord Rahl, you have had a hard ride,' Berdine said. 'I think you should be resting. We should go back. So you can rest, I mean.'

The massive rampart, lit by the mellow light of the low sun, spread out before the three of them like a broad road. He wanted to be out of the Keep before dark. Not that the light of day would save him from dangerous magic, but somehow being in the Wizard's Keep after dark seemed worse.

Raina leaned past him to speak. 'It was your idea, Berdine.'

'My idea? I never suggested any such thing!'

'Quiet, both of you.' Richard murmured.

He was considering the feel of magic against his skin. They had advanced halfway across the long rampart toward the First Wizard's private enclave before the distinct caress of magic began tingling against his flesh. Both Mord-Sith had balked at its feel.

Kahlan had told him about this place, about the First Wizard's private enclave. She said that she used to come up to this rampart because it provided a beautiful view of Aydindril, and indeed there was that, but there was also the magic of powerful shields. Those shields kept everyone out of this small corner of the Wizard's Keep.

Kahlan had told him that in her life there had never been a wizard with enough power to pass these shields. Wizards had tried, but failed. The wizards living and working in the Keep as Kahlan was growing up simply didn't have the magic required to enter this part of it. Zedd was the First Wizard; no one had been in the First Wizard's enclave since before Kahlan and Richard were born, when Zedd had left the Midlands.

Kahlan had said that these shields exerted more magic as you got closer, that they made your hair stand on end and made it difficult to breathe. She had also said that if a person didn't have enough magic of their own, just getting too close to the shields could be deadly. Richard didn't discount in the slightest what she had said, but he had need to go in there.

Kahlan had also said that to enter required placing your hand on the cold metal plate beside the door, something no wizard she knew had ever been able to do. Richard had encountered shields like this one at the Palace of the Prophets, ones passed by touching a metal plate, but as far as he knew none of those were potentially deadly. He had been able to pass those shields, and he had been able to pass others in the Keep that required magic only he possessed, so he reasoned that he might be able to pass this one. He needed to get in there.

Berdine rubbed her arms, distressed by the tingle of the magic. 'Are you sure you aren't tired? You rode all that way.'

'It wasn't that hard a ride,' Richard said. 'I'm not tired.'

He was too worried to rest. He had thought Kahlan would be back by now. He had been sure he would find her back home when he returned from Mount Kymermosst. She should have been back by now.

But she wasn't.

He would wait only until morning.

'I still don't think we should be doing this,' Berdine muttered. 'How is your foot? I don't think you should be on it.'

Richard finally looked down at her. She was pressed up against his left side. Raina was pressed to his right. Each held her Agiel in her fist.

'My foot is just fine, thank you.' He shifted his body to force them away a bit to give himself breathing room. 'I only need one of you. No loss of face if you wish to remain here. Raina can go, if you don't want to.'

Berdine scowled up at him. 'I didn't say I wasn't going. I said you shouldn't be doing it.'

'I have to. It wasn't anywhere else. It has to be here. I was told that important things, things not meant to be seen by just anyone, were kept in the First Wizard's enclave.'

Berdine rolled her shoulders, easing the tension in her muscles. 'If you insist on going, then I'm going, too. I'll not let you walk in there without me.'

'Raina?' he asked. 'I don't need both of you. Do you want to wait here?'

Raina gave him a dark, Mord-Sith glare in answer.

'All right, then. Now, listen to me. I know that the shields here are dangerous, but that's all I know about them. They may not be like the others I've taken you through.

'I have to touch that metal plate down there on the wall. I want you two to wait here while I go see if I have the proper magic to open the door. If it opens, then you both can come the rest of the way.'

'This isn't a trick, is it?' Raina asked. 'You tricked us one other time to keep us out, to keep us from going where there was danger. Mord-Sith are not afraid of danger.'

The wind lifted his gold cloak. 'No, Raina, it's not a trick. This is important, but I don't want either of you risking your lives needlessly. If I can open the door, then I promise to take you both with me. Satisfied?'

Both women nodded. Richard gave them each an appreciative squeeze on the shoulder. He absently adjusted the metal bands on his wrists as he gazed at the towering bastion waiting at the end of the rampart.

A cold wind buffeted him as he started across. He could feel the pressure of the shield, like the weight of water when you swam toward the bottom of a pond. The fine hairs at the back of his neck stiffened as he progressed. The pressure made it difficult but not impossible to draw a breath, as Kahlan had said she had experienced.

Six immense columns of variegated red stone stood to each side of the gold-clad door, holding up a protruding entablature of dark stone. The architrave was decorated with brass plaques. As Richard approached it, he recognized some of their symbols as the same ones on his wristbands, belt, and boot pins. The frieze held round metal disks with other of the more circular symbols. The more linear of symbols he wore were also carved into the stone of the cornice.

Seeing the symbols he recognized reassured him, even though he didn't know their meaning. He wore these things by obligation, duty, and right – he was born to them, that much he knew. Why, he didn't know. Even if he wished it could be otherwise, it wasn't; he was a war wizard.

Distracted by the uncomfortable pressure and tingling of the shields, he reached the door almost before he realized it. The door was at least twelve feet tall, and a good four feet wide, gold-clad and embellished in the same symbolic motifs.

Embossed in the center was the more prominent of the symbols he wore: two rough triangles, with a sinuous double line running around and through them. Richard rested his left hand on the hilt of his sword as he fingered the symbol with his other hand, tracing its oval, undulating outer margin.

With the act of touching it, tracing it, following its pattern, he understood. The spirits who had used the Sword of Truth before him passed their knowledge on to him as he used the sword, but they didn't always convey that knowledge in words; in the heat of combat there wasn't always time.

Sometimes it came to him in images, symbols: these symbols.

This one on the door, like the ones on his wristbands, was a kind of dance used for fighting when outnumbered. It conveyed a sense of the movements of the dance, movements without form.

The dance with death.

It made sense. He wore the outfit of a war wizard. Richard had learned from Kolo's journal that in Kolo's time the First Wizard, named Baraccus, had also been a war wizard, as was Richard. These symbols had meaning to a war wizard. Much as a tailor painted shears on his window, or a tavern sign had a mug on it, or a blacksmith nailed up horseshoes, or a weapons maker displayed knives, these symbols were signs of his craft: bringing death.

Richard realized that his fear had vanished. He stood in the Wizard's Keep, which had always before set his nerves on edge and worse, stood now before the most restricted and protected place in the Keep, yet he felt calm.

He touched a starburst symbol on the door. This symbol was an admonition.

Keep your vision all-inclusive, never allowing it to lock on any one thing. That was the meaning of the starburst symbol: look everywhere at once, see nothing to the exclusion of all else – don't allow the enemy to direct your vision, or you will see what he wishes you to see. He will then come at you as you become bewildered, looking for his attack, and you will lose.

Instead, your vision must open to all there is, never settling, even when cutting. Know your enemy's moves by instinct, not by waiting to see them. To dance with death meant to know the enemy's sword and its speed without waiting to see it. Dancing with death meant being one with the enemy, without looking fixedly, so that you could kill him. Dancing with death meant being committed to killing, committed with your heart and soul. Dancing with death meant that you were the incarnation of death, come to reap the living.

Berdine's voice drifted across the rampart. 'Lord Rahl?'

Richard looked over his shoulder. 'What? What's wrong?'

Berdine shifted her weight to her other foot. 'Well, are you all right? You've been standing there for a long time, staring at the door. Are you all right?'

Richard wiped a hand across his face. 'Yes. I'm fine. I was just … just looking at the things written on the door, that's all.'

He turned, and without thinking, slapped his hand to the cold metal plate in the polished gray granite wall. Kahlan had told him it was said that to touch that metal plate was like touching the cold, dead heart of the Keeper himself.

The metal plate warmed. The gold door silently swung inward.

Dim light came from beyond. Richard took a careful step into the doorway. Like a wick on a lamp being slowly turned up, the dim light coming from inside brightened. He took another step, and the light brightened more.

He scanned the inside as he motioned the two waiting Mord-Sith forward. Whatever magic prevented people from approaching apparently was now withdrawn; Berdine and Raina walked to him without any difficulty.

'That wasn't so bad,' Raina said. 'I didn't feel anything.'

'So far, so good,' Richard said.

Inside, there were glass spheres, about a hand-width in diameter, set atop green marble pedestals against the wall to his left and right. Richard had seen glass spheres similar to these before, down in the lower reaches of the Keep. Like those, these too provided light.

The inside of the First Wizard's enclave was an immense cavern of ornate stonework. Four columns of polished black marble, at least ten feet in diameter, formed a square that supported arches just beyond the outer edges of a central dome dotted by a high ring of windows. Between each pair of columns a wing ran off from the vast central chamber. He noticed that much of the stonework repeated the palm-leaf pattern that adorned the gold capitals atop the black marble columns. The polish of the marble was so high that it reflected images like glass.

Finely worked wrought-iron sconces decorated with the same palm-leaf pattern held candles. Fluidly worked iron formed railings at the edge of the expansive, sunken central floor.

This was not the sinister lair Richard expected. This was a place of grand splendor to match any he had seen. The place was so beautiful that it left him awestricken.

The wing in which the three of them stood, the entry hall, appeared to be by far the smallest of the four wings. Six-foot-tall white marble pedestals marched in a long double row beside the walkway laid with a long red carpet over a gold-flecked dark brown marble floor.

Richard wouldn't have been able to touch fingers were he to put his arms around one of the pedestals. The ribbed, barrel ceiling thirty feet overhead made the fat pedestals look miniscule.

Sitting atop some of the pedestals were objects Richard recognized: ornate knives, gems set in brooches or at the ends of gold-worked chains, a silver chalice, filigree bowls, and delicately worked boxes. Some sat on squares of cloth trimmed with gold or silver embroidery, others on stands carved from burled wood.

Other pedestals held contorted objects that made no sense to him. He would have sworn that they changed shape when he looked at them. He decided it would be best not to look directly at such things of magic, and warned the other two.

The distant wing opposite them, across the central area under the huge dome, ended at a round-topped window that had to be thirty feet tall. Before the window was a huge table piled with a clutter of objects: glass jars, bowls, and coiled tubes; a massive but simple iron candelabrum covered with ages of wax; stacks of scrolls; several human skulls; and a chaos of smaller items Richard couldn't make out from such a distance. The floor all around the table was similarly cluttered, along with things stacked up and leaning against the table.

The wing to the right was dark. Richard felt uncomfortable even looking in that direction. He heeded the warning, and looked to the left. In that wing, he saw books. Thousands of them.

'There,' Richard said, as he gestured to the left. 'That's what we're here for. Remember what I told you. Don't touch anything.' He glanced at them both as they looked about with wide eyes. 'I mean it. I don't know how to save you if you get in trouble touching something in here.'

Both pairs of eyes looked back at him.

'We remember,' Berdine said.

'We know better than to tempt magic,' Raina said. 'We're just looking around, that's all. We wouldn't touch anything.'

'Good. But I suggest that you don't even look at anything, either, except what we need to look at. For all I know, simply looking at something in here could trigger its magic.'

'Do you think?' Raina asked in astonishment.

'What I think is that I'd rather not find out after it's too late. Come on. Let's get this over with so we can get out of here.'

Oddly, even though he had said the words, and knew they made sense, he didn't really feel like leaving. As potentially dangerous as he knew the place to be, he found that he liked the First Wizard's enclave.

Berdine smirked. 'Lord Rahl fears magic as much as we do.'

'You're wrong, Berdine. I know a little about magic.' He started down the red carpet. 'I fear it more.'

Ten broad steps at the end led down into the central area. An expanse of cream-colored marble covered the floor. A border of darker brown marble ran around the floor near the edge. When Richard reached the bottom step and his foot touched the floor, it hummed and began to glow. He quickly retreated back up onto the red carpet. The glow extinguished.

'What now?' Raina asked.

He pried her fingers from his arm. 'Did either of you put your foot to the floor?' They both shook their heads. 'Try.'

As Richard waited on the step, Berdine gingerly tried to test the marble. She withdrew her foot.

'I can't. Something stops my foot before I can get it on the floor.'

Richard stepped out onto the marble again. Again it glowed and hummed.

'It must be a shield, then. Here, take my hand and try again.'

Holding Richard's hand, Berdine was able to step onto the marble with him. Raina took his other hand and followed.

'All right,' he said, 'since it's some kind of shield, don't let go of my hand while we're on this part. We don't know what would happen. For all I know, if you let go of my hand you could fry like bacon on a griddle.'

Their grips on his hands tightened. As they stepped onto the steps up to the wing with the books, the floor went silent. Without Richard to hold their hands on the way out, they would be trapped inside this place, unable to return across the central floor.

The wing with the books wasn't the kind of library he had expected. There were rows of shelves, but they were in disarray, with books stacked every which way. Chunks of rock served as bookends for the few standing upright among the disorder.

Here and there books were in piles, as if someone had pulled them from the shelves and simply tossed them in a heap. Most were closed, but a significant number lay open, some face up, some face down. But that wasn't the biggest surprise.

Everywhere, it seemed, there were books stacked up on the floor. A few stacks were short, maybe three or four feet tall, but many more were tall pillars of books. Some of the irregular stacks towered twelve or fourteen feet. They looked as if the mere act of breathing could make them topple. The columns of books were everywhere, creating a maze. Richard couldn't fathom the reason for the books being stacked in such disarray, but the mystery of it made him sweat.

Richard took an arm of each woman. 'My grandfather told me that there were books in the Keep that were extremely dangerous. Kahlan told me that the most dangerous things were kept in here, where no one could get to them, not even the wizards she knew.'

Berdine shot him a look. 'You mean, you think that the books themselves could be dangerous? Not just the information in them, but the actual books?'

Richard thought of the description of a book that Sister Amelia had used to start the plague. 'I'm not sure, but we had better treat them as such. Look, but don't touch.'

Berdine's brow drew down with a dubious frown. 'Lord Rahl, there must be thousands of books I can see just standing here. There are bound to be more down the aisles. It will take us weeks to find the one we want – if it's even here.'

Richard took a deep breath. Berdine was right. He hadn't expected to find so many books in here. He thought the libraries held most of the books, and there would only be a few in here.

'If you want to be out of here before dark, we don't have long,' Raina said. 'We might as well come back tomorrow and get an early start.'

Richard was beginning to feel intimidated by the task ahead. 'We'll just have to stay after dark. We'll stay all night if we have to.'

Raina rolled her Agiel in her fingers. 'If you say so, Lord Rahl.'

Richard's heart sank as he stood staring at the forest of books. He needed information, not a search for one leaf in a forest. If only he could use magic to find that one leaf.

He idly adjusted the bands at his wrist. Under his fingers he felt the starburst pattern on one of them.

Look without fixing your sight.

'I have an idea,' he said. 'Wait here. I'll be right back.'

Richard returned to the pillars. He went to one that held a crackled-glass bowl upon a large square of black cloth.

'What good is that going to do?' Raina asked, when he came back holding the cloth out for them.

'There's too much to see. I'm going to use this as a blindfold, so I won't see all the things I don't want to see.'

Berdine's face twisted with incredulity. 'If you're blindfolded, then how are you going to see the thing we're looking for?'

'With magic. I'm going to try to let my gift guide me. Sometimes it works that way – through need. All these books are too confusing. If I'm blindfolded, I won't see them, and I'll be able to feel the one I'm looking for. At least, that's what I hope.'

Raina gazed out over all the books. 'Well, you are the Lord Rahl. You have magic. If it has a chance of getting us out of spending the night in here, then I say do it.'

Richard placed the black cloth over his eyes and began tying its tails behind his head. 'Just guide me and keep me from touching anything. Don't forget what I said about you two not touching anything, either.'

'Don't worry about us, Lord Rahl,' Raina said. 'We're not about to touch anything.'

When he finished tying the blindfold over his eyes, Richard turned his head this way and that, testing to make sure that he couldn't see. He rubbed a finger over the starburst on his wristband.

His world was pitch-black. He sought the inner peace, the inner calm, where dwelled his gift.

If the plague was started by magic from the Temple of the Winds, then maybe they had a chance to halt it. If he did nothing, then untold thousands of people were going to die.

He needed that book.

He thought about the boy he had watched die. About the little girl, Lily, who told him about the Sister of the Dark showing her the book. That was how the plague started. He knew it was.

That precious child had the tokens on her. Richard hadn't inquired, but he knew that she, at least, would be dead by now. He couldn't bear to inquire.

He needed that book.

He put a foot out. 'Nudge me with your fingers if I'm about

to run into anything. Try not to talk, but if you must, don't be afraid to speak up.'

He felt their fingers lightly touch his arm as he stepped forward. They guided him with that touch, keeping him from colliding with the towering stacks of books as he waded deeper into the maze.

Richard didn't know what it was he should feel. He didn't know if it was magic, a hunch, or his imagination guiding him. By the way he seemed to be winding up and down aisles and snaking through the stacks, he feared it was no more than his imagination. He tried to ignore the things that kept his thoughts skipping about and running in every direction.

He tried to concentrate on the book and his need to find it.

Thinking of the sick children, he was able to focus better. They needed him. They were helpless.

Richard felt himself jerk to a halt. He wondered why. He turned left when he expected that he was going to turn right. It had to be the gift. With that thought, his thoughts scattered in every direction again. He focused once more.

The two Mord-Sith forcibly snatched his arm to halt him. He understood. Another step, and he would have collided with a stack.

Wondering which way he would be turned, he found himself squatting instead. His arm lifted and he reached out.

'Careful,' Berdine whispered. 'It's a big, irregular stack. Be careful, or you'll knock it over.'

Richard nodded, not wanting to distract himself by answering with words. He was concentrating on feeling the object of his need. He felt it near. His fingers lightly brushed the books, running down the stack, touching the bindings of some and the pages of others because they were turned around the other way.

His fingers stopped on a binding.

'This one.' He tapped the leather binding. 'This one. What does it say?'

Berdine propped a hand on his thigh to support herself as she leaned in. 'It's High D'Haran. Something about the Temple of the Winds – "*Tagenricht ost fuer Mosst Verlaschendreck nich Greschlechten*" '

'*Temple of the Winds Inquisition and Trial*,' Richard translated in a whisper. 'We've found it.'

CHAPTER 47

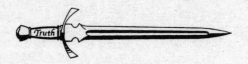

Breathe, the sliph said.

Kahlan let go the silken essence and pulled a deep breath of the alien air. The dim world of the sliph's well down in the Keep whirled around her. Stone of the walls and floor finally settled in her vision. The dome overhead seemed to slow its spinning.

Something unexpected waited in the sliph's room.

Tilted back in the chair, with her feet propped up on the table, sat a figure in red leather. Kahlan sat down, dangling her feet over the edge of the stone wall, to gather her senses.

The front legs of the chair thunked down. 'Well, well, the wandering Mother Confessor returns at last.'

Kahlan hopped down onto the floor. She almost lost her footing with the way it seemed to twist and tilt.

'Cara, what are you doing down here?'

Cara gripped Kahlan under her arm. 'You better sit down until you regain your feet.'

'I'm all right.' Kahlan glanced over her shoulder to the silver face behind her. 'Thank you, sliph.'

'Do you wish to travel?' The sliph's haunting voice echoed off the walls and dome overhead for a long moment.

'No, I've had enough traveling for the time being. I'm going to stay here.'

'When you wish to travel, call me, and we will travel. You will be pleased.'

'I don't know about that,' Kahlan muttered as the sliph seemed to melt back into her well.

'She's a spooky companion to have down here,' Cara said. 'She invited me to travel with her, too, and then told me I didn't have the magic required. She comes and stares at me with that eerie smile.'

'Cara, what are you doing down here?'

Cara leaned Kahlan back against the sliph's well. She gave Kahlan the strangest look as she shook her head to herself.

'When Lord Rahl read your letter, it didn't take him long to figure out what you had done. Berdine told him how you had brought us here to look for that book on the trial record. He came down here, but the sliph wouldn't tell him where she had taken you.

'Lord Rahl said that now that he knew the sliph was not sleeping, as he had thought, it wasn't safe to leave her alone. He said that others, like the Sister and Marlin, could come through.'

Kahlan hadn't thought about that, about another one of Jagang's minions coming to Aydindril through the sliph. The sliph seemed to have no loyalty. She would travel with anyone who had the required price of magic.

'So, Richard left you here?'

'He said he couldn't remain down here all the time to guard the sliph.' Cara's chin lifted with pride. 'He said that a Mord-Sith must guard the well at all times, since we have the power to stop someone with magic. The Lord Rahl has always used the Mord-Sith to protect him against magic.'

The wizards of old obviously had this same problem with the sliph, and had left wizards like Kolo down here to guard her. Kolo said that the enemy sometimes arrived suddenly by way of the sliph, and that only the quick reactions of the one on guard had prevented disaster.

'You mean he brought you down here and just left you?'

'No. He searched for hours until he found a way without magic so we could get down here on our own. He didn't want to have to bring each of us down here for our turn, and he didn't want us trapped down here, either. We have to take shifts. I don't like it, because we should be close to Lord Rahl in order to guard him, not this ... silver thing, but I guess that we are guarding Lord Rahl by doing this, so I agreed to it.'

Kahlan found her feet steady at last. 'If we had known the

sliph was awake, and had been guarding her before, then Marlin wouldn't have been able to come to try to assassinate Richard, and the Sister wouldn't have been able to start the plague.'

Kahlan's chest constricted with a hot, cutting pang of regret. They could have prevented the whole thing. All the awful things she had learned would not be threatening her people, her world, and her love. The realization of the chance lost left her nauseous.

'Lord Rahl also wanted us to wait until your return from the witch woman, in case you needed help.'

'Richard knew where I went?'

'The sliph wouldn't tell him, but he said he knew anyway. He said you went to the witch woman.'

'He knew, and he didn't chase after me?'

Cara pulled her long blond braid over her shoulder. 'I was surprised, too. I asked him why he wouldn't go after you. He said that he loved you; he did not own you.'

'Really? Richard said that?'

'Yes.' A smirk tightened Cara's lips. 'You are training him well, Mother Confessor. I approve. And then he kicked a chair. I think he hurt his foot, but he denies it.'

'So, Richard is angry with me?'

Cara rolled her eyes. 'Mother Confessor, this is Richard we are talking about. The man is fool in love with you. He wouldn't be angry with you if you told him to marry Nadine instead of you.'

Kahlan swallowed at the renewed twist of pain. 'Why would you say that?'

Cara frowned. 'I only meant he could never be angry with you, no matter what. You were supposed to laugh, not jump like I had poked you with my Agiel. Mother Confessor, he loves you; he is worried sick, but he is not angry with you.'

'What about kicking the chair?'

Cara stroked her long blond braid and smirked again. 'He claimed the chair gave him just cause.'

'I see.' Kahlan couldn't seem to find pleasure in Cara's sense of humor. 'How long have I been gone?'

'Not quite two days. And I expect you to tell me how you

managed to slip past those D'Haran guards out there by the bridge.'

'It was snowing. They didn't see me.'

Cara didn't look to believe it. She was giving Kahlan that odd look again.

'And did you kill the witch woman?'

'No.' Kahlan changed the subject. 'What has Richard been doing while I was gone?'

'Well, first he asked the sliph to take him to the Temple of the Winds, but she said she didn't know that place and couldn't take him there, so he rode to Mount Kymermosst –'

'He went there?' Kahlan snatched Cara's arm. 'What did he find?'

'Nothing. He said that there was nothing to find. He said that if the Temple of the Winds was once there, it is now gone.'

Kahlan released Cara's arm. 'He went to Mount Kymermosst, and he's back already?'

'You know Lord Rahl; when he gets something in his head, he charges after it. The men who went with him said they rode hard. They slept little and rode much of the night. Lord Rahl expected you to return last night and wanted to be back for you. When you did not return as expected, he paced and fretted, but still he did not go after you. Whenever he looked like he was about to change his mind, he read your letter again, and went back to pacing instead.'

'I guess my letter was a little strong,' Kahlan said as she glanced down at the floor.

'Lord Rahl showed it to me.' Cara's face was unreadable. 'Sometimes it is necessary to threaten men, or they get to thinking that they are the ones who say what will be. You dissuaded him of that idea with your threats.'

'I didn't threaten him.' Kahlan thought that her tone sounded too much like a plea.

Cara watched Kahlan's eyes for a moment. 'You are probably right. The chair must have given Lord Rahl cause, as he said.'

'I did what I had to do. Richard would understand that. I guess I'd better go explain it to him.'

Cara gestured behind, to the door. 'You just missed him. He was here not long ago.'

'He came to see if I was back? He must be worried sick.'

'Berdine told him about the book you were searching for. He came here and found it.'

Kahlan blinked in astonishment. 'He found it? But we looked. It wasn't there. How did he find it?'

'He went to a place he called the First Wizard's enclave, and found it there.'

Kahlan's jaw dropped. 'He went in there? He went into the First Wizard's enclave? Alone, without me? He shouldn't have gone there! That's a dangerous place!'

'Really.' Cara folded her arms. 'And of course you would never do anything so foolish as to get it in your head to go run off alone to a dangerous place. Maybe you should reprimand Lord Rahl for his impulsive behavior, since you are so prudent and above such reckless conduct yourself.'

The echo of Cara's voice lingered uncomfortably before it died out. Kahlan understood. Even though Richard did as she had asked by not coming after her, Cara had tried. Even though she didn't like magic, Cara had tried to go to protect Kahlan.

'Cara,' she said in a meek voice, 'I'm sorry I tricked you, too.'

Cara shrugged, but still showed no emotion. 'I am just a guard. You have no obligation to me.'

'Yes, I do. You are not "just a guard." You may be our protector, but you are more. I consider you my friend. You are a sister of the Agiel. I should have told you what I was doing, but I feared that if I did, Richard would be angry with you for not stopping me. I didn't want that.'

Cara said nothing. Still, she showed no emotion. Kahlan breached the uncomfortable silence. 'Cara, I'm sorry. I guess I was afraid you would try to stop me. I tricked you. You're a sister of the Agiel; I should have trusted you and taken you into my confidence. Please, Cara, I was wrong. I beg you forgive me.'

A smile finally spread on Cara's face. 'We are sisters of the Agiel. I forgive you.'

Kahlan managed a small smile. 'Do you think Richard will be as understanding as you?'

Cara let out an amused grunt. 'Well, you have better ways to persuade him to forgive you. It is not so difficult to melt a man's frown.'

'I only wish I had good news, so I could bring a smile to his face, but I don't.' She paused at the doorway. 'What has Nadine been up to while I've been gone?'

'Well, I've been down here guarding the sliph much of the time, but from what I've seen, she has been giving the staff herbs to try to protect them, and to use in smoking the palace. It's a good thing the place is made mostly of stone or it would have been burned down by now. She has been conferring with Drefan and helping him in talking to the staff and others who come for advice.

'Lord Rahl asked her to go out to visit herb sellers and such, to make sure they are not hucksters out to swindle people who are in fear for their lives. The city seems to be sprouting shameless mountebanks the way the sudden warmth seems to be bringing green grass. Nadine also gives reports to Lord Rahl, but he has been gone much of the time, and as busy as she seems to be trying to help people, the visits since he returned are short.'

Kahlan tapped the side of her fist against the doorway.

'Thanks, Cara.' She looked into the other's blue eyes. 'There are rats down here. Are you all right?'

'There are worse things than rats.'

'Indeed there are,' Kahlan whispered.

CHAPTER 48

It was late, and with the dark, people on the streets didn't recognize her. Without her usual escort of guards, they had no reason to give her a second look, no reason to suspect she was the Mother Confessor out among them. Just as well; there were some people who wished the Mother Confessor harm. Mostly, people kept their distance from her, as they did with everyone else, hoping to keep the plague from themselves.

As Cara had said, there were hucksters everywhere, hawking potions to ward off the plague, or to cure your loved ones already stricken. Others strolled the streets with trays, held up on straps over their shoulders, neatly laid out with amulets possessing magic to protect against the plague. Kahlan remembered seeing some of these same people not long ago selling the same amulets as magic to find a husband or wife, or to enthrall an unfaithful spouse. Old women with small carts or simple wooden stands sold carved spell-invested plaques made to hang over the door to a home as a sure way to keep the plague from entering the house. As late as it was, business seemed brisk. Even the vendors selling meats and produce extolled the healthful virtues of their goods and their value in promoting continued health, if eaten regularly, of course.

Kahlan would send the soldiers out to put a stop to some of these swindlers, but she knew that such intervention would likely be viewed with hostility on the part of the buyers. If she tried to use the army to stop such foolish practices, desperate people would concoct theories about those in power wanting to stop the cures so that the decent, working folk would get the plague. Despite common sense, or evidence to the contrary, many people believed that those in power were always scheming to harm them; if they only knew the truth.

If Kahlan were to order the sale of these items stopped, the 'cures' would be sold in secret, and for a higher price. No matter how insupportable the claims of these cures, their benefits would be vehemently supported as self-evident truth.

Wizard's First Rule: people would believe any lie, either because they wanted to believe it was true, or because they feared it was. These people were desperate, and would become more so, yet. Many wanted to believe.

Kahlan tried to imagine what she would do if Richard had the plague. Would she be despairing enough to put her faith in such trickery, hoping against hope that it would save him? Sometimes hope was all people had. Groundless as it was, she couldn't take that hope away from them; it was all they had, and all they could do.

It was up to Kahlan and Richard to do that which would help these people.

As she made her way through the familiar splendor of the Confessors' Palace, on her way to find Richard, Kahlan paused at the open double doors to a large room used for formal receptions. The room was a calming blue color, with dark blue drapes over the tall, narrow windows. The granite floor had a starburst pattern of darker and lighter stone radiating out from the center. Lamps on cherrywood stands around the edge of the room lent a mellow light to the gathering hall. The table where small foods were sometimes set out for guests now held only an array of candles.

Kahlan's attention had been drawn by the sound of Drefan's voice. He stood to the right, before the table with the candles, speaking to perhaps fifty or sixty people. They sat cross-legged on the floor before him, listening with rapt attention as he spoke of the way of health, of keeping the body sound by being in touch with the inner self.

Most of the people nodded absently as they listened to Drefan explaining how, by defiling their bodies with unhealthy thoughts and actions, people opened the pathway for sickness to enter. He told them that the Creator had endowed them with the ability to fight off things such as the plague, if only they would do as nature provided, by eating the right foods that would strengthen the auras that defended the body, and by using inner reflection to direct the vigor of various energy fields to their proper function in harmony with the whole.

Many of the things he said made sense: not eating foods that you knew gave you headaches, because it interfered with the mind's ability to regulate the body; not eating foods that you knew caused pains and cramps in the gut, because it interfered with the body's ability to digest the good foods you needed; not eating heavy meals right before sleeping, because it interfered with your body getting the rest it needed to remain strong, and how all of these things disrupt the auras that give us strength and protect health.

People marveled openly that Drefan could make it all so simple for them to understand. They spoke as if they had been blind, and now for the first time had vision. They watched with unblinking eyes as he went on, telling them that we had within us the power to control our own bodies, and that disease could only afflict us if we allowed it to. He spoke of herbs and foods that purged poisons from the body and left people truly healthy for perhaps the first time since their birth.

These people weren't listening to Lord Rahl's brother, they were listening to Drefan Rahl, High Priest of the Raug'Moss.

As one, they followed the High Priest's instructions when he told them to close their eyes and draw the breath of life and healthy steams through their noses and down into their inner core by using the muscles low in their bellies. He explained how to let it reach deep into the source of the power of each person's unique aura, to draw out the poisons from the furthest, darkest corners of their beings and expel it out through the mouth, to be replaced with a renewing breath of life drawn in again through the nose.

Better, Kahlan guessed, that these people would come to Drefan for advice that might help them, and at least sounded like it could do no harm, than spend their savings on false hope from the hucksters in the street. Paying attention to their body's needs with things like proper food and rest seemed sound advice.

As they all drew the slow, deep breaths in through their noses, Drefan turned his head and locked his Darken Rahl eyes on Kahlan, as if he had known all along that she had been standing there outside the doorway. He gave her a kind-hearted smile that sparkled benevolently in his blue eyes. She could see why these people put their trust in him. She made herself return a little smile.

Kahlan remembered the talk she had had with Shota about how difficult it was to banish unpleasant memories. Kahlan wished she could forget Drefan's hand between Cara's legs.

Drefan was trying to help people. He was doing everything he could to halt the plague. He was a great healer – the High Priest of the Raug'Moss. She tried to put the image of him comforting those sick children in place of the memory of him forcing his big hand down between Cara's legs.

Drefan had explained, at the time, why he had done that to Cara. He had saved Cara's life. A Mord-Sith, screaming in pain, then unconscious, and Drefan had brought her back. Richard found comfort in Drefan, as did everyone else. Kahlan broke eye contact with him and continued on her way to find Richard.

Tristan Bashkar, the Jarian ambassador staying at the Confessors' Palace while he waited for further signs from the stars, further word from above, before surrendering, paused at a balcony as she passed below. As was his habit, he drew back his coat and rested his hand on his hip. It displayed the wicked dagger he wore at his belt. Oftentimes, in conversation, he would also put a boot up on a chair or stool and casually rest his forearm on his knee. It provided those in conversation with him the opportunity to see also the knife he kept in his boot.

The more she saw Tristan in the palace, watching her with his cunning eyes, the more she disliked his presence. If there was a man who acted more childish, Kahlan didn't know him.

Tristan watched silently as she hurried on her way. Kahlan was glad he was up on a balcony, so that she wouldn't have to waste time playing word games with him.

Ulic and Egan gave Kahlan an odd look as she greeted them before whisking through the door to the small room Richard liked to use to study Kolo's journal. He was sitting with his head in his hands, his fingers buried in his hair, as he read from another book that lay open on the table. Two candles and a lamp on the table beside him provided light, and a small, fragrant fire of birch logs added warmth to the cozy room. His cloak lay over a nearby chair, but he wore his sword.

Richard looked up. When he saw her, he shot to his feet. Without the gold cloak, he was like a big, black shadow gliding across the room. Before he could speak, Kahlan rushed into his arms.

Kahlan pressed the side of her face to his chest as she hugged him. 'Please, Richard, don't yell at me. Please, just hold me.' Tears choked her voice. 'Please, don't say anything – just hold me.'

It was ecstasy being with him again. It never failed to astound her, whenever she saw him, just how much she needed and loved him.

Richard's arms enclosed her in comforting shelter. She listened to the fire crackle, and the sound of his heart under her ear. She could almost imagine, in the safety of his strong arms, that everything was fine, and that they had a future.

She remembered her mother's words.

Confessors don't have love, Kahlan. They have duty.

Kahlan clutched his black shirt as she fought a losing battle to hold back tears. He held her and stroked her hair. She had asked him to hold her and not speak, and he was doing just that. That only made her feel worse.

He must have questions. He must want to say something to her, to tell her how relieved he was to see her safe, to tell her how worried he had been, to ask her where she had been and what she had found out, to tell her what he had found, to yell at her; but he didn't. Instead, without protest, he did as she had asked, relegating his own desires to secondary, after hers.

How would she go on without his love? How would she draw a breath? How would she manage to make herself go on until she was old and could finally finish her duty and at last die?

'Richard … I'm so sorry I made that letter sound threatening. I didn't mean to threaten you, I swear. I just wanted you to be safe. I'm so sorry if I hurt you.'

He squeezed her a little tighter and kissed the top of her head. Kahlan wished she could just die in his arms, now, and not have to face her duty, not have to face the finality of the future, the finality of losing him.

'How's your foot?' she asked.

'My foot?'

'Cara said you hurt it on a chair.'

'Oh. My foot is fine. The chair died, but I don't think it suffered.'

Against all odds, Kahlan laughed. She looked up through her tears into his gentle smile.

'All right, I think your hug has revived me. You can yell at me now.'

He kissed her instead. The feeling of being pulled up in his arms was rapture. Being in the sliph didn't even come close.

'So,' he finally said, 'what did our ancestors' spirits have to say?'

'Our ancestors' … how did you know that I went to the Mud People?'

Richard's brow curved into a bewildered cast. 'Kahlan, your face is all painted so the ancestors' spirits could see you in a gathering. Did you think I wouldn't notice?'

Kahlan touched her fingers to her forehead, to her cheek. 'I was in such a hurry, I never even gave it any thought. No wonder people have been giving me such odd looks.'

As she had raced through the palace looking for him, three different women on the staff had offered to draw her a bath. Everyone must have thought she had gone mad.

Richard's expression turned serious as he settled his arms around her waist. 'So, what did the ancestors' spirits have to say?'

Kahlan steeled herself. She tilted her head, indicating the bone knife on her arm.

'Grandfather's spirit called me, through his bone knife. He had to speak with me. He told me that the plague isn't confined to Aydindril. It's spread all over the Midlands.'

Richard tensed. 'Do you think it's true?'

'Elder Breginderin had the tokens on his legs. He's probably dead by now. Some children reported that they saw a woman near the Mud People's village. She showed them something with colored light, just like what Lily told us she saw. One of those children has already died. Sister Amelia was there.'

'Dear spirits,' Richard whispered.

'It gets worse. The spirit showed me other places I know in

the Midlands. He said that the plague has spread to all these places, too. The spirit showed me what will be if the plague isn't stopped. Death will sweep the land. Few will survive.

'The spirit told me that magic stolen from the Temple of the Winds started the plague, but that the plague itself isn't magic. Jagang has used magic more powerful than he understands. If allowed to rage unchecked, the plague could eventually sweep into the Old World, too.'

'Small consolation. Did the spirit say how Jagang stole this magic from the Temple of the Winds?'

Kahlan nodded as she looked away from his eyes. 'You were right about the red moons. It was a warning that the Temple of the Winds had been violated.'

Kahlan told him about the Hall of the Betrayer, and how Sister Amelia had been able to tread that path. Kahlan recounted the rest of her meeting with the spirit of Chandalen's grandfather, as best as she could remember it, including the part about the temple being at least partially sentient, as Richard had suspected.

Richard leaned an arm against the mantel as he stared into the fire. He pinched his lower lip as he listened patiently.

Kahlan told him how the spirit had told her that to stop the plague, they must get into the Temple of the Winds, how it existed in both worlds at the same time, and how both the good and the evil spirits were involved and had a say in this.

'And the ancestor's spirit could give you no indication how we were to get to the Temple of the Winds?'

'No,' Kahlan said. 'In fact, he wasn't interested in that part of it. He said that the temple would reveal what must be done. Shota said the same thing.'

Engrossed in thought, Richard nodded while he considered her words. Kahlan twisted her fingers together while she waited.

'What about Shota?' he asked at last. 'What happened with her?'

Kahlan hesitated. She knew she had to tell him at least some of it, but she was reluctant to tell him all of what Shota had said.

'Richard, I don't believe Shota was trying to cause trouble.'

He looked back over his shoulder. 'She sends Nadine to

marry me, and you don't think that kind of interference trouble?'

Kahlan cleared her throat into her fist. 'Shota didn't send Nadine, exactly.' Richard's hawklike gaze continued to fix on her, so she went on. 'The message about the winds hunting you was not her idea. The Temple of the Winds was sending you a message, through her, just as it was sending you a message through that boy who died. Shota wasn't trying to harm us.'

Richard's brow lowered. 'What else did the witch woman tell you?'

Kahlan interlocked her fingers behind her back. She looked away from his penetrating glare.

'Richard, I went there to put an end to Shota's interference. I was prepared to kill her, if she threatened you or tried to harm me. I thought the worst of her. I did. I was convinced she was trying to harm us.

'I talked with her. Really talked. Shota isn't as … malicious as I thought. She admitted she doesn't want us to have a child, but this isn't about trying to keep us apart.

'She has a talent for seeing the future, and she is only telling us what she sees – to try to help you. She's just the messenger in this. She's not directing these events. She said the same thing as the ancestor's spirit, that the plague was started by magic, and not of its own accord.'

With three strides, Richard closed the distance between them. He seized her by the upper arm.

'She sent Nadine to marry me! She sent Nadine to keep us apart! She's trying to put a wedge between us, and you are taken in by her tricks?'

Kahlan backed away from him. 'No, Richard, you have it wrong, as did I. The spirits sent you a bride. Shota was only able to influence who it would be. She used that influence so that the bride sent would be Nadine. Shota says she sees that you will marry this bride sent by the spirits, and so she wanted it to be someone you knew. She was only trying to ease your pain in this.'

'And you believe her? Have you lost your mind!'

'Richard, you're hurting my arm.'

He released her. 'Sorry,' he muttered, as he withdrew to the hearth. Kahlan could see the muscles in his jaw flexing as he ground his teeth.

'You said she told you the same as the ancestor's spirit. Do you remember her words?'

Kahlan tried frantically to separate what she knew she had to tell him from what she didn't want him to know. She realized how unwise it was to try to hide information from Richard, but she reasoned that if she had to, she could always tell him everything. If she could get away with withholding some of it, though ...

'Shota said we have not heard the last message from the winds. She said we will receive one more, involving the moon.'

'Involving the moon? How?'

'I don't know. Just like the spirit, the "how" didn't seem to be important to her. What she did say was that this message from the moon will be the "consequential communion," as she called it. She said we must not ignore or dismiss it.'

'Did she, now. And did she say why, exactly?'

'She said our future – and the future of all those innocent people – will hinge on this event. She said it would be our only chance to carry out our duty to save the innocent lives of all those who depend upon us to do what they cannot.'

Richard turned to her. It was like death itself rounding on her. His eyes had that look, like Drefan's. Like Darken Rahl's.

'She told you something else that you're holding back. What is it?' he growled.

It wasn't Richard speaking, it was the Seeker. She knew in that instant why a Seeker was so feared: he was a law unto himself. Those gray eyes were looking right into her.

'Richard,' she whispered, 'please leave it at that.'

His glare cut to her soul. 'What did she tell you?'

Kahlan swallowed as she panted with dread. She could feel hot tears coursing down her face.

'Shota saw the future.' Kahlan heard herself speaking, even though she had intended to remain silent. 'She saw that you will wed another. She used her influence to make it someone you knew.' Under his glare, she found remaining silent impossible. 'She could not influence who I am to wed. I will be married, too. It will not be you who becomes my husband.'

Richard stood frozen for a moment, a boiling thunderhead gathering. He yanked the baldric off over his head and tossed it and the scabbard holding the sword on a chair.

'Richard, what are you doing?'

And then he was moving. He went for the door. Kahlan put herself in front of him. It was like stepping in front of an enraged mountain.

'Richard, what are you going to do?'

He grasped her by the waist, picked her up, and set her aside as if she were no more than a child in his way.

'I'm going to kill her.'

Kahlan threw her arms around his waist from behind, trying to drag him to a halt. It slowed him no more than if she had been a gnat. He was leaving his sword because he couldn't travel in the sliph with the magic of the Sword of Truth.

'Richard! Richard, please, stop! If you love me, stop!'

He halted and turned his wrathful glare on her. His voice came like a crack of thunder.

'What?'

'Richard, do you think I'm stupid?'

'Of course not.'

'Then do you believe I want to marry someone else?'

'No.'

'Richard, you have to listen to me. Shota said she saw the future. She isn't making the future, she just saw it. She told me these things so that what she saw might help us.'

'I've had all of the "help" from Shota I intend to have. I'll have no more of it. She has taken one liberty too many. It will be her last.'

'Richard, we have to figure out what to do. We have to do what we can to stop this plague. You saw those sick, dying children. The spirit of Chandalen's grandfather showed me countless other dead children – dead people of all sorts. That will be the future if you do this. Do you want those children and their parents to die because you refuse to use your head?'

His fist was gripping some sort of ornament on an elaborate necklace. She realized she had never seen it before.

Even though he wasn't wearing his sword, its magic drove him. He was a cauldron of lethal rage. Death was dancing in his eyes.

'I don't care what Shota says, I'll not marry Nadine. Nor will I stand by while you –'

'I know,' she whispered. 'Richard, I know how you feel. How do you think this makes me feel? But use your head. This is not the way to change what Shota says. You always said before that the future is not yet decided, and that we couldn't act on what Shota says. You always said that we couldn't allow ourselves to put our faith in what she says, and let it direct our actions.'

His eyes shone with deadly wrath. 'You believe her.'

Kahlan took a calming breath, trying to regain her composure. 'I believe she saw the future. Richard, don't you remember how she also said that I would touch you with my power? Look at how that turned out. She was right, but it wasn't the calamitous event I feared. It was what brought us together, and allowed us to have our love.'

'How can your marrying someone else turn out good?'

Kahlan abruptly realized what this was really about: he was jealous. She had never seen him this jealous before. But that's what it was a – jealous rage.

'I would be lying if I told you I knew.' Kahlan gripped his broad shoulders. 'Richard, I love you, and that's the truth. I could never love anyone else. You believe me, don't you? I trust in your love for me, and I know that you don't love Nadine. Don't you believe in me? Don't you trust me?'

He visibly cooled. 'Of course I do. I do trust you.' Frustration replaced the rage in his eyes. He released the amulet in his fist. 'But –'

'But nothing. We love each other, and that's all there is to it. Whatever happens, we have to believe in each other. If we don't believe in each other, then we are lost in this.'

At last, he pulled her into his arms. She knew his anguish. She felt it, too. Hers, though, was worse, because she didn't believe there was a way out of Shota's prediction.

Kahlan lifted the strange amulet at his neck. In the center, surrounded by a complex of gold and silver lines, was a teardrop-shaped ruby as big as her thumbnail.

'Richard, what is this? Where did you get it?'

He lifted the gold and silver object from her fingers to peer down at it. 'It's a symbol, like the others I wear. I found it in the Keep.'

'In the First Wizard's enclave?'

'Yes. It was part of this outfit, but unlike the rest of it, this was left in the First Wizard's enclave. The man who wore it was the First Wizard in Kolo's time. His name was Baraccus.'

'Cara told me that you found the record of the trial. What did it look like in there?'

Richard stared off. 'It was … beautiful. I didn't want to leave.'

'Have you found out anything from the book yet?'

'No. It's in High D'Haran. Berdine is working on Kolo's journal; I'll work on this one. I've only had an hour or so to start translating it. I haven't really done much yet; I was too worried about you to be able to think about anything else.'

Kahlan touched the amulet hanging around his neck. 'Do you know what this symbol represents?'

'Yes. The ruby is meant to represent a drop of blood. It is the symbolic representation of the way of the primary edict.'

'The primary edict?'

His voice turned distant, as if speaking to himself more than to her.

'It means only one thing, and everything: cut. Once committed to fight, cut. Everything else is secondary. Cut. That is your duty, your purpose, your hunger. There is no rule more important, no commitment that overrides that one. Cut.'

His words chilled her to the bone as he went on.

'The lines are a portrayal of the dance. Cut from the void, not from bewilderment. Cut the enemy as quickly and directly as possible. Cut with certainty. Cut decisively, resolutely. Cut into his strength. Flow through the gaps in his guard. Cut him. Cut him down utterly. Don't allow him a breath. Crush him. Cut him without mercy to the depths of his spirit.

'It is the balance to life: death. It is the dance with death.

'It is the law a war wizard lives by, or he dies.'

CHAPTER 49

Clarissa sat curled up in a chair, sewing the hem of a new dress Nathan had bought for her. He had wanted to let the seamstress do the work, but she had insisted on doing it herself, mostly to have something to do. Nathan had smiled and told her that if it would please her, then it was all right with him. She didn't know what she would do with all the dresses he kept buying for her. She had told him to stop, but he just kept doing it.

Nathan returned from the door, having had a long discussion with a soldier named Bollesdun about the movements of Jagang's expeditionary force. They were the men who had attacked her home of Renwold, Clarissa had learned. She tried not to listen to Nathan's talks with his soldier friends who showed up from time to time.

She didn't like to think about the nightmare of Renwold. Nathan told her that he wanted to end the killing, so there would be no more Renwolds. He called it a waste of life.

Clarissa touched Nathan's leg when he came close. 'Is there anything I can do to help?'

His blue eyes turned toward her, watching her for a long moment. 'No, not yet. I must write a letter. I'm expecting someone soon. Don't go into the bedroom to answer the door when they come. Stay in here. I don't want them to get a look at you. You don't have magic, so they won't know you're in here.'

Clarissa caught the tone of disquiet in his voice. 'Do you

think they will cause trouble? They won't try to hurt you, will they?'

A sly smile took his face. 'That would be the last mistake they ever made. I've laid so many traps around this place that the Keeper himself wouldn't dare to try to take me here.' He winked at her, as if to reassure her. 'Watch through the keyhole, if you wish. It may be good for you to remember the faces of these people. They're dangerous.'

Her stomach churning with anxiety, Clarissa began embroidering little vines and leaves along the hem of the dress, because she thought they would be pretty, and to pass the time while Nathan wrote his letter. When he finished, he clasped his hands behind his back and paced.

When the knock finally came, he looked toward the bedroom, where stood the door to the hall. He turned to her and crossed his lips with a finger. Clarissa nodded. He shut the door to the sitting room as he went to answer the knock. She set aside her needlework and knelt at the door to peek through the keyhole.

She had a good view of the hall door as Nathan pulled it open. Two attractive women, about Clarissa's age, stood in the hall. Two young men waited behind them. The scowls on the women could have cut stone.

Clarissa was astonished to see that each woman had a small gold ring through her lower lip, as did Clarissa.

'Well, well,' one of the women said contemptuously, 'if it isn't the prophet himself. We thought it was probably you, Nathan, messing about in things that aren't your business.'

Nathan grinned as he bowed dramatically from the waist. 'Sister Jodelle. Sister Wiliamina. How nice to see you again. And that's Lord Rahl. Even to you, Sister Jodelle.'

'Lord Rahl,' Sister Jodelle said in a flat, mocking voice. 'So we've heard.'

Nathan waggled his fingers in greeting to the two young men standing out in the hall behind the two women. 'Vincent, Pierce, how good to see you two boy wizards again. Still trying to master prophecy, are you? Come for some advice? Maybe a lesson?'

'In a little over your head, aren't you, old man?' one of the young men asked.

Nathan's amusement vanished. He flicked his finger. The young man cried out and dropped to the floor.

'I told you, Pierce, it's Lord Rahl.' Nathan's voice turned as deadly as Clarissa had ever heard it. 'Don't test me again.'

Sister Willamina scowled back at Pierce, whispering a harsh admonishment as he staggered to his feet.

Nathan held his arm out in invitation. 'Won't you ladies please come in? Bring your boys, too.'

Clarissa didn't think they really looked like boys, as Nathan called them. She thought they looked to be in their late twenties, at least. The four warily stepped inside and stood in a bunch, hands clasped before them, while Nathan shut the door.

'Pretty risky, Na ... Lord Rahl, to let the four of us get this close,' Sister Jodelle said. 'I wouldn't think you would be this careless, now that you've somehow convinced some feeble-minded Sister to take pity on you and remove your Rada'Han.'

Nathan slapped his knee and howled with laughter. None of the other four so much as cracked a smile.

'Risky?' he asked, as his fit of laughter died out. 'Why, what have I to fear from the likes of you four? And I'll have you know that I took off the Rada'Han by myself. I think it only fair to tell you that while you foolishly chose to view me as a crazy old man, I was studying things you can't even fathom. While all of you Sisters –'

'Get to the point,' Sister Jodelle growled.

Nathan held up a finger. 'The point is, my fine people, that I have no ill will toward you or your leader, but I can weave webs you couldn't even understand, much less defend against, should you wish me harm. For example, I'm sure you detect the simple shields I've placed here and there, but there is more, hidden beyond those things you sense. Should you –'

Sister Jodelle lost her patience and cut him off again. 'We didn't come here to listen to the babble of a doddering old man. Do you think us stupid? We detected the pathetic magic you have so proudly laced about this place, and I can tell you with confidence there's not a bit of it that one of us alone couldn't slice apart with ease, while at the same time enjoying a bowl of soup!'

Vincent shoved the two Sisters aside. 'I've heard just about enough from this dried-up old jackass. He always was full of himself. It's about time he learned just who he's dealing with!'

Nathan made no move to defend himself as Vincent lifted his hands. Clarissa's eyes went wide in fright as the young man's fingers curled and his face twisted with hate. Clarissa covered her mouth in terror as light shot from Vincent's hands toward Nathan.

A brief whine sang through the air. The light from the young man scattered. There was a thump that Clarissa could feel in the floor as light flared through the other room.

When the sound and light cleared, Vincent was gone.

On the floor, where he had stood, Clarissa could see a small pile of white ash.

Nathan went to the wall and retrieved a broom leaned there, just behind a curtain. He opened the door and swept the ash out through the door into the hall.

'Thank you for coming, Vincent. Sorry you have to leave now. Let me show you out.'

With a flourish, Nathan swept the last of the ash out into the hall, creating a small cloud as he did so. He shut the door and turned back to the gaping gazes of the three people left.

'Now, as I was saying, you will be making the last mistake of your lives if you underestimate me or what it is you think me capable of. Your negligible intellects couldn't even understand it if I showed it to you.' Nathan's brow drew down in a way that frightened even Clarissa. 'Now, show proper respect and bow to the Lord Rahl.'

Reluctantly, the three people bowed, each touching a knee to the floor.

'What is it you want?' Sister Jodelle asked after she had straightened. Her voice had lost some of its edge.

'You can tell Jagang that I'm interested in peace.'

'Peace?' Sister Jodelle fussed back some of her dark hair. 'What position are you in that you could make such an offer?'

Nathan lifted his chin. 'I am Lord Rahl. I will soon be Master of D'Hara. I will be in command of the New World. I believe it is a war with the New World in which Jagang is embroiled.'

Sister Jodelle's eyes narrowed. 'What do you mean, you are soon to be the Master of D'Hara?'

'Just tell Jagang that his daring plan is about to be successfully completed; he will soon have eliminated the present Lord Rahl. Jagang has made a mistake, though. He forgot about me.'

'But … but …' Sister Jodelle sputtered, 'you aren't the Lord Rahl.'

Nathan leaned toward them with a sly smile. 'If Jagang succeeds, which as a prophet I can foresee he will, then I will be the Lord Rahl. I am a Rahl, born with the gift. All D'Harans will become bonded to me. As you know, that bond will prevent the dream walker from using his talent to take the New World.

'Jagang has made a mistake.' Nathan thunked Pierce on the head. 'He's been using amateur prophets, like this witless tadpole.'

Pierce turned red. 'I'm no amateur prophet!'

Nathan regarded him with a look of contempt. 'Really? Then why didn't you warn Jagang that by using prophecy to eliminate Richard Rahl, it would get him nowhere but into a worse predicament, because it would leave me to become the Lord Rahl, Master of D'Hara and most of the major powers in the New World? Did you warn him about that result? While Richard may be determined, he knows next to nothing about magic, whereas I know a great deal about it. A very great deal.'

Nathan towered over Pierce. 'Just ask Vincent. A real prophet would have realized the danger lurking behind my simple shields, waiting to be triggered if anyone attacked. Did you?'

Sister Willamina put out an arm, forcing Pierce back, and just in time, it appeared to Clarissa, as Nathan looked to be about to make another pile of white dust.

'What is it you want, Lord Rahl?' she asked.

'Jagang can either listen to my terms, or he can have really big trouble on his hands. Trouble a lot worse than Richard Rahl.'

'Terms?' Sister Jodelle drew the word out suspiciously.

'The present Lord Rahl is young and idealistic; he would never surrender to Jagang. I, on the other hand, am older and wiser. I know the foolishness of a war that would take the lives

552

of countless people. And to what purpose? Just for the right to put a name to the one who is the leader?

'Richard is a young fool who doesn't know how to use his power. I am not a young fool, and, as you saw, I know how to use my gift. I'm willing to entertain the possibility of letting Jagang rule the New World as he wishes.'

'And in return?'

Nathan casually flicked his hand. 'I simply want some of the spoils for myself – in return for my assistance. I will have the rule of D'Hara. Under his leadership, of course. I will be his man, running the affairs of D'Hara. Other than Jagang, no one will outrank me. Quite fair I think.'

The young Pierce was still white as a sheet, and trying to look invisible behind the two women. The two Sisters, on the other hand, were looking suddenly a lot less unhappy. They wore small, interested smiles.

'How would Jagang know that you could be trusted?'

'Trusted? Does he think I'm as stupid as the young Lord Rahl leading the New World right now? I saw what was done to Renwold. If I didn't rule D'Hara as Jagang wished, allowing him generous tribute, he might come in and try to crush us. Wars are expensive. I'd rather have the wealth for myself.'

Sister Jodelle smiled politely. 'And in the meantime? How do we know you really mean this?'

'So, it's assurance you want?' Nathan rubbed his chin as he stared up at the ceiling. 'There is a D'Haran army, of close to a hundred thousand men, north of here. You'll never find them without my help, until they descend on Jagang's expeditionary force. When Jagang finishes eliminating the present Lord Rahl, then this army's bond will transfer to me. They will be loyal to me. As soon as that happens, I will surrender that army to his, giving him even more men at arms. D'Harans have a long tradition of warring for plunder. They'll fit right in with Jagang's force.'

'Surrender an army,' Sister Jodelle said in a reflective tone.

'You see, my kind Sisters, Jagang is trying to use prophecy to win this war. In that, he has made a mistake; he is using wizards who are not real prophets. I could provide the expert service of a real prophet. His alternative is to have a real prophet as his enemy, and amateurs to aid him. The aid of amateurs is what got him into this … predicament, don't you see?

'For a small, insignificant slice of the spoils, I can get him out of it. I'm sure you can understand that after all those years under the care of you fine Sisters, I'd like to spend my few remaining years enjoying the pleasures of life.

'With my help, there will be no more resistance from the New World than that offered by Renwold. If Jagang should choose to be unreasonable, well, who knows, with a real prophet on the side of the New World, they might even win.'

Sister Jodelle studied Nathan's eyes. 'Yes. I see what you mean.'

Nathan held out his letter. 'Here. Give this to Jagang. It explains my proposal and terms, in return for my surrender of the New World. As I said, I'm sure he will find me much more reasonable than the present Lord Rahl; I know that there is no profit in war. One leader or another, it means little. Why should hundreds of thousands of people die over the name put to that leader?'

Both Sisters glanced around the luxurious room and smiled conspiratorially at Nathan.

'Why, you crafty old man,' Sister Jodelle said. 'And here, all this time, we thought you were just an old fool, living out your life down in your apartments. Well, Lord Rahl, we will pass your words along to Emperor Jagang. I think he will find them most interesting. Had the present Lord Rahl been so reasonable, he wouldn't be in his present, fatal difficulties.'

'All those years do give a man time to think.'

Sister Jodelle turned back from the door. 'I can't speak for the emperor, Lord Rahl, but I think he will be most pleased with this news. I think we can dare to see the end to this war, and the victory that will result in Jagang being the name put to the leader of all people.'

'I just want the killing to stop. It would profit us all, Sister. Oh, and tell Jagang that I am sorry about Vincent, but the boy wasn't really serving him well, anyway.'

Sister Jodelle shrugged. 'You're right, Lord Rahl, he wasn't.'

CHAPTER 50

Richard ran his fingers through his hair as he rested his forehead in his palms. He looked up when he heard someone enter the room. It was Kahlan.

His heart lifted at her smile, her bright green eyes, the lush fall of her thick hair, at how beautiful she was. He marveled at her beauty, and that she loved him.

The safety he felt in that love was something he had never imagined he would feel. He had always imagined being in love with someone, but he had never imagined the feeling of security and peace it would bring to his soul. If Shota ever did anything to harm that security ...

Kahlan carried a steaming bowl of soup. 'I thought you might like something to eat. You've been at this for a hand of days now; I think you need to get more sleep, too.'

He glanced at the big white bowl in her hands. 'Thanks.'

Her brow wrinkled. 'Richard, what's wrong? Your face is white as ashes.'

He leaned back in his chair and sighed. 'I feel a little sick.'

She turned white as ashes, too. 'Sick. Richard, it isn't –'

'No, it's not that. It's this book on the Temple of the Winds inquisition and trial. I almost wish I'd never found it.'

Kahlan leaned over as she set down the bowl. 'Here. Eat some of this.'

'What is it?' Richard asked, as he watched the lush curve of her cleavage rise and fall above the square neckline of her white Confessor's dress.

'Lentil porridge. Eat some. What have you found out?'

Richard sucked in through his mouth to cool the spoonful of porridge. 'I haven't translated much yet, it's taking forever, but from just the little bit I've been able to figure out, these people, these wizards … they … they executed all the wizards who sent away the Temple of the Winds. The temple team, they called them. Almost a hundred men.' He pulled a finger across his throat.

Kahlan sat on the edge of the table opposite him. 'What did they do to warrant death?'

Richard stirred the porridge. 'Well, for one thing, they left a way into the Temple of the Winds, as they were directed to do, but they made it so hard to get back into the temple that when these people wanted to get back in to retrieve some magic, in order to fight the war, they couldn't.'

'Kolo said that there were the red moons, that the temple sent the warning. You mean, the wizards of old were never able to answer the warning?'

'That wasn't the way it worked. They did get back in.' He waved his spoon for emphasis. 'In fact, that was the reason for the red moon. It was the second attempt to get in, to answer the red moons caused by the first person sent, that they failed at.'

Kahlan leaned toward him while Richard ate a spoonful of porridge. 'But this first person got in?'

'Oh yes, he got in. In that was the problem.'

Kahlan shook her head. 'I'm not following this.'

Richard set down his spoon and leaned back in his chair. He met her gaze.

'The temple team, who sent away the Temple of the Winds, were also the ones who placed the magic in it. You know about some of the terrible magical creations that were made in the war? Things made out of people? Like the mriswith? Like the dream walkers?

'Well, the people of the New World were fighting the people of the Old World, who wanted to eliminate magic, much as Jagang does today. These wizards who took the things of power to the safety of the temple were somewhat in sympathy with those in the Old World who wanted to eliminate magic. They thought that using people to create these terrible weapons was as evil as some of the very things they fought against.'

Fascinated, Kahlan leaned toward him. 'You mean they turned to the side of the enemy? They were really working for those in the Old World, to eliminate magic?'

'No, they weren't working to defeat the New World, or to stop all magic, but they felt that they viewed the whole matter on a wider scope than just the war, unlike the wizards in charge, here, at the Keep. They sought the middle ground. They decided that, to an extent, the war, and all their troubles, were related to the misuse of magic.

'They decided that something had to be done.'

Kahlan hooked some hair behind her ear. 'Done? Like what?'

'You know the way the Keep used to be full of wizards? The way wizards used to have both sides of the magic? The way the wizards of old wielded much more power than even Zedd does now as First Wizard? The way those born with the gift are more and more rare all the time?

'I think these wizards used the Temple of the Winds to withdraw some of the magic's power from this world – they locked it away in the underworld, where it couldn't be used to cause harm, as they saw it, in this world.'

Kahlan put a hand to her chest. 'Dear spirits. What gave them the right to decide this? They are not the Creator who gave all things, including magic.'

Richard smiled. 'The head of the inquisition said much the same thing. He demanded to know exactly what they had done.'

'And have you found the answer?'

'I haven't translated much, yet, and I don't understand the way the magic worked, but I think that what the temple team did was to lock away the Subtractive portion of the wizards' magic. It's the Subtractive part that was used to turn people into these weapons; with it, they took away parts of who these people were, the parts these wizards didn't want, and then with Additive Magic, the wizards added in the things they did want, so they could use these people as weapons.'

'What about you? You were born with both sides. If the power was locked away, how does that explain your gift? I, too, have an element of Subtractive Magic to my Confessor's power. Darken Rahl used Subtractive Magic, as do some of the

557

Sisters. There are creatures yet today who have some of this element to their magic.'

Richard wiped a weary hand across his face. 'I don't know. I'm not even positive about what I've told you. There's still most of this book to translate. I've only just begun.

'Even when I translate it all, I'm not sure it will provide the answers we want. This was an inquisition and trial; they weren't trying to teach me history. It was common knowledge at the time. They didn't need to explain it.

'What I'm beginning to think the temple team did was to halt Subtractive Magic's ability to be passed on to the offspring of wizards. Your magic isn't passed on from a wizard, so perhaps that's why it wasn't affected. Darken Rahl learned to use Subtractive Magic; he wasn't born with it. Therein, perhaps, lies the difference. Maybe they miscalculated how taking Subtractive Magic out of those born with the wizard's gift would affect the balance, and so didn't anticipate the way it would cause fewer and fewer to be born with the gift.

'Maybe they did know. Maybe that's what they wanted. Maybe that's why they were executed.'

'What about the red moons?'

'Well, when those in charge found all this out, they sent someone to undo what these wizards had done. They needed one with tremendous power, and conviction, hoping he would have enough strength to succeed. They sent the most zealous proponent of magic among them, a fanatic – the head prosecutor, a powerful wizard named Lothain – to the Temple of the Winds to undo the damage.'

Kahlan drew her lower lip between her teeth. 'What happened?'

'He got in, through Betrayer's Hall, just like you told me. It worked just as you said; Lothain entered, but in so doing, he betrayed them. I'm not sure what it was that he did; many of the words, I think, have to do with specific magic that I don't understand. But from what I gather, he reinforced what the wizards who sent the temple away had done, and made it even worse.

'He betrayed those in the New World. Because he had to

558

alter the way the Temple of the Winds held this magic, it set off the warnings of the red moons.

'When the Temple sent the red moons, and the call for aid, a wizard was sent. Because the temple was sending for help, the wizards were glad for the call, since it meant that they wouldn't have to enter through Betrayer's Hall. They thought they would be able to get in and at last remedy the problem. He never came back. They sent another, more powerful and experienced wizard. He never returned, either.

'Finally, in view of the seriousness of the situation, the First Wizard himself went to the Temple of the Winds.' Richard lifted the amulet at his chest. 'Baraccus.'

'Baraccus,' Kahlan breathed in wonder. 'Did he get into the temple?'

'They were never sure.' Richard pushed his thumb back and forth along the edge of the table. 'Baraccus came back in a dazed stupor. They followed after him, but he didn't react or respond to anything they said or did.

'He went into the First Wizard's enclave – his retreat – and left this there.' Richard held up the amulet at his chest, showing it to her. 'He came out, removed the rest of his outfit – these things I wear – and then walked to the edge of the rampart and jumped off the side of the mountain to his death.'

Kahlan sat back up straight while Richard cleared his throat and gathered his voice before going on.

'After that, the wizards abandoned any further attempt to get into the Temple of the Winds, to answer the call of the red moons, as impossible. They were never able to get in to undo the damage the temple team and then Lothain had done.'

Kahlan watched him with a sober look as he stared off at nothing. 'How did they know all this?'

Richard's fist tightened around the amulet at his chest.

'They used a Confessor. Magda Searus. The first Mother Confessor herself.'

'She lived in that time? She was there, in this war? I never knew that.'

Richard rubbed his fingertips across the furrows on his brow. 'Lothain wouldn't tell them what he had done. The wizards conducting the trial were the ones who ordered the creation of the Confessors. Magda Searus was the first. They knew that they wouldn't be able to torture the truth out of Lothain – they tried – so they took this woman, Magda Searus, created the magic of the Confessors, and instilled the power in her.

'She touched Lothain with her power and got the truth out of him. He confessed the extent of what the temple team had done, and what he had done.'

Richard looked away from her green eyes. 'The wizard who did this to Magda Searus, created the Confessors' power, was named Merritt. The tribunal was so pleased with the results of Merritt's conjuring that they commanded an order of Confessors to be created, and wizards assigned to safeguard them.

'Merritt became protector to Magda Searus, her wizard, in return for the life, the duty, to which he had condemned her, to which he had condemned all the descendants of Confessors to follow.'

The room fell silent. Kahlan was wearing her Confessor's face: the blank expression that showed nothing of her feelings. He didn't need to see an expression on her face to know her feelings. Richard pulled the porridge back and ate some more. It had cooled considerably.

'Richard,' Kahlan finally whispered, 'if these wizards, with all that power, with all that knowledge … if even they couldn't get into the Temple of the Winds after it sent its warning with the red moons, then …'

Her voice trailed off. Richard put words to the rest of it.

'Then how can I hope to?'

Richard ate lentil porridge as the uncomfortable silence dragged on.

'Richard,' Kahlan said in a quiet voice, 'if we don't get into the temple, then what the spirit showed me will come to pass. Death will sweep the land. Untold numbers of people will die.'

Richard nearly leaped to his feet and screamed at her that he knew that. Nearly screamed, asking what she expected him to do. Instead, he swallowed back the screams along with the porridge.

'I know,' he whispered.

He went back to eating his porridge in silence. When he had finished, and was sure he had composed himself, he went on.

'One of the temple team, a wizard named Ricker, made a

statement before they executed him.' Richard pulled the piece of paper with the translation out of the disorderly stack and read it to her. ' "I can no longer countenance what we do with our gift. We are not the Creator, nor are we the Keeper. Even a vexatious prostitute has the right to live her life." '

'What was he talking about?' Kahlan asked.

'I think that when the wizards used people – destroyed them – to create the things they needed to fight the war, I think they used people who were troublesome for one reason or another – people they didn't mind destroying. I've heard it said that a wizard must use people. I doubt they knew the ghastly origin of the maxim.'

He saw dismay haunting her eyes.

'Richard, do you think then, from what you've read, that it's hopeless? Do you think we can do nothing, then?'

Richard didn't know what to say. He reached over and clasped her hand. 'The temple team, before they were executed, said in their own defense that they hadn't sealed the temple away for good, as they might have easily done, but instead left a way in to answer the call. They said that if the need was truly great enough, it could still be entered.

'I will get in, Kahlan. I swear it.'

A small measure of relief came briefly to her beautiful eyes, but the haunted look settled back into them. Richard knew what she was thinking. It was the same as he'd wondered himself as he read of the madness that was the war, and of what people had done to each other.

'Kahlan, we don't use magic to destroy people for our own purposes. We use it to fight against a cause that murders helpless children. We fight for freedom from terror and killing.'

A small smile returned as she squeezed his hand.

They both looked up when they heard a knock on the open door.

It was Drefan. 'Can I come in? I'm not interrupting anything, am I?'

'No, it's all right,' Richard said. 'Come in.'

'I just wanted you to know that I ordered the carts, like you wanted. It's gotten to that point.'

Richard rubbed his fingertips across his forehead. 'How many?'

'A little over three hundred last night, if the reports are all in. As you suspected might be the case, the people can't handle that many dead anymore, and the numbers grow each day.'

Richard nodded. 'We can't let the dead wait. It could spread the plague even faster to have them rotting in the open air. They have to be buried as soon as they die. Tell the men I want the dead-carts sent out just as soon as they have it organized. I give them until sunset.'

'I already told them. As you say, we can't allow bodies infected with the plague to go untended; it could make the plague worse.'

'It can get worse?' Richard mocked.

Drefan didn't answer.

'I'm sorry,' Richard said. 'That wasn't called for. Have you found anything that is of any use?'

Drefan tugged down the sleeves of his white shirt. 'Richard, there is no cure for the plague. At least, I know of none. The only hope is to stay healthy. Speaking of which, it isn't healthy to sit in here all day and most of the night. You aren't getting enough sleep, again. I can see it in your eyes. I've warned you about that before. And you need to walk around, get some air.'

Richard was sick of trying to translate the book, and sick of the things he found out when he succeeded. He flipped it closed and pushed back his chair.

'This is doing no good, anyway. Let's go for that walk you suggested.' Richard yawned as he stretched. 'And what have you been doing to keep busy,' he asked Kahlan, 'while I've been shut up in this stuffy room?'

Kahlan cast a furtive glance at Drefan. 'I – I've been helping Drefan and Nadine.'

'Helping them? Helping them do what?'

Drefan smoothed the ruffles on the front of his shirt. 'Kahlan has been helping with the staff. Some of them are … ill.'

Richard looked from Kahlan's eyes to Drefan's. 'The plague is in the palace?'

'I'm afraid so. Sixteen of them have come down sick. A few are common illnesses, the rest –'

Richard heaved a weary sigh. 'I see.'

Raina was standing guard outside his room. She straightened when Richard came through the door.

'Raina, we're going for a walk. I suppose you'd better come along, or I'll never hear the end of it from Cara.'

Raina smiled as she brushed back a wisp of dark hair. She knew he was right, and was obviously glad he was cooperating.

'Lord Rahl,' Raina said, 'I didn't want to disturb you while you were working, but the captain of the city guard came by with a report.'

'I know. I heard. Three hundred people died last night.'

Raina's leather creaked as she shifted her weight. 'That, too, but they wanted me to tell you that they found another woman last night. She was cut up like the other four.'

Richard closed his eyes as he wiped a hand across his mouth. He noticed that he hadn't remembered to shave that day. 'Dear spirits. Don't we have enough people dying without some madman going around killing more of them?'

'Was this one a prostitute, like the others?' Drefan asked.

'The captain said he wasn't positive, but he was pretty sure she was.'

Drefan shook his head with disgust. 'You'd think he'd be worried about the plague, if not getting caught. The plague is running wild among the prostitutes, more so than among the populace at large.'

Richard caught sight of Berdine coming up the hall. 'As much as I'd like to do something about it, we have bigger worries.' He turned to Raina. 'When we get back, tell the captain that I want his men to spread the word among those women that there's a killer among them, and that for their own safety we hope they will cease their profession, at least for the time being.

'I'm sure the soldiers will know where to find all the prostitutes,' he added under his breath. 'Have them get the word out at once. If these women don't stop selling their bodies, they're likely to find themselves in the company of the wrong customer. Their last customer.'

Richard waited until Berdine reached them. 'Aren't you supposed to be up in the Keep taking your turn guarding the sliph?' Richard asked her.

Berdine shrugged. 'I went up there, to relieve Cara, but she said she wanted to stay for another watch.'

Richard raked back his hair. 'Why would she want to do that?'

Berdine shrugged again. 'She didn't say.'

Kahlan took his arm. 'I think it's the rats.'

'What?'

'I think she's trying to prove something to herself.' Kahlan hesitated. 'Cara doesn't like rats.'

'I don't blame her,' Raina muttered.

'Filthy creatures,' Drefan put in. 'I don't blame her, either.'

'If any of you tease her about it,' Kahlan warned, 'you will answer to me – when Cara's done with you. It's not funny.'

No one looked in the mood to challenge Kahlan, nor were any of them in a mood to see anything as funny.

'Where are you going?' Berdine asked.

'We're going for a walk,' Richard said. 'You've probably been sitting as much as I have. If you'd like, come along.'

Nadine came around the corner and caught sight of them just as they started out. 'What's going on?'

'Nothing,' Richard said. 'How are you doing, Nadine?'

Nadine smiled. 'Fine, thank you. I've been busy smoking sick rooms, as Drefan asked.'

'We were just going out for a walk,' Kahlan said. 'You've been working hard, Nadine. Why don't you come along with us?'

Richard frowned at Kahlan. She didn't look back at him.

Nadine studied Kahlan's eyes for a moment. 'Sure. I'd like that.'

The six of them made their way through the marble halls, past imposing tapestries and elegant furniture, and across sumptuous carpets on their way toward the main palace gates. Soldiers on patrol bowed or clapped fists over heart as the six of them passed. The staff Richard saw going about their business seemed to be in a state of shock. He saw people weeping as they hurried about their tasks.

Before they made the door, they encountered Tristan

Bashkar. Richard was in no mood to speak with the Jarian ambassador. Tristan sauntered to a halt before them. There would be no avoiding him this time.

Tristan bowed his head. 'Mother Confessor, Lord Rahl, I'm glad I ran into you.'

'What do you want, Tristan?' Kahlan asked in a level tone.

He watched her cleavage as she spoke. His gaze moved to Richard. 'I want to know –'

Richard cut him off. 'Did you come to offer Jara's surrender?'

Tristan pulled his coat back and rested his fist on his hip. 'The time I was allotted is not yet expired. I'm concerned about this plague. You're Lord Rahl. You're supposed to be running everything, now. I want to know what you're going to do about the plague.'

Richard restrained himself. 'What we can.'

Tristan glanced to Kahlan's chest again. 'Well, I'm sure that you can understand that I need assurance.' His gaze returned to Richard. A sly smile spread on his face. 'After all, how can I, in good conscience, surrender my land to a man overseeing what may prove to be the greatest cataclysm in the history of the Midlands? No offense intended. The skies speak the truth to me. I'm sure you can understand my position.'

Richard leaned toward the pompous ambassador. 'You are rapidly running out of time, ambassador. You had better be prepared to surrender Jara soon, or I will see to it – my way. Now, if you'll excuse us, we're going to get some fresh air. It suddenly stinks in here.'

Tristan Bashkar's expression darkened.

When his eyes turned toward Kahlan again, Richard yanked the knife from Tristan's belt scabbard before he could so much as blink. Everyone froze.

Richard pressed the point to the man's chest.

'And if I ever again catch your lecherous eyes anywhere on Kahlan but her face, I'll cut out your heart.'

Richard turned and loosed the knife, burying it in a round oak ball atop a nearby newel. The *twang* echoed through the marble halls. Without waiting for a response, he took Kahlan by the arm and marched away, his golden cloak billowing out behind. Kahlan's face was red. The two Mord-Sith followed, grinning broadly. Drefan smiled, too, as he followed after. Nadine showed no reaction.

CHAPTER 51

In the distance, a dog barked as Richard led them up the cobbled alley. He brought his escorts to a halt outside the small yard behind the Anderson family's home. The yard was still cluttered with cutoffs, wood scraps, shavings, stickered lumber, and the two carving benches.

Richard heard neither the sound of wood being worked nor voices. He swung open the gate and made his way through the clutter. The workshop remained silent. A knock produced no response. Richard pushed open one of the double doors and called out. There was no reply.

'Clive!' Richard called again. 'Darby! Erling! Is anyone home?'

Old chairs and templates still hung from pegs on the dusty walls, and the cobwebs still hung in all the corners. Upstairs, instead of the aroma of meat pies and boiling turnips, like the last time Richard had been to the Anderson home, there was the heavy stench of death.

In one of the chairs he had made sat Clive Anderson. He was dead. In his arms, he was holding the stiff corpse of his wife.

Richard stood stunned at the sight. Behind, he heard Kahlan let out a mournful cry.

Drefan went to the bedrooms. After a brief look, he returned and shook his head.

Richard stood staring at the dead husband and wife. He tried to imagine Clive's misery as he sat there, sick with the plague, holding his dead wife in his arms – his dreams and hopes dead in his arms.

Drefan eased a hand under Richard's arm and pulled him away.

'Richard, there's nothing to be done. We'd best go and have a dead-cart sent.'

Kahlan pressed her face against his shoulder as she wept. He saw the stricken look on the faces of Berdine and Raina. He saw their fingers find one another and curl together – a furtive comforting touch. Nadine glanced away from the rest of them. Richard felt sudden sorrow for her; she was alone among them. Thankfully, Drefan rested a comforting hand on her shoulder. The room droned with painful silence.

Richard held Kahlan to him as they went down the stairs. The others followed behind. When they reached the workshop, he took a breath, at last. The stench upstairs had nearly gagged him.

Just then, Erling, the grandfather, walked through the door. He started at seeing the six people standing in his workshop.

'I'm sorry, Erling,' Richard said. 'We didn't mean to invade your home. We came to check. We came ...'

Erling nodded distantly. 'My boy's dead. Hattie, too. I had to ... go out. I couldn't carry them by myself.'

'We'll have a cart sent right away. There are some soldiers on the next street over. I'll send them right away to help you.'

Erling nodded again. 'That would be kind of you.'

'The ... rest of them? Are they –'

Erling's bloodshot eyes turned up. 'My wife, daughter, son, his wife, Darby, and little Lily – all dead.' His mouth worked as his eyes watered up. 'Beth, she recovered. Got well again, she did. I couldn't care for her. I just now took her to Hattie's sister. So far, their home is still sound.'

Richard laid a hand gently on Erling's arm. 'I'm so sorry. Dear spirits, I'm so sorry.'

Erling nodded. 'Thank you.' He cleared his throat. 'Long as I've lived, you'd think it would be me, not the young'uns. The spirits weren't fair in this. Not fair at all.'

'I know,' Richard said. 'They're at a place of peace now. We all go there, sooner or later. They'll be with you again.'

Out in the alley, after they had made sure that Erling didn't need anything, they all paused to gather their wits.

'Raina,' Richard said, 'please run over to the next street, where we saw those soldiers. Get them over here right now. Tell them to get those bodies out of there for Erling.'

'Of course,' she said before dashing away. Her dark braid flew behind as she ran.

'I don't know what to do,' Richard whispered. 'What do you do for someone who has just lost his whole family? Everyone he loved? I felt a fool. I didn't know what to say.'

Drefan squeezed Richard's shoulder. 'You said the right things, Richard. You did.'

'He took comfort in your words, Richard,' Nadine said. 'That was all you could do.'

'All I can do,' Richard repeated as he stared off.

Kahlan squeezed his hand. Berdine's hand touched his. He gripped it. The three of them stood linked in shared sorrow.

Richard paced as he waited for Raina to return. The sun was almost down. It would be dark before they got back to the palace. The least he could do was wait until Erling had help getting his dead son and daughter-in-law out of the house.

Kahlan and Berdine stood close together, leaning against the wall beside the Andersons' yard. Drefan, hands clasped behind his back, looking to be lost in thought, strolled a ways back down the alley. Nadine went to the other side of the alley, alone, and leaned against the clapboard wall.

Richard paced as he thought about the Temple of the Winds and the magic stolen by Jagang's order. Richard could think of no way to stop this slaughter. When he thought about Tristan Bashkar's eyes on Kahlan, Richard's blood boiled.

Richard paused. His head came up. Nadine was behind him. He had the oddest sensation.

The hair on the back of his neck stiffened.

Richard heard the air whine as he spun.

The world slowed. Sound dragged. He floated as he moved. The air felt as thick as mud. Everyone seemed a statue in his vision.

Time was his.

His arm stretched out as he drifted ahead. He commanded

the thickness of the air. In the eerie silence, he could hear the feathers singing. He could hear the hiss of blade.

Time was his.

Nadine's startled blink took forever.

He closed his fist.

With a slam of sound, the world crashed back with a wild rush.

In his fist, Richard held a bolt from a crossbow.

The blade wasn't three inches from Nadine's wide eyes.

A fraction of a second more and it would have killed her. That fraction of a second had been an hour to him.

'Richard,' Nadine panted, 'how did you catch that arrow? I hope you can understand that it gives me the creeps. Not that I'm complaining,' she was quick to add.

Drefan was there, his jaw hanging open. 'How did you do that?' he whispered.

'I'm a wizard, remember?' Richard said as he turned, looking in the direction from which the arrow had come. He thought he saw movement.

Kahlan clutched a trembling Nadine. 'Are you all right?'

Nadine nodded and let out a belated, frightened cry as Kahlan pulled her to her in a reassuring embrace.

Richard's eyes locked on a movement as his fist snapped the arrow in half. He took off, running. Berdine raced after him.

Richard turned as he ran. 'Find some soldiers! I want this whole area closed off! I want him caught!'

Berdine cut down a street, going after soldiers. Richard ran like the wind on a storm. Rage inundated him. Someone had tried to kill Nadine.

In that instant, Nadine wasn't a woman sent by Shota to marry him, a woman who was causing him trouble; in that instant, she was simply an old friend from home. The full fury of the magic took him.

Buildings flashed by. Dogs barked as he raced past. People in the alley cried out and dived for safety. A woman screamed as she cowered against a small, crooked storage building.

Richard vaulted the low board fence where he had seen the movement. In mid-leap, he drew his sword. The air rang with the unique sound of steel.

He rolled as he landed, coming to his feet with the sword in both hands. He found himself face-to-face with a white goat. There was no man there. A crossbow lay on the ground, between the board fence and a squat goat shed.

Richard looked around in all directions. Sheets and shirts hung from lines. A woman, her hair wrapped in a blue scarf, stood on a balcony beyond the flapping laundry.

Richard slid his sword back into its scabbard and cupped his hands around his mouth. 'Did you see a man here?' he yelled up at the woman.

She lifted her arm, pointing off to her right. 'I saw someone running that way,' she called from the distance.

Richard dashed off in the direction the woman had pointed. The alley narrowed. Beyond the tunnel of buildings, the passageway opened onto a street. He looked both ways.

He seized the arm of a young woman. 'A man came through here. Which way did he go?'

In fright she tried to pull away, at the same time holding her hat on with her other hand. 'There be people all about. Which man?'

Richard released her arm. Up the street to his left, he saw a man righting an overturned handcart full of fresh greens. The man looked up when Richard skidded to a panting halt before him.

'What did he look like? The man who ran through here – what did he look like?'

The man straightened his broad-rimmed hat. 'Don't know.' He pointed. 'I was looking for a good spot. I heard the sound as my cart fell over. I saw a dark shape, running up that way.'

Richard ran on. The ancient part of the city branched into a warren of alleys, streets, and twisting passageways. Only by keeping track of the golden glow in the western sky could he keep his bearings. That didn't mean, though, that the man he chased had run in a specific direction. He was probably just running, trying to get away.

Richard came across a patrol of a dozen soldiers. Before they had time to salute, he was talking.

'A man came running through here, somewhere. Did any of you see him?'

'We saw no one running. What did he look like?'

'I don't know. He attacked us with a crossbow and then ran. I want him found. Spread out and start searching.'

Before they could be on their way, Raina came running up the street with a good fifty men.

'Did you see where he went?' she asked, gasping for breath.

'No. I lost him in here somewhere. I want all of you to spread out and find him.'

One of the soldiers, a sergeant, spoke up. 'Lord Rahl, a man who wants to escape would make himself obvious by running. A man with any sense at all would simply round a corner and walk away.'

The sergeant gestured back up the street to make his point. There were people everywhere going about their business, although a good many were staring at the excitement on their street. Any number of them could have been the man he was chasing.

'Any idea at all what this assassin looks like?'

Richard shook his head in frustration. 'I never got a look at him.' He raked back his hair as he caught his breath. 'Split up. Half of you go back in the direction we came from. Question everyone you can find, to see if anyone got a look at him, at a man running. He may be walking now, but until he got somewhere along in here he was running.'

Raina, Agiel in hand, took up her defensive position close beside him.

'The rest of you come with me,' Richard said. 'We'll pick up some more men. I want to keep searching. Maybe we'll come across someone walking and he'll panic and try to run again. If he does, I want him. Alive.'

It was late in the night by the time they returned to the Confessors' Palace. Soldiers there were already on high alert. Men stood with swords and battle-axes to hand, arrows nocked, and spears leveled. Others patrolled the expansive grounds. A mouse wouldn't have escaped their intense scrutiny.

As Kahlan, Berdine, Raina, Drefan, and Nadine accompanied him into the gathering hall inside, Richard saw Tristan

Bashkar waiting there, hands clasped behind his back as he paced. He halted and looked up when he heard them coming.

Richard drifted to a stop as the contrite-looking ambassador approached. Those escorting Richard gathered in a knot behind him, except Kahlan, who stood close at his side. With a hand in the air, Tristan hailed them.

'Lord Rahl, may I have a word with you, please?'

Richard swept his gaze over the man, noticing that he didn't rest his hand on a hip so as to show off his fancy knife.

Richard held up a finger. 'One moment, please.'

Richard turned a little to the rest of them. 'It's late. We have a lot of work to do, so I want you to get some rest. Berdine, I want you to go up to the Keep and stand guard with Cara tonight.'

Berdine frowned. 'Both of us?'

Richard scowled. 'Isn't that what I said? Yes, both of you. With this trouble, I don't want to take any chances.'

'I will guard the Mother Confessor's room, then,' Raina said.

'No,' Richard lifted a thumb. 'I want you guarding Nadine's room. She was the one who was attacked.'

'Yes, Lord Rahl,' Raina stammered. 'I'll see to setting up a guard of soldiers outside the Mother Confessor's room, then.'

'If I wanted soldiers around Kahlan's room, I'd have told you so, now wouldn't I?' Raina's face reddened. 'I want all the soldiers doing their jobs patrolling the entrances, the palace grounds, and a perimeter around the grounds. Every one of them! The danger is from out there, not in here. Kahlan is perfectly safe inside the palace. I don't want men who should be guarding outside instead sitting on their bottoms around Kahlan's room inside. I'll not have it, do you hear me?'

'But, Lord Rahl –'

'Don't question me. I'm not in the mood.'

Kahlan touched his arm. 'Richard,' she whispered, 'are you sure that –'

'Someone tried to kill Nadine. They nearly succeeded. Or did some of you miss the significance of that? I'll not take any more chances. I want her protected, and I don't want to hear any more arguments. Drefan, I want you to start carrying a sword at once. Healers are a target.'

Everyone stared at the floor in silence.

'Good.' Richard turned his glare on Tristan. 'What is it?'

Tristan spread his hands. 'Lord Rahl, I just wanted to say that I'm sorry. I realize I seemed insensitive, but I've been worried about the people here who are sick and dying. It set my nerves on edge. I meant to cause no ill will between us. I hope you will accept my apology.'

Richard studied Tristan's eyes. 'Yes, of course. Apology accepted, and I'm sorry that I lost my temper. I, too, have been out of sorts.' Richard put a hand on Nadine's shoulder. 'Someone tried to kill one of my healers – a person devoted to helping others. People are beginning to blame healers because the plague continues to spread. I can't allow harm to come to people who are only trying their best to help.'

'Yes, of course. You are most kind to accept my apology. Thank you, Lord Rahl.'

'Just don't forget, ambassador, that your time runs out tomorrow.'

Tristan bowed. 'I realize that, and you will know my stand by tomorrow, Lord Rahl. You have my word. Good night, then.'

Richard rounded on the rest of them. 'We have a lot of work to do tomorrow. It's very late. As Drefan is constantly reminding me, we need to get some sleep. You all have your orders. Any questions?'

Each answered with a silent shake of the head.

Two hours after they had returned to the palace, and Richard had sent them all to bed, Kahlan thought she saw something move in her room.

The lamp on the far wall was turned down low. The clouds hid the moon, so there was no light coming in the glassed doors to the balcony. The thick carpets silenced the sound of footsteps, if there were any. The weak flame from the lamp was all that betrayed the shape she thought she saw.

Another motion came from across the room – a hint of shadowed movement. She hadn't seen a person enter her rooms; it could be nothing other than her imagination. The day had left her in an edgy state.

With the next silent step, there was no doubt: there was someone in her room. Someone slipped ever closer to her bed. As furtive as the movements were, he had closed the distance in remarkably short order.

Kahlan didn't move a muscle as she saw the knife glint in the dim lamplight. She held her breath.

A powerful arm stabbed hatefully into her bed. The arm rose and fell, stabbing in quick succession.

With a finger, Richard pushed on the balcony door. It swung open on silent hinges. Berdine glided across the room the instant Richard gave her a hand signal. When she was in place, he tapped the glass once. Berdine turned up the wick on the lamp.

Tristan Bashkar straightened beside Kahlan's bed, knife in hand, panting with the effort of what he had just been doing.

'Toss down the knife, ambassador,' Richard said in a quiet tone.

Tristan spun the knife in his fingers, seizing the blade in preparation to throw it.

Berdine's Agiel to the back of his neck dropped him instantly. She pressed the Agiel down on his shoulder to support herself as she bent and picked up the knife. Tristan howled in pain.

Berdine straightened, coming up with three knives.

'You were right, Richard,' Drefan said from behind.

'I can't believe it,' Nadine said as she stepped up into the lamplight.

'Believe it,' General Kerson said as he, too, came in from the balcony. 'I'd say Tristan Bashkar has nullified his immunity as a diplomat.'

Richard put two fingers between his lips and whistled. Raina charged through the door ahead of a large contingent of D'Haran soldiers bristling steel. Two of them lit more lamps.

Richard hooked his thumbs behind his belt as he stood beside Kahlan, a towering black form defined with gold trim on his tunic and silver ornaments, buckles, and wristbands, watching the soldiers haul Tristan to his feet.

'You were right, Richard,' she said. 'He attacked Nadine to draw the guard off me. It was me he was after all along.'

For a while, she had thought he had lost his mind. His performance had convinced everyone, including Tristan.

'Thanks for believing me,' Richard whispered.

When he had first told her what he was doing, Kahlan had suspected that Richard had accused Tristan because of the incident earlier. Kahlan had not put words to it, but she had wondered if Richard was simply acting out of jealousy.

Since she had told him what Shota said, he had now twice displayed jealousy, something she had never before seen from him. He didn't have any reason to be jealous, but Shota's words played on his mind, casting in doubt.

Whenever she looked at Nadine, Kahlan understood his feelings. Whenever she saw Nadine so much as standing near him, Kahlan felt the hot claws of jealousy rake through her insides.

She knew that Shota and the spirit had told her the truth. She knew that she would not have Richard. Her mind tried to put rational thought to it, to tell her that it would work out, that they would be together, but her heart knew better. Richard would marry Nadine. Kahlan would marry another man.

Richard refused to believe it. At least, he said he refused to believe it. She wondered.

In her mind's eye, Kahlan saw Clive Anderson, sitting dead in his chair, holding his dead wife. In comparison to the tragedy that had befallen the Anderson family and so many others, what price was an unhappy marriage? Wouldn't it be worth that price, if it would stop the appalling suffering and death?

Nadine slipped up next to Richard on the other side. 'Drawing the guard off Kahlan or not, I'd have been dead. Thank you, Richard. I've never seen anything like the way you caught that arrow right in front of my face.'

Richard gave her a quick, one-armed hug. 'Nadine, you've said thank you enough times. You'd have done the same for me.'

Kahlan felt those hot claws again. She suppressed the feeling. As Shota had said, if she loved him, she would want him to have at least the small comfort of it being someone he knew.

'But what if he had killed me? I mean, if he just wanted to

draw the guard away from Kahlan, what if he had killed me? What good would that have done him?'

'He knows I have the gift, and counted on that. If he had happened to kill you, it might still have worked, or he could have faked something similar with Drefan, reinforcing our belief that the target was healers and not Kahlan.'

'Why didn't he just shoot Kahlan with the arrow?'

Richard watched the one-sided struggle on the other side of Kahlan's bed. 'Because he likes to use that knife of his. He wanted to feel it when he killed her.'

His words gave Kahlan a chill. She knew Tristan; Richard might be right. Tristan would have gotten pleasure from it.

The soldiers wrestled Tristan's arms behind his back as they hauled him to his feet. He was still full of fight, but he was grossly overpowered. More lamps were lit as the room filled with soldiers.

Kahlan felt embarrassed to have all those people in her bedroom. She guessed it was because the Mother Confessor's rooms had always been a private sanctuary. A safe place.

A man had invaded that sanctuary. A man intent on stabbing her to death.

'What's this all about?' Tristan shouted.

'Oh, we just thought we'd like to watch a man stabbing a nightdress stuffed with tow,' Richard said.

General Kerson inspected the prisoner to assure himself that Berdine had found all his weapons. When he was satisfied, he turned to Richard.

'What would you like done, Lord Rahl?'

'Behead him.'

Kahlan turned in shock. 'Richard, you can't do that.'

'You saw him. He thought he was killing you.'

'But he didn't. He only stabbed my empty bed. The spirits mark a difference between intent and deed.'

'He tried to kill Nadine, too.'

'I did no such thing!' Tristan shouted. 'That wasn't me – I haven't even left the palace tonight!'

Richard turned a cold glare on Tristan. 'You have white hairs on your knees. White goat hairs. You knelt behind that fence while you aimed the crossbow, and got the goat hairs on you.'

Kahlan glanced down, and saw that Richard was right.

'You're crazy! I never did!'

'Richard,' Kahlan said, 'he didn't kill Nadine, either. He may have tried, but he didn't. You can't execute him for intent.'

Richard closed his fist around the amulet at his chest, the amulet representing the dance with death. No mercy.

The general's eyes left Kahlan and returned to Richard. 'Lord Rahl?'

'Richard,' Kahlan insisted, 'you can't.'

Richard glared at Tristan. 'He killed those women. He sliced them up with his fancy knife. You like to cut people, don't you, Tristan?'

'What are you talking about? I never killed anyone – except in war!'

'No,' Richard said, 'and you didn't try to kill Kahlan, and you didn't try to kill Nadine, and there aren't white goat hairs on your pants.'

Tristan's panicked brown eyes turned to Kahlan. 'Mother Confessor, I didn't kill you, I didn't kill her. You said it yourself, the spirits mark a difference between intent and deed. I didn't kill anyone. You can't let him do this!'

Kahlan recalled the whispers about Tristan, the whispers that when he went into battle he drew his knife instead of his sword, and that he got sadistic pleasure from cutting people.

Those women were killed for sadistic pleasure.

'What was it you told me, Tristan? That you often had to resort to the charms of coin for the company of a woman? And that if you broke our rules, you would expect to be subjected to our choice of punishment?'

'What about a trial? I've killed no one! Intent is not the same as deed!'

'And what was your intent, Tristan?' Richard asked. 'Why did you intend to kill Kahlan?'

'It wasn't because I wanted to. It wasn't for pleasure, as you think. It was to save lives.'

Richard lifted an eyebrow. 'Killing to save lives?'

'You've killed people. You don't do it for the pleasure of killing, but to save the lives of innocent people. That's all I'm guilty of – trying to save innocent lives.

'The Imperial Order sent representatives to the royal palace in Sandilar. They told us to join with them, or die. Javas Kedar, our star guide, told me I must watch the skies for a sign.

'When the red moons came, and the plague started, I knew what they meant. I was going to kill the Mother Confessor in order to try to gain favor with the Order, so that they wouldn't send the plague to us, too. I was only trying to save my people.'

Richard's eyes turned to Kahlan. 'How far is Sandilar?'

'A month, there and back. Maybe a few days less.'

Richard looked back at the general. 'Get some officers together to take command of the Jarian forces and capital. Have them take Tristan's head to the royal family and tell them that he was executed for attempting to kill the Mother Confessor.

'The officers are to offer Jara surrender to D'Hara under the peaceful terms already offered. It's a month, there and back. The king himself is to return with the surrender documents. I expect him, and the D'Haran guard sent to accompany him, back here within one month from tomorrow.

'Tell the king that if they don't surrender, and our men don't return safely, I will personally ride into Sandilar at the head of an army and I will behead every member of the royal family. We will then conquer Jara and occupy the capital. The occupation will not be friendly.'

General Kerson clapped a fist to the chain mail over his heart. 'It will be as you say, Lord Rahl.'

'Richard,' Kahlan whispered, 'what if what he says is true – that he didn't kill those women? I could touch him with my Confessor's power, and we would know for sure.'

'No! I'll not have you touching him, or hearing the things he did to those women. He's a monster; I don't want you to have to touch him.'

'But what if he's telling the truth? What if he didn't kill those women?'

Richard's fist gripped the amulet at his chest. 'I'm not having him put to death for the murder of those women. He tried to kill you. I saw it. As far as I'm concerned, the intent is the same as the deed. He is going to pay for the intent, the same as he would have paid for the deed.'

Richard turned a cold, dark glare back to the soldiers. 'Last night alone, three hundred people died of the plague. He would have joined with the murderers who caused it. I want the men on their way to Jara first thing in the morning, and I want his head to go with them. You have your orders. Get him out of here.'

CHAPTER 52

When she saw Drefan coming from the other direction, Kahlan set down the basket of clean bandages and rags she was carrying. Even though Richard had only ordered it as part of his ruse to convince Tristan that his plan was working, Drefan was still wearing a sword. Perhaps it wasn't such a bad idea. Some people were beginning to resent healers because they spoke out against the potions and cures being sold on the streets.

She brushed back her hair. 'How are they?'

Drefan sighed as he glanced back up the hall. 'One died last night. Most are worse. We have six new ones today.'

'Dear spirits,' she whispered, 'what is to happen to us?'

Drefan lifted her chin. 'We will persevere.'

Kahlan nodded. 'Drefan, if so many of the staff are coming down sick, and so many have died already, what good is this infernal smoke doing? I'm sick of breathing it.'

'The smoke is doing no good for the plague.'

Kahlan blinked up at him. 'Then why must we keep doing it?'

Drefan smiled sadly. 'The people think it helps keep the plague from being worse. It makes them feel better that we're doing something, and that there is hope. If we stop, then they will think there is no hope.'

'Is there? Is there any hope?'

'I don't know,' he whispered.

'Have you heard last night's report yet?'

He nodded. 'In the last week the number of dead has continued to rise. Last night it was up to over six hundred.'

Kahlan looked away despondently. 'I wish we could do something.'

Shota had told her that a way would come. The spirit had told her that a way would come. She couldn't bear the thought of losing Richard, but she also couldn't bear the thought of all the people who were dying.

'Well,' Drefan said, 'I'm going to make my rounds through the city.'

Kahlan clasped his forearm. He flinched. It was a reaction that she, as a Confessor, was used to. She took her hand back. 'I know you can do nothing to stop it, but thank you for all your aid anyway. Just your words help those living to have hope.'

'A healer's best aid, words. Most of the time it's all we can do to help. Most people think being a healer means healing people. That actually happens rarely. I learned a long time ago that being a healer means living with pain and suffering.'

'How's Richard? Have you seen him this morning?'

'He's in his office. He looked fine. I made him get some sleep.'

'Good. He needed rest.'

Drefan's blue eyes searched hers. 'He did what he had to with that man who tried to kill you, but I know that despite how resolute he appeared, it was a terribly hard thing for him to do. Killing a man, even one who richly deserves it, is not something that comes easily to Richard.'

'I know,' Kahlan said. 'I know that condemning a man to death weighs heavily on him. I, myself, have had to order the deaths of people. In a time of peace, you have the luxury of order, but in war you must act. Hesitation is death.'

'And have you told that to Richard?'

Kahlan smiled. 'Of course I have. He knows he did what he had to, and that those of us close to him understand. In his place I would have done the same, and I told him so.'

'Someday, I hope to have a woman of half your strength.' Drefan smiled. 'To say nothing of your beauty. Well, I must be off.'

Kahlan watched him walk away. His trousers were still too tight. She blushed at the thought, and turned back to her work.

Nadine was in the sick room, tending to people in two rows of beds. The infirmary held twenty beds, and they were all full, with more people on blankets on the floor. There were others sick in other rooms.

'Thanks,' Nadine said, when Kahlan set down the clean things she had brought. Nadine was putting herbs in pots, making teas. Other women who tended the sick were changing sheets, cleaning and wrapping open sores, or serving tea to the patients.

Nadine plucked a cloth from the basket, dipped it in a basin of water, wrung it out, and laid it across the forehead of a moaning woman. Nadine patted the woman's shoulder.

'There you go, dear. How does that feel?'

The woman managed only a weak smile and nod.

Kahlan did the same for several more people, dabbing a cool, damp cloth to their sweaty faces, offering soft words of comfort.

'You could be a healer,' Nadine said as she paused beside Kahlan. 'You have a kind touch.'

'That's the only thing I know to do. I couldn't heal anyone.'

Nadine leaned close. 'And do you think I am?'

Kahlan glanced around the room. 'I see what you mean. But at least you have devoted your life to helping people. My life is devoted to duty. To fighting.'

'What do you mean?'

'In the end, I am a warrior. My duty is to hurt people in order to save others. It is left to people like you to heal those remaining, when people like me are finished fighting.'

Nadine stood close to her. 'Sometimes, I wish I was a warrior, and could fight to end the suffering, so that there wouldn't be so many wounded for the healers to tend to.'

Kahlan finally had to leave the room. She couldn't stand the stink, and the smoke was making her sick. Nadine felt the same, and went with her. They both slid their backs down the wall and sat on the floor.

'I feel helpless,' Nadine said. 'Back home, if someone had a headache, I'd give him something and he'd get to feeling better. If a woman was pregnant, I'd help settle her stomach, or

I'd help deliver the baby when it was time. It seemed I was always helping people.

'This is different. All I do is comfort people who are going to die, and wonder the whole time if it will be me on the bed tomorrow. I don't know what to do for any of them. I feel totally useless. I wish I'd come here to help these people, instead of watching them die.'

'I know,' Kahlan whispered. 'It must have been a lot more satisfying to help a woman deliver a baby.'

Nadine stared off in thought. 'Sometimes a woman would tell me that it seemed like it would never happen, that it seemed unreal. She'd wait, knowing it would happen, but never really believing it, dreading the things she'd heard about how hard it would be. Dreading the pain. Sometimes they think things will change, like they'll wake up one day and not be pregnant, or something.

'Then, the baby would come. Suddenly, she'll be in a panic. The time has come. She'll be terrified that it's really happening, at last. Sometimes they'll scream just from that fear, the fear of the pain. That's when I can help them. I'm there with them. I reassure them that it will be all right.

'For the first time, for some of them, they finally believe it's happening. I guess it's only natural to dread such a profound change in their lives. Until it's over, until the day is upon them, some of them are miserable with dread.'

Together, in the silence of the hall, they sat, resting, listening to the moans from the sick room.

'Nadine, you still think you will end up marrying Richard, don't you?'

Nadine glanced over, scratching her freckled nose, but she didn't answer.

'I didn't ask that to – to start in on you, or anything. I just meant, well, like you said, you might end up on one of those beds in there. I was just thinking … it could be me, too. I could get the plague, or something.'

Nadine watched her. 'You won't. Don't say that. You won't get it.'

Kahlan ran her thumbnail along a joint in the floorboards. 'But I could. I was just thinking that if I did, or something, well, what about Richard? He'd be alone.'

'What are you saying?'

Kahlan looked into Nadine's soft brown eyes. 'If for some reason you ended up being the one with him, instead of me, you'd be good to him, wouldn't you? You'd always be good to him?'

Nadine swallowed. 'Of course I would.'

'I'm serious, Nadine. There's so much happening. I want to know that you wouldn't ever hurt him.'

'I'd never hurt Richard.'

'You hurt him before.'

Nadine turned away and scratched her shoulder. 'That was different. I was trying to win him. I would have done anything to get him to be with me. I already explained it to you.'

'I know.' Kahlan picked at a little stone stuck in the crack between the floorboards. 'But if something happened, and it turned out that you were ... the one, the one to marry him, I want to know that you'd never do anything like that to him again.

'I'd like to hear it from you, that you would never do anything to hurt Richard. Anything.'

Nadine met Kahlan's eyes for a moment before glancing away.

'If I ever ended up with Richard, I would make him the happiest man in the world. I'd take the best care of him that any woman ever took of any man. I would love him better than – well, I'd do my very best to make him happy.'

Kahlan felt the familiar pain gnaw at her insides. She endured it. 'Do you swear that that's the truth?'

'Yes.'

Kahlan looked away and wiped at her eyes. 'Thanks, Nadine. That's what I wanted to know.'

'Why are you asking me such a thing?'

Kahlan cleared her throat. 'As I said, I'm worried that I might get the plague, too. If anything happens, I could bear it better if I knew that there was someone who would take care of Richard.'

'Near as I can figure, Richard pretty much takes care of himself. Do you know that that man can cook better than me?'

Kahlan laughed. Nadine laughed with her.

'Isn't that the truth?' Kahlan said. 'I guess, where Richard is concerned, a woman can only hope to go along with him for the ride.'

'Lord Rahl!'

Richard turned to see General Kerson calling out for him. He let go of Kahlan's hand. Cara glided to a stop behind Kahlan.

'Yes, what is it, general?'

The general came to a halt, waving a letter. A dusty, tired-looking soldier followed behind, along with the general's usual guard.

'A message from General Reibisch, with his army to the south.' The general lifted a thumb. 'Grissom here just rode in.'

Richard glanced to the young soldier, still panting to get his breath. He smelled like a horse. Richard thought he would much rather smell like a horse and be out riding than sitting in a little room day after day translating the mad account of a trial and execution. He guessed that if his labors were doing him any good, he might feel differently.

He broke the seal and opened the letter. When he finished reading it, he handed the letter to Kahlan.

'Take a look.' While Kahlan read the letter, Richard turned to the messenger. 'How is our army to the south doing?'

'Fine when I left them, Lord Rahl,' Grissom said. 'The Sisters of the Light caught up with us, as they said you told them to do. They're all together with our men. We're awaiting orders.'

The letter had said much the same thing. When Kahlan had finished reading, Richard took the letter and handed it to General Kerson. The general idly scratched his graying hair as he read the letter. He looked up when he had finished.

'What do you think, Lord Rahl?'

'Makes sense to me. I don't think we should bring all those men back up north right now. As General Reibisch says, they would be in a position to know about it if the Order moves very far into the New World. What do you think?' Richard asked, as he passed the letter back to Cara.

The general hiked up his trousers. 'I agree with Reibisch. I'd want to do the same if I were him. He's already down there, why not put him to good use? As he says, it would be best to know what the Order is up to, and if the enemy does come up north to attack us, he will be in a position to bite their ass.' He winced. 'Sorry, Mother Confessor.'

Kahlan smiled. 'My father was a warrior, general, before he was king. It brings back memories.' She didn't say if they were good memories. 'I also agree about the strategic advantage of having an army in that position.'

Cara handed the letter back to Richard. 'He's right about one other thing, too. If he abandons his position, and the Order went to the northeast, they would be able to sweep into D'Hara unopposed. We wouldn't even know about it. That part of D'Hara is sparsely populated. The Order could drive north and we would never know it until they cut west, back into the Midlands.'

'Unless they pushed straight for the People's Palace,' the general said.

'That would be a fatal mistake – attacking the heart of D'Hara,' Cara said. 'Commander General Trimack of the First File of the Palace Guard would show the enemy why no army has ever attacked the palace and had so much as a single soldier live to recount the tale of their bloody defeat. The cavalry would cut them to pieces out on the Azrith Plains.'

'She's right,' the general said. 'If the enemy goes there, the vultures will feast – Trimack will see to that. If they did go northeast up into D'Hara, it would be to flank us. Best to have Reibisch guarding the gate.'

Richard had another reason to want General Reibisch's army to stay south.

'Lord Rahl,' the messenger asked, 'may I ask a question?'

'Of course. What is it?'

Grissom fussed with the hilt of his short sword. 'What's going on in the city? I mean, I saw men hauling carts with dead people, and I saw others going through the streets calling for people to bring out their dead.'

Richard took a deep breath. 'That's the other reason we want General Reibisch to stay down south. The plague is loose in the Midlands. Last night, seven hundred fifty people died.'

'The spirits preserve us.' Grissom wiped his palms on his hips. 'I was afraid it might be something like that.'

587

'I want you to take my reply back to General Reibisch. Having been here, I don't want you to carry the plague to him, too. When you get back, you are to pass my message along verbally.

'Don't approach any of his men, or any people for that matter, any closer than you must in order to be heard. When you get to their sentries, tell them to pass the message on to the general. Tell him that I find his reasoning to be sound. All of the command here agrees with him. Tell him to carry on with his plans and to keep us informed.

'Now that you've been here, you can't return to those men. You'll have to come back here, when you've delivered the message. I want you to take a good-sized patrol with you to make sure you get our instructions through, then all of you come back here.'

Grissom saluted with a fist to his heart. 'It shall be as you command, Lord Rahl.'

'I wish I could let you return to your men, soldier, but we're trying to keep the plague from getting to the army. We have the soldiers here spread out around the city so they don't come down sick. You can tell them that, too.'

General Kerson scratched his face. 'Ah, Lord Rahl, I have to talk to you about that. I just found out myself.'

Richard frowned at the general's sudden wincing expression. 'What is it?'

'Ah, well, the plague has gotten to our men.'

Richard felt his heart in his throat. 'Which group?'

The general wiped a hand across his mouth. 'All of them, Lord Rahl. Seems that the prostitutes have been visiting the camps. The women thought it would be safer than plying their trade in the city, what with those murders. I don't know anything about how sickness spreads, but Drefan told me that that might have been the way it happened.'

Richard squeezed his temples between his thumb and second finger. He wanted to give up. He wanted to simply sit down on the floor and give up.

'I should never have had Tristan Bashkar put to death. I should have let him kill all those women. In the end, it would have saved countless lives. If I'd have known this, I'd have killed them all myself.'

He felt Kahlan's hand touch his back in sympathy.

'Dear spirits,' he whispered. He could think of nothing else to say. 'Dear spirits, what are we doing to ourselves? Those women have just unwittingly struck a blow for Jagang.'

'Do you want them executed, Lord Rahl?' General Kerson asked.

'No,' Richard said in a quiet voice. 'The deed is done. It would serve no purpose, now. They didn't do it intentionally to cause harm. They were just trying to keep themselves safe.'

Richard recalled the words of one of the temple team before he was put to death. *I can no longer countenance what we do with our gift. We are not the Creator, nor are we the Keeper. Even a vexatious prostitute has the right to live her life.*

'Grissom, get a patrol together, and as soon as you've had some food and rest, get my message back to General Reibisch.'

Grissom saluted again. 'Yes, Lord Rahl. I'll get some food and supplies and be on my way within the hour.'

Richard nodded. The messenger took his leave.

'Lord Rahl,' the general said, 'if there's nothing else, I'd better see to my duties.'

'Yes, general, there is one more thing. Cut the sick soldiers out of the camps. Put them in a separate camp. Let's see if we can limit the extent of the outbreak. Who knows, maybe we can even contain it.

'And I don't want any prostitutes in the camps. None. Maybe we can keep the distemper lighter, that way. Have all the women warned to stay away under penalty of death. Post archers with the sentries. If they continue to approach after being challenged, have the archers cut them down.'

The general heaved a sigh. 'I understand, Lord Rahl. I'll also separate out the men who have been with those women and have them tend to the sick soldiers.'

'Good idea.'

Richard put his arm around Kahlan's waist as he watched the general and his guard hurry to their tasks. 'Why didn't I think of that before? I might have kept the plague from the soldiers if only I'd thought of it.'

Kahlan didn't have an answer.

'Lord Rahl,' Cara said, 'I'm going up to the sliph to relieve Berdine.'

'I'll go with you. I want to see if Berdine has learned anything from the journal. Besides, I need to get out of here for a while. You want to go, too?' he asked Kahlan.

Her arm tightened around him. 'I'd like that.'

Berdine was bent over the journal, reading. The sliph looked Richard's way before Berdine did.

'Do you wish to travel, Master? You will be pleased.'

'No,' Richard said when the echo of the eerie voice had died out. 'Thank you, sliph, but not now.'

Berdine leaned back and yawned as she stretched her arms. 'Glad to see you, Cara. I can't stay awake any longer.'

'You look like you could use some sleep.'

Richard gestured to the open journal on the table before her. 'Anything new?'

Berdine glanced to the sliph as she stood. She picked up the journal and turned it around, offering it to him. She leaned closer and lowered her voice.

'You remember telling me about what that man said before he was put to death. What he said about even a vexatious … woman having a right to her life?'

Richard knew what Berdine was talking about. 'Yes. You mean Wizard Ricker.'

'That's the one. Well, Kolo mentioned it briefly.' She tapped a place in the journal. 'Read here.'

Richard studied the sentence a moment until he had it translated in his head. ' "Ricker's vexatious prostitute is watching me as I sit here pondering what damage the team has done. I heard today that we have lost Lothain. Ricker has had his revenge." '

'Do you know who Lothain is?' Berdine asked.

'He was the head prosecutor at the Temple of the Winds trial. He was the one who went to undo the damage done by the team.'

Richard looked up. The sliph was watching him. He stepped closer. It had never occurred to him before. Why hadn't he thought of it before?

'Sliph.'

'Yes, Master? You wish to travel? Come. You will be pleased.'

Richard stepped closer. 'No, I don't wish to travel, but I would like to talk to you. Do you remember the time, long ago, when there was a great war going on?'

'Long? I am long enough to travel. Tell me where you wish to go. You will be pleased.'

'No, I don't mean traveling. Do you remember any names?'

'Names?'

'Names. Do you remember the name Ricker?'

The silver face watched without expression. 'I never betray my clients.'

'Sliph, you were a person, once, weren't you? A person like me?'

The sliph smiled. 'No.'

Richard laid a hand on Kahlan's shoulder. 'A person like this?'

The silver smile widened. 'Yes. I was a whore, like her.'

Kahlan cleared her throat. 'I think Richard meant to ask if you were a woman, sliph.'

'Yes, I was a woman, too.'

'What was your name?' Richard asked.

'Name?' The sliph frowned, as if puzzled. 'I am the sliph.'

'Who made you into the sliph?'

'Some of my clients.'

'Why? Why did they make you into the sliph?'

'Because I never reveal my clients.'

'Sliph, could you explain that better?'

'Some of the wizards here, in this place, were my clients. The most powerful of them. I was a very exclusive whore, and very expensive. Many of the wizards contended for power. Others tried to use me to displace some of those who were my clients. Some wished to use me for their pleasure, but not the kind of pleasure I offered. I never reveal my clients.'

'You mean they would have been pleased if you told them the names of the wizards who visited you, and maybe a little more about those visits.'

'Yes. My clients feared these others would use me for this pleasure, and so they made me the sliph.'

Richard turned away. He raked his fingers back through his hair. Even as they fought the enemy, they fought among themselves. When he finally gathered his wits, he turned back to the beautiful silver face.

'Sliph, those men are all dead now. There is no one alive who knows these men. There are no wizards anymore to vie for power. Could you tell me a little more?'

'They made me, and told me that I would be unable to speak their names as long as they lived. They said that their power would prevent it. If it is true that their spirits have passed from this world, then it will no longer matter and I will be able to speak their names.'

'It was this man, Lothain, who was one of your clients, wasn't it? And this other wizard, Ricker, thought he was a hypocrite.'

'Lothain.' The quicksilver face softened as she seemed to test the name. 'Wizard Ricker came to me, and said that this man, Lothain, was the head prosecutor, and that he was a vile beast, who would turn on me. He wanted my help to depose Lothain. I refused to name my clients.'

Richard spoke into the silence. 'And Ricker's words proved true. Lothain turned on you, and made you into the sliph so that you couldn't speak out against him.'

'Yes. I told Lothain that I did not reveal my clients. I told him that he had no need to fear me speaking. He said that it didn't matter, that I was only a whore, and the world would never miss me. He twisted my arm and hurt me. He used me for his pleasure without my permission. When he finished, he laughed, and then I saw a flash of light in my mind.

'Ricker came to me after, and told me that he would put an end to Lothain, and wizards like him. He wept at the edge of my well, and said he was sorry for what they did to me. He told me that he would put a stop to the way magic destroyed people.'

'Were you sad?' Berdine asked. 'Was it sad to be made into the sliph?'

'They took sadness from me when they made me.'

'Did they take happiness, too?' Kahlan whispered.

'They left me with duty.'

Even in this, they had made a mistake. They left some of

who the sliph had been so that they could use her. The part they left would submit to anyone with the price required: magic. They had been tripped up by her nature. They used her, but had to guard her, because she would offer herself to anyone – even the enemy – who had the required price.

'Sliph,' Richard said, 'I'm so sorry that we wizards did this to you. They had no right. I'm so sorry.'

The sliph smiled. 'Wizard Ricker told me that if any Master said those words to me, I should tell them these words from him: "Ward left in. Ward right out. Guard your heart from stone." '

'What does that mean?'

'He did not explain the words to me.'

Richard felt sick. Were they going to die because of a three-thousand-year-old fight for power? Perhaps Jagang was right; perhaps magic had no place in the world any longer.

Richard turned back to the others.

'Berdine, you need to get some sleep. Raina has to be up early to relieve Cara. She needs to get to bed, too. Set a guard for Kahlan's rooms and then both of you get some rest. I've had enough of this day, too.'

Richard was in a dead sleep when he awakened to a hand pushing at him. He sat up and rubbed at his eyes, trying to gather his senses in a panic.

'What? What is it?' His voice sounded to him like gravel being poured from a bucket.

'Lord Rahl?' came a tearful voice. 'Are you awake?'

Richard squinted up at the figure holding a lamp. At first, he couldn't make out who it was.

'Berdine?' He had never seen her in anything but her leather uniform before. She was standing in his room in a white nightdress. Her hair was down. He had never seen Berdine without her hair in the single braid. It was a disorienting sight.

Richard swung his legs over the edge of the bed and pulled his pants on in a rush. 'Berdine, what is it? What's wrong?'

She wiped at the tears on her face. 'Lord Rahl, please, come.' She let out a sob. 'Raina is sick.'

CHAPTER 53

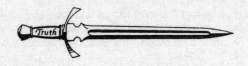

Verna shut the door as silently as she could after Warren dragged the flailing woman back into the darkness. His hand was clamped just as tightly over her mouth as his web was clamped around her gift. Verna wouldn't have been able to control the woman's magic as well as could Warren. The gift of a wizard was stronger than a sorceress's – even Verna's – gift.

Verna lit a small flame above her upturned palm. The woman's eyes widened, and then filled with tears.

'Yes, Janet, it's me, Verna. If you promise not to cry out and betray us, I will have Warren release you.'

Janet nodded earnestly. Verna gripped her dacra in her other fist, held out of sight, just in case she was wrong. She gave a nod to Warren, signaling him to release the young woman.

When she was free, Janet flung her arms around Verna's neck. She rejoiced with a soft sob. Warren held up his palm, letting a small flame dance above it so they could see. The tiny room was made of huge blocks of dark stone, as was the rest of the stronghold. Milky water seeped through some of the joints, leaving trails of crusty stains down the walls.

'Oh, Verna,' Janet whispered, 'you have no idea what a joy it is to see your face.'

Verna embraced the trembling woman as she wept softly while clutching at Verna's cloak. Verna still had the dacra in her fist, behind Janet's back.

Verna eased her away to smile at the tear-stained face. She

wiped away some of the tears, and smoothed back Janet's dark locks.

Janet kissed her ring finger – an ancient gesture beseeching the Creator's protection. Even though she had been reasonably sure Janet was loyal to the Light, Verna was relieved to see such confirmation.

A Sister of the Dark was sworn to the Keeper of the Underworld, and would never kiss her ring finger. It was an act that represented a Sister's symbolic betrothal to the Creator.

It was the one thing that a Sister of the Dark could not do. A Sister of the Dark could not hide her loyalty to her true master, the Keeper, by kissing her ring finger, for kissing that finger would invoke her dark master's wrath.

Verna slipped the dacra back up her sleeve as Janet glanced back at Warren. They exchanged smiles.

Both Verna and Warren took in Janet's bizarre garb. She was barefoot. The baggy garment, cinched at the waist with a white cord, covered her from ankles to neck to wrists, but was so sheer that the woman might as well have been naked.

Between a thumb and finger, Verna tugged out some of the diaphanous material. 'What in the name of Creation are you doing wearing this?'

Janet glanced down at herself. 'Jagang makes all his slaves dress like this. After a while, you don't even notice anymore.'

'I see.' Verna could see that Warren was doing his best to avert his eyes.

'Verna, what are you doing here?' Janet asked in a demure voice.

Verna grinned and pinched Janet's cheek. 'I came to get you out of here, silly. I came to rescue you. We're friends – did you think I'd leave you here?'

Janet blinked in astonishment. 'The Prelate let you come after me?'

Verna lifted her hand, showing the woman the sunburst-patterned ring of the Prelate. 'I am the Prelate.'

Janet's jaw fell open. She dropped to the floor and began kissing the hem of Verna's dress.

Verna gripped Janet's shoulder and urged her to her feet. 'Stop that. There's no time for that.'

'But – but, how? What happened? How can this be? What has happened?'

'Verna, those webs won't hold for long,' Warren cautioned in a thin whisper. 'We've already overstayed our welcome.'

'Janet, listen to me. We can talk later, after we get you out of here. The things we had to do to get in here only give us a brief time to get back out. It's dangerous for us to be here.'

'I should say so,' Janet said. 'Prelate, you must –'

'Verna. We're friends. It's still Verna.'

'Verna, how in Creation did you ever get into Jagang's stronghold? You must get out at once. If you are found –'

Verna frowned and touched the ring through Janet's lower lip. 'What's this?'

Janet paled. 'It marks me as one of Jagang's slaves.' She started shivering. 'Verna, save yourself. Get out of here. You must get out!' she whispered urgently.

'I agree,' Warren whispered through gritted teeth. 'Let's go!'

Verna pushed her cloak back over her shoulders, out of the way. 'I know. Now that we've got you, we can go.'

'Dear Creator, you have no idea how much I'd like to go with you, but if I did – you can't imagine what Jagang would do to me. Oh, dear Creator, you can't imagine.'

Her eyes flooded with tears at the very thought. Verna embraced her for a moment.

'Janet, listen to me. I'm your friend, you know I wouldn't lie to you.' She waited until the other nodded. 'There is a way to keep the dream walker from your mind.'

Janet clutched Verna's dress at the shoulders. 'Verna, don't torment me with hope that I know is false. You have no idea how much I'd like to believe you, but I know –'

'It's true. Listen to me, Janet. I'm the Prelate, now. Don't you think Jagang would take me if he could? Why do you think he hasn't taken the others? He can't, that's why.'

Janet was shivering again, tears running down her cheeks.

Warren put a hand to her back. 'What Verna says is true, Sister Janet. Jagang can't get into our minds. Come with us, and you will be safe. Hurry.'

'How?' Janet whispered.

Verna leaned close. 'You remember Richard?'

'Of course. Trouble and wonder in one person.'

Verna smiled at the truth of that. 'He has the gift, that's why I went after him, but there is more to it. He is born with both sides of it. More than that, though, he is a Rahl.

'Three thousand years ago, in the great war, Richard's ancestor created a magic to block the dream walkers of that time from his people's minds. That magic was passed down to his descendants who have the gift.'

Janet's fists tightened on Verna's dress. 'How? How does it work?'

Verna smiled. 'It's so simple that it's hard to believe. The most powerful magic is sometimes like that. All that is necessary is to be sworn to him, in your heart, and his magic protects you from the dream walker. As long as Richard is alive and in this world, Jagang will never again be able to enter your mind.'

'I swear allegiance to Richard, and I'm free of Jagang?'

Verna nodded at the woman's stunned face. 'It's true.'

'What do I have to do?'

Verna held up a finger to forestall Warren's objections. She went to her knees, pulling Janet down with her.

'Say the words with me, and mean them in your heart. Richard is a war wizard, and leads us in our fight against Jagang. We believe in him, in his heart, with all our hearts. Say the words with me, and believe, and you will be free.'

Janet nodded as she clasped her hands prayerfully. Tears coursed down her cheeks. Verna whispered the devotion, pausing so Janet could repeat the words after her.

'Master Rahl guide us. Master Rahl teach us. Master Rahl protect us. In your light we thrive. In your mercy we are sheltered. In your wisdom we are humbled. We live only to serve. Our lives are yours.'

Janet's whispered words echoed Verna's until she was finished.

Verna kissed Janet's cheek. 'You are free, my friend. Now hurry, let's get out of here.'

Janet snatched Verna's sleeve. 'What about the others?'

Verna hesitated. 'Janet, I would like nothing better than to rescue the rest of our Sisters, too, but I can't, not now. We will try to get them later. If we try now, Jagang will have us.

'I came to get you because you are my friend, and I love you. The five of us all swore to always protect each other. Phoebe is with us already. There is only you left.

'As much as I want to rescue the rest of our Sisters, it must be left until later. I promise you, I won't forget them, or leave them, but we can't do it all now, all at once.'

Janet's head lowered, and she stared at the floor. 'Jagang killed Christabel. I saw him do it. Her screams still haunt my nightmares. Her screams, and Jagang.'

Verna felt as if she had been punched in the gut. Christabel had been her best friend. She didn't want to know the details. Christabel had turned to the Keeper.

'That's why I have to get you out of here, Janet. My fear for you, and for what Jagang has done to you, haunts my nightmares.'

Janet's head came up. 'What about Amelia? She was one of us five. We can't leave her.'

Verna gave Janet a level look. 'Amelia is a Sister of the Dark.'

'Was,' Janet said. 'No longer.'

'What?' Verna whispered.

Warren leaned over. 'Once you're sworn to the Keeper, you can't change your mind. You can't trust what she says, Sister Janet. Now, let's get out of here. She's sworn to the Keeper.'

Janet shook her head. 'No longer. Jagang sent her on some sort of mission, involving magic, and in order to accomplish her task, she was forced to betray the Keeper.'

'Impossible,' Verna said.

'True,' Janet insisted. 'She's back. She has re-sworn her oath to the Creator. I've talked to her. She sits and weeps, kissing her ring finger half the night, praying to the Creator.'

Verna leaned closer, looking into Janet's eyes. 'Janet, listen to me. Have you seen her kiss her ring finger? Have you seen it with your own eyes? Are you absolutely sure she wasn't kissing another finger?'

'I've sat with her, trying to comfort her. I've watched her.' Janet kissed her own finger with a whispered supplication that if she wasn't telling the truth she would be struck dead.

'Just like that? She kisses her finger just like that?'

'Yes. She kisses her finger and cries and prays that the Creator will kill her for the horror of what she has done.'

'What has she done?'

'I don't know. When I ask, she practically goes crazy with screaming and weeping. Jagang won't let her kill herself. He has control of her mind, as he does with the rest of us. He wouldn't let any of us kill ourselves; we must continue to serve him.

'Verna, we can't leave Amelia here. We have to take her with us. I won't leave her here. I'm the only comfort she has in this world. The things Jagang does to her ...'

Verna turned away. Her stomach roiled at the thought of leaving Amelia if indeed she had abandoned the Keeper. The five of them had been best friends for close to one hundred fifty years, since they were young novices.

The life of a Sister of the Light was a difficult one. They had sworn oaths always to protect one another.

'Verna, she is one of us, a Sister of the Light, again. She is one of us five. Please, Verna, I'd rather stay with her than leave her here alone.'

Verna glanced back to Janet's haunted eyes.

'Verna, we must call him Excellency,' Janet said in a shuddering whisper. 'If we displease him for any reason at all, we have to serve a week in the tents.'

Warren spoke Verna's name with rising inflection. Verna waved him to silence. 'The tents? What are you saying?'

Janet's eyes flooded with tears again. 'He gives us to his soldiers for a week. We have gold rings, so they won't kill us, because those with gold rings belong to Jagang, but they can do whatever else they want. They pass us from tent to tent for a week. Even the old Sisters are sent to the tents. Jagang calls it a lesson in discipline that all must learn.'

Janet fell to her knees, convulsing in sobs as she covered her mouth with both hands. Verna sank down beside her and hugged her.

'You don't know what Jagang's men do to us,' Janet cried. 'You don't know, Verna!'

'I understand,' Verna whispered. 'Hush now. It's all right, now. We'll get you away from here.'

Janet shook her head against Verna's shoulder. 'I won't

leave Amelia here. I'm all she has. I'm a Sister of the Light. The Creator would never forgive me if I abandoned her. If I leave her, I'd be leaving my duty to the Creator. She's my friend. She came back to the Light. She came back to the Creator.

'Jagang sent her to the tents, again. If I'm not here when she comes back, she'll go crazy. No one else will tend her. The Sisters of the Dark won't go near her, and the Sisters of the Light won't forgive her. I'm her only friend. I'm the only one who forgave her and accepted her back to the Light.

'She'll be a bloody mess when she gets back. You don't know what Jagang's men are like. Except for broken bones, Jagang won't allow us to use the gift to heal one another when we come back from the tents. He says it's part of the lesson, that our souls may belong to the Creator when we die, but in this life, Jagang owns our bodies.

'We can have our broken bones knitted by the gift when we come back, but until them, we have to suffer the agony of that along with everything else. If I'm not here, no one else will heal that much for her, or comfort her.'

Janet was nearly hysterical. 'I won't leave without Amelia.'

Verna felt dizzy and sick to her stomach. Her heart pounded in terror. Bile rose into her throat.

Verna's voice broke. 'How do you endure it?'

Janet held her fists to her heart. 'We are Sisters of the Light; we must endure for the Creator.'

Verna shared a long look with Warren's troubled eyes. 'Do you know where we can find her? Maybe we could go find her and take her with us.'

Janet shook her head. 'We're passed among the tents. She could be anywhere. The army is spread out for miles and miles in every direction.

'Not long ago, more captured women were sent back here. The screams are everywhere, so you can't simply follow the sounds of screams. Besides, if we went out among the tents, we wouldn't last five minutes before we were dragged into one of them.'

'How long?' Verna asked. 'How long until Amelia is back?'

'Five days, but she won't be able to walk for at least a day after that, maybe two.'

Verna held a tight grip on her rage. 'There's nothing saying I can't use my gift to cure her once she's back.'

Janet looked up. 'That's true. Five days, then. Tomorrow night is the full moon. The fourth day after the full moon.'

'Are you able to leave this place? In order to meet us? I don't think we can get back in here again.'

'Not very far. I can't even imagine how you could have gotten in here.'

Verna showed the woman a tight smile. 'I'm not Prelate for nothing. Warren helped, too. We'll come back, four nights after the full moon.'

'Verna, there's one other thing. If Jagang can't enter my dreams, he will know something is wrong.'

Verna pressed her hands to her face. 'But you've already given the oath. You can't take it back, or it would mean nothing. You have already given your heart to Richard.'

'Then I'll have to be careful.'

'Can you do that? Can you get away with it?'

Janet touched her fingers to her lips. 'What choice do I have? I'll have to.'

Verna held out her dacra. 'Here. At least you can protect yourself.'

Janet pushed it away as if it were poison. 'If I was caught with that thing, I'd be sent out to the tents for a year.'

'Well, at least you can use your gift, now that Jagang can't enter your mind to prevent it.'

'It won't do any good here. Jagang has total control over all those with the gift who are here – Sisters and wizards. It would be spitting into a storm to try to use my gift against them.'

'I know. That's why we can't try to take the others right now. We'd never make it. The Sisters of the Dark would fight us, and with their use of Subtractive Magic, they would cut us to pieces.' Verna pressed her lips together. 'Janet, are you sure about this?'

'If I don't help a Sister in dire need, then what good is my oath as a Sister of the Light? One has come back to us from the Keeper; perhaps she can teach us how to bring the others back.'

Verna had never thought of that. Warren was making

impatient eye signals. She could see the muscles in his jaw flexing.

Janet saw, too. She gripped Verna by the shoulders and kissed her cheeks. She turned and hugged Warren.

'Please, Verna, get out of here before it's too late. I'll be able to endure five days. I know how to bow and scrape for Jagang. He's been busy; maybe I can stay out of his sight for that long.'

'All right. Where? We came down the coast to Grafan Harbor, and I don't know the lay of the land.'

'The coast? Then you would have passed the watch house, near the docks.'

'Yes, I saw the place, but it had guards in it.'

Janet leaned close. 'As you said, there's nothing stopping you from using your gift. The guard changes around sundown. Wait until you see the guard change, and then silence them. That will give you a safe place to wait until nearly dawn. Sometime in the night, I will be there with Amelia.'

'The watch house, then. Fourth night after the full moon.'

Janet gave her a quick hug. 'Five nights, and we're free. Hurry. Get out of here.'

Warren snatched Verna's arm and pulled her through the door.

CHAPTER 54

Soon after he awoke, just before dawn, Richard stood outside his bedroom, reading the morning report. For the first time, the number of dead in one night had climbed over one thousand. A thousand tragedies in one night.

Ulic, standing not far away with his massive arms folded, asked the number. A rare event, Ulic asking a question. Richard couldn't speak. He handed the report to his bodyguard. Ulic sighed heavily when he read the number.

The city was in shambles. Trade had been disrupted to the point that food was getting scarce. Firewood, used for both heat and cooking, was hard to come by. Services of every kind were difficult to secure, either because people were afraid to bring their wares into the city, they had abandoned their homes and fled the city, or they were dead.

Only the cures in the streets were in abundance.

Richard paused beside a long tapestry of a city market scene as he was headed for his office. His shadow glided to a silent halt behind him. The thought of going back to translating the book made him nauseous. He was finding nothing new, anyway. He was mired in a long report on an inquiry into the dealings Wizard Ricker had had with a people called the Andolians. It was boring and made little sense to him.

Richard couldn't face the book again this early in the day. Besides, he was worried sick about Raina. In the last week she had only gotten worse. Nothing could be done for her, any more than anything could be done for the thousand people who had died the night before.

Shota had told Kahlan that the Temple of the Winds would send another message, would send a way to get in. The spirit had told her the same thing. Why hadn't it come? Would they all be dead before the winds sent word?

Richard glanced out an east window and saw the first rays of the morning sun coming from between two mountains. With the gathering clouds he had already seen coming in from the west, he knew that they wouldn't be seeing the full moon that night.

He headed for Kahlan's room. He had to see her face, see something that could lift his spirits. Ulic took up station beside Egan at the corner of the hall. Egan had been with Kahlan's guard the night before.

Richard was greeted by Nancy, just coming out the door.

'Is Kahlan up?'

Nancy pulled the door closed behind herself. She glanced up the hall to see Ulic and Egan. They were too far away to hear.

'Yes, Lord Rahl. She is just a little slow, this morning. She isn't feeling well.'

Richard gripped the woman's arm. He thought that Kahlan had looked out of sorts for the last few days, but she had steadfastly dismissed his concerns. Richard could feel the blood draining from his face.

'What's wrong? Is she … sick? She doesn't –'

'No, no,' Nancy insisted, suddenly realizing that she had frightened the wits out of him. 'Nothing like that.'

'Then what's wrong?' Richard pressed.

The woman patted her lower belly and leaned close. She let her voice drop to little more than a whisper. 'It's just her cycle of the moon, that's all. It'll be over in a couple more days. I wouldn't say anything, mind you, but with the plague, I don't want you to worry yourself to death. Just don't tell her I told you, or she'll bite off my head.'

Richard sighed as he smiled with relief. He squeezed Nancy's hand in appreciation.

'Of course not. Thank you, Nancy. You don't know how much that eases my mind. I couldn't endure it if she …'

Nancy touched his arm as she gave him a warm smile. 'I know. That's the only reason I said anything.'

After Nancy had trundled off down the hall, Richard

604

knocked on the door. Kahlan had been just about to open it, and was surprised to find him standing there.

She smiled up at him. 'I was wrong.'

'About what?'

'You are more handsome than I remembered.'

Richard grinned. She had lifted his spirits. He gave her a quick kiss when she rose on her toes and puckered her lips.

Richard gathered up her hand. 'I'm on my way to check on Raina. Want to come with me?'

She nodded, the mirth ghosting away from her face.

Berdine met them not far from their room. Her eyes were red and leaden. She wore red leather. Richard didn't ask why.

'Lord Rahl, please … Raina is asking for you.'

Richard enclosed her shoulders with one arm. 'We were on our way there. Come on.'

Richard didn't ask how Berdine was. It was obvious she was sick with worry.

'Berdine, some people have recovered from the plague. No one is stronger than Raina. She is Mord-Sith. She will be one of the ones who recovers.'

Berdine nodded woodenly.

Raina was lying on her bed. She was wearing her red leather.

Standing in the doorway, Richard leaned toward Berdine and whispered, 'Why is she dressed?' He left the obvious question of why she was wearing her red leather unasked.

Berdine clutched his arm. 'She asked me to dress her in the red leather of a Mord-Sith' – Berdine stifled a wail – 'for the final battle.'

Richard sank to his knees beside the bed. Raina's half-open eyes rolled toward him. Sweat ran from her face. Her lower lip quivered.

Raina gripped Richard's arm. 'Lord Rahl … please, take me out to see Reggie?'

'Reggie?'

'The chipmunks … please take me out to feed Reggie. He's the one missing the end of his little tail.'

His heart breaking, he smiled for her. 'It would be my honor.'

He scooped her up in his arms. She had lost a lot of weight. She hardly weighed anything.

Raina wrapped a weak arm around his neck as she cuddled her head to his shoulder while he carried her through the halls.

Berdine walked beside them, holding Raina's other hand. Kahlan walked at his other side. Ulic and Egan marched behind.

Soldiers along the way silently stepped clear, eyes to the ground, giving a salute of fist to heart as Richard and the procession passed.

The salute was for Raina.

Outside, Richard sat on the stone court, in the light of the dawning sun, holding Raina in his lap. Berdine sat on her heels by her head. Kahlan sat on his other side. Ulic and Egan, hands clasped behind their backs, stood not far to the rear. Richard saw a tear or two wend its way down each of their stony faces.

'Over there,' Richard said to Kahlan, pointing with his chin. 'Give me that box.'

Kahlan turned and saw what he meant. He kept seeds in a box under a stone bench. She wiggled off the lid and held out the box.

Richard scooped out a handful of seeds and tossed some on the ground before them. He trickled the rest into Raina's bony hand.

It wasn't long before two chipmunks, tails twitching, scampered across the lawn. Richard had fed them enough so they knew that the appearance of people might mean food. They stuffed seeds in their cheeks, as best they could, between sudden, chattering bouts of trying to chase each other away.

Raina watched, her eyes only half opened.

Her Agiel dangled from the chain on the wrist of the hand that Berdine held.

The two chipmunks, their cheeks full, scurried for their burrows to store their booty.

Raina opened her arm out and rested her hand on the paving stone. She uncurled her fingers. Each shallow breath rattled.

Berdine tenderly stroked Raina's forehead.

Another chipmunk appeared from under a bush. He came partway toward them, froze stiff while he checked for threat, and then dashed the rest of the way. He was missing the end of his tail.

'Reggie,' Raina breathed.

Raina smiled as Reggie climbed into her open hand. He sat there, pressing his little feet against her fingers as he popped seeds into his mouth with his tongue. He paused, sitting up in her hand, to rearrange the seeds stuffed in his cheeks. Satisfied, he dropped back down, putting his little feet to Raina's fingers again.

Raina let out a soft giggle.

Berdine kissed her forehead. 'I love you, Raina,' she whispered.

'I love you, Berdine.'

Richard felt Raina's muscles go slack as she died in his arms while Reggie sat eating seeds from her hand.

CHAPTER 55

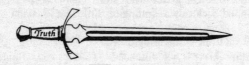

Kahlan stood behind Richard as he sat in his chair in his office, her arms circled around his neck, her cheek laid against the top of his head as she wept.

Richard rolled Raina's Agiel in his fingers. Berdine said that Raina had wanted him to have it.

Berdine had asked for permission to go up to the Keep to tell Cara. She also asked if she could take her turn at watch over the sliph, as Cara had been up there for the last three days.

Richard told her that she could do whatever she wished, for as long as she wished, and that if she wanted him to take her watch, or to come sit with her, he would. She had said that she wanted to be alone for a while.

'Why hasn't the temple sent its message?'

Kahlan smoothed his hair. 'I don't know.'

'What are we going to do?' he asked. It wasn't a question for which he expected an answer. 'I just don't know what to do.'

Kahlan rubbed her palms up and down the sides of his shoulders. 'Do you think you might find an answer in the trial record?'

'For all I know it could be the very last line I translate that gives me any information I can use.' He slowly shook his head. 'Long before I can translate every line, we'll all be dead.'

Richard hooked Raina's Agiel on the chain along with the

amulet at his chest. The red color of the Agiel matched the ruby.

Silence hung in the air for a time before he said, 'Jagang is going to win.'

Kahlan turned his head toward her.

'Don't say that. Please don't say that.'

He forced a smile. 'You're right. We'll beat him.'

A knock came to the door. Ulic stuck his head in when Richard called to ask who it was.

'Lord Rahl, General Kerson wanted to know if he could talk to you for a minute.'

Kahlan patted Richard's shoulder. 'I'm going to go tell Drefan and Nadine about Raina.'

Richard walked to the door with her. General Kerson was waiting outside with his usual fistful of reports.

'I'll catch up with you in a few minutes,' Richard said.

As Kahlan left Richard to hear the general's reports, Egan fell in with her. It felt odd to be guarded by Egan alone, without a Mord-Sith. One of them had always seemed to be around.

'Mother Confessor,' Egan said, 'some people just arrived at the palace and wanted to see you and Lord Rahl. I told them that everyone was busy. I didn't want to burden Lord Rahl.'

'Petitioners' Hall must be packed with people who want to see us, what with all the trouble.'

'They aren't in Petitioners' Hall. The guards stopped them as they went into one of the reception rooms. They aren't exactly arrogant, like some of the representatives I've seen, but they are insistent, in an odd sort of way.'

Kahlan frowned up at the huge, blond D'Haran. 'Did they say who they were? Did you find out that much, at least?'

'They said they were Andolians.'

Kahlan jerked to a halt, seizing Egan's massive arm. 'Andolians! And the guards let them in? They let Andolians in the palace?'

Egan's brow drew down. 'I didn't hear how they got in. Only that they were here. Is this a problem, Mother Confessor?'

The man's hand was already on his sword. 'No, it's not that. It's just that ... dear spirits, how do you explain the

Andolians?' She searched for the right words. 'They aren't exactly – human.'

'What do you mean?'

'There are creatures of magic that live in the Midlands. There are people with magic who live in the Midlands. It is sometimes difficult to know where to place the line separating them. Some of these people with magic are part creature – like the Andolians.'

'Magic?' Egan asked with obvious distaste. 'Are they dangerous?'

Kahlan heaved a sigh as she changed her mind about where she was going and instead started out for the reception hall. 'Not exactly. At least, not usually. Not if you know how to treat them.

'No one knows a great deal about the Andolians. We leave them alone. Most people of the Midlands have a strong dislike for them. The Andolians steal things. Not for the wealth of the object, but simply because the Andolians are fascinated by things. Shiny things, mostly. A piece of glass, a gold piece, or a button – it's all the same to them.

'People don't like them because the Andolians look much like you and I, and so people think they should behave like people, but they aren't people, exactly.

'They usually show up in places out of simple curiosity. We don't allow them in the palace because they cause such a disruption. It's best to simply keep them out. With the magic they have, if you try to discipline them, they can turn nasty. Very nasty.'

'Perhaps I should have the soldiers get rid of them.'

'No. That could get ugly. Dealing with them requires a very special kind of protocol. Fortunately, I know the protocol. I'll get rid of them.'

'How?'

'The Andolians like to carry messages. They like that more than anything – more than shiny objects, even. They love to carry messages for people. I guess it makes them feel more connected to their human side to be involved in human affairs.

'Some people in the Midlands use them for that purpose. Andolians will carry a message more faithfully than any

610

courier. They will do it for a shiny button. They would even do it for no compensation. They live to convey messages.

'All I have to do is give them a message to carry, and they will be off to deliver it. That's the easiest way to get rid of an Andolian.'

'Will it get rid of all of them?' Egan asked as he scratched his head.

'All of them? Dear spirits, don't tell me that there are more than a couple?'

'Seven. Six women who all look alike, and one man.'

Kahlan lost a stride. 'I don't believe it. That would be the Legate Rishi and his six wives, all sisters. The six sisters were all born of the same … litter.'

The Andolians believed that only a litter of six females were worthy to be the legate's wives. Kahlan's head spun as she tried to concentrate through the depression over Raina's death, over all the deaths. She had to think of a place to send the Andolians, and a message for them to carry.

Maybe something about the plague. She could send them somewhere with a warning about the plague. Maybe down into the wilds. Most of the people of the wilds tolerated the Andolians better than most other people in the Midlands.

A throng of guards bristling with weapons filled the halls all around the reception room. Two guards with pikes opened the tall, mahogany-paneled doors as Kahlan and Egan approached.

The reception hall, where waited the Andolians, was one of the smaller ones, without windows. Sculptures of every sort, from rulers' busts to a farmer and oxen, most done in pale marble, rested on square granite blocks placed back against the dark walls. Behind each sculpture, ornamental drapery of a rich maroon was swagged back to half-columns of dark violet marble set against the walls between each sculpture. It lent each piece the air of being displayed on a stage, with curtains opening for them.

Four separate clusters of ornate lamps with cut-glass chimneys hung on silver chains. Because of the dark decor, the dozens of lamps were unable to bring anything brighter than a somber atmosphere to the room. Three heavy, dark tables sat on the black marble floor.

The Andolians stood before one of these tables. The six

sisters were tall and slender, and Kahlan couldn't tell one from another. Their hair was dyed a bright orange with the berries of a hasset bush that grew in the Andolians' homeland. Their homeland wasn't close; they had made a long journey to get to Aydindril.

Their big, round black eyes watched Kahlan approach. Their orange hair, woven into hundreds of small braids, made the women look as if they wore wigs of orange yarn. Woven into the yarnlike hair were small, shiny things – buttons, pieces of metal, gold and silver coins, shards of glass, chips of obsidian – any scrap that they found shiny enough for their taste.

All six were dressed in simple but elegant white robes of a lustrous, satiny material. Despite what Kahlan knew about the Andolians – such as the way a simple storm could send them puling for protection under a bush or a hole in the ground – they had a noble air. Kahlan guessed that made sense; they were, after all, the wives of the legate, the leader of the Andolians.

The legate himself was shorter than his wives, and much older. Other than his round black eyes, he looked to be nothing more than a distinguished official, a bit on the stocky side. A bald pate shone above his fringe of white hair. Some kind of grease had been rubbed on it so as to make it glossy.

He wore robes similar to his wives', but of gold material trimmed with rows of shiny objects sewn on. Each finger had at least one ring. From a distance, all the shiny objects made him look opulent. Closer up, he looked more like a crazy beggar who had dug through a midden heap to pluck out worthless items discarded by normal people.

Legate Rishi's eyes were red-rimmed and leaden-looking. He wore a doltish grin and swayed on his feet. Kahlan saw him infrequently, but she didn't remember him this way.

The six sisters formed into a line before him. They straightened, putting their shoulders back with pride.

'We share the moon,' one of the six said.

'We share the moon,' Kahlan said in their traditional greeting among females. Her waning cramps reminded her that the greeting had more than one meaning.

The rest spoke the greeting in turn. The way those big black eyes blinked as they watched her gave Kahlan shivers. When they had finished with the official greeting, the six split into two groups of three and backed to either side of their husband.

The legate lifted a hand, as if a king greeting a crowd. He grinned moronically. Kahlan frowned at his odd behavior, although she wasn't at all sure that for an Andolian it was odd.

'We share the sun,' he said in a slur.

'We share the sun,' Kahlan answered, but he ignored her as his attention was diverted by something behind her.

Kahlan turned and saw Richard striding across the room, a glower heating his expression.

'What's this about the moon?' Richard asked as he came up beside Kahlan.

She took his hand. 'Richard,' she said in a tone of warning, 'this is Legate Rishi and his wives. They are Andolians. I have just given them their traditional greeting, that's all.'

His expression slackened. 'Oh, I see. When they said something about the moon – I thought.'

The blood suddenly drained from Richard's face.

'Andolians,' he whispered to himself. 'Wizard Ricker was doing something with the Andolians ...' He seemed lost in a confusion of thought.

'We share the sun,' Legate Rishi said through his grin. 'The females share the moon. A female and a male share the sun, but not the moon.'

Richard rubbed his brow. He looked engrossed in recollection, or confusion. Kahlan squeezed his hand, hoping he would get the message to let her handle this. She turned back to the legate.

'Legate Rishi, I would like you to –'

'Our husband has been drinking things that make him happy,' one of the wives said, as if it were a fascinating bit of news. 'He has been trading some of his prizes for this drink.' Her expression turned perplexed. 'It makes him slow, too, or we would have been here sooner.'

'Thank you for telling me this,' Kahlan said. One had always to thank an Andolian for any information they offered about themselves. Information about themselves so given was considered a gift.

Kahlan turned her attention once more to the legate. 'Legate Rishi, I would like you to carry an important message for me.'

'Sorry,' the legate said. 'We can carry no message for you.'

Kahlan was dumbfounded. She had never heard of an Andolian refusing to carry a message.

'But, why not?'

One of the six leaned toward Kahlan. 'Because we already carry a message of great importance.'

'You do?'

Her big black eyes blinked. 'Yes. The greatest of all honors. Husband carries a message from the moon.'

'You what?' Richard whispered as his head came up.

'The moon sends a message from the winds,' the legate said in a drunken slur.

Kahlan felt as if the world had frozen.

'We would have been here sooner, but husband had to stop many times to have the drink of happiness.'

Kahlan felt her whole body tingle with icy dread.

'Been here sooner,' Richard repeated. 'While all those people died, you've been drinking?' His voice boomed like thunder. 'Raina died, because you've been out getting drunk!'

Richard exploded in a blur of movement, his fist striking Legate Rishi so hard that the man tumbled back over the table.

'People are dying, and you're out getting drunk!' Richard roared as he vaulted over the table.

'Richard, no!' Kahlan shrieked. 'He has magic!'

Kahlan saw a blur of red racing in from the side. Cara came at a dead run and dived over the table, knocking Richard sprawling across the floor.

Legate Rishi rose up in a rage. Blood frothed at his mouth. Strings of it whipped from his chin.

Wavering flares of light and undulating flutters of darkness radiated up his arms, gathering at his chest as he rose up. He was gathering his magic, preparing to unleash it against Richard. Richard went for his sword.

Cara shoved Richard again and rebounded back at the legate, backhanding him across his bloody mouth. The legate whirled, redirecting his rage at her.

Cat-quick, Cara spun past him, striking him again, turning his attention away from Richard as he followed her.

His magic already gathered, he unleashed it at her.

The air thumped and at the same time seemed to oscillate.

The legate went down with a grunt of pain. Cara was on him before he hit the ground. She pressed her Agiel to his throat.

'You are mine, now,' she sneered as he gagged in agony. 'Your magic is mine, now.'

'Cara!' Kahlan yelled. 'Don't kill him!'

The six sisters were squatted down in a shivering clump, hugging one another in terror. Kahlan put a hand to the frightened sisters, reassuring them that they wouldn't be harmed.

'Cara, don't hurt him,' Kahlan said. 'He carries a message from the Temple of the Winds.'

Cara's head came up. She had a disturbing look in her eyes.

'I know. It came to him with magic. His magic is mine, now. The message he carries is embedded within his magic.'

Richard let his sword drop back into its scabbard. 'You mean, you know the message?'

Cara nodded, her blue eyes filling with tears.

'I know it with him. I share his magic, his knowledge of the message.'

'Ulic, Egan,' Richard said, 'clear the soldiers out. Shut the doors. Keep everyone out.'

As Ulic and Egan were ushering the soldiers out, Richard seized the legate by the robes at his throat and lifted him. He heaved him into a chair. Richard towered over the suddenly meek-looking, panting Andolian leader.

His chest heaving, Richard gripped the amulet and Raina's Agiel in a fist. The muscles in his jaw flexed as he pointed at the legate's face.

'Let's have the message. And you had better tell it true. Thousands of people have already died while you delayed your arrival to get drunk.'

'The message from the winds is for two people.'

Richard looked up. The words had come not only from the legate, but also from Cara. She had spoken the words along with him.

'Cara, do you know the message, too? Just as he does?'

Cara looked as surprised as Richard. 'I ... it came to me, as it came to him. I knew only that he carried a message. He didn't know it until he spoke it. I knew it when he did.'

'Who is the message for?'

Kahlan knew.

'For Wizard Richard Rahl, and for Mother Confessor Kahlan Amnell.' Once again, both had spoken the words.

'What is the message?' Richard asked.

Kahlan knew. She went to Richard's side, taking his hand in hers, holding it for dear life.

The room was empty of everyone except Richard, Kahlan, Cara, Legate Rishi, and the six sisters, cowering under a table. The lamps around the room dimmed, as if their wicks had been turned down. It cast them all in an eerie, wavering light.

The legate, his face gone blank, looked to have gone into a trance. He rose from the chair, blood still dripping from his chin. His arm lifted, pointing at Richard. Only he spoke, this time.

'The winds summon you, Wizard Richard Rahl. Magic has been stolen from the winds, and used in this world to cause harm. You must wed in order to enter the Temple of the Winds.

'Your wife is to be one named Nadine Brighton.'

Unable to speak, Richard brought Kahlan's hand to his heart, holding it there in both of his hands.

Cara's arm lifted, pointing at Kahlan. Only she spoke, this time, in a frigid, heartless voice.

'The winds summon you, Mother Confessor Kahlan Amnell. Magic has been stolen from the winds, and used in this world to cause harm. You must wed in order to help Wizard Richard Rahl enter the Temple of the Winds.

'You husband is to be one named Drefan Rahl.'

Richard dropped to his knees. Kahlan sank down beside him.

She thought she should feel something. She felt only numbness. It seemed a dream.

She had thought it would never come. Now that it was happening, it seemed too fast, as if she were tumbling over a cliff, grasping for a handhold, but finding nothing to stop her fall as she plunged into icy blackness.

It was over. Everything was over. Her life, her dreams, her future, her joy, was over. It only remained to act it out until the end.

Richard's ashen face looked up from Cara's feet.

'Cara, please, I'm begging you, don't do this to us.' His voice broke. 'Dear spirits, please don't do this to us, Cara.'

Cara's cold blue eyes stared back.

'I do not do this to you. I only bear the message from the winds. You must both agree to this, if you wish to enter the Temple of the Winds.'

'Why must Kahlan marry?'

'The winds require a virgin bride.'

Richard's eyes darted to Kahlan. He looked back to Cara. 'She isn't a virgin.'

'Yes, she is,' Cara said.

'No! She's not!'

Kahlan put her forehead against the side of Richard's face as she gripped his muscular neck, hugging herself to him.

'Yes, Richard. I am,' she whispered. 'In this world, I am. Shota told me that that was all that mattered to the spirits. In this world, in our world, the world of life, I am a virgin. We were together in another world. It doesn't apply here.'

'That's crazy,' he whispered in a hoarse voice. 'That's just crazy.'

'It fulfills the requirements of the winds,' Cara said.

'This is the only chance you will be offered,' the legate said. 'If you do not take it, then the obligation of the winds to remedy the damage will be ended.'

'Please, Cara,' Richard whispered. 'Please … don't do this. There has to be another way.'

'This is the only way.' Cara, in her red leather, towered above them. 'It is up to you whether you will repair the damage. You must agree. If you fail to answer the call, it will not come again, and the magic released will run free.'

'The winds wish to know your answer,' the legate said. 'You must both agree to this of your free will. It must be a true marriage in all aspects. It must be for life. You must both be of honest intent in your marriages, and faithful to the ones you wed.'

'He speaks the truth of the winds. What is your answer?' Cara asked in a voice like ice.

Kahlan looked through the watery blur into Richard's eyes. She could see him dying behind those eyes.

'It is our duty. Only we can save those people, but I will say no if you wish it, Richard.'

'How many more Rainas must die in my arms? I couldn't ask you to have me at the cost of another life.'

Kahlan swallowed the wail. 'Is there anything … do you know of anything we could do to stop the plague?'

Richard shook his head. 'I'm sorry. I have failed you. I haven't found a way around this.'

'You haven't failed me, Richard. I couldn't bear to think we were the cause of more death, like Raina's, today.' She threw her arms around his neck. 'I love you so much, Richard.'

Richard's big hand held her head to him. 'We are agreed, then. We must do this.'

Richard brought her to her feet with him. There was so much she wanted to say to him. No words came. When she looked into Richard's eyes, she knew words weren't needed.

They turned to Cara and the legate.

'I agree. I will marry Nadine.'

'I agree. I will marry Drefan.'

Kahlan fell into Richard's arms as she lost control of her tears. She sobbed in agony. Richard embraced her, nearly squeezing the life out of her.

Cara and the legate were suddenly there, pulling them apart.

'You are each promised to another,' Cara said. 'You may not do this now. You must each be loyal to your mates.'

Kahlan looked past the legate into Richard's eyes, each of them knowing that they had embraced for the last time.

In that moment, her world ended.

CHAPTER 56

Kahlan and Richard sat apart, with the legate and Cara between them. Kahlan heard the doors open. It was Nadine and Drefan. After Ulic had let them in, he closed the doors.

Richard raked his hair back as he rose. Kahlan didn't want to test her legs, yet. It had all slipped through her fingers. Everything was lost to duty.

Nadine eyed everyone in the room: the legate, his six wives, Cara, Kahlan, and finally Richard as he walked haltingly to her.

Richard stared at the floor. 'You both know that the plague was started with magic. I told you both how it was stolen from the Temple of the Winds. The temple has sent its requirements if I am to be allowed to enter and stop the plague.

'The temple requires that both Kahlan and I wed. The temple has named who it is it requires we wed. I'm sorry that both of you have been … tangled in this. I don't know the reason. The temple will not explain why it must be so, only that this is our only chance to halt the plague. I can't force either of you to be part of this; I can only ask.'

Richard cleared his throat, trying to steady his voice. He lifted Nadine's hand. He couldn't look her in the eye.

'Nadine, will you marry me?'

Nadine's gaze immediately went to Kahlan. Kahlan wore her Confessor's face, as her mother taught her. Duty, as her mother had taught her.

Nadine glanced to the others, and then back to the top of Richard's head.

'Do you love me, Richard?'

Richard finally looked up into her eyes. 'No. I'm sorry, Nadine, but, no. I don't love you.'

She was unruffled by the answer. Kahlan was sure that she had expected it.

'I'll marry you, Richard. I'll make you happy. You'll see. You'll come to love me, in time.'

'No, Nadine,' Richard whispered, 'I won't. We will be husband and wife, if you agree to this, and I will be faithful to you, but my heart will always belong to Kahlan. I'm sorry to say such a harsh thing to you when I'm asking you to marry me, but I won't deceive you.'

Nadine thought a moment. 'Well, many marriages are arranged, and they turn out well in the end.' She smiled at him. To Kahlan, it looked a sympathetic smile. 'The spirits have arranged this one. That means something. I will marry you, Richard.'

Richard glanced back at Kahlan. It was her turn. She saw in those dead gray eyes a glimmer of something: rage.

Kahlan knew that his insides were being torn apart the same as were hers.

She found herself before Drefan before she realized it. The first time she tried, her voice wouldn't come out. It simply wouldn't. She tried again.

'Drefan, will you … be … my husband?'

His blue, Darken Rahl eyes appraised her without emotion. For some reason, she recalled his hand between Cara's legs, and she almost vomited.

'As Nadine said, I could do worse than a marriage arranged by the spirits. I don't suppose there's any chance you will ever come to love me?'

Kahlan's jaw trembled as she stared at the floor. Her voice wouldn't work. She shook her head.

'Well, no matter. We may still have some good times. I'll do it. I will marry you, Kahlan.'

She was glad that she had never told Richard about what Drefan had done to Cara. If she had, Richard might have lost control when Drefan said he would marry Kahlan and pulled free his sword.

Cara and the legate stepped forward. 'It is agreed, then,'

they said as one. 'The winds are pleased to have the consent of all involved.'

'When?' Richard asked in a hoarse voice. 'When will we … when do we …? And when can I get into the Temple of the Winds? People are dying. I have to help the winds put a stop to it.'

'Tonight,' Cara and the legate said as one. 'We will leave immediately for Mount Kymermosst. You will be wed tonight, as soon as we arrive there.'

Kahlan didn't ask how they would get to a place that wasn't there anymore. It didn't really matter to her. The only thing that really mattered to her was that they would be wed that very night.

'I'm sorry about Raina,' Nadine said to Richard. 'How is Berdine doing?'

'Not well. She's up at the Keep.'

Richard turned to Cara. 'Can we stop up there on our way? I must tell her what has happened. She will have to stay to guard the sliph until I return. I have to tell her.'

'And I'd like to give her something to help her feel better,' Nadine said.

'It is permitted,' Cara said in that awful, icy voice.

Berdine looked terror-stricken when Richard told her. She threw her arms around him and wept with twin misery. The sliph watched from her well, frowning with curiosity.

Nadine mixed things from pouches in her big bag, giving Berdine instructions on when to take them, promising that it would help her get through her grief. Richard tried to tell Berdine everything he could think of that she might need to know.

Kahlan could almost feel time tingling against her flesh as it flew past, as she plunged and plunged into the black depths.

'We must go,' Cara said, cutting off the stalling. 'We must ride hard to arrive before the full moon rises.'

'How will I find the Temple of the Winds?' Richard asked.

'You do not find the Temple of the Winds,' Cara said. 'The Temple of the Winds will find you, if the requirements are met.'

Nadine lifted her bag before Richard. 'Can I leave this here, then? It's heavy to carry if we're coming back here anyway.'

'Of course,' Richard said, his voice a dead monotone.

Kahlan was made to walk behind Richard and beside Drefan as they returned to the horses. Nadine touched Richard's back as she walked beside him. She was doing a fair job of restraining her joy over her triumph, yet it was a touch meant to send a message: he belonged to her, now.

At the bottom of the Keep road, as they turned away from the city, Kahlan could hear the men with the dead-carts, calling out for people to bring out their dead. Soon, that would be ended, as the suffering and death of the plague was ended. Only in that did she find any solace. The children, their parents, would live.

If only it had come in time for Raina. Berdine hadn't said that, but Kahlan knew that that thought was screaming in her head.

Richard had ordered all their guards to remain. When Ulic and Egan had seen the look on his face, they hadn't argued. Only Richard and Nadine, Kahlan and Drefan, Cara, the legate, and his six wives rode out for Mount Kymermosst.

Kahlan didn't know how any of it was going to work, getting into the Temple of the Winds, nor did Richard. She didn't have the slightest curiosity about it. The only thing she could think about was Richard marrying Nadine. Kahlan was sure that Richard could think of nothing but her marrying Drefan.

As they rode, Drefan told stories, trying to keep everyone entertained, trying to lift their spirits. Kahlan didn't hear much of it. She watched Richard's back; her only need was to be looking when he glanced back at her, as he did from time to time.

She couldn't bear not to look at him, yet meeting his eyes was like a hot knife searing into her heart.

She took no joy in the mountainous country they rode into, the greening grass, unfurling ferns, budding trees. The day was warm, compared to what the weather had been for spring, so far, but the sky brooded with dark clouds. Before the day was out, she expected they would encounter a storm. The Andolians cringed every time their eyes turned up.

622

Kahlan pulled her cloak tighter around herself. She thought about her blue wedding dress back in her room that she had planned to wear when she married Richard.

She felt herself getting angry at him. He had seduced her into thinking she could have love, could have happiness. Seduced her into forgetting she had only duty. Seduced her into loving him.

When she realized she was angry at him, the tears came again, running down her face in a silent torrent. This wasn't happening just to her, it was happening to him, too. They shared this torment.

She thought about the first time she saw him. It seemed so long ago that she had been running from Darken Rahl's assassins, and Richard had helped her. She thought about all the things they had done together, all the times she stood watch while he slept, and she gazed at him, imagining being just a normal woman who could fall in love, instead of a Confessor who had to keep her feelings secret and live a loveless life of duty.

Richard had found a way, though, found a way that she, a Confessor, could have love. And now it was in ashes.

Why would the spirits do this to them? The answer came when she remembered her talk with Shota, and with the spirit. There were not only good spirits, but evil spirits, too. Those evil spirits had a hand in this. They were the ones who wanted this, who demanded it as the price of the path.

The spirits who demanded that price were worse than evil.

Late in the morning, they stopped to rest the horses and eat. Nadine and Drefan talked with their mouths full. The legate sat back as his wives fed him. He had a hard time, what with his cut lip. They rubbed their legs against his, giggling as he took food from their fingers. They ate between offering him bites. Cara ate in silence. Kahlan didn't notice what any of them had to eat.

She and Richard didn't eat. They both sat on the sunny rocks like deadwood, silent, sullen, staring at nothing.

When the others had finished with their meal, Richard watched as they all mounted up again. Even though none of the others noticed it, Kahlan could see the smoldering rage in his eyes. The spirits had chosen Drefan to wound him. They could have done nothing worse.

'How's the arm?' Nadine asked Drefan as they all started out again.

Drefan held it up and flexed his fingers in demonstration. 'Nearly good as new.'

Kahlan ignored their conversation. All morning, they had chattered. In her silent world, it was barely noticed.

'What is wrong with your arm, master Drefan?' one of the six sisters asked.

'Oh, some miscreant didn't like the way I try to purge the world of sickness.'

Big black eyes blinked at him. 'What did he do to you?'

Drefan straightened haughtily in his saddle. 'Cut me with his knife. Tried to kill me, the filthy scum.'

'Why did he not succeed?'

Drefan dismissed the incident with an arrogant wave. 'Once I showed him some steel, he ran for his life.'

'I sewed his wound,' Nadine told the amazed sisters. 'And a deep one it was, too.'

Drefan cast a glance at Nadine that seemed to make her shrink in her saddle. 'I told you, Nadine, it's nothing. I don't want sympathy. A lot of people are in much greater need than I.'

He relented when he saw the sheepish look on her face. 'But you did a good job. As fine as any of my healers would have done. You did a fine job, and I appreciate it.'

Nadine smiled as they rode on.

Drefan pulled up the broad hood of his flaxen cloak. *Dear spirits,* she thought, *that is to be my husband. For the rest of my life, this is to be my partner in life.*

Until she could die, and be with Richard again.

Sweet death could not come soon enough.

Clarissa wiped her sweaty palms together as she peered through the keyhole and listened to Nathan speaking with the Sisters in the other room.

'I'm sure you can understand, Lord Rahl,' Sister Jodelle said. 'This is for your own safety, too.'

Nathan chuckled. 'How good of the emperor to consider my well-being.'

'If, as you say, Richard Rahl will be eliminated tonight, then you have nothing to be concerned about. We will bring it afterwards. Surely, this would be satisfactory.'

Nathan shot them a hot glare. 'I told you, Jagang's plan has worked. Richard Rahl will be eradicated tonight. You will learn not to question me after tonight, I pray.'

Clarissa had to strain to see Nathan through the keyhole as he turned away from the two Sisters while he considered. He turned back to them.

'And he has agreed to everything else?'

'Everything,' Sister Willamina assured him. 'He looks forward to having you as his plenipotentiary in D'Hara, and is most agreeable to your offer of aid with the books of prophecy he has collected over the years.'

Nathan grunted. 'Where are they? I don't know that I'm amenable to traveling all over the Old World just to have a look at worthless volumes. I have business in D'Haran, after all. As the new Lord Rahl, I will need to consolidate my authority.'

'His Excellency has anticipated that this would be inconvenient for you, and so has suggested that he will have his wizards pull out things of interest and have them sent to you for your analysis.'

Clarissa knew what the Sister was talking about. Before they had arrived, Nathan had told her that he probably wouldn't be allowed to have a look at the prophecies Jagang possessed, much less be told where they all were. Jagang would want Nathan to see only selected volumes that had been screened by others, first.

Nathan finally turned his full attention to the two Sisters.

'In due time, in due time. Once we have worked together and brought the New World to task, and have come to fully trust one another's word, then I will happily accept visits by Jagang's lapdogs, but until then, I'm sure our emperor understands that I am leery of allowing those with the gift to know exactly where I am. That is why I will be leaving at once.'

Sister Jodelle sighed. 'As I said, he would be happy to have it brought to you. But you can understand that he would have cause for concern to have a wizard of your power, whose mind is a mystery to him, approach too closely. While he is eager for this arrangement, he is a man who takes precautions.'

'As am I,' Nathan said. 'That is why I can't allow the book to be brought to me. Having you meet me here again today is the last risk I intend to take. In the meantime, I want that book. Until I have it, I have no way of knowing if it's safe for me to go to D'Hara.'

'His Excellency understands, and has no disagreement with your request. His objective will soon be complete, and he therefore has no further need of the book. Besides, a world without people to work for him would be of little value.

'The book only works for Sister Amelia, since she was the one who went to the Temple of the Winds to recover it. He has offered to let you have either the book, or Sister Amelia. If you wish, we will send her to you.'

'So Jagang will know where I am? I don't think so, Sister. I'll take the book.'

'That, too, is agreeable with His Excellency. We can send it, or have someone meet you, to deliver it to you. He objects only to you, yourself, coming to get it, for safety reasons, as I've already explained.'

Nathan rubbed his jaw as he thought. 'What if I sent someone back with you? A representative, someone with my interests in mind? Someone loyal to me, so I had no need to fear that Jagang would delve into their mind and find where I was to be? Someone without the gift? He would have no need to fear them.'

'Without the gift?' Sister Jodelle thought a moment. 'And we could test them, without your shields around them, to insure that they in fact did not have the gift?'

'Of course. I want this relationship with Jagang to work for both of us. I wouldn't jeopardize it by trying to deceive him. I want to build trust, not destroy it.' Nathan hesitated, clearing his throat. 'But you understand, though, that this person is … valued, to me. If anything were to happen to her, I would view it in the harshest light.'

Both Sisters smiled.

'Her. Of course,' Sister Willamina said.

'Why, Nathan' – Sister Jodelle rocked on her heels as she smiled – 'you really have been enjoying your freedom.'

'I mean it,' Nathan said in a level tone. 'Anything happens to her, and the entire agreement is ended. I'm sending her as a show of my faith in Jagang, in our agreement. I'm taking the first step of trust, so that the emperor will see that I am sincere.'

'We understand, Nathan,' Sister Jodelle said, more serious now. 'No harm will come to her.'

'When she leaves with the book, I want her escorted to safety, beyond Jagang's troops, and then left to be on her way. If she is followed, I will know it. If she is followed, I will view it in the most unfavorable light – as a sign of hostility toward me, and an attempt on my life.'

Sister Jodelle nodded. 'Understood, and very reasonable. She comes with us, gets the book, and returns safely to you, without being followed, and we are all happy.'

'Good,' Nathan said decisively, as if closing the deal. 'After tonight, Jagang will be rid of Richard Rahl. When I have the book safely in hand, then I will have the southern army surrender to Jagang's expeditionary force, as my part of the bargain.'

Sister Jodelle bowed. 'We have an agreement, Lord Rahl. His Excellency wishes to welcome you to the empire as his second.'

Nathan turned toward the door Clarissa was kneeling behind. Clarissa jumped up and rushed to the far window. She drew back the drapes with a hand and pretended to be gazing out when she heard the door open.

'Clarissa,' Nathan called.

She turned to see him standing in the doorway, holding the doorknob. Beyond him, she could see the two Sisters watching.

'Yes, Nathan? You wish something?'

'Yes, Clarissa. I would like you to go on a small journey for me – a bit of business. I need you to go with my friends out here.'

Clarissa guided her full skirts around the writing table and followed him out into the other room. Nathan introduced her to the two Sisters.

The two women wore knowing, smug smiles. They glanced to her cleavage and then at each other. Clarissa had that feeling of being judged as a whore, again.

'Clarissa, you will leave at once, with these ladies. When you reach your destination, they will give you a book. You will then return with it. You remember where I told you we would be off to, tomorrow?'

'Yes, Nathan.'

'You will meet me there, after you have the book. No one, no one at all, is to know where it is you will be meeting me. Do you understand?'

'Yes, Nathan.'

'I'll go see to getting her a horse,' Sister Willamina said.

'A horse?' Clarissa gasped. 'I've never ridden a horse in my life. I can't ride a horse.'

Nathan waved patience at the sudden hitch in their plans. 'I have a carriage. I'll have it brought around, and Clarissa can take that. There, is that satisfactory to all?'

Sister Jodelle shrugged. 'Horse, carriage, it makes no difference to us, as long as we can test her for the gift, first.'

'Test her all you want. I will order the carriage while you test her, and then Clarissa can pack a few things.'

'Agreed.'

'Good. That's settled then.'

Nathan turned to Clarissa, putting his back to the two Sisters. 'It won't be long, my dear, and we'll be together again.' He adjusted the locket hanging from a fine gold chain, straightening it for her. He looked into her eyes. 'I will be waiting for you. I've told these friends of mine that if anything happens to you, I will be more than unhappy.'

Clarissa stared into his wonderful eyes. 'Thank you, Nathan. I will bring the book, as you ask.'

Nathan kissed her cheek. 'Thank you, my dear. That's good of you. Safe journey, then.'

CHAPTER 57

Even with the gathering dark, brooding clouds, an eerie calm hung over the summit of Mount Kymermosst. The Andolians cast uneasy glances skyward. As Kahlan watched Richard dismount, his golden cloak hung limp in the unnaturally still air. Drefan offered her his hand to help her down. Kahlan pretended not to see it.

In the fading light, the ruins were only ghostly shapes, the bones of some long extinct monster, waiting to come back to life and swallow her up. Though this was the night of the full moon, the leaden clouds would totally obscure it. When the last of the daylight soon left, it would be black as death atop the forsaken peak.

Nadine stood close to Richard as he stared off toward the edge of the cliff. Drefan stood nearby, not wanting to look too forward to the woman who would shortly be his wife, but not wanting to ignore her, either. Like Nadine, he didn't seem to view this as the end of his happiness.

After the horses were secured, the legate and Cara ushered the brides and bridegrooms to a crumbling, circular garden structure made up of curved stone benches on one side and broken columns on the other. The top piece, connecting the columns, was mostly missing, joining only four of the ten stone columns.

In the distance, in the fading light, Kahlan could still see the knife edge of the cliff, and the black swath of mountains beyond. Somewhere out there was the Temple of the Winds.

Kahlan was directed to sit on a curved stone bench beside

Drefan, and Richard, two benches away, was told to sit beside Nadine. Kahlan glanced over, and saw Richard looking back; but then Drefan leaned forward and blocked her view of Richard. She turned her attention to the legate and Cara standing before them. The six sisters stood behind their husband.

'We are gathered here,' the legate and Cara said as one, 'to wed Richard Rahl and Nadine Brighton, and to wed Kahlan Amnell and Drefan Rahl. This is the most solemn of rites; it binds in the most earnest of vows, and commits these mates for life. This marriage is sanctioned and witnessed by the spirits themselves.'

Kahlan stared at the weeds sprouting from the cracks in the disintegrating stone floor as she only partly listened to the words about loyalty, fidelity, and obligation. It was so warm and muggy that she could hardly breathe. Her white Mother Confessor's dress was sticking to her back. Sweat trickled down between her breasts.

Kahlan's head came up when Drefan started lifting her with a hand under her arm. 'What? What is it?'

'It is time,' he said. 'Come.'

And then she was standing before the legate and Cara, with Drefan beside her, and three of the legate's wives at her other side as her attendants. She looked past Drefan to see Richard standing beside Nadine, with the other three Andolians serving as her attendants. Nadine wore a smile.

'If anyone has any objections to the wedding of these people, they must speak now, for once it is done, it cannot be undone.'

'I have an objection,' Richard said.

'What is it?' the legate asked.

'The winds said that this had to be of our own free will. It is not. We are being coerced into this. We are being told that people will die if we don't do this. I don't do this of my own free will; I do this only to save lives.'

'Do you wish to save the lives of the people who will die if the magic stolen from the Temple of the Winds is not stopped?' the legate asked.

'Of course I do.'

'This wedding is part of that attempt. If you do not go

through with it, then they will die. You wish to save them. This qualifies as your free will as far as the spirits involved are concerned.

'If you wish to withdraw your agreement to this, then it must be now, before the vows. Afterwards, you may not change your mind.'

Muggy silence hung in the air.

She was plummeting helpless into the inky depths. It was all happening too fast. Too fast for her to get a breath.

'I wish to speak with Richard, if I am to do this. Before I do this,' Kahlan said. 'Alone.'

The legate and Cara stared at her a moment. 'Then hurry,' they said as one. 'There is not much time. The moon rises.'

They both walked far enough away from the circle that Kahlan could be reasonably sure they couldn't be heard. She stood close, facing him.

She wanted Richard to save them from this. He had to save them. He had to do something, now, or it would be too late.

'Richard, we're out of time. Is there anything? Can you think of anything at all to stop this? Any way we can still save those people and not have to do this?'

Richard stood close to her, and yet a world away. 'I'm sorry. I don't have any other solution. Forgive me,' he whispered. 'I have failed you.'

She shook her head. 'No, you didn't. Don't ever think that, Richard. I don't. The spirits have made it impossible for us to win. They wish this, and have put us in a double bind.

'But at least, if we go through with this, Jagang will not win. That is more important. How many lovers, like us, will be able to have a life, now, have happiness, now, have children, now, because of the sacrifice we make this night?'

Richard smiled that smile that melted her heart. 'That's one reason I love you so much: your passion. Even if I never see you again, I've known true happiness with you. True love. How many ever experience even this small taste?'

Kahlan swallowed. 'Richard, if we do this, we have to be true to our vows, don't we. We can't … still be together … sometimes, can we?'

The way his jaw trembled, and his eyes filled with tears, was more than answer enough.

Just before they fell into each other's arms, Cara was there, between them.

'It is time. What are your wishes?'

'I have a lot of them,' Richard said with sudden venom. 'Which do you want to hear?'

'The winds wish to know if you will do this, or not.'

'We will do it,' Richard growled. 'But the spirits had better know that I will have revenge.'

'The winds are simply doing the only thing they can do to stop the death caused by what was stolen from them,' Cara said with sudden compassion, but still with that haunting quality that told Kahlan that it wasn't Cara speaking, but the winds. 'They do not do this out of animosity.'

'A wise man once told me that dead is dead, no matter the how,' Richard said.

He defiantly took Kahlan's hand and walked with her back to the circle of stone, where they each took their places beside their chosen.

Kahlan wore her Confessor's face as she stood beside Drefan. She felt pain for Richard; he had not grown up being taught how to subjugate his emotions, his longings, his desires – for duty. She had had a lifetime to prepare for this final torment. He had had a lifetime to prepare for the opposite, expecting he would have happiness. Kahlan had only briefly felt the warmth of that flame.

With deliberate care, she ignored the words spoken to Nadine, and then to Drefan, words of loyalty and devotion to their mate. Kahlan instead focused her mind on Richard, hoping to pass to him some strength, hoping that he could get through this, so that they could save those stricken and stop the plague. Richard still had to get into the Temple of the Winds. He needed strength.

Soon, the ceremony would be over, and they would head back to Aydindril. Perhaps they would have to wait until Richard went into the temple, and did what he had to do, and then they would return to Aydindril. In any event, it wouldn't be long, and she would be going home, home to the place she had grown up, to a life of duty to which she had been bred.

'Yes or no?' the legate said.

Kahlan looked up. 'What?'

He glanced up at the threatening clouds and then took a hurried breath. 'Do you swear to honor this man, to obey him as the master of your home, to care for his needs when he is well, and when he is ill, and to be his loyal wife in this life as long as you both live?'

Kahlan glanced up at Drefan. She wondered what he had sworn to.

'I swear to whatever it is that is required of me to stop the plague.'

'Yes or no?'

Kahlan let out an angry sigh. 'Is this what is required of me to stop the magic stolen from the winds from killing people?'

'It is.'

In her mind, she swore the oath, but to Richard, not Drefan. She would swear words aloud to Drefan, but her heart would always be Richard's. Kahlan's fists tightened. 'Then, yes, I swear to do what is required to stop the plague. I swear not one stitch more, nor for one breath longer, than that required of me.'

'Then in full view of the spirits, and by the power of the spirits, you are now pronounced husband and wife.'

Kahlan doubled over in sudden pain. It felt as if her insides had been torn apart. She tried to pull a breath. It wouldn't come. She saw swirling color before her wide eyes.

Drefan put his arm around her waist. 'What is it? Kahlan, what's wrong?'

Her legs buckled, but he held her up.

'It is the spirits,' came the legate and Cara's voice together, 'they have bound her power. She is to live this marriage as any woman wed to a man. Her power would have interfered.'

'You can't do that!' Richard screamed. 'She'll be defenseless! You can't take her power!'

'Her power was not taken, but walled away so she cannot use it for the term of her vows to her husband, Drefan Rahl. It is done,' the two said together. 'You will now swear to the vows, or you will lose your chance to help the winds.'

Kahlan stared at the ground, feeling a swirl of emptiness, feeling the void between her mind and her power, as she listened to similar words spoken before Richard. She couldn't hear his answer, but he must have said what was required

633

because the legate pronounced him and Nadine husband and wife.

They had not only taken her love, but her Confessor's power, as the price of the path. The emptiness threatened to smother her. The profound and sudden sense of loss clouded her mind with blackness darker than the falling night.

Drefan took her arm. 'Here, you'd better sit down. Even in this light, as a healer I can see that you are not well.'

Kahlan let him guide her back to a bench and help her to sit.

'Your wife will be fine,' the legate said. He looked up at the boiling sky. 'Richard Rahl, Drefan Rahl, come with me.'

'Where are we going?' Richard wanted to know.

'We are to prepare you to consummate the marriage.'

Kahlan's head came up. Even in the darkness, she could see that Richard was near to exploding in rage. His hand was on his sword.

Drefan rubbed Kahlan's back in sympathy. 'You will be all right. Everything will be all right. Don't worry, I will take care of you, as I promised.'

'Thank you, Drefan,' she managed through the anguish.

Drefan left her and strode to Richard. Drefan gripped Richard's arm and bent close, speaking to him in a whisper. Kahlan could see Richard rake his hands back through his hair and nod occasionally. Whatever Drefan was saying was cooling Richard.

After Drefan and Richard parted, the legate and Cara looked back to Nadine and Kahlan. 'You two will wait here.'

Kahlan huddled on the stone bench as Richard and Drefan were led off in the darkness toward the cliff, toward the two buildings, one to either side of the road that ended abruptly at the edge. It was becoming so dark that Kahlan could hardly make out Nadine's face as she sat down beside her on the stone bench. The six sisters had gone back to the horses, sucking their fingers as they watched the sky.

'I'm sorry. About your magic, I mean. I didn't know they would do that to you. I guess you'll be like any other woman, now.'

'I guess.'

'Kahlan,' Nadine said, 'I won't lie to you and tell you that

I'm sorry that I'm the one who married Richard, but I will tell you that I'll do my best to make him happy.'

'Nadine, you just don't understand, do you? You can be as kind as pudding to him, or you can be as mean as nettles, and it won't make any difference. With the pain he's in, if you do your worst, it would be a bee sting after a beheading.'

Nadine giggled uncomfortably. 'Well, I know a poultice for a bee sting. Richard will see. I will –'

'You have already promised me that you would be kind to him, Nadine. I appreciate that you will be kind to him, but at the moment, I'm not in the mood to hear the details of just how kind you are going to be.'

'Sure. I understand.' Nadine picked at the stone on the bench. 'Not the way I had my wedding pictured in my head.'

'Me neither.'

'Maybe I can make the rest of it the way I pictured.' Her tone had turned cold and vindictive. 'You've made me to feel a fool for wanting Richard, for thinking I might have him. You've taken the pleasure out of my wedding day, but you won't take the pleasure out of the rest of it.'

'I'm sorry, Nadine, if you think that I have –'

'Now that I have him, I intend to show him how a woman can really please a man. He'll see. He'll see that I can be just as good a woman for him as you. You think I can't, but I can.'

Nadine leaned close. 'I'll have Richard's eyes spinning in his head before this night is out. Then we'll see who the better woman is, and how much he misses you. When you're lying there with Richard's brother, listen close, and you'll hear my screams of pleasure. The screams of pleasure Richard gives me. Not you – me!'

Nadine stormed away to stand with her arms folded in a huff. Kahlan put her face in her hands. The spirits weren't content to destroy her, they had to twist the knife.

Cara and the legate returned. 'It is time,' they said as one.

Kahlan rose woodenly, to stand, waiting to be told what to do next. The legate turned to Cara.

'This storm is going to break soon.' The legate turned to peer up at the blackness. 'My wives and I must be off this mountain.' He gripped Cara's arm. 'The winds speak to you the same as they speak to me. Can you take them?'

'Yes. It is nearly done. I can finish it,' Cara said. 'The winds will pass the message through me as well as through you.'

Without further word, he scurried off into the darkness.

Cara's strong fingers gripped under Kahlan's arm. 'Come with me,' she said in that icy voice of the winds.

Kahlan dug in her heels. 'Cara, please. I can't.'

'You can, and you will, or the chance will pass and the plague will rage on.'

Kahlan pulled back. 'No, you don't understand. I can't. I'm having my moon flow. It isn't finished yet. I can't … do this. Not now.'

Cara's sinister glare drew close. 'It will not prevent you from consummating your marriage. You will do this, or all hope of stopping the plague is lost. It is not finished, yet. You must do your part in this – indulge in this. It must be now. Tonight. Or would you rather the dying continue unabated?'

With Nadine on one side of her, and Kahlan on the other, Cara led them down the road, through the darkness, toward the edge of the cliff.

Standing in the black night at the edge of the cliff, Kahlan felt numb and lost. She didn't know how long Cara was gone with Nadine, taking her to Richard in the crumbling building to the right. She felt Cara's hand under her arm again.

'This way,' came the icy voice.

Kahlan let the woman lead her to the ruins on the left. Kahlan could hardly see a thing. Cara, led by the winds, had no trouble negotiating the halls and rooms in the wreck of a building.

They came to a doorway. Kahlan could just make out Drefan's sword standing up against the wall outside. Her fingers rested on its leatherbound hilt. Inside, she could just discern the rectangles where windows once stood. Beyond was the edge of the cliff, and the emptiness where the Temple of the Winds had once been.

'This is your wife,' Cara said with that icy, horrid voice as she spoke into the room. 'Here is your husband,' she said to Kahlan.

'This marriage must be consummated. It is now your duty to

do so. The winds have requirements. You may ask no more questions. Do not speak. The winds have reasons, and it is not for you to know them, only to obey, if you wish to end the death.

'As the test narrows, it becomes more intense.

'You must now lie as husband and wife. If either of you utters so much as one word, the test will end, and entry into the Temple of the Winds will be denied. There can be no appeal. The stolen magic will rage on, as will the death caused by it.

'Only after you have fulfilled the requirements of the consummation will the winds come. After the winds come – and you will have no doubt that it has happened – you may then speak to one another. Not before.'

Cara turned Kahlan around and helped her out of her dress and the rest of her things. It wasn't hard for Kahlan not to speak; she had nothing to say.

Kahlan felt the black night air on her naked flesh. She glanced down at Drefan's sword, thinking briefly that when it was over, she could always use it on herself. If not, if he denied her access to it, there was always the cliff.

Cara gripped Kahlan by the wrist and led her forward. Forcefully, Cara made her kneel down, and then lean forward until Kahlan felt the edge of the pallet.

'Your husband awaits you here. Go to him.'

Kahlan heard Cara's footsteps fade into the distance.

Then she was alone with Drefan.

CHAPTER 58

As Kahlan felt her way, her hand brushed Drefan's hairy leg.
She moved off to the side, to lie down beside him. There was a
blanket over straw, or something softer than bare wood,
anyway. At least it didn't hurt her back as would have the hard
ground.

She lay on the pallet, staring up into the blackness with wide
eyes. She couldn't see anything, other than the vague
indication of the windows before them. She made an effort to
slow her breathing, although she could do nothing to slow her
panicked pulse.

This wasn't the worst thing, she told herself. Not the worst
thing in the world. Not at all. This wasn't rape. Exactly.

After a time, she felt Drefan's hand settle on her belly.
Kahlan shoved it away as she stifled a cry.

She shouldn't have done that, she told herself. What was a
hand, compared to the plague? How many people in agony
with the plague would gladly have traded places with her? Not
the worst thing at all, a gentle hand.

Drefan's hand found hers, trying to give it a squeeze of
reassurance. She yanked her hand away as if a snake had
touched her. She didn't want his reassurance. She had not
vowed to hold his hand. She had not vowed to accept his
reassurance. She had committed to being his wife, not to
holding his hand. She would let him do to her what she must
let him do to her, but she didn't have to hold his hand.

Kahlan frantically tried to reason with herself. Richard had
to get into the Temple of the Winds. The Temple of the Winds

demanded this as the price of the path. The spirit of Chandalen's grandfather had warned her that she must not shirk her duty. She remembered his words all too well:

I have not been shown the price, but I forewarn you that I do know that there is no way for you to circumvent or avoid it. It must be as it will be revealed to you, or all will be lost. I ask that when the winds show you the path, you take it, lest what I have shown you comes to be.

Kahlan remembered the scenes of mass death the spirit had shown her. If she failed to do as the winds asked, what she had been shown would come to pass.

She had to let Drefan do this. Stalling would not make it any easier.

This couldn't be easy for Drefan. Couldn't be easy at all, what with the way she shoved away his attempts at tenderness. That made her angry all over again. She didn't want his tenderness.

What did she want? Did she want him to be rough? Of course she had to let him touch her. How could he do this if he didn't touch her? Richard had to get into the Temple of the Winds. She had to let Drefan do this.

Kahlan reached over and took Drefan's wrist. She put his hand back where he had tried to put it before, on her belly. She let go of his hand. It stayed there.

What was he waiting for? She wanted to scream at him to get it over with, to do it and be done. To take what was his brother's by heart if not by vow.

She lay there, with Drefan's hand on her, listening to the dead silence of the night. She realized that she was listening for sounds coming from Nadine and Richard. She shut her eyes.

Drefan's hand moved to her breast. Fists at her sides, she forced herself to remain still. She had to let him. She tried to think of other things. She silently recited rote language lessons of her youth, trying to ignore his hand. But she couldn't.

He was being gentle, but that was no consolation. Even his touch was a violation. How gently he did it made no difference, didn't make it right. That he was now her husband made no difference to her. She knew in her heart it was wrong, and that made it a violation.

In her mind, she screamed at herself. She was being worse than childish. She was the Mother Confessor, and had faced much worse than this, much worse than a man for whom she had no feelings being this close, this intimate.

But she was no longer the Mother Confessor. The Temple of the Winds, the spirits, had taken that, too, from her.

Kahlan gasped in a breath and held it tight as Drefan's hand roamed down her belly and finally settled between her legs. She remembered Drefan doing that to Cara. Now he did it to her.

She hated him. She was married to a man she hated.

Cara had felt it, the same as Kahlan could feel it, now. Cara hadn't been so childish about it. Cara wouldn't be this foolish. Kahlan let Drefan's hand do what it would.

This was to save lives. She had to save all those innocent people from the plague sent by Jagang. Her people couldn't be saved without her. It was her duty.

Drefan suddenly rose up. The dark shape of him hovered over her. His knee pushed gently between her thighs, urging her to open her legs. It would be over soon, she told herself, as he put his other knee between her legs, too.

The hulking shape of him lowered over her. He was big, as big as Richard. She feared he was going to crush her, but he didn't. He held himself up on his elbows, so he wouldn't hurt her. He was being tender, and she was only making it harder for him. He had to do this, and she had to let him.

Kahlan grimaced. She wasn't ready. She held her breath. It was too late not to be ready; Drefan was there. She bit her lower lip as she winced.

She felt as helpless as she had ever felt in her entire life. She was married to Drefan, not Richard, and Drefan, not Richard, was having her. Everything was lost.

Her eyes squeezed shut, Kahlan pressed her fists to her shoulders as he moved in her. Tears trickled from the corners of her eyes. Her nose stuffed up as she wept silently, and she had to open her mouth to breathe. She wanted to wail in anguish, but she instead had to remind herself to breathe. She couldn't seem to stop holding her breath.

It took longer than she had hoped, but not as long as she feared.

Finished at last, Drefan rolled off her, onto his back. He had accomplished his task, but he seemed not to have relished it. She was somehow relieved that he hadn't enjoyed it. He lay there, recovering his breath, as she finally let hers out. It was over.

She told herself that it hadn't been so bad. It was nothing, really. She hardly felt anything. She had foolishly balked, and here it was, over already. It wasn't so bad as she had feared. It was nothing, really.

But it was. She did feel something. She felt defiled.

Drefan reached out, his fingers tenderly, sympathetically brushing a tear from her cheek. She shoved his hand away. She didn't want his sympathy. She didn't want him touching her. She hadn't agreed to him touching her, just to consummating the marriage. His touch wasn't part of it.

She remembered being with Richard. She remembered her hot need of him. She remembered the wild passion. She remembered her screams of sheer pleasure.

Why was this so different?

Because she didn't love Drefan, that was why. In fact, she was beginning to realize that she loathed him. There was something about him that she didn't like, and it was more than just that memory of his hand on Cara. There was something deceptive about him, something devious. She hadn't consciously realized it before, but she could see guile in his blue eyes.

Kahlan wondered why she would think that. He had just consummated their marriage, and he had been as gentle as he possibly could be while still doing it. He could easily have done anything he wanted; her power was locked away. She couldn't stop him. Yet he had tried to be sympathetic, understanding.

Still, it seemed a wonder to her that it could be so different from when she had been with Richard. She would give anything, almost, to have that pleasure again. She longed for that fulfillment, that satisfaction. The sating of lust.

Drefan's breathing evened out after a time. Kahlan lay there, in the darkness, beside him, beside her new husband, waiting. Why hadn't the Temple of the Winds come? She had done her part.

Maybe Richard hadn't. Kahlan wondered if he could. After all, she had only to lie there. Richard had to be aroused. How could he be aroused, over there, knowing that his brother was over here, having his way with the woman Richard loved?

Kahlan had seen the look in Richard's eyes, the look of wild jealousy, at the mere mention of what Shota said – that Kahlan would marry another. Kahlan had never seen such a look in his eyes before, and at the time there hadn't really been a reason for it. Now there was.

No, Nadine would see to it that Richard did what he needed to do. If there was one thing Kahlan had confidence in, it was Nadine's desire to consummate that marriage.

Nadine was a beautiful woman. She was more than enthusiastic. How could Richard not be aroused? He knew he had to do it. He would have no reason to try to resist her urging. Maybe Richard was thinking of it as revenge against his brother, Michael, for taking Nadine. Perhaps that was how he would get through it.

Kahlan knew that Nadine was having the time of her life. This was Nadine's dream.

This was Kahlan's nightmare.

The dark sky she could just perceive out the windows seemed to boil, as it had all day and all night. The air remained dead still and sticky. The storm wouldn't break. It threatened, but it would not come.

Kahlan laid her wrist over her forehead as she rested, waiting. Her legs hurt, and she realized that it was because she was pressing her knees together. She let her legs relax. Drefan had done his duty. He was finished. It was over. She could relax.

Kahlan shut her eyes when she heard Nadine's distant laughter drifting through the night air. The woman was as good as her word. Did Richard have to make her laugh? Couldn't he just do his duty? No, Richard would not make Nadine laugh. Nadine laughed for Kahlan's benefit.

The night dragged on endlessly. Where was the Temple of the Winds? Drefan made no attempt to touch her again, and she was thankful for that. He lay there, on his back, waiting with her.

Each hour that passed brought no change. From time to

time, Kahlan drifted off to sleep. Nadine's throaty laughter brought her awake with a jolt.

Kahlan wanted to slap Richard. How long was he going to make this go on? He could have had Nadine three times by now. Maybe he had. Maybe when the Temple of the Winds didn't come, he kept trying. Nadine would like that. Kahlan felt her cheeks burning.

Drefan was silent as he lay beside her. The winds had said that they couldn't talk. She guessed that Nadine's laughter didn't count; she used no words. Her laughter carried message enough.

Kahlan sighed. Sooner or later, the winds would come. They had all done as required.

Had she, though?

What was it Cara had said?

You must do your part in this – indulge in this.

Drefan had indulged. He had been satisfied. Nadine certainly was indulging. Richard must have.

Kahlan hadn't. She hadn't 'indulged.'

She dismissed the idea. It had to be something else. Maybe the winds were just waiting for Nadine to finally have enough. That would fit the way the Temple of the Winds had done everything else, twisting the pain for Richard and Kahlan. Making them suffer.

As the night dragged on, and recollecting Cara's words about indulging, Kahlan thought again about the time she had been with Richard in that place between worlds. She had felt the kind of pleasure that other woman felt – the indulgence not only in love, but in lust.

Kahlan had been so frustrated lately, waiting to be with Richard, waiting for that closeness again, waiting to be married to him so they could be together as husband and wife. Waiting for that satisfaction again. It was so near, she had been so close, so ready, and then it all fell apart, leaving her hopes dashed and needs unfulfilled.

Now, for the first time, she was free of her Confessor's power, free to take pleasure from a man, not for love, but for the sheer indulgence of pleasure. She was free to enjoy what other women enjoyed. Here she was, lying next to her husband, and not an unattractive man at all, and she was feeling frustration for the need of Richard.

Was she to live the rest of her life being denied a simple pleasure of life that she was now free to indulge?

But she didn't love Drefan. Without love, the passion was empty.

Still, it was passion, and if not ideal, at least she could have that much satisfaction. The spirits had taken everything else from her. They had taken Richard, the only thing she really wanted out of life. Would she let them take simple pleasure, too?

What else had she, now?

This was her husband. She was condemned to live the rest of her life with him. Must it be without at least some small release of pent-up need? Wasn't she entitled to at least that much after all she had sacrificed? They had taken everything else from her: her only love in life; her Confessor's power.

You must do your part in this – indulge in this.

What if that was why the winds hadn't come? What if it was because she hadn't indulged?

Drefan rolled over on his stomach and sighed. He was frustrated by the wait, too. Or maybe he was tending to his auras.

She thought about Drefan's tight trousers, and the way she caught herself looking. Drefan was a handsome man; he was built like Richard. Drefan was her husband.

Her anger at the spirits for taking everything from her was what finally made something inside her snap. This was all she had. She was entitled to this much – to release.

When her hand touched Drefan's back, he jumped. Kahlan smoothed her hand across the muscles of his back, and he settled. She let herself feel his muscles, as she used to feel Richard's muscles, feel his shape. She took a deep breath, and she let herself go.

Kahlan's hand moved down Drefan's back. She gritted her teeth as she gripped his buttocks. They were as tight as they looked in his trousers. She was lucky, she guessed; the spirits could have insisted that she marry a repulsive man. Instead, they had insisted that she marry Drefan, and he was far from repulsive. He wasn't as handsome as Richard, no one was as handsome to her as Richard, but women were always fawning over Drefan. Now, he was her husband. He had pledged to be loyal to her. She had pledged to be loyal to him.

This was the only pleasure she was to be allowed. This was all the spirits had left her. At least she could have this much – have what she was entitled to.

Kahlan seized Drefan's hip and rolled him over, toward her. She hooked her leg over his, and let her hand roam over his chest. Drefan didn't react. Maybe he was surprised by her change of behavior. Maybe he was confused. She would have to unconfuse him. She gently pinched one of his nipples, then let her hand slide across his flat stomach, and down.

Kahlan found that Drefan was in no condition to do her any good. If she wanted to have her pleasure, she would have to change that.

She kissed his chest. She trailed wet kisses down his stomach. His breathing seemed slow. Kahlan felt frustrated anger that he wasn't taking the hint. She was tired of being frustrated, while everyone else wasn't.

She decided that if she wanted to have satisfaction, it was up to her to see to it that she got what she wanted. No one would give it to her – she would have to take it. Kahlan let her tongue, her kisses, glide the rest of the way down Drefan's taut belly.

When she took him in her mouth, she tasted her own blood. She forced herself to ignore the taste as she urged him to react.

At first she thought he wasn't going to, but when she lost herself in the erotic nature of what she was doing, he finally did. He came back as strong as before.

By the time Drefan was fully ready, Kahlan was panting with need. Once she had decided to have her pleasure, she became insistent. Drefan was her husband now. It was his duty to fulfill her needs, too, not just his own.

Kahlan's head was spinning with the want of release. That it was Drefan no longer mattered. In her mind, she imagined it was Richard. At that thought, she moaned with longing and climbed atop him, straddling his hips.

This time, she was ready to accept him. This time, she wanted him. She shut it out of her mind that this was Drefan and imagined it was Richard. Since she couldn't see Drefan's blue eyes, it wasn't hard to envision it was Richard, instead.

She remembered the things she did with Richard, and did those things. She relived that experience in her imagination. Her mouth gaped. She gasped for air. Sweat ran down her body as she moved atop him, writhing forcefully against him.

Drefan was panting now, too. She needed to have release from all the frustration that had built up for so long – all the times she had kissed Richard, and wanted to do more; all the times he had touched her, and she had wanted him to do more. Now, he was.

Kahlan leaned forward, to kiss him. Drefan turned his face away. She scooped her arm under his head, and held him to her chest, instead. His face felt hot against her breasts. The roughness of his unshaved face excited her as she slid her sweaty flesh against him. It made her pant all the more.

She was just about to scream at him to put his hands on her, when she remembered that she wasn't allowed to utter so much as a word. She seized his wrist and put first one hand where she wanted it, and then the other, to hold her bottom while she moved – so she could imagine it was Richard holding her again, needing her. She wanted to feel him gripping her in his big hands while she moved.

For the first time since she had last been with Richard, she felt wild pleasure, wild lust, a wild, desperate need. That it was with Drefan no longer mattered to her. She wanted only release.

It came with stunning, ridged shivers. Her sharp moan shook her shoulders. Her legs stiffened to stone. Her toes clawed. She slammed herself down on him as the wanton fulfillment of lust inundated her. She gave herself over to it completely, and with helpless, unbridled abandon let it run free. She gasped sharply again, the cry following in the echoing wake of the first. It seemed that it lasted an eternity, as if it was almost too much to endure. With a final convulsion, it subsided. At last, it was over.

For one twisting moment, she had been free. There was no plague, no people dying, no responsibility, no duty, no marriage to Drefan, no Nadine. For that one moment, she had been free of it all, and she had been immersed in gratification.

For that one moment, her heart and her lust had been with Richard again.

Kahlan collapsed to the side of Drefan, panting, getting her wind back, pushing her wet hair back off her face. It occurred to her that he hadn't reached any satisfaction this second time. She didn't care. She had. At the moment, that was all that mattered: sweet release.

For a wonderful moment, she had been free of everything, and had been with her love, if only in her imagination. Kahlan realized that she was weeping with the joy of it.

She lay on her side, turned away from Drefan, as she recovered. She wiped the tears of pleasure from her face. In the absence of need, she unexpectedly began to feel ashamed.

Dear spirits, what had she just done? She had enjoyed herself, that was all. She had needed the release. Then why did she suddenly feel so dirty?

Distant thunder rumbled toward them. A hint of embedded lightning flickered in the sky. Kahlan looked up, out the windows. Another flash, closer, ripped through the insides of the roiling clouds, briefly lighting the mountaintop.

From the other building, Kahlan heard a long scream from Nadine. Kahlan blocked it from her mind. As much as Nadine's scream rankled Kahlan, it at least didn't leave her as frustrated as it had before.

Three more screams came from Nadine. Short, piercing, urgent. Kahlan pressed her hands to her ears. Nadine had made her point, couldn't she just let it be, now?

The wind came up, abruptly, as if a great, huge door had opened. The blast of air hit like an avalanche. The building shuddered. The entire mountain quaked.

Kahlan propped herself up on her elbows, peering out the windows. Distant lightning flickered through the turbulent clouds. Thunder rumbled, reverberating through the mountains. Each strike came a little closer.

The Temple of the Winds was coming – there was no doubt in her mind. That took her thoughts back to Richard, because it was coming for him. She felt sudden shame. How could she so easily lose track of her heart? How could she find such pleasure from another man? What was she thinking?

She had never felt so dirty in her whole life as she suddenly did now. With Richard, she had felt wonderful afterward. Now, she was feeling worse by the moment. If Richard ever found out, he would never understand.

Richard would never know. There was no way for him to find out. Unless Drefan told him. Her heart pounded. She thought about the guile she thought she had seen in Drefan's eyes. No, he wouldn't tell Richard.

But what if he did?

With a sudden, close strike of lightning, Kahlan sat up straight. She saw something out the window – a structure. As the winds had said, there was no doubt. She could talk, now.

She spun back to Drefan. She had to secure his silence in this before they left this place. If Richard ever found out …

The wind lashed at the mountaintop. The thunder boomed.

In the darkness, she reached out and clutched his arm.

'Drefan, listen to me. You must promise. You can never tell what just happened, what I just did with you.' Her hand tightened. Her fingernails dug into his arm. 'I'll do whatever you tell me to do for the rest of my life, but you must promise me that you will never tell' – ribbons of lightning lit the room – 'Richard …'

Thunder crashed, jarring the ground. Lightning snaked along the bottoms of the clouds, lighting the room with a harsh glare.

In the flickering flashes, gray eyes were fixed on her.

'I think "Richard" already knows.'

Kahlan screamed.

CHAPTER 59

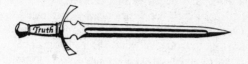

Kahlan froze. Thoughts crashed through her mind in a confusion of thundering terror.

Her scream came again, ripping through the night, loud enough to be heard over the sound of the thunder. She couldn't make herself blink. She couldn't tear her eyes from Richard's face.

She couldn't understand, couldn't make sense of it. The world felt as if it had turned upside down. Everything tumbled around in her mind, making it impossible to think.

As the lightning lit the room again, she knew only one thing: this was Richard, not Drefan.

No look she had ever seen on Richard's face was as terrifying to Kahlan as the one she saw now. There was nothing in his eyes. Not rage, not lethal commitment, not determination, not a deadly calm countenance, not jealousy, not even empty disinterest.

There was no ... soul, in those gray eyes. No heart.

Kahlan covered her mouth with both trembling hands. She backed away until her back smacked into the stone wall.

He had known from the first instant she had come into the room. Richard could tell it was her coming into a room. He had known it was her the whole time – from the first instant Cara had led her in here.

He knew. He had tried to squeeze her hand, to reassure her, to let her know. She had pushed his hand away. He had been as gentle as he could. He had tried to brush her tears away,

649

after. She had pushed his hand away. She hadn't let him show her that it was him.

Kahlan collapsed to the floor with a wail of horror.

'No! Dear spirits, no!'

Richard didn't rush to her, didn't speak words of comfort, didn't yell. Instead, he went to where his clothes were lying, near the door, and began getting dressed.

Kahlan scurried to her things nearby. She raced to pull on her underthings, suddenly feeling the humiliation of her nakedness, its reminder of what she had just done.

She scooped up her dress. She paused, tears streaming down her face. She reached around the outside of the doorway and brought the sword and scabbard up before her face. It had a leather handle, just as she remembered seeing, not a wire-wound hilt. It wasn't the Sword of Truth, Richard's sword. It was Drefan's sword.

Kahlan gripped Richard by his wrist as he picked up his pants. 'How … this is Drefan's sword, not yours. It's Drefan's sword!'

Richard took it from her and leaned it against the wall. 'They took your power. You have no way to defend yourself. Drefan will be the one near you, now, not me. I gave him the Sword of Truth so that he could protect you.' His eyes finally met hers. 'I guess this one finds the truth just as well as the other.'

Richard stuffed his leg into his pants. Kahlan snatched his arm again.

'Richard, don't you see? It was you. It was you in here with me, not Drefan. The spirits mark a distinction – between intent and deed. It wasn't him, it was you all along!'

He pulled his arm away. The spirits might mark a distinction, but he didn't. To Richard, the intent was the same as the deed.

'Richard, you don't understand. It wasn't what you think.'

He shot her a glare of such power that it staggered her back a step. He waited as she stood frozen, unable to find any words to explain. He went back to dressing.

Kahlan pulled on her white Confessor's dress. Outside, the lightning was coming closer. During some of the closer strikes, she could see an immense structure rising up at the edge of the cliff: the Temple of the Winds. When the flash extinguished, the temple vanished again, and she could see the distant mountains beyond, lit by the lightning farther away.

'Richard,' she wept as he pulled on a boot, 'please, talk to me. Say something. Ask me to explain. Tell me there can be no explanation. Yell at me. Call me a whore. Tell me you hate me. Hit me. Do something! Don't ignore me!'

He turned and picked up his black sleeveless undershirt. As he pulled it on over his head, she scooped up his black shirt and held it to her breast, hoping to halt his dressing.

'Richard, please! I love you!'

His gaze again rose to hers. She thought he was going to say something, but instead he turned away and retrieved his belt with the leather packs on it. He snapped on his wristbands.

Kahlan held his shirt to her chest and shook as she watched him hook his belt together. She didn't know what to do. He picked up Drefan's sword and buckled it on.

'Richard, please talk to me. Say something. This is the doing of the spirits. Don't you remember what I told you that grandfather's spirit told me? *The winds have decided that you are the path of the price.* They did this to us!'

He shot her a look again. The intensity in his eyes extinguished. He saw that she wasn't going to surrender his shirt, so he threw his golden cloak around his shoulders.

As he turned toward the door, Kahlan seized his arm with both her hands and turned him back to her.

'Richard, I love you. You've got to believe me. I'll explain this in here to you later, but for now, you have to believe me. I love you. No other. My heart is yours alone. Dear spirits, please believe me.'

Richard gripped her jaw in his hand and wiped a thumb across her lips. He held his thumb up for her to see in the pandemonium of lightning.

'... for the one in white, his true beloved, will betray him in her blood.'

His words ripped her heart.

Kahlan covered her scream with his shirt as he swept out the door. The one thing she had sworn she would never do, she

651

had done; she had betrayed him. It could have been no worse betrayal. It was a betrayal that had destroyed his heart.

Crying hysterically, Kahlan raced after him, out into the wild night. She had to do something to mend that heart. She couldn't let him endure the pain she had caused him. She loved him more than life itself, and she had done the worst thing possible to him.

Outside, the wind howled across the mountain. She could see his black shape, his bare arms, in the flashes of lightning as he headed for the road.

As he reached the edge of the cliff at the end of the road, Kahlan threw herself on him, dragging him to a halt.

The sky was a savage show of violent discharges. Thunder thumped in her bones. Lightning ripped across the sky followed by deafening booms. Beyond the edge, when the most powerful of those bolts struck, the Temple of the Winds was there – but only during those fierce strikes. Between those strikes, there was nothing but empty space.

'Richard, what are you going to do?'

'I'm going to stop the plague.'

'When will you be back? I'll wait here. When will you be back?'

He stared into her eyes a long moment as the storm raged around them.

'There is nothing here for me.'

Kahlan clutched at him. 'Richard, you have to come back. Come back. I'll be here, waiting. I love you. Dear spirits, I need you. Richard, you have to come back to me!'

'You have a husband. You have given him an oath … and everything else.'

'Richard, don't leave me alone,' Kahlan wailed, on the edge of hysteria. 'If you don't come back, I'll never forgive you.'

Richard turned to the edge of the cliff.

'Richard, you have a wife! You have to come back!'

Thunder shuddered the mountain.

He looked back over his shoulder. 'Nadine is dead. I am no longer bound by my oath to her. You have a husband, and an oath. There is nothing here for me.'

Brutal cords of lightning slammed into the road beyond the

edge of the cliff, bringing the Temple of the Winds into full view.

Golden cloak billowing out behind, Richard leaped into the lightning.

'Richard! I'm here! I'm here for you! We can find a way! Please come back to me!'

When the frenetic flash cut off, the temple was gone. Another flash came, and the soaring towers were back for a second, weaker this time, and then gone again.

Kahlan dropped to the ground, clutching Richard's black shirt to herself. She had destroyed him.

From the side, Kahlan saw a streak of red. It was Cara, racing for the edge of the cliff. She leaped just as another flash erupted, lighting the Temple of the Winds into the world of life. She landed on the road in the sky, and when the flash was gone, so was the Temple of the Winds, Richard, and Cara.

Devastated, Kahlan stared silently at the rampaging storm, seeing from time to time the towering, phantom temple in another world. It never looked solid enough again, or she would have jumped across. She should have. She couldn't understand why she hadn't. Why had she just stood here?

Because Richard didn't want her. She had betrayed him.

How could he do this to her? He said he would always love her. He said they would be together in the next world. He made her promises. He swore his eternal love.

So had she, and she had betrayed him.

From somewhere out in the storm, Kahlan heard the distant sound of laughter. The malevolent chuckle made her skin crawl.

Drefan strolled up beside her. He was alone.

'Where's Nadine?' Kahlan asked.

Drefan cleared his throat. 'When the lightning came, and she saw it was me, and not Richard, she screamed. She went crazy. She leaped over the edge of the mountain.'

Kahlan stared up at him. Richard knew. He told her Nadine was dead. Richard was a wizard. She had seen that, too, in his eyes, at the end, before he jumped across. She saw magic in his eyes.

'Where's Richard?'

Kahlan stared out at the empty air, at the black wall of night. 'Gone.'

*

On the road to the Temple of the Winds, in the eerie silence, Richard drew his sword. Its alien feel surprised him for an instant, until he recalled whose sword it was.

He was no longer the Seeker of Truth. He had had all the truth he could stand.

It wasn't night, here, nor day, yet there was light. It wasn't like sunlight – more like an overcast day, with no hint of exactly where the sun was. But he knew that there was no sun here. This was not the world of life.

This was a part of the underworld – an isolated, remote, obscure niche in the world of the dead. It was as if the wizards had found an out-of-the-way hole in which to hide the Temple of the Winds. It had been similarly hidden when in the world of life.

The dark walls of the immense Temple of the Winds rose up before him, the twin towers soaring up into trailers of mist. The entire side of Mount Kymermosst was here – the whole part that was missing in the world of life.

Richard knew where he was going. He knew more than he had ever known before. Knowledge was flooding into his mind. He was a war wizard. The Temple of the Winds had opened a floodgate into his mind. It was feeding him all he needed to know, and more.

He felt as if he were sentient for the first time.

Recompense, for the price demanded.

'Lord Rahl!'

A breathless Cara ran up beside him. Agiel in hand, she took up a defensive position. Her Agiel would be useless here. For that matter, it would be useless back in the world of life now.

Richard turned to the winds and started out again. It wasn't far. Not far at all. He knew the way in.

'Cara, go home. You don't belong here.'

'Lord Rahl, what happened? I –'

'Go home.'

She scowled at him as she pushed past to clear his way of any danger. She had no concept of the dangers here.

'I am Mord-Sith. I am here to protect the Lord Rahl.'

'I am no longer the Lord Rahl,' Richard whispered.

She gazed up at the huge black stone pillars beside the

entrance ahead. Beside them on walls of inky stone banded with copper-colored caps, frozen in raven-black granite, stood the skrin, guardians of the boundary between worlds. Frozen only to Cara's eyes, not to his.

Cara lifted a hand, bidding him to stay back as she peered down the passageway to the distant entry, checking for danger. There were bones at their feet.

'Lord Rahl, what is this place?'

'You can't go in here, Cara.'

'Why not?'

Richard turned and looked back toward the way he had come – at everything he was leaving behind. At nothing.

'Because this is the Hall of the Betrayed.'

Richard glanced up at the twin skrin, guardians that had left the bones of two wizards here on this walkway, at their feet.

Richard remembered well the message the sliph had passed on from Wizard Ricker: *Ward left in.* Richard now knew what that meant.

He lifted his left arm, fist out, toward the skrin perched on the stone wall at the right. Ward left told him which arm to use and which skrin to ward. The wrong arm would have denied him entry into this place in the world of the dead. One of Ricker's traps for the enemy.

His wristband heated. The leather pad protected his flesh from the power he focused in that band. A green glow enveloped his fist. The skrin to the right, to which he directed his birthright of authority, glowed in sympathy with his fist, immobilized for now, to allow Richard to enter.

Richard glanced up at the guardian of raven-black granite to his left. Richard called out its name, a guttural sound to which it answered. Black stone cracked and crumbled as the skrin turned to its master, awaiting instruction.

Richard made the sound of its name again. He lifted his hand to Cara.

'This one does not belong here. Ward her back to the world of life. Do not harm her. After, return to your post.'

The skrin sprang from the stone wall, enveloping Cara.

'Lord Rahl! When will you be home?'

Richard gazed into her blue eyes. 'I am home.'

Light flared and silent thunder shook the soundless world as the skrin vanished on its journey with Cara, back to the world of life.

Richard turned to the winds. The four winds and the seer watched from their place up on the wall. Richard scanned the solid gold runes running up each side of the wall beside the entrance to the hall, reading the messages and warnings placed there by wizards past.

In a world without wind, Richard's cloak billowed out behind, a telltale in a place with eddies of power and currents of force, as he strode onward, into the Hall of the Betrayed.

Kahlan threw up an arm before her face as lightning suddenly cracked before her. The road into the Temple of the Winds lit for an instant. In the distance, Kahlan could see Richard's back as he strode resolutely into a passageway.

Cara tumbled to the ground on the road at the edge of the cliff, at Kahlan's feet.

With the boom of thunder, the temple, and Richard, were gone.

Cara rolled to her feet. With wild fury, she seized Kahlan by the shoulders.

'What have you done!'

Kahlan hurt too much to speak. She stared at the ground.

'Mother Confessor, what have you done! I fixed it for you. What did you do to him?'

Kahlan's head came up. 'You what?'

'I swore an oath. We are sisters of the Agiel. I swore an oath to you that if anything ever happened, if anything went wrong, I would see to it that it was you, and not Nadine, who was with Richard.'

Kahlan's mouth fell open. 'Cara, what did you do?'

'What you wanted! I spoke the words of the winds as they came to me, but when I took you and Nadine to the buildings, I switched you both. I took Nadine to Drefan, and I took you to Lord Rahl.

'I wanted you to be with the man you truly loved. I took you to Richard! Didn't you trust in me? Didn't you have faith in me?'

Kahlan fell into Cara's arms. 'Oh, Cara, I'm sorry. I should have believed in you. Dear spirits, I should have trusted you.'

'Lord Rahl said he was going into the Hall of the Betrayed. I asked when he would be coming home. He said he was home. He isn't coming back! What have you done!'

'The Hall of the Betrayed ...' Kahlan crumpled to the ground. 'I have fulfilled the prophecy. I have helped Richard get into the Temple of the Winds. I have helped him stop the plague.

'In so doing, I have destroyed him.

'In so doing, I have destroyed myself.'

'You have done more than that,' Cara whispered.

'What do you mean?'

Cara lifted her Agiel in her fist. 'My Agiel. It has lost its power. The power of a Mord-Sith works only in the presence of the bond to our Lord Rahl. It exists to protect the Lord Rahl. Without a Lord Rahl, there is no bond. I have lost my power.'

'I am Lord Rahl now,' Drefan said as he strode up behind Kahlan.

Cara sneered at him. 'You are no Lord Rahl. You do not have the gift.'

Drefan met her glare. 'I'm all the Lord Rahl you have, now. Someone has to hold the D'Haran empire together.'

Kahlan clutched Richard's black shirt to her stomach. 'I am the Mother Confessor. I will hold the alliance together.'

'You, my dear, have lost your power, too. You are no longer a Confessor, much less the Mother Confessor.' He reached down and gripped Kahlan under her arm. His powerful fingers tightened painfully as he lifted her. 'You are my wife, now, and you will do as I tell you to do. You have sworn an oath to obey me.'

Cara reached out to force him to let go of Kahlan. Drefan backhanded her across the mouth, knocking her to the ground.

'And you, Cara, are a toothless snake now. If you wish to stick around, then you will have to obey me. If not, I have no use for you. For now, only we know that your Agiel doesn't work. Keep it that way. You will protect me as any Lord Rahl.'

Cara gave him a venomous look as she wiped the blood from her mouth. 'You are not the Lord Rahl.'

'No?' He lifted the Sword of Truth, Richard's sword, and let it drop back into its scabbard. 'Well, I am the Seeker, now.'

'You are not the Seeker, either,' Kahlan growled. 'Richard is the Seeker.'

'Richard? There is no Richard anymore. I am now Lord Rahl, and the Seeker.' Drefan pulled Kahlan against him, his Darken Rahl eyes burning into her. 'And you are my wife. At least you will be, once we consummate the marriage. But this is neither the time nor place. We have to get back. There is work to be done.'

'Never. If you ever touch me, I'll cut your throat.'

'You have sworn an oath before the spirits. You will do as you have sworn.' Drefan smiled. 'You're a whore. You'll enjoy it. I want you to enjoy it, to be pleased, I really do.'

'How dare you call me that! I am no whore, especially yours!'

His smile widened. 'Really? Then how did you betray Richard? Why would he walk away without even looking back? My guess would be that you enjoyed it, when you thought it was me. I'd say Richard saw you for the whore you are. When it really is me, you will find pleasure in it, then, too. I'll like that.'

CHAPTER 60

Verna gently shoved Warren. 'Wake up. Someone is coming.'

Warren knuckled his eyes. 'I'm awake.'

Verna glanced back at the other windows, to make sure that the dead guards were still propped up to make it appear they were on watch. A light from a lamp on the table was just enough to show those outside the guards at the windows, but it would provide enough light to see her and Warren, too, so they stayed away from the windows.

'How do you feel?' she asked.

'Better. I think I'm all right, now.'

He had been unconscious earlier. The headaches caused by the gift were coming closer and closer together. Verna didn't know what to do for him. She didn't know how long it would be before his gift killed him. The only thing she could think to do was to stick to her plan. Warren had said that prophecy had told him that his only chance was to be with her.

Out the window, in the darkness, she could see two shadowed figures approaching up the road. In the distance, on the hills, campfires by the thousands made the countryside look like a lake's reflection of the starry sky.

Verna shuddered to think of the hundreds of thousands of brutes in those tents. The sooner they left this place, the better. She was thankful they weren't going up into Jagang's stronghold again. They wouldn't be able to pull off that kind of magic twice. The spells Warren had used would not trick the guards again.

Thankfully, once was enough. This time, her friends, Janet

and Amelia, were coming out to meet her and Warren. If that was, in fact, Janet and Amelia she saw approaching.

It had to be. This was the fourth night after the full moon. This was where they were to meet. Janet had said that Amelia would be back from the tents by now.

Verna feared to think of what kind of shape Amelia would be in. She would probably need to be healed. Verna hoped that it wouldn't take long; it was close to dawn.

She and Warren had taken turns at short naps. They had a lot of traveling to do, to get back to General Reibisch and his army, and they needed to be rested for the journey. Verna wanted to be as far away from this place as she could get in case an alert rose from the stronghold.

Verna hoped that Janet had already told Amelia about the bond to Richard so that she wouldn't have to waste time with that, too. As soon as Amelia was sworn to Richard, the bond would protect her, too, from the dream walker. Then they could escape.

Verna dearly wanted to rescue the rest of the Sisters, but she knew that presumption was a road to ruin. On her twenty-year journey away from the cloistered life of the Palace of the Prophets, Verna had learned that out in the world, a Sister had to do her work with care if there was to be any hope of success. Rescuing the rest of the Sisters would be worse than tricky, and it would do them no good if Verna got herself caught while trying to rescue them all at once. Best be aware of your limitations and take it one step at a time. She would get the rest of the Sisters safely away from the dream walker, in due time.

Right now, it was most important to get her two friends out, get information from them that would help her to rescue the rest, and get Warren some help. Without Warren, their cause would be jeopardized; Warren was a prophet, just beginning to come into his talent – if that talent didn't kill him before they could get him the help he needed.

One step at a time, she reminded herself. Use care, use your head, and you have the best chance of success.

A knock came at the door. Verna cracked it open and peeked out as Warren called out like a guard for them to announce themselves.

'Two of His Excellency's slaves, Sister Janet and Sister Amelia.'

Verna pulled open the door, reached out, snatching the cloak of one, yanked her in, and then the other. Verna flattened them both against the wall so they couldn't be seen from the windows.

'Thank the Creator,' Verna said with a sigh. 'I thought you two would never get here.'

Both women stood with wide eyes, trembling like frightened rabbits. Sister Amelia's face was bruised, cut, and swollen.

Warren moved close to Verna. She took his hand as she looked from one white face to the other. Her heart ached for Amelia's obvious pain. But there was something more in her eyes: terror.

'What's wrong?' she whispered.

'You lied to us,' Janet said in a pained whisper.

'What are you talking about?'

'The bond. The bond to protect us from His Excellency. I told Amelia about it. She swore the oath to Richard, as you told it to me.'

Verna frowned and leaned closer. 'What in Creation are you saying? I told you, it will keep Jagang from entering your mind.'

Janet slowly shook her head. 'No, Verna, it won't. Not from my mind, not from Amelia's ... not from Warren's ... not from yours.'

Verna laid a comforting hand on Janet's arm, trying to calm the frightened woman. 'Yes, it will, Janet. You must only believe, and you will be protected.'

Janet slowly shook her head again. 'Before I swore the oath to Richard, Jagang was in my mind. He knew my thoughts. He knew what you told me. He knew it all.'

Verna covered her mouth in horror. She hadn't considered that possibility.

'But you swore the oath. That protects you, now.'

Again, Janet slowly shook her head. 'It did, for the first day, but four days ago, on the night of the full moon, His Excellency returned to my mind. I didn't know it. I told Amelia about the oath. She swore, as had I. We thought we were safe. We thought that when you came back, we would escape with you.'

'You will,' Verna assured her. 'We all will escape right now.'

'None of us is going to escape, Verna. Jagang has you. He has Warren. He told us that he slipped into the cracks of your minds while you slept, the first night after the full moon.' Tears filled Janet's eyes. 'I'm sorry, Verna. You should never have come here to rescue me. It is to cost you both your freedom.'

Verna smiled through her rising panic. 'Janet, that just isn't possible. The bond protects us.'

'It would,' Janet said in a suddenly gruff, suddenly sinister voice, 'were Richard Rahl still alive. But Richard Rahl departed the world of the living four nights ago, on the night of the full moon.'

Janet laughed a hearty belly laugh, even as tears ran down her face.

Verna couldn't draw a breath. 'Richard … is … dead?'

Warren slapped his hands to the sides of his head as he let out a cry of anguish. 'No! No!'

Verna clutched at him as he sank toward the floor. 'Warren! What is it?'

'His Excellency … His Excellency has tasks for me.'

'Tasks? Warren, what's wrong? What's happening?'

'His Excellency has a new prophet!' Warren cried out. 'Please, stop the pain! I will serve! I will serve as I am commanded!'

Verna crouched over him. 'Warren!'

It felt as if a white-hot steel rod slammed through her skull. Verna cried out as she clamped her hands to her head. Nothing in her entire life of one hundred fifty-six years had prepared her for the fount of pain erupting in her mind. The room went black. She felt the floor smack her face. Her arms and legs twitched with the agony.

Baleful laughter danced through the hot torture, like flames through a ruin.

Verna prayed to the Creator that she would black out. Her prayer went unanswered.

Above her, she heard a voice. Janet's voice.

'I'm so sorry Verna. You should never have come here to try to rescue us. You will serve His Excellency, now, as his slaves.'

The blond one, Cara, followed him into the reception room. She stayed three paces behind, as he had ordered. She always wore her red leather, now, as he had ordered. He liked the way the red leather made them look like they were sheathed in blood. One of them was always there, with him, a bloodred reminder of the slick, sticky debauchery to come.

Her blue eyes turned away when he glanced back over his shoulder. He knew that she stayed only to be near Kahlan. That was fine by him. That she stayed was all that mattered. She was harmless, now, but it looked better if the Lord Rahl had an escort of guards like her – a proper accoutrement of his rank.

And he was the Lord Rahl, now, as the whispers from the ethers had promised him. Only he had the intellect to perceive the voices, the wisdom to hear them, the acumen to heed them. It had brought him triumph. Attention to detail had brought him his rewards. His extraordinary insight had brought him to the place of power he had always deserved. His gift was his genius, and it would serve him better than mere magic.

He was a man above others, and for good reason. He was superior to others – a man of rare understanding, instinct, and rare ethics, unadulterated by the twisted excuses women put to their vulgar pleasures.

His own virtue intoxicated him.

Kahlan glanced up when she saw him striding into the room. Her face showed a blankness, an expression she wore almost constantly. She only thought it showed nothing. To him, it revealed a panoply of emotion. Immersed in the details of her bewitching face, he could discern the rich flux of emotions she tried to hide.

He saw the way she looked at him. He had caught her glances at his body in the past. He knew: she wanted him. She hungered for him. She wanted pleasure from him.

That she tried to deny it only excited him all the more. That she covered her hunger for him with harsh words only proved it to him. That she pretended revulsion only showed him the extraordinary depths of her need.

When she finally gave in to her lust, it would be all the more glorious for the wait, for the abstinence, for the yearning, for the delayed fulfillment. Then, at long last, he would give her what she wanted. Then he would hear her screams.

The general with Kahlan bowed. 'Good morning – Lord Rahl.'

'What's this?' he asked. He didn't like it when the soldiers brought things to Kahlan without seeing to informing the Lord Rahl first.

'It's just the morning reports, Drefan,' Kahlan said in that flat tone of hers.

'Then why wasn't I informed? Reports should come to the Lord Rahl first.'

General Kerson stole a glance at Kahlan. He bowed again. 'As you wish, Lord Rahl. I just thought –'

'I do the thinking. You do the soldiering.'

The general cleared his throat. 'Of course, Lord Rahl.'

'So, what do the morning reports have to say?'

The general glanced to Kahlan again. Drefan saw the slight nod. As if the general needed permission from the Lord Rahl's wife to report. Drefan let it pass, as he always did. He enjoyed her games, the way she thought he missed things. It amused him.

'Well, Lord Rahl, the plague is nearly over.'

'Describe 'nearly over,' if you would, please. As a healer, vagueness hardly does me any good.'

'In the last week, the deaths from the plague have dropped to only three confirmed cases last night. Nearly everyone who was sick when Lord' – he caught himself – 'when Richard left has recovered. Whatever Richard did –'

'My brother died, that's what he did. I am the healer. I am the one responsible for the plague ending.'

Kahlan lost the calm look. Her expression twisted to tightly controlled rage. He wondered how her face would twist were it pain, were it terror. He would know, in the end.

'Richard went to the Temple of the Winds. He sacrificed himself to save everyone. Richard! Not you, Drefan, Richard!'

Drefan dismissed her tirade with a casual flip of his hand.

'Nonsense. What did Richard know of healing? I am the healer. It is Lord Rahl who has saved his people from the plague.' Drefan raised a finger to the general. 'And you had better see to it that everyone knows it.'

Kahlan gave her slight nod to the general again.

'Yes, Lord Rahl,' the general said. 'I will personally see to it that everyone knows that it was Lord Rahl himself who stopped the plague.'

Kahlan's face showed the slightest hint of a smile at the general's ambiguous response. Drefan let it go. He had more important business than her disrespect for her husband.

'And what else have you to report, general?'

'Well, Lord Rahl, it seems that some of our units are ... missing.'

'Missing? How can troops be missing? I want them found. We must have the army together to defend against the Imperial Order. I won't have the D'Haran empire fall to the Imperial Order because my officers fail to maintain discipline!'

'Yes, Lord Rahl. I have already sent scouts to find the troops who have ... wandered off from their stations.'

'It's the bond, Drefan,' Kahlan said. 'The D'Harans aren't bonded to you. The army is breaking up, wandering off aimlessly because they have lost the bond, lost their leader. They don't know what to do. They are without a Lord Rahl –'

He struck her. The sharp sound reverberated through the room. 'Stand up!' He waited until she regained her feet. 'I'll not have insolence from my wife! Do you understand?'

Kahlan pressed her fingers to her nose, trying to halt the flow of blood. The crimson tide flooded over her fingers and lips and down her chin. The sight of it nearly drove a gasp from him. The sight of the Mother Confessor with blood on her made his hands shake. He longed for the slicing, for the sight of blood everywhere on her, for her screams, for her terror.

But he could wait until she begged for it. As had Nadine. He had enjoyed Nadine's perverted hunger. He had relished her surprise, her terror, her agony, before he cast her over the side of the mountain, still alive, so she could think about her vile nature all the way down. It had sated him – for now.

He could wait until the Mother Confessor's true corruption

665

finally surfaced once again, as it had the first night. Richard must have been horrified to discover how much she really wanted his brother, that the woman he had loved was as impure as any whore. Poor, innocent, stupid Richard. He never even looked back over his shoulder as he walked away.

Drefan could wait. She would need time to recover from the shock of causing Richard's death. Drefan could wait. It wouldn't take her long, as badly as she wanted him.

He swept Kahlan up in his arms. 'Forgive me, my wife. I didn't mean to hurt you. Forgive me, please. I was only worried for our safety from the Order – distraught that these worthless soldiers won't follow orders and in so doing endanger us all.'

Kahlan wrenched herself out of his arms. 'I understand.'

She lied so poorly. From the corner of his eye, he could see the coiled form in red leather. If she moved to strike, he would slice her down. If she didn't, he still had use for her.

Kahlan twitched a finger in caution to Cara. Cara reluctantly relaxed. Kahlan thought she was so clever, thought he didn't see the way she gave orders to people. For now, it didn't matter.

'General Kerson,' Drefan said, 'I want those derelict troops found. We must have discipline in the army, or we are lost to the Order. When they are found, I want the officers executed.'

'What? You want me to execute my own men because they have lost the bond –'

'I want you to execute them for treason. When the rest of the men learn that we won't tolerate such negligence to duty, they will think twice about joining with our enemy.'

'Our enemy, Lord Rahl?'

'Of course. If they don't do their duty as D'Harans, to serve and protect the D'Haran empire, to say nothing of their Lord Rahl, then they are aiding the enemy. That makes them traitors! It endangers the life of my wife! Of everyone!'

He glided his fingers over the raised gold letters on the hilt of the Sword of Truth – his sword. He wielded it by right. 'Now, do you have anything else to report?'

The general and Kahlan surreptitiously shared a look.

'No, Lord Rahl.'

'Good. That will be all, then. Dismissed.' He turned to

Kahlan and held out his arm. 'Come, my dear. We will have breakfast together.'

CHAPTER 61

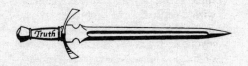

In a daze, Richard stepped down off the wizard's throne at the head of the Hall of the Winds. His footsteps echoed into the distance. It was his rightful place, the wizard's throne; he was the only war wizard, the only wizard with both Additive and Subtractive Magic.

The inside of the Temple of the Winds was beyond colossal. It was almost beyond comprehension. There was no sound in this soundless place, unless he put one there, or willed it into being.

The arched ceiling enclosing the lofty heights overhead could have contained eagles, and they hardly would have been aware that they were captive inside a structure. Mountain hawks, were there any, could soar and dive under that aerial arch, and feel at home.

To the sides, massive columns supported walls that ascended into the remote curve of the ribbed ceiling. In those side walls, enormous windows let in more of the omnipresent diffused light.

At least he could see the side walls. The far distant end of the hall simply faded out of sight, into a haze.

Nearly everything was the color of a pale afternoon mist: the floors, the columns, the walls, the ceiling. They almost seemed made of the filmy light.

Richard was a flea in a vast canyon. Even so, the place was not limitless, as it was outside the walls.

Before, he would have been stunned and awed by this place. Now, he was neither. He was simply numb.

Here, time had no meaning, other than that which he brought with him. Time had no place to anchor in eternity. He could have been here a century, rather than a mere couple of weeks, and only he would note the difference, and then, only if he so chose. Life had little meaning here, a concept as distant as the other end of eternity; he brought that, too, to this place. Yet the Temple of the Winds had perception, and sheltered him in its wizard-crafted, stone embrace.

To the sides, as he strode the hall, there were alcoves under each arch, beyond each pair of columns. In each alcove resided the things of magic stored here for safekeeping – sent here from the world of life, for the safekeeping of the world of life.

Richard understood them and could use them. He understood how dangerous these things were, and why some had wanted them locked away for all time. The knowledge of the winds was his, now.

With that knowledge, he had halted the plague. He didn't have the book that was used to start the plague, but it wasn't necessary to have the book to render it impotent. The book was stolen from this place, and so was still yoked to the winds. It was a simple matter of switching the fluxes of power emanating from the winds which enabled the magic of the book to function in the world of life.

In fact, it was so simple that he was ashamed that he hadn't realized the way to do it before. Thousands of people had died because he had been so ignorant. Had he known then what he knew now, he could have merely cast a web spun with both sides of his power and the book would have been useless to Jagang. All those people dead – and it had been so simple.

At least he was able to use his healing powers to halt the sickness among most who were afflicted before he had interrupted the currents of magic. At least the plague was ended.

It had only cost him everything. What price, for all those lives. What price the spirits had set. What price, indeed.

It had cost Nadine her life. He felt profound sorrow for her.

He would have eliminated Jagang, and the threat from the Old World, too, but he couldn't do so from this place. That was the world of life, and he could only affect those things taken from this place to the world of life, and the damage they caused.

He had touched the core of power in this place, though; there would be no more entry through Betrayer's Hall. Jagang would not twice accomplish the same feat.

Richard paused. He drew his sword, Drefan's sword. He held it out in his palms, staring at it, watching the light catch it. This wasn't his sword – the Sword of Truth.

He let his will flow from the core of his soul, carrying his birthright of power with it. His gift came as easily as a sigh, where before he had struggled to bring forth the most insignificant shred of his power. Force flowed outward, through his arms, and into the object he held.

His mind guided its elements, balancing each to the desired sequence and result, until the sword in his hands transmuted into the twin of the one he knew so well. He held the twin to the Sword of Truth, although without its attendant impressions of those past souls who had used his real sword. In every other way, though, it was the same. It held the same power, the same magic.

Wizards had died in the attempt to make the Sword of Truth, until some were finally successful. Once they had succeeded, that knowledge was borne to this place, and it was therefore Richard's for the taking, as was all the knowledge here.

He seized the hilt and held the blade aloft. Richard let the power, the magic, the rage of the sword inundate him, storm through him, just to feel something. Even wrath was something.

He had no need of a sword, though. The wrath winked out, to be replaced again by the emptiness.

He tossed the sword high into the air and held it there, where it rotated slowly on a bed of force. With a pulse of power, he shattered the sword he had made into a cloud of metallic dust, and with another thought, evacuated the dust out of existence.

He stood empty again. Empty and alone.

A presence caused him to turn. It was another spirit. They came, from time to time, to see him, to speak with him, to urge him to return to his world before it was too late, before he lost the thread back to the world of life.

This form, this spirit, rooted him to the floor in rigid shock.

It looked like Kahlan.

The soft, glowing apparition hovered before him, radiating with a glow the same color as everything else in this place, only with more intensity, more definition.

It looked like Kahlan. For the first time in weeks, his heart pounded.

'Kahlan? Have you died? Are you a spirit, now?'

'No,' the spirit said, 'I am Kahlan's mother.'

Richard's muscles went slack again. He turned away and continued on through the hall. 'What do you want?'

The spirit followed, as they sometimes did, interested in him, a curiosity, perhaps, in their world.

'I have brought you something,' the spirit said.

Richard turned. 'What?'

She held out a rose. The green of the stem and the red of the petals were stunning in this colorless world, a ripple of pleasure to his eyes. The fragrance filled his lungs with its pleasant aroma. He had almost forgotten the pleasure of such a thing.

'What am I to do with this?'

The spirit held it out, urging him to take it. He had no fear of the spirits who came to see him. Even those who hated him could not harm him. He knew how to protect himself.

Richard took the rose. 'Thank you.' He slid the stem behind his belt.

He turned and continued on. The spirit of Kahlan's mother followed. He didn't like looking into her face. Though she was a spirit, and her features were indistinct in that glow they had, she still looked too much like Kahlan.

'Richard, may I talk with you?'

His footsteps echoed through the vast hall. 'If you wish.'

'I wish to tell you about my daughter. Kahlan.'

Richard stopped and turned back to the spirit. 'Why?'

'Because she is part of me. She was of my flesh, just as you are of your mother's flesh. Kahlan is my connection to the world of life, the place I once was. Where you must return.'

Richard started out once more. 'I am home. I have no

intention of returning to that bitter world. If you wish me to carry a message to your daughter, I'm sorry, I can't. Leave me.'

He lifted his hand to banish her from the hall, but she raised her hands, pleading for him to stay his power.

'I do not wish you to carry a message. Kahlan knows I love her. I wish to talk to you.'

'Why?'

'Because of what I did to Kahlan.'

'Did to her? What did you do to her?'

'I instilled in her a sense of duty. *"Confessors don't have love, Kahlan. They have duty."* That was what I told her. To my shame, I never explained what I meant by that. I fear I left her no room for life.

'More than any Confessor I knew, Kahlan wanted to live life, to relish it. Duty denied her much of that. That is what makes her such a good protector of her people. She wants them to have a chance at their joy, because she sees so clearly what she was denied. She is left to take small pleasures as she can.'

'Is there a point to this?'

'Don't you enjoy life, Richard?'

Richard walked on. 'I understand about duty. I have been born to duty. I am now done with it. I am done with everything.'

'You, too, misunderstand what I meant about duty. To the right person, the person who is truly born to it, duty is a form of love, through which all is possible. Duty is not always a denial of things, but an expansion of them to others. Duty is not always a chore, but is best carried out with love.

'Will you not return to her, Richard? She needs you.'

'Kahlan has a husband, now. I have no place in her life.'

'You have a place in her heart.'

'Kahlan said she would never forgive me.'

'Richard, have you never said something you didn't mean, in desperation? Have you never wished you could take back the words?'

'I can't return to her. She is married to another. She has given an oath, and she has ... I won't go back.'

'Even if she is married to another, even if you cannot be

672

with her, even if it breaks your heart to know you can't have her, don't you love her enough to mend her heart? To put her heart at peace? Is it all you, and none of it her, in this love you have?'

Richard glared at the spirit. 'She has found happiness in my absence. She doesn't need anything from me.'

'Do you find enjoyment in the rose, Richard?'

Richard walked on. 'Yes, it's very nice, thank you.'

'Will you consider going back, then?'

Richard wheeled to the spirit of Kahlan's mother. 'Thank you for the rose. Here are a thousand in repayment, so you may not say I owe you anything in return!'

Richard cast out his hand and the air filled with roses. Rose petals flew and swirled in a red blizzard.

'I'm sorry I could not make you understand, Richard. I can see that I only bring you pain. I will leave you.'

When she vanished, the floor was bespattered with red petals, looking like nothing so much as a pool of blood.

Richard sank to the floor, feeling too sick to stand. Soon, he would be one of them, a spirit, and he would not have to endure this limbo where he twisted between worlds. He had food, when he wanted it, he had sleep, when he wanted it, but he couldn't maintain life here indefinitely. This was not the world of life.

Soon enough, he would be one of them, and finished with this emptiness that was his life.

Kahlan had once filled that emptiness. She had once been everything to him. He had trusted her. He had thought his heart had been safe in her care. He had imagined more than was true. How could he have been such a fool? Was it all such illusion?

Richard's head came up. He peered across the hall. He went through a mental inventory of the items stored here. The gazing font. It was there, across the hall. He knew how to use it.

He rose and crossed the hall, going between two of the columns, to find the stone gazing font. It had two basins, in two tiers, the lower one waist-high, and the upper just above his head. Each basin was a long rectangle. Carved into the glittering charcoal-gray stone were ornate symbols of instruction and power. The lower basin was brimful of a silver liquid, appearing similar to the sliph, but very different, he knew.

Richard lifted the silver ewer from the shelf below and dipped it in the lower basin. He emptied the ewer into the upper basin. He continued, until the upper basin was loaded with its charge of the gazing liquid.

Richard leaned across the lower basin to place his hands on the proper symbols, spread wide to each side. He read the ancient words before him as he leaned in, hands pressed to the gazing keyways. When the words were said, he focused his mind on the person he wished to gaze upon. As he did this, he let slip a small cord of power to release the liquid in the upper font.

Across the entire knife-edge front of the upper basin, the silver liquid spilled out in a thin, silvery sheet before his face. In that waterfall of gazing liquid, Richard saw the person he called in his mind: Kahlan.

His chest tightened at seeing her. He almost gasped, almost called out her name in anguish.

She was in her white Confessor's dress. The familiar contours of her face made him ache with longing. She was near her rooms, her bedroom, in the Confessors' Palace. It was night, there. Richard could feel his heart hammering against his ribs as he watched her glide to a halt at the door.

Drefan slipped up behind her. He put his hands on her shoulders, giving them a squeeze as he leaned close, putting his mouth by her ear.

'Kahlan, my wife, my love. Are you ready to go into bed? I've had a hard day. I so look forward to a night of your lustful passion.'

Richard released the font. He lifted his fists as he staggered back. The gazing font exploded apart, heavy pieces of rock driven ahead of huge gouts of flame and smoke. Shards of stone whistled through the hall, disappearing into the distance. Massive chunks of stone wailed as they rose up into the air, lifted on a raging inferno, until they lost their upward momentum and dropped back down, to shatter into fragments and dust. The gazing liquid flooded the floor.

In each droplet and pool, Richard could see Kahlan's face.

He turned his back and stalked away. A furnace of flame blasted the floor, evaporating each droplet, yet he could still perceive her face in the tiniest mist of it filling the air. He cast up his fists. Every droplet, every infinitesimal bit of mist, winked into nothingness behind him.

In the center of the hall, in a daze, Richard slumped to the floor, staring out at nothing.

A malicious chuckle drifted through the winds. Richard knew who it was. His father was back to torment him again.

'What's the matter, my son?' Darken Rahl said in his derisive hiss. 'Aren't you happy with my choice of a husband for your true love? My own son, my own flesh and blood, Drefan, wed to the Mother Confessor. I think it a good choice myself. He's a good boy. She seemed pleased. But then, you already know that, don't you? You should be pleased that she is pleased. So very pleased.'

Darken Rahl's laughter cavorted through the hall.

Richard didn't bother to banish the luminous form standing over him. What did it matter?

'So, what do you say, my wife? Shall we have a night of wild passion? Like you showed my brother when you thought it me?'

Kahlan used all her strength to ram her elbow into Drefan's sternum. She had caught him off guard. He hadn't expected that. He doubled over in pain, unable to get his breath.

'I told you, Drefan, if you touch me, I'll cut your throat.'

Before he could recover to laugh at her anger, or to taunt her with his threats of force, she slipped into her room, slammed the door, and threw the bolt.

She stood trembling in the near darkness. She had felt something. For a moment, it had felt as if Richard was there with her. She had almost called out his name – screamed she loved him.

She clutched her abdomen in agony. When would she ever stop thinking about him?

Richard was never coming back.

Kahlan crossed the thick carpets in her sitting room and

went back into the bedroom. She dropped into a defensive crouch when someone stepped out in front of her.

'Sorry,' Berdine whispered. 'I didn't mean to frighten you.'

Kahlan sighed as she unclenched her fists and rose to her feet. 'Berdine.' She threw her arms around the woman. 'Oh, Berdine, I'm glad to see you. How are you doing?'

Berdine hugged Kahlan with a desperate need for comfort. 'It's been a few weeks, but it seems as if Raina died only yesterday. I'm so angry with her for leaving me. And then when I get angry at her, I cry because I miss her so. If she would only have held on for a few more days, she would be alive now. Just a couple of days.'

'I know, I know,' Kahlan whispered. She parted from Berdine, keeping her voice low. 'What are you doing here? I thought you went up to the Keep to relieve Cara.'

'I did, but I had to come down to talk to you.'

'You mean the sliph is unguarded?' Berdine nodded. 'Berdine, we can't leave her alone. We would never know if someone slipped into Aydindril – someone with dangerous magic. That was what –'

Berdine shushed her. 'I know. This is important, too. Besides, what difference does it really make? Cara and I have lost our power. We couldn't stop someone with magic, now, if they did come through the sliph.

'I have to talk to you, Mother Confessor, and I can never do it in the day because Drefan is always showing up.'

'Don't let him catch you calling him anything other than Lord Rahl, or he –'

'He isn't Lord Rahl. He isn't, Mother Confessor.'

'I know. But he's all the Lord Rahl we have.'

Berdine looked Kahlan in the eye. 'Cara and I have been talking. We decided we should kill him. We need you to help us.'

'We can't do that.' Kahlan gripped Berdine's shoulder. 'We can't.'

'Sure we can. We'll hide out on the balcony, you get him out of his clothes so that he's away from those knives of his, and while you … distract his attention, we'll burst in and end it.'

'Berdine, we can't.'

'Well, all right, if you're skittish about that plan, we can easily think of another. The point is, we have to kill him.'

'No, the point is, we can't kill him.'

Berdine scowled. 'Do you want to be married to that pig? Sooner or later, he's going to insist on his rights as your husband.'

'Berdine, listen to me. Even if he does that, I will have to endure it. I can endure rape if it means saving lives. We can't kill Drefan. He's the only Lord Rahl we have. Until we can figure out what to do, he is the only thing holding the army together.

'Right now, they're confused by his aggressive command. D'Harans are used to being told what to do by Lord Rahl. Drefan is acting as if he is the Lord Rahl and, for the moment, the army is scratching their heads, wondering if they're sure he isn't.'

'But he isn't,' Berdine insisted.

'But at the moment, that's all that is holding the whole thing together. If it falls apart, then the Imperial Order will be able to roll right over the Midlands. Drefan is right about that much of it.'

'But you are the Mother Confessor. General Kerson is loyal to you. Even without the bond, he sticks around because of you. Most of the officers do the same. Because of you, not Drefan. You could hold things together as well as Drefan. Maybe it would work.'

'And maybe not. I may not like Drefan, but he has done nothing to earn assassination. As much as I don't like his ways, he's doing his best to keep us all together. With him, and me, we may be able to keep everyone together in this.'

Berdine tilted her head closer. 'It won't last, and you know it.'

Kahlan wiped a hand across her face. 'Berdine, Drefan is my husband. I have sworn an oath to him.'

'An oath, is it? Then why haven't you let him in your bed?'

Kahlan opened her mouth, but couldn't find the words.

'It's because of Lord Rahl, isn't it? You still think he's coming back, don't you? You want him to come back.'

Kahlan put her fingertips to her lips. She turned away. 'If Richard was going to come back, he'd have done so by now.'

'Maybe it's the plague, maybe he isn't finished ridding the magic of the plague. Maybe when he's finished, he will return.'

Kahlan hugged her arms to herself. She knew that wasn't it.

'Mother Confessor, you do want him to return, don't you?'

'I'm married to Drefan. I have a husband.'

'That isn't what I asked you. You do want him to return. You must want him to come back.'

Kahlan shook her head. 'He said he would always love me. He said his heart would always be mine. He promised.' Kahlan swallowed the anguish. 'He walked away. I may have – hurt him, but if he really loved me, he wouldn't do this to me. He'd have given me a chance ...'

'But you still want him back.'

'No. I don't want ever to go through this kind of pain again. I don't want ever to leave myself open to this much hurt. I was wrong ever to let myself fall in love with him in the first place.' Kahlan shook her head again. 'I don't want him to come back.'

'I don't believe you. You're just upset, as I get because Raina died. But if she came back, I'd forgive her for dying and take her back in a heartbeat.'

'Not Richard. I'll not trust my heart to him again. Regardless of what I did, that doesn't make it right for him to hurt me as he did. He just walked away from me, and after he'd made promises of always loving me no matter what. He failed me in that test.

'I never thought he would hurt me like that. I thought my heart was safe with him, no matter what, but it wasn't.'

Berdine turned her around and gripped her shoulders.

'Mother Confessor, you don't mean that. You don't. Trust works both ways. If you really loved him, then you must trust in him, no matter what, just as you expected him to always trust in you.'

Tears trickled down Kahlan's cheeks. 'I can't, Berdine. It hurts too much. I'll not put myself through it again.

'It doesn't matter anyway. It's been weeks. The plague is long over. Richard is never coming back.'

'Look, I don't know exactly what happened up on the

mountain, but you just ask yourself this: If the situation were reversed, if you were in his place, how would you feel?'

'Don't you think I do that every moment of every day? I know how I'd feel. I'd feel betrayed. I'd never forgive me, if I were him. I'd hate me, just as I know he does.'

'No,' Berdine soothed, 'that isn't true. He doesn't hate you. Lord Rahl may be confused, or hurt, but he could never hate you.'

'He does. He hates me for what I did. That's the other reason I can never take him back – I hurt him too much. How could I ever look him in the eye again? I couldn't. I could never ask him to trust me again.'

Berdine circled an arm around Kahlan's neck and drew her to a shoulder. 'Don't close your heart, Kahlan. Please don't do that. You are a sister of the Agiel. As your sister, I beg you not to do that.'

'It makes no difference,' Kahlan whispered. 'I can't be with him anyway, no matter what I might think or wish or hope. I must forget him. The spirits have forced me into marrying Drefan. I have given my oath to Drefan and to the spirits in trade to save lives. I must respect the oath I've given. Richard, too, must respect my oath.'

CHAPTER 62

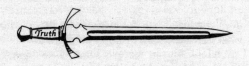

Wake him! the voice in her head commanded.

Verna cried out. It felt as though she was covered with wasps, and they were all stinging her at once. She frantically swiped at her arms, her shoulders, her legs, her face. She screamed in panic, swatting, swatting.

Wake him! came the voice in her head again.

His Excellency's voice.

Verna snatched the cloth from the bucket. She turned Warren's head. He was sprawled forward on the table, unconscious. She dabbed the wet cloth on his cheeks, his forehead. With trembling fingers, she smoothed back his hair. He hadn't been out long, so she had a better chance to bring him around.

'Warren. Warren, please wake up. Warren!'

He moaned in delirium. She pressed the wet cloth to his lips. She rubbed his back with her other hand as she kissed his cheek. It broke her heart to see him so afflicted with the pain, not only of the dream walker but of the gift out of control. She pressed her fingers to the back of his neck and let a warm flow of Han seep into him, hoping it would give him strength, hoping it would bring him around.

'Warren,' she cried, 'please wake up. Please, for me, wake up, or His Excellency will be angry. Please, Warren.'

Tears streamed down her face. She didn't care. She needed only to wake Warren, or His Excellency would make them both suffer. She had never known that resistance could be so futile. She had never known that she could so easily be made to betray everything in which she believed.

She couldn't even protect those she loved by killing herself. She had tried. Oh, how she had tried. He wouldn't allow it; he wanted them alive so that they could serve him. He wished to use their talents.

She now knew that it had to be true: Richard had to be dead. The bond to him was broken, and they were defenseless against the dream walker. He intruded into her mind at will. With frightening ease, Jagang bent her to his wishes. It was as if she were no longer in control of the simplest of actions. If Jagang willed it, her arm lifted, and she could do nothing but watch. He controlled her use of her Han, too. Without the bond, she was powerless.

Warren let out another groggy groan. He moved of his own accord, at last. Only Verna seemed able to wake him when he passed out from the gift. That was the only reason Jagang hadn't sent her to the tents.

Only his heart's connection to her was enough to stir Warren. She knew that it was harmful to wake him when the gift wanted him unconscious – it did that as a way to stretch his endurance until he could get proper help – but she had no choice. She was using their love to wake him, and in so doing, was bringing him closer to death; but Jagang didn't care, as long as Warren did as ordered.

'Sorry,' Warren mumbled. 'I … I couldn't …'

'I know,' Verna comforted, 'I know. Wake up, now, Warren. His Excellency wants us to keep working. We have to keep working.'

'I … can't. I can't, Verna. My head –'

'Please, Warren.' Verna couldn't control the tears. The pain of a thousand wasps stinging her everywhere at once made it impossible to hold still. She flinched constantly. 'Warren, you know what he'll do to us. Please, Warren, you must go back to the books. I'll carry them down. Just tell me which ones you need. I'll get them for you.'

He nodded as he pushed himself up. He was becoming more alert. Verna slid the lamp near him and turned up the wick. She pushed close the volume he had been reading when he had passed out, and tapped the page.

'Here, Warren. Here. This is where you were. His Excellency wants to know what this means.'

Warren pressed his fists to the sides of his head. 'I don't know! Please, Excellency, I don't know. I can't make the visions of prophecy come at will. I'm not a prophet yet. I am only beginning.'

Warren cried out, squirming in his chair.

'I'll try! I'll try! Please, let me try!'

Warren panted as his agony subsided. He bent over the book, licking his lips. Fingers shook as he set them to the book, following along the line of words, the line of prophecy.

' "Patronizing past," ' he muttered as he read to himself. ' "Patronizing past carries forward the same disfavor twisted to new use, for a new master. ..." Dear Creator, I don't know what it means. Please, let the vision come.'

Clarissa peered out into the darkness as the coach rocked to a stop. Dust hung in the air, their ghostlike escort. A stone fortress rose up just outside the coach's window. It was dark, and she couldn't see the whole thing, but what she could see made her heart pound out of control.

She waited, twisting her fingers together, until the soldier opened the door.

'Clarissa,' he whispered. 'This is the place.'

Clarissa took his hand as she stepped out into the inky night. 'Thank you, Walsh.'

The other one of Nathan's soldier friends, a man named Bollesdun, waited up in the driver's seat, keeping tight the reins.

'Hurry, now,' Walsh told her. 'Nathan said he doesn't want you in there for more than a few minutes. If anything happens, the two of us aren't going to be able to fight much of a battle to get you out.'

She knew the truth of that. They had ridden past so many tents that it left her stunned by their numbers. The hoard who had overrun Renwold had been nothing compared to the numbers of men here.

Clarissa pulled up the hood on her cloak. 'Don't you worry, I know better than to dally. Nathan told me what to do.'

She clutched her cloak together in her fist. She had promised Nathan. He had done so much for her. He had saved her life. She would do this for him. She would do this so others wouldn't die.

As terrified as she was, she would do anything for Nathan. There was no better man in the whole world. No kinder man, no more compassionate, no braver.

Walsh walked beside her as they passed under an iron portcullis, and then into an entryway under a barreled roof. Two brutish guards, wearing hide mantles and hung with grisly-looking weapons, stood beside a hissing torch.

Clarissa kept her cloak tightly drawn and her hood pulled forward. She hung her head so that the guards couldn't see her face in the shadow. She let Walsh do the talking, as she had been instructed.

Walsh flicked his hand toward her. 'The representative of His Excellency's plenipotentiary, Lord Rahl,' he said in a gruff voice, as if unhappy that this assignment had fallen to him.

The bearded guard grunted. 'So I've been told.' He lifted a thumb toward the door. 'Go on in. Someone is supposed to be waiting for you.'

Walsh adjusted his weapons belt. 'Good. I have to drive this one back tonight. Can you believe it? Won't even let us wait until morning. That Lord Rahl is as demanding as they come.'

The guard grunted, as if he well understood the annoyance of night duty.

'Oh,' Walsh added, as if in afterthought, 'Lord Rahl also wanted to know if his representative could pay the Lord Rahl's respects to His Excellency.'

The guard shrugged. 'Sorry. Jagang took out of here this morning. He took most everyone with him. Just left a few behind to mind things.'

Clarissa's heart sank with disappointment. Nathan had been hoping that Jagang would be here, but he had said that even though he hoped it, Jagang would likely be smarter than that. Jagang wasn't one to trust his life to the unknown abilities of a wizard as powerful as Nathan.

Walsh took Clarissa's arm and pushed her on ahead as he gave the guard a good-natured slap on the shoulder. 'Thanks.'

'Yea, just go on in down the hall. There's one of the women

waiting there for you. Last I saw her, she was pacing by the second set of torches.'

Walsh and Bollesdun were Imperial Order soldiers, and they had had no trouble with any of the other soldiers, either. Clarissa dreaded to think what would have happened to her without those two the times their coach had been stopped by troops to query its mission. Walsh and Bollesdun also had little trouble ushering her through checkpoints.

Clarissa remembered all too well what happened to the women in Renwold. She still had nightmares about what she had seen happening to Manda Perlin when the Order's troops captured Renwold. And right there, on the floor beside her murdered husband, Rupert.

Their footsteps echoed as they hurried down the stone corridor. It was a dark, dank, and depressing place. It looked to Clarissa to have no comforts other than a few wooden benches. This was a place for soldiers, not a place for families to live.

As the guard had said, the woman was waiting near the second set of torches.

'Yes,' the woman asked, 'what is it?'

As Clarissa came to a stop before the woman, she could see in the torchlight that her face was badly battered. She had horrid-looking cuts and bruises. One side of her lower lip was swollen to twice normal size. Even Walsh moved back a little when he got a good look at her.

'I am to meet Sister Amelia. His Excellency's plenipotentiary sent me.'

The woman slumped with relief. 'Good. I am Sister Amelia. I have the book. I hope never to see it again.'

'His Excellency's plenipotentiary also told me that I am to pay his respects to an acquaintance of his, Sister Verna. Is she here?'

'Well, I don't know if I should –'

'If I'm not allowed to see her, His Excellency will be most unhappy when his plenipotentiary reports how his request was so rudely treated by a slave. As a slave myself, serving His Excellency, I can tell you that I will not be the one to take the blame.'

Clarissa felt foolish saying such words, but as Nathan had told her, they seemed to work magic.

Sister Amelia's eyes fixed on the gold ring through Clarissa's lip. Her hesitation vanished. 'Of course. Please follow me. That is where the book is kept, anyway.'

With Walsh close at her side, and his hand near the hilt of his short sword, Clarissa followed Sister Amelia deeper into the gloomy fortress. They went down a long hall, and then took a turn. Clarissa was paying careful attention as they went, so that if they had to get out fast, she wouldn't take a wrong route and be caught in here.

Sister Amelia stopped before a door, glancing to Clarissa for just an instant before she lifted the lever and led them in. A woman and a man were in the room, he sitting at a simple plank table, reading a book laid open on the table, and she looking over his shoulder.

The woman glanced up. She was a little older than Clarissa, and attractive, with curly brown hair. She looked to Clarissa to be a woman of authority crushed by humiliation. She looked in agony. Whether it was physical, or emotional, Clarissa didn't know.

Sister Amelia held out a hand. 'This is Verna.'

Verna straightened. She had a gold ring in her lip, the same as Sister Amelia, the same as Clarissa. The man, his curly blond hair in disarray, didn't look up. He seemed frantically absorbed in his book.

'Pleased to meet you,' Clarissa said.

Verna turned back to the man and the book he was studying.

Clarissa pushed back her hood as she turned to Sister Amelia. 'The book?'

Sister Amelia bowed. 'Of course. It's right here.'

She scurried to a shelf. The room wasn't large. One of the stone block walls had a crudely built shelf holding books. There were perhaps no more than a hundred. Nathan had been hoping there would be a great many more. As Nathan had expected, though, Jagang wouldn't keep many of his prizes together in one place.

Sister Amelia pulled a volume from a shelf and placed it on the table. She looked to be uncomfortable even touching it.

'This is it.'

The cover was as Nathan had described it to her, a strange

black that seemed to absorb the light from the room. Clarissa flipped open the cover.

'What are you doing?' Sister Amelia cried out as she stepped closer.

Clarissa looked up. 'I was instructed how to make sure it is the right book. Please leave it to me.'

Sister Amelia stepped back, wringing her hands together. 'Of course. But I can tell you only too well that it's the right book. It's the one His Excellency agreed to.'

Clarissa carefully turned over the first page as Sister Amelia nervously licked her lips. Verna watched from the corner of her eye.

Clarissa reached inside her cloak and pulled out the little leather pouch of powder Nathan had given her. She sprinkled it over the open page. Words began to appear.

Assigned to the Winds by Wizard Ricker.

It was the book she had come for. Nathan hadn't known the name of the wizard, but he had told her it would say 'Assigned to the Winds' and then a name. She flipped the cover closed.

'Sister Amelia, would you leave us for a moment, please?'

The woman bowed and quickly scurried out of the room.

Verna frowned as she straightened again. 'What's this about?'

'May I see your ring, please?'

'My ring?'

Verna finally sighed and held out her hand, showing Clarissa the ring on her third finger. It had the sunburst pattern as Nathan had described.

'Why do you want to see –' For the first time, Verna noticed Clarissa's guard. Her eyes went wide. She jostled Warren's shoulder while she spoke. 'Walsh?' Warren's head came up.

Walsh smiled. 'How you doing, Prelate? Warren?'

'Not very well.'

Clarissa stepped closer. The man, Warren, was looking very puzzled.

'I was sent by Lord Rahl to get this book.' Clarissa gave Verna and Warren both a meaningful look. 'I am bonded to Lord Rahl.'

'Richard is dead,' Verna said in a flat whisper.

'I know. But I was sent by Lord Rahl. Nathan Rahl, the master of D'Hara. He wanted me to pass along his regards.'

Verna's mouth fell open. Warren's chair skidded across the floor as he rushed to his feet.

'Do you understand?' Clarissa carefully asked. 'If you do, then you had better be quick about it.'

'But, Nathan, we couldn't …'

'Well,' Clarissa said, 'I must be getting back to *Lord Rahl*. He's waiting for me. I have a coach, and I must be leaving at once.'

Verna's eyes turned up to Walsh. He gave her a nod.

Verna fell to her knees. She snatched Warren's violet robes and yanked him down beside her.

'Do it, Warren!' She folded her hands together as she bowed her head. Her words spilled out. 'Master Rahl guide us. Master Rahl teach us. Master Rahl protect us. In your light we thrive. In your mercy we are sheltered. In your wisdom we are humbled. We live only to serve. Our lives are yours.'

Warren spoke the words, too, just a little in her wake.

Verna knelt frozen for a moment, her hands still folded together prayerfully. She suddenly let out a cry of joy. She laughed like a madwoman.

'Thank the Creator! My prayers have been answered! I'm free! He's gone! I can feel that he's gone from my mind!'

Clarissa sighed in relief. Nathan had warned her that if Verna failed to do as they had hoped, she would have to die here.

Verna and Warren hugged as they wept with joy. Clarissa seized them both and urged them up.

'We have to get out of here, but Lord Rahl wants me to do something else, first. I need to look for some books.'

'Books?' Warren asked. 'What books?'

'*Mountain's Twin, Selleron's Seventh Task, The Book of Inversion and Duplex*, and *Twelve Words Left for Reason*.'

Warren turned to the book on the table. '*Twelve Words*, that's this one, here. I think I saw a couple of the others.'

Clarissa went to the shelves. 'Help me look. Nathan wants to know if they are here. He needs to know.'

They all scanned the titles on the spines, and had to pull out

687

several that weren't marked so as to check their titles. They found all but *The Book of Inversion and Duplex*.

Clarissa brushed the dust from her hands. 'That will have to do. Nathan said that they might not all be here. With only one missing, that's better than we could have hoped.'

'What does Nathan want with these books?' Warren asked.

'He doesn't want Jagang to have them. He says that they're dangerous for Jagang to have.'

'They all could be dangerous,' Verna said.

'Let me worry about that,' Clarissa said, as she slipped the book from the table back into an empty slot. 'Nathan just needed to know which were here. Now, we can leave.'

Verna clutched Clarissa's sleeve. 'I have two friends here. We have to get them out with us. You said you have a coach. We can all go.'

'Who?' Walsh asked.

'Janet and Amelia.'

Walsh let out a knowing grunt as Clarissa glanced to the door. 'But Nathan said –'

'Look, if they give their oath to … to Lord Rahl, also, they can escape.' Verna touched the ring in Clarissa's lip. 'You don't know what they do to the women here. Did you see Amelia's face?'

'I know what they do,' Clarissa whispered, remembering the scenes in Renwold. 'Will they take the oath?'

'Of course. Wouldn't you, if it would get you away from here?'

Clarissa swallowed. 'I'd do anything.'

'Hurry, then,' Walsh said. 'There's room in the coach, but we have to hurry.'

Verna nodded and then slipped out the door.

While Verna went to get the other two, Clarissa unhooked the clasp on the fine gold chain around her neck. Warren watched with a frown as Clarissa pulled a book from a lower shelf and then set it on the table.

Clarissa placed the locket on the shelf, in the empty slot. Carefully, she laid open the locket. With a finger, she gently pushed it all the way back against the wall. She wiggled her fingers at Warren. He handed back the book she had removed. Clarissa slid it back into its place.

'What did you do?' Warren asked.

'What Nathan wanted me to do.'

Verna burst back into the room, holding the hands of two beaming women. One was the one with the battered face, Sister Amelia.

'They've given the oath,' Verna said in a breathless voice. 'They are bonded to Lord Rahl. Let's get out of here.'

'About time,' Walsh said. He had a little smile on his face for Verna. It was obvious to Clarissa that they knew each other.

Walsh took ahold of Clarissa's arm and the two of them led out the rest, to retrace their route back through the fortress. The dark, dripping stone smelled of rot. They saw only a few guards inside the stronghold, most people having left along with Jagang, gone to his huge tents.

Nathan said that Jagang traveled with a large contingent of people and that he had big, round tents with all the comforts of a palace. Of the people left behind, there seemed to be a scattering of officers and guards, and a few of the women who were slaves to Jagang and his army.

As they came around a corner, one of those slaves was coming the other way, carrying two steaming kettles of what smelled like lamb stew. She was dressed the same as the other women Clarissa had seen, except Verna. The clothes they wore, like Janet and Amelia, were not clothes as far as Clarissa was concerned. The women might as well have been naked, for all the good those transparent garments did.

When the woman looked up and saw them coming, especially Walsh, she immediately stepped to the side of the hall, out of their way.

Clarissa jerked to a halt, staring at the woman, whose gaze fixed on the floor.

'Manda?' Clarissa whispered. 'Manda Perlin, is that you?'

Manda looked up. 'Yes, mistress?'

'Manda, it's me, Clarissa. From Renwold. I'm Clarissa.'

The young woman looked up the length of Clarissa, at her expensive gown, at her jewelry, at her hair all done in ringlets. Manda's gaze met Clarissa's, and her eyes widened.

'Clarissa, is it really you?'

'Yes.'

'I don't hardly ... recognize you. You look so ... different. You look so ...' The spark went out of her expression. 'Were you captured back home, too, then? I see the ring.'

'No. I wasn't captured.'

Manda's eyes filled with tears. 'Oh, good. I'm so glad they didn't get you, there. It was –'

Clarissa hugged the young woman. Manda had never spoken this many words to her in all the years Clarissa had known her, and the words she had spoken hadn't been decent. Clarissa had always hated Manda for the cruel words, the cruel smirks, the condescending glances. Now, Clarissa felt sorrow for her.

'Manda, we have to go. Would you like to come away with us?'

Verna snatched Clarissa's arm. 'We can't do that.'

Clarissa glared at Verna. 'I came here to rescue you. I let you take your friends with us. I want to take my friend out of here, too.'

Verna sighed and let go of Clarissa's arm. 'Of course.'

'Friend?' Manda whined as her face twisted with untold sorrow.

'Yes,' Clarissa said. 'I could get you out of here, too.'

'You would do that for me? After all the times I ...' Sobbing, Manda threw her arms around Clarissa. 'Oh, yes. Oh, Clarissa, please! Oh, Clarissa, please let me go with you!'

Clarissa gripped the woman's wrists and pushed her away. 'Then listen carefully. I give you only one chance. My master has magic to protect your mind from the dream walker. You must swear an oath to him. You must be loyal to him.'

Manda fell to her knees, clutching at Clarissa's dress. 'Yes, I swear.'

'Then say these words, and you must mean them with all your heart.'

Clarissa spoke the devotion, pausing to let Manda repeat the words. When she finished, Verna and Clarissa helped the sobbing woman to her feet.

Clarissa had always been so intimidated by Manda, always so afraid of her scorn. How many times had Clarissa crossed the street, her head bowed low, as she tried to avoid Manda's attention?

'Hurry, now,' Walsh said. 'Nathan told us to get out of here fast.'

At the entrance, Walsh had to make up a story about His Excellency's plenipotentiary wanting some women. The guard eyed the nearly naked women, smiled knowingly, and slapped Walsh on the back.

They all piled into the coach as Walsh climbed up into the driver's seat with Bollesdun. As the coach lurched and then started out, Clarissa pushed Janet and Manda to the floor, in the center, so she could lift the leather-covered seat. She pulled out a long cloak. She only had one extra; they had expected to rescue Verna and Warren. Since Verna had a cloak, Clarissa gave the extra cloak to Manda, and retrieved blankets for Janet and Amelia. All three women were immensely grateful to be able to cover themselves, at last.

Clarissa sat at the end of the seat, holding the strange black book Nathan had sent her for, with Amelia at the other end, and Manda in the center, clutching at Clarissa for comfort.

Manda kept weeping on Clarissa's shoulder, and thanking her profusely. Clarissa put an arm around Manda and told her that she had expressed her gratitude enough times. It did feel good, though, to have the beautiful Manda Perlin looking up to Clarissa for a change, rather than looking down on her. All because of Nathan. How he had changed her life – changed everything.

They had to stop three times, while soldiers checked the coach. Once, the soldiers made them all get out and line up for a look. The blankets and cloak had to remain in the coach as Janet, Amelia, and Manda climbed out for inspection.

Walsh explained, in very crude terms, what he was doing with these slaves – how he was taking them for the pleasure of His Excellency's plenipotentiary. The soldiers were satisfied by Walsh's explanation, and allowed them to continue on their way.

They turned north at the harbor, and headed up the coast road. Clarissa sighed in relief as she saw the last of the fires and tents finally fade into the distance behind them. It wasn't until they crested a hill, nearly an hour's ride out after leaving the last of the soldiers, that the flash lit the sky behind.

Clarissa heard a cheer from up on the driver's seat. Walsh

leaned down, gripping a rail with one arm, and stuck his face, nearly upside down, partly into the window.

'Good job, Clarissa! You did it!'

Clarissa grinned. He swung back up, and he and Bollesdun hooted into the night air. It was then that the sudden boom reached them, making Manda jump with fright.

Verna, sitting in the center, opposite, produced a flame above her upturned palm and leaned toward Clarissa. 'Job? What is it that you have done?'

Clarissa patted the inky black book in her lap. 'Nathan sent me for this book, and he wanted the ones left behind destroyed. He said that they were dangerous, what with you, and especially Warren, telling Jagang the meaning of the prophecies in them. Nathan didn't want Jagang to be able to use the information.'

'I see,' Verna said. 'Lucky for us that we agreed to swear loyalty to … *Lord Rahl,* and go with you.'

Clarissa nodded. 'Nathan said I was to offer you the chance, but in either case, I was to open that locket and leave it hidden there. He said that Jagang having both Warren and the prophecies together could ruin everything, if you told Jagang anything important.'

Verna pressed her lips together as she let out a breath. She shared a look with Warren.

'I can't believe that after all this time, I'm finally going to get to meet the prophet himself,' Warren said. 'Not long ago I had given up hope, and now … I will be meeting Nathan.'

Verna harrumphed. 'Out of the rain and into the lake. I can't believe I've sworn loyalty to that crazy old man.'

Clarissa leaned forward. 'Nathan is dashing. He isn't old.'

Verna barked a laugh. 'You have no idea, child.'

'And he isn't crazy, either. Nathan is the kindest, most wonderful, most generous man I've ever met!'

Verna glanced down at Clarissa's cleavage, and back up to her eyes. She had that look that Clarissa was used to seeing.

'Yes,' Verna murmured. 'I'm sure he is, my dear.'

'You could have no better man to swear loyalty to,' Clarissa said. 'Besides being thoughtful and kind, Nathan is a powerful wizard. I saw him turn another wizard to a pile of dust.'

Verna's brow creased. 'Another wizard?'

Clarissa nodded. 'Named Vincent. Vincent and another wizard and two Sisters, Jodelle and Willamina, came to see Nathan. They tried to hurt him. Nathan turned Vincent into a pile of ash.'

Verna's eyebrows rose.

'After that,' Clarissa said, 'they were very polite to Nathan, and Jagang agreed to give the book' – she tapped the book in her lap –'to Nathan. Jagang said Nathan could have either the book, or Sister Amelia. Now, Nathan will have both. Nathan has great plans. Nathan will rule the world, one day.'

Verna and Warren shared a sidelong glance. She looked at Amelia.

'What is this book, Amelia?'

'I stole it from the Temple of the Winds,' Amelia said in a hoarse voice. 'I'm the only one who can use it. I started a plague. Thousands have already died because of what I did. It was how Jagang eliminated Richard Rahl.

'Thank the Creator that we still have Nathan Rahl to protect us with the bond to him.'

'Dear Creator,' Verna whispered, 'what have we agreed to with our oath to the likes of Nathan?'

CHAPTER 63

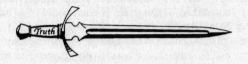

Richard rose from the wizard's chair when he recognized the spirit gliding toward him. He couldn't call a specific spirit, and he didn't always know the ones who came, but he knew this one. With this one, he had a deep connection.

The person this spirit once was, he had loathed, he had feared. Only once he understood her, and only after he had forgiven her for what she had done to him, was he able to gain his release. This one he had killed, and in so doing, he freed her from her torment.

This spirit was the one who had later brought Kahlan and Richard together in that place between worlds.

'Richard,' the spirit said as she seemed to smile.

'Denna.'

'I see you wear an Agiel. It is not mine.'

Richard slowly shook his head. 'It is that of yet another Mord-Sith who died because of me.'

'Raina. I knew her in the world of life, and I know her here. Since she passed into the spirit world after the violation of the winds, she may not come to you, here. She is not one of those who holds sway over the forces involved as they pertain to you and the winds. Know that her spirit is at peace. You gave her peace, in life, and so she asked me to come to you.'

Richard rolled the red Agiel in his fingers. 'I gave your Agiel to Kahlan. As I promised you, one time, only she is able to give me more pain than you.'

'Only you, Richard, are able to give yourself more pain than I could give you.'

'Have it your way. I care not to argue. It is good to see you, Denna.'

'You may disagree, after I am finished with you.'

Richard smiled at her nature showing through, even in her spirit form. 'You cannot harm me here, Denna.'

'You think not? I may not be able to harm your body, but I can still hurt you.' She nodded to herself. 'Oh, yes, Richard, I can hurt you.'

'And how is that?'

Denna lifted an arm. 'I can make you remember – remember and make it real again. You and I have a past.'

Richard spread his hands. 'And to what purpose?'

Denna spread her luminous arms. 'That is for you to decide, Richard.'

With a flash of light in his mind, the Temple of the Winds was gone, fading from his consciousness, and he was in a place he remembered: the castle in Tamarang.

He was there again.

He could taste the terror. Denna had captured him. She had tortured him for days. He was delirious and weak.

Every step was painful as he followed Denna through the grand dining hall. His wrists were cut and swollen from the manacles she used to shackle him up to a beam. When Denna stopped and spoke to people, Richard kept his eyes to her braid as he silently waited behind her.

Denna controlled his life, his destiny. He was allowed only that which she granted. He hadn't eaten since she had captured him. He longed to eat something. Anything.

All around, the jumble of talking and laughter from the queen's guests droned in his head. Denna, too, was a guest of the queen. Richard, at the end of a chain running from his mistress to a collar around his neck, was Denna's prisoner.

She hadn't let him eat during those days of torture, and he needed food. As she sat at the dining table, Denna snapped her fingers, pointing at the floor behind her chair. Richard sank to the floor, relieved to be allowed that small comfort. He could rest. He wasn't hanging from the shackles; he wasn't being made to stand all night; he wasn't being tortured.

All of the guests were eating. The varied aromas tormented him. He ached with hunger. Everyone else was eating, but he

695

had to sit on the floor behind Denna, watching what others enjoyed – what he was denied.

Richard thought about the times he had been with Kahlan, at camp, eating rabbit cooked over the fire or porridge sweetened with berries. He licked his lips thinking about the succulent, hot, tender meat, brown and crunchy on the outside from the fire. He had so enjoyed those meals with her. The food and the company were the best.

Now, he was denied that life, and was yoked to another.

After everyone else had been eating for a while, a server brought a bowl of gruel. Denna had him hand it down to Richard. He held it in trembling hands. Almost any time before, he would have cast it aside in disgust, but now, it was all he had.

He was made to put it on the floor and to eat it like a dog, while laughter from the guests filled his ears. He didn't care. He was being allowed to eat at last.

Gruel was all he was allowed, but at that moment, in his state of tormented need, it was wonderful – it was freedom from the ache of hunger, freedom from the misery of seeing others eat while he starved, fulfillment of a simple but long denied need.

He slurped at it, relishing it, gulping it down. He could not escape his imprisonment in his new life, over which he had no say, and so he decided that if gruel was all he would be allowed, then he would have to accept that fact, and sate his hunger with what he was given.

The light flashed in his head.

Color bled from his sight, vanishing almost painfully, and he saw again the muted mists of the Temple of the Winds around him.

Richard was on his hands and knees on the floor, panting in terror. The glowing white spirit of Denna towered over him.

Denna was right. She could hurt him, still. This pain, though, she had given him out of love.

Richard staggered to his feet. How could he have thought he was ignorant before, and that the knowledge of the Temple of the Winds had brought him new sight? He had had sight all along, but had failed to see. Knowledge without heart was empty.

Wizard Ricker had left, with the sliph, a message for him, but he had ignored it.

Ward left in. Ward right out. Guard your heart from stone.

He had failed to guard his heart from stone, and it had almost cost him everything.

'Thank you, Denna, for that gift of pain.'

'It has taught you something, Richard?'

'That I have to go home, back to my world.'

'Thank you, Richard, for living up to what I expect of you.'

Richard smiled. 'Were you not a spirit, I'd kiss you.'

Denna smiled a sad smile. 'The thought is the gift, Richard.'

Richard shared a gaze with her for a moment, a gaze between worlds.

'Denna, please tell Raina that we all love her.'

'Raina knows this. Feelings of the heart cross the boundary.'

Richard nodded. 'Then you know how much we love you, too.'

'That is why I came to vouch for you in your quest to the winds.'

Richard held his arm out. 'Would you escort me to the passageway? I would find peace in your company before I leave this empty place. The worst is yet ahead of me.'

Denna glided along at his side as he headed for the passageway out, striding the Hall of the Winds for the last time. They didn't speak; words were too paltry to touch what was in his heart.

Near the great doors, the spirit of Darken Rahl waited.

'Going somewhere, my son?' The sound of his words echoed painfully through the hall.

Richard glared at the spirit of his father. 'Back to my world.'

'There is nothing for you there. Kahlan, your true love, is married to another man. She has sworn an oath to him before the spirits.'

'You could never understand why I'm going back.'

'Kahlan is married to my son, Drefan. You cannot have her now.'

'That is not why I'm going back.'

'Then why leave this place? The world of life will be empty for you now.'

Richard stalked past the spirit of his father. He didn't have to explain his reasons to the one who had caused so much grief. Denna glided along beside Richard.

At the doors, Darken Rahl appeared again, blocking the way.

'You may not leave.'

'You can't stop me.'

'Oh, yes, my son, I can.'

'You must let him pass,' Denna said.

'Only if he agrees to the terms.'

Richard turned to Denna. 'What's he talking about?'

'The spirits set the requirements for your path into our world. Because it was your unique path here, Darken Rahl was called upon and given commensurate sway over your price for coming here, your sacrifice to come here. Darken Rahl set the more onerous of the sacrifices, such as Drefan marrying Kahlan. If one who participated in your coming so chooses, this spirit also has the right to set requirements if you are to leave.'

'I will simply banish him,' Richard said. 'I know how to do that, now. I can banish him from the winds, and then leave.'

'It is not that simple,' Denna said. 'You traveled from the world of life, through the underworld, to this place within the world of souls. You must return through the underworld. The spirits can set a price. It must, however, be one that is fair, in view of the forces and worlds involved, and it must be a price within your ability to satisfy.'

Richard ran his fingers back through his hair. 'And I must pay?'

'If he names a price within the edicts, then you must, if you are to return to your world.'

Smiling that vile smile of his, Darken Rahl glided closer.

'I only have two small, insignificant requirements. Meet them, and you may return to your brother, Drefan, and his wife.'

Richard glared. 'Name them, but if you set the price too high, and I choose not to pay it and remain here instead, then I swear I will devote my eternity to making your soul twist in torment. And you know I can do it – the winds have taught me how.'

'Then I guess you will have to decide just how important this is to you, my son. I think you will pay it.'

Richard didn't want to tell him how important it was, or the price would climb.

'Name the price, and I will decide if I will pay it. I was willing to stay here, I may yet decide to do so.'

Darken Rahl came closer, close enough that the pain of his spirit coruscation was almost enough to make Richard back away. He willed himself to hold his ground, without a shield of magic.

'Oh, the price is going to be high, indeed, but I think you will pay it. I know you, Richard. I know your foolish heart. Even this price, you will pay for her.'

Darken Rahl did indeed know Richard's heart. Darken Rahl, after all, was the one who had almost destroyed it.

'Name the price or be gone.'

'First, the knowledge of the Temple of the Winds was not yours before you came to this place. You will return as you came – without the knowledge you acquired here. Back in your world, you will be as you were before you left it.'

Richard had expected as much. 'Agreed.'

'Oh, very good, my son. How eager, how earnest, you are. Will you agree to the second requirement so readily?' His smile seemed as if it would strip flesh from bone. 'I wonder.'

His voice went on in a lethal hiss.

When Darken Rahl named the second requirement, Richard's knees nearly buckled.

'Can he do that?' Richard could manage no more than a whisper. 'Can he demand that?'

Denna stared back with somber, spirit eyes.

'Yes.'

Richard turned away from the two spirits. Head bent, he pressed his hand over his eyes. 'It is that important to me,' he whispered. 'I agree to the price.'

'I knew you would.' Darken Rahl's malevolent laugh echoed the length of the Temple of the Winds. 'I knew that even this, you would pay for her.'

Richard gathered his senses. He slowly turned, lifting his hand toward the evil spirit.

'And with this price, you have shown me your barren spirit. In that, dear father, you have made a mistake, for I can now use that emptiness against you.'

The laughter died out. 'You have agreed to the price I have set within my right and power. You can do nothing but banish me from the winds, and that will not negate the price; the world of souls will enforce it, now that it is named and accepted.'

'So they will,' Richard said. 'But you will taste my revenge for all you have done, including the price you have demanded, when you could have stopped with the first as fair.'

Richard freed a pristine flow of Subtractive Magic, uncontaminated by so much as a scintilla of the Additive. It was the force of the void unleashed.

Total oblivion of Light engulfed the spirit of Darken Rahl.

A wail came from that deep forever as Darken Rahl was plunged into the unmitigated shadow of the Keeper of the Underworld, where not the slightest trace of Light from the Creator shone.

It was the pain of denial of that Light that was the true torture of the Keeper's dark eternity.

When he was gone, Richard turned once more to the passageway back to the world of life.

'I am sorry, Richard,' came Denna's tender voice. 'None but he would have demanded this of you.'

'I know,' Richard whispered as he called the lightning to take him back. 'Dear spirit, I know.'

CHAPTER 64

Drefan hooked his hand under her arm and pulled her shoulder against him. At the white ruffles of his shirt hung two red Agiel.

'Isn't it about time you ended this pretense, my wife? Isn't it about time you gave in to your desires, and admitted your hunger for me?'

Kahlan glared into his blue, Darken Rahl eyes. 'Are you really mad, Drefan, or do you just pretend it? I agreed to wed you to save lives, not because I wanted it. When will you ever admit it to yourself? I do not love you, nor will I ever.'

'Love? When have I ever mentioned love? I speak of passion.'

'You are delusional if you think I will ever –'

'You already have. You want it again.'

It cut her to the heart that he had so easily deduced what had happened with Richard. He pointed it out constantly. He taunted her for it. It was her eternal punishment for what she had done, a stain she couldn't annul.

Distant thunder rumbled through the mountains as the spring storm that had come so suddenly moved on, away from the city. The wild lightning had reminded Kahlan of Richard. She had stood at the window, watching the violent flashes, remembering.

'Never.'

'You are my wife. You have sworn an oath.'

'Yes, Drefan, I have sworn an oath, and I am your wife. I will live by my words, but the spirits are satisfied with what I

701

have given. They demand no more, or the plague would not be gone.' She pulled her arm away. 'If you want me, then you will have to rape me, for that is what it will be. I will not go to your bed willingly, nor easily.'

His smile was maddening. 'I can wait until you finally give in to your lust. I want you to enjoy it. I long for you finally to admit it, to ask for it.'

He stalked away, but turned back when she called his name.

'What are you doing with Cara and Berdine's Agiel?'

Touching an Agiel was painful only if it was one that had been used against you in the past – if you had been the prisoner of a Mord-Sith. Agiel were weapons only in the hands of the Mord-Sith to whom they belonged, but without the bond to a true Lord Rahl they no longer functioned. For Drefan, they were nothing more than obscene decoration.

He lifted the red rods away from his chest to have a look at them. 'Well, I thought that since I am the Lord Rahl now, I should wear these, as a symbol of my authority. After all, Richard wore one. You wear one.'

'The Agiel we wear are not symbols of authority. They are symbols of our respect for the women to whom they belonged.'

He shrugged as he let them drop back down. 'The army seems quite intimidated to see me wearing them. That will do. Good night, my dear. Sleep well.' His sly smile returned. 'Call out if you have need of anything.'

Muttering a curse under her breath, Kahlan shouldered open the door to her rooms. She was exhausted, and wanted only to fall into bed, but she knew that her racing mind would deny her sleep.

Berdine was waiting for her.

'Is he gone to bed?' she asked, referring to Drefan.

'Yes,' Kahlan said, 'as I am about to do.'

'No, you can't. You have to come with me.'

Kahlan frowned at the serious look on Berdine's face. 'Where do you want me to go?'

'We have to go up to the Keep.'

'What's wrong? Is it the sliph? Has someone tried to come through the sliph?'

Berdine waved dismissively as she stepped closer. 'No, no, it's not the sliph.'

'Then what is it?'

'I just want you to come up there with me, that's all. I want some company.'

Kahlan stroked her hand down the woman's shoulder. 'Berdine, I know how lonely you are, but it's late, I have a headache, and I'm tired. All afternoon and evening I've been in meetings with Drefan, General Kerson, and a number of officers. Drefan wants to move the troops back to D'Hara – for us all to go to D'Hara. He wants to abandon the Midlands to the Order and concentrate on defending D'Hara. I've been arguing myself blue.

'I need to go to bed and get some rest so I can get up in the morning and try again to convince them of the folly of Drefan's plan. The general isn't so sure that Drefan isn't right. I am.'

'Sleep later. You are coming up to the Keep with me.'

Kahlan gazed into the Mord-Sith's eyes. And that was what they were: Mord-Sith eyes. This was not Berdine speaking, it was mistress Berdine, as cold and demanding as any Mord-Sith came.

'Not until you tell me why,' Kahlan said in a level tone.

Berdine seized Kahlan's arm. 'You are going up to the Keep with me. You can either go sitting in the saddle, or lying over it – your choice – but you are going, and you are going *now*.'

Kahlan had never seen such a look of determination in Berdine's eyes. It was frightening. That was the only word for it: frightening.

'All right, if it's that important to you, let's go. I just want to know why.'

Instead of answering, Berdine tightened her grip on Kahlan's arm and forced her to the door. Berdine cracked the door, checking, then opened it enough to stick her head out for a look.

'It's clear,' she whispered. 'Come on.'

'Berdine, you're scaring me. What's going on?'

Without answering, Berdine shoved her through the door. They took the service stairs and avoided the passageways that were heavily patrolled. Berdine must have spoken with the

703

guards they did encounter, because when the two of them approached, the guards turned the other way, looking off as if they had seen no one.

Two horses waited, both army horses, big bay geldings.

Berdine tossed a soldier's cloak at Kahlan. 'Here, put this on to cover that white dress of yours so people won't recognize you, or Drefan will hear about it.'

'Why don't you want Drefan to know where we're going?'

Berdine seized Kahlan's ankle and stuffed her foot into the stirrup. The stirrup was big and loose, made for a man's boot. Berdine smacked Kahlan's bottom.

'Get it up there.'

Kahlan abandoned her resistance. Berdine obviously wasn't going to tell her what the urgency was about. The ride to the Wizard's Keep was silent, as was the march through the empty halls, passageways, and rooms.

Before they turned down the last stone corridor to the sliph, they encountered Cara standing guard outside a door. Cara, like Berdine, was unreadable in her stern demeanor as she watched Berdine and Kahlan hurry toward her.

At the door, Berdine seized the lever with one hand and Kahlan's arm with the other.

The look in Berdine's eye was unequivocal sobriety. 'Don't you *dare* disappoint me, Mother Confessor, or you will find out exactly why Mord-Sith are so feared. Cara and I will be with the sliph.'

Without looking back, Cara started out toward the sliph while Berdine, without further word, opened the door and roughly shoved Kahlan into the room. Kahlan stumbled, catching her balance as she glanced back to see Berdine pull shut the door.

Kahlan turned, and found herself looking into Richard's eyes.

Her heart seemed to stop along with her breathing.

A half dozen candles in an iron stand reflected little points of light in his gray eyes. He seemed bigger than life. Every detail was as she remembered. Only his sword was missing from that of her mental image of him.

Ambivalence kept her breath locked in her lungs.

Finally, she found words. 'The plague is ended.'

'I know.'

The room felt so small. The stone so dark. The air so heavy. She labored to breathe, to slow her suddenly racing heart.

His forehead was beaded with sweat, even though it was cool in the depths of the Keep. A drop rolled down over his cheekbone, leaving a wet trail.

'Then what are you doing here? There can be no point to it. I have a husband. We have nothing to say to each other ... not after ... not here, like this, alone.'

His gaze left hers at hearing the cool tone of her voice.

She had hoped it would force him to say it.

Dear spirits, let him say he forgives me.

He said instead, 'I asked Cara and Berdine to bring you here so I could talk to you. I came back because I must speak with you. Will you grant me that much?'

Kahlan didn't know what to do with her hands.

'Of course, Richard.'

He nodded his thanks. He looked in pain. He looked in anguish. His eyes had the dull gloss of distress.

She wanted nothing so much as for him to say that he forgave her. Only that would mend her broken heart. Those were the only words that would mean anything to her. She wanted him to say it, but he just stood there, while his gaze focused beyond the cold stone of the walls.

She decided that if he was going to say it, to forgive her, then the only way was to force him into it.

'So, have you come to forgive me, Richard?'

His words came softly, but with great resolve.

'No, I did not come to forgive you. I can't forgive you, Kahlan.'

She turned away. She finally found something to do with her hands; she pressed her fists against her stomach.

'I see.'

'Kahlan,' he said from behind her, 'I can't forgive you because it would be wrong of me to come here to forgive you.

'Would you have me forgive your humanity? Shall I forgive you slaking your thirst? Shall I forgive your eating when you hunger? Shall I forgive you for the feel of warm sunlight on your face?'

Kahlan wiped at her cheeks and then turned to him. 'What are you talking about?'

The stem of a rose was stuck behind his belt. Richard lifted the rose and held it out to her.

'Your mother gave this to me.'

'My mother?'

Richard nodded. 'She asked if I found enjoyment in it, and when I told her that I did, she asked if I would then return to you. It took a long time for me to understand what she meant.'

'And what did she mean?'

'What she meant is that we have the capacity to enjoy such things. Is it wrong for you to find pleasure at the sight of a rose, in its fragrance, if I am not the one who gave it to you? How can I forgive you that?'

'Richard, this is far different from finding pleasure in the fragrance of a rose.'

He sank to one knee. He put a fist to his abdomen. 'Kahlan, I was once connected to a woman by my flesh, as you were connected to your mother. That is the only connection of flesh we have in this life.'

His fist moved to his chest. 'It is here that we connect ever after that. We can be connected only in our hearts. You did not give him your heart. That was mine and mine alone.

'The winds, the spirits, took their price from you. They left you with little, and you chose to take what was left and to live. You chose to be human. You chose to live life as best you could with what you had left of yourself. You fought for life. You simply took pleasure to which you were entitled.

'I do not own you. You are not my slave. There is nothing for me to forgive. You did not betray me in your heart. It would be presumption of the worst order if I came with an offer of forgiveness when you never betrayed me with your heart.'

Kahlan could feel herself trembling as she drew a breath.

'You hurt me, Richard. I thought my heart was safe with you, always, no matter what, and you walked away from me. You promised it was. You wouldn't even let me try to explain.'

'I know,' he whispered.

His other knee touched the floor as he bent at her feet. His head bowed.

'That is why I have returned. I have come to beg *your* forgiveness. I am the one who was wrong. I am the one who caused the true pain. I am the one who betrayed our hearts, not you. It is the worst sin I could commit, and I alone am guilty of it.

'I am without defense. There can be no excuse.

'I'm so sorry for what I've done to you, Kahlan. I cannot undo the wrong I have done. I have wounded your heart, and for that, I throw myself before you, and beg your forgiveness. I do not deserve it, and so cannot ask it; I can only beg it.'

The way he knelt at her feet, she towered over him.

'Will you forgive me, Richard?'

'There is no room in my heart to hold anything for you but love, even though we cannot be together. Though I am free of my oath, you are sworn to another, and I must respect that, but I cannot help that I can love no other but you. If your heart wishes it, then I forgive you.

'Please, Kahlan, all I can have in this life, if you will grant it, is your forgiveness.'

Mere moments before she had had doubts, been uncertain as to her true feelings about him. Now, absolute conviction avalanched through her.

Kahlan sank down to the floor before him. She put her hands to his shoulders and urged him to look up at her.

'I forgive you, Richard. With all my heart, I love you and I forgive you.'

He smiled a sad smile. 'Thank you.'

She could feel the miracle of her heart mending, of joy flooding into the emptiness, like life itself returning.

'At the ceremony, when I was being married to Drefan, I said the words aloud that they demanded, but in my mind, in my heart, I was saying the oath of marriage to you.'

Richard wiped a tear from her chin. 'I did the same.'

She squeezed his arms. 'Richard, what are we going to do now?'

'There is nothing to do now. You are sworn to Drefan.'

She touched her fingers to his face. 'But what about you? What about you and me?'

His smile left. He shook his head. 'It doesn't matter. I have what I needed – what I came for. You have returned my heart.'

'But, how can we go on like this? Not only that, but we have to do something, and fast. Drefan wants to withdraw the troops back to D'Hara and make a stand against the Order there.'

Anger flashed in Richard's eyes. 'No. You can't let him do that, Kahlan. If you let Jagang divide the New World, he will take it one piece at a time, with D'Hara the last to fall. You can't let Drefan do that. Promise me you won't.'

'I don't need to promise. You are Lord Rahl. You can stop it, now. I am the Mother Confessor. We'll do it together.'

'You must do it, Kahlan. I can't help you.'

'But why not? You've returned. Everything will work out. We'll think of something – find a way. You are the Seeker, you always find a way.'

'I'm dying.'

Ice flashed through her. 'What? What … do you mean, you're dying? Richard, you can't die, not now. Not after … No, Richard, no, it's all right now. You're back. Everything is going to be all right.'

She saw it then, the pain in his eyes, and realized, when he slumped to a hip, that he was unable to stand.

'In order for me to return, the spirits demanded a price.'

He coughed, wincing in pain. She clutched at him.

'What are you talking about? What price?'

'When I was there, at the Temple of the Winds, I gained all the knowledge there. I understood my power. I could use it. I used it to stop the plague. I somehow interrupted the flow of power from the winds that made the book of magic work in this world.'

'You mean that you no longer know how to do it? You mean the plague will come back?'

He lifted a hand to allay her fear. 'No, the plague will not return. But as the price of returning to this world, I was not allowed to keep the knowledge of the winds. I had to come back as I was before.'

'But … you mean that you are simply mortal, like before?'

'No. They demanded more. They demanded that if I was to

return, I had to take the magic of the stolen book into myself to keep it from the rest of the world of life.'

'What?' Kahlan breathed, wide-eyed. 'You don't mean –'

'I have the plague.'

She gripped his shoulder with one hand, and felt his forehead with the other. He was burning with fever.

'Richard, why didn't you tell me before?'

He smiled through the pain. 'Forgiveness was all I needed, all I wanted, but I had to know it was true, and not granted out of pity.'

'Richard, you can't die. Not now. Dear spirits, you can't die!'

'The dear spirits had nothing to do with this. It was Darken Rahl who chose Drefan to be your husband, as the price of the path into the winds, and Darken Rahl who demanded this as the price of my return.'

'Your return. Don't tell me that you only came back to die? Oh, Richard, why would you do such a foolish thing?'

'If I had stayed at the Temple of the Winds, I would eventually have died, but without your forgiveness. I chose, instead, to return and hope that a part of you still loved me enough to forgive me, so I could die with that much at least. With your love back. I couldn't go on, knowing what I had done to you, knowing how I had hurt your heart.'

'And you don't think this hurts my heart! Richard, there has to be something we can do. What can we do? Please, you must have known!'

Richard fell onto his side, holding his stomach. 'I'm sorry, Kahlan. There is nothing. I am absorbing the magic from the book that was stolen. When I die, the magic will die with me.'

Kahlan crouched over him, clutching at him, as the tears overwhelmed her. 'Richard, please don't do this. Please don't die.'

'I'm sorry, Kahlan. I can't stop it. I gladly paid the price. My heart is at peace, now.' He reached up and touched the Agiel hanging from the chain at her throat. 'There was never a moment's hesitation, once I understood. Denna helped me to understand.'

Kahlan hugged him as he rolled onto his back. 'Richard, there must be something. You would have known what to do, before they took the knowledge from you. Try to remember. Please, Richard, try to remember.'

His eyelids drooped. 'I need ... to rest. I'm sorry. I used all my strength. I need to rest a bit.'

Kahlan gripped his hand in both of hers as she wept. It was all too overwhelming to endure. To have him back, only to lose him was too crushing to endure.

She opened his limp hand, to press it to her cheek, and saw something in his palm. She pulled back his fingers, and through the tears, she saw writing in the palm of his hand.

It said, *Find book, destroy it to live.*

Kahlan sprawled over his unconscious form and grabbed his other hand. It, too, had writing in it. *Pinch of white sorcerer's sand on third page. One grain of black sorcerer's sand tossed on.*

There were three other words, but in her mind's state of chaotic disorder, she couldn't think of how to pronounce them.

He knew he was going to forget, and before he did, he wrote a message to himself. He had even forgotten that he had written it.

The book. She had to have the book.

And then she was running, screaming as she went.

'Cara, Berdine! Help me! Cara! Berdine!'

Both women dashed out of the sliph's room, out onto the walkway beside the inky pool, when they heard Kahlan screaming their names as she raced into the tower room.

Kahlan grasped at their leather as she tried to explain. They each seized one of Kahlan's arms and pressed her up against the wall.

'Slow down,' Berdine said.

'We can't understand you,' Cara said. 'Get your breath. Stop crying and get your breath.'

'Richard –' She tried to point but they held her arms. 'Richard has the plague ... I need the book.'

Berdine leaned in close. 'Lord Rahl ... has the plague?'

Kahlan nodded frantically. 'I have to get the book. The book that was stolen from the Temple of the Winds. I have to get it or he will die.' Kahlan tore her arms away from them. 'Please help me. Richard has the plague.'

'What do you need us to do?' Cara asked.

'I'm going to the Old World. Protect him.'

'The Old World!' Berdine gasped. 'Do you know where the book is? Did he tell you where to find it? Did he give you any hint?'

Kahlan shook her head. There wasn't time. She had to hurry. She had to go.

'I don't know where it is! But it's the only chance he has. He took on the magic of the plague in order to return to this world. In order to beg my forgiveness. He wanted to tell me he was sorry for hurting me. If we don't destroy the book, he'll die – just so he could say he was sorry. He'll die! I have to go!'

'But, Mother Confessor,' Berdine said, 'the Old World is a big place. If Richard has the plague … how can you hope to find the book?'

In time. That was what she meant. How could she hope to find the book in time? Before Richard died.

Kahlan gripped a fistful of red leather. 'I have to try! Protect Richard. Don't let Drefan know that Richard is back. I don't know what Drefan would do. Don't tell him!'

Cara was shaking her head. 'Don't worry about that. We won't tell Drefan. We'll take care of Richard while you're gone. We'll hide him here in the Keep. But hurry. If you can't find it, please come back before –'

Kahlan rushed into the room with the sliph. She raced to the sliph's well. The sliph smiled at seeing her.

'Do you wish –'

'Travel! I need to travel! Now!'

'To where do you wish to travel?'

'The Old World!'

'Where in the Old World? There are a number of places I know there. We can go to any you wish. I will take you. You will be pleased.'

Kahlan pressed her hands to her head, growling in frustration as the sliph started naming places Kahlan had never heard of.

'The place you came to with Richard, with your Master, when he went to get me! The first time I traveled with you!'

'I know the place of which you speak.'

Kahlan hiked up her white dress and clambered up onto the

wall of the well. 'That place! Take me there! Hurry! Your master's life is at stake!'

'Protect Richard,' Kahlan called out to Cara and Berdine.

'What should we tell Drefan when he wants to know where you are?' Berdine asked.

'I don't know. You'll have to think of something!'

'We will care for Richard until you return,' Cara said. 'May the good spirits be with you.'

'Tell him I love him. If ... tell him I love him!' she called out as the sliph's silver arm swept Kahlan from the top of the wall.

Her voice was still echoing off the stone walls when Kahlan was plunged into the quicksilver froth. She gasped in the sliph, praying to the good spirits that they would help her find the book. With frantic effort, she swam into what in the past had been the silver rapture.

Now, there was only dark terror.

CHAPTER 65

Ann leaned toward him. 'This is your fault, you know.'

Zedd, sitting on the floor in the center of the room with her, glanced over. 'You broke her prized mirror.'

'That was an accident,' Ann insisted. 'You are the one who ruined their shrine.'

'I was simply trying to get it clean. How was I to know that it would catch fire? They shouldn't have put all those dried flowers around it. You were the one who spilled that berry wine on her best dress.'

Ann turned her nose up. 'The pitcher was too full. You're the one who filled it. Besides, you broke his prized knife handle. He won't ever be able to find a burled wassen root like that one again. He was understandably upset.'

Zedd harrumphed. 'What do I know about sharpening knives? I'm a wizard, not a blacksmith.'

'That would explain the incident with the elder's horse.'

'They can't blame that on me. I didn't leave the gate open. At least, I'm pretty sure I didn't leave it open. Anyway, there is bound to be another horse that fast he can buy. He can afford it. What I want to know is how you managed to turn his number three wife's hair that color green.'

Ann folded her arms. 'Well, it was an accident. I thought those herbs would make her hair smell good. I wanted to surprise her. But the elder's prized rabbit skin headdress – that was no accident; that was plain laziness. You should have checked it sooner, instead of leaving it to dry unattended over the fire. That headdress was a work of art, what with those thousands of beads. He won't easily replace such a nice headdress.'

Zedd shrugged. 'Well, we never told them that we were any good at domestic tasks. We never told them that at all.'

'Quite right. We didn't. It's not our fault if we didn't work out. We could have told them, if they'd asked.'

'We certainly could have.'

Ann cleared her throat into the silence. 'What do you think they are going to do with us?'

Both of them were sitting back to back, bound together with a coarse rope, while the meeting across the room dragged on. They still wore the wristbands that kept them from using their magic.

Zedd glanced across the room, where a heated discussion was being conducted. The bareheaded elder, his number one wife, several influential members of the Si Doak community who had claimed rights to use the services of the captives, and the Si Doak shaman, were all complaining to one another about troubles they had had. Zedd couldn't understand all of the words, but he could understand enough to follow the deliberations.

'They've decided they want to cut their losses and rid themselves of their domestic slaves,' Zedd whispered to Ann.

'What's happening?' Ann asked, when the chattering finally came to an end. 'What have they decided? Are they going to set us free?'

The eyes across the room all turned to the captives. Zedd made a warning sound to Ann.

'I think maybe we should have been a little more attentive to our chores,' Zedd whispered over his shoulder. 'I think we're in a great deal of trouble.'

'Why, what are they going to do,' Ann mocked, 'return us to the Nangtong and demand their blankets back?'

Zedd shook his head as the Si Doak rose up. The shaman's necklaces jangled together. The elder thumped his staff.

'I wish they would. They want to get back all their costs and something toward the damages. They are going to take us on a journey.

'They have just decided that they can get the best price for us by selling us to cannibals.'

Ann's head swung around. 'Cannibals?'

'That's what they said. Cannibals.'

'Zedd, you were able to take the collar off your neck. Can't you get these confounded bracelets off our wrists? I think that now would be the time.'

'I'm afraid we may end up in a cook pot with them still on us.'

Zedd watched an angry elder and a seething shaman stalking toward them.

'Well, it's been fun, Ann. But I'm afraid the fun is over.'

Verna put an arm around Warren's waist, trying to help him as he stumbled along, as she followed behind Clarissa, who was following behind Walsh and Bollesdun. Janet hurried to the other side of Warren and lifted his arm, draping it over her shoulder.

'Are you sure?' Verna whispered to Walsh. 'Here? Nathan wanted us to meet him in the Hagen Woods?'

'Yes,' Walsh said over his shoulder.

'That was the name he told me, too,' Clarissa added.

Verna let out an annoyed breath. It was just like Nathan to make them go into the Hagen Woods. Even if Richard had cleared the mriswith from this place, she still didn't like it. Verna always suspected Nathan of being dangerously unbalanced, and that he would want her to meet him here only confirmed it.

Trailers of moss hung down, like gauzy rags of the dead. Roots tripped their feet as they moved through the darkness. Unpleasant odors wafted in on the warm, humid air. Verna had never been this deep into the Hagen Woods before – and for good reason.

'How are you doing, Warren?' she whispered.

'Fine,' he mumbled in a groggy voice.

'It won't be long, Warren. It won't be long, now. Just a little farther, and then it will be over. Nathan will help you.'

'Nathan,' he mumbled under his breath. 'Must warn him.'

They came upon a massive stone block that was obviously worked by man; it was square. It was nearly covered with snaking tendrils and gnarled roots. More stones, like white bones in the moonlight, jutted up from the thick vegetation. She saw the low, jagged remains of a wall, and columns, looking like the ribs of a monster.

Light shone through the undergrowth. The way it flickered it appeared to be the light of a campfire. Walsh and Bollesdun held aside the branches for the rest of them. The fire was set in a circle of rocks placed on the stone floor of old ruins. Beyond the fire Verna could see the round wall of a large well, or something like a well. She had never known that this place was hidden in the Hagen Woods, but as infrequently as anyone went into the Hagen Woods, that wasn't surprising.

Nathan, dressed like a rich nobleman, rose to greet them. He was tall, and intimidating, especially without a Rada'Han around his neck. When he saw them all, he grinned that confident Rahl grin. Walsh and Bollesdun laughed aloud, and received good-natured slaps on the back.

Clarissa ducked under an arm, throwing hers around Nathan's midsection. He grunted when she squeezed with all her might and ardor. When she proudly held out the book, he took it from her. He gave her a private smile, laden with meaning. Clarissa's eyes sparkled. Verna's eyes rolled.

'Verna!' Nathan called out when he saw her. 'Glad you could make it.'

'How good to see you, *Lord Rahl*.'

'You shouldn't scowl like that, Verna. You'll get wrinkles.' He scanned the others. 'Janet, so you have joined us, too.' His brow tightened a bit. 'And Amelia.' He looked to the other woman, standing off to the side. 'And who have we here?'

Clarissa held out an arm, wiggling her fingers, urging Manda forward. From underneath, Manda's fists tightened the cloak at her throat. She timidly stepped forward.

'Nathan, this is a friend of mine, Manda. From Renwold.'

Manda put a knee to the ground as she bowed deeply. 'Lord Rahl. My life is yours.'

'Renwold.' Nathan's brow twitched again as he glanced briefly at Clarissa. 'Yes, well, glad you escaped from Jagang, Manda.'

'I owe it all to Clarissa,' Manda said as she came to her feet. 'She is the bravest woman I've ever seen.'

716

Clarissa giggled as she pressed herself to Nathan. 'Nonsense. I'm so thankful that the good spirits put you where they did, or I'd never have even known you were there.'

Nathan turned his attention back toward Verna. 'Who have we here? The young Warren, I presume?'

Verna did her best to smooth her own brow. 'Nathan –'

'Lord Rahl.' His grin cracked through the scowl. 'But we are old friends, Verna. I am still Nathan to you, and all my old friends.'

Verna dipped her head as she bit the inside of her cheek.

'Nathan,' she began again, 'you're right; this is Warren. Can you help him? He's just coming into prophecy, just starting to have them. I took his collar off a while back and there is nothing to protect him from the gift. He's having the headaches. Nathan, he's in a bad way. I'll follow you anywhere if you will help him.'

'Help him?'

'Please, Nathan. I'm begging you.'

'Nothing to it, Verna. I'd be delighted to help the boy.' Nathan gestured. 'Bring him over here by the fire.'

Warren mumbled, trying to introduce himself, but he was nearly unconscious. Verna and Janet helped him down where Nathan pointed, and balanced him upright.

Nathan hiked up his trousers at his knees and lowered himself to the stone floor of the missing building, sitting crosslegged. He set the book beside him. His brow drew down in that Rahl frown as he studied Warren's face. He waved his hand at Verna and Janet, ordering them away. With a web, Nathan held Warren upright. He inched forward, until their knees touched.

'Warren,' Nathan called in that deep, commanding voice of his. Warren's eyes opened. 'Hold up your hands.'

Fingers extended, both Warren and Nathan held up their hands. They pressed their fingers together. Their eyes fixed on each other.

'Let your Han flow into my fingertips,' Nathan said in gentle prompting. 'Open the seventh gateway. Close the others. You know of what I speak?'

'Yes.'

'That's a good lad. Do it then. It will make it easier if I have your help.'

A warm, mellow glow enveloped both men. The night air hummed with the power from that light. It was neither flame nor heat. Verna didn't know what Nathan was doing. She was somewhat astounded that Nathan did.

Nathan had always been something of a enigma at the Palace of the Prophets. He had seemed an old man to her even when Verna was a young girl. He had always been regarded as, at the least, unbalanced, even by the most magnanimous of the Sisters.

There were those at the palace who didn't believe that Nathan had more than the slightest hint of the gift in anything but prophecy. Others suspected, but were never sure, that he was capable of much more than he ever showed them. There were others who were so terrified of him that they feared going to the rooms where he was confined, even though he had a Rada'Han around his neck. Verna had always considered Nathan trouble on two feet.

Now, she watched as this troublesome old lecher of a wizard did his best to save the life of the man Verna loved. At times, the light glowed more strongly in one man than the other, before passing away, and then coming back, as if it had forgotten something and then returned for it.

Walsh and Bollesdun loafed near the round stone wall behind Nathan, but the rest of the party watched transfixed. Verna had no more idea what Nathan was doing than did Manda.

What unnerved Verna the most was when both men, their knees touching, their fingers pressed together, floated a few inches off the ground. She was relieved when they at last settled back down.

Nathan clapped his hands together once. 'There!' he announced. 'That should do it.'

Verna couldn't see how that could have possibly been enough to set the gift right in Warren.

Warren, though, wore a wide grin. 'Nathan, that was – marvelous. The headache is completely gone. I feel so clearheaded – so alive.'

Nathan picked up the inky book and stood. 'I enjoyed it,

too, my boy. Took that gaggle of Sisters near to three hundred years to do for me what I have just done for you. But then they were a misguided lot.' He glanced Verna's way. 'Sorry, Prelate. No slight intended.'

'None taken.' Verna rushed to Warren's side. 'Thank you, Nathan. I was so worried for him. You have no idea what a relief this is.'

Warren's face was losing the joyous look. 'Nathan, now that you have done this for me, I can see more clearly that … we have inadvertently given Jagang insight into prophecy that –'

Nathan cried out. Clarissa cried out. Verna froze. She could feel something sharp pressed to her back.

Amelia had a dacra stabbed in the back of Nathan's thigh. Manda had a knife at Clarissa's throat. Janet was holding a weapon at Verna's back. Warren stiffened when Janet held a warning finger to him and then to the two soldiers.

'Don't you move a muscle, Nathan,' Amelia said, 'or I let flow my Han, and you are instantly dead.'

'Warren is right,' Janet said. 'He did, in fact, give His Excellency some very valuable information.'

'Amelia, Janet!' Verna cried out. 'What are you doing?'

Amelia turned a wicked smile on Verna. 'His Excellency's bidding, of course.'

'But you swore the oath.'

'We swore the oath in word only, not in our hearts.'

'But you can be free of him! You don't need to serve Jagang!'

'Had you told us true the first time, maybe, but once we tried, and failed to hold the bond when Richard died, His Excellency punished us. We'll not take the chance again.'

'Don't do this,' Verna pleaded. 'We're friends. I came to save you. Don't do this, please. Swear the bond, and you will be free!'

'Oh, darlin, I'm afraid she can't do that.' It was not Amelia's voice alone, but more. It was the voice Verna had heard in her own head: Jagang. She felt herself suddenly trembling, just at hearing his tone and inflection in Amelia's voice.

'Now, my loyal and faithful plenipotentiary, hand over the book. Sister Amelia and I have more use of it.'

Nathan held it out to the side. With her other hand, the one not on the dacra in his leg, Amelia snatched back the book.

'Well,' Nathan said, 'are you going to kill me, or not?'

'Oh, yes, I intend to kill you,' Amelia said in Jagang's voice. 'You betrayed our bargain, Lord Rahl. Besides, I don't like having subordinates who won't allow me into their minds.

'Before you die, I thought I'd let you watch how a real slave obeys orders. I thought you'd like to watch me cut your little darlin Clarissa's throat.'

Breathe.

Kahlan expelled the sliph from her lungs, and with frantic need, sucked in the alien air. Night crashed in around her. She refused to spare the time to fear the sudden vision, the sudden sound, to give it time to settle into place in her mind, and instead seized the stone wall to hoist herself out.

A frightening sight – to match the words she had already heard – greeted her. With her vision enhanced by the sliph, she took in the whole scene at once, in one slamming jolt.

The instant she saw him, Kahlan knew this was Nathan. He looked like a Rahl, and Richard had told her about Nathan – tall, older, with long white hair to his shoulders. A woman had stabbed a dacra into his leg, and was holding it there. Kahlan had heard her name: Amelia – the one who had started the plague. Kahlan saw Verna, with a woman at her back. A young man stood frozen. Kahlan saw a beautiful young woman holding another woman by a fistful of hair done in ringlets – it could only be Clarissa. The woman's other fist held a knife at the terrified Clarissa's throat.

As Kahlan had emerged from the sliph, she was conscious of the last part of the conversation that had just taken place, and knew well the voice coming from the woman holding the dacra in Nathan's leg. Kahlan knew well the word 'darlin.' She remembered hearing that voice from the wizard, Marlin, who had come to assassinate Richard. It was Jagang's voice.

The image of the amulet Richard wore came unbidden into Kahlan's mind. *It means only one thing, and everything: cut. Once committed to fight, cut. Everything else is secondary. Cut.*

720

Her training at the hands of her warrior father had been much the same. Kill or be killed. Never yield. Never wait. Attack.

Richard was near death – near his last breath. She had no time to spare, no time to consider. She was committed. Cut.

In one fluid movement, she erupted from the sliph, dived out of the well, yanked a short sword free of the scabbard on the soldier standing right there, ducked her head, tumbled forward, and came up with the sword already whipping down.

In the span of a heartbeat, before anyone had time to flinch, Kahlan was there. She had to stop Amelia before she released her magic into the dacra in Nathan's leg, or he would be dead. Like lightning, her sword descended, severing Sister Amelia's arm at the crook of her elbow.

And then, everything moved in a painfully slow dance. Kahlan could see the expression on every face. The woman Kahlan had just cut, Sister Amelia, was falling back with a cry. Already, Kahlan's sword was whirling, to reverse her hand-hold, as she followed her quarry down. Verna was spinning, a dacra in her own hand, toward a surprised woman behind her. The young man was diving toward the woman with the knife. Nathan's hands were coming up toward Clarissa. His scream cut through the night.

Clarissa was reaching toward Nathan. The young woman holding her by the hair snarled with a vicious sneer, and savagely cut through Clarissa's throat.

Kahlan saw the spray of blood for only an instant before the night exploded with lightning from both Nathan and the young man.

Her left hand now joined with her right, Kahlan slammed her sword down through Sister Amelia's heart, pinning her to the ground before the second soldier had his sword clear of his scabbard.

Verna's dacra expeditiously dispatched the woman behind her at the same time as the young woman with the knife took two bolts of lightning, shattering her in a red horror as Clarissa's body still collapsed toward the ground.

The violence was over before comprehension could catch up with it.

In a daze, Nathan staggered toward Clarissa's body. Kahlan

rushed past him and knelt beside Clarissa. The sight that greeted her brought a gasp.

Kahlan sprang up and put her hands against Nathan, stopping him. 'It's too late, Nathan. She's with the spirits, now. Don't look. Please don't look. I saw in her eyes the love she had for you. Please don't look at her like this. Remember her the way she was.'

Nathan nodded. 'She had a good heart. She saved so many people. She had a good heart.'

Nathan lifted his arms. He held his palms out toward Clarissa's body. Intense light flared forth, flooding the dead woman with a brilliant blaze so radiant that the body couldn't be seen at its center.

'From the light of this fire, and into the Light. Safe journey to the spirit world,' Nathan whispered. When the light was gone, only ash remained.

Nathan slumped. 'The vultures can have the rest of them.'

Verna tucked her dacra back up her sleeve. One soldier retrieved his sword from Amelia's body as the other sheathed his.

The young man looked in shock. 'Nathan, I'm so sorry. I gave Jagang the meaning of prophecy that helped him. I didn't want to, but he made me. I'm so sorry.'

Nathan's doleful, azure eyes turned toward the young man. 'I understand, Warren. You didn't do it out of malice; the dream walker was in your mind and you had no choice. You are free of him now.'

Nathan yanked the dacra from his leg. He turned to Verna.

'You brought traitors to me, Verna. You brought assassins to me. But I realize you had not intended it. Sometimes prophecy overwhelms our attempts to outwit it, and catches us unaware. Sometimes we think we are more clever than we are, and that we can stay the hand of fate, if we wish it hard enough.'

Verna straightened her cloak on her shoulders. 'I thought I was saving them from Jagang. I never had any idea that they would give the oath to you without committing their hearts.'

'I understand,' Nathan whispered.

'I don't know what goes through that head of yours, Nathan. Lord Rahl indeed.' Verna glanced to where Clarissa's body had been, and where now there was only white ash. 'And I see that you haven't changed your ways, Nathan. Once again, you've gotten another of your little whores killed.'

The impact of Nathan's fist lifted Verna clear off the ground. Her jawbone shattered with a loud crack. Strings of blood sailed out into the night air. Warren cried out as Verna landed flat on her back. She didn't move.

Warren, crouched at Verna's side, looked up with frantic eyes. 'Nathan! Dear Creator, why would you do this? You've broken her jaw. Why would you try to kill her?'

Nathan flexed his fist. 'If I was trying to kill her, she would be dead. If you want her to live, then I would suggest you heal her. I've heard that you are talented at healing, and with what I have done for you tonight, you should be able to accomplish it in short order. Put some sense in her head, while you're at it.'

Warren bent over Verna, pressing his hands to the unconscious woman's face. Kahlan said nothing. She had seen love in Nathan's eyes when he had looked at Clarissa. She had just seen rage, too.

Nathan bent and retrieved the inky black book lying on the ground beside Sister Amelia's body. He straightened and turned those Rahl eyes on Kahlan. He held out the book.

'You could be none other than Kahlan. I have been expecting you. Prophecy, you know. I'm glad I was not late. You don't have much time. Give this to Lord Rahl. I hope he knows how to destroy it.'

'He knew when he was at the Temple of the Winds, but he said he had to give up his knowledge to leave. But he wrote a message in the palms of his hands. It says, 'Pinch of white sorcerer's sand on third page. One grain of black sorcerer's sand tossed on.' And then there were three words, but I don't know what they mean.'

Nathan laid a big hand on her shoulder. 'The words are the three chimes: Reechani, Sentrosi, Vasi. I don't have time to teach you about the three chimes, but know that they must be spoken after the white and before the black. That's what is important.'

'Reechani, Sentrosi, Vasi,' Kahlan repeated, trying to commit the words to memory. She said them over again in her head.

'Richard does have both white and black sorcerer's sand, does he not?'

Kahlan nodded. 'Yes. He told me about it. He has both.'

Nathan shook his head, as if considering some private thought. 'Both,' he muttered. Nathan squeezed her shoulder. 'I know from prophecy some of what he has been through. Stand by him. Love is too precious a gift to lose.'

Kahlan smiled. 'I understand. May the good spirits bring it to your heart, Nathan. I can't thank you enough for helping Richard, for helping me.' Her voice broke. 'I didn't know what I was going to do. I only knew I had to come here.'

Nathan hugged her, she thought more for his own need than hers. 'You did the right thing. Maybe the good spirits guided you. Get back to him, now, or we will lose our Lord Rahl.'

Kahlan nodded. 'The killing is over.'

'The killing is just about to begin.'

Nathan turned and held both fists skyward. An awesome flare of light ignited at his fists and shot into the night sky. Kahlan watched as it streaked northwest, so bright that the stars vanished in the glare.

Kahlan saw Verna sitting up, with Warren's help. He was wiping the blood away from her newly healed jaw.

'What have you done?' Kahlan asked Nathan.

He looked down at her a long moment, and then a sly smile spread on his lips. 'I have just given Jagang a nasty surprise. I have just given General Reibisch the signal to attack.'

'Attack? Attack who?'

'Jagang's expeditionary force. They destroyed Renwold. They are up to other trouble in the New World, too, but are unaware of who shadows them. It will be a short battle. The prophecy says that the D'Harans will fight as fiercely as they have ever fought, and will, before this night is over, destroy the enemy in the traditional D'Haran fashion: without mercy.'

Verna was coming to her feet. Kahlan had never seen Verna looking so meek. 'Nathan, I beg your forgiveness.'

'I'm not interested –'

Kahlan laid a hand on Nathan's arm and whispered up at him. 'Nathan, please, for your own sake, listen to her.'

Nathan gazed into Kahlan's eyes a moment before he turned his glare on Verna. 'I'm listening.'

'Nathan, I've known you a long time. My whole life. I've seen things before that … perhaps I didn't understand. I thought you were doing this to seize power for yourself. Please forgive me for lashing out at you for my own guilt at my friends turning against me – against us. I sometimes … jump to judgment. I can see that I have mistaken what was truly going on with you and Clarissa. She adored you, and I thought – I beg you to forgive me, Nathan.'

Nathan let out a grunt. 'Knowing you, Verna, that must have been the hardest thing you have ever had to say. Forgiveness granted.'

'Thank you, Nathan,' she sighed.

Nathan bent and kissed Kahlan's cheek. 'May the good spirits be with you, Mother Confessor. Tell Richard I give him back his title. Maybe I will see him again someday.'

With his hands on her waist, he boosted Kahlan up onto the sliph's wall.

'Thank you, Nathan. I can see why Richard liked you. Clarissa, too. I think she saw the real Nathan.'

Nathan smiled, but then turned serious. 'When you get back, you must offer Richard's brother what he truly wants, if you are to save Richard.'

'You wish to travel?' the sliph asked.

Kahlan's stomach roiled. 'Yes, back to Aydindril.'

'Is Richard truly alive?' Verna asked.

'Yes,' Kahlan said with revived panic. 'He's sick, but he will be fine once I get this book back to him and it's destroyed.'

'Walsh, Bollesdun.' Nathan gestured as he started away. 'My coach awaits. Let's be off.'

'But, Nathan,' Warren said, 'I want to learn about prophecy. I would like to study with you.'

'A true prophet is born, Warren, not made.'

'Where are you going?' Verna called after him. 'You can't leave. You're a prophet. You can't be left to run … I mean, we must know where you will be – in case we need you.'

Without looking back, Nathan pointed. 'Your Sisters are that way, Prelate. To the northwest. Go to them, and save yourself the trouble of trying to follow me. You won't succeed. Your Sisters are safe from the dream walker; I had them transfer their bond to me while Richard went to the world of the dead. If Richard lives, you all can transfer it back to him. Good-bye, Verna. Warren.'

Kahlan pressed a fist to her stomach. If he lives? *If?* 'Hurry,' she said to the sliph. 'Hurry!'

A silver arm swept her from the wall and down into the quicksilver froth.

CHAPTER 66

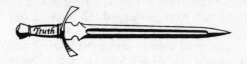

He smiled at the way she struggled. He liked the way she had fought him. He enjoyed teaching her how useless it was to fight a person of his superior strength, superior intellect. He watched in fascination as blood ran from her mouth and nose. The gash on her jaw oozed.

'You are only succeeding at making your wrists bleed,' he taunted. 'You can't break the ropes, but keep at it, if you wish.'

She spat at him. He smacked her again. He dug his thumb across the cut on her jaw, spellbound by the pattern of blood flooding down the side of her neck.

He knew her auras. He'd felt them before. He knew just which ones to touch to cripple her. It hadn't taken long to overpower her. Not long at all.

Her teeth gritted as she growled with effort, straining against the ropes. She was strong, but she was not strong enough. Without her power and her weapon, she was a mere woman. No mere woman was a match for him. Not in any way.

When his fingers began unbuttoning the row of buttons along the side of her ribs, she tugged violently at the ropes holding her wrists and ankles. He liked that. He like to watch her struggle. To watch her bleed. He punched her face again.

He was intrigued that she didn't cry out, that she didn't beg for mercy. That she didn't scream. She would. Oh, how she would scream.

His punch had stunned her for the moment. Her eyes rolled

as she fought to remain conscious. He threw back the front of her outfit, exposing her breasts and the upper half of her torso.

He hooked his fingers under the tight waist of her red leather pants and, with a quick pull, yanked them down enough for what he was going to do to her.

Her entire belly was exposed. He felt it. Tight. Hard. There were scars on her. They riveted him. He tried to imagine what had caused such scars. As jagged and white as they were, it would have been bloody.

'I've been raped before,' she sneered. 'More times than I can remember. I can tell you from experience that you're not very good at it. You haven't even gotten my pants down enough, you stupid pig. Get on with it, if you even can. I'm waiting.'

'Oh, Cara, I'm not going to rape you. That would be wrong. I have never raped a woman. I only have women who want it.'

She laughed at him. Laughed. 'You are one twisted bastard.'

He resisted his urge to smash her face. He wanted her awake for this. Alive for this.

But he shook with rage.

'Bastard?' His fist tightened. 'Because of women like you!'

He hammered a fist down on her breast. Her eyes squeezed shut and her teeth clenched as she winced in pain, trying to curl up in a ball, but unable to, stretched out in the ropes as she was.

He took a settling breath, regaining his control. He wouldn't let her divert him with her filthy mouth.

'Now, I'm going to give you one last chance. Where is Richard? The soldiers are going wild with talk of Richard being back, of the bond being back. Where are you whores hiding him?'

The voices from the ether had told him, too, that Richard was back. The voices had told him that if he wished to assume his rightful place, he must eliminate Richard.

'And where is my loving wife? Where has she gone to?'

The voices told him that she was in the sliph, but the sliph wouldn't tell him where she had gone.

Cara spat at him again. 'I am Mord-Sith. You are too stupid to even imagine what has been done to me before. You couldn't fill the boots of the meekest trainer of Mord-Sith. Your puny torture will pry nothing from me.'

'Oh, Cara, you have never encountered one of my talents.'

'Do what you want with me, Drefan, but Lord Rahl – the real Lord Rahl – is going to cut you up into little pieces.'

'And just how would he be able to do that?' He lifted the hilt of the Sword of Truth clear of its scabbard, so she could see the gold lettering that spelled out the word TRUTH. 'I'm the one who is going to be doing the cutting into little pieces. Little tiny Richard pieces. Where is he!'

When she spat at him again, he couldn't resist fisting her across her cut and swollen lip. The blood gushed anew.

He turned and retrieved one of the items he had brought: an iron pot. He put it on her belly, upside down.

'I'm too big to cook in that pot, you stupid pig. You will have to cut me up. Do I have to explain everything to you?'

He liked the way she tried to antagonize him, to make him lose his temper. She wanted him to kill her. He would, but she would talk, first.

'Cook you? Oh, no, Cara. You have the wrong idea. The wrong idea entirely. You think me some maniacal murderer. No murderer, I. I am the hand of justice. I am the hand of mercy. Come to bring eternal virtue to those who have none.

'This pot isn't to cook you.

'It's to cook the rats.'

He was watching. He saw the way her blue eyes flicked toward him. He had been waiting for just that reaction.

'Rats. I hope you aren't stupid enough to think that I am afraid of rats just because I'm a woman. I'm no woman like you have ever seen before. I used to keep rats as pets.'

'Really? You lie so poorly. My dear, loving, passionate wife explained to me how afraid you are of rats.'

She didn't answer. She was afraid of showing her fear. But he could see it in her eyes.

'I have a sack of rats, here. Nice, fat rats.'

'Just get on with this rape. I'm growing bored.'

'I told you, I don't rape women. They want it from me. They ask for it. They beg for it.' He tugged down his ruffled cuffs. 'No, Cara, I have something else in mind for you. I want you to tell me where I can find my loving brother.'

She turned her face away. 'Never. Get on with the torture before I fall asleep and miss it.'

'You see? As I told you, women always ask me for it.'

He pressed the iron pot to her belly and wound a chain around her middle, to hold down the pot. He forced a finger under the rim, checking, to make sure that it was tight enough.

He then loosened the rough knot in the chain, so he could get the rats under the pot. Cara showed no reaction when he shoved the first under the pot.

Holding the second by the scruff of its neck, he held it before her face, letting her see it squirm and squeak. 'See, Cara? As I promised you. Rats. Big rats.'

Sweat beaded on her forehead. 'I kind of like it. It feels fuzzy against my stomach. I may fall asleep.'

He stuffed the second, and then a third under the pot. There was room for no more. He took the slack from the chain, and tightened the knot of links.

'Fuzzy,' he mocked. 'I think they will keep you wide awake, Cara. Wide awake, and eager to talk, eager to betray Richard. Whores have no honor. You will betray him.'

'Berdine is going to be here soon. She will skin you alive.'

He lifted an eyebrow. 'You relieved Berdine. I saw you. After she left, I took you down. She won't be back for quite a while, but when she does come back, she will get the same as you.'

With tongs, he retrieved a big, glowing coal from the pan over the mass of candles. He plunked the red-hot coal down inside the rim of the footed bottom of the iron pot.

'You see, Cara, the coals are going to heat this iron pot – get it very hot.' He looked at her eyes. 'The rats aren't going to like that. They are going to want out.'

Her breathing quickened. Sweat rolled down her face. Where were her brave words now? She was silent, now.

'And how do you suppose the rats are going to get out, Cara? Once they start to get hot? Once the iron pot starts burning them? Singeing their tender noses?'

'Just cut my throat and kill me, you bastard.'

'When the rats get hot enough under there, they'll panic. They'll be frantic to get out. Guess how they'll get out, Cara.'

She had no haughty answer to fill the silence.

He pulled his knife and with the handle, tapped the iron pot. 'How are you doing in there, my little rat friends?'

Cara flinched. He smiled when her eyes turned to him, watching him. He could see fear in those eyes. Real fear. He plunked down a half dozen more glowing coals on the iron pot.

'Where is Richard?'

She had nothing to say. He piled on more coals, into a nice, round hump. That was all the pot's bottom would hold.

He bent over and looked into her eyes. Her skin was as white as chalk. Sweat glistened on her face, on her breasts.

'Where are you whores hiding Richard?'

'You are crazy, Drefan. I don't like this, but if this is how I am to die, then I will die. But I will never betray Lord Rahl.'

'I am Lord Rahl! When I get rid of my brother, there will be no one to challenge my rule! I am the son of Darken Rahl, and the rightful master of D'Hara.'

She turned her face away. He saw her swallow. Her feet were trembling. Her smooth breathing was interrupted now and again, caught up short.

He chuckled. 'I'll ask again, when the rats start gnawing their way through you, to get away from their hot, iron prison. When their sharp little claws start digging into your belly. When the rats start tunneling into your guts, trying to get out.'

Cara's whole body jerked. It jerked again. Her eyes widened as she stared up at the ceiling, trying to keep the moan from escaping her throat. He glanced back and saw a drop of blood run from under the rim of the bowl, down her side.

'Well, looks like they already want out. Ready to talk, yet?'

She spat at him, and then gasped sharply. Her wide blue eyes fixed on the ceiling. She was trembling all over now.

Her whole body stiffed. Every muscle strained. She started to pant. Tears filled the corners of her eyes, to run down the side of her face.

She was feeling every little thing the rats did – every frantic bite, every desperate digging, ripping of their claws.

Cara let out a short little cry. Sharp, shrill, clipped.

It was rapture. He knew it was only the beginning. Even if she talked, he had no intention of stopping this. He longed to hear screams. Real, from the gut screams.

731

Cara obliged him, and let out her first.

Because of his singular perception, another detail caught his attention. His vigilance had again rewarded him. Smiling, he turned to the sliph's well.

Breathe.

Kahlan expelled the sliph, but she knew something was wrong. even before she sucked a breath of air.

A piercing scream echoed around the stone room. Kahlan thought the shriek would make her ears bleed.

As she erupted from the sliph, before she could brace herself to react, big, strong hands reached down and seized her. She struggled to get her bearings, to make sense of what was happening as the sudden light and sound whirled in around her.

The hands tore the book from her grasp. An arm clamped around her neck, its big fist gripping her arm. She felt rope being wound around her wrist.

A nightmare came to life in her vision as she was dragged from the well, kicking and twisting and trying to get away. She went limp when a fist in her gut drove the wind from her lungs. Her knees smacked the stone floor. Her arms felt as if they were being wrenched from her shoulder sockets as they were twisted behind her back.

She fought to reach her Confessor's power – only to remember when she couldn't touch it that the spirits had walled it from her so she could be married to Drefan. She was defenseless. It was Drefan attacking her.

Cara was there, on the floor, her wrists bound above her head, the rope fastened to a pin in the wall. Her ankles, likewise secured with rope, were stretched toward the opposite wall. She had an iron pot chained over her middle. The smell of hot coals and burning flesh assailed Kahlan's nostrils, gagging her.

Drefan pressed his knee to her arm as he knotted rope around her wrists. Kahlan tried to bite his leg. He backhanded her across the face so hard that her vision narrowed to a tiny spot. She fought to keep that vision, to stay conscious. She knew that she was lost if she passed out.

Her arms bound behind her, unable to break her fall, she smacked into the stone floor face-first. Drefan pounced on her back, sitting on her, holding her down, as he bound her legs together. Kahlan struggled to pull a breath against the weight of him. Blood gushed from her nose. The rope around her wrists was so tight that already her fingers were tingling.

Cara screamed. It was the loudest scream Kahlan had ever heard. It sent icy needles stabbing into her head. It made her face hurt.

Blood was running from under the rim of the iron pot. Cara shook and thrashed. She stiffened and screamed again.

Drefan lifted Kahlan's head by her hair. 'Where's Richard?'

'Richard? Richard is dead.'

Kahlan grunted at a punch in her kidney. She couldn't get her breath. Drefan turned his attention to Cara.

'Ready to talk yet? Where did you hide Richard?'

Cara's only answer was another shuddering scream. When it ended, she panted in pain.

'Why did you tell him?' Cara wept. 'Why did you tell him about … the rats? Dear spirits, why did you tell him about the rats?'

Terror locked Kahlan's breath in her lungs.

Blood, vivid red against white skin, ran in rivulets from under the pot's rim, and down Cara's side. Smoke curled up from the hot coals atop it. And then Kahlan saw the bloody claw wriggling from under the rim of the pot on Cara's stomach. Kahlan suddenly understood. It took all her force of will to keep from vomiting.

Cara cried hysterically, thrashing at the bloody ropes holding her.

Kahlan furiously squirmed forward, going for the chain, to try to undo it with her teeth – to try to get the iron pot off Cara. Drefan lifted Kahlan by her hair.

'Your turn will come, wife.'

He heaved her back. Kahlan smacked into the wall and slid down onto something hard and sharp. The pain brought stinging tears to her eyes. It was Nadine's bag, full of all those horn containers. She lurched and wrenched herself until she was able to slip to the side, off the bag, and get her breath back.

Drefan turned his Darken Rahl eyes on her. 'If you tell me where Richard is, I'll let Cara go.'

'Don't tell him!' Cara screamed. 'Don't tell him!'

'I couldn't if I wanted to,' Kahlan called out to Cara. 'I don't know where you hid him.'

Drefan picked up the book Kahlan had brought. 'What's this?'

Kahlan's gaze locked on the sinister black book. She had to have that book, or Richard would die.

'Well, no matter, you won't be needing it anymore.'

'No!' Kahlan screamed when she saw what Drefan was going to do with the book. 'Please!'

He looked back at her as he held the book out over the sliph's well. 'Tell me where Richard is.' He smiled, lifting an eyebrow. 'No?'

He dropped the book down the well. Kahlan's heart sank with the book. The sliph, who liked to watch the people in the room, was nowhere to be seen now. She probably had been frightened away by the screams.

'Drefan, let Cara go. Please. You have me. Do what you want to with me, but please let her go.'

Drefan smiled as wicked a smile as Kahlan had ever seen. It was a twin to Darken Rahl's smile. 'Oh, don't you worry, I intend to do what I want with you. When it is time.'

He turned back to Cara. 'How are the rats doing, Cara? Ready to talk yet?'

Cara cursed him through clenched teeth.

Drefan reached into a sack and brought out a rat, holding it by the scruff of its neck. He shook it in her face as she tried to turn away. He lowered it against her. Squeaking and twisting, its claws scratched and dug as it tried to get away from Drefan's grip, leaving red streaks along Cara's cheeks, chin, and lips.

'Please,' Cara wailed. 'Please, get them away!'

'Where's Richard?'

'Dear spirits, help me. Please help me. Please help me,' she mumbled over and over.

'Where's Richard?'

Cara's body jerked violently. 'Mama!' She shrieked. 'Help me! Mama! Get them off! *Mamaaaaa!*'

Cara was alone in a cage with rats, in the grip of terror and pain. She was a helpless child again, begging for the comfort and protection of her mother, wailing for her mother.

Kahlan gasped in tears. This was her fault. She had told Drefan that Cara was afraid of rats.

'Cara, forgive me! I didn't know!'

Cara thrashed at her ropes, a little girl, frantically begging for her mother to get the rats away.

Kahlan strained to pull a hand free. If she could only get a hand free of the ropes. But they were so tight. She tugged and pulled. Her fingers tingled. The coarse rope cut into her wrists.

Kahlan pressed her wrists against Nadine's bag, searching for something sharp to cut the ropes. The bag was cloth, the handle smooth wood.

The bag. Kahlan bent to the side, her fingers feeling for the button that held the bag closed. She found it. She struggled to undo the button, but her fingers were numb and at the angle that her arms were twisted, she couldn't make her fingers work properly. She dug at the button with her thumbnail, trying to hook it to the side, trying to rip it off. It was sewn on with heavy thread to stand up to the rigors of use and weight. At last, the button popped through its hole.

Kahlan scooped at the contents in the bag, trying to sling them out where she could see them. Every shrill wail from Cara made Kahlan flinch. Every time Cara cried for her mother to save her from the rats, Kahlan had to hold back a sob of her own.

When she glanced up, she saw Drefan wiping a rat across Cara's face. He had broken the back of another and draped it across her throat. Kahlan gritted her teeth and fingered the horn containers out of the bag.

Cara was her sister of the Agiel. Kahlan had to do something. Cara's only hope was Kahlan. She twisted her neck, trying to see the markings on the horns. She couldn't find the one she wanted.

She used her fingers, groping at the symbols scratched into the horn. She felt one that she thought was the right one, and her hopes soared, only to be dashed when she felt that there were three circles. She flicked each horn out of the way when she determined that it was not the one she needed.

735

She rooted in the bag and found another. Her fingers blindly felt the scratches. They went in a circle. She slipped her fingers along the horn and found another circle. She felt a heavily scratched straight line between them.

Kahlan held the horn in her fingertips and twisted, trying to see if she was right. Cara screamed and Kahlan dropped the horn. She scooted to the side so she could see it on the floor.

It had two circles scratched into the patina of the horn. A horizontal line ran through both circles. It was the right one: canin pepper.

Nadine had warned her about taking off the wooden stopper, warned her about getting it in your face, your eyes. It would immobilize a person for a time, Nadine had said. Make them helpless, for a time.

Kahlan worked the horn back into her fingers. She wiggled the wooden stopper, trying to loosen it. It was cut to fit tightly, to keep the dangerous substance from leaking out.

Kahlan's fingers were so numb they had no strength. She gritted her teeth as she tried to work the stopper loose. She didn't want it off, yet, but she had to know she could get it off.

With her hands behind her back, she couldn't throw it. She frantically tried to think of what she was going to do. She had to do something. If she didn't, Cara would soon be dead. And then Drefan would start in on his loving wife.

Cara wailed in agony.

'Please, mama, get the rats away from Cari. Please, mama, please. Help me, please help me.'

The pleading cries of hopeless terror ripped at Kahlan's heart. She could wait no longer. She would just have to figure out what to do when the time came. She had to act.

'Drefan!'

His head twisted around. 'Are you ready to tell me where Richard is?'

Kahlan remembered something Nathan had told her. *You must offer Richard's brother what he truly wants, if you are to save Richard.* Maybe it would save Cara.

'Richard? What would I want with Richard? You know that it's you I want.'

He smiled a knowing, satisfied smile. 'Soon, my dear. In a little while. You can wait.'

He turned back to Cara.

'No, Drefan! I can't wait. I need you now. I want you now. I can't resist any longer. I can't pretend any longer. I need you.'

'I said –'

'Just like your mother.' He froze at her words. 'I need you like your whore of a mother needed your father.'

His expression darkened. Like a provoked bull, he turned toward her, his piercing eyes riveted on her. 'What do you mean?'

'You know exactly what I mean. I need to be taken, like your father took your mother. I want you to take me like that. Only you can satisfy me. Do it. Do it now. Please.'

He rose up, huge and imposing. His muscles rippled and knotted. His brow drew down in that grim Rahl glare.

'I knew it,' he breathed. 'I knew it. I knew you would finally give in to your filthy perversion.'

He hesitated, looking back at Cara.

'Yes. You're right. You're always right, Drefan. You're smarter than me. You were right all along. I can't fool you any longer. Give me what I want. Give me what I need. Please, Drefan, I'm begging you. I need you.'

The look on his face was frightening. It was madness. If she could have shrunk back into the stone, she would have.

Drefan slipped free the knife at his belt as his tongue wet his lips. He started toward her.

She had had no idea just how effective her words had been. In sudden panic, Kahlan wiggled the wooden stopper. Drefan's whole face, the whole way he carried his body, changed. He was a seething monster coming at her. His eyes narrowed with bestial loathing, savage hatred. Hatred for her.

Kahlan swallowed back the sudden terror welling up in her throat. Dear spirits, what had she just done? She scuffed her feet against the stone floor, trying to back away. She was already against the wall.

How was she going to get the powder in his face?

Dear spirits, what do I do?

Kahlan wiggled the stopper with all her might. It popped off. Drefan went to a knee beside her.

'Tell me how much you want me to please you.'

'Yes! I want you. Now. Give me the pleasure only you can give me.'

He brought the knife up as he leaned toward her.

Kahlan heaved herself toward him, twisting, rolling to the side as hard as she could, flinging the horn full of powder at his face as she rolled onto hers.

She couldn't see, facedown on the stone. She didn't know if she had missed, if the oily powder had come out, if she had the horn turned the right way, if he was close enough. She held her breath, bracing for the thrust of his knife, imagining it coming, knowing it was coming. She could almost feel the sharp edge slicing her. She struggled against the panic of not knowing just where he was going to cut her.

Drefan staggered back. She turned her face and saw him fall on his back, writhing, gasping for breath.

Kahlan flipped herself over and started scooting toward Cara. She tried to move around Drefan, but she didn't have much room to maneuver. His groping hand caught her ankles. She kicked, trying to pull away from his grip.

His fingers tightened around her ankles. His powerful arm dragged her toward him. He gasped for air, his other hand flailing about, trying to feel what was around him. He was blind.

Kahlan saw yellow powder on his cheek and neck. She hadn't gotten it in his eyes as she had hoped. She hadn't gotten it directly in his mouth, or nose. Just the side of his face. Most had missed. She didn't know how long that would stop him, but she didn't think for long.

Dear spirits, let it be enough.

The horn was on the other side of him. She couldn't get to it.

With all her strength, when he tugged on her leg, she used his pull to add momentum and kicked as hard as she could at his face. She caught his ear, tearing it partly away from his head. He bellowed and released her ankle.

Desperately, Kahlan pushed with her feet, to get away from his grasping fingers. She made it out of his reach. She bumped into Cara. Kahlan sat up and scooted back toward the woman.

'Hold on, Cara. Please hold on. I'm here. I'm going to get them off you. I swear I'll get them off you.'

738

'Please, mama,' Cara wailed, 'It hurts so much … It hurts. It hurts.'

Kahlan pulled her feet under herself so she could raise up enough. She craned her neck, looking over her shoulder, trying to see what she was doing. She seized the chain. It burned her fingers, making her recoil. She made herself grab the chain again. She tugged on the iron knot, shaking, twisting, pulling.

Through burning fingers, she felt a link slip and the chain loosen. She stole a quick glance. Drefan was still struggling to breathe, but he had straightened his legs. He put his arms at his sides. What was he doing?

Kahlan felt a link pull past resistance. She wiggled the chain to loosen the knot, to give it more room to come undone. Another link slipped free. The chain loosened further. She tugged at it, refusing to let go, even though the hot iron was burning her fingers.

Drefan's breathing was evening out. He was laying perfectly still. What was he doing?

Kahlan cried out with joy when the chain rattled off the side of the pot. With her back to Cara, Kahlan hooked her fingers under the rim of the scalding pot and heaved it up and back, flipping it off Cara.

Bloody rats tumbled to the floor, squirming and wriggling, trying to get their feet as they scurried away.

Kahlan was near tears with joy. 'I got them off, Cara. I got them off you.'

Cara's head lolled from side to side. Her eyes rolled. She mumbled incoherently. When she looked over her shoulder and saw Cara's stomach, Kahlan had to look away, or be sick.

She scooted up toward Cara's hands. With frenzied effort, Kahlan dug at the knot of rope, but the knots were pulled impossibly tight from Cara's thrashing. Kahlan couldn't budge them. She wasn't going to be able to untie them. She would have to cut them.

Drefan's knife lay on the floor, near him. He was lying there, perfectly still. She had to hurry. She had to get the knife and cut Cara's ropes. She had to cut her own. Before he recovered.

Kahlan dug in her heels and scooted toward the knife. She turned around, feeling for it with her fingers.

Drefan rose up and seized her. Holding her around the middle, he lifted her as if she weighed nothing. He brought the knife around in front of her face.

'Nasty stuff, powdered canin pepper. Lucky for me I know how to use my auras to overcome it. Now, my whore of a wife, it's time you paid the price for your perversion.'

CHAPTER 67

Richard staggered toward the sliph's room. From a room not far away, where Cara and Berdine had put him, he had heard the screams. He had no idea how long he had been insensate, no idea how long it had been since they had taken him there, but the screams had brought him awake.

Someone needed help. And the last scream, he knew – Kahlan.

His head pounded in violent pain. He hurt everywhere. He hadn't thought he would be able to stand, but he did. He hadn't thought he would be able to walk, but he did. He had to.

He was barefooted, and without a shirt. He had on only his pants. He knew that the lower Keep was cool, but he was covered in a sheen of sweat, hardly able to breathe through the heat he felt.

He used all his willpower to force himself to move.

He straightened, put a hand to the side of the door into the sliph's room, and walked in.

Drefan looked up. He had his arm around Kahlan's middle. He had a knife in his other hand. To the side, Cara was lying on the floor, tied in ropes. Her middle was ripped open. She was still alive, but shivering in agony.

Richard couldn't make sense of it.

'What in the name of all that's good is going on, Drefan?'

'Richard,' he sneered. 'Just the man I'm looking for.'

'Well, now I'm here. Let Kahlan go.'

'Oh, I will, dear brother. Soon. It is you I need.'

'Why?'

Drefan's eyebrows lifted. 'So that I can be reinstated as Lord Rahl. It's my rightful place. The voices told me. My father told me. I am to be Lord Rahl. I was born to it.'

The plague was a far distant drone in Richard's mind and body, yet this all seemed a dream, too. 'Drop the knife, Drefan, and give up. It's over. Let Kahlan go.'

Drefan laughed. He threw his head back and roared with laughter. When it died out, Drefan's eyes narrowed with frightening resolve.

'She wants me. She begs for it. You know the truth of that, my dear brother. You saw what she is. She is a whore. She is just like all the others. Just like Nadine. Just like my mother. She must die, like all the rest.'

Richard looked into Kahlan's eyes. What was going on? Dear spirits, how was he going to get her away from Drefan?

'You're wrong, Drefan. Your mother loved you; she took you to a place where you would be safe from Darken Rahl. She loved you. Please, let Kahlan go. I'm begging you.'

'She is mine! My wife! I will do with her what I will!'

Drefan slammed the knife into Kahlan's lower back. Richard flinched at hearing it hit bone. Kahlan grunted with the impact, her eyes going wide in shock. Drefan released her. She dropped to her knees and crumpled to her side.

Richard tried with all his might to make sense of this. He couldn't decide if this was real, or a dream. He had been having so many dreams, so many nightmares. This seemed like all the rest, but different. He didn't even know if he was alive anymore. The whole room swam before him.

Drefan drew the Sword of Truth. The ring of steel that Richard knew so well echoed around the stone room, a chime that seemed to awaken him into a nightmare. Richard could see the rage from the sword, the magic, take Drefan's eyes.

'I'm all right, Richard,' Kahlan panted as she stared up at him. 'You don't have a weapon. Get out of here. Get away. I love you. Please, for me. *Run.*'

The rage in Drefan's eyes was nothing to match the rage thundering into Richard's heart.

'Drop the sword, Drefan, now. Or I will kill you.'

Drefan swept the sword around. 'How? With your bare hands?'

Richard vividly remembered what Zedd had told him when first giving him the Sword of Truth: the sword was only a tool; the Seeker was the weapon. A true Seeker didn't need the sword.

Richard started forward. 'And with hate in my heart.'

'I will enjoy killing you, at last, Richard. Even if you don't have a weapon.'

'I am the weapon.'

Richard was running. The distance between them shrank at an alarming rate. Kahlan screamed for him to get away. He hardly heard her. Richard was committed.

Drefan lifted the sword overhead, pulling a breath in preparation to cleave Richard.

That was the opening. Richard knew that a thrust was faster than a cut.

He was in the iron grip of deadly determination.

Richard was lost in the dance with death.

Drefan bellowed in rage as the sword started down.

Richard dropped to his left knee, through the opening, using his forward momentum and a twist of his torso to add force to his strike. Fingers straight and stiff, he drove his arm ahead with all his might.

Before the sword could touch him, Richard struck like lightning, driving his hand through Drefan's soft middle. In the blink of an eye, he had seized Drefan's spinal column and yanked it back out, ripping it apart.

Drefan pitched backward, crashing against the sliph's well, slumping down in a spreading, crimson flood.

Richard bent to Kahlan, cupping her face with his left hand. He didn't want to touch her with Drefan's blood. She was panting in pain. From the corner of his eye, Richard could see Drefan's arm move.

'I can't feel my legs. Richard, I can't feel my legs. Dear spirits, what did he do to me?' Her voice quivered with panic. 'I can't make them move.'

Richard was already lost in need. He had forgotten how to use his power as the price of returning from the Temple of the Winds, but he had used it before. He had healed before. He was a wizard.

He ignored his dizzy head, his sick stomach; he couldn't allow that to stop him.

From Nathan, Richard had learned that his power was called through need, if the need was great enough, or through anger, if the anger was great enough. He had never had more need than he had at that moment, nor more anger.

'Richard. Oh, Richard, I love you. I want you to know, if we, if we ...'

'Hush,' he said in a gentle voice. Her face was cut and bloody. It made him ache to see her pain, her panic. 'I will heal you. Lie still, and I will make you whole again.'

'Oh, Richard, I had the book. I lost it. Oh, Richard, I'm so sorry. I had it. I had it, but it's gone.'

With a sinking feeling, he grasped what she was saying; he was going to die. There was nothing to be done, now. He was lost.

'Richard, please, heal Cara.'

'No. I don't think I have enough strength to heal both of you.' To heal, he had to take the pain from the one injured. Killing Drefan had taken nearly all the strength he had. 'I must heal you.'

Kahlan shook her head. 'Please, Richard, if you love me, do as I ask. Heal Cara. It's my fault – what he did to her. My fault.' A tear ran down her cheek. 'I lost the book. I can't save you. Heal Cara.' She stifled a cry. 'We will be together soon, for all time, then.'

He understood. They were both to die. They would be together in the spirit world. She didn't want to live without him.

Richard kissed her brow. 'Hold on. Don't give up. Please, Kahlan, I love you. Don't give up.'

Richard turned to Cara. He already felt so sick that the sight didn't affect him the way it normally would have. Her suffering, though, bent him with pain for her.

He laid his hands across Cara's bloody, torn middle.

'Cara, I'm here. Hold on. For me, hold on, so I can help you.'

She didn't seem to hear his words as she mumbled, her head lolling from side to side.

Richard closed his eyes and opened his heart, his need, his

soul. He released himself into the current of empathy. He wanted nothing but to make Cara whole again. She had given her all for them. He didn't know if he had strength enough, but he gave all of himself over to it.

He descended into the swirl of her agony. He felt everything she felt, suffered with her. He gritted his teeth, held his breath, and pulled her pain into himself, onward, ever onward, without sparing anything to protect himself.

He shook with the suffering, and his mind wailed with it. He absorbed it into himself, and then asked for more. He asked for all of it. He demanded it.

The world was liquid, twisting, coursing pain. He was swept away in a molten river of it. Its fiery heat consumed his being.

Time lost all meaning. There was only the pain.

When he felt it all gathered into himself, he let flow his empathy, his power: healing strength; healing heart.

He didn't know how to direct it, he just let it flow into her. It felt as if his whole self drained away into her need. She was baked, barren earth, soaking in life-giving rain.

When at last he opened his eyes and lifted his head, his arms were lying across the smooth skin of her midriff. She was whole again. Though she seemed still unaware of it, she was whole.

Richard turned. Kahlan was lying on her side, her breath coming in short, sharp pants. Her face was ashen and covered with sweat and blood, her eyes half closed.

'Richard,' she whispered when he bent to her, 'free my hands. I want to be hugging you, when ...'

When she died. That was what she was going to say.

Richard snatched up a knife lying nearby, and sliced through the ropes. The anger was back, but only as a distant glow now. He could hardly see the room anymore. Hardly hear her. Hardly see her.

Her wrists finally free, she threw an arm over his neck and drew him to her. Richard struggled to keep from falling on her.

'Richard, Richard, Richard,' she whispered. 'I love you.'

Richard went to embrace her, and saw the pool of blood spreading under her.

His rage ignited anew. His need ignited anew.

He took her up in his arms, begging the spirits to spare her.

'Please give me the strength to heal this loved one,' he whispered in choking tears. 'I have done everything required of me. I have sacrificed everything. Please, losing this loved one should not be part of it. I'm dying. Give me the time. Help me.'

It was all he wanted, all he needed, as he held her to him. He wanted her to live, to be well, to be whole.

Holding her in his arms, he once again released himself into the torrent. He pulled the pain onward, heedless of it, welcoming it, drawing it with all his might.

At the same time, he let flow his love, his warmth, his compassion.

Kahlan gasped.

Richard could see that his arms were glowing, as if a spirit were sharing his body with him. Perhaps, he was already a spirit, but he didn't care. He cared only that he would heal her, and cared not at what cost. He would pay any price.

Kahlan gasped with the feel of it, the feel of the power surging into her. Her legs began to tingle. It was the first time she had felt anything in them since Drefan had stabbed her.

Richard seemed to glow around her as he hugged her in his arms, held her in his warm, loving embrace.

The rapture of the sliph, by comparison, was torture. This was beyond anything she had ever felt in her life. She could feel his warm, healing magic coursing through every fiber of her.

It was like being born anew. Life and vitality welled up in her. Tears of bliss flooded from her eyes as she hung in Richard's arms, his magic completely overwhelming her.

When at last he parted from her, she moved without pain. Her legs moved. She felt whole. She was healed.

Richard wiped the blood from her lips as he gazed into her eyes.

Kneeling on the floor together, Kahlan kissed him, tasting their salty tears.

She parted, gripping his arms, looking into his eyes, seeing him as if in a new light. She had just shared something with him that was beyond words, beyond comprehension.

Kahlan stood, holding out her hand to help him up. Richard lifted his hand toward hers.

And then he toppled over onto his face.

'Richard!' She dropped down, rolling him over onto his back. He was hardly breathing. 'Richard. Please, Richard, don't leave me. Please don't leave me!'

She clutched at his shoulders. He was burning with fever. His eyes were closed. He struggled for each shallow breath.

'Oh, Richard, I'm so sorry. I lost the book. Please, Richard, I love you. Don't die and leave me alone.'

'Here,' came a voice that echoed around the room.

Kahlan's head came up. The voice seemed unreal. She couldn't understand it. Then realization hit her.

Kahlan spun around and saw the quicksilver face of the sliph looking down at her. A liquid silver arm held out the black book.

'Master needs this,' the sliph said. 'Take it.'

Kahlan snatched the book. 'Thank you! Thank you, sliph!'

Kahlan dropped down to get the sorcerer's sand that Richard carried in the leather packs, but he wasn't wearing his big over-belt.

She rushed to Cara, still tied in the ropes. Cara's head rolled from side to side as she mumbled, as if she didn't know that Richard had healed her. She was still lost in a prison of her own private terror.

Zedd had told Kahlan that the gift couldn't heal maladies of the mind.

'Cara! Cara, where were you keeping Richard? Where are his things?'

Cara didn't respond. Kahlan snatched the knife off the floor and sliced through the ropes. Cara just lay there.

Kahlan pressed her hands to Cara's face, making the woman look at her. 'Cara, it's all right, now. The rats are gone. They're gone. You're safe. Richard healed you. You're all right.'

'Rats,' Cara mumbled. 'Get them off me. Please. Please …'

Kahlan hugged her. 'Cara, they're gone. I'm your sister of the Agiel. I need you. Please, Cara, come back to me. Please.'

Cara only mumbled.

'Cara,' Kahlan wept, 'Richard will die if you don't help me.

747

There are thousands of rooms in the Keep. I need to know where you kept him. Please, Cara, Richard helped you. Now he needs your help – or he will die. There's no time. Richard needs you.'

Cara's eyes focused, as if she were coming awake. 'Richard?'

Kahlan wiped the tears from her face. 'Yes, Richard. Hurry, Cara. I need the belt Richard wears. I need it or he will die.'

Cara brought her hands down, rubbing her wrists, now smooth where they had been cut before. She felt her stomach. Even the old scars were gone.

'I am healed,' she whispered. 'Lord Rahl healed me.'

'Yes! Cara, please, Richard is dying. I have the book, but I need the things he keeps in his belt.'

Cara abruptly sat up, pulling the red leather across her chest. She buttoned two of the buttons to hold it closed.

'His belt. Yes. You stay with Lord Rahl. I will get it.'

'Hurry!'

Cara stood, swaying for a moment as she steadied herself, and then she dashed from the room. Kahlan hugged the inky black book to herself. She bent over Richard. He was hardly breathing. She knew that any one of those breaths could be his last. He had given them, Cara and Kahlan, the rest of his strength.

'Dear spirits, help him. Give him just a little more time. Please. He has suffered so much. Please just give him a little time, until I can destroy this vile book.'

Kahlan bent over him and kissed his lips. 'Hold on, Richard. Hold on for me, please. If you can hear me, we have the book. I know how to destroy it. Please, just hold on.'

Kahlan knelt down on a clear spot closer to the door and laid open the book to the third page so she would be ready when Cara returned.

She gazed into a vision of a wasteland. There was sand, blown into dunes, stretching into the distance of the phantasm emanating from the book. Kahlan stared into that barren place, and saw runes on the sand – lines drawn in geometric patterns.

Her sight was drawn into the pattern of lines that swirled and twisted around. There, in the runes, was light. It flared forth, every color, shining out toward her, calling to her.

'Mother Confessor!' Cara yelled, shaking Kahlan's shoulders. 'Didn't you hear me? I have Lord Rahl's belt.'

Kahlan blinked, shaking her head, trying to clear her mind. She snatched the belt and undid the bone holder on the flap of the pack where Richard kept the sorcerer's sand. Inside, she found the leather pouch of white sand.

With Cara standing behind her, touching her shoulder, Kahlan cast a pinch of the white sand into the book.

The color boiled and twisted, tumbled and turned. Kahlan pulled her eyes away and stabbed her hand back into the pack, pulling out the other leather pouch, the one with the black sorcerer's sand. With two fingers, she carefully pulled the top open. Inside, she could see the inky black sand.

Troubled, Kahlan paused. There was something else, something tickling at the back of her mind.

The words. Nathan said to say the words, the three chimes, before using the black sand. Three words. What were they?

She couldn't remember them. Her mind raced after them, but they kept going around dark corners, and when she turned, they were gone again. Her thoughts mired in staggering fright. She ached in desperate thought, but the words wouldn't come to her.

Richard had them written in the palm of his hand. Kahlan turned, to go to read them from his palm, and froze.

Drefan, leaning up against the well of the sliph where he had fallen, somehow still hanging to a thread of life, was holding up the sword. Richard was lying right there, on the floor, within reach. Drefan was going to kill him.

'No!' Kahlan screamed.

But the sword was already sweeping down. Faint, maniacal laughter drifted on the air.

Kahlan threw her fist up, calling the blue lightning to protect Richard. It didn't come. She was blocked from her power.

Cara was already diving toward Drefan, but she was too far away. She wasn't going to make it. The sword was halfway there.

A silver arm swept down and seized Drefan's arm, holding it tight. Kahlan held her breath.

Another liquid silver arm enveloped Drefan's head. '*Breathe*,' the sliph cooed, a voice promising the sating of bestial lust, a voice promising rapture. '*I wish you to please me. Breathe.*'

Drefan's chest rose as he inhaled the sliph.

He went still, holding the sliph in his lungs. The sliph freed him, and he slumped to the side. His breath left him, releasing the sliph he had inhaled.

It drained from his mouth and nose, not silver, but red.

Kahlan felt something inside her part, a profound unraveling, and all at once, she joined with her power, a sweet reclaiming that brought a gasp of euphoric, inner union.

Drefan was dead. *As long as they both live.* Those were the words.

Her oath was ended. The winds had returned her power.

Kahlan was brought out of her daze when she heard Richard gasp for a breath. With renewed panic, she scrambled across the floor and scooped up his right hand, where Richard had written the message. She pried open his fingers.

The words were gone. The act of stopping Drefan, and his blood, had scoured away the writing.

Kahlan screamed in frustrated rage. She scrambled back to the open book. She couldn't remember the words. Her mind ached with frustration; she couldn't make the words come.

What was she going to do?

Maybe if she just threw in the grain of black sand anyway.

No, she knew better than to disregard what a wizard like Nathan said to do.

She squeezed her head between the heels of her hands, as if trying to press the words out. Cara knelt down, grasping her by her shoulders.

'Mother Confessor, what's wrong? You must hurry. Lord Rahl is hardly breathing. Hurry!'

Tears ran down her face. 'I can't remember the words. Oh, Cara, I can't remember them. Nathan told me, but I can't remember them.'

Kahlan clambered back across the floor to Richard. She smoothed a hand down his face.

'Richard, please, wake up. I need to know the words. Please, Richard, what are the words? The three words?'

He struggled to draw a breath, gasping with the effort. He wasn't going to wake. He wasn't going to live.

Kahlan rushed back to the book. She snatched up the leather pouch of black sand. She would have to do it without the words. Maybe it would work. It would work. It had to work.

She couldn't make her hands move. She knew better. It wouldn't work unless she said the words. She knew it wouldn't. She had grown up around wizards and magic; she knew better than to disregard what Nathan had told her. Without the words, it wouldn't work.

She fell forward with a wail, beating her fists against the stone floor. 'I can't remember the words! I can't!'

Cara put an arm around Kahlan, making her sit up, holding her in a gentle embrace. 'Calm down. Take a breath. Good. Let it go. Take another. Now, picture in your mind this man Nathan. Picture him telling you the words, and how happy you were that you could save Richard's life.'

Kahlan tried. She tried so hard she wanted to scream.

'I can't remember them,' she wept. 'Richard's going to die because I can't remember three stupid words. I can't remember the three chimes.'

'The three chimes?' Cara asked. 'You mean, Reechani, Sentrosi, Vasi? Those three chimes?'

Kahlan stared in disbelief. 'That's them. The three chimes. Reechani, Sentrosi, Vasi.'

'Reechani! Sentrosi! Vasi! I remember! Thank you, Cara, I remember!'

Kahlan pulled out a grain of black sorcerer's sand between her thumb and finger.

'Reechani, Sentrosi, Vasi,' she said again, for good measure.

She tossed the grain of black sand into the book.

She and Cara both held their breath.

A hum slowly built in the room. The air seemed to dance and vibrate. Light of every color flared forth, twisting and tumbling, pulsing and throbbing. It grew with the hum, until Kahlan had to turn her eyes away.

Rays of light swept across the stone walls. Cara put a hand up before her face. Kahlan did the same, so bright was the light that just turning away was not enough.

And then darkness began gathering, like the inky black of a night stone, or of the book's cover itself, pulling the light and color back into the book. It drew all the light from the room, until all fell into darkness.

In that depth of sightless obscurity, there came such terrible moans that Kahlan was thankful she couldn't see their source. The wails of souls filled the room, scattering about in a blind, mad frenzy, swirling through the air, lost, frantic, wild.

The sound of distant laughter that Kahlan knew all too well died into a wail that stretched into eternity.

When the light of the candles returned, the book was gone, only a stain of ash to show where it had been.

Kahlan and Cara rushed to Richard. He opened his eyes. He still didn't look well, but he looked more alert. His breathing was stronger, and even.

'What happened?' he asked. 'I can breathe. My head isn't pounding.'

'The Mother Confessor saved you,' Cara announced. 'As I have told you so often, women are stronger than men.'

'Cara,' Kahlan whispered, 'how did you know the three chimes?'

Cara shrugged. 'The Legate Rishi knew the words, with the message from the winds. When you said "the three chimes," they just came to me, through his magic, as the other messages from the winds came to me.'

Kahlan pressed her forehead to Cara's shoulder in relief, in wordless gratitude. With equally silent empathy, Cara stroked Kahlan's back.

Richard blinked and scrunched his eyes, as if clearing his head. When he sat up, Kahlan leaned to hug him, but Cara held her back.

'Please, Mother Confessor, may I be first? I fear that once you start, I may never again get a chance.'

Kahlan grinned. 'You're right about that. Take all you want.'

As Cara threw her arms around Richard and squeezed for all she was worth, whispering private, heartfelt words in his ear, Kahlan stood and faced the sliph.

'I can't thank you enough, sliph. You saved Richard. You are a friend, and I will honor you as long as I live.'

The silver face warped into a satisfied smile. She looked down at Drefan's body.

'He had no magic, but he was using his talent to stop the flow of blood so that he might live long enough to kill master. It is death to breathe me if you have no magic. I am pleased I could take him on a journey, a journey to the world of the dead.'

Richard stood on wobbly legs and slipped an arm around Kahlan's waist. 'Sliph, you have my gratitude, too. I don't know what it is I could ever do for you, but if it is within my power, it's yours for the asking.'

The sliph smiled. 'Thank you, master. I would be pleased to have you travel with me. You will be pleased.'

Even though he was unsteady on his feet, Richard's eyes had the sparkle back. 'Yes, we would like to travel. I need to rest for a time first, to finish recovering and get my strength back, and then we will travel, I promise you.'

Kahlan took up Cara's hand. 'Are you all right? I mean, are you really all right … everything?'

Cara nodded with a haunted look in her eyes. 'I still have the ghosts of the past with me, but I am all right. Thank you, sister, for helping me. It is not often that a Mord-Sith can depend on anyone else for help, but with Richard as Lord Rahl, and you as Mother Confessor, all things seem possible.'

Cara glanced to Richard. 'When you healed the Mother Confessor, you seemed to glow, as if a spirit was with you.'

'I believe the good spirits helped me. I do indeed.'

'I recognized the spirit. It was Raina.'

Richard nodded. 'It felt like Raina. When I was in the spirit world, Denna told me that Raina was at peace, and knows that we love her.'

'I think we should tell this to Berdine,' Cara said.

Richard slipped his other arm around Cara's waist, and started them all toward the door.

'I think we should, too.'

CHAPTER 68

Several days later, when Richard was almost fully recovered, Tristan Bashkar's uncle, King Jorin Bashkar, the king of Jara, rode into Aydindril at the head of his company of king's lancers. On the point of each of the hundred lances was a head.

Kahlan watched from a window as the lances, under the watchful eye of D'Haran soldiers, were deployed in an arrow-straight double row along the entrance to the Confessors' Palace. Flags of state flew from poles held by the first opposing pair of Jarian soldiers. Jorin Bashkar, with his star guide Javas Kedar behind him, waited until the lancers were lined up perfectly, their armor gleaming in the sun, before he strode regally, between the row of heads, toward the entrance.

As she peered out the window, Kahlan touched Cara's arm. 'Go get Richard. Have him meet me in the council chambers.'

Cara was out the door and on her way before Kahlan could turn to be on her way, too.

Kahlan Amnell, Mother Confessor, sitting in the first chair under the figures of Magda Searus, the first Mother Confessor, and her wizard, Merritt, painted across the expanse of the dome above the council chambers, waited for her wizard.

Her heart lifted when she saw him sweep into the room, golden cloak billowing out behind, dressed in the gold-trimmed black outfit of a war wizard, the gold and ruby amulet on his chest gleaming in the streamers of sunlight through which he strode, his silver wristbands burnished and bright. The Sword of Truth at his hip caught the light, sending out a starburst of sunlight to glitter across the polished marble.

'Good morning, my queen!' he called out, his voice echoing around the huge room. 'How do you fare this, your last day of freedom?'

Kahlan rarely laughed in the council chambers. It had always seemed improper. She laughed, now, the lilting sound echoing around the cavernous room, bringing a smile to the guards.

'I fare well, Lord Rahl,' she said as he ascended the dais.

Cara and Berdine followed in his shadow, along with Ulic and Egan, taking up places to either side.

'What's going on?' he asked, more seriously. 'I heard that some king just rode in with a hundred heads on pikes.'

'The king of Jara. Remember? You sent him Tristan's head, demanding his surrender?'

'Oh, that king.' Richard slid down into a chair beside her. 'Whose heads are they?'

'I guess we're about to find out.'

The guards pulled open the double doors. Light stabbed in through the doorway, silhouetting the two figures as they approached.

Once before the dais, the king spread his violet cape, trimmed in spotted white fox, and went to one knee in a deep bow. Behind him, the star guide went to both knees, in his bow.

'Rise, my children,' Kahlan said in formal response to the bow.

'Mother Confessor,' King Jorin said, 'how good to see you again.'

His trim figure, his graying hair meticulously cut so that it swept back as if he were facing the wind, his elegant scabbard and sword, his ribbons, his sash, his red and blue and gold-embroidered coat, and his jeweled pins, made him look one of the most grand of kings, Kahlan had always thought.

'And you, King Jorin.' Kahlan lifted an introductory hand. 'This is Lord Rahl, Master of the D'Haran empire, and my husband to be.'

The king lifted an eyebrow. 'As I have heard it told. My congratulations.'

Richard leaned forward. 'I sent you a message. What is your reply?'

Kahlan thought that she had a lot of work to do, teaching Richard proper diplomatic decorum.

The king let out a belly laugh. 'It will be a pleasure being part of an empire led by a man who doesn't gibber jabber me to death.' He lifted a thumb, indicating the star guide behind him. 'Like some people.'

'And does that mean that you surrender?' Richard pressed.

'It does indeed, Lord Rahl, Mother Confessor.

'A large delegation from the Imperial Order came to Sandilar and invited us to join the Imperial Order. We had been waiting for a sign, as requested by Javas Kedar, here. Tristan thought to take matters into his own hands, and try to strike a favorable deal with the Order.

'When the plague came, we thought it showed the power of the Order, and we feared that, I must admit, but when you swept the plague from the land, that was sign enough for me. Javas, here, will no doubt soon find the appropriate sign in the sky to confirm my decision. If not, there are other star guides.'

A red-faced Javas Kedar bowed. 'As I told you, Your Highness, as your star guide, I will be able to confirm your decision without difficulty.'

The king scowled over his shoulder. 'Good!'

'And the heads?' Richard asked.

'The delegation from the Imperial Order. I brought you their heads to show you my sincerity. I wanted you to see that this is a choice I make with conviction. I thought it a fitting answer to the likes of people who would cast a plague into the land, to kill indiscriminately. It shows their true nature, putting the lie to all the things they say.'

Richard bowed his head to the king. 'Thank you, King Jorin.'

'Who ordered the beheading of my nephew, Tristan?'

'I did,' Richard said. 'As I stood on a balcony watching, with the Mother Confessor at my side, Tristan entered the Mother Confessor's bedroom and stabbed a nightdress stuffed with tow that we had placed there. He thought he was killing her.'

The king shrugged. 'Justice befits all, no matter his station. I bear no grudge. Tristan did not serve our people well, either. I look forward to the day we can be rid of the threat from the Order.'

'As do we,' Richard said. 'With your help, we are that much closer to that day.'

As the king went to see to the signing of papers, and to discuss logistics with the D'Haran command, Richard and Kahlan rose to leave, but were interrupted by a guard.

'What is it?' Kahlan asked.

'There are three men asking to see Lord Rahl.'

'Three men? Who are they?'

'They did not give their names, Mother Confessor, but they said they were Raug'Moss.'

Richard sat back down. 'Send them in.'

Under the desk, Kahlan reached over and curled her fingers around his hand, giving him a reassuring squeeze as three figures in flaxen cloaks, with broad hoods pulled up onto their heads, and with their hands folded before them, glided up to the dais.

'I am Lord Rahl,' Richard said.

'Yes,' the one in front said, 'we feel the bond.' He lifted a hand out to his side. 'This is Brother Kerloff, and this is Brother Houck.' He pushed his hood back to reveal a heavily creased face and a head of thinning gray hair. 'I am Marsden Taboor.'

Richard warily eyed the three men. 'Welcome to Aydindril. I hear you wanted to see me. What is it I can do for you?'

'We are searching for Drefan Rahl,' Marsden Taboor said.

Richard rubbed his thumb along the edge of the desk as he watched the three men. 'I'm sorry, but your High Priest is dead.'

The two in back shared a look.

Marsden Taboor's expression darkened. 'High Priest? I am the High Priest of the Raug'Moss, and have been since before Drefan was born.'

Richard frowned. 'Drefan told us he was the High Priest.'

Marsden Taboor stroked his temple as he searched for words.

'Lord Rahl, I'm afraid that your brother was … given to delusion. If he told you that he was the High Priest of the

757

Raug'Moss, then he was deceiving you for reasons I fear to imagine.

'He was left with us by his mother, when he was a young boy. We raised him, knowing what his father would do should he come to discover a son without the gift. Drefan could be – dangerous. Once we realized this, we kept him confined, within our community, to prevent him from hurting anyone.

'He was talented at healing, and we always hoped that he would come to be at peace with himself. We hoped that through healing he could find a way to prove his worth, in his own right.

'A while back, he vanished. Several of our healers were found dead. They had been killed in a most unpleasant fashion: torture. We have been searching for Drefan since. We have been to several places where he had been, and found women who had been murdered in a similar way.

'Drefan had an unsavory attitude toward women. His father, too, was not inclined to be kind toward women. Though he escaped his father in body, I think he failed to escape him in spirit.

'I pray he has not caused harm to anyone here.'

Richard was silent for a time before he spoke.

'We had a plague. A terrible plague. Thousands died. Without regard for himself, Drefan, upholding the noble ideals of the Raug'Moss, worked to help those stricken. He shared his knowledge, and in that way may have prevented yet more from dying.

'My brother, in his own way, helped stop the plague, and in so doing, he died.'

Marsden Taboor folded his hands before him again as he studied Richard's eyes. 'Is this the way you wish it remembered?'

'He was my brother. Partly because of his being here, I learned the power of forgiveness.'

Kahlan squeezed Richard's hand under the table.

'Thank you for seeing me, Lord Rahl.' Marsden Taboor bowed. 'In your light we thrive.'

'Thank you,' Richard whispered.

The three healers started away, but Marsden Taboor turned back. 'I knew your father. You do not take after him. Drefan did. Not many will mourn the passing of your father, or your brother.

'I can see in your eyes, Lord Rahl, a healer, a true healer, besides a warrior. A wizard, as a healer, must be in balance, or he is lost. D'Hara is well served, at long last. Call on us if you have need.'

Ulic let out a sigh when the doors closed. 'Lord Rahl, there are other representatives also wishing to see you.'

'If you are well enough,' Cara added.

'Someone always wants to see us.' Richard stood and held out his hand to Kahlan. 'General Kerson can see them. Don't we have something more important to do?'

'Are you sure you are well enough?' Kahlan asked.

'I've never felt better. You haven't had a change of mind, have you?'

Kahlan smiled as she took his hand and stood. 'Never. If Lord Rahl is fully recovered, what are we waiting for? My things are ready.'

'About time,' Berdine muttered.

As they waited for Richard to return, Kahlan put a reassuring hand on Cara's back. 'She wouldn't lie to us, Cara. If the sliph says you can travel, you can travel.'

The sliph had tested Cara, Berdine, Ulic, and Egan, all of them thinking that, as guards, they should go along to protect Richard and Kahlan.

Only Cara had passed the sliph's test. Richard guessed that it was because Cara had linked with the Andolian leader, Legate Rishi, and he must have an element of both sides of the magic. Cara didn't like anything to do with magic, and the sliph was definitely magic enough to give her pause.

Kahlan leaned close, and whispered in Cara's ear. 'You have passed bigger tests than this, in this room. I am a sister of the Agiel; I will hold your hand the whole way.'

Cara eyed Kahlan, and then the sliph.

'You have to do it, Cara,' Berdine pleaded. 'You will be the only Mord-Sith at the wedding of our Lord Rahl and Mother Confessor.'

Cara's brow twitched as she leaned toward Berdine. 'Lord

Rahl healed you one time.' Berdine nodded. 'Since then, have you felt a … special bond with him?'

Berdine smiled. 'Yes. That is why I want you to go. I'll be all right. I know Raina would want you to go, too.' She gave Ulic a backhanded slap on his stomach. 'Besides, someone has to stay here and keep Ulic and Egan in line.'

Ulic and Egan, together, rolled their eyes.

Cara put a hand on Kahlan's arm as she leaned close and whispered, 'Since Lord Rahl healed you, have you felt … have you felt it, too?'

Kahlan smiled. 'I felt it before he healed me. It is called love, Cara. Truly caring about someone else, not only because you are bonded to them, but because you share something in your heart. When he healed you, you felt his love for you.'

'But I knew before that.'

Kahlan shrugged. 'Maybe it was just a more vivid way of feeling it.'

Cara lifted her Agiel, rolling it in her fingers. 'Maybe, he is a brother of the Agiel.'

Kahlan smiled. 'With all we've been through together, I guess we are all as close as family.'

Richard strode into the room. 'I'm ready. Shall we travel?'

Richard couldn't take the Sword of Truth into the sliph; its magic was incompatible with life being sustained while traveling. He had gone up to leave his sword in the First Wizard's enclave, where it would be safe, where no one but he could get to it. Except Zedd, of course. But Zedd was no longer living. At least, Kahlan didn't think he was alive. Richard refused to doubt that he was.

Richard rubbed his hands together. 'So, Cara, are you going, or not? I would really like you to be there. It would mean a lot to us.'

Cara smiled. 'I must go. You are incapable of protecting yourself. Without a Mord-Sith, you would be helpless.'

Richard turned to the silver face watching them. 'Sliph, I know that I put you to sleep before, but you didn't stay asleep. Why?'

'You did not put me into the deep sleep from which only one such as yourself can call me. You put me – at rest. Others can call me if I am only at rest.'

'But we can't allow those others to use you. Can't you refuse? Can't you just not go to them if they call? We can't have you taking Jagang's wizards and such all over Creation to cause trouble.'

The sliph regarded him with a thoughtful expression. 'Those who made me the sliph made me this way. I must travel with those who ask, if they have the price of power required.' She moved to the edge of her well, closer to him. 'But if I was asleep, only you have the power to call me, master, and then the others could not use me.'

'But I tried to put you to sleep before, and it didn't work.'

The sliph's smile returned. 'You did not have the silver required, before.'

'Silver?'

The sliph reached out and touched his wristbands. 'Silver.'

'You mean, when I crossed my wrists to put you to sleep before, it didn't work because I didn't have these? And now, if I put you to sleep, it will work?'

'Yes, master.'

Richard thought a moment. 'Does it – hurt, or anything, when you are put into this sleep?'

'No. It is rapture, for me, when I sleep, because I am with the rest of my soul.'

Richard's eyes widened. 'When you sleep, you go to the world of souls?'

'Yes, master. I am not to tell anyone how it is that they can put me into the sleep, but you are the only master, and since you wished to know, you will not be angry that I tell you.'

Richard sighed with relief. 'Thank you, sliph. You have given us a way to prevent the wrong people from using you. I'm glad to know that you will be pleased to go into your sleep.'

Richard hugged Berdine. 'Take care of everything until we get back.'

'I am to be in charge, then?' Berdine asked.

Richard frowned suspiciously. 'All three of you are in charge.'

'Are you sure you heard that, mistress Berdine?' Ulic asked. 'I don't want you to later say that you heard no such orders.'

Berdine made a face at him as Richard helped Kahlan up

onto the well. 'I heard. All three of us are to take care of things.'

Kahlan adjusted the bone knife on her arm, and the pack on her back. She took Cara's hand as she climbed up.

'Sliph,' Richard said with a big grin, 'we wish to travel.'

CHAPTER 69

Breathe.

Kahlan let go the silken rapture and drew in a breath, and the world.

As they sat up on the edge of the sliph's stone wall, Kahlan smacked Cara on the back.

'Breathe, Cara. Come on, let it go. Let out the sliph, and breathe.'

Cara finally bent forward and released the sliph from her lungs, reluctantly pulling a breath. Kahlan remembered how hard it was the first time, not only to breathe the sliph, but to then breathe the air again. Cara had held on tightly to Richard and Kahlan's hands the whole time they traveled.

Cara looked up with a silly grin. 'That was – wonderful.'

Richard gave them both a hand down. Kahlan adjusted the bone knife on her arm, and the small pack on her back. It felt good to be in her traveling clothes again. Cara thought that Kahlan looked odd in pants.

'This is where you wished to travel,' the sliph said. 'The Jocopo Treasure.'

Richard looked around the cave, having to duck down because the ceiling was so low. 'I don't see any treasure.'

'It's in the next room,' Kahlan told him. 'Someone must be expecting us. They left a torch burning.'

'Are you ready to sleep?' Richard asked the sliph.

'Yes, master. I look forward to being with my soul.'

The thought of what the sliph was, what the wizards had made her into, gave Kahlan shivers.

'Will it make you – unhappy, when I need to wake you again?'

'No, master. I am always ready to please.'

Richard nodded. 'Thank you for your help. We all are in your debt. Have a good … sleep.'

The sliph smiled at him as Richard crossed his wrists, closing his eyes, calling the magic.

The shiny silver face, reflecting the dancing torchlight, softened, melting back into the pool of quicksilver. Richard's fists began to glow. The silver wristbands he wore brightened to such intensity that Kahlan could see the other side of them through his flesh and bone, and the way they touched, they formed into endless twin loops: the symbol for infinity.

The pool of sparkling silver took on the glow as the sliph sank down into her well, slowly at first, and then with gathering speed, until she vanished into the far darkness below.

Richard took the reed torch and the three of them moved out through a wide, low passageway, following the twisting, turning route through dark brown rock, until they came at last to an expansive room.

Kahlan gestured around the room. 'The Jocopo Treasure.'

Richard held the torch up. Torchlight reflected back in thousands of golden sparkles from the room filled with gold in nearly every form, from nuggets and crude ingots to golden statues.

'Well, it isn't hard to see why it's called the Jocopo Treasure,' Richard said. He pointed toward the shelves. 'Looks like something is missing.'

Kahlan saw what he meant. 'When I was here before, those shelves were packed full of rolled vellum scrolls.' She sniffed the air. 'Something else is missing, too. This room was filled with foul air before. It's gone now.'

She remembered how it made her gag and cough, and her head spin, having to breathe the stench. On the floor of the cave was a smoldering heap of ash.

Kahlan swiped the toe of her boot across the ash. 'I wonder what happened here.'

The flame of the torch whipped and fluttered as they followed the twisting tunnel up and out into a golden dawn.

Thin bands of violet clouds drifted across the sunrise. Luminous gold, more stunning than the Jocopo Treasure, edged the clouds.

Verdant grasslands spread out before them, smelling clean and fresh.

'It looks like the Azrith Plains in spring,' Cara said, 'before the high heat of summer bakes it barren.'

Broad swaths of wildflowers at their feet led in the general direction of the Mud People. Kahlan took Richard's hand. It was a beautiful morning for a walk through the spring grasslands of the wilds. It was a beautiful day to be married.

Long before they reached the Mud People's village, they could hear the sound of drums drifting out onto the plains. Laughter and song filled the morning air.

'Sounds like the Mud People are having a banquet,' Richard said. 'What do you think that's about?'

His voice sounded uneasy. She felt the same; banquets were usually held to call the spirit ancestors, in preparation for a gathering.

Chandalen met them not far from the village. He was wearing the coyote hide of an elder. His hair was slicked down with sticky mud. He was barechested and had on his ceremonial dress of buckskin pants and his finest knife, and he carried his best spear.

Grim-faced, Chandalen strode forward and slapped Kahlan.

'Strength to Confessor Kahlan.'

Richard caught Cara by the wrist. 'Easy,' he whispered. 'We told you about this. It's the way they greet people.'

Kahlan returned the slap, a show of respect for a person's strength. 'Strength to Chandalen and the Mud People. It is good to be home.' She fingered the coyote hide. 'You are an elder, now?'

He nodded. 'Elder Breginderin died of the fever. I was named elder.'

Kahlan smiled. 'A wise choice, them picking you.'

Chandalen stood before Richard, appraising him a moment. The two men had once been foes. Chandalen finally slapped Richard, harder than he had Kahlan.

'Strength to Richard with the Temper. It is good to see you again, too. I am happy that you are to marry the Mother Confessor, so that she will not pick Chandalen.'

Richard returned the slap in kind. 'Strength to Chandalen. You have my gratitude, for protecting Kahlan on your journey together.' He lifted a hand. 'This is our friend and protector, Cara.'

Chandalen was a protector of his people, and the term had special meaning to him. He lifted his chin as he looked into her eyes. He slapped her harder than he had slapped either Richard or Kahlan.

'Strength to protector Cara.'

It was fortunate that Cara wasn't wearing her armored gloves. As hard as she punched him, she would have broken his jaw. Chandalen grinned when he straightened his neck.

'Strength to Chandalen,' she said to him, and then to Richard, 'I like this custom.'

Cara reached out and ran a finger over a few of Chandalen's scars. 'Very nice. This one here is excellent. The pain must have been exquisite.'

Chandalen frowned at Kahlan and spoke in his language. *'What does that last word mean?'*

'It means that it must have been intense pain,' Kahlan told him. She had taught Chandalen her language, and he did very well, but he still had some to learn.

Chandalen grinned with pride. 'Yes, it was very painful. I wept for my mother.'

Cara lifted an eyebrow to Kahlan. 'I like him.'

Chandalen looked Cara up and down, taking in the red leather, and the shape of her.

'You have fine breasts.'

Her Agiel flicked up into her fist.

Kahlan put a restraining hand on Cara's arm. 'The Mud People have different customs,' she whispered. 'To them, it means that you look like a healthy, strong woman, able to bear children and raise them to be healthy. To them, this is a strictly proper compliment.' She leaned closer, lowering her voice so that Chandalen couldn't hear. 'Just don't tell him that you would like to see him with the mud washed out of his hair, or you will be inviting him to give you those children.'

Cara took in all this, considering Kahlan's words with care. Finally, she turned and, bending over a little, lifted her red leather to expose a nasty scar.

'This one was very painful, like the one you have.' Chandalen grunted with knowing appreciation. 'I had more, on my front, but Lord Rahl made them disappear. It is a shame; some were quite remarkable.'

Richard and Kahlan followed behind Chandalen and Cara as he showed her his weapons, and they discussed the worst place to be wounded. She was impressed with his knowledge.

'Chandalen,' Kahlan asked, 'what's going on? Why has a banquet been called?'

He looked over his shoulder as if she were deranged.

'It is a wedding banquet. For your wedding.'

Kahlan and Richard shared a look. 'But, how did you know we were coming to be married?'

Chandalen shrugged. 'The Bird Man told me.'

As they entered the village, they were surrounded by a flood of people. Children swept in around them, touching the wandering Mud People, as they called Richard and Kahlan. People they knew came to give them gentle slaps in greeting.

Savidlin was there, clapping Richard on the back, and his wife, Weselan, was hugging and kissing them both. Their son, Siddin, threw his arms around Kahlan's leg, jabbering up at them in his language. It felt so good to ruffle his hair again. Richard and Cara didn't understand any of it; only Chandalen spoke their language.

'We have come to be married,' Kahlan told Weselan. *'I brought the beautiful dress you made for me. I hope you remember that I asked you to stand with me.'*

Weselan beamed. *'I remember.'*

Kahlan saw a man with long silver hair, dressed in buckskin pants and tunic, approaching. She leaned toward Cara. 'This is their leader.'

The Bird Man greeted them with the gentle slaps customary in the village proper.

He embraced Kahlan in a fatherly hug. *'The fever is over. Our ancestor's spirit must have been a help to you.'* Kahlan nodded. *'I am glad you are home. It will be good to wed you and Richard with the Temper. Everything is prepared.'*

'What did he say?' Richard asked.

'Everything is prepared for our wedding.'

Richard scowled. 'It makes me nervous when people know things that we haven't told them.'

'Richard with the Temper is upset? He is not happy with our preparations?'

'No, it's not that,' Kahlan said. *'Everything is wonderful. It's just that we don't understand how you could know we would be here to be married. We're puzzled. We didn't know ourselves until just a couple of days ago.'*

The Bird Man pointed to one of the open pole structures shaded under a grass roof. *'That man over there told us.'*

'Really,' Richard said, after Kahlan translated, his scowl growing. 'Well, I think it's about time we go see this man who seems to know more about us than we do.'

As they turned away, Kahlan caught the Bird Man scratching a cheek to screen a smile.

They had to work at making their way through the throng. The entire village was out in the open area, celebrating. Musicians and dancers entranced children and adults alike. People paused to talk to Richard and Kahlan as they passed. Young people, especially young girls, who were always painfully shy in the past, now boldly offered congratulations. It was as festive an event as Kahlan had ever seen.

At various open pole structures where food was being prepared, people, beguiled by the different aromas, crowded around to sample the fare. A contingent of young women carried bowls and platters, and passed around food.

Kahlan saw special women at one of the cook fires preparing a singular offering served only at gatherings. No one congregated to sample it. This dish was presented only by those women, according to strict protocol, and by invitation only.

Cara didn't like how close people crowded in around her charges, but she did her best to remain tolerant while at the same time watchful and prepared to react. She wasn't gripping her Agiel, but Kahlan knew that it was never more than a flick away.

Young women were carrying platters of the more traditional food to and from the pole building where the Bird Man had pointed them. Richard, holding Kahlan by the hand, pushed his way through the crowd around the platform.

They finally made it to the head of the crowd, at the platform. Richard and Kahlan froze in shock.

'Zedd –' Richard whispered.

Reposing in his splendid violet and black robes, the regal effect somewhat diminished by the way his wavy white hair stuck out in its typical disarray, was Richard's grandfather. The rawboned old wizard glanced up from the platform as young women offered him platters of food to sample. A squat woman in a dark dress and cloak sat cross-legged beside him.

'Zedd!' Richard bounded onto the platform.

Zedd smiled and waved. 'Oh, there you are, my boy.'

'You're alive! I knew you were alive!'

'Well, of course I'm –'

That was all he got out before Richard scooped him up, squeezing so hard that Zedd lost his wind with a whoosh.

Zedd's fists beat on Richard's shoulders. 'Richard!' he squeaked. 'Bags, Richard! You're going to crush me! Leave go!'

Richard set him down, only to have Kahlan rush to embrace him. 'Richard kept saying you were alive, but I didn't believe him.'

The woman rose up. 'Good to see you, Richard.'

'Ann? You're alive too!'

She smiled. 'No thanks to your fool grandfather.' Her knowing eyes turned to Kahlan. 'And this could be none other than the Mother Confessor herself.'

Richard hugged her before the introductions. Zedd took a bite of a rice cake while he watched.

Richard brought Cara forward. She spoke before he had a chance. 'I am Lord Rahl's bodyguard.'

Richard looked to her eyes. 'This is Cara, and she is more than a guard. She is our friend. Cara, this is my grandfather, Zedd, and Annalina Aldurren, Prelate of the Sisters of the Light.'

'Retired Prelate,' Ann said. 'Pleased to meet a friend of Richard.'

Richard turned back to Zedd. 'I can't believe you're here. This is the best surprise we could possibly have. But what's this about you knowing we were coming to get married?'

Zedd spoke with his mouth full. 'Read it. Read all about it.'

'Read it? Where?'

'In the Jocopo Treasure.'

Kahlan leaned in. 'There's writing on all that gold?'

Zedd waved the rice cake. 'No, no, not the gold – the Jocopo Treasure. The prophecies. All those scrolls. They were the Jocopo Treasure. We burned them to keep them out of the hands of the Imperial Order. I read a few, before I destroyed them. That's where I read the prophecy about you two being married. Ann figured out the day. She's quite knowledgeable about prophecy.'

'Well, it wasn't a difficult prophecy,' Ann said. 'None of them were. That was why they were so dangerous, if Jagang had captured them. He nearly did.'

'So, you two came to destroy the prophecies?' Richard asked.

'Yes.' Zedd threw up his hands with a huff. 'Oh, but a terrible time of it we've had, though.'

'Yes, just terrible,' Ann confirmed.

Zedd shook a sticklike finger at Richard. 'While you've been larking about in Aydindril, we've had real trouble.'

'Trouble? What sort of trouble?'

'Awful trouble,' Ann said.

'Yes,' Zedd agreed. 'We were captured, and held in the most horrid of conditions. It was awful. Simply awful. We barely got away with our lives.'

'Who captured you?'

'The Nangtong.'

Kahlan cleared her throat. 'The Nangtong? Why would the Nangtong capture you?'

Zedd tugged his robes straight. 'They were going to sacrifice us. Human sacrifices, we almost were. We were in mortal danger the entire time.'

Kahlan squinted skeptically. 'The Nangtong are daring to engage in their forbidden rites?'

'Something about red moons,' Zedd offered. 'They feared the worst, and were only trying to protect themselves.'

Kahlan cocked her head. 'Nonetheless, I will have to pay them a visit and see to this.'

'You could have been killed,' Richard said.

'Piffle. A wizard and a sorceress are smarter than a wandering band of Nangtong. Aren't we, Ann?'

Ann blinked. 'Well –'

'Well, yes, as Ann says, it was more complicated than that.' Zedd turned away from her. 'But it was just awful, I can assure you. And then we were sold into slavery.'

Richard's brow lifted. 'Slavery!'

'Indeed. To the Si Doak. We were forced to labor as slaves. But the Si Doak didn't like us, for some reason, something about Ann being unsatisfactory, and they decided to sell us to cannibals.'

Richard's jaw dropped. 'Cannibals?'

Zedd grinned. 'Fortunately, the cannibals turned out to be the Mud People. Chandalen was the one they approached. He knew me, of course, from when we were together before, so he played along, and bought us to get us away from our bondage to the Si Doak.'

'And why couldn't you get away from the Si Doak?' Kahlan asked. 'You're a wizard. Ann is a sorceress.'

Zedd pointed at his bare wrists. 'They put magic wristbands on us. We were helpless.' He looked up. 'Quite helpless. It was terrible. We were helpless slaves under the lash.'

'That sounds dreadful,' Richard said. 'Then how did you get the bands off?'

Zedd threw his arms up. 'We couldn't.'

Richard pressed one hand to his forehead and held the other up. 'Well, they're off now.'

Zedd scratched his chin. 'Well, now they are. The bands are held on with magic. I – we – were smart enough to know better than to try to use magic. That would have bound them on even harder. We just had to wait, without using magic, until they lost their power. Once we were away from the Si Doak, and were burning the scrolls, they came undone, and fell off.'

'So, that was your plan all along?'

'Of course it was!'

Ann nodded. 'Trust in the Creator to reveal His plan.'

Zedd shook a finger up at Richard. 'Magic is dangerous,

Richard. As you will learn, someday, the hardest part of being a wizard is knowing when not to use magic. This was one of those times.

'We had to find the Jocopo Treasure. With all the currents of trouble about, I knew our best chance would be to do it without magic.' He folded his arms. 'And it worked, too, thus proving my point.'

Chandalen stepped forward. 'Many soldiers came toward us.' He pointed off toward the southeast. 'A large scouting party of men came to get these things that Zedd burned. While he and Ann were burning them, my men and I fought off the enemy.

'A great battle was fought to the west, against the main force of the enemy. This army of the Order was destroyed.

'I went and spoke with a man called Reibisch, and he said that one named Nathan had sent him to destroy our enemy.'

Richard shook his head. 'This is all very confusing.'

Zedd flicked a hand. 'Ah, well, you'll learn, someday, Richard. This wizard business is very complicated. Someday, when you decide to do something with your gift, other than sit around with your intended while I'm out risking my neck, then you will see. By the way, what have you been up to, while all the important work has been going on?'

'What have I been up to?' Kahlan smiled as she put a hand on his shoulder while Richard tried to think how to begin. 'Ah, well, I'm the Lord Rahl, now, and all.'

Zedd grunted and flopped down on the wooden platform. 'Lord Rahl, indeed.' He scooped up a roasted pepper. 'The paperwork must be grueling.'

Richard scratched his head while Ann sat down. 'Zedd, can you answer something for me? Why are the books in the First Wizard's private enclave stacked up in wobbly columns?'

'It's a telltale, of sorts. I remember how they're stacked, so that if anyone has touched them, I'll know it.' Zedd's hazel eyes opened wide. 'What? Bags, Richard, what were you doing in there? That's a dangerous place! And how did you get in there?' Zedd pointed at Richard's chest. 'That amulet! It's from in there. How did you get in there? Bags, Richard! Where's the Sword of Truth? I entrusted the sword to you! You weren't foolish enough to give it to someone?'

'Uh, well … I couldn't travel in the sliph with it, so I had to leave it in the First Wizard's enclave, so no one could get at it.'

'Sliph? What's a sliph? Richard, you're the Seeker. You have to have your sword – it's your weapon. You can't just leave it lying about places.'

'When you gave it to me, you told me that the sword was just a tool, and that it is the Seeker that is the true weapon.'

'So I did. But I didn't think you were listening.' Zedd peered up at him. 'You didn't mess with the books, I hope. You don't know enough to be allowed to read any of them.'

'Just one. *Tagenricht ost fuer Mosst Verlaschendreck nich Greschlechten.*'

'That's High D'Haran.' Zedd dismissed the matter with a wave. 'No one knows High D'Haran anymore. At least you can't get into trouble with a book you can't read.' Zedd shook his finger. 'And you still haven't said how you got in there!'

'It wasn't all that hard to get in.' The mirth melted from Richard's face. 'It was a lot easier than it was getting into the Temple of the Winds.'

Both Zedd and Ann shot to their feet.

'The Temple of the Winds!' they said as one.

'*Temple of the Winds Inquisition and Trial* – that's what the book was. I've kind of had to learn High D'Haran.' Richard put his arm around Kahlan's shoulders. 'Jagang sent Sister Amelia there. She entered through something called Betrayer's Hall. She betrayed the Keeper to get in.

'She came back with magic and started a plague. It killed thousands of people. She started it among children – at Jagang's instruction. We watched, helpless, while children and friends died.

'There was no other way. I had to go there to stop the plague, or it would have been a firestorm that would have consumed nearly everyone.'

One of the women who prepared the special meat approached, carrying a tray of neatly arranged dried strips. She offered the tray to Chandalen first; he was an elder, now. Chandalen tore off a bite as he looked up at Richard.

Richard knew what the meat was. He took a big piece.

Kahlan had always refused to eat this dish in the past. This

773

time, when offered, she took a piece. Chandalen watched her pull off a bite.

Zedd took a piece, and then the tray was offered to Ann. Kahlan was going to say something, but Zedd shot her a silencing glance.

They ate in silence a moment before Richard asked, 'Who is it?'

'The commander of the men of the Order who came here and attacked us to get the Jocopo Treasure that Zedd burned.'

Ann's eyes came up. 'You mean... ?'

'We fight a battle for our existence,' Richard said. 'If we lose, we all die, and the man who started a plague among children will rule those still alive. All magic will be eliminated. Those left will be his slaves. The Mud People do this so that they might know the hearts of their enemy, and save their families.'

Richard glared at her. 'Eat it, so that you, too, may know the enemy better.'

It was not Richard but Lord Rahl who had spoken.

Ann watched his eyes for a moment, and then started chewing. They all ate the strip of their enemy's flesh to know him better.

'Sister Amelia,' Ann finally whispered. 'If she has been to the Temple of the Winds ... she will be beyond dangerous.'

'She's dead,' Kahlan said, haunted by the memory of it all. When Ann's questioning eyes looked at her, Kahlan added, 'Yes, I am sure. I put a sword through her heart. She had a dacra in Nathan's leg. She was going to kill him.'

'Nathan!' Ann said. 'We must soon be off to find him. Where was this? Where is he?'

Zedd scowled over at Ann. 'We?'

'It was in Tanimura, in the Old World, just after Richard came back from the Temple of the Winds. Nathan helped me save Richard's life by telling me the three chimes.'

Zedd and Ann's eyes widened. They looked as if they had stopped breathing. They finally glanced to each other.

'The three chimes,' Ann said in a cautious voice. 'You mean, he just mentioned "the three chimes." He didn't actually tell them to you? He didn't speak them to you?'

Kahlan nodded. 'Reechan –'

Zedd and Ann threw their hands up. *'No!'* they yelled together.

'Didn't Nathan tell you that no one without the gift may speak the three chimes aloud?' Ann's face had gone red. 'Didn't that crazy old man tell you that!'

Kahlan scowled back. 'Nathan is not a crazy old man. He helped me save Richard's life. Without the three chimes, Richard would have died when he came back from the Temple of the Winds. I owe Nathan a great debt. We all do.'

'I owe him a collar around his neck,' Ann muttered. 'Before he causes who knows what catastrophe. Zedd, we must find him. And soon.' She lowered her voice to a private whisper. 'And we must do something about … this business.'

Zedd's eyes turned to Kahlan. 'You said them silently, when you did this. You said the three chimes silently. You didn't actually say them aloud. Tell me that you didn't say them aloud.'

'I had to. Cara remembered them, and said them. Then I said them aloud a couple of times.'

Zedd winced. 'More than once?'

'Zedd,' Ann murmured, 'what are we going to do about this?'

'Why?' Richard asked. 'What's the problem?'

'Nothing you need be concerned about. Just don't say them aloud again. Any of you.'

'Zedd,' Ann whispered under her breath, 'if she has freed –'

Zedd lifted a hand out to the side, touching her, silencing her.

'What was I supposed to do?' Kahlan asked defensively. 'Richard had absorbed the magic from the book Sister Amelia brought back from the winds. He had the plague. He was a breath or two away from death. He would have died within minutes, at the most. Would you have had me let him die instead?'

'Of course not, dear one. You did the right thing.' Zedd lifted an eyebrow to Ann as he leaned close. 'We will discuss this later.'

Ann folded her hands. 'Of course. You did the only thing you could. We are all grateful, Kahlan. You did well.'

Zedd was looking more serious by the moment. 'Bags,

Richard, the Temple of the Winds is in the underworld. How did you get in?'

Richard looked out over the celebration. 'We need to tell you both the story. Some of it, anyway. But this is the day Kahlan and I are to be married.' Richard smiled. Kahlan thought it looked forced. 'It's a hard story to tell. I'd rather tell you about it on another day. I can't, just now ...'

Zedd stroked a thumb down his smooth jaw. 'Of course, Richard, I understand. And you are quite right. Another day. But, the Temple of the Winds ...' He lifted a finger, unable to resist asking a question. 'Richard, what did you have to leave at the Temple of the Winds in order to return?'

Richard shared a long look with his grandfather. 'Knowledge.'

'And what did you take away with you?'

'Understanding.'

Zedd encircled a protective arm around both Richard and Kahlan. 'Good for you, Richard. Good for you. Good for both of you. You two have earned this day. Let's put this other business aside for now, and let us celebrate the joy of your marriage.'

CHAPTER 70

They enjoyed the company of friends and loved ones the whole day, talking and laughing, celebrating together with the Mud People. Kahlan did her best to try to ignore the way her low-cut blue wedding dress displayed her breasts. It was hard, with the way people kept coming up to her and telling her that she had fine breasts. Richard wanted to know what they were saying all the time. She thought it best to lie; she told him that they were saying that her dress was beautiful.

As the sun turned the sky golden, it was at last time.

Kahlan gripped Richard's hand as if it were the only thing holding her on the ground. Richard had trouble keeping his eyes off her in her blue wedding dress. Every time he looked at her, a helpless smile took him.

Kahlan's heart swelled with joy, seeing how much he liked the dress Weselan had made for her. She had for so long dreamed of wearing it, dreamed of this moment. She had hoped so often, with all her heart, that this day would come. She had feared so often that it never would. So many times, something had happened, delaying this moment. Now, it was happening.

Richard mimicked the Mud People's words, not realizing that he was saying how fine he thought her breasts looked; he thought he was telling her how beautiful her dress looked. Everyone grinned with satisfaction when he spoke the words in their language, happy that he agreed with them. Kahlan could feel her face turning red.

Richard looked magnificent in his black and gold war

wizard's uniform. Every time Kahlan looked at him, a smile took her. She was marrying Richard. At last. Her knees trembled under the blue dress.

Cara, standing behind, gave her a reassuring touch. Weselan, at Kahlan's side, beamed with pride. Savidlin stood to the far side of Richard, beaming just as much. Zedd and Ann stood behind. Zedd was eating something.

Kahlan silently prayed to the good spirits that, this time, nothing would go wrong, and that it would at last happen. She couldn't help worrying that it would be taken from her, yet again.

The Bird Man straightened before them, clasping his hands. Behind him, the entire Mud People village spread out before the wedding party to hear the vows.

When all had fallen silent, the Bird Man began, and Kahlan's fear began to melt away, to be replaced with joyous anticipation. As the Bird Man spoke, Chandalen, at his side, said the words in the language Richard and some of the others could understand.

'These two people have not been born Mud People, but they have proven themselves to be one of us, in their strength, and in their hearts. They have bound themselves to us, and us to them. They have been our friends, and our protectors. That they would wish to be wedded as Mud People proves their hearts.

'As members of our people, these two have chosen not only to be wedded before those of this world, but before the next, and in so doing, have called the spirits of our ancestors to be with us on this day to smile on this joining. We welcome our ancestors into our hearts to share our joy.'

Richard's hand tightened around hers, and she realized that he was sharing her thoughts: it was real, at last, and it was as they both had always dreamed – except it was better than she could ever have imagined.

'Both of you are Mud People, and are bound not only by your words before your people, but by your own hearts. These are simple words, but in simple things, there is great power.'

He met Richard's eyes.

'Richard, will you have this woman as your wife, and will you love and honor her in all ways for all time?'

'I will,' he said in a clear voice that rang out over the gathering.

The Bird Man looked into Kahlan's eyes, and she had the most profound sense that he was speaking not only as a representative of his people, but for the spirits, too. She could almost hear their voices echoing in his.

'Kahlan, will you have this man as your husband, and will you love and honor him in all ways for all time?'

'I will,' she said, a clear chime matching Richard's.

'Then before your people, and before the spirits, you are now wedded for all time.'

All the gathered people were dead silent, until Richard took her in his arms and kissed her, and then they went wild.

Kahlan hardly heard them.

It seemed a dream. A dream she had dreamed so often that it had finally come to life.

To be in Richard's arms. To have him. To be his wife, and he her husband. For all time.

And then everyone was hugging them. Zedd and Ann. The Bird Man and the elders. Weselan and the other wives.

Cara, with tears in her eyes, hugged Kahlan. 'Thank you both for wearing an Agiel at your wedding. Hally, Raina, and Denna are all watching because of that. Thank you for honoring the sacrifice of Mord-Sith.'

With a thumb, Kahlan wiped the tear from Cara's cheek. 'Thank you for braving the magic of the sliph to be with us, my sister.'

Everyone in the village crowded in to greet the new couple. Kahlan thought they might be crushed. People brought food and flowers, and sincere, simple offerings of every sort.

The celebration resumed around the wedding platform. Kahlan tried to talk to everyone, and to thank everyone, as did Richard, until, as Richard was asking some of Chandalen's hunters about the battle that they had witnessed, his golden cloak billowed out.

There was no wind.

Richard straightened. His raptor gaze swept out over the heads of the people gathered before the wedding platform. He instinctively reached for his sword. It wasn't there.

The crowd, in the back, fell silent. Zedd and Ann both

stepped up beside Richard and Kahlan. Cara had her Agiel in her fist as she pushed between them to get in front. Richard gently pushed her behind.

The entire village fell silent, the people parting for two approaching figures. Some people grabbed their children and moved farther back as worried whispers rippled through the crowd.

As the two solitary figures, one tall and one short, came closer, Kahlan saw that it was Shota, and her companion, Samuel.

The witch woman, looking as stunning as ever, strode up onto the platform, her ageless almond eyes staying on Kahlan the whole time.

Shota took up Kahlan's hand. She kissed Kahlan's cheek.

'I have come to congratulate you, Mother Confessor, on your accomplishment, and on your marriage.'

Throwing caution to the winds, Kahlan hugged the witch woman. 'Thank you for coming, Shota.'

Shota smiled, staring into Richard's eyes as she ran a lacquered nail along his jaw. 'Hard fought, Richard. Hard fought. And well earned.'

Kahlan turned to the silent gathering. She knew that the Mud People feared the witch woman so much that they wouldn't even speak her name. Kahlan could understand; she had felt nearly the same way herself.

'Shota has come to offer her best wishes to us on our wedding day. She has helped us in our struggle. She is a friend, and I hope you will welcome her to this celebration, for she deserves to be here, and I wish her to be here.'

Kahlan turned to Shota. 'I told them that –'

Smiling, Shota held up a hand. 'I know what you told them, Mother Confessor.'

The Bird Man stepped forward. *'Welcome to our home, Shota.'*

'Thank you, Bird Man. You have my word that we will bring no harm this day.'

Shota glanced to Zedd. 'A truce, for a day.'

Zedd smiled a sly smile. 'A truce.'

Samuel's long arm reached up, grabbing for the Bird Man's carved bone whistle he wore around his neck.

'Mine! Gimme!'

Shota thunked him on the head. 'Samuel, behave yourself.'

The Bird Man smiled. He pulled the thong and whistle over his head and held it out to Samuel.

'A gift, for a friend to the Mud People.'

Samuel gently took the whistle. A grin split his face, showing his wickedly sharp teeth.

'Thank you, Bird Man.' Shota said.

Samuel blew the silent whistle. He seemed able to hear the sound, and was pleased by it. People began chuckling and talking again. Kahlan was relieved that vultures didn't appear in response to the silent whistle. Fortunately, Samuel didn't know how to call specific birds. Samuel grinned at his gift and hung it around his neck. He took up Shota's hand again.

Shota's arresting gaze took in Richard and Kahlan. In that moment, there was no one else there. The three of them were as good as alone, in that gaze.

'Do not think, either of you, that just because I congratulate you, I will forget my promise to you.'

Kahlan swallowed. 'Shota –'

Shota's eyes were both beautiful and frightening as she held up a silencing finger.

'You both have earned this joyous wedding. I am happy for you both. I will honor your vows, and protect you in any way I can, out of respect for all you have done for me, as long as you remember what I have warned you about. I will not allow a male child of this union to live. Do not doubt my word in this.'

Richard's gaze was heating. 'Shota, I'll not be threatened –'

Again, the finger rose, silencing Richard this time.

'I do not make a threat. I deliver you a promise. I do not do it out of animosity for either of you, but out of concern for everyone else in the world. There is a long struggle ahead of us all. I will not allow any chance at victory to be clouded by what you two would bring upon the world. Jagang is worry enough.'

For some reason, Kahlan's voice wouldn't work. Richard didn't seem to have words, either. Kahlan believed Shota; she wasn't doing this out of malice.

Shota lifted Kahlan's hand and placed something in it. 'This is my gift to you both. I do this out of love for you both, and for everyone else.' She smiled a strange smile. 'An odd thing for a witch woman to say?'

'No, Shota,' Kahlan said. 'I don't know that I believe what you tell us about a son, but I know that it is not said in hate.'

'Good. Wear the gift, always, and all will be well. Mark my words well – never take this off when you are together, and you will always be happy. Disregard my request, and suffer the consequences of my vow.' She looked into Richard's eyes. 'Better you battle the Keeper himself, than me.'

Kahlan opened her hand and saw a delicate necklace. A small, dark stone hung from the gold chain.

'Why? What is this?'

Shota put a finger under Kahlan's chin as she stared into her eyes. 'As long as you wear it, you will bear no children.'

Richard's voice, strangely, seemed gentle. 'But what if we –'

Again, Shota's raised finger silenced him. 'You love each other. Have joy in that love, and in each other. You have struggled hard to be together. Celebrate your union and your love. You have each other, now, as you always wanted. Don't throw it away.'

Richard and Kahlan both nodded. Somehow, Kahlan didn't feel any anger. She felt nothing other than relief that Shota wasn't going to do anything to harm their marriage. It had a dreamlike quality, like a formal settlement over an obscure, remote tract of ground claimed by two lands, like agreements in the council chambers over which she had so often presided. There seemed no emotion to it. A simple settlement.

Shota turned to go.

'Shota,' Richard said. She turned back. 'Won't you stay? You've come a long way.'

'Yes,' Kahlan said. 'We really would like it if you stayed.'

Shota smiled a witch woman smile as she watched Kahlan fasten the chain around her neck.

'That you would ask is pleasure enough, but it is a long journey, and we must be on our way.'

Kahlan ran down the steps and scooped up a pile of tava bread. She wrapped it in a square of cloth from the table. She met Shota at the bottom of the steps.

'Take this for your journey, as our thanks for coming, and for the gift.'

Shota kissed Kahlan's cheek and then took the bundle. Samuel didn't try to grab it; he seemed content. Richard was suddenly there, beside Kahlan. Shota smiled a small smile and kissed his cheek, too. She had a strange, wistful look.

'Thank you. Both of you.'

And then she was gone. Simply, gone.

Zedd and Ann were still up on the platform, along with Cara and the rest of the people. Zedd turned to Richard and Kahlan.

'What happened to Shota? We make a truce, and then she just leaves without a word?'

Kahlan's brow tightened. 'She spoke to us.'

Zedd glanced about. 'When? She was gone before she had a chance to say anything.'

'I had intended to speak with her, too,' Ann said.

Kahlan looked up at Richard. He looked back at Zedd. 'She said some nice things to us. Maybe she just didn't want you to hear her saying nice things.'

Zedd grunted a laugh. 'No doubt.'

Kahlan touched the dark stone on the necklace. She put an arm around Richard's waist and pulled him close.

'What do you think?' she whispered.

Richard stared out in the direction Shota had gone.

'For now, she's right; we're together. That's what we wanted. I think that, for now, we should be happy that our dream has at last come true and we can be together. I'm so tired of trouble, and there is still Jagang to worry about. I'd just like to be with you for now, and love you.'

Kahlan put her head against him. 'I think you're right. For now, let's not complicate matters.'

'We can worry about this another time.' He grinned at her. 'Right?'

Kahlan forgot all about Shota and the future and grinned back, thinking about the now. 'Right.'

The celebration went on until well after nightfall. Kahlan knew it would likely go on all night. She whispered to Richard that she would be happy not to have to remain for the whole thing. Richard kissed her cheek, and then asked the Bird Man if they could be excused. They wanted to go to the spirit house. The spirit house had special meaning to both of them.

The Bird Man smiled. 'It has been a long day. Sleep well.'

Richard and Kahlan said their thanks to everyone, and then, in the quiet of the spirit house, in the soft glow of the low fire that always burned there, they were at long last alone.

As they stared into each other's eyes, words were too small.

Berdine stood tall and straight as she watched the double doors burst open. Like a gout of flame they stormed into the Confessors' Palace – a dozen Mord-Sith in red leather.

Soldiers scrambled across the slick marble, falling back out of the way, while at the same time trying not to look hurried. They quickly established new guard positions at a safe distance. The twelve women paid them no attention. The existence of D'Haran soldiers hardly registered on the mind of a Mord-Sith – unless they gave her trouble.

The group came to a halt. Silence once again settled in the entrance hall.

'Berdine, how good to see you.'

Berdine let a small smile touch her lips. 'Welcome, Rikka. But what are you doing here? Lord Rahl left you at the People's Palace, awaiting his return.'

Rikka's eyes swept the area before her steady gaze settled on Berdine. 'We heard that he is here, now, and we decided that we should be closer so that we could protect him. We left the others at the palace, should he return unexpectedly. We will return with him when he goes home.'

Berdine shrugged. 'He sort of considers this home, now.'

'Whatever he wishes. We are here, now. Where is he, so that we may announce ourselves, and protect him?'

'He has gone to be married. Some distance to the south.'

Rikka's brows drew together. 'Why are you not with him?'

'He ordered me to stay here and see to things in his absence. Cara is with him.'

'Cara. Good. Cara will not let anything happen to him.' Rikka considered a moment, her dark frown returning. 'Lord Rahl is getting married?'

Berdine nodded. 'He is in love.'

The other women glanced at one another as Rikka put her fists on her hips. 'In love. A Lord Rahl, in love. Somehow, I can't picture it.' She huffed. 'He's up to something. Well, never mind; we will figure it out. What of the others?'

'Hally was killed awhile back. In battle, protecting Lord Rahl.'

'A noble death. What of Raina?'

Berdine swallowed, and forced her voice to stay level. 'Raina died a short time ago. Killed by the enemy.'

Rikka searched Berdine's eyes. 'I'm sorry, Berdine.'

Berdine nodded. 'Lord Rahl wept for her, as he did for Hally.'

Silence echoed around the entryway as all the other Mord-Sith stared at Berdine in disbelief.

'This man is going to be trouble,' Rikka muttered.

Berdine smiled. 'I think he would say a similar thing of you.'

Kahlan growled at the insistent knock. It appeared that ignoring it would not make it go away. She kissed Richard and wrapped a blanket around herself.

'Don't move, Lord Rahl. I'll get rid of them.'

Barefoot, she crossed the dim, windowless room. She squinted at the sudden light when she opened the door.

'Zedd, what is it?'

He was eating a piece of tava bread. He had a platter of it in his other hand. He offered her the tray.

'I thought you might be hungry.'

'Yes, thank you. Very thoughtful.'

He took a bite of tava bread as his gaze roamed over her hair. He pointed at it with the rolled-up tava bread.

'You will never get those tangles out, dear one.'

'Thank you for your fashion advice.'

She started to close the door. He put his hand against it.

'The elders are becoming concerned. They would like to know when they can have their spirit house back.'

'Tell them that when I'm done with it, I'll let them know.'

Cara, scowling her best Mord-Sith scowl, stepped up behind

him. 'I will see that he does not bother you again, Mother Confessor.'

'Thank you, Cara.'

Kahlan shut the door in his smiling face.

She hurried across the floor, back to Richard. She set the platter aside, laid down, and enfolded Richard in her blanket.

'A pesky in-law,' she explained.

'I heard. Tava bread and tangled hair.'

'Now, where were we?'

He kissed her, and she remembered; he was showing her some magic.